AUTHOR'S NOTE

This book is a work that comes from an incredibly personal place; it is also a work that features fairly heavy subject matter that may be difficult/potentially triggering for some readers. It is vitally important that we destigmatize the discussion of mental health, depression, and suicide, especially among our youth. While books are one of the safest spaces we have in which to talk about these very real and serious issues that affect so many of us, it is also crucial that you—the reader—be fully aware of and consenting to that exploration. As such, please be advised of the content warnings listed below, provided for your discretion.

Content Warnings: anger, arson, blood/gore, depression, grief (loss of loved one), miscarriage (past, off-page), parental abuse/neglect, psychopathy, self-harm (past, moderate description), suicide (past, off-page), suicide (present, on-page, moderate description), suicidal ideation

A CRUEL AND FATED LIGHT

ALSO BY ASHLEY SHUTTLEWORTH

A Dark and Hollow Star

A CRUEL AND FATED LIGHT

ASHLEY SHUTTLEWORTH

HODDER

First published in Great Britain in 2022 by Hodder & Stoughton
An Hachette UK company

1

Copyright © Ashley Shuttleworth 2022

A CIP catalogue record for this title is available from the British Library

Paperback ISBN 978 1 529 36627 3
eBook ISBN 978 1 529 36623 5

Printed and bound in Great Britain by Clays Ltd, Elcograf S.p.A.

Hodder & Stoughton policy is to use papers that are natural, renewable
and recyclable products and made from wood grown in sustainable
forests. The logging and manufacturing processes are expected to
conform to the environmental regulations of the country of origin.

Hodder & Stoughton Ltd
Carmelite House
50 Victoria Embankment
London EC4Y 0DZ

www.hodder.co.uk

to Celadon

Alecto

~~~~~

The Mortal Realm—North Atlantic Ocean

THE *DIRGE* WAS A ship that served many a whim, so long as those whims all served woe.

Poaching, piracy, trafficking, whaling—there was little in which its all-sorts crew of folk wouldn't dabble, no depravity too obscene. Decades of wicked delights stained its planks, left them reeking of torture and tears; of violence and fish-guts and sour sweat, lechery and vice; of frightened youths destined for black market auction and magical creatures butchered for parts. Death swarmed like flies to this festering carcass. Rage haunted its heart. The *Dirge* cried out for justice—this wasn't the glory her magnificence deserved—and Alecto . . . she understood.

Standing in the darkened cabin of the man who captained these terrible deeds, Alecto could hardly *breathe* for how fiercely she *understood*.

The *Dirge*'s anger mirrored her own.

Its howling echoed what screamed inside her heart, what shook her bones like tremors through earth, as though her entire being were on the brink of cracking open wide enough to swallow the world down whole.

Yes, Alecto understood.

The *Dirge* deserved better . . . Tisiphone had deserved better too—and there, the man, asleep in his cot, the root cause of it all. He looked so *peaceful*; it was terribly unfair.

"Heulfryn . . ."

Quiet as a guttering ember gasping for air, Alecto called Heulfryn's name. Once upon a time, it might have been amusing, the way he jolted awake at her voice. He was quick to blink through the fog of sleep and scan his chamber for what had disturbed him.

Moonlight spilled through the salt-crusted windows that sprawled at Alecto's back. Shadows warped the room. But every sound out of place would be loud as thunder to Heulfryn's sidhe fae senses. Alecto's magic on its own would have been enough to conceal her from him, but she'd taken extra precaution, regardless.

Tonight, she'd worn her cloak, the only thing even immortals couldn't see through.

Her cloak, the glittering swatch of midnight Eris had given her when she'd ascended from her nameless rank of A-12 to the coveted role of "Alecto." She'd been the very first Fury to have earned so much of a Hunter's esteem, to be gifted such a prized possession as this lighter-than-smoke bit of silk that was so much more than it seemed—like her, Eris had told her upon its gifting.

Eris . . . leader of the Wild Hunt . . . This cloak had always been security to Alecto. *Eris* had always been security. He'd been like a father to her, the only parent apparently willing to try to make things better, make things *right*, and yet . . .

I will give you this man, Alecto.

And yet . . .

I will register his name for death, and you will satisfy your grief on that, and we'll put this behind us. Do you understand me, Alecto? The deities are beginning to tire of your anger. They're growing angry themselves . . .

And yet it wasn't enough.

It would *never* be enough.

"I'm sorry," Alecto apologized to the night, to the bond she was about to betray. Reaching up, she unclasped her cloak and stepped forward, letting it fall to a shimmering pool at her feet.

Skeletal, towering, obsidian-clawed, and molten silver–eyed, Alecto was a *terrible* sight to behold in her unglamoured glory. The red and orange and yellow fire that seethed in the veins of her wings crackled as she spread them wide enough to fill the room, high enough to blot out that pale moon behind her. Her hair flickered like white-hot flame around her face. In her boney hand she clasped a vial so tightly her knuckles threatened to break through her skin, and she could feel the conflagration contained in its enchanted glass, its heat already blistering her palm.

The pain was nowhere near enough to make all the screaming stop, to distract from the rage that built and built and *built* inside her.

It would *never be enough*.

"Alecto," Heulfryn breathed, but not in fear. "I wondered when you'd appear."

He thought himself so perfect, this mortal maggot. It was in the very way he looked up at her from his bed through heavy lashes, in the casual way he slid his long legs over its edge and dared to rise like an equal before her. Lithe and lean but strongly built, his black hair raven soft and curling around his pointed ears, Winter-blue eyes glacier-bright—yes, he thought himself perfect. His confidence poured out in waves. Tisiphone had loved him . . . *Many* folk had loved him . . .

No. This man was not a maggot but a *spider*, whose paralytic bite was his beauty, distracting his victims as he drained them of their life.

"Here I am," Alecto spat, and took another step forward.

Heulfryn squared his jaw in a poor attempt at affecting calm.

"I'm sorry about Tisiphone. Your sister and I . . . we just didn't work."

"You're *sorry*."

"I am." Heulfryn nodded, falsely earnest down to the flash of per-formative pity in his eyes. Did it even hurt him to tell such lies any-more? He played the role of poor romantic hero well, but his remorse was purely that: an act. Alecto wasn't fooled. "I hope, in time, she'll find someone who better deserves her. I wish that could have been me, but my heart took to another. Iliana, she—"

"Tisiphone is dead."

It was the first time she'd ever spoken the words aloud. There were all so many euphemisms to gloss over her sister's "absence," and here, in the gloom, on the cusp of revenge and whatever resulting ruin awaited its completion, Alecto had finally said it.

Tisiphone was dead.

She could barely hear herself as she spoke, but whatever lurked in her voice, it was deadly enough to make Heulfryn's snowy complexion pale even further. She supposed she would have once been happy to see that, however little comfort it was now.

"I'm . . . I'm *sorry*, Alecto."

"Sorry for what, I wonder—for what you drove her to, or that she's no longer a shield to protect you from me?"

She'd known all along what sort of *vermin* this fae really was. Tisiphone wouldn't listen, didn't care that he'd never once been faithful to her or anyone previous, didn't care what he got up to, so long as he kept telling her *he loved her*, this thing she craved above all else.

She wouldn't entertain Alecto's caution, the warning that underneath Heulfryn's inability to lie was still deceit—the unspoken truth that what he loved about Tisiphone was her worship of him . . . and what she could help him get away with.

Tch . . .

Alecto swept out her hand. From dense black smoke assembled her obsidian blade: Erebos, fashioned from Darkness itself. It had surprised many when she'd picked that element to forge her weapon over the fire from which she'd been made. She'd enjoyed that surprise— flame burned brightest against the dark, she'd been all too happy to remind them in her juvenile arrogance. Back then, she'd seen death as merely a concept, something she delivered, nothing that could ever affect *her* or the ones she loved. With this Darkness-wrought blade, she'd intended to burn brighter than any Alecto ever before.

And she was going to still, even if the *how* of this had changed.

"Please," Heulfryn rasped. He dropped a bit of composure now, desperation peeking though as his eyes darted quickly around to see what he could use for defense, now that he knew his *untruths* wouldn't save him as they normally did. "Please let me explain. I never meant for this to happen!"

"I don't care."

He threw a hand up between them—with so much moisture in the air, all it took was a flick of his fingers for shards of the ice he wielded to form and hurl her way. Alecto stumbled, and Heulfryn took his chance, lunged for his dresser and the dagger he kept there, as though that could ever kill her.

"Listen to me, you insane bitch, your sister was a gods-damned *misery*. Always moping, always tired, jealous as all fucking hell, and never sodding happy about anything, least of all *me*. She's dead? Good for her. Sounds like she did us all a *favor*—"

Alecto snarled, baring her teeth, cutting Heulfryn off in his poorly chosen rant. Miserable, was her sister? Alecto would show him misery. Advancing toward him, she twitched her blade and disarmed him of his dagger as easily as though he'd been a child brandishing a stick. It clattered on the wooden floor and snapped in two when she trod across it to walk Heulfryn flat against the door behind him. The tip of her blade pressed into the soft flesh under his chin, just enough for a pearl of blue to well up around it and trickle down its length, and she was sorely tempted to press even further, *just a little more* . . .

But no, she had other plans for this mortal.

"You can't hurt me." Heulfryn spoke with all the care of a man on the verge of impalement, but *still* was there that *arrogance*. "Your sister told me everything. I haven't done anything wrong by the Law. None of the folk on this ship have, either. It goes against your rules to hurt me, so this is all for show. I'm not afraid of you."

Alecto's mouth fell open, and a rush of air came out. It might have been a laugh, if she could hear it over the *screaming* to tell. "You should be," she choked out.

The things this mortal had pulled from her sister with honeyed words and clever half-truths. The Mortal Realm remembered so little about the Others who'd once lived here too—even less about the Furies still permitted to walk among them. Alecto and her sisters, they kept to themselves, part of the conditions of their freedom. That Heulfryn knew so much about them was more insult than anything, but Eris had used it as grounds to convince the higher-ups he couldn't be allowed to live, and oh, he would be *very* afraid before the end.

But it wasn't enough.

She wanted more than Heulfryn's fear. She wanted more than his death.

"You should be, but you're really quite stupid, aren't you."

"Your sister was stupid too." The door at Heulfryn's back gave way. He'd found its knob at last and turned it to tumble through. "HELP!" he cried, tearing out into the hall. "HELP, WE'RE UNDER ATTACK!"

The chaos was immediate.

Doors sprung open; men shouted threats as they stumbled from their posts or out of bed, arming themselves with whatever they could grab quickest. Heulfryn fled—Alecto pursued. She'd only come for one tonight, but if others wanted to die, so be it. She had no intention of coming back from this, so what did she have to lose? One life or all, so long as she made Heulfryn pay . . .

Down the hall Heulfryn ran and up the stairs, out onto the *Dirge*'s deck, and Alecto followed close on his heel. For all the screaming inside her head—and outside of it now too, shouting and roaring and the gurgle of sapphire life spilling out at her feet—she hardly registered the people she cut down.

One . . . two . . . four . . . seven . . .

Out onto the deck she burst. "HEULFRYN!"

Eight . . .

"A demon!" men shouted. They'd never seen a Fury to recognize what she was.

"Abandon ship!"

"You fucking *cowards*," Heulfryn bellowed after them as crewman after crewman took one good look at Alecto's claws and wings and vicious teeth, and dove for the *Dirge's* rails.

"*Heulfryn*," Alecto seethed.

On he fled.

Nine . . . ten . . . more souls joined the others, folk too slow to clear her path. A kindness—Heulfryn would have company in the torment of his very long afterlife because the souls of folk could not depart until collected by a Hunter, and it would be far too late by the time any arrived tonight to save them from what Alecto had planned.

Company . . . This was all so much *better* than what her sister's *murderer* deserved.

On the prow of the ship now, nowhere left for him to go, Heulfryn wheeled around. "Leave me the fuck alone, you *hag*!" He threw his hands up once again. More shards of ice shot at Alecto, this wave so thick and sharp they cut her like hundreds of tiny knives. In her wake trailed splashes of sapphire-blue blood; the fire in her wings oozed and hissed and spluttered in droplets beside it, blooming into burning pools as soon as it hit the wood. Heulfryn was a talented fae—it was part of his charm—but strong as he was, he was mortal. Alecto still could have dodged this onslaught if she'd wanted.

She simply didn't care.

She stalked through the thick of this lethal-edged storm, undeterred, advancing on the man, whose eyes grew wider the closer she drew . . . "Nowhere left to go, Heulfryn."

The screaming in her head grew louder.

There was almost a crooning quality to it now, as though it could sense that the revenge it craved was nigh.

Heulfryn dropped his hands. He pulled himself tall, inflating his chest, one last show of arrogance as he squared his jaw at Alecto. Something about the hardness in his smirk made her freeze as she watched him reach into the collar of his shirt and pull out a chain, on the end of which hung a sliver-thin strip of pure, gleaming silver.

A whistle.

Hells, Alecto recognized *that*.

That whistle had once belonged to Tisiphone. She wouldn't have given it to him, not of her own volition. Another thing this man must have stolen from her, along with her time and her life.

"Let's see what your family has to say about that." He lifted the whistle to his lips and blew. A singular, shrill note cut so precisely through the night that every other sound deferred, if only for a ringing moment.

Even the screaming stopped in her head.

Then . . . "No," she breathed.

Then . . . "*NO!*" she bellowed.

Rage swept through her—*rage*, like nothing she'd ever known. Rage, the sort that rattled stars.

Heulfryn laughed as the heavens began to swell. The whistle was a summons. Alecto had made it for Tisiphone out of moonlight; if she'd ever found herself in trouble and needed help, it would call to her other sisters. It would call to the Wild Hunt. It would summon the people Alecto had trusted most to care for her, and now . . . they were coming.

And they would *stop* her—stop her *revenge,* collect Heulfryn's soul and save him from the only thing that would make any of this even a little better . . .

"NO!" She shot forward. Heulfryn tried to leap overboard, but Alecto wouldn't allow this escape, not now—his death was hers, and his suffering was the only thing she had left to give Tisiphone to try to make amends.

His suffering was her very last purpose in this deities-forsaken life.

Dropping her sword into the sea—she needed a free hand, and there was no point in spending precious seconds on vanishing a weapon she'd no longer require once her revenge was complete—she spread her wings, took to the air, and caught Heulfryn before he could hit the water.

"*No.*"

Upward they soared, higher and higher.

Heulfryn clawed at her. He begged and pleaded when Alecto stopped and heaved him up right to face her. "Please, don't do this!"

She laughed in his face.

She continued laughing as she plunged her hand through his chest and tore it back out clutching his still-beating heart.

She laughed and laughed until laughter turned to something else, and finally—*finally,* at long last—all the noise inside Alecto's head found its way out.

The only thing was, now that it had, there was no way of making it stop.

As Alecto's laughter turned to *screaming,* she hurled Heulfryn's body back to the ship. He hit its deck with a sickening crack of bone, and Alecto squeezed the vial she'd held through all of this until finally the glass broke.

And as she did, she screamed.

Starfire—what she'd done to get this fiercely guarded substance. . . . It was another betrayal of Eris, who'd told her in confidence long ago where and how it was kept. The vial slipped out of her grasp and fell, shattering on the ship below—Heulfryn's grave. Immediately, the *Dirge* erupted into flame that would never extinguish. It would burn away Heulfryn's body, then burn even fiercer on his ghost and the eleven other souls Alecto had managed to trap in its clutches, as well. The heat was so great that she could feel her skin melt off her face faster than it could regenerate. Joy, relief, gratitude, vengeance—*thank you*, the ship seemed to sing to her as it crumbled apart and sank below the waves, and still Alecto could only scream.

She tasted salt. Blood or tears, it didn't matter.

One by one, the men who'd jumped overboard were pulled beneath the sea's surface as merfolk flocked to the scene to feast; as Fate rewrote the crew's gruesome ending to keep with what Alecto had now set in stone.

Their screaming joined hers, but theirs was short-lived.

"ALECTO!"

She screamed . . .

"SISTER!"

And screamed . . .

"Tsk, tsk, *tsk*."

And *screamed*.

CHAPTER 1

Arlo

~~~~~~

Toronto—The Palace of Spring, Present Day

THE REVERDIE WAS QUIET—UNUSUALLY so. Arlo had never seen its reception so entirely deserted. Even on weekends, when most of the palace's government services were closed to the public, folk still made use of things like the Tim Hortons off to her left and the Falchion Police Headquarters beside it.

Today, there was no one, not even staff.

No one sat at the information booth in the center of the room, and no one patrolled the moss-and-marble floor. No one posed for pictures around the gilded statues of former High Sovereigns or by the enormous waterfall across the way. Where normally the budding forest canopy magicked onto the vaulted ceiling would rustle and sway in some illusory breeze, at the moment it was perfectly still. The only signs of the hummingbird faeries that tended to the palace's flora were glimpses of their vibrant rainbow plumage peeking out from the dark-leafed ivy that climbed the walls, from the lilac and rose and rhododendron bushes that flourished between ornate fixtures, and from the handsome oaks growing in place of random soapstone pillars with bluebells, crocuses, snowdrops, and black-eyed windflowers gathered around their bases.

This silence was eerie.

This all-around *emptiness* was practically unheard of.

Not once in Arlo's eighteen years had the Palace of Spring been shut so tightly to what seemed like *everyone* save a handful of its guards, and she couldn't help but wonder why the High King had chosen to do so now—and knew this meant nothing good for the meeting that called her and her mother here.

"Explain." Thalo, as always, got straight to the point.

Oren—the burly ogre who'd seen Arlo and her mother through the doors—was quick to supply an answer to what Thalo demanded. "Order from the High King himself, Commander. Effective immediately, the palace is closed until tomorrow morning."

"But *why*?"

"I . . ." Oren grimaced. "I'm sorry, Sir. I can't tell you that. I'm not permitted to speak it."

The frown on Thalo's face etched deeper.

Oren wasn't one of the Reverdie's usual guards—in fact, he wasn't a guard at all. As a Falchion officer, it wasn't his normal duty to mediate the palace's comings and goings, and that had been Arlo's first clue that something was going on today beyond the High King's requested debriefing. The fact that Oren very clearly *wanted* to tell his superior exactly what was happening here but *couldn't* meant he'd been ordered not to say by the only person whose command ranked higher than Arlo's mother's, and that didn't bode well for today at all.

Arlo felt her anxiety ratchet even higher.

"Commander."

Head snapping in the direction of this newest voice, Arlo saw the Lieutenant Commander making quickly for them. Klair Cardale, second to Thalo in the ranks of the Falchion and a few years her senior, had exited the FPF Headquarters so silently that he was almost right beside them by the time Arlo registered his presence.

Thalo—with her acute fae senses—was less surprised.

Handsome as any other fae Arlo had ever encountered, Klair was also immaculate down to his perfectly pressed Falchion uniform of black trousers and a sage button-down shirt with the crescent moon and windflower sigil of UnSeelie Spring emblazoned in dark emerald thread on its back. He was one of the rare few who'd supported Thalo as both Commander of the Falchion and the High King's Sword and

Shield right from the beginning, a fact even more surprising to Arlo given how obsessed she knew him to be with rules and traditions. He was a no-nonsense sort of person. Arlo honestly couldn't say whether he liked *her*, but he liked Thalo . . . or at least tolerated her.

Although his stoic mannerisms made that difficult to tell sometimes.

"Lieutenant Commander." Thalo faced her subordinate, eyeing him warily, clearly apprehensive of what he had to say on this troubling mystery. "Please tell me this isn't what I think it is."

Arlo looked between them, curious.

She was too used to keeping herself in her mother's shadow by now, small and silent whenever they were together at the palace, to ask anything outright. Thalo, of course, had never requested that of her. She'd never once given Arlo reason to suspect she was embarrassed of her ironborn daughter in any way, never made it a secret how much she enjoyed being a mother, even if she'd taken to the role with the same intensity she brought to being the High King's Right Hand, which had made everything from bedtime stories to school bake sales just a *touch* dramatic.

But Arlo knew how incredibly hard her mother had been forced to work to get where she was, harder than she would have if she'd been born a male, and many of her personal choices—such as taking a human for a partner instead of a well-to-do fae—hadn't helped that along. Jealousy looked for any ammunition it could find to knock people from their highly envied pedestals, and Arlo was determined not to lend it any more than it already had.

She was already a significant reason Thalo couldn't live at the palace with the rest of her family, Arlo's ironborn status conflicting with the strict tradition that declared only fae could hold permanent residence here. She was already a significant reason their relationship with the many Viridians was fraught with tension.

Her mother would have already been fully apprised of whatever situation had put the palace on lockdown this morning if she'd been here around the clock as she should be—if she didn't have to hand over her duties to Klair at the end of the day just to return to her separate residence with her daughter. Arlo *wouldn't* allow herself to be the reason Thalo lost this job altogether.

"Sorry, Sir." Klair shook his head. "I can't tell you this isn't what you think it is, as that would be a lie. Official protocol has been enacted. We can't be certain. She didn't give a reason for her visit on arrival, only said she's here for the meeting. We thought it best to take precautions, because if she's here for what we fear, we'll now have a few hours to control how that gets out to the Courts."

Thalo's mouth pressed into a fine line. She drew a deep, steadying breath through her nose.

Arlo's stomach twisted, because really . . . it could only be one person.

The meeting today was a private affair, meant to fill the High King in on what had happened mere days ago in the cavum factory. It had been held off in respect for the injuries Nausicaä sustained while protecting Arlo, but now that she was recovered, they couldn't postpone this any longer. Arlo would have to tell her great uncle everything they'd learned about the ironborn deaths, the abducted humans used to sew together a monstrous undead army, and the philosopher's stones he'd been thoroughly unwilling to entertain were being made.

Of course, there was absolutely *no* way she was going to tell him she'd made a deal with a *Titan* to become their Hollow Star, nor that she was waiting on Luck to train her in a magic that would definitely be just as forbidden as alchemy, if the Courts knew about it. As for *when* that training was going to happen, well, Arlo had been waiting . . . and waiting . . . and waiting. Luck hadn't shown themself once over the last few days, and Arlo already had enough to worry about even without this monumental promise hanging over her head.

So she wouldn't say a word about any of *that* today, if she could help it. But very possibly, she was going to have to admit to using alchemy to get them inside the factory so they could catch the evil scientist responsible for all the murders and mayhem.

Just thinking about betraying *that* secret sent Arlo's nerves into hyperdrive, especially considering the not-at-all kind warning the High King had given her the last time they'd come together like this—that he'd punish Arlo if she ever dared use that forbidden magic again. She didn't like her chances of the High King's mood being any more forgiving than last time, even less if the one person in the whole of the Courts who could put him on edge was including herself in this meeting.

"Walk with me," said Thalo to the Lieutenant Commander, setting off toward the carved oak doors that marked the throne room's entrance.

Klair followed immediately after Thalo. Arlo did too, trailing close behind, watching the hem of her mother's thick emerald cloak as it snapped around her legs.

"Tell me what we *do* know," Thalo continued. "His Majesty?"

"Tense, to put it mildly," Klair replied, falling into step beside her.

"*Damn it.* Of all the days, she chooses this one. The Wild Hunt?"

"Present. Minus one."

Lethe.

When Arlo had filled Nausicaä in on what she'd missed after being stabbed by Hieronymus Aurum and slipping into some sort of healing coma, the ex-Fury hadn't said much. That in itself was odd; Nausicaä had something to say about *everything*, constructive or otherwise. But when Arlo had mentioned that a *Hunter* had come to their rescue in the lab—one who admitted not only to working with Hieronymus but also with the person behind the philosopher's stones as well—she'd fallen silent. Grim. Contemplative. All kinds of things that weren't Nausicaä at all, and the only thing Arlo had been able to wheedle out of her was the Hunter's name.

"Good. He actually *listens* to Eris, so at least there's that. And if nothing else, for Cosmin's sake, I hope he'll remember he can call on Eris to serve as Champion if—"

Champion.

And there it was.

"The queen," Arlo groaned, then instantly dipped her chin to her chest in sheepish apology for interrupting Klair and her mother. But Arlo knew without a doubt now who they were talking about. She knew who was here, causing a stir, because it was pretty near *clockwork* for this particular fae to make her appearance.

After all, she had come at the same time every year for about a decade.

They approached the doors, and the stone-faced fae on duty snapped to attention, saluting Thalo and Klair. At a wave of Thalo's hand, the throne room's doors swung open, and all Arlo's shorting-out brain could think as she followed them through was that she was very possibly about to witness the beginning of the end.

Riadne Lysterne, Queen of Seelie Summer, had come to issue her annual Challenge for Azurean Lazuli-Viridian's Crown, and there was no doubt in Arlo's mind (or anyone else's, it seemed) that *this* time, she'd follow through with it.

CHAPTER 2

Nausicaä

～✦～

THE PALACE OF SPRING'S throne room was beautiful, Nausicaä supposed, with its marble floors and soapstone pillars carved into the likeness of towering oak trees; with the happy little springtime flowers that clustered around their trunks, and the dark-leafed ivy that grew like tapestries up the walls and dripped from the branchlike network of beams overhead. She hadn't been in much of a mood to appreciate the aesthetic the first time she'd been dragged here, and if she was being perfectly honest, wasn't any more interested in it now. Nausicaä was getting *bored*, and nothing was *happening* despite all the fucking tension in the air, and she was *trying*, damn it, to be on her "best behavior," as Arlo had begged of her in a series of texts this morning at the hellscape-crack-of-dawn, but that was getting harder and harder to do the longer all this silent *nothing* wore on.

A rustling in Nausicaä's periphery caught her attention.

She turned her gaze from the high-flung ceiling where it had wandered—where dozens of brightly colored hummingbird faeries sat watching her curiously—to the person who'd stolen everyone else's attention already, but whom Nausicaä had been dutifully ignoring.

Riadne Lysterne, Queen of Seelie Summer.

Riadne looked nothing like her son, Vehan, Nausicaä observed, for all that they shared the same electric bright blue eyes and raven black hair. Her beauty was almost frigid, much like what people said of her late, UnSeelie Winterborn father—jutting sharp bone under icy white skin that reminded Nausicaä of a wraith she'd once encountered in the wilds of Eastern Europe.

At the moment Riadne stood perfectly composed against the far wall, hands clasped in casual grace in front of her, as though she weren't in the thick of "enemy territory" with no one but herself for support, and fully aware she was under even closer scrutiny than Nausicaä was. There wasn't a single strand of feather-soft hair out of place in the glossy sheet that fell to her hips; there wasn't even a *hint* of a wrinkle in the white silk and gold-embroidered robe she wore over an ivory blouse so sheer it was almost transparent, and tucked into tight-fitted pants so dark a bronze they were almost black. The crown on her head—shocking yellow shards of jagged-cut sapphire, quartz, and garnet set into a gleaming circle of gold—was polished and perfectly centered on her head.

And what *would* Riadne have to be concerned about?

Azurean might wear the Bone Crown, that coveted amplifier of magic that all knew full well Riadne wanted for her own, but *she* was easily the most dangerous person in this room—and when that room contained Nausicaä and three members of the Wild Hunt, that was saying something.

It meant nothing good that Riadne was here.

Nothing good . . . but interesting. Very, *very* interesting, to Nausicaä at least, even if the rest of the room looked like they'd swallowed whole bolts of the lightning that the Seelie Queen of Summer commanded.

Given her son's involvement in what they'd been gathered to discuss today, it wasn't as though anyone could deny Riadne's attendance for this meeting, even if she *was* likely here to issue a Challenge to the High King, which they couldn't deny her either. The fae and their convoluted rules. *Hoisted by their own petard*, Nausicaä thought with a snort, but she'd bet her shiny gold right arm—souvenir from her encounter with Scumbag Hieronymus and the philosopher's stone he'd touched to her skin—that the *true* reason Riadne had come today wasn't what anyone would guess. Until Riadne played her cards, whatever she was here to accomplish, it was only she who knew.

"The *Dark Star*, I presume?" said Riadne in a tone so soft and clear and careful that it might have been a pleasant sound if it weren't for the total and disturbing lack of emotion behind it.

They were the first words anyone had spoken in the twenty-some odd minutes they'd been gathered here, waiting; if there was anyone not already paying attention to the Seelie Queen before, they were now.

"Yuuuup," Nausicaä replied, popping the final consonant and mentally congratulating herself for showing none of the surprise she felt at being so suddenly and directly targeted for conversation by the last person she thought would try to speak to her today.

They'd never met in person before this moment, she and Riadne, but it wasn't too long ago that Nausicaä had unleashed a bull troll on her foyer for the queen's audacity to accuse Nausicaä of being responsible for the recent deaths of ironborn children. With the Solstice celebration just around the corner, it had been a fitting punishment, Nausicaä thought—deep annoyance for deep annoyance.

Riadne smiled serenely. Nausicaä was just a little envious of how terrifying that must look to someone *other* than her, too generally terrifying a person herself to be much affected. But still, Nausicaä had to hand it to her, it was an impressive amount of *I could destroy your whole life and I know it.*

"Curious." Riadne's bright blue gaze shimmered with the other, far less *diplomatic* words she left unspoken. "For some reason I was picturing someone . . ."

"Older?" Nausicaä supplied in a bored tone. "Taller? *Scarier?*"

"No . . ."

"Hmmm." Nausicaä made a show of thinking this over, a little more invested now. "Someone with fangs, maybe? Or snakes for hair? You know, I've always wanted snakes for hair, but that's already been done. Hate disappointing my fans though, so if you really want, I could probably swing some . . . worms? No—slugs! No, that's stupid. Or is it? We'll come back to the slugs thing, but *scorpions,* now that's a statement—"

"Yes, that's it," Riadne interrupted, smiling still but sounding a little smug. "I'd always imagined you as someone a bit more concerned about *appearances*." She looked Nausicaä pointedly over, from her unbrushed hair and gray Hello Kitty sweater to her black leggings and boots, all gifts from Arlo's closet that she'd brought for Nausicaä to wear while recuperating in the hospital wing, and which Nausicaä appreciated immensely, thank the fuck you very much. When getting dressed today, Nausicaa had felt this ensemble nicely encompassed how little she actually cared for the High King's authority right now in his fancy-ass glorified playroom.

Arms folded across her chest, back against the wall, one foot crossed ever so casually over the other, Nausicaä was the picture of insouciance, and she eyed the Seelie Summer Queen with enough hard dislike for this statement that a couple of the UnSeelie Spring guards shifted uneasily, as though anticipating things might turn physical at any moment and unsure of how to respond.

Because really, was Nausicaä liked any more than Riadne by the people here? By the High King on his wood-and-ivy throne, or his solemn but proud queen beside him, or his children at their flanks: the Crown High Princess Cerelia; her twin, Serulian; and the youngest, Celadon, whom she had only just started to get to know. The Wild Hunt—that infamous cadre of the four most elite Hunters, best of their kind, which Cosmin had made a *ton* of over the years, all from the souls of the fiercest mortal warriors—had now dwindled to three, and would remain as such until either Lethe was forced to return by the higher-ups or someone was able to defeat him to claim his place. Regardless, they stood as silent and watchful as ever behind the throne, and Nausicaä had done enough damage there to know that they'd be happy to let her go at the Seelie Summer Queen and risk the outcome. And at the base of the dais, to the far left and right, the highest clearance Court officials were gathered, grim-faced and stiff, poised to defend their king from any threat, which Nausicaä was undoubtedly still considered.

Please please please don't get into a fight with anyone before mom and I get there.

Nausicaä sighed.

Such promises she'd made, and she wouldn't go back on her word to Arlo so easily. "I think that's called projection," she drawled, and left it at that to look away again.

A rude gesture in any culture, really, but doubly so for the fae, who all had such hard-ons for pretense and etiquette that flatly ignoring one of them (especially one of the pissy, royal sidhe elite like Riadne Lysterne) was probably tantamount to murder or something, but Nausicaä had promised Arlo she'd *behave*—she hadn't promised to be a deities-damned saint.

Her gaze wandered to the High King, who'd remained silent through this entire exchange. Azurean had eyes only for Riadne. He watched her fixedly, as he'd done since she'd arrived, so much distance in that old jade gaze that Nausicaä wondered what he was really seeing. Before she could ponder this any further, though, the heavy oak doors at the far end of the room creaked loudly open.

And *finally* . . .

"Arlo!" Nausicaä cheered.

Arlo's familiar red head was only just visible behind a tall, willowy woman with tightly bound russet hair, blue-tinted fair skin, and jade-green eyes—Commander Viridian-Verdell, Arlo's mother. At her side was an ashen-haired someone who Nausicaä didn't know but was no doubt also important, given the theme of this morning.

She waited until Arlo drew level with her to peel away from the wall and fall into step beside her. Latching onto her arm, Nausicaä pitched her voice in a whisper and said, "*Thank you*. I was starting to think I'd died in that hospital wing and this was the hell so many people keep suggesting I visit."

"Mm-hmm, yeah, hell. That would explain the *pajamas*, at least," Arlo practically moaned in despair as she side-eyed Nausicaä's chosen outfit, but at this, Nausicaä only beamed.

Red looked different today, she noticed in return. A little more scrubbed and groomed to royal fae standard. Her long hair blazed as fiery as ever, but there was a healthy amount of product in it to tame its easily tangled thickness and the way the growing humidity outside made it curl, which Nausicaä much preferred, even if *this* was still nice. A little paler white than usual—no doubt owing to nerves—and sporting an emerald green dress over black tights and glossy Mary Janes, Red's overall impression screamed cute-but-slightly-nauseated porcelain doll.

What struck her, though, in this room where the High King's presence stripped all of their glamour, was Arlo's *faeness*. Quiet, yes, that was Red all over—the point of her ears and cut of her facial structure wasn't anywhere near as pronounced as it was for the gathered others, and while a tinge of something bluer blushed her skin tone, she still possessed that copper-red warmth of human blood. But outside of this room, it was almost impossible to tell at a glance that Arlo was one of the folk, her glamour was so expertly woven (and oh, but Nausicaä had some thoughts on why that might be, why this eager-to-please girl so desperate to belong to at least *one* community might have subconsciously hidden herself behind so *precise* a human mask . . .)

Outside of this room, Arlo was Arlo.

Inside . . .

Nausicaä snorted. How any of them could look at this girl and *miss all these damned signs* . . .

"None of that," she said, giving Arlo's arm a squeeze. "Stop stressing. This isn't a trial, you'll be all right. And I'm right here with you—a dark and hollow star, remember?"

The way Arlo squeezed her arm back saved this entire morning from being designated in her mental diary as *completely* awful.

"Your Majesty," Commander Viridian-Verdell greeted, coming to a halt in the middle of the room and folding her fist over her heart. Her companion mirrored the action. Nausicaä made no move to reverence like the others—Azurean was lucky she was even doing this at all, considering how shitty he'd been to her the last time around—but she loosened her hold on Arlo so that Arlo could greet the High King too. "Your Highness," the Commander continued to Queen Reseda and her children each in turn. "Queen Riadne," she added, turning to the Seelie Summer Queen, and it amused Nausicaä right down to the charred remains of her soul to note how much harder her tone had grown.

Thalo and Riadne—two extremely badass women, accomplished and formidable despite everything working against them. They were both single mothers, both masters of the sword, both nobility of very old houses that wouldn't have let them come this far if it weren't for their strength of character. They might have been good friends, if circumstances were different.

Nausicaä couldn't help wondering which one would come out the winner, should it ever come down to a duel.

"Your Majesty?" the Commander repeated, when the High King made no reply.

His attention was still fixed on Riadne, and it wasn't until his wife nudged his side that he blinked, stirred, and looked to Reseda, who whispered something in his ear before he turned his attention on the rest of the room at last. His daze seemed to linger; he regarded his Commander with a hint of surprise, as though he hadn't heard her—or anyone else, for that matter—enter the room and speak to him.

In fact, to Nausicaä, he looked a little surprised to find himself in the throne room at all.

"Commander," Azurean greeted, finally recovering to sit a little straighter and dip his chin in a respectful nod to Arlo's mother.

"Apologies for keeping the Court from proceedings," said the Commander, as though nothing about the High King's behavior had been unusual.

"No matter." Azurean waved a hand, and was it Nausicaä's imagination, or did he look a little *older* than even the last time they'd tried to have this conversation? Their first meeting—in which she'd done him the immense favor of pointing out that, yes, ironborn *were* being hunted down, by an alchemist no less, who was using them to grow philosopher's stones in their chests, and the High King had been a complete jackass about it, repaying that favor by slapping her with an arrest warrant—it hadn't been more than a couple of weeks ago, but already a little more gray was streaked through the High King's wavy russet hair than before; a few more lines had etched their wear around jade green eyes that had lost a bit of verdure.

Nausicaä shook her head.

Fools.

The price people were willing to pay for power . . .

"We are present and accounted for," the High King continued. "The meeting can begin. Arlo Jarsdel—good morning."

Commander Viridian-Verdell and the fae man she'd entered with stepped aside to allow Arlo forward. "Good morning, Your Majesty," Arlo replied, steady enough but soft as the windflowers growing around the High King's chair, and Nausicaä could feel the tension she radiated despite the fact that they were no longer touching.

"The Seelie Queen Riadne has requested inclusion on this meeting. I have assented—Prince Vehan was enough involved in what you have to tell us that I see no reason to bar her from further information unless you wish otherwise. So, I ask you, before we begin: Is there anyone present you'd rather be removed?"

Arlo looked around, more for show than anything, Nausicaä suspected. Her reply was a touch shakier than her greeting had been. "N-no, it's fine. Thank you, Your Majesty."

"Very well, then, let's get this underway." He relaxed back against his throne—easy, calm, elegant as any fae king, and the way he angled his jaw just so . . . Hells, his son Celadon really was a younger little carbon copy of him. Nausicaä had spent enough time with Arlo's cousin this past week, plastered at Arlo's side as he'd been, to spot it now: the same build, same angular features, same hair and eyes and complexion and even tone of voice. They looked more alike than any of Azurean's other children. It was actually *creepy* how much so. Maybe he was a clone? Nausicaä needed to pay attention. "—has already explained as much to me as she knows. And I've gathered a good deal from my own investigation of the place. But in your words, I'd like you to share with me exactly what happened in Hieronymus Aurum's factory the night we found you."

"Well . . ." Arlo took a deep breath, quite obviously psyching herself up for whatever speech she'd prepared ahead of time. Nausicaä kept quiet, listening for the details Arlo deemed safe enough to share and the ones she didn't. "It started, I guess, with Prince Vehan's visit to the Palace last week. I . . . uh . . . heard he was here and that he wanted to talk about what was going on with the ironborn, and . . ."

She continued for a while, explaining in a mixture of truth and omission what had gone down: the four of them meeting (though she kept to herself the location of that meeting, no doubt to protect the Assistance); their decision to investigate the factory Vehan had discovered in the desert (though she kept to herself the disastrous drug deal that had led to this, as well as the revenge the goblins involved had tried to take on Vehan in the Hiraeth); their teleporting to the Nevada desert, and encounter and defeat of the cava—those monstrous dolls of sewn-together human flesh given life by foul alchemy—and then at last their infiltration of Hieronymus's illegal alchemical factory (though she kept to herself the alchemy she used to get them inside).

Finally, Arlo explained that it was Lethe who'd killed Hieronymus, turning on the man he'd been working with to save them. "I tried to get as much as I could out of him before he took off. It wasn't a lot, but he more or less admitted that someone *was* trying to use ironborn children to host and grow philosopher's stones, and that Hieronymus *had* been in on it but wasn't the true culprit."

"Hmmm," was all Azurean replied to this. He stared at Arlo for a very long minute, intensely at first, as though he knew full well she'd left things out and might just be able to piece together what. But the shrewdness in his gaze was short-lived. His attention drifted back to Riadne. Was it better or worse that the High King was clearly too lost in his thoughts right now for this conversation? Nausicaä wondered.

"And how did you get into this factory, Miss Jarsdel?"

The High King startled; this new voice had spoken so sharply it must have broken him from his returning daze before it could take proper hold.

Nausicaä searched out the fae who'd spoken: a sidhe man with carefully groomed brown hair and sun-tanned skin beneath that fae tinge of sapphire blue that was considerably fainter than the others around him, but Nausicaä supposed that was just the High King's magic grown too weak to strip this man's glamours completely, because it couldn't be that he wasn't fully fae. The robes he wore, splendid material of emerald and turquoise, were such that only a member of the Fae High Council would wear—the Seelie Spring Councillor, if Nausicaä's extremely vague memory of the Court color schematics could be at all trusted—and enough prejudice remained among the upper echelons of this society for that to be a pretty sidhe fae–exclusive club.

Judging by the glimmer of contempt in the look he fixed on Arlo, he wasn't all that fond of her.

"I'm . . . I'm sorry?" Arlo stuttered.

The Councillor stepped forward from his huddle at the base of the throne and bowed to the High King. "Apologies for speaking out of turn, Your Majesty. I mean no disrespect, only that you combed that underground factory yourself. By the reports, it seemed to be the focus of considerable dangerous alchemy. Arrays on everything— every*where*—including the door that sealed it." He turned his gaze back on Arlo, positively *glittering* now with dark delight, as though he'd been waiting for something like this moment, as though Arlo was someone he not only disliked but wanted to *punish*. "How did you get in, Miss Jarsdel? Who deactivated a Grade Two alchemical seal to let you into that factory?"

Arlo grew, if possible, even paler.

"It couldn't have been the Seelie Summer Prince, a full-blooded sidhe fae."

"I . . ."

"It couldn't have been his retainer, Lord Aurelian, a full-blooded lesidhe fae."

"It's not what—"

"Very doubtful it was your new little friend, the Dark Star, an immortal wanted for quite a number of crimes in every Court under our command and surely the ones outside of it, too. Questionable company, I might well add, but company not capable of alchemy. So who let you into that factory?" The smile on the Councillor's face grew vicious in anticipated victory, and thank you the fuck no, that was quite enough of *that*. "Who performed considerable illegal magic and—"

"Oh, it was Arlo," Nausicaä interrupted, folding her arms across her chest as casually as though she'd just announced the day of the week.

It was hard to tell whether Arlo was going to throw up or pass out or slap Nausicaä like she'd slapped Meg for what Nausicaä had just said. The rest of the room exploded into murmurs. The Councillors shifted, turning in on themselves to discuss. The High King sat straight once more in his throne, budding outrage creeping into his expression.

Celadon stiffened, his face falling from the fury that had clenched his jaw at the Councillor's accusation to horror.

Commander Viridian-Verdell stepped forward, hand hovering over the pommel of the sword she carried strapped to her side (and glamoured invisible to anyone without the Sight, no doubt) as though she expected one of the spectators to break away and launch an attack on her daughter, and any who dared would be skewered.

It was only Riadne who maintained her ease. A fine black brow had quirked a little higher, Nausicaä noticed when she'd glanced to check the room's reaction. But other than this, perfect composure.

Riadne wasn't surprised at all. Perhaps Vehan had told her everything, no details withheld; perhaps he hadn't, and Riadne had her own source of information, which was just as likely.

Why are you here? There was too much about Riadne that was a mystery for Nausicaä's liking.

Out loud, she continued, "Yup, Arlo. Pretty impressive, right? An eighteen-year-old ironborn girl managed to deactivate a *Grade Two* alchemic array easy as flicking on a light switch, and with absolutely no training whatsoever." She glared down the Councillor who'd spoken, now peeking through his coterie to regard Nausicaä. His perceived triumph was still painted across his face, but Nausicaä didn't miss the way it had started to dim—he couldn't quite work out where this was going but was smart enough to detect the hint of a coming counterattack.

"Even more impressive," Nausicaä continued, "when you consider what she's demonstrated over the past few days. All that intelligence and cunning . . . Aren't those the things UnSeelie fae prize most? Plus, she outran the Reaper that attacked the Danforth—*outran* a *Reaper*. I'm going to let that just . . . sink in for a moment, because even *I* can't catch up to one of those things when it gets going, and I can *teleport*."

"Arlo?" the Commander interrupted, her sternness a touch faint for her motherly concern showing through. "What is she talking about? The Danforth . . . the Reaper . . ."

Ah. Another secret revealed. Too bad, but too late, and too necessary to what Nausicaä was after. It was the reason she'd agreed to be here at all, actually. Whoever the hells this damn Councillor guy thought he was, he had no idea the opportunity his pathetic attempt against Arlo had presented, and Nausicaä was all about capitalizing on others' foolishness.

"Swiftness—a windborn gift. You're all over here so keyed up about who's not allowed to do what that you're missing the fact that Arlo Jarsdel is eighteen years old and right on the cusp of her deities-damned Maturity—and it *is* deities-damned, all right. By one deity in particular. In any case, I want to propose a trade."

The Councillor, his triumph melted in agitation, wheeled around to the High King. "She admits it! Arlo Jarsdel performed illegal magic to get inside that factory, Your Majesty—"

"Yeah, because none of *you* could be assed to do anything about it when we tried to pass this off to you, and if she hadn't, your Courts would be royally *screwed* by the army Hieronymus Aurum almost got away with. So, thanks, but you can take this attitude you're popping off and shove it up your—"

"Your *Majesty!*" the Councillor cried, his residual glamour malfunctioning spectacularly it seemed, because for a moment, iron red and fae blue bled brightly together to flush him a splotchy purple in the face.

Azurean stood from his throne so quickly the room fell silent. "Enough, Councillor Sylvain." He took a step forward. Nausicaä squared her jaw at the fathomless expression on his age-lined face, holding her ground, but she uncrossed her arms and grabbed hold of Arlo's once again, prepared to teleport them both right the hells out of here if Nausicaä's gamble didn't pay off in the way she hoped.

"Is this true, Arlo, what the Dark Star claims of you? Did you perform alchemy to get inside that factory? After I specifically warned you that any further practice would see *strict* consequences?"

Nausicaä felt a tremble shudder through Arlo's entire body. She probably wasn't all that happy with her right now for revealing these things she'd gone out of her way to withhold, but she stood just as surely beside Nausicaä, jutted her chin in the exact same show of defiance, and faced down the High King's building ire with all the stubborn determination that had helped her stare down the Reaper, too, and slap a *Fury* across the *face*.

Arlo was worth a hundred of the Azureans in this world, Nausicaä thought in a sudden and fierce swell of pride.

"I did," she replied. "It was the right thing to do."

"You think so, do you?" Azurean began to swell with rage, eyes flashing dangerously. "You know better than I do about what's good and right for the Courts, little girl? You'd like to make the decisions, would you, and sit on this throne? I suppose *you* want my Crown, too?" His hand flew to his head at this, to the twist of bleached antler bone that shaped the circlet there, and for a moment looked so convinced of this absurd accusation that his features twisted in visible fear.

Confusion . . . irritability . . . paranoia . . . The sands that measured the High King's time in this world were down to a mere palmful of grains, and his burnout wouldn't be pretty, as was the case for High Sovereigns who went unchecked for too long. For now, though, this behavior was exactly what Nausicaä had been counting on; she fully intended to use it to their advantage.

"Oh, you don't want the High King's Crown, do you, Arlo?" she asked, slanting Arlo a casual glance.

Arlo—whose eyes had grown saucer-wide—shook her head a fervent *no*, first at Nausicaä, then at her great uncle. "I-I don't!" she stammered. "Honest! I was just—"

Nausicaä gave Arlo's arm another squeeze of reassurance before releasing her hold and letting her hands fall clasped behind her back. She smiled. "But I can tell you who *does* want it, if you're interested."

The High King's gaze cut sharply to Riadne, who finally looked something other than composed, the way her mouth pinched slightly tighter and her shocking blue eyes gained a darker sort of gleam to them. She glared at Nausicaä when she turned to look at the Seelie Summer Queen as well, but Nausicaä merely increased the wattage of her smile and shook her head; to the High King, she added, "Well, yeah, I think we *all* know *she* wants it."

It was secret to precisely no one that Riadne Lysterne's sight was fixed on obtaining the Bone Crown, the legendary circlet given to mortalkind by Cosmin, one of the three main deities of Western worship. The Bone Crown was many things to mortals and immortals alike; here, it made its possessor sovereign over the Eight Great Courts of Folk. According to gossip, Riadne had wanted it to a point of near obsession her entire life, and it would have been hers, too, if it hadn't been for Azurean—a fact just as well-known as her hatred for the UnSeelie Spring's current Head, so the High King's paranoia wasn't *completely* unfounded. But . . .

"But that's not who I was talking about."

Azurean's focus shifted to Nausicaä. He regarded her almost as though seeing her for the very first time, and while some of the madness that had stolen over him had calmed a little, he didn't look any happier for hearing that the Seelie Summer Queen wasn't the only threat to his continued rule.

His eyes narrowed in suspicion. "You?" he asked, tone grown darker. "My Hunters explained a bit of your circumstances to me. Perhaps your banishment here was your intention. Perhaps you figured it was—"

"Better to reign in hell than serve in heaven?" Nausicaä waved a dismissive hand. "This finger-pointing is getting really old, really fast. No, I don't want your stupid-ass Crown and never did. Put some respect on my name—if you knew what I know about it, you wouldn't want it either. You honestly think that was given to you lot as a *gift*? As a kind gesture? You murder and bleed and *bicker* over the damn thing so much, and it's never occurred to even one of you that this might have been the intention all along?"

A heaviness weighed on the High King's brow now that had nothing to do with his ailing mental state. In fact, he seemed a little more alert, a little more conscious of himself and his surroundings, a little more like what he would be if it weren't for the Crown wrapped around his head. Azurean Lazuli-Viridian had always been considered intelligent even among the fae, and right now it was evident to Nausicaä that he was once again sifting through things left unsaid.

"I'm proposing a trade," she repeated, slowly and pointedly now that she had him in a better frame of mind to pay attention. "The folk like trades, yeah? Fae even more—nothing for nothing, isn't that the saying on the streets? And I told you before, there's a whole lot more going on here than you know. The Bone Crown . . . the philosopher's stones . . . Immortals play a very long game. Everything that's going on? It's all connected, and you can bet every one of your shiny palaces that my people haven't forgotten you like you've forgotten them, or *forgiven* you at all, either, for what you took away from them."

Azurean drew himself up to full height. There was a curiosity in those eyes—none of the folk could help their interest in striking bargains with one another—but wariness, too. He didn't trust her, that Nausicaä could tell, but he knew she knew things he didn't. "It sounds to me like you're *suggesting* the immortals have been plotting against us. That's a serious accusation."

"Is that what I'm saying?" Nausicaä's smile spread razor sharp across her face. "Well, I imagine that would be information tagged with a pretty price. I won't hand it over for anything less than your promise to train Arlo in alchemy."

The room, which had been watching this exchange in avid silence, erupted.

"Your Majesty!"

"Sire!"

"Absolutely not!"

The Fae High Council buzzed like a nest of wasps, but the High King raised his hand for silence. When he said nothing, merely held steady Nausicaä's gaze, she pressed on. "I want you to train her. You don't have to make her into some superpowered alchemist, don't worry. You don't have to reopen the universities and give her a fucking degree. But *train* her. Get her a teacher. There's a deep well of magic inside this girl, and I'm telling you—you didn't listen before, but listen to me now, because *I'm telling you*—if you don't give her power an outlet, it's going to Rebound."

The Commander issued a gasp. Arlo looked at Nausicaä, shocked.

"Plus," Nausicaä continued, undeterred, "I think you'll want to have someone with her potential on your side when shit hits the fan. You give Arlo training, and I'll let you in on some very big secrets—secrets even your Hunters won't tell you."

The Hunters in question made no move to signal they were bothered by what she was saying, but Nausicaä knew them far too well to mistake their silent stillness for apathy. She had their attention right now—she had their tension.

Will she betray us again, they probably wondered, and unfortunately that answer was *yes*.

For Arlo, that answer would always be *yes*—and she was far too busy right now to marvel over that sudden realization, but later . . .

"Secrets," Nausicaä added, dangling this promise like the greatest temptation—and indeed, to the fae it was. "Secrets I wasn't too sure I even had to trade until Arlo told me *Lethe* was in on these stones being made."

The room leaned in, if only a little. Even Riadne reacted—her own stillness in the offing grew just as preternaturally stiff as what froze the Hunters. Death threats, political intrigue, bargaining, and secrets; it was a very good day for the fae in this room, Nausicaä suspected. The palace would be gossiping about this for months to come; pockets would be full of precious info to trade.

"Arlo gets a tutor to teach her alchemy, and you'll allow her to practice it from here on out, the bare minimum to keep her safe at *least*. That's the terms of my trade."

Azurean stared down at her from his dais. There was nothing mild about the sternness tightening his jaw, the hardness in his bright eyes. He looked down at her, assessing, weighing the risk in agreeing against the risk in denying her what she wanted.

"Your High Majesty."

It was Riadne who'd spoken, firm and clear but just as benign as the smile that had returned to her flawless face. All attention in the room transferred to her as she stepped from the wall and practically glided to the center of the room. She came to a rest at Nausicaä's side, but it was the High King she watched all the way, and Nausicaä didn't trust this meek deference for a minute.

It didn't look like the High King did, either.

"If I might, perhaps it's time I illuminate my true reason for coming here today."

Nobody moved. Everyone listened. Commander Viridian-Verdell's hand remained poised over the hilt of her sword, though her target of this threat had changed.

Azurean lifted a brow, his gaze flicking briefly to his side . . . to Celadon, curiously. "Oh?" The flatness to his tone betrayed his lack of surprise. "And here I believed you when you said you wanted only to listen in."

"I wanted that, yes." Riadne inclined her head without dropping her gaze or blinking. It was a bit like watching a tigress stalk a proud old stag. "But my true aim was to beg of you something, too. And apologize. I feel quite terrible, if I'm being honest, that my own son nearly caused such grievous harm to come to a niece of our estimable High King. I thought perhaps the best way to convey said regret would be to extend a personal invitation to young Miss Jarsdel. I would like her to join me and Vehan for the summer at our palace, and as my honored guest to the Solstice celebration, too."

She turned her attention briefly on Arlo, and Nausicaä felt her chest constrict; she didn't like this, not at all. This was kindness. This was *normal*. This was the *very opposite* of what the Seelie Queen of Summer was known to be, and what Nausicaä hated most of all was that she was probably *helping*.

"Our royal children are expected to spend time abroad, are they not?" Riadne continued, her smile growing and now directed at Arlo. "If it's as you say, if Arlo is coming into her fae Maturity, then my invitation should be considered welcome custom! It would be my honor to host her, and I would see to it—with your permission, of course, Your Majesty—that we find her a suitable tutor to train her in alchemy."

"Nausicaä."

Nausicaä tore her attention from Riadne to look up at the High King.

"This secret you possess, it's to do with this philosopher's stone business."

Nausicaä nodded.

"It's to do with why one of my Hunt has betrayed me."

She nodded again.

"Arlo."

Arlo jolted. She'd probably preferred it when they'd been ignoring her, talking about her as though she weren't here—probably would prefer it if she actually *weren't* here at all—but tried to hold herself a little taller now that everyone was looking at her.

"Do you wish to be trained in alchemy?"

Looking a bit like a mouse unsure whether the cheese it was being presented was poisoned, Arlo nodded. "If Nausicaä says I should be, then yeah. Yes! Your Majesty. I trust her."

"If I permit this, it would be done in the strictest secrecy. It will not be public knowledge, and any who must know will be sworn to silence on the matter. Whoever is chosen as your tutor, in return for their absolution from the crime they've committed in even being able to pass on this knowledge—knowledge that is *forbidden,* I will remind you—they are to cease their own practice of it outside of your lessons. Furthermore, Arlo Jarsdel's service as a *Court-Appointed Alchemist* will be tied indefinitely to the aid and protection of UnSeelie Spring. These are *my* terms."

A geas.

All promises made to the High King were geasa—promises bound by magic that would inflict all manner of dangerous and potentially lethal consequences on those who broke their conditions. As the life force of the Courts he ruled, Azurean's word was more than law.

Indefinitely.

Nausicaä opened her mouth.

She wanted to object, not necessarily to his strict stipulations, or the fact that this was going well, damn it, much better than she'd anticipated, but that it was shaping up that the High King was going to permit Riadne's "request" as well.

Was she the only one who saw what this was? Was she the only one who suspected this might be some sort of plot to hold Arlo hostage over the High King—Riadne, who'd never once opened her doors to any of the UnSeelie Spring, was now doing so for ironborn Arlo, who was barely recognized by her *own family* as a royal?

She wanted to protest.

But her argument died on her tongue.

Arlo looked pale, close to tears, highly uncomfortable, and so achingly used to being talked over. Here was a girl who tried so hard—always, *always*—to live up to others' expectations of her . . . but there, beneath it all, was a glimmer of genuine delight.

Arlo was *happy.*

She was being offered something that wouldn't have been such a big deal if people treated her the way she deserved, if she'd been *accepted* by those she most cared about and shouldn't have had to work to impress. She was happy, and Nausicaä didn't have the heart to take this rare reward of inclusion away from her.

"Of . . . of course, I would agree to any of your terms," said Arlo.

"Do you want to spend the summer with the Seelie Queen of Summer and her son, Prince Vehan?"

"*Yes.*" The reply was instant, breathless for fervor.

"Permission granted."

The room stood stunned for all of a moment.

Then . . .

"Your Majesty!"

"Sire!"

"Absolutely not!"

"I SAID, PERMISSION GRANTED!" Azurean bellowed, his poise at last cracking to show he wasn't as collected as he appeared to be. In a flurry of movement, he swept around, his emerald robe fanning out about him, and stomped back to his throne. At the heel of his boots sprang even more bluebells and crocuses and delicate snowdrops—flowers of spring, none of them looking all that healthy the way they drooped.

He threw himself into his seat and rubbed at his temples, knocking his Crown askew.

How much longer?

It was on everyone's mind.

How much longer would the High King last?

"Father, I wish to go with her."

Celadon stepped forward, every bit as anxious about this as Nausicaä, judging by the pallor of his face. Thank goodness for that. Celadon moved in front of the king and bent to his right knee to make his very formal request. "Your terms. Allow me to go with Arlo to ensure she's well taken care of and *safe*. She is a member of the Viridian household. She should have an UnSeelie Spring escort when abroad, and I volunteer."

There was silence again, and this time, Azurean's gaze lingered *hard* on his youngest son.

A moment ticked by.

Another.

The expression on Riadne's face was a little *too* unreadable right now. Nausicaä couldn't gauge at all what she felt about this pending compromise. But the way she *stared* at Celadon . . . She hadn't allowed her gaze to drift at all from the High King until now, but the way it devoured this perfect Azurean look-alike . . .

And then, Azurean sighed—*deflated*. "Yes, yes, permission granted."

He dropped a hand, and Celadon sprung forward to kiss the back of it, grateful. "Nausicaä," the High King continued when Celadon slid back into position, ignoring the glower his older brother directed at him.

"If you think I'm going to kiss you too, you can bet the fuck not—"

Azurean ignored her. "We will talk. Later. I will send for you, and you will tell me *everything* you know about the situation we're in."

"Fine." So long as he honored his promise, Nausicaä could deal with the rest. So long as Arlo received some deities-effing training, and Celadon was there to protect her when Nausicaä couldn't, everything would be okay.

Vehan was a spoiled brat, but he wouldn't let anything happen to Arlo.

Aurelian was an aggravating dick, but she could trust him to keep Arlo safe.

And Nausicaä would be there herself when she could be, and she would make sure Arlo was well warned about what she was walking into. Whatever Riadne was playing at, she wasn't going to touch a hair on Arlo's head.

Fine.

"Fine," the High King echoed wearily. "The room is dismissed. Rigel, escort Queen Riadne back to the Egress. Forgive me if I don't accompany you, Your Majesty."

Riadne inclined her head once more, tearing her eyes from Celadon at last and turning to sweep from the room that was slowly starting to sift apart.

Rigel, a blue-haired and pinched-faced fae, hurried forward from the sidelines where he and the other handful of personal attendants had been waiting. He made to escort Riadne from the room, but on its threshold she paused and turned around . . .

"One more thing."

Azurean lifted his head. The gathered officials all halted, as did their breath. Nausicaä's jaw twitched in the spike of her own bit of tension.

"I suppose it *is* that time—forgive me, I've been so busy with Solstice preparations that I almost completely forgot. But I wouldn't want to disappoint you." Riadne smiled, with so much malice that even Nausicaä had to fight a shiver. "I Challenge you, Azurean Lazuli-Viridian. I Challenge you for the Bone Crown, and all privileges and obligations that come with it."

"Challenge accepted," Azurean rumbled tiredly. It was a sound more appropriate to distant thunder. "Two moons full cycle, as usual, to name your Champion and date. Unless you wish to act on your Challenge here and now?"

Riadne shook her head, and the relief in the room was palpable.

"You will hear from me." Riadne bowed. "Lovely—as ever, Your Majesty," she said in parting, and swept from the room, and Nausicaä couldn't be the only one who felt like whatever game they'd just taken part in, they'd lost that round spectacularly.

Riadne stood beside her mother, her gaze on the floor with her spirits. Attendants flew around them, fussing over last-minute touches to the Luminous Palace's foyer in preparation for the High King's arrival.

All the white marble had been scrubbed and polished, almost as much as Riadne had been this morning, the streaks of gold that shocked through it like fresh bolts of lightning beneath her feet. Sunlight streamed from the newly washed stained-glass windows. Every recently buffed, yellow-toned jewel and gilded ornament winked in cheerful anticipation of such an honored guest. Fizzling, bright balls of electric light—enchanted to mirror the room's level of excitement—*danced* in place of the bulbs in the crystal chandelier above.

So much commotion.

So much *effort*.

It was Riadne's sixteenth birthday, but today she waited to celebrate someone else; no matter how she tried to keep her disappointment from showing, she couldn't help the hurt that whispered this was a touch unfair—as much as she actually liked when he and his son came to visit, the High King could have chosen *any* other day to make his annual rounds of the Courts.

"But he's chosen *this* day, so smarten yourself and stop pouting. Stand up straight. You want the world to revolve around you, silly child? Become the High Queen."

Become the High Queen.

This was something her mother told her often, whenever the opportunity arose and sometimes even when it didn't, just when Arina Lysterne felt like mocking her daughter, reminding her how dissatisfied she was that Riadne had been born a girl and not a boy.

No girl is ever going to be able to contend with High Prince Azurean to claim the Bone Crown for their Court, was her mother's second favorite reminder, because the folk might value their women better than humans did, but they were far from lacking in prejudice.

Riadne straightened her posture and composed herself as commanded. Her long black hair had been brushed through with a hot comb and ginger-scented oil, pinned tightly behind her head to match Queen Arina's strict, favored style. Her skin felt raw from an equally hot, lily-perfumed bath, the flower of Seelie Summer. Her stark white dress, overlaid with pretty glass beads and intricate golden lace, was fitted and bound so tightly around her that the butter-soft fabric did nothing to ease her discomfort. In appearance she looked very little like her mother, who was copper-haired and golden-toned and radiated warmth despite the subzero cold in her heart; in fashion they were twins, not that Riadne had any say in the matter.

She wasn't overly fond of dresses.

"They're here, Your Highness," said Garren, the teal-haired, fawn-toned, navy-eyed fae man who served as Queen Arina's steward. In his voluminous ivory and lemon-yellow robes, it was a little surprising to Riadne that he could dart up the marble staircase so quickly.

"Then open the doors," Arina hissed.

The guards scrambled to comply.

"Arina!" boomed the jovial High King of UnSeelie Spring, the first to step over the palace's threshold.

Enfys Viridian was a bear of a fae both in girth and height, his wild, russet beard and hair a bit like a mane around a face that was always smiling, always laughing, always pleasant, and covered in so many freckles that his deep sapphire flush and royal twilight glow had to work extra hard to be seen over them.

On his arm was Iris Lazuli, his queen, a beautiful fae woman, soft and plump in figure, a smile on her full face that made her blue-rose cheeks swell prettily, her hair so deep and glossy a black it shone like a rainbow in slants of the palace foyer's light.

And there, just beside them . . . the High Prince Azurean.

Riadne stood a little taller.

The Lysternes and the Viridians had always been close, given the proximity of their Courts, and Enfys and Nikolai—Riadne's late father—had been best of friends growing up. Azurean had been present for Riadne's birth celebration, only three years old at the time. He came every year on his father's visit to Seelie Summer and had been forced on Riadne when they were young, their fathers looking on in eager encouragement for them to become the same best of friends as they were.

And it had worked . . . of sorts.

Azurean was the only person Riadne didn't . . . hate to spend time with, and Riadne . . . well, she was the one fae girl he'd never dared to chase in his very long list of conquests, despite the fact that he confided in her almost everything and revolved around her when they were together like she was the very sun her Court worshipped.

Best friends—as much as they would ever be allowed to be; as much as Riadne was friends with anyone.

Quite unlike either parent, Azurean was tall and leanly toned, the handsome fairy-tale prince that human fantasy twittered about, with his windswept and slightly curling russet hair; jade green eyes framed by heavy, dark lashes; angular features and charming airs and a smile that bloomed like a flower.

It helped that he was stunningly powerful, too. Even more talented in his element and the Gift that determined the next head of their Court. People fawned over him wherever he went, and Riadne didn't exactly want *that* for herself, but the power to make people stop, to make them pay attention, to make them actually *see* her? *This* she could use a little more of.

Azurean was glowing today, even more so than usual, no doubt owing to the woman on his arm which . . . discombobulated Riadne to see, if only for a moment. Azurean, she knew, both from gossip and personal experience, having walked in on a number of his *dalliances* in the past few years, was quite a voracious fae when it came to romantic partners. But the shapely, blond, and blue-eyed Reseda Fleur—very pretty, even Riadne had to admit—was a first.

First to ever capture the High Prince's attention enough to secure a proposal.

And the High Prince couldn't take his eyes off her for more than a minute—Riadne noticed *that*, as well.

Arina and Enfys exchanged pleasant greetings. Iris extended a hand for Arina to kiss. Azurean took Arina's to do much the same. Riadne stood in silence through it all, maintained her graceful poise, the perfect porcelain doll that a princess was "supposed to be," according to her mother.

She stood, and she *observed*.

Did Azurean really love this young woman fixed to his side, she wondered, or was there truth to the other bits of gossip that floated around about him, to the one thing he didn't talk to even *her* about—that this marriage was one of arrangement, designed to temper the amorous High Prince of Spring and keep him from "sowing his oats" as widely as he'd been doing?

And why did Riadne even care?

"This beautiful young lady, she can't be my little Ria?"

A carefully concealed nudge to Riadne's shoulder—Garren prodded her forward, and Riadne pulled immediately out of her thoughts to bow her head to the High King. "Hello, Your High Majesty," she greeted politely. "It's good to see you again."

Enfys clapped a hand on her shoulder, and though Riadne's knees almost buckled, she didn't mind.

"You look like your father more and more every year—may Darkness keep him." Maybe not what a normal young girl wanted to hear, but Riadne felt the corner of her mouth twitch upward. She didn't mind Enfys one bit, even if he *had* chosen today for his grand arrival. He was the only person who held her up to her common, UnSeelie

Winter father—a man whom Riadne had loved dearly and missed terribly after his passing a few years back—and with kindness instead of the judgment with which she was often compared to her mother.

"Lovely." Enfys grinned. "As ever, my dear."

"Hello, Riadne," said Azurean, untangling himself at last from his fiancée. His father fell back to allow him forward, and Azurean strode to the head of the group, grinning ear to ear.

"Hello, Azurean."

Arina clicked her tongue, dismayed no doubt by the lack of due reverence. As High Prince, it was expected of *all* to use that title in addressing him, but Azurean had never demanded it of her—he was her *best friend*, after all, and lately it made something trill inside her that she had his personal permission to treat him so intimately.

No, instead of offense, his grin grew impossibly wider, a little more mischievous—an intimacy he seemed to reserve just for her. "It's your birthday today, don't think I've forgotten." He reached behind him to unclasp what turned out to be a sword strapped to his back, and held it out between them.

Riadne's eyes widened.

It was the most exquisite thing she'd ever seen, its hilt made of twists of gold and sapphire more vibrant a yellow than the jewels that adorned her mother's crown. Its sheath was solid gold as well, and the moment Azurean transferred it into her outstretched hands, she pulled out the sword to marvel at its electric-white glass blade.

"Be careful, it's sharp," Azurean warned with a wink.

"Azurean!" scolded Queen Iris. "That is no suitable present for a sixteen-year-old *lady*."

Enfys, meanwhile, barked a laugh. "I'm sorry, Lady Arina. It's all combat and pretty lasses in my useless son's head."

Arina shrugged her indifference. "She'll either learn to use it or hurt herself trying. Riadne, thank the High Prince for his gift."

Riadne looked up at her mother.

She looked down at her sword.

It was so big and so heavy that she wouldn't be able to wield it properly until she was physically stronger, but it was *beautiful* and it was *hers* and it was a better present than she would have received if the Viridians *hadn't* imposed themselves on her birthday. It was something she actually *wanted*, so they were thoroughly forgiven now, of course, for coming today—and *Azurean* . . .

She opened her mouth, intending to thank Azurean as instructed, gazing up at him like he'd just handed her the heavens . . . as though he *knew*—did he? It wouldn't surprise her that Azurean would be the one to even care to remember this custom when no one else so far seemed to, that sixteen was the age the fae boys of Winter were presented with their first blades, and if Nikolai were still alive, he would have certainly given this blade to her himself, the fact that she was a girl be damned.

She'd been so miserable, waking up this morning, knowing her mother would *never* gift such a thing to her herself. Her mother, who still pretended not to care in the least about the rival Court her own late husband had been born to . . . that her own daughter half belonged to, and loved.

Riadne had been so miserable . . . and now . . .

The sincerest *thank you* she'd ever said to anyone was on the tip of her tongue, but what she said instead was, "Will you teach me?"

Arina clicked her tongue.

Azurean laughed, as joyous and light as garden chimes. It was a nice sound, Riadne noted absently, and blushed a little when she caught how she'd just thought that sentiment—different than ever before.

"It would be my honor," he replied.

Enfys shook his head and chuckled. "Ah, but if only things were different and Reseda a little less wonderful. These two are quite the pair. They'd have made a good couple."

Longing—Riadne would swear that was what had flashed across Azurean's face just then, the briefest but no less intense flare of desire, which she'd caught a handful of times before, when her attention had turned to him quicker than he'd expected in random moments. And just like those times, when he realized Riadne had seen it now as she had then, his gaze cut away; he hid himself entirely behind his carefully manicured, bland smile; Riadne was left with wondering after what had consumed his thoughts.

"If only." Arina frowned, oblivious to what had just passed between her daughter and the High King's son, and as though this situation was Riadne's fault, that she was her mother's only child, the one to inherit the Summer Gift that marked succession; as though the one use she could have served as a girl was now wasted—this match between their houses that would have elevated the Lysternes in the hierarchy of Court aristocracy if it weren't for the fact that such unions were forbidden between Heads of the Courts directly, and their succeeding heirs.

Another disappointment for her mother to tally under Riadne's name.

"Well, Your Majesty, it's been a long trip. I'm sure you'd like to see the rooms we've prepared for your stay? Goodness, but it's been almost a full *year* since we've had the honor of receiving you."

"The ruddy Goblin Rebellion. I tell you, Arina, I never miss your husband more than when there's a head or twelve that need cleaving right from the shoulders . . ."

Attendants poured forth as the High King and Queen of Seelie Summer spoke, joining the ones Enfys had brought with him. Arina swept out an arm, and the High King started forward, launching into further conversation about the war that was high on the list of everyone's concerns of late.

Queen Iris followed, demure at his side, but the hard glint in her eye when she scowled at Azurean remained. He'd misstepped somehow, had perhaps been a little too good to Riadne in gifting her such an exquisite thing that would undoubtedly strike up a rumor or two by morning.

Rolling his own eyes, Azurean wrapped himself back up in Reseda and followed his parents, ruffling Riadne's head on the way by, and that was . . . tolerable. He'd given her an excellent gift, after all.

Clutching tightly to her sword lest someone try to take it away, she turned and trailed silently after the Eight Great Courts' Highest nobility, already envisioning her very first lesson with her present, and the way Azurean might look at her *then*, when she became the best swordswoman the Courts had ever known.

CHAPTER 3

Vehan

———⌇———

"GATHER 'ROUND, CLASS, GATHER 'round!" Emiradian Gaumond, the Nevada Fae Academy's illustrious professor of the Elemental Arts, beckoned his students closer with a singular wave of his hands.

Vehan stepped forward. His classmates followed far more hesitantly, shuffling only a few extra steps toward the broad, hard-jawed sidhe fae who was quite old even by folk standards. His close-cropped hair had gone from black to completely gray, and age had stamped itself into the deep lines in the earthen-brown skin around his quartz eyes.

A war hero famous for his role in securing Court victory in the long-ago Goblin Rebellion, Professor Gaumond was a popular fae at their school. His many years meant he also had quite a number of stories, and some of Vehan's favorite memories of his time at the Academy were the classes when they'd managed to coax their professor into sharing tales from his past. Unfortunately, Emiradian Gaumond was also quite intense. And sometimes he forgot what it was like to not have centuries of advanced military training to mediate the dangerous situations his *slightly* very unorthodox lessons *occasionally* often put his students in.

Vehan had to wonder if this was one of those times.

A thick cover of dark clouds weighed on the sky above. The way they churned and rumbled threatened an impressive storm building in their depths, and Vehan could already smell the sweet, earthy scent of ozone in the air. He could feel static energy against his skin that made the hairs on the back of his neck and arms stand at attention, could taste the rain that the heavens were moments away from dumping on their heads.

The sweeping view from the peak of Yosemite National Park's Half Dome mountain might be better appreciated if they weren't a group of children standing around in a brewing thunderstorm on a massive slab of slippery granite jutting thousands of feet above sea level. But Vehan doubted they were here to appreciate the scenery anyhow.

"Come on, snap to it!" Professor Gaumond barked, indifferent to the gusts of wind that whipped his hair and sunny-gold robes around him. "Seelie Summer fae afraid of a little lightning? To think I've lived to see the day."

Heaving a sigh, Vehan took another couple of steps toward the center of the peak. The rest of the class moved more boldly now to crowd in closer too, as though determined to prove they weren't the cowards their professor suggested—all except Theodore Reynolds, heir to the second of three Seelie Summer royal families. An arm slipped through and locked around Vehan's, and only Theo would be so bold as to latch onto him like this. Sure enough, when Vehan looked to his side, he found short black curls and deep amber eyes framed by long lashes, high-flung cheekbones and finely crafted features, and a copper-warm complexion with a faint morning glow about it, indicative of an undiluted royal bloodline. Theodore was exceptionally pretty.

He was also currently scowling.

"As your possible future husband," said Theo, his tone as dark as the day had grown, "if I die here today, you're contractually obligated to rip out all your hair and wail through the streets in mourning."

Vehan nodded solemnly. "Of course, that sounds perfectly reasonable."

"*And* the person you marry in my stead can't be hotter than I am."

"That would be impossible anyhow. There's no higher rating than you, a ten, after all."

Theo sniffed and patted Vehan's arm. "Make sure to mention that in your eulogy."

"You two should be paying attention."

Vehan's head turned to his left, where Aurelian stood, arms folded across his chest, the tattooed foliage that covered every inch of skin on his right arm, from shoulder blade to fingertips, peeking out from under the short sleeve of his stark white NFA polo.

His was another pretty face that was also scowling at Vehan, lightly tanned and paired with strong, sharply-carved features and brown hair shaved to a stubble around ears that sported multiple silver piercings. Normally, the longer, lavender top of his hair fell like a curtain over his molten gold eyes, but the wind was currently giving Vehan an unobstructed view of their ever-gleaming intensity.

As a lesidhe fae, whose magic was different from that of the sidhe, this class wasn't mandatory for Aurelian to take. In fact, it was a complete waste on him, because even if he *could* command the elements like the sidhe fae were able to do, he was Autumn-born. He wouldn't have been able to bend lightning in the first place. But as Vehan's retainer and future steward, it was expected that they do pretty much everything together. There were two thickly built palace bodyguards standing back by the portal that had brought them here, but Vehan knew without needing telling that Aurelian had been tasked as additional protection whenever they were outside the palace.

Aurelian was here because he had to be.

Theo leaned in. "I will, however, permit you to marry another ten," he added suggestively in Vehan's ear, and Vehan felt his face flare hot with embarrassment. He jerked his elbow into Theo's side to shut him up, knew full well without looking that Theo was waggling his brows at Aurelian, who rolled *his* eyes and frowned even deeper in response, and looked pointedly away.

"Reynolds! Lysterne! Eyes forward," Professor Gaumond snapped. Vehan quickly drew himself straight, still a touch blue in the face. "Now, as I was saying, your final examinations are soon at hand. They won't be easy. You're a senior, graduating class, and both bar and expectations are high for each of you—some more than others."

The professor paused to fix his gaze back on Vehan, to which Vehan squared his jaw, relaxed his shoulders, tried to stand even taller to show that he knew exactly how many eyes would be on his performance and was nothing but *encouraged* by the challenge. "It is my duty to ensure that those of you who are of age come graduation are prepared to face one of the most important tests you'll ever undertake: your registration as lightning wielders of the Seelie Summer Court."

He held up a large hand and curled his fingers into a fist. The sky gave an ominous, bone-rattling *boom* that echoed off the rock, and fissures of crackling electricity zipped through the clouds. Several of the students exclaimed in awe over the effect; a few of them shrank back, even more skittish now than before.

Not every sidhe fae could exert control over the elements, and in the ones whose magic was strong enough to manage it, there were varying degrees. Given how dangerous even a sliver of this power could be, it was required throughout the Courts for sidhe fae to be registered upon Maturity (or after graduation, if Maturity occurred while in school), and after that, reassessed every handful of decades that passed.

As the Crown Prince of Seelie Summer and heir to the ruling royal family, if Vehan couldn't achieve a classification of at least a Three on the five-scale ranking, his ascension would be called into serious question. He wasn't too concerned about that—a key component to Class Three element wielding was the ability to take the electricity one absorbed and bend it into a different shape, like a weapon, which Vehan had already perfected.

"It won't be easy," Professor Gaumond repeated, almost as though he could read Vehan's mind. "The examination of your elemental control will test many things: How much electrical current you can safely wield. What you can do with it. Which sources you can successfully draw from. There's a considerable difference between drawing on the electricity made readily available to us by human invention, and . . ." He paused, grinned, and once he was sure he had everyone's attention, pulled down his fist as though yanking on some invisible lever.

And with his hand came down a fat, sizzling bolt of lightning.

". . . being able to pull raw energy from the air."

There were several more oohs and aahs. Fina shrieked in alarm and jolted backward, colliding with Kine, her brother. Vehan's eyes widened as though that lightning had called out directly to him, and a sudden insatiable hunger filled him with a desperation to touch it too, as their professor had done. Professor Gaumond and Vehan's mother—these were two of the very few Class Four lightning wielders Vehan had ever met. There hadn't been a registered Five in over a millennium, and it was true what his professor had said, that there was a massive jump between what separated the top tier classifications from the three lower ranks.

Because lightning was difficult to harness. It was firm defiance, had a will of its own, and much like its counterpart *fire* possessed great potential for harm if the wielder's control slipped even a little. They'd been studying the theory of this particular art their entire senior year and had been forbidden to practice on their own or with anyone other than a licensed wielder. And now that the time had come for some genuine training, Vehan could hardly keep still for how he *itched* to take this next step.

Professor Gaumond flexed his hand.

Vehan could see the charge he'd absorbed running like pale yellow veins beneath his skin.

"As you've learned in class, a single thunderstorm can contain the potential energy equivalent of up to *ten* of humankind's atomic bombs. I expect that of the few of you who are already Mature, fewer will be able to coax even a spark of your element from the sky—which at bare minimum will be required of you to register as a Class Three element wielder, I'll remind you—let alone absorb and return it." Professor Gaumond lifted his hand once more, and with a flourish of his fingers, sent all the electricity he'd just absorbed into the air above them. Everyone watched in rapt attention as it burst apart and scattered like a fireworks display. "You will all be tested the same, though, and in an environment similar to this. I thought it best you get some *real* experience, none of the quaint and cushioned practice rooms they'd have you faff around in instead. Well? How about it? Who will be the first to show their classmates how it's done?"

Vehan's hand shot high in the air so quickly he almost struck Aurelian in the face.

His was one of only two that did, of the eleven who were already Mature, of the twenty-two who made up this class. The other belonged to Theodore, whose hand had risen only a fraction slower.

"Enthusiasm! That's what I like to see. And from our two young royals, no less! Excellent, excellent—Reynolds, you first, if only because I think this is the first time in all the years I've been teaching you that you've ever *volunteered* for participation."

Apparently no longer fearful of slipping off the mountain, Theo extracted himself from Vehan and sauntered to where their professor stood. He turned and bowed dramatically at his classmates. Vehan rolled his eyes and booed the display, but clapped along with everyone else regardless.

"All right, young man, enough posturing. Remember what I taught you in class?" Professor Gaumond moved aside, falling back to his students to watch as Theo drew in a deep breath and relaxed himself on its exhale. "It's all in the stance. Good tall posture, steady breathing—loosen up those shoulders a little more, that's it! The less tension you carry, the better your magic will flow. Now raise your dominant hand straight above your head, fingers splayed. No curling that fist just yet."

Theo did as instructed.

In the time it took for him to get into proper position, rain had finally begun to fall. Nothing more than a scatter of droplets, but Vehan now wished he'd listened to the professor's warning to bring their waterproof windbreakers.

Something slipped around his shoulders, catching him by surprise.

Vehan looked down at himself, at the uniform-issue ivory white jacket someone had just draped across him. He saw the emblazoned *Bessel* in shimmery gold letters just visible on the left sleeve and frowned, lifting his gaze to Aurelian. "Thank you, but . . . this is yours; *you* should wear it. I'll be okay."

Aurelian gave him a pursed sort of look that Vehan could almost *hear* saying: *I would if you'd brought your own.* His smile more of an apologetic grimace, Vehan nodded his gratitude and turned back to observing Theo; there was often no arguing with Aurelian, and in the past few days, things had been almost *decent* between them, so he was keen to keep him happy.

"Good, *good*, excellent form," the professor went on saying, and Vehan forced himself to focus on the lesson again instead of the fallen-leaves and mossy-forest scent of Aurelian's jacket as he shrugged it properly on. "Take note of this, those of you who wish to try this yourselves today. *That's* how you want to look."

Several of Vehan's classmates snickered. Theo grinned cheekily back at them. He dropped a wink at Vehan, and Vehan made a show of shaking his head. Professor Gaumond clapped his hands together to regain control of his class. "Yes, yes, no doubt young Reynolds is all too used to people wishing they looked like him in general. If you're more interested in playing around, I can bring you all to a park instead? No? That's what I thought. Reynolds, close your eyes."

Theo closed his eyes.

"All right, now I want you to block out everything but my instruction. Ignore the wind, the rain, your classmates. Forget you're standing on a mountain. I want you to concentrate only on breathing and relaxation and the core of all that magic inside you. Picture yourself able to touch it. Give it texture, weight. Is it cool to the touch or hot? Don't tell us—just concentrate, until the only thing that exists in this moment is you and your bond with your element."

Most of the class had abandoned their anxiety and hesitation now. Many had crept closer, curious to see if Theo could actually do what was so rare even among registered wielders; probably they also hoped that Theo would get himself zapped in the process, but Vehan wasn't paying much attention to any of that. He was so enraptured by the sight before him that he'd near forgotten how to breathe. He could almost see himself standing in Theo's place, his hand raised just as his friend's currently was, could *feel* the core of his own power already beginning to stir in anticipation.

"Good, good. Now, in your own time, once you've a good feel for the energy inside you, I want you to picture yourself letting a bit of it go. Slowly, just a little, let your magic trickle out and reach for the current above you. You'll have to direct it—picture it flowing upward, the electricity in the clouds reaching down to meet it. It will take however long it needs to take, and remember, slow and steady! I'll be here to catch anything you can't control, so worry not for yourself or your fellow students. It's just you and your power. Once you can feel the lightning reach back, once you can see it make contact in your mind, close your fingers around it and *pull.*"

Theo's eyes remained closed, and for a solid minute longer, nothing happened.

The raindrops grew a little fatter, a little more frequent, and the tang of ozone heavier on the tongue. But the clouds remained unresponsive, until . . .

A loud *crack* split the day once again.

A singular thread of lightning—thin and there and gone in a flicker—shot from the sky toward Theo's fingers. It didn't quite make contact, but this was still much more than perhaps even their professor had expected from any of them today, let alone on a student's first "official" try. Vehan's eyes grew wide in awe.

His weren't the only to do so. Fina actually exclaimed, her shriek a bit more delighted this time, and Kine was muttering something that sounded a lot like disappointment. A handful of students vocalized their amazement over Theo's achievement, too. Professor Gaumond gave a fierce roar of approval, so loud even the fresh clap of thunder was quiet in comparison, and he broke into wild applause that everyone was quick to join.

When Theo opened his eyes, he looked a bit confused. He clearly had no idea how close he'd come to touching *real lightning* and on his *very first attempt*.

"You could look a bit happier!" Vehan teased, shooting forward. He laughed and grinned as he raised both hands in the air. Theo, dazed but brightening quickly, raised his, too, to clap them together. It was then that a few of their other classmates surged forward to offer their own congratulations.

"Well done, Lord Reynolds, well done!" Professor Gaumond was more than delighted, actually *proud*, to be using a title at all for Theo when normally he refused to address even Vehan with one unless absolutely necessary. "That was quite the impressive display. You've Class Three registration in the bag with that! Oh, *well* done." He strode forward, shooing everyone else back. "There's a glowing report for your parents on the way, son. You should be *very* pleased with yourself right now, more than you usually are, even! All right, go on back to the others—Lysterne, you're up. Let's see what stuff *you're* made of."

"If you die, I'm stealing your throne," said Theo very sweetly.

"Yeah, yeah, get in line," Vehan muttered, aiming a playful blow at his friend, who laughed and dodged it easily before darting off back to the class.

Vehan moved quickly to occupy the exact place where Theo had stood. His every nerve was alight with excitement, the magic inside him sparking and eager to prove it, too, could do this. He shook himself out, trying to burn off some of his adrenaline and force himself to relax. To breathe. He thrust his dominant hand in the air and willed himself to scrap together some semblance of calm.

Professor Gaumond stepped away, circling Vehan to examine his form. "Very good, yes, excellent posture, minimal tension, nice deep breathing. Now close your eyes. Picture yourself safe and alone. It's only you out here, you and your power. Reach for it. Give your element tangible shape inside you. Focus on it and it alone. Nothing else matters right now but you and the energy in your core."

It took a moment longer for Vehan's breathing to even out, for his jitteriness to pass and his thoughts to settle. At last, he sank into a more tranquil state of being. He'd always been able to feel his magic warm and fizzling and incredibly malleable whenever he reached within himself to touch it, but he was a little more aware of it now . . . even if it required stretching just a little deeper than what he was used to.

The well of his power ran deep; this was already known by himself and his mother *and* his professors. It was deepening by the day, it seemed, requiring constant upkeep and refilling, thanks to his recent Maturity, and more and more it felt like he was perpetually running on low. Until the well plateaued and he was practiced and comfortable with what he carried, he supposed he'd just have to continue getting used to extending himself further to touch it, recharging himself more often—and of course, exercising caution when attempting to utilize it.

If he didn't, he ran the risk of Surging.

He'd only *just* come of age and into his power properly, narrowly escaping the Rebound that all those with considerable stores of magic were in danger of succumbing to, where it might turn against them and destroy them from the inside out. Over the next decade, his aging would start to slow to a crawl; the features that marked him as fae would grow more pronounced; his well of magic would extend deeper and deeper and necessitate more and more lessons on how to control it, and until then would be easily provoked by outside influences as well as Vehan's own emotions.

A Surge could be just as dangerous as a Rebound. A Rebound was magic with nowhere to go, turning on its host to shred through flesh and blood in desperation for escape. A Surge was magic forgetting to *pace* itself, pouring forth all at once to empty one's core in a single burst, and in someone like Vehan, with so *much* to give, the mere shock of such a drastic hollowing-out could kill him easily. And all that power unleashed could just as easily kill others around him.

But Vehan was a Lysterne and a *prince*; his considerable potential was more a cause for celebration than concern.

Everyone expected greatness from him, after all.

Vehan expected it too.

He could do this—*would* do this—and tick every other box in the Class Three registry, and Class Four as well, and his mother would be *proud*. A true light of the Courts, they'd call him, a legend just as the Seelie Summer Founder had been—fated for greatness.

"When you're ready, Lysterne. When you can feel your magic in the tips of your fingers and picture clearly it making contact with its natural source, close your fist around it and pull."

Vehan did.

He could see it in his mind's eye, his magic—however oddly sluggish—reaching up in a tendril of electric-yellow energy. He could feel it—however oddly dulled—a fizzling warmth in his hands. It took a moment or so longer than usual, but soon enough his magic was ready to burst from the tips of his fingers, and he'd always been more than good both with its use and control; this felt natural—*right*. This was what Vehan had been born to do; it should be easy.

But for some reason, even in his mind he couldn't coax the storm above to answer his call.

It wasn't reaching *back*.

Not a glimmer. Not a flash. Not a here-and-gone *zap* as what Theo had managed.

Mouth pressing flat in determination, Vehan dug down deeper, gutted into his core for a little more magic. It was a little like rooting out a tooth and maybe even hurt a little, if he was being honest, but once a bit more of his power gave way to his command, it flowed effortlessly through him, up to his fingers, no trouble at all . . . So what was the problem? The lightning remained unresponsive, and Vehan felt his calm begin to curdle.

A horrible thought occurred to him, creeping in with his anxiety—what if he *couldn't* do this?

He hadn't practiced *this* at home yet with his tutors. His mother had *wanted* him to, of course, but Vehan had been so insistent on fairness, on waiting until their first real lesson with natural lightning before practicing at home because he'd been so sure it would be so easy, and he'd wanted to impress everyone with his "raw talent," give them no question he was meant to fill his mother's role as Head of Seelie Summer—and now . . . *now* he was making a *fool* of himself.

Please, he begged his magic. *Everyone's watching, just give me a flicker, something.* Any*thing*.

His magic crackled and churned in his hand. It continued to spark in his veins. Vehan could still feel it, buzzing and eager to charge at the sky, a building pressure ready to burst forth at any moment, but the sky simply wasn't having it.

And what did *that* mean, this blatant rejection by the natural source of his power?

He tried not to think about it. Biting his lip, his confidence wavering, Vehan pushed himself a little harder.

More of his magic welled up in his hand.

He ignored the ache in the pit of his core, the little flare in the back of his mind that warned him to *stop*. All the while, his palm grew from warm to hot, his power from fizzling to sharp, angry jolts that weren't exactly painful but shocked unpleasantly across his nerves.

Still the sky ignored him.

"Take your time, Lysterne, there's no rush," said Professor Gaumond.

"Is he having trouble?" Vehan heard a student hiss.

"Is he not able to do it?"

"*Theodore* did it . . ."

"*Oooh*, how *embarrassing*."

The whispers sounded delighted.

Screwing his eyes closed even tighter, Vehan tried to focus, tried to shut them out, but that was getting harder to do.

A moment became another, became another.

He tried to reach deeper within, to pull more of his magic forward, because this couldn't be it, it couldn't be all he had to give, not when he'd thrown around so much more in mere sparring sessions so many times before. He'd stand here all day if that's what it took. He'd stand here all night. He'd break past whatever damned barrier had thrown itself up inside him that was blocking him from accessing his full potential, channel everything he had into this and risk a deities-damned Surge to prove himself . . . to prove he could summon lightning . . . could be the prince he needed to be to keep the Lysternes on the throne and his mother happy. "*Damn it*," he swore under his breath.

And he had to admit it now, the shocks in his veins actually stung. His magic was beginning to splutter and—was it possible? Was it about to *give out* over so little?

Vehan gritted his teeth—no, he was *going to do this*. This was nerves and nothing more.

Someone's hand wrapped around his arm and forced it down to his side.

Vehan's eyes flew open. He blinked at Aurelian, who stood in front of him, glaring not at Vehan but their professor as though irritated with him for not stepping in himself. "Let *go*," Vehan growled, incensed by the interruption, *angry* to what would be a surprising degree if he had it in him to care right now. He tried to shake himself free of Aurelian's grip, but lesidhe strength was greater than sidhe, and Aurelian wouldn't yield. "Aurelian, I said let go of me. I almost have it!"

Aurelian's glare shifted to him.

He lifted his free hand and wordlessly wiped at something on Vehan's upper lip. When he then held that finger up for Vehan's inspection, and Vehan saw the smear of sapphire there from what surely had to be the barest perceptible rivulet of blood trickling from his nose, for some reason it only made him angrier. "It's *fine*," he hissed, sounding so unlike himself. "Let me *go*."

He was Vehan Lysterne, Crown Prince of Seelie Summer; he couldn't possibly be this *weak*. This was only a test, his first attempt. It didn't mean he couldn't manipulate lightning at all—he knew this in the part of him that was still rational. And . . . this wasn't the first time Vehan had noticed that ever since the cavum factory, ever since encountering whatever alchemic magic had knocked his powers out of commission inside that facility, his magic had been acting strangely. But if he gave up now, it would be in front of his entire class. In front of the children of Seelie Summer's most influential dignitaries, the one-day elite of this Court who'd remember this moment as a *failure* when they were older, and the only thing keeping them in line was their respect for his power.

Failure, right after the success of a rival Seelie Summer heir . . .

What was his mother going to say?

A chuckle, low and darkly amused.

A voice that could almost be Vehan's, but wasn't . . .

What's wrong, Little Light? Have you lost your spark?

"*Enough*," Aurelian rumbled back. The gold of his eyes flared dangerously bright. They searched Vehan's own, alarm shining in their depths, as though he had just seen something disturbing that was there and gone too quickly to say for certain it was truly there. "That's enough, Your Highness. You need a break."

Vehan felt his eyes begin to sting now, too. He sneered, because it was this or cry, and if he did *that* he might as well go home and put a bow on the throne he'd be just *giving* away. "I don't need a deities-damned—"

"Take one anyhow."

Clapping his hands loudly together, Professor Gaumond strode forward. The air between Vehan and Aurelian was tense in a different sort of way than was usual these days. Vehan wasn't the picture of composure like Theo or High Prince Celadon, but he could count on one hand the amount of times he'd ever bared his teeth like this at *Aurelian*. He didn't like it. It wasn't fair to Aurelian. It wasn't even Aurelian he was angry at—his frustration and irritation was purely at himself—but the fact that Aurelian was bearing the brunt of it anyhow and didn't even seem to mind only made Vehan's sour mood worse.

"Not to worry, Lysterne," said Professor Gaumond, placing a hand on Vehan's shoulder. Despite his words, Vehan detected a note of disappointment in his tone. "It's no competition. It was remarkable that Reynolds even managed it at all, and I have faith you'll astound us soon enough in this department."

Vehan was certain his eyes sparked as hotly as the charge that had just been in his hand.

It's no competition.

Except that it was.

He continued to glare at Aurelian. If at all bothered by this, nothing in Aurelian's face hinted as much, but he still seemed caught on examining Vehan's eyes, like there was something wrong with *them*, too.

"Back to the group with you," the professor commanded. "Both of you. You can give it another go, Lysterne, once the rest have had their shot."

"No need," Vehan snarled. "I'm done."

Extracting himself from Aurelian's jacket, he tossed it to him in a ball and stormed back toward the portal.

He heard the professor call after him. "Where are you going, young man? Class isn't over!"

He heard Aurelian scoff at his behavior.

He was acting childishly, throwing such a tantrum over nothing, but he also didn't care. He strode through the group, which parted like a shoal of fish before him, and pointedly ignored making eye contact with anyone. It wasn't until he'd returned to school and barred himself up in the bathroom, until he was bent over the sink and scrubbing his face of the blood that was now streaming from his nose that he realized just how close he'd actually pushed himself to breaking.

And it hadn't been enough.

"*Stupid*," he hissed at his pale, blood-smeared reflection—and winced when a sudden, violent throb rippled through his chest.

Clawing at the hem of his polo, he rucked it up enough to reveal the array etched into the skin over his heart, and was it just his imagination or did the intricate, pearly scarring there look a little darker blue than normal, too? Like it was aggravated.

He released his shirt and slammed his palms against the sink.

Another chuckle in the back of his head . . .

Once again the parody of Vehan's voice taunted him.

How long this time until you figure it out, I wonder . . .

The marble cracked.

Vehan wondered in a detached sort of way how much longer until he did the same.

CHAPTER 4

Aurelian

~~~~~

AURELIAN WASN'T SUPPOSED TO be here. He wasn't supposed to use the Endless Egress without permission, and certainly not to whisk himself back to Autumn territory. But thanks to his high-ranking status in this new life of secrets and pretend, Aurelian had figured out how to work Riadne's specialized portal, able to access any place its user could picture, at just about the same time he figured out that the guards who patrolled this space could be bought for the right price.

Never their silence; Riadne was always apprised of what he did, and he was always punished in some way for flouting the rule, but she still allowed him to break it again and again, probably because she enjoyed the way it crushed his spirit each time he had to return.

Escape was an illusion, and every excursion reinforced that, but it was worth it because it meant that whenever Aurelian was feeling particularly troubled or just missed home so strongly he could no longer bear it, he could come to this patch of the German countryside, "not supposed to" be damned.

The effects of being here were almost instant.

Much of whatever tension drove Aurelian to this spot melted away simply for the change in scenery, for the woodsmoke-scented fresh air and the black and red-brown rooftops of his former sleepy village, the rolling emerald hills and distant gray mountains and verdant trees scattered all around.

Given the time difference between here and Nevada, it was currently well past midnight, the perfect time for brooding, as Vehan liked to call it. Sitting beneath his favorite oak tree on the top of a modest hill that overlooked the handful of houses below, Aurelian was doing just that. No one would spot him up here in the dark, and if one of the humans who made up the majority of this village woke for any reason and happened to glance outside, they'd assume him an elf of some sort and leave him to his business.

European sensibilities—Aurelian missed that, too.

"Do you mind if I sit with you?"

Aurelian said nothing.

He wasn't surprised by this sudden question—had heard the air's tinkling shiver as it admitted another through from the palace—and made no move to show he was listening, but neither did he intimate that he wanted the speaker to leave.

He never minded Vehan's presence, even when he was angry with him.

In his periphery, he saw Vehan lower himself to the grass. No longer in his uniform, he was dressed in loose pants of heavy gold linen and a plain white tank, baring the strength of his sun-tanned arms. There was an artificial ginger and lily-floral scent to him, and his inky black hair was damp, which meant he'd showered recently and therefore must have spent the rest of his day in physical training with his combat instructor, Zale.

One mystery solved, then.

Aurelian had been in too much of a mood himself to track down where the prince had fled to after his dramatic exit from class.

"I owe you an apology."

There was a beat in which neither of them said anything.

"Was that the apology?" Aurelian asked, still keeping his sight forward.

Vehan released a sigh. "I shouldn't have snapped at you like that earlier. I'm sorry. I was frustrated, and . . . I don't know. It's no excuse, but . . ." He trailed off, folding his arms around his knees to hug them closer to his chest.

To be perfectly honest with himself, it *had* stung that Vehan had turned his temper on him like that. It wasn't as though they'd never fought before. Even in their happy youth they'd found plenty to argue over, a lesidhe born to human customs and a sidhe raised on the peak of fae extravagance. But ever since Aurelian had grown wise to Riadne's scheming and why she'd brought him here to begin with, he couldn't help but notice the meaner edge their disagreements had acquired.

Sitting out here like a ghost haunting a past he couldn't let go of, it was hard not to dwell on the fact that all the hard work he was putting into pushing Vehan away was paying off. Aurelian had poured his all into forcing distance between them to ensure that Vehan's value of him depreciated enough that his mother couldn't use him as a weapon against them *both*.

This was what he'd wanted.

This was exactly what he'd been steeling himself to endure.

But still, this *hurt*.

He'd expected that, but there was the theory of a thing and then reality, and no matter what lies Aurelian told himself *or* Vehan, it was painful to see them growing apart.

But that wasn't what had upset Aurelian the most.

"I'll apologize to Professor Gaumond, too," Vehan finally continued. "It was childish of me to storm out of class like that."

"It was," Aurelian replied, mirroring Vehan to draw his knees to his chest and rest his chin on his arms. Still he refused to look at the prince. "But I'm glad you did. I'll take theatrics over watching you kill yourself to impress a bunch of spoiled sidhe fae."

And however much . . . *sharper* Vehan's anger had been today, it hadn't been as concerning to him as what he thought he'd seen: a flash of red, consuming the prince's electric-blue eyes; as what he thought he'd felt: a distinct and wholly *not Vehan* darkness bleeding into his aura.

But it had just been his imagination, Aurelian told himself.

That flash . . . it had just been Aurelian's anxiety keyed up by the situation.

Vehan turned his face to him, his cheek pressed flat where his chin had just been. He smiled softly, a simple quirk of his mouth that was far too attractive for the irritation Aurelian wanted to hold onto right now, and there was no trace of that red anywhere in him.

Vehan was safe.

Aurelian could breathe—it was going to be okay, for a little longer, at least.

"Do you think maybe we're *both* dramatic?" Vehan arched a dark brow. "That wasn't going to kill me, Aurelian."

"You could have Surged." Aurelian did *not* pout, but his tone was just shy of sulky, because the crux of the problem was that Vehan had demonstrated a recklessness Aurelian had thought—*hoped*—he'd long grown out of, a recklessness Aurelian had been seeing more and more lately, little signs he'd been trying to write off as anything else. Skulking through a Goblin Market for clues, chasing after drug-dealing goblins in the Nevada desert for information on forbidden magic and disappearing humans, investigating mysterious factories responsible for both, and this whole business with philosopher's stones that really didn't involve them, and yet . . . Aurelian's glance flickered first to Vehan's eyes, and then his chest, where he knew that deadly array was etched into his skin. He cleared his throat and returned his eyes forward. "You're the Crown Prince of Seelie Summer; it *matters* what happens to you. And it's my duty to keep you safe."

"Your duty," Vehan echoed, his tone falling distinctly flat. It recovered quickly—the prince as good as any fae at shielding his truer thoughts—but Aurelian hadn't missed it. "Can I be candied for a moment?"

That *almost* won a twitch of amusement. Aurelian's determination to learn human English without the need for magic to act as translator meant the inevitable, initial difficulty with certain words that sounded too similar. "Candid" and "candied" had given him trouble, much to Vehan's amusement as children. His use of it now was an olive branch Aurelian wanted very much to accept, but really shouldn't.

Not if he wanted to maintain this current rift between them.

"What *happened* to us?"

Aurelian stiffened.

"We were *friends*, Aurelian. We did *everything* together. I even . . . well . . ." The prince stumbled over his words now, suddenly awkward in a way that made Aurelian curious as to what he'd been about to say, and at the same time horrified because he was pretty sure he knew.

Of course he knew.

Riadne knew, too, and this was exactly why Aurelian had put extra effort into pulling away. He didn't think he could handle rejecting any love confessions tonight on top of everything else.

"The point is," Vehan continued, and Aurelian released a small, quiet sigh of relief, "we barely talk anymore or spend any time together that isn't school, or training, or *duty*, and I get that you're kind of pissed my mother roped you into being my steward when you had other things planned for your life, but is it honestly *that* bad? To be my partner in this?"

Aurelian opened his mouth. He had no idea what he was about to say, but thankfully, Vehan held up a hand. "You know what, don't answer that. You don't have to justify yourself. I'm sorry for that too, that you've had to give up your whole way of life for one you wouldn't have picked if you had the choice. I'm not stupid, I know you're unhappy here. Or, well . . ." He gestured around. "Not *here*, but in Nevada. Just . . . can we have it out for a moment? No dodging the subject or confusing half-truths, just straight out, are we still friends? Do you even still like me? Because *honestly* . . ." His voice trembled, and Aurelian couldn't help himself; he turned to face Vehan fully at last.

He regretted it for the way moonlight made Vehan's perpetually messy hair even darker than black and his Seelie royal glow even cooler in his skin; for the way shadows enhanced his sharpening features to throw across his face a glimpse of the man he'd grow to be, and those too-bright blue eyes watching him back as though the answer he gave now would determine their entire future.

Aurelian could see it, like the deities descending to point out the two paths down which his life could conceivably go.

He could lie to Vehan, outright lie to him, and the enormity of that lie would make him sick for days, he suspected, but he could tell him *no*. He could tell him they were no longer friends and finally put an end to the feelings Vehan harbored for him, even if he doubted he could forget his own. The prince would turn to Theodore, then, as he was already starting to do, and Theodore—whom Aurelian had his own suspicions about that would one day need to be addressed—had wealth and power and family far more able to protect Vehan from the queen. It was a better match by far. Theodore would be good to him, and Riadne would lose interest in toying with Aurelian. Maybe she'd even let him go. Maybe she'd let him and his family escape back here to the countryside, where they'd been safe and happy and . . . without Vehan, the boy Aurelian loved so much he'd been willing to play the Seelie Summer Queen's games in the first place.

Or . . .

He could tell Vehan the truth. That they *were* still friends. Vehan would fight even harder for the scraps of affection Aurelian dared to let show (and more often, couldn't help but let slip), and Aurelian would continue to be trapped in this purgatory of pretending he didn't care that everything was unravelling around him, that something wasn't just a little bit off with Vehan's mental health, and that the Seelie Summer Queen wasn't plotting to overthrow the *world*, for all he knew. She'd brought him to her Court to *die*, and he would if he didn't keep up with her. But if he told the prince this one great truth, they'd still be Aurelian and Vehan—the two of them against it all as it had always been before and as he desperately wanted it still to be.

"Honestly," continued Vehan, "I think you kind of *hate* me now."

"I don't."

The words were out of his mouth before he could think any more on his answer.

He still had no idea what to say, felt caught between what he *should* do and what he *wanted* to do. But he knew he didn't want Vehan to think he hated him. If he didn't say anything too obvious one way or another, could he circumvent this terrible ultimatum? Defer it, if only for a little while longer?

"You don't?" Vehan echoed warily.

Aurelian shook his head, returning his gaze to the village, which was a far safer sight right now than the tentative spark of hope on Vehan's face. "I don't hate you."

This was all he could give. It would have to do.

"All right," said Vehan, quiet and a touch resigned. He rocked himself to bump against Aurelian's shoulder, and Aurelian knew him too well to read that as anything other than an attempt to cover his disappointment with levity. "I guess that's better than nothing, hmm?"

He stood, and Aurelian's gaze followed before he could think better of it. Moonlight highlighted Vehan's profile now in a way that rendered him stunningly ethereal, and when the prince turned to smile at him—that lazy, roguish half grin of his that always seemed to win him his way—Aurelian's heart clenched to see it. "Want to hunt some moss folk?"

Vehan extended a hand.

Aurelian fought a smile. Moss folk—Moosleute, as they were called out here—were a type of faerie that were short and gray and stocky, with moss for beards and hair, and the clothes they wore were a mismatch of things they took in payment for keeping the village tidy. Otherwise known as forest-folk, they belonged to Wild folk—faeries who'd rejected the elemental fae Court system and chose instead to keep to their old way of being. They spent their days hard at work tending to the patches of heavily wooded and picturesque areas they claimed for their own. By night they reveled, and it had been one of Aurelian's and Vehan's favorite pastimes when they were younger to sneak out here and try to catch one before it could curl up like a hedgehog into a mossy, unmovable boulder.

Thankfully, the Moosleute had always been gracious enough about this bit of fun.

"You're trying to avoid your mother, aren't you," Aurelian accused. He batted aside Vehan's hand and rose unassisted, wiping dirt and bits of grass off his beige uniform trousers, which he hadn't bothered to change out of yet.

"Yes!" Vehan confirmed, his smile brightening to a slightly manic degree, his electric gaze aglow with mischief and just a flicker of underlying fear. "I have no idea how her meeting with the High King went today, but they never put her in a very good mood afterward. Plus, I'm sure she's heard by now that her only child and heir threw a tantrum in his professor's classroom and stormed out to sulk like a toddler, *so* . . . yeah. I'm thinking of maybe running away. That's the mature way to deal with this, right?"

Aurelian shook his head, dipping his chin to hide a laugh. "Very."

"I thought so. And since you don't hate me, I've decided *you* can be the one to keep Arlo company in my stead when she arrives."

Aurelian's gaze shot upward once more, amusement fading quickly—at first into confusion, but the longer and closer he searched the prince's face for clarification, the more that confusion began to curdle. "Arlo?"

Vehan nodded. "Yes? Arlo Jarsdel, you know—yea high, red-haired, quiet on the outside, big ball of stubborn fae fierceness underneath? Again, I haven't met with Mother to hear this from her, but word travels quickly. *Apparently* she's invited Arlo to spend the summer with us! Or, rather, with you, because—you know—the whole *I'm running away* thing, and I've also decided to change my name to Uranus Von HugeShaft, a quiet human man who doesn't know anything about your Vehan Lysterne, thank you very much, and doesn't have a theatrical bone in his entire body. He used to be a priest, but then fell in forbidden love! So he left the church to marry the girl of his dreams, but then she *died*, and left him with—"

"Vehan."

Aurelian cut him off, gripping the prince by the shoulders and fixing him with every ounce of seriousness he could manage, because if this was *true*, it was the first he was hearing of it. If this was true, and the queen herself had indeed invited Arlo to join them, it couldn't mean anything good. "Arlo Jarsdel is coming to the Luminous Palace. When?"

"I don't know." Vehan shrugged. "Before the Solstice, I would assume, because she's also been invited to that as our guest." The prince eyed him warily as he spoke, not at all as concerned as he should be that his *mother*—who never did anything without a thoroughly planned and often vindictive reason—had for all intents and purposes lured a very vulnerable, very nice, very clueless *Viridian* out from the protection of her Court and into the clutches of someone who despised her family.

"*Just* Arlo?"

"Mmm, the High Prince Celadon, too, I think. Which is—Aurelian, *hey!*"

But Aurelian was already halfway to the pocket of air that gleamed like slightly warped glass: the portal back to the palace.

Arlo Jarsdel and Celadon Fleur-Viridian were coming any day. The Solstice was just over a month away. Riadne was plotting, and here was Aurelian *moping* as though any step she advanced without his knowledge wasn't an edge she gained in their deadly game.

Arlo was coming.

Aurelian had a text to send.

He didn't particularly want to talk to the person he needed to speak to, but the queen had made a move. Aurelian had to make his before the turn was over.

CHAPTER 5

Arlo

———

WE'LL HAVE TO TELL your father something, of course," said Thalo, head bent, attention divided by the text she was simultaneously writing on her phone. "He'll want to know where you're going for a whole summer. I'll call him—which I'm sure will be an absolute joy, as always—but when *you two* talk, all you need to say is that Celadon's visiting a friend of the family, and you've been invited to go along. He likes Celadon."

Arlo nodded.

After what had happened at the cavum factory, her mother had more or less let go of her anger with Arlo's older cousin. Arlo's grounding had been forgiven too, but between Nausicaä's recovery and Celadon's involvement in the numerous exhausting council meetings the High King had been hosting lately, Arlo had barely noticed her returned freedom.

"I have no idea what His Majesty was thinking in agreeing to all this." Thalo set her phone back on the dark-stained wood of their dining room table. It was another late dinner for another late night that had kept Arlo's mother away much longer than usual. The palace had been in an uproar after Queen Riadne's visit. On top of everything else, it wasn't surprising that already her phone screen kept lighting up with messages in dire need of Thalo's input on something or other.

Arlo sighed, and poked at one of the potatoes on her plate.

"Surely there had to be a better way of doing this. I *really* don't approve of your dabbling in alchemy."

"I know," Arlo started. "But—"

"It's dangerous."

"I *know*, but—"

"And it's illegal. How does the High King expect us to handle this? One of his own family members, allowed to practice a magic he's banned throughout the Courts? If word gets out about this, the folk will call for blood. Favoritism will be the *least* they'll accuse us of, and—"

Arlo's fork clattered on her plate. She could feel her irritation starting to warm her face. "Can you take off the Commander pants for a second, please? I want to talk to my *mom*."

It was Thalo's turn to sigh. A little softer, she replied, "Arlo, this *is* me talking to you as your mother. I'm *worried* about you."

"Okay, but to me it sounds like you're more worried about how this looks for the family."

"That's out of line."

Arlo bit her lip.

It wasn't, really. Everything Arlo did was about how it looked for the family. How she dressed, where she went to school, who her father was, her magic—it was all about the Viridian name that she didn't even get to wear. "I'm sorry," she replied, swallowing down what frustration wanted her to say. "It's just . . . you heard Nausicaä. If I don't get my alchemy under control, I could Rebound. Which almost always results in, you know, *death*. And *so far*, the only thing you seem to be upset about is the stupid law I have to break just to keep that from happening."

A beat of silence passed between them in which Thalo's face flared splotchy blue.

The phone beside her on the table lit up once more with another message.

Thalo narrowed her gaze into an almost glare, ignoring it. "Don't you take that tone with me, young lady. You think I don't care about you?" Her jade eyes grew a little glassy for the emotion she kept behind her words. "I carried you. I gave birth to you. I've had my heart broken *every* time someone says something nasty about you,

74

to you; felt it freeze whenever you get hurt; every cough, every fever, every nightmare, every tear, every*thing* that's ever happened to you I have felt because I'm your *mother*. There is *nothing* in this world more important to me than you, Arlo, so do not mistake my concern over your involvement in dangerous magic for lack of *caring*."

Arlo's eyes watered.

It might have pained her mother to feel any of that, but Arlo was still the one against whom all their family's unkindness was directed. Thalo would never truly understand.

"This is the first time I've been invited to participate in something fae," Arlo replied, her voice worn soft on her own swelling emotion, admitting to the other half of what they weren't saying. She blinked down at her plate, nowhere near as good at keeping a stoic face as her mother. "I'm sorry. I know you love me. I know alchemy is dangerous and that you're worried, but I'm worried, too. And you know what, I *want* to go to the Seelie Summer palace, to the Solstice ball. I've never been allowed at any of the official Court parties before. This is my *chance*, Mom. My chance to be *something* that's anything like the rest of you. It might not be in the way you want, but . . ."

It was her chance to prove she truly belonged with the magical community.

Thalo's phone lit up again, and Arlo didn't miss the way it snatched a bit more of her mother's attention.

She drew a shaky breath and held it—a moment, two—then released it along with the rest of her frustration. "I'm sorry. I didn't mean to turn this into a fight."

"I'm sorry too, Arlo. That I made you feel like your safety isn't always my first priority."

Arlo shook her head, not because she didn't agree that this was exactly how it had come across, but because the easier thing to do right now was dismiss this argument altogether. "You didn't. I'm just being . . . dramatic, I guess."

"That's allowed, you know. You're a teenager. A *sidhe fae* teenager."

Thalo's eyes glittered, referencing the other thing Nausicaä had mentioned: Arlo's possible Maturity that might be close at hand. "Listen, why don't we—" The small, hand glass–sized mirror mounted on the wall beside their apartment's kitchen intercom flared brilliant blue, indicating an incoming call from the palace.

Magic mirrors—they'd begun as a tongue-in-cheek Kickstarter for the eccentric faerie who craved a jazzier alternative to video calling but with all the same perks. It had caught on like wildfire, and in the course of a year, every folk household had one. The ones in Arlo's apartment were all privately connected to the palace, and as neither Arlo nor Thalo had any friends outside of that who'd actually call on them, it had to be Klair, or the High King's steward, Lord Morayo.

"You should get it." Arlo nodded toward the open concept kitchen across the way. "I'm pretty much finished with my dinner. I'll just go to my room and game."

It would have been nice if they could have a proper, uninterrupted conversation. But Arlo was accustomed to sharing her mother's attention like this. Thalo was busy, and Arlo understood, even if she was also a little disappointed by the fact that they hadn't been able to share a full meal together in days.

Thalo sighed. "It's been arranged that you'll go to the Luminous Palace the day after graduation. June 1st, all right? Prince Vehan's Classification Registration has been set for July, so that gives you a good month to spend with each other before his schedule fills up with extra duties."

Nodding, Arlo pushed back from the table, even less hungry now at the mention of graduation, her indecision on what to do after still weighing on her with everything else. "Sounds good," she mumbled, and grabbed her plate. Thalo pushed up from the table as well, taking up her phone as she hurried into the kitchen to accept the incoming call.

Half-eaten dinner wrapped and placed in the fridge for later, Arlo left her mother to it and padded down the hall.

It bothered her more than she wanted to admit, what Nausicaä had said.

She could Rebound played on repeat in her head. Ever since the Good Vibes Only café, where Arlo had watched a young ironborn girl die before her very eyes, death trailed Arlo wherever she went, whatever she did. Would she ever get used to it?

Pushing open her bedroom door, she was so absorbed in her thoughts that she didn't notice at first that there was already someone inside.

Two someones.

"It kills me that Buff Daddy's special skill is survival and all Not Vehan can do is *fish*. No wonder his garbage kingdom failed."

Arlo blinked at the sight before her.

Her bedroom was divided into sections, one half devoted to her princess-netted bed and pastel wardrobe. The other half was fashioned a bit like Celadon's private sitting room, with bookshelves lining cherry-blossom pink walls, a compact bathroom through the far door, and a large, plush sofa situated in front of an even bigger television. It was here that Nausicaä and Arlo's youngest cousin, Elyas, were seated, Nausicaä upside down with her legs draped over the back of the couch and Elyas beside her, controller in hand, expertly kicking MT butt in the Final Fantasy game he was still trying to Platinum.

She had a point with the "Not Vehan" comment, Arlo noted distractedly. She hadn't noticed until now how much Prince Vehan looked like the game's princely main character.

Shaking her head, Arlo refocused on the root matter of the moment: neither of these two had been here before dinner, and they weren't expected to be here at all.

"Uh . . ."

"Hi, Arlo," Nausicaä greeted without getting up, in a tone as though Arlo shouldn't be as surprised as she was to see them here, despite the fact that she hadn't invited them. "I've been freed. Your cousin sprang me from the hospital in exchange for my teleportation services." Then, with zero remorse, Nausicaä added, "Also, I snooped through all your stuff."

With a sigh, Arlo turned to peer out into the hall, listening intently for a sign that her mother had overheard them. But Thalo's voice could still be heard in the kitchen, and none of her words were directed at Arlo. How Thalo had missed any of this with her fae hearing, Arlo had no idea, but she seemed distracted still, and that was probably for the best.

"What are you doing here?" she proceeded to ask, closing her bedroom door. Nausicaä slid around, righting herself to pop her messy head up over the back of the couch and grin.

"Killing time," she replied too innocently to be believed. "His High Prime Majestic Lordship has yet to extend the *indubitable* honor of meeting with him to talk the shop he traded for your soul." She shrugged a shoulder. "And I was bored. What, did you get enough of me in the hospital wing? Did you fill your friendship quota for the month? Am I doomed to spend eternity with Thing One and Thing Two, your extremely annoying cousins, to fill the barren nothingness that will now become my life without you?"

Burnished gold skin, wicked-sharp silver eyes, white sand hair cut jagged at her shoulders, all long limbs, sweeping curves, firm muscle, and easy, immortal grace—Nausicaä was so *very* gorgeous. Arlo noticed this every time they met after a parting like it was the first time seeing her. She was also wholly recovered now—save the gold that leafed her wrist and lower arm—obvious by the return of all that typical fiery energy, which was good. It upset Arlo more than she could really comprehend, to see Nausicaä lying in that hospital wing bed, unconscious and startlingly pale. And when Nausicaä had awoken, she'd been unusually subdued. Quiet.

Arlo had explained what had happened after her loss of consciousness, that Hieronymus had tried to activate the array he'd carved on the floor that would effectively drain Arlo of all her powers and siphon it to *him*; that he'd failed, because Arlo had disrupted this array too, just like the one that kept the laboratory sealed; that in order to secure their escape from this entire mess, she'd agreed to become Luck's Hollow Star; and that Lethe had turned up at the end, collected Hieronymus's philosopher's stone, and whisked off again after gifting her a ring Arlo still couldn't figure out the importance of.

And even after all this, for the first time in their admittedly short acquaintance, Nausicaä had nothing to say . . . about *anything*.

All she'd done was watch Arlo with a mixture of pity and concern and something bright that Arlo couldn't place, and Arlo hadn't understood what any of it meant until the meeting this morning.

But a small thread of something inside her worried that what was weighing on her friend wasn't *only* that Arlo's magic might potentially Rebound if she wasn't given this alchemical outlet. It was starting to seem to Arlo that she was a little more connected to everything going on than she was being allowed to know.

Later—she'd question this *later*; for now, it was enough to see Nausicaä here and acting like her old self again.

"Has anyone ever told you you're super dramatic?"

Nausicaä nodded, her grin spreading wider. "Frequently. I'm very proud of it."

And with that, she launched herself up and over the couch with about as much effort as jumping a crack in the sidewalk. Elyas, still completely absorbed in his video game, grumbled at the disturbance. "So . . . sounds like things got pretty heated out there. I take it the good Commander isn't all that thrilled about your alchemy lessons?"

No keener to have this conversation either, Arlo shook her head and crossed the room to drop onto her bed. "She's not, but . . . you know. I'd like to *not* die, and she can't say no if the High King's allowed it, so . . ." Looking back to Nausicaä, she frowned and asked at last the other question she'd been mulling over since the meeting. "What *is* it you have to tell him that made him agree to this? All that talk about the immortals not forgetting or forgiving us, about the philosopher's stones and how someone who is not Queen Riadne is after the High King's Crown—what's happening?"

Dropping all hint of humor to fold her arms over her chest, it was Nausicaä's turn to sigh. "Listen, I *want* to tell you, Arlo. I do. But I—"

"But you can't? Or you won't." Arlo frowned even deeper and gave Nausicaä a slightly harder look, because there was very little Nausicaä allowed herself to be limited in doing. "You said something else at the meeting. That my Maturity was 'deities-damned' by one in particular. If that's true, I'd like to know. I feel like I probably *deserve* to know, since it's about *me* . . ."

"You *do* deserve to know," Nausicaä replied, guilt flickering briefly across her face, along with something that might almost be . . . fear? "And I *will* tell you, but there's a difference between spouting off immortal secrets to the High King versus to someone I actually care about. I want to make sure the things I tell you are actually *true* before I paint an even bigger target on your back than what I suspect is already there. Because yeah, it *does* concern you. Everything that's been going on *is* connected. Fate damned you to a pretty shitty situation in making it possible for you to meet Luck and become their Hollow Star. But there's also someone else who . . . might make their appearance, if you're attractive enough a tool to them, and even just knowing who that is could put you at more risk than I want you in. So all I can say right now is that it's all a bit more complicated than just the immortals using you and the philosopher's stone as a way to stir up dissent here to allow them to return to this realm."

Even Elyas had turned to look at Nausicaä now, his mouth agape, his game paused in the background.

Arlo blinked, then blinked again. "I'm sorry, they want to *what?*"

Nausicaä shook her head. "Give me some time, Arlo. I need to talk it over with the others first. With Eris. I might be wrong—again, I *hope* I'm wrong, which isn't really a thing I'm accustomed to wanting. Usually, I'm pretty determined to be *right*. It's just . . . things I remember from when I lived in the Immortal Realm, and what I know about . . . certain individuals who'd do anything to snag the Crown Cosmin left here. And then there's Lethe, and . . . Just a little more time. I promise I'll fill you in on *everything* once I have a chance to figure some of this shit out. Right now, the less you know, the better. And you've got Luck on your side, yeah? You agreed to become their Hollow Star."

She had.

To secure their survival in the cavum factory, Arlo had to announce her decision to take Luck up on their offer. That very same night, in the quiet of the UnSeelie Spring palace's hospital wing, Nausicaä fast asleep in her healing trance, Luck had appeared to Arlo with her die in hand, and she'd confirmed the trade.

Her previous fate for that of a Hollow Star's.

Arlo wasn't any clearer on what that meant nor what her previous fate had even been, and all Luck had said was that they'd come to her later to explain what she needed to know, teach her how to use her die and embrace this new role properly. But *later* had passed, and passed, and passed, and Luck still hadn't returned.

Had they forgotten?

Had something happened?

Had they changed their mind?

"I did . . . ," she replied aloud, more questions than she could keep up with flying through her mind.

"Then you're safe for now. You're still in the Padawan stage—no one's going to try jack shit right under *Luck's* nose." Nausicaä shook her head again and made for the bed now, too. She sat down beside Arlo, watching her closely, such a fierce, unreadable promise in her gaze that part of Arlo wanted desperately to look away, overwhelmed. "Just focus on learning alchemy, okay? And remember, you said it yourself back at the factory, we're in this together. I won't let anything happen to you. I won't keep you in the dark, either. Just give me a little more time while we still have it to spare."

Arlo couldn't help it—her attention drifted downward to Nausicaä's lips.

She recalled the feel of that wide mouth against her own—like kissing fire, Arlo imagined, searingly hot and all-consuming. She'd forgotten *everything* in that too-brief moment, and when Nausicaä had pulled away, Arlo had felt her world *shift*.

Oh, she'd thought in that elevator.

Oh, she thought, sitting here on the bed, the focus of so much affection.

Her face flared bright and warm again, and Arlo did look away now. She had no idea what to do with this feeling inside her, impossible to ignore when she was around Nausicaä. It built and changed by the day, it seemed, and she had no idea what it meant, either—was she interested in girls? Was she *only* interested in girls, or did she like boys, too? Did she only feel this for Nausicaä? Was she making a bigger deal out of this than she should? Maybe they were just friends; maybe that kiss in the elevator had just been a thing people did— really, Arlo didn't have friends, so she supposed that could be the case. Maybe Arlo just *admired* Nausicaä's ease and confidence and beauty— the way her thighs squished wider as she sat here beside Arlo; the curve of her neck when she threw her head back to laugh at the things that really amused her; the way she snapped and growled at everyone, but with Arlo she was incredibly gentle—and maybe Arlo saw all this and just wanted to be *like* her, not with her.

It was confusing.

Everything in her life was *confusing* right now, and scary, and she just wanted things to go back to normal even for a moment.

"Besides," Nausicaä added, in a lighter tone, perhaps sensing Arlo's troubles. "You have other things to worry about. Riadne's invited you for a summer-long sleepover, and maybe you don't know this, but she's kind of . . . What's the word I'm looking for?"

"Evil? Terrifying beyond all reason?" Elyas supplied. He'd abandoned his game truly now to bend over the back of the couch, watching Arlo and Nausicaä with his chin propped on his palm and amusement in his Viridian green eyes, as though he was perfectly aware of the very thing Arlo couldn't figure out herself.

Arlo scowled at him—or tried to, at least. A bubble of laughter escaped, despite this. "I *have* heard, thanks. But seriously . . . *evil*?" She shook her head. "This is Vehan's *mother*. She's not evil. How could anyone with a son like Vehan be evil? And, okay, so she might be a bit scary and cutthroat, like pretty much everyone in the magical community, FYI. I don't know if you've noticed, but *my* mom is *also* a scary, cutthroat person. I'm pretty sure most women in power have to be."

She'd heard plenty about Riadne Lysterne, much of it from Celadon's own mouth, and she trusted him implicitly. Nausicaä wouldn't label her a threat if she wasn't one, but . . .

But . . .

"What do you think she's going to do to me? What sort of ingenious plan would pick *me* as the hostage, anyhow?" Arlo continued, shaking her head. "I think she really just wants to make amends for what happened—not that she needs to! But, well . . ." She bit the inside of her cheek, giving voice to the truth of the matter at last. "What you said about me maybe having a Gift? It's kind of . . . flattering. To be the person the fae want around for once instead of out of the way. If Riadne's willing to take a chance on me regardless of what everyone says, the very least I can do is take that same chance back. And I don't know, maybe I *will* Mature, and this could be the start of a renewed alliance between our families. Seelie Summer hasn't accepted *anyone* from UnSeelie Spring on exchange for years."

"Yeah, maybe. And maybe she'll fry you with lightning and use your bones as utensils for the Solstice," Nausicaä countered in a matter-of-fact tone, and there was something in her gaze that made it seem like her opinion hadn't changed a bit but that Arlo's tone kept her from pressing any further. "Which would suck, but also be pretty badass."

"Maybe Celadon's the hostage," Elyas chimed in with his own, more likely suggestion. "He's going with you, after all."

Arlo snorted. "Doubtful. And I'd like to see someone try. I have a feeling they'd keep him for all of a day before they send him right back. If anyone could annoy their way out of danger, it's Cel."

"True." Elyas laughed. "And I dare someone to try anything with *you* that he doesn't approve of. So when are you going?"

"After graduation."

"Soon, then. Are you going to prom first?"

Prom—this was a hilariously mundane concept in the midst of philosopher's stones and plotting immortals and dangerous fae queens. Arlo wanted a bit of normalcy, but right now, it was her human high school prom that felt the most *ab*normal and again served as an uncomfortable reminder of yet more life-altering choices she'd have to make. "No." She shook her head.

"Excuse me, *what?*"

It was Nausicaä who'd spoken, looking up from the phone she'd pulled out of her pocket, alight with a string of texts that had seemed to irritate her before alarm swept that expression away. Both she and Elyas looked aghast.

"You're not going to prom?"

"Why would I?" Arlo shrugged, nonchalant. "It's not like I really know anyone there. It's not like I particularly *liked* high school or have anyone to go with to celebrate it ending."

"*I* would go with you," Nausicaä practically *breathed* this reply, she was so appalled, and so *excited* by what Arlo suspected she saw as an opportunity to terrorize drunk human teenagers. She tossed her phone behind her on the bed. It landed face up. In a glance, Arlo saw she'd been texting *Aurelian*, of all people, and could probably guess it was along the lines of the warning he'd first sent Arlo telling her not to accept Riadne's invitation.

No one trusted the Seelie Summer Queen. Arlo wasn't sure she did, either—except even thinking that made her more determined to prove that, just like Arlo wasn't what rumors made her out to be, neither was Riadne Lysterne.

"I would *love* to go with you," Nausicaä carried on. "I look *amazing* in party attire."

"I'm sure you do." Arlo nodded with a soft laugh. "But you'll come visit me at Vehan's, won't you? And there's the Solstice ball. You . . . you can come to that. With me. If you want." She tacked on the last part as casually as her awkwardness would allow. She had no idea how she felt about Nausicaä, but she couldn't pretend like it didn't make her happy to see Nausicaä's glee tear razor sharp across her face . . .

Wait, perhaps she shouldn't have offered this.

Unleashing Nausicaä on a bunch of rowdy teenagers was one thing. Unleashing her on the largest fae social of the year . . .

"If I want?" She grinned, and she *grinned*, and Arlo might as well start formulating apologies now for what she'd just done to the fae Courts. "The most anticipated Solstice celebration in recent folk history and the offer to pose as arm-candy for its stunning guest of honor?" Nausicaä held out a hand, palm upward. "A celebration thrown by Riadne Lysterne, one of the Mortal Realm's most talented swordmasters, rumored to be in possession of the biggest collection of fae-forged weapons in all the Eight Mc-frickin' Courts?" She held out the other hand, then clasped them together, the parody of earnest supplication.

If only her eyes weren't *glowing* with dark delight.

"Yes, Arlo. I very much want."

Arlo was never getting invited anywhere again after this.

CHAPTER 6

Celadon

~~~~~~

CELADON DUCKED—A NARROW MISS as the crystal decanter, lobbed at the space where his head had just been, sailed out the open doors of his father's private quarters and shattered on the hallway floor behind him.

. . . always sets him off . . .

. . . have to quit, if this keeps up. He's getting more and more dangerous . . .

. . . and it does make me wonder why Father is oh so reliant on him *in these moments—what poison our* charming *younger brother might be whispering in his ear, under the pretense of help . . .*

With a sigh, he pulled himself straight once more, ignoring the whispers that swarmed him the moment he entered the room.

It was habit by now to listen for fragments of conversations in any new space he occupied, trawling the air for information like a fisherman for fish. Oh, what Celadon's special Gift had helped him learn over the years, the *secrets* it had helped him uncover . . . His mother; his sister, Cerelia; his brother, Serulean—they were always so quick with unkindness and judgment when it came to Celadon. They had no idea how grateful they should be to him for the things he'd learned and wielded in their favor, for the things he guarded for their protection.

No one did.

No one but the man glaring him down by the fireplace mantel, graying russet hair in wild disarray around a tired face that was twisted into an even wilder expression.

Fever was bright in his green eyes—distance, too. Caught in the grips of wherever his mind had taken him, by voices only he could hear, all courtesy of the twist of bone on his head that Azurean never removed anymore, not even to sleep. Here, in his private rooms, Celadon's father was nothing like the formidable image he usually struck.

At the moment he was rumpled sleep robes and too many years, a tired old tree that had weathered a few storms too many.

"The state he works himself into over that hideous woman," Celadon's mother scathed from the hall, where she'd taken refuge with the guards on duty a safe distance away from her husband's tempest. She transferred her glare from the shattered decanter up to her son's face, but it didn't much soften for the change in target. "Quickly, Celadon—I'm sure Lord Morayo has called in the Commander by now, but goodness knows *you're* the only one of us he listens to in these moments."

Us. Azurean's family. And the way his mother said this, the faintest trace of sour disdain that only Celadon's ears could detect—disdain, as though it were an *honor* to be the one they called on to manage Azurean when Thalo wasn't around; as though it was Celadon's *fault*, something to be ashamed of, that he was closer with his father than his siblings were and therefore more often in his better graces.

Frowning, Celadon turned, reached for the heavy oak doors still open behind him.

Reseda Fleur had been celebrated far and wide as one of the loveliest folk the Mortal Realm could boast from a very early age. A noble daughter of a well-respected Unseelie Spring family, Reseda had been elegance and poise her entire life, as clever as she was coy. She had a way of speaking that teased at some private joke and a rare ability to make anyone feel like the center of the universe should her attention fix on them even for a moment. She was a doting wife and a good mother. Celadon couldn't fault her that, even if he could never exactly say that she loved *him* . . . not like she loved Cerelia and Serulean, his older twin siblings—both of them blond and lovely in exactly the same way as Reseda was, whereas *Celadon* . . .

He never missed the way she examined him in glances meant to be fleeting, in comments meant to be offhand, prodding at this image that was so incredibly *Azurean Lazuli-Viridian* and nothing at all like the woman who was supposed to have given birth to him . . . as though she might be convinced to love him a little more if she could see even a sliver of herself in the son who too much resembled the man who'd so grossly betrayed her.

But that was another secret.

Another chain tying him down.

Another threat held at his throat . . . *But still, what an* honor *I've been given in holding the High King's favor*, he thought a touch bitterly.

"Thank you, Mother," was all he said aloud, swallowing once again—like so many times before—the words he'd like to say instead, always the question, always the plea, always *please, I'm your son, could you even just once try to love me, too* . . . "I'll take it from here. Send Thalo in when she arrives," he added gently before pulling the doors closed between them.

A moment . . . two . . . drawing a breath, he gathered himself for whatever scenario he'd have to play out, whatever role in his father's reality he'd be designated tonight . . .

He was only twenty years old, but sometimes he felt like those years numbered centuries.

"Your Majesty," he said, turning back around. All charm and grace, shoulders back, chin level, as nonchalant as he'd trained himself to be in any situation . . . just like the mother who thought he bore no resemblance to her at all. "Whatever has upset you, please tell me—"

"Oh, enough of you, *boy*," Azurean growled, tearing away from the fireplace.

Celadon was used to his father's magical outbursts at this point, but it never failed to unnerve him, this evidence of just how powerful Azurean truly was—and how quickly that power was growing out of control.

As one of the two Heads of Spring, the boost to his magic that this title alone granted was not insignificant. Headship in the Courts had always been determined by the one who demonstrated the Blessing of their Season.

Magic was a living force, after all. The Elements and Seasons, too—and all could dole out Gifts at their choosing. No one knew how or why this power was bestowed. But just as Celadon was born with his Element's Blessing to hear past conversations in the air, so too could people be born with the Blessing of their Season. Azurean had been born with the ability to spring greenery in his wake, to suffuse his surroundings with verdant *life*, as had his daughter, Cerelia. As had a handful of others with UnSeelie Spring blood, and if no one of royal blood had inherited what was generally referred to as the Crowning Gift of their Season when it came time for Headship to pass to new shoulders, and no other royal family usurped them with a contender of their own, one of those "others" would be adopted into the family, rebranded, remade, their entire previous life stripped from them to make them into the next suitable Head. But that happened rarely, even if the Viridian line was the only one of the remaining Founding families still in control of their respective Courts to be "fertile" enough to ensure a direct heir was born with their Season's Crowning Gift.

Azurean was strong, and as High King of all eight Courts, that strength was made almost infinite.

And in madness, that infinity was *frightening*.

The enormous sitting room in which Celadon currently stood watching his father bluster toward him was normally a splendid sight. It was mossy carpets and vibrant blooms and sheets of ivy growing up and around jade, and gold, and obsidian fixtures, all of it such a green as only spring could paint, rich and lovelier than any emerald that accented the decorations here.

There were numerous handsome pieces of furniture to fill the space made from polished, dark-stained wood and smooth black stone and sage brocade fabric. The fireplace off to the right was taller than Celadon and wider by several fae abreast, and cabinets of favored trinkets and bookcases filled with private knowledge lined the walls.

The windows beyond overlooked a spectacular view of Toronto just as Celadon's did, the cityscape at this time of night a glittering jewel as precious as the ones that adorned Azurean's rings. So much happiness filled Celadon's memories of his younger years spent sitting with his father in front of the glass. Just him and Azurean—Celadon, his father's favorite child, it was often pointed out, and he'd once taken great pride in knowing this, too—reading together, talking together, innocent things that were far preferable to *this* . . .

Boy—so he was either himself tonight, or he was . . .

"And you can wipe that simpering look off your damned face, too," the High King added, grabbing Celadon by the front of his nightrobe once he reached him, tugging him forcibly closer, their faces now inches apart.

And Celadon allowed it, concealing his wince only barely, because it would upset Azurean further if he showed anything like fear or discomfort, or tried to pull away.

"I'm sorry, I—"

"You're *sorry*?" Azurean laughed, a mean sound that was wholly unlike anything he ever directed at *anyone*, let alone Celadon, normally. "We're sorry, are we? You couldn't leave well enough alone, you couldn't stop it. You couldn't put your duty over your *weakness* for her, and look what it's brought you."

It was . . . difficult to keep up with Azurean's narrative at times; the best way to navigate these situations was to play along until his father's lapse in memory passed, but there were times (like now) when Celadon could only flounder. They'd dipped into this specific conversation before—not often, oh no, this was something Azurean didn't speak about at all, to anyone, a secret even Celadon only held a minuscule portion of, and one of the few he didn't *want* to know any further of.

Because . . .

Because . . .

"How long until they find out, do you think?"

Azurean pressed his advantage, tightened his grip on Celadon's robes, walked him backward into the doors, and Celadon could only allow it.

"F-father—"

"How long can you keep this secret? She hates you even more for this, for what you took from her. . . . Azurean, what have you done? She . . . your *wife* . . . They hate you, and he will too, when he finds out . . ."

Azurean. Your wife—so Celadon was Azurean in this scenario. His younger self, by the sound of it, and this was definitely the conversation he wanted never to have, the knowledge he wished to never possess. He screwed his eyes closed, as if the simple action could shut it out, his heart hammering in his chest all the while. *Don't tell me, don't tell me, don't make it true!*

"Father, *please*—"

"Good luck, Azurean, when that precious boy of yours you love so *dearly* realizes *exactly* who he is . . . and what you did, to him, to *her*, to yourself, all for *the good of the Courts* . . ." He spat on the ground as though the very words were foul in his mouth, and Celadon's eyes fluttered open in time to see a raised hand—but Azurean had never struck him before, not even in the worst of these moments . . . He wouldn't now, would he?

All of a sudden, Celadon was tumbling backward.

The doors behind him had opened swiftly, and Celadon fell through, Azurean releasing him in surprise as there in the space stood Thalo, shock scrawled clear across her face; his father's steward, High Lord Morayo, his own expression twisted in horror; a Hunter shrouded in his cloak, those pure, all-consuming white eyes of his almost . . . *concerned* as they took in Celadon rumpled and sprawled on the carpet; Reseda looking on behind them all in alarm—but not for Celadon.

Never for Celadon.

Why don't you love me, I'm your son . . .

"Celadon?" Thalo breathed, recovering just as soon as she spoke to stoop and attempt helping him up.

Celadon brushed the assistance away. "I'm all right," he said, over and over, a little choked on tears that would *not* fall, gods damn it! He would not lie on the floor crying over his own pathetic misery like a child who'd fallen and scraped his knees, hoping the sound would draw someone who cared . . . but that someone would never come. "I'm all right. See to Father."

Azurean, meanwhile, deflated.

Withdrew into himself.

As Celadon scrambled to pull himself off the floor and emulate a bit of Reseda's poise, that image he was *so careful* to maintain, he caught in a glimpse the look on his father's face: pity, regret, horror, himself again and realizing now what he'd almost done.

"Celadon . . . ," he whispered, and the ache of it pierced Celadon's heart, but he couldn't be here right now. "*My boy* . . . I'm so sorry, I—"

He couldn't see this.

He needed air.

"Celadon—wait!" Thalo tried to call after him, but Celadon turned on his heels and fled, past the mother who continued to stare and nothing more; past the guards who pitied him, too; past *Serulean*, who'd apparently arrived in the minutes Celadon was in with Azurean, just in time to sneer at him as Celadon slammed on the elevator's button.

"Do you ever get tired of scraping around for our father's attention, *brother?*"

It wasn't until the elevator doors closed between them that Celadon allowed himself to cry.

The sound of metal striking glass reverberated around the room as Riadne's blade caught Asurean's only *just* in time. Locked in place, their swords crossed like a clash of wills above their heads, she gritted her teeth and *glared*.

"You're getting better," the High Prince teased, his jade eyes bright with exhilaration . . . and behind it, a flicker of something a little more *intimate* that she couldn't exactly name.

Light poured in through the stained glass that stood in place of every wall and spanned the entire vaulted ceiling of the Luminous Palace's Crystal Atrium. It bathed both Riadne and her opponent in a rainbow wash of red and yellow and green and blue, and splashed color across the crystal floor, which gleamed like liquid silver beneath their feet. Only the white marble pillars marking out the room's borders and the stark white arches that framed the numerous panes of glass provided definition in what otherwise seemed to Riadne like the disorienting interior of a human child's kaleidoscope toy.

But her mother had always enjoyed a spectacle—even more, a challenge.

It had been no surprise to Riadne when she'd remodeled this once simple battle arena into a veritable nightmare of tinted light.

Azurean didn't give her the opportunity to respond to this taunt. Extending a hand between them, he forced Riadne back with a powerful burst of the wind he controlled, aimed directly at her gut. She staggered, giving Azurean the opening he needed to gain the upper hand and disarm her, and Riadne watched in horror as *Perun*—the sword Azurean had gifted her all those years ago on her birthday, with its gold and yellow-sapphire hilt and its translucent, diamond-strength blade—clattered onto the ground and out of reach.

Horror quickly morphed back into irritation.

Riadne growled.

She threw herself forward, lunging at Azurean with a crackle of blue-white sparks gathering in the palms of her hands.

He dodged the electricity she shot at him—left and right and right again—leaped over the bolt she aimed at his feet and parried with a sweeping gesture that sent more wind like a scythe at her head.

She dodged that just as easily. Tumbled to her side and reclaimed her weapon, then threw her whole body into the swing of it, blocking Azurean's following blow.

There was clapping on the sidelines.

It was Riadne's turn to smirk.

She'd lost track of how long they'd been at this, but every time Azurean came to visit anymore, he was just as eager as she to indulge her with these training sessions—to spend time with her in general, more so than their usual. Their matches had always been popular entertainment for her folk in waiting too, and attendants, and Azurean's pretty new wife, whom he didn't seem quite so absorbed in these days, Riadne noted with a touch of satisfaction she couldn't quite explain.

This match Riadne's mother had come to watch, and Riadne wasn't foolish enough to think it had been *her* applauding such a minor victory, the ease with which Riadne had thwarted Azurean's win. But it sent a thrill of satisfaction through her that Arina was bearing witness to her daughter doing something others deemed impressive.

"That would explain it, then," Riadne replied, slightly winded, but her smile curved no less sure and mocking than the High Prince's. "For a moment I thought you were getting *worse*."

Azurean released a garden-chime laugh, dropped a wink at her with that same sort of *indecency* Riadne had seen directed at others enough to recognize it as *flirtation*—flirtation he'd been directing at her more and more over the years, ever since she'd Matured six years ago at nineteen, when Azurean had been twenty-two.

Harder to discern was whether he actually meant it—as the traitorous flutter of Riadne's heart seemed to suggest she was hoping. The winking, the pretty compliments here and there, the extra and undivided attention he paid Riadne whenever he came to call—or whether that was just Azurean, a bit of a gallant by everyone's estimation, amorous by nature, and not to be taken seriously.

After all, there was Reseda, *lovely* as the flowers Spring prided themselves in producing. Azurean would be a fool to let his affections stray, but yet . . . she could almost swear . . .

At the moment, though, this wink was all the warning she received before he spun with his blade. Using the flat of it, Azurean slapped the metal against her back with enough force that she toppled to the ground.

His wife cheered loudly.

Azurean kissed his hand and waved it off in her direction, all smiles and charm and insufferable confidence, and Reseda made a show of snatching that disgusting display of affection out of the air, like she, too, hadn't noticed these sorts of affections for her had started to wane as they waxed for a certain other.

One of the queen's folk leaned in to whisper something into Arina's ear, and Riadne saw her scoff, shake her head, heard perfectly clearly the intentionally loud, "I doubt she'll *ever* win against him," and glowered.

In mock battles such as this, combatants wore lightweight, flexible leather magically reinforced to soften sharp-edged blows. In this faerie-made armor, there was much less chance of their weapons accidentally slicing through to injure or even kill.

Unintentionally.

Riadne tightened her gloved hand around Perun's hilt and shot from the ground.

His back turned to her—more fool him, for dropping his guard, as there was no such thing as cheating when it came to war—Azurean presented an easy mark.

She wouldn't *kill* him, goodness no; she didn't even want to hurt him. It was just a stab, a wound that would heal in a blink and leave only the lesson to take her threat more seriously from here on out—more than any of his other sparring partners would dare.

And there was that unexplainable satisfaction again at the additional, none-too-insignificant thought that it would also serve to steal his diverted attention back to *her*.

But Azurean wasn't to be taken unaware.

With speed only a windborn fae could manage, he angled about and one-handedly deflected Riadne's blade.

Another gust of wind blew her back.

Riadne collided with one of the pillars, sent cracks spidering up its length with the force of her impact. She ignored the way this smarted, and countered with another bolt of the electricity she kept stored inside her, a trick she'd learned from the lightning wielders that served in the Seelie Summer military, who frequently portaled themselves to wherever a storm was raging to harvest a bit of its energy.

A *dangerous* trick.

Hoarding electricity was one thing—hoarding *lightning* was perilous and ran the risk of overloading one's core and sending them into a Surge. It could also make one too accustomed to carrying large amounts of electricity, could make them dependent on it, crave it, and then run the additional risk of withdrawal should the voltage of one's core dip too low to sustain the addiction. But Riadne was neither a coward nor a *weakling*, and Azurean needed reminding that she wasn't a little girl anymore, either.

Azurean stiffened and groaned when instinct made him catch Riadne's bolt on his blade, and the shock traveled up through his arm, leaving him temporarily paralyzed, just long enough for Riadne to regain her ground.

She grinned as she flew forward—as Azurean had finally lost his advantage.

They rained down blows on each other then, whipping around the room in a violent dance.

Riadne struck, and dodged, and parried, and with every swing built more and more force until—at last!

Azurean stumbled.

She took her opening and slammed the flat of her blade to Azurean's unguarded side, then swept his legs out from under him before he could recover. With an echoing yell, Riadne *threw* herself at him, Perun raised, the tip of her mighty sword angled to meet the High Prince's throat and claim her victory.

And then, before she could even comprehend what had happened, Azurean rolled . . .

. . . was behind her.

. . . had her *pinned* on all fours.

The point of his sword pressed just enough into the back of her neck that a pinprick of blood welled up and trickled down around her throat.

Applause broke out, louder than before.

"Oh, Zure, you did it!" Riadne heard Reseda gush, her clapping the fiercest as she rushed forward to hug her *darling* husband.

Riadne remained on the floor, panting, struggling to keep tears of frustration from gathering in her eyes lest anyone see and mistake them for anything like embarrassment or disgrace—anything other than *rage*.

Azurean's sword-point had long slipped away. A gloved hand appeared in her periphery. "You fought well," the High Prince conceded graciously. "You fought *very* well, Riadne. Goodness, to think how far you've come since we started this. You'll get there, Ria, you're *good*, and soon enough not even I will be able to best you, I think."

Growling, Riadne slapped his hand away. "I don't need your *pity*," she clipped, and lifted her head at last.

Her mother was gone.

She didn't know what bothered her more, that Arina might have stuck around just long enough to witness her daughter's defeat, or that more likely she'd left before it had happened, so sure it wouldn't end any other way.

Still blinking against the stinging in her eyes, Riadne rose as gracefully as she could manage, snatched Perun, and turned her biting blue gaze on Azurean. "I hope you enjoy being High Prince. The next time we spar, I'm going to beat you, and then I'll beat your father, and you'll never get to know how it feels to be High *King*."

They were all too used to her making this threat, to hearing her vow to win the Bone Crown and become the first High Queen in Court Sovereign history. Reseda regarded her coolly for this declaration, and probably for the low tactic Riadne had employed to impale Azurean while his back had been turned. Riadne hardly cared; it was Azurean's shuttered expression she watched, eyes trained on *her* and not his fawning wife, as though for a moment it was only the two of them . . .

As it should be, a traitorous voice in her head whispered.

But the moment passed, and Azurean recovered from whatever had stolen over his thoughts, merely shook his head and chuckled, his pale face flush with blue and spirits high, jade eyes gleaming good humor and sport.

He was so unshakable, so sure of his glorious future.

. . . so very handsome, the first and only man she could ever truly attribute that word to. Which was . . .

Ridiculous.

Riadne felt whatever softer feeling had just tried to settle over her shrivel back into irritation even deeper than before.

Irritation, because Azurean had *everything*; like hells he would have her simpering over him as well. Irritation, because there were moments, like just now, when he looked at her like he might genuinely *crave* that from her.

And *that* simply couldn't be.

"Good luck, Your Highness," Azurean bid, inclining his head, eyes as bright as ever, a coyness in his smile like a secret just for her. And if Riadne could figure out what it meant . . . if she even *wanted* to . . .

Riadne scoffed, and turned to leave. "Keep your luck," she called over her shoulder. "You're going to need it more than I ever will."

"Why do you want it?"

Riadne woke with a start.

She hadn't been fast asleep. It hadn't been all that long since she'd retired to her room after dinner. But still, she was a powerful sidhe fae, future queen of Seelie Summer—*no* one should have been able to slip so deep into her room unheard, to sit themself on her bed for goodness only knew how long, hunched over in the moonlight that seemed to make her intruder *radiant* in exactly the same way sunlight did her.

"Azurean," she half whispered, half hissed, and relaxed the hand she'd primed in an instant with enough electricity to stop a heart. "*What* are you doing here?"

In her *bedroom*.

In the deep of *night*.

She glowered at him, jutted her chin in as much defiance as she could muster in this situation, because here she sat in her white-silk nightclothes, barely dressed and as vulnerable as it was possible for her to ever be, and if any of the waiting staff came in to witness this *extreme* impropriety . . .

But there Azurean sat. His back to her, so at least he hadn't been *looming* over her while she slept. His back was tight, though, full of tension despite the way he almost curled in on himself, elbows resting on his legs, hands hanging between them.

For a moment, Riadne forgot her irritation with him, her alarm, and the not-small desire to shock him anyhow for his brazen disregard of her *integrity*, the only thing that seemed to matter of a woman in this world. She stared.

The way moonlight washed those russet locks to glittering gold and fueled the royal glow in his skin to a soft halo of greenish-steel light was nothing short of ethereal.

Azurean could have anyone he wanted—*had* had a *great deal* of the people he'd wanted before his parents took him to task over his "rakishness," as they'd called it, reminded him of his obligations as a High Royal, and paired him with a good, sweet girl no one could say a lick of wrong about, pretty enough that they no doubt hoped to keep him content.

Monogamy . . . the folk weren't all that fussed about it, but the High Royals had to be careful about who they empowered with their affairs—and Urielle forbid, a *child*.

Riadne was the very last person Azurean could *ever* let himself have relations with, but here he was . . . on the edge of her bed . . . and there was something in her that wanted to reach out; wanted to wrap her arms around him from behind like this was a thing they did, like they *were* lovers; like he was hers, and she was his, and that was absolutely ridiculous—

"*Why?*" he repeated, and turned to face her.

His jade eyes were so bright in this lighting that they gleamed almost luminescent.

"Why do you think?" she said, instead of *get out*, which was what she should be insisting. "Why do you think I could possibly want it—me, the *daughter* of a woman with such strict standards that I might as well not exist for all I can ever do right by her. Me, a young woman in a world that only puts chairs at the table for *men*, why do *I* want the Bone Crown?"

Because that's what this was about.

Finally, they were having the conversation he'd been asking after in his gaze but had never been able to bring himself to give voice to when the topic came up.

Azurean drew a heavy breath. It sounded as though he'd drawn the air from his very core. "If you knew what I know about it—"

"*Pah*," Riadne scoffed, leaning back in her bed. She let her blankets fall—because if Azurean didn't care that she was in such a level of undress as she was currently, she wouldn't either—and folded her arms across her chest. "Oh, I've heard all about the insanity it's said to feed into the mind and the energy it drains from its host in years. As though I haven't been living the past twenty-five of them in madness. As though I don't have extra to spare for *power*."

"Riadne." Azurean leaned in.

Now she was aware—that her shoulders were bare save modest straps, the silk of her nightdress so transparent Azurean could undoubtedly see through it to her bosom. *Now* she was aware that her hair was unbound and sleep-mussed and knotted around her face, and night sapped her radiance down to so little she probably looked like a street urchin next to how Reseda undoubtedly *glowed* in these hours.

"If I could have one thing in this life, it would be for that Crown to *never* touch your head. If I could have one thing . . . What it would do to you, in exchange for that power . . ."

Now she was aware, and at the moment, for all that her heart *galloped* in her chest, she didn't care.

She wetted her lips, dropped her gaze to Azurean's, which had grown so much closer.

"*That's* the one thing you would ask for, if you could have anything in the world?" she heard herself ask, and barely recognized her voice for how low it was pitched in *desire*—an emotion so foreign to her tone that it was almost as surprising to her as this entire situation.

"And if I asked for *you* instead?"

Riadne bit her bottom lip, wetting it anew.

Azurean's hand came up to her face like inevitability, his fingers skating along her jaw to sink into her hair at her nape. "Do you know how brightly you shine to me?" he continued, his own voice like the sweetest, darkest honey. "Do you know how impossible I find it to look away from you even for a moment? Every time I see you, you get lovelier and lovelier, *fiercer* and *fiercer*. Every time I come to you, I find it harder to leave." He looked her deep in the eye, and Riadne shivered with how the intensity there dropped warmth down to her core.

"Should I start a war for you, Riadne?"

It would.

The future Court Head of UnSeelie Spring and the future Court Head of Seelie Summer. They'd be breaking so many laws to strike up even the briefest of clandestine affairs. The Court Heads were not to indulge in relations of any degree of intimacy beyond platonic—it was forbidden, and even more so for the offending parties to be the *High Prince* and a crown heir of a differing Court, and worst of all was that *Riadne* would be the one to bear the blame.

They'd discover her secret.

They'd pin this on her, accuse her of enchanting the High Prince into her arms, and this wasn't worth it, this wasn't wise, this was foolish and reckless and— "You could start with a kiss," she breathed out, because once, just once, she wanted to *win* something.

Right now, she wanted more than anything for that something to be Azurean.

Azurean leaned in.

CHAPTER 7

Arlo

~~~

FOR EVERYTHING THAT HAD happened in the last two weeks, it was the second half of May that seemed to pass in a blur to Arlo. Nausicaä had taken up residence in her bedroom, and together with Elyas and Celadon, spent the remainder of the month on Arlo's couch gaming, and binge-watching *Miraculous Ladybug* on Netflix, and ordering food from Uber Eats while Arlo studied for and then took her final exams.

And now, finally, June had arrived.

"You'll send me a text when you get there safely, right?"

Arlo unfastened her seat belt and smiled at her father. "Don't worry, Dad, will do."

From behind the wheel of his small blue Ford Focus, Rory frowned, regarding Arlo with the deep skepticism he'd had for this entire thing from the start. It was quite obvious he knew there was something amiss with the spontaneous visit to a family friend he'd never heard of before, something his daughter wasn't telling him, but he just couldn't put his finger on what.

"And Celadon will be there?"

"For the last time, Dad—*yes*. He'll be there. I'm going to visit a friend in Nevada, not . . . hike up an active volcano or something. I'll be okay!"

The frown on Rory's face etched a little deeper, concern touching the light in his pale eyes. "I'm allowed to worry about you. I'm your father. I don't know this Vehan Lysterne at *all*—you've never mentioned him before. If he's a friend of your mother's family, he's probably wealthy. Entitled. Is he good-looking?"

Alarmed by the direction in which this conversation had

turned, Arlo's hand paused on the car door. "I . . . what?"

"Is he good-looking?"

"What does *that* have to do with anything?"

"I'll take that as a yes, then. This Vehan Lysterne sounds like all the makings of a boy who's used to getting what he wants. You tell him your father is a man who certifiably knows how to dissolve a body in acid and has a youth of activism under his belt that's desensitized him to the threat of jail."

Arlo stared. "A youth of activism?" she repeated in bewilderment.

Rory Jarsdel was as mild-mannered as he was exceptionally intelligent. He was soft around the middle, liked Earl Grey with his elevenses and oolong for his afternoon tea, took nature walks and trips to the Science Center, and didn't so much as have a parking ticket to his name as far as Arlo knew. A youth of activism? This was the first Arlo was ever hearing of *that*, and it struck her as humorous, so completely out of character for her perfectly ordinary father that she wanted to laugh.

Except something about it also struck her as vaguely familiar too.

In that moment, she could swear she recalled a memory of her father when she'd been young enough that her parents were still together, and her father was holding her on his hip, smiling, introducing Arlo to a bear of a man with wild black hair and a matching beard and pointed fae ears . . . Was that Nikos?

You must be Rory Jarsdel's daughter.

"Dad," Arlo asked, turning serious. She dropped her hand from the door and faced him fully now. "Did you ever know someone named Nikos Chorley?"

Nikos Chorley, the founder and leader of the Assistance, a humanitarian group of folk who risked expulsion from the magical community and even their very *lives* to go against Court decree that forbade the use of their powers to aid in the protection of humankind. Arlo had met him only weeks ago when Nausicaä had brought her to Vehan and Aurelian in his headquarters on the Danforth, and the way he'd reacted to Arlo, as though recognizing her by her *Jarsdel* name instead of her Viridian ties . . .

A youth of activism . . .

Nikos had told Arlo that her father hadn't been an Assistant, but Nikos was *ironborn*. It hadn't occurred to her then, but just as Arlo could lie without consequence, so could he. Was this all a weird coincidence? Was Arlo reading too much into things? She had to be. She was pretty sure she'd remember something more substantial if her father had once been in league with an illegal folk organization, especially given her mother's job and family.

Someone would have said *something* to her, would have used this as one more mark against her in the multitude of reasons so many had to dislike her.

"Nikos Chorley . . ." Rory mused on the name. His face screwed up in thought, eyes trained forward to look through the car windshield, but whatever he saw, Arlo doubted it was Success Tower's front courtyard, where they were currently idling. "Can't say I do."

Was it Arlo once again seeing things that just weren't there, or did her father both seem and sound a touch unconvinced by his own words?

He turned then to look at Arlo—really *look* at her—for such a long moment that she started to feel uncomfortable. The fire-red brows over his eyes knitted together in deep concentration, and it was odd, but for all of a second there was so much clarity in his gaze that Arlo had the impression that he was seeing her for the first time in a while. For the first time since—

"Why, is he going to be on this vacation too?" Whatever had fallen over her father, it passed in a blink. Rory was back to frowning and eyeing Arlo with sulky disapproval. "You tell him the same thing, then. I want a FaceTime call with all of them!"

Shaking her head—the feeling of meeting Nikos well before mere weeks ago sank back into obscurity, and with it, Arlo's sense of wrongness—she hugged her overnight bag close to her chest and reached again for the car door. "No, he won't be there. But okay, I'm sure Vehan will be thrilled to talk to you. I'll call you tonight, yeah? After I get settled in." It wouldn't take half that long; she was portaling over through the palace Egress, but as far as her human father knew, she was taking a flight that was leaving in a few hours. "Probably around eight or nine p.m. your time," she added.

"Right, okay. I . . . might be a little late getting home tonight, so don't panic if I don't pick up right away."

Arlo looked back at him for the second time in confusion. "Late getting home?"

"Just a thing I said I'd do tonight with someone." He gave a nervous chuckle and waved her off. "Nothing to fuss about. Text me when you get in and also maybe post something on your Instagram, so I know you aren't being serious about that hiking up an active volcano thing. And the photo should preferably be with this Vehan fellow so that I have a visual."

"*Bye*, Dad." Arlo rolled her eyes as she threw open the door to step out onto the curb.

"Safe travels!" Rory called after her. "Remember—chemical warfare. I'm a trained scientist who knows how to end people in highly gruesome ways. Love you!"

With another shake of her head, and a snort of amusement, Arlo replied, "I love you too," and closed the door. She watched her father drive away, waving him off, then once he pulled out of the circuit and back onto the road, she turned to head inside.

And made it all the way to the glass front doors of her complex before she saw it—a black cat, seated on the pavement as though guarding Success Tower's entrance. A gorgeous black cat too, with glossy fur and a long tail lazily flicking against the ground. It was also quite large, as though it were some sort of miniature panther. Given the sort of people who could afford to live in this building, Arlo wouldn't rule that out completely as a possibility.

"Hello, cat," she greeted cheerfully, and it was definitely someone's well-cared-for pet, the way it didn't so much as tense when she got close enough with an outstretched hand to try to pat it.

The cat turned its head to stare up at her, though. Its eyes were as wholly obsidian and glittering dark as space.

Hello, mortal, said a deep, measured, slightly rumbling voice in her head, and it took Arlo a moment to realize what was going on.

"*Ah!*" she screeched, jerking upright and retracting her hand as though the cat had bitten it. "*Talking* cat!"

There were all sorts of faeries in Toronto, many of whom could shift their shape at will. A phooka was her most obvious guess for who this was. These mischievous nature sprites were better known for taking horse-like forms, but in cities favored those of cats and dogs, pure black and larger than ordinary. And they were harmless, really. More of an annoyance. Most of what they did was trick unwary travelers off their path and lead them on twisting, lengthy journeys through the phooka's perceived territory until the phooka tired of the sport and brought their traveler back to the beginning of their loop.

Arlo didn't have time to play around right now, and given who lived here—the Commander of the Falchion—it was incredibly bold of this particular faerie to try a bit of "fun" here of all places.

Something iron—she was supposed to carry at least a piece of this metal on her always, because even though the Courts protected their people from its poison, faeries still detested to have it touch them. But Arlo hadn't been thinking about this protective measure when packing to head to her father's for the night.

The phooka's tail twitched a little more irritably. *What's that human saying? Lord, what fools these mortals be,* they drawled in her head, an unusual talent for any faerie to possess, let alone this one, but she'd never met another phooka before to compare. *Have you forgotten about our deal already?*

Their deal?

"Wait a minute . . ." Arlo took a closer look at the cat. The cat peered back. Those cosmic black eyes . . . "*Luck?*" she cried, incredulous.

It was eerie to see a cat grin, especially one with such perfectly white fangs.

Indeed. Luck stood—on all fours they reached to Arlo's knees in height—and circled her legs, weaving between them as deftly as smoke and nearly knocking Arlo off-balance. *You thought* I *forgot about* you. *Is that it?*

Untangling herself from the titan playing at her feet, Arlo sighed. "Not really," she lied, then looked around to make sure no one was watching their interaction. "If you're here to start my training, though, you picked a not-great time. I'm about to—"

Leave for the Seelie Summer Court as Riadne Lysterne's guest to the Solstice celebration, yes, I know. Luck sat once again in front of her, head tilted and fathomless black eyes gleaming with some unspoken amusement. It made Arlo shiver despite the day's building heat. *And I will go with you.*

They'd explained it before, in the hospital wing when they'd come to return Arlo's die. As a descendant of one of the original eight fae who'd banished the immortals to a separate realm and crafted the peace treaty keeping them out of the Courts those eight had proceeded to form, Arlo was able to excuse an immortal from the treaty's restrictions to a certain degree. Anywhere she went, Luck was able to follow, so long as it was at Arlo's invitation—which technically she'd given in agreeing to become Luck's Hollow Star and had never revoked, and most likely (she assumed) this was why they'd been able to appear at her doorstep just now as they willed. But Arlo had to wonder if this perhaps had something to do with what Nausicaä had refused to tell her about. Because surely this wasn't widespread knowledge. Arlo hadn't known she could do this herself until Luck had told her, and neither Celadon nor Elyas had ever mentioned that they could call on any of the Immortal Realm to invite them down for a visit. Only the High Sovereign had that permission, was the general consensus.

"You're . . . going to train me as a cat?" was what Arlo said aloud. Folding her arms across her chest, she gave Luck a skeptical look.

For now, they confirmed. *I'm much less conspicuous in this form, much freer to go about my business undisturbed. Just as you'll find that being outside the immediate watch of the High King's inner circle allows for fewer restrictions, so what better time than now to begin your instruction, hmmm?*

"Right." She wasn't too convinced a massive black panther-cat with twin voids for eyes was "less conspicuous" than a normal mortal guise, but they had a point, she supposed. And Luck sounded rather firm on this decision—who was she to complain? In the very least, they were finally here, proving she hadn't dreamed the entire thing. At long last, she'd get to ask her questions and learn how to play the utterly mysterious role she'd traded her original fate to assume. "Well, come on, then. You can help me pack."

Help you pack? Luck sounded just about as aghast as Arlo imagined a cat would sound about that. They regarded her coolly, ears pressed flat against their head, and when Arlo laughed, flicked their tail and prowled off for the door that led into her building.

Alchemy lessons . . . Hollow Star training . . . a vacation spent in the fae palace with people who actually *liked* her—if anyone had told Arlo at the start of the year that this was how her summer was going to go, she wouldn't have believed them for anything. And when she thought about her future after the next few months, it wasn't with dread at all but anticipation.

That was new.

Finally, after eighteen years of feeling she wasn't enough for almost everything in her life, after spending so long terrified of the unknown that sprawled after graduation, there was genuine hope on the horizon, a real possibility for happiness. Luck padded into Success Tower's reception and passed the concierge, who regarded the sight with a raised brow, but nodded to Arlo when she waved at him.

To the elevator, up the floors—Arlo spent a good portion of their trek rehearsing what she was going to say to her mother about her apparent out-of-the-blue adoption of her new "pet."

Out into the hall, through her front door— "Mom, I'm home!" she called as she toed off her shoes, Luck trailing close at her side. Thalo had told her last night that she'd leave work early to pick Arlo up and escort her through the Egress, which was a large part of why Arlo's anxiety wasn't through the roof right now. "Also, don't freak out, but there's a cat. My cat. I've sort of . . . taken them in, but don't worry! I'll bring them with me to the Luminous Palace, so you won't have to look after them while I'm gone. That should be fine, right?" She chuckled awkwardly, stepping through the front foyer into the kitchen. "Queen Riadne wouldn't be upset about that, would she? Mom?"

"Arlo."

"*Ah!*" Arlo startled again, clutching her chest. The answering voice hadn't been her mother's as she'd been expecting but *Celadon's*, and when she whipped her head to the left, there he was. In skin-tight black trousers and a sheer sage blouse, his emerald cloak emblazoned with UnSeelie Spring's sigil draped over his shoulders, and his royal golden circlet—made to resemble a vine that sprouted exquisite jade leaves—nestled in slightly curling russet hair, he looked more like a fae prince than usual.

As Celadon had been permitted to join Arlo's stay at the palace, it wasn't so much that he was dressed like this that surprised her as it was the fact that he was here at all. "Celadon? I thought we were meeting you at the palace." She peered at him, eyes narrowing in suspicion, and added, "Nausicaä isn't here too, is she? I thought she was meeting with the High King today."

The High King had finally summoned her for the chat she'd bargained in trade for Arlo's lessons. She'd actually seemed keen about it too, having complained several times over the last handful of days that he was "taking his sweet time" to do this, but Arlo wouldn't put it past her to blow it off in a mood.

Celadon was no longer looking at her, though. Leaning against the white-painted frame of the archway leading out into the hall he'd just appeared from, arms folded casually across his chest, he peered bemusedly down at Luck and said, "Hello, cat."

Celadon Fleur-Viridian, greeted Luck with another flick of their tail. Their tone was even more unreadable than before, and it wasn't until she saw Celadon cock his head and furrow his brow in confusion that Arlo realized he'd been able to hear them too—Luck's voice, at least for now, had been projected to them both. *How very much not like your mother you look.*

"Uh . . . huh." Celadon glanced to Arlo. "Arlo, you're aware that your cat's a phooka, right?"

"Yeah, yeah, it's fine, they're fine." She waved off the question. Fae kept all sorts of creatures and folk alike as pets, so a phooka wasn't that outlandish. Celadon wouldn't press it too much. She didn't know fully why she was keeping the truth of Luck from her cousin or her mother. From what she could tell, Elyas had kept the little *he* knew of this secret to himself, as had Nausicaä, and Vehan, and Aurelian, and she was grateful; a not small part of her wanted to be sure of what she was doing before she started advertising it. She wanted to know who she was going to become and what this really meant before she caused any unnecessary worry.

And maybe Luck didn't want her talking about it at all? She hadn't had the chance to ask them yet how much of this she could share with others.

"Where's Mom?" she repeated, changing the subject. Dropping her bag on the island countertop beside where Luck had leaped to sit, she craned her head to check the digital clock on the oven. "Is she not back from 'the office' yet? It's almost noon—she's cutting it kind of close . . ."

Celadon peeled off the wall with a sigh. "I'm sorry, Arlo, there's been a change of plans."

"She's . . . going to meet me at the palace?" Arlo hedged, hopeful despite the way her heart had already begun to sink.

"No," Celadon replied gently, "she's not going to be able to see you off at all." His eyes were full of sympathy as he moved to stand in front of her and placed his hands on her shoulders, and the smile he gave tried at reassuring but didn't quite hit the mark. "Something came up with work, I'm told. Something important. She didn't say exactly what, but you know Thalo wouldn't miss this if she didn't absolutely have to."

Something important . . . more important than Arlo.

It was unfair of her to latch onto that part. Arlo *knew* her mother loved and valued her immensely. But it didn't hurt any less, the birthdays, recitals, parent-teacher interviews, playdates, meals, and whole vacations Thalo had been forced to cancel or not attend because *something came up with work*. And now this. Her mother wasn't going to be there to say goodbye at all? Arlo was leaving for the entire summer—this would be the longest she'd ever been away from both her parents at once in her life—and her mother was too busy to even drop by for a hug?

Are you upset right now or hungry? Apologies, I often can't tell with mortal emotions. You all feel things like wildfire—immediate, fierce, and all-consuming.

Arlo glared at Luck.

Celadon regarded them with deep suspicion, having apparently heard this too. "You're a strange sort of phooka. What's your name?"

In response to this, Luck merely yawned. If Celadon was offended that a faerie had just ignored the command of their High Prince, he didn't show it, but he did shoot a look at Arlo that told her he didn't exactly approve of her new companion.

"Their name is Luck," Arlo answered for them. "And all right, well, I guess that's that, then. Mom isn't coming. *You're* still coming with me, right?"

"Of course!" Celadon replied, entirely radiant now, glad it seemed that Arlo wasn't as dejected as he'd obviously feared she might be over this change in their plans (though, truthfully, she was). "I would never pass up this opportunity."

With a groan, Arlo slipped away from the island and started toward the hall for her room. "That had better be an *opportunity to strengthen the bonds of unity* and not an *opportunity to get us banned from an entire Court,* because I swear to Cosmin, Cel—"

"Who do you take me for?" said Celadon, following, with the airiness of extreme affront. "I have every intention of being perfectly lovely in the home of the Viridian family's greatest nemesis."

"Oh my deities, Mom was right. I need better friends."

"Maybe so," Celadon replied, with a solemn nod of his head. "But could better friends do *this*?"

They'd arrived at her bedroom. He reached around her and opened the door. Revealed was the interior, cleaned of all trace of the three additional people who'd been practically living in it the past little while. It had taken Arlo an entire day to restore it to that point.

Just Arlo.

The three miniature hurricanes responsible for the majority of her room's destruction had conveniently taken off to other "business" as soon as she'd started.

"My bedroom," Arlo observed flatly.

"Your *clean* bedroom," replied Celadon.

"Yes, I know. I cleaned it."

"And it's *stayed* that way."

There was a heavy *thud* from the kitchen—Luck leaping down from the counter to no doubt begin snooping around her apartment.

Arlo shook her head with a laugh. "Okay, yes, thank you for not trashing the place in the whole ten minutes you must have been here ahead of me. I know that was probably challenging for you. Now come on, you can help me pack, too."

Wrinkling his nose in similar disgust to what Luck had shown for this chore, Celadon breezed past Arlo and into the room, calling, "Fine, but I get power of veto on every outfit you choose to bring," over his shoulder, as though he didn't always and wasn't the one who'd picked out the majority of the clothing Arlo owned.

Arlo sighed and entered after him. She supposed there were worse things in life than having a fae fashion icon for overly invested family.

CHAPTER 8

Nausicaä

~~~

The Wishing Well—noon

THIS WAS ALL THAT had been written on the folded piece of black parchment that had appeared in Arlo's mailbox just this morning, sealed with a dollop of pearlescent white wax and addressed quite plainly to *Nausicaä*.

Hunters weren't exactly the letter-writing type. Nausicaä had never known the Wild Hunt to send out their High Sovereign's summons like party invitations, either—much like her, they were a bit too dramatic for something so mundane—so this scrap bit of paper had been more than enough to raise her suspicion right from its delivery. But it was the fact that she'd received a letter identical to this once before that made her certain it wasn't what it pretended to be.

UnSeelie Spring's Goblin Market existed under permanent nightfall, a gentle wash of deep navy blue and rose quartz pink, purple, and marigold light.

It was nowhere near as grand as the others the folk had built throughout the Courts, with its broken-stone paths overgrown with moss; its shops built up like mounds in the ground, their roofs littered with bioluminescent flowers and poison-bright toadstools, and covered in thick blankets of lush green grass; wooden stalls painted a rainbow array of colors, overgrown by weeds and vines, as were the numerous lampposts dangling lanterns, which on first glance looked to be made of paper but were actually iridescent insect wings, overlapping like papier-mâché, with greenish-blue will-o'-the-wisps contained within like glowing hearts.

A birch-tree forest surrounded everything, Toronto's Kensington Market (where the entrance to the Goblin Market was hidden) completely transfigured by the illusion. It was impressive to Nausicaä that even the air had been magically filtered to a cleaner, sweeter taste, when the human city's iron pressed so heavily in on this bubble from all around; it was probably owing to this that some of even the Wild folk were present, in addition to the *hundreds* from the Fae Courts that packed the seemingly endless, twisting branches of streets today.

Nausicaä spent a lot of her time in all manner of faerie markets. She hadn't been to this one in particular since before her banishment and was actually a bit curious to see how it had changed, and that was part of why she'd come anyhow, even though she'd known full well the High King wouldn't actually be here.

This summons wasn't the talk she'd been meant to have—*wanted* to have, damn it. She wanted to compare her notes with Eris's, at least, even if the High King would probably be worse than useless in this necessary discussion—but one hundred and sixteen years ago, when she'd first arrived in this realm under banishment, she'd ignored her first receipt of: *The Wishing Well—noon.*

She wasn't going to make the same mistake twice.

In the Market's crowded courtyard entrance, leaning against a massive stone well the folk all believed emptied out into a magical void—and for a rare change, actually hit the bullseye on one of their many rumors—Nausicaä waited for the letter's *mysterious* sender to arrive.

"You're late."

A chill iced down her spine, spread like frost through her body, and made her shiver—she knew that voice, knew its equally cool, still-water tone, the vaguely accented lilt of it unmistakably *Lethe*.

"Excuse you, I am *not*," Nausicaä growled, though . . . yes, technically she was. She'd been as positive back when she received the first letter as she was when she received the second—Lethe had been waiting quite some time for this meeting. She hadn't been in the mood back then to entertain whatever he wanted, but now . . . Forcing down the shock over being snuck up on (it was never something she'd get used to, so few were actually able to do it), she whipped her head to the side. "I've been—"

But her words died on her tongue.

Lethe wasn't beside her—no one was, and no one was behind her, either. There were plenty of folk milling about in lively, chattering groups. They were a varied collection of wings and horns and fur-tipped ears, hulking and sliver-thin bodies, gigantic and short and everything in between, just as colorful as the shops they visited. It was the perfect place for blending in. A mortal, even one of their fae Trackers, would have had difficulty spotting the silvery-white immortal hiding amongst this throng. But there, just ahead: long arms folded across a painfully narrow torso, the driftwood-warped build of him bent further out of shape by the casual way he was leaning against the corner of a frost-sprite's ice cream parlor.

He still had on his Hunter's cloak, despite his betrayal; still the high-laced boots he favored and the tight black leather pants, and his black tunic that was more wicked silver fastenings, buckles, chains, and glittering pins than fabric.

Lethe watched Nausicaä with a grin that grew a little wider across his pale face. His antifreeze-green eyes gleamed bright with the promise of whatever game he was about to set in motion. He tilted his head—the half of his waist-long gunmetal-black hair that hadn't been shaven to his skull spilled around him with the motion. It was clear he was moments from fleeing and that he expected Nausicaä to give chase, that he knew she *would*, because ever since Arlo had told her that he'd been involved with Hieronymus Aurum, and in some way the entire philosopher's stone business, it was *Lethe* who Nausicaä wanted to speak to most.

Lethe, who never did a thing without a reason or personal gain. But *why*?

What had he wanted to talk to Nausicaä about so badly that he hadn't let it go after so much time? More important, what part did he play in the plot unfolding oh so quietly behind the distraction of alchemy and stones? What did he know . . . and why had he come to their rescue so many times over the last few weeks—Arlo's and Vehan's in particular?

Why, why, *why*—there were too many questions piling up in Nausicaä's life. She didn't appreciate that stress.

"It must be rough being older than dirt," she drawled. She knew he could hear her, that she wouldn't receive a single answer she wanted without a price, so there was no point asking yet, and honestly, as much as she hated to admit it, it was Lethe she probably understood the best. The fallen Fury . . . and the fallen Hunter. "You must be so fucking *bored*."

Lethe's smile gained a sharper, slightly manic edge. "You were always my favorite. So much smarter than the others . . . so much more *perceptive* of the truth of things." It was all the warning she received before Lethe fell back from the parlor and sank into the crowd.

The truth of things, huh . . .

She shot forward, snaking and shoving her way through the masses of folk. Lethe was nowhere in sight when she finally reached where he'd been standing a blink of a moment ago. Nausicaä hadn't expected him to be. If Lethe's game was wanting to be caught, he wouldn't make it simple.

There—just up ahead, a flash of silver and gunpowder black.

Nausicaä took off once more. If she had to chase this irritating-as-all-hells immortal around this entire Market, she would. Plus, she'd texted Arlo this morning that she'd be tied up with her talk with the High King—a slight lie, but she hadn't wanted Arlo to worry. No one expected her anywhere for hours.

Up the street, in and out of crowds, hunting down a Hunter was an exhilaration she hadn't felt in a while. More instinct than anything drove her on, leading her from one place to the next, turning her abruptly around corners and down the winding web of streets.

When Nausicaä heard an icy chuckle, she slammed to a halt in the middle of one of the Market's quieter side streets. Even darker than the main strip, it was considerably less packed, but her sudden stop made the folk behind her plow directly into her back.

She ignored their grumbling.

Lethe was nowhere in sight, but something else had stolen her focus. *The truth of things . . .*

The stall beside her, it was a shabby, dilapidated thing, the purple paint faded and peeling over deeply cracked wood. A fairy mound rose up behind it, all browning grass and thorny bramble and snarls of weeds. No sign hung above its door like the others around it, and Nausicaä didn't have to look to know the door was made of solid iron. The message was clear: keep out.

Interesting . . .

But not nearly as interesting as what the stall in front displayed for sale, the large, dull rock among the heap of other *highly* illegal folk parts. The large, dull rock that was actually an ironborn's *heart*, a failed *philosopher's stone* . . . "How did you get this?" Nausicaä demanded. When she'd approached the stall and picked the stone up to weigh it in her hand, she couldn't recall.

The faerie vendor—green and toadlike in shape, a soft pink kerchief tied over his bald, warty head—looked as harmless as an old man, almost adorable, and peered out from behind the stall with large pale eyes made even bigger by his thick glasses.

In Nausicaä's experience, none of the folk were as meek as they might try to seem.

"Don't ask, don't tell—you know the rules of the Market, dear," the faerie vendor croaked.

"Uh-huh. Do you know what this is?"

The faerie's face brightened into a toothless grin. "Oh, but you have a very keen eye! Not many would see this rock for its worth among my other treasures."

His *other treasures*.

Nausicaä looked down at the stall, at the unicorn horn, the sphinx tongue, the manticore spines; plumes of phoenix tail feathers; scales plucked from some poor mer's tail; thick chunks of what she could only assume were pieces of a dryad's dried, bark-like skin pried right off their body.

She raised a brow.

"Yes, yes." The faerie nodded eagerly, looking around as though what he had to say was secret—and really, it was, but how did *he* know? "This stone, it doesn't look like much, but it actually possesses great power. Power that will amplify your own—any in possession of *it* will find their magic significantly stronger! A *very* good eye you have. It's a terrible wrench to sell it; I'm tempted to keep it for myself. But for the right price—*ack*!"

Reaching out with her gold-leafed arm, Nausicaä snatched the faerie by the front of his floral-print dress and hauled him half over his stall. "Me and my very good eyes would like to know where you got this," Nausicaä repeated, and this time, immortal sharpness shaped her tone, making the faerie flinch.

His face began to swell. The green in his skin flared to a neon shade of yellow and the warts all over his body began to secrete an acidic substance that hissed when it dribbled on his stall and immediately began to eat through the wood. No doubt, if Nausicaä had been mortal, it would have burned and forced her to let go. But she had once held *Starfire* in her palm—this self-defense mechanism was no more felt than droplets of water.

She tightened her fist, hauling the faerie a little farther off the ground, and leaned in to glare into eyes that were shocked, then confused, then fearful. "If I have to ask you one more time, you're going to wish you decided to keep this after all—and *still* it wouldn't help you for *shit*."

She held up the stone in the scant space between them.

"Through the door," the faerie hissed, and bared his vicious set of now-unsheathed teeth. He jerked his head to the shop behind him. "You want to know where I got it, bitch? See for yourself."

The truth of things . . .

Oh, this was definitely a trap.

The truth of things . . .

Lethe wanted to talk.

He'd wanted to talk one hundred and sixteen years ago, and he sure as shit wanted to talk now, but his phrasing echoed in Nausicaä's ears because it was no longer the simple game of chase. No; Lethe wanted her to see something. He wanted her to see *the truth*. Of what, exactly, she couldn't say, but he'd known *this* was here. She remembered enough about her chaotic asshole "older cousin" to be sure of that. If she wanted answers from him, she'd have to play through his little scavenger hunt first.

Nausicaä was almost . . . delighted.

Boredom. She knew a thing or two about *that*.

With an even sharper glare, she let the vendor go. He dropped back to his feet, still swollen and toxic bright in outrage, his glasses askew on his face. But whatever other insult he'd like to say or act on, he wisely refrained from it—Nausicaä hadn't let enough of who she really was show in front of him for him to gather she was immortal, but he was likely smart enough to realize she wasn't something he could mess with and walk away unscathed.

She pocketed the stone.

"Hey—" the vendor started, but Nausicaä flicked her thumb like flipping a coin, and from the interdimensional plane where she kept her extensive inventory of crap, filled with years' worth of treasures of her own, tossed him an apple-shaped ruby.

Nothing for nothing, the saying indeed went.

The moment the faerie caught this ruby between his hands, it changed from vibrant red to ocean blue, and when he tilted it for inspection, it shifted to peacock green. Another tilt, and it was an apple gold as the blazing sun—an Otherworld gem, an immortal jewel, fruit from one of their coveted trees, with skin that would break a mortal's teeth to bite, but if they could manage to split it open, the flesh inside would be the sweetest thing they'd ever taste . . . and, incidentally, they would crave nothing but forever after.

"A pleasure doing business," the faerie sneered, not at all about to question how Nausicaä had come by this peculiar item and tucked it out of sight before she could change her mind about the trade. He probably thought she'd far overpaid what this ironborn heart was worth—had to, because if he really knew anything about this stone, he wouldn't have let it go for a bit of curious sparkle, even to her.

Nausicaä sneered right back at him. "Uh-huh. Call me bitch ever again and I'll show you a *real* good time."

Walking around the stall, she made for the iron door.

The faerie would no doubt whisk himself away while she was occupied with whatever lurked within, but he was useless to her anyhow, and dragging him along would just be a pain. She could track him down later if she really needed—no, for now, her focus was on this mysterious mound and whatever she'd find within.

She pushed on the door.

A bit of immortal strength was all that was needed to break through the lock, and the slab of iron fell with a resounding *slam* on the cement floor within.

"Another day, another secret underground investigation," Nausicaä sighed, stepping over the threshold.

Darkness pressed in all around her, obscuring the room's depths. That was no matter; her eyes adjusted quickly to the gloom and could see better than the night-vision goggles humans had invented to supplement their terrible sight.

She noticed immediately the change in temperature, much cooler than the heat outside, and the damp moisture dripping from the tangles of roots that hung from the earthen ceiling.

The air smelled strongly of mold and soil.

Worms wriggled through the dirt above, and beetles skittered across the floor.

Nausicaä lifted a hand to absently bat away a spider that had begun to descend on a thread by her ear, and she walked toward another iron door, this one in the ground.

There weren't any symbols carved into its surface; it wasn't protected by alchemy. However strongly this reminded Nausicaä of their murder factory back in the Nevada desert, something about this place seemed . . . different.

Wrong.

"Nausicaä."

She startled, again, for the second time today, as someone else had managed to creep up behind her without her noticing. Much like when Lethe had first spoken, she whipped around to face the owner of that rich baritone, much deeper than Lethe's frigid sea-water alto. "Eris?"

It *was* Eris, standing behind her.

She'd recognized him the moment he'd spoken, but for some reason, still wasn't expecting what she saw—the leader of the Wild Hunt, in full Hunter garb, standing just a few steps away. He was so tall he had to stoop to fit inside the mound, his deathly presence so tremendous that it filled the entire room. His bone-white eyes were stark and disturbing the way they gleamed, peering at her through the dark.

"I received a summons," Eris explained, holding up his own letter between them. Nausicaä didn't have to read it to know what it said—a twin inscription to her own. "I thought perhaps its sender was you."

"And then realized it couldn't possibly be me, because why the fuck would I even do that? *Tch*—" She turned around. Like burning hells was she was going to let *Eris* see the spark of hope she felt over the fact that he'd actually come, even when he thought *she*—in all her disgrace—could be the one to have called him. "Sorry, invites to my tea parties are always delivered in person, and with much more style."

Eris didn't respond to her sarcasm. He moved shadow-silent to her side, and it felt as though the world shifted with him when he bent and traced his fingers over the door in the ground.

"There is wrongness here."

Nausicaä rolled her eyes and snorted. "A disturbance in the Force, Obi-Wan? No shit." She summoned the stone she'd slipped into her interdimensional pocket and handed it over when he reached to examine it. "You know, how cool would it be if we were all on the same page with things?" she hinted, changing the subject, watching Eris's expression closely for any hint of what he thought, but Eris was unreadable even at the best of times. "You're shackled to this realm just like I am, but the other immortals still speak to *you*, at least. Cosmin still speaks to you. You've got to have a better idea than I do about what the flipping frick is going on here."

Eris unfurled himself to stand again.

The stone in his starlight shimmery, bronze-black hands was just as lifeless as it had been in Nausicaä's, but somehow seemed even smaller, even more fragile.

A low, rumbling growl behind her tore Nausicaä's attention back to the doorway she'd come from, where a massive, moonlight-pale Rottweiler was slinking into the room. It padded across the floor to sit beside Nausicaä and sniff at the gold encasing her forearm; gold that honestly wasn't so much of a setback, given the way everything seemed to readily bend as it normally did, if perhaps a touch more stiffly.

More than anything, that it was an irritation—a reminder that what she was up against was dangerous even to her; that if Hieronymus, powered by his Greed-fueled philosopher's stone, had held on any longer, her arm would have turned gold to the bone, and maybe her whole body, which would have been a fuck-off way to die.

Death licked her arm as though irritated that it couldn't get this off her as well.

At times a dog, at other times a terrible, monstrous steed, and sometimes nothing more than the shadow at Eris's heels, Death was a powerful creature. It trailed Eris everywhere he went and answered only to Eris the way War did Vesper, and Famine did Yue, and Pestilence did Lethe. The fact that it was visible for Nausicaä to see meant that Eris was treating this situation as official duty, not just by the High King's standards, but by what Cosmin demanded, too.

"Are the immortals instructing the alchemist creating the philosopher's stones?" Nausicaä asked then, cutting directly to the chase.

Eris shook his head. It almost surprised her, how readily he answered her question, given how angry he still seemed to be with her on their last meeting a few weeks ago. "To my knowledge, they are not. Not the immortals together, at least. I suspect this is more *Lethe's* role, but he must be doing it at the behest of another. The why of it eludes me—"

"Does it?" Nausicaä cocked her head with a wry grin. "We all know Cosmin gave his Crown to the mortals *specifically* because he knew it would weaken them. They'd fight over it just like they fight over everything, and the unity that once made them strong—made them able to stand against the entire cohort of deities and *win*—would be broken. The Mortal Realm would be divided. Some might even start wondering if they'd gain an edge by throwing their lot in with one of their former oppressors. They'd *certainly* start wondering about calling off the treaty and inviting the immortals back if, say, the Sins and their Big Bad Master were drawn back into this world to wreak total destruction." She raised a brow, her smirk drawing deeper. "Opportunity. That's all the immortals have been waiting for. And here it is."

Every citizen in the Immortal Realm knew what Cosmin had done and why—he'd told them. They knew all it would take for their return was enough mortals praying to them, sacrificing to them, offering to them and tending to their temples and *believing* in them as *fiercely* as they'd once done.

Megaera's strange protection of the Reaper keeping the philosopher's stones from discovery . . .

The Immortal Realm's suspicious silence when, under normal circumstances, they'd at least inform the High King that he should be taking a bit more care . . .

"I know what Lord Cosmin has *said* he's sown into this world," Eris replied, his tone as ambiguous as his phrasing. "I'm not so sure it is the truth, at least in full. The amount of attention on his Crown . . . the *whispers* of who might be interested in collecting it for their own . . ." A bold statement, and a curious one—one that made Nausicaä wonder something *else* now: what Cosmin could possibly stand to gain in pretending he'd done this for Immortal benefit. "But yes, I do know what is commonly believed," Eris continued, "and I've even surmised our sovereigns' plan for using this current situation to their advantage. It's not the first time a mortal has tried to unleash Ruin, and certain deities knew they'd only have to wait for them to attempt as much again. What *eludes* me is what Lethe gets out of helping them. He has never done anything for no return."

"Who knows, more shiny belt buckles? Someone should really teach him how to use Etsy. He'd be in his glory." Frowning, Nausicaä nudged the door in the ground with her foot. With her boots and black leather pants and equally black tank top, the two of them could almost pass for colleagues; all she was missing was the cloak Eris had taken back from her upon expulsion. "Seriously though, Lethe's a walking game of Russian roulette, a *whole* grab bag of wild instability. I wouldn't put it past him to be doing this for the fun of it, except . . ."

"If Lethe's hate could be measured in levels, the Hunt's Lord Father would rank at the top. Yes, that is what Yue and Vesper believe as well—that he's doing this out of revenge, for freedom from Cosmin's control. And he's certainly made no secret of his contempt for both his immortal role and Lord Father, but . . ."

Cosmin.

Lethe had never forgiven Cosmin for confining him to the role of Hunter instead of letting him move on to the afterlife. That was one of the few things Nausicaä knew about him, too.

Lifting her foot, she slammed it down against the square of iron floor, knocking it clean off its hinges. It clattered loudly down a set of stone steps descending into yet more gloom and a flickering, sickly fluorescence below.

"—*but* I'm sure we'll find out when he's ready to reveal it, in extremely dramatic and silver-fastened fashion," she finished for him. "For now, time to find out what my darling unhinged cousin wants us to see, I guess." Because whatever Lethe's motivation for doing any of this, it was definitely personal. He'd tell them, one way or another, when he decided the time was right. "Also, can I just say that I'm getting *real* tired of secret underground hideouts? Just once I'd like to investigate a tree-fort."

Choosing once more to refrain from answering, Eris glided past Nausicaä and descended the steps.

Death remained sitting, watching Eris disappear from sight with wholly white eyes, the exact match to Eris's gaze—it didn't need to follow to see what its master saw.

But Nausicaä did.

Down the steps she went too, straight into a cloud of pain.

Every nerve lit up in prickling discomfort. Despair weighed on her chest. Nausicaä issued an audible gasp—however "wrong" things had felt up above, down in this pit it was so much worse.

And so very familiar.

More cement paved the floor of this cavernous room, a strip of metal grating down its center so the dark, sticky substance caked around its edges could run into a foul sewer below. Around her was a collection of operating tables. On the walls and the metal trays between them were gleaming knives and saws and scalpels, clamps and rods and chains with wicked hooks on their ends, as though to string up livestock for butchering. Past all this, rows of cages piled up to the ceiling, and Nausicaä knew what she'd find inside them, but continued to follow Eris as he recovered from his own shock to peer into them.

There were the rotting remains of the ironborn child the faerie vendor had harvested his failed stone from, dumped without care back into a cage crammed with other too-young, starved, and filthy bodies—emaciated kids who sat so frighteningly still and glassy-eyed they were little better than corpses.

There was the mermaid whose scales had been plucked, limp and rotting like the skeletal body of a dead fish washed ashore.

There was the flayed dryad, the dismembered manticore, so many other faeries and creatures and folk and *people* in varying states of pieces and decomposition.

Nausicaä covered her nose.

The urge to vomit struck her so overwhelmingly and suddenly that she almost succumbed to it, and it had nothing to do with the sight and stench around her—as sad as it was, she was too used to seeing such horror for it to affect her so deeply.

But this . . . What was Lethe playing at?

What "truth" did he want her to find here?

This was *exactly* what Heulfryn's ship had smelled like—she'd never forget this scent. These were exactly the sort of horrendous crimes he and his crew had partaken in, and no one had ever done anything because the Laws were effectively *bullshit*. The immortals only cared about themselves and their precious magic, and even then, they were selfish. "And you all thought I was *overreacting* for wanting to set this shit on fire," she hissed around her hand.

Eris halted.

Nausicaä paused as well.

She was tempted to read the tension in his broad shoulders as impending admonishment, but Eris didn't turn on her to shout her down as he had the first time they'd seen each other after her expulsion. He flung out an arm.

Nausicaä pushed it down. "Thanks, but it's a little too late for all this parental concern. What's—"

She didn't need to finish that question. *What's going on* was clearly evident by the faerie standing mere feet away. Nausicaä had been too distracted by the cages to pay much attention to the group of faeries who undoubtedly thought they were well hidden at the back of the room, that the gloom would be enough to give them the upper hand.

She'd seen the one that had broken ranks to quietly inch forward—but she hadn't realized who they were until just now.

The Pied freaking Piper.

Tall and scarecrow-thin, with porridge-pale skin the texture of rag-doll cloth, this faerie was technically an imp, one of many varieties of that species, dressed in a threadbare jacket, half crimson red and half moldering yellow. Wisps of oily, straw-blond hair hung from under a tattered, wide-brimmed hat. His cherubic face was distorted by bulbous, button-black eyes and a smile that sliced from ear to pointed ear. In appearance, the Piper was a twisted mixture of juvenile comedy and creepy-as-all-fucking-hells horror, and it was proof that human-kind remembered *something* of the magic that time and the Courts had stripped from their memories given that this particular scum had become a legend and had earned himself his very own nursery rhyme.

The Piper laughed at them from the shadows, a chittering sound like an insect clicking pincers, and his voice was disturbingly childish. "More toys to play with? How fun, how *fun*!" He skittered closer—bouncing, disjointed movements that made Nausicaä's skin crawl—and cocked his head, a bit like a mantis sizing them up for devouring. "How fun, how fun, a bit too *old* for my tastes, yes, but the others! Oh, they'll be so *pleased*."

Nausicaä blew out her cheeks. "Wow. Okay, so, we're definitely beating up Pedophile Gollum, right? I mean, I know you have your *rules*, but—"

A cloud of thick black smoke burst around Eris's outstretched hand, and in it appeared the adamant bow he wielded, the Reaper's Weapon he used to hunt down souls and harvest them for Cosmin's Starpool. A similar cloud of smoke at his back equipped him with a quiver of silver-fletched arrows, the points of which were made of the same legendary metal as his bow.

"Law precludes me from dealing death to any unmarked for it. There is quite a lot of flexibility, however, around the ones who have been."

Ah, so that's why he'd come.

The Piper's name must have appeared in the small black books that the Wild Hunt carried, siphoned from the original copy, the Book of the Dead, where all lifespans were recorded by Fate and watched over by Cosmin. Nausicaä, now a free agent in the Mortal Realm and able to terrorize at will, and her decision to heed Lethe's letter, must have locked in the Piper's time of death, and for whatever unfathomable reason, Eris had claimed this reaping as his.

Tch—it figured.

Eris had only come to keep her in line.

But the Piper was despised enough by so many of the folk for his methods and "tastes" that even the cold, unflinching leader of the Wild Hunt wouldn't begrudge Nausicaä this kill . . . or deny himself the sport in joining in.

Fine.

"Just try not to get in my way, old man," she scoffed, and threw out her left hand.

Diminished as she was from what she'd once been, Nausicaä wasn't completely without magic. The veins that traveled from her shoulders to her fingers began to burn. They glowed, hotter and hotter, a fiery, molten red. Sparks gathered in her palm. They sprouted into flickering flame. Those flickers of flame contorted into a ball—the sidhe fae of UnSeelie Summer were the only ones in this realm who could bend and wield fire anywhere close to what Nausicaä could, but none of them could produce it from nothing, as she could.

None of them were *made* from fire, as Nausicaä had been.

"Such disrespect," said Eris, a singular curl of amusement in his otherwise grave tone.

It was almost—*almost*—as though the last one hundred and sixteen years hadn't occurred at all.

The Piper cocked his head the opposite way. They knew who he was, but did he know them? The bravado in his manner and tone suggested not, but the Piper was *old*. He'd remember the Furies. He'd remember the Hunters, when both had been free to roam around in their natural forms. He'd recognize true Fire and the glittering, deadly arrow Eris had nocked and trained directly at his heart.

And then . . . the click of recognition.

Nausicaä could *see* the moment when he realized who they were.

Baring his vicious teeth, he hissed at them, and the fingers he flung wide sprouted claws like knives. His face hollowed out, grew bone-sharp and dark around his flashing eyes.

Eris loosed his arrow.

A whistling pierced the air as it sailed, up and over the Piper's head and straight through the skull of the Arachnid creeping toward them on the ceiling. The spider-faerie fell to the ground, convulsing, her eight legs twitching and curling inward on her bulbous red-and-black abdomen, her parody of a human female face gone completely slack in her nearly instant death.

The room stood stunned.

"A surprise party just for me . . ." Nausicaä raised her hand, and the fireball in her palm illuminated the darkness behind the Piper—the six burly redcaps who lurked against the wall, glinting silver scythes in their hands. A mean-looking bunch, these particular redcaps, a collection of talons and tusks, and one even had spikes protruding from every node of his spine. Any of the folk could call themselves a redcap, could join their murderous ranks with nothing more than a hood stained red with human blood and a taste for killing on contract. But it wasn't only humans they terrorized—that was just the joining fee. "It's not even my birthday. You really, *really* shouldn't have."

The Piper and his comrades *lunged*.

One.

That's all they'd managed to rescue from the depravity of the fairy mound that was currently burning behind them. One was all that had been left alive by the time Nausicaä and Eris had executed the redcap crew, because of course it had all come too late.

Of course, a few of that disgusting collection of faeries had broken away from the fight, had taken it upon themselves to deliver the cruelest, pettiest blow against her and Eris. Of course they'd attempted to dispatch their *stock* rather than allow any of them their freedom.

Just as Nausicaä had suspected he would, the vendor outside had long since taken off, and the rest of the folk in the street tried very hard to ignore both the actual Hunter among them and the giant flames that licked the sky and reduced the nightmare fairy mound to ash. It wouldn't spread. Nausicaä was far too good with her fire for it to burn out of control. It would douse itself once the warehouse was no more, and there would be one less horror in a world that choked on them.

"I would like your help."

"Pardon me?" Nausicaä stared at Eris. It was odd to see him so composed, with the unconscious child he had cradled in his arms, pulled from the cage that had kept the poor boy, and it wasn't the first time she got the impression that whoever else Eris had been in life, he'd also been a father. A good one.

Shifting the child into the crook of one arm, he reached into a pocket in his cloak and tossed something Nausicaä's way.

The failed philosopher's stone.

"I would like your help," he repeated, with steady graveness. "There is too much I don't understand about this situation. Cosmin has told me I need not concern myself with it, but one of my cadre is involved in this matter. I concern myself with *that*."

He waved his hand, and the same cloud of smoke that had called out his bow and arrow draped something over Nausicaä's arm that was light as air, black as starry midnight; Nausicaä simply *stared* at it, unable to breathe, let alone speak.

"You must know as I do that it was Lethe who sent us those letters. He must have been chosen as champion of this cause by one of the immortals after the Bone Crown, chosen to guide the mortal alchemist behind this and see them through to the seven stones' completion. That is none of my business. I care only about *Lethe*. He has been through much more than you know, and has a better heart than you would guess . . . however deeper down and more fiercely guarded than any other. I will not leave one of my own to the deities' wrath if he should fail what he's been tasked, not if I can help it. And the uncompleted stones are making their way into the hands of the folk. They may not be fully functional, but they do give their possessors enough power to cause serious harm, and they feed like a parasite on their host's better nature. As a former Fury, and one of the rare few immortals I've personally trained, I request *your* help in tracking Lethe down for questioning. In exchange for this, I return to you your Hunter's cloak."

Nausicaä could only continue to stare.

"Arlo," she said at last, her voice cracking through emotion. She cleared her throat. "Arlo Jarsdel is a Wild Card. Fate dressed her up real attractive with immortal-grade magic and dangled her in front of Luck as a fucking Wild Card, and *of course* they took her and made her their scion. Who wouldn't? And when Luck is finished *broadening her horizons*, the other deities will make their play to get her to align herself with one of them. That's what I was going to tell the High King—and I'm right, aren't I?"

Nausicaä shook her head, as if that one action could erase the enormous weight Arlo had no idea she carried . . . not yet. She didn't need this burden, not when she was only just starting to come into herself. "Arlo Jarsdel was always going to be a pawn in this game. I don't know everything, but based on what I *do* know, I'm willing to bet that Fate originally had her primed to play the hero for the Courts. But here comes Luck, and there goes Arlo, trading her original purpose for endless, shitty *possibility*. Now she's up for grabs, a hero for whoever manages to claim her, a *villain* to everyone else, and the wrong person winning her favor once Luck has trained her up could easily mean the end of the fucking mortal *world* . . . in the very least, the end of that fucking girl."

There were too many immortals Nausicaä didn't trust not to break Arlo beyond repair, to use her up and discard her once they got what they wanted from her. It was anathema to Nausicaä, the idea of Arlo treated as no more than a means to an end by anyone, a tool instead of flesh and blood and vibrant life.

She had to repress a shudder just imagining some of the ways the worst of immortalkind could abuse their power over such an innocent, good-hearted person.

"If her family wants the Courts to survive what's coming, Azurean should meet with Luck to discuss a new pact. He should *certainly* devise a better way of keeping Arlo aligned to the Mortal Realm more than the clever little *alchemy devoted to UnSeelie Spring* he slipped in there—"

Eris arched a brow, but whatever he thought about this new information was otherwise unreadable. "The High King has quite forgotten you even promised to give him this warning at all."

Yeah . . . she'd figured as much. Azurean Lazuli-Viridian was no longer Court sovereign in any way that truly mattered. Ensuring Arlo kept one foot in his Court was probably the best and last thing he was going to do for the war ahead.

"But I will tell him," Eris added, inclining his head once more. "I will give him your message and fulfill your bargain. And I will remind you that whatever Arlo becomes, no role has ever been straightforward or simple. Hero or villain . . . each is more than what it seems, and defined in different ways. Do not yet fret for your friend. Now, will you lend me your help, Nausicaä Kraken?"

"Permission to bring along said *friend*?"

Eris's brow arched even higher. "You mean Arlo?"

Nausicaä tried to feign some semblance of her normal indifference, but her shrug was a little too stiff for even her to believe she was unaffected by this entire exchange. "Listen, I have no idea if Arlo is even interested in girls, but I'll be damned if I don't try my hardest to find that out, and I literally don't know any other way to woo someone than by showing off in front of them."

"Very well." Eris nodded. Slipping both arms back under the boy he carried, he shifted him a little closer, as though his deathly cool body could provide some warmth. "That's wise, regardless. Look out for Arlo Jarsdel, Nausicaä. No matter what, I do believe she'll need you by her side. And look out for yourself. Luck is one of the better of our kind, but they *are* a titan—their nature is of different airs, and the same hand that delivers fortune is just as capable of the opposite. Do not go out of your way to earn their ire."

Trying her best to ignore the emotions clawing desperately at her—the relief, the joy, the anger, the pain, the fear for the first real sort-of friend she'd made in so many deities-forsaken years; her cloak returned; another step with Eris toward forgiveness she couldn't decide whether she actually wanted; another step back to the Hunt that had been her family just as much as Megaera and Tisiphone had been—Nausicaä laughed.

Her cloak evaporated into a cloud of pitch-black smoke.

"What could I *possibly* do to piss off the upper management that I haven't already tried?"

CHAPTER 9

Celadon

H E HADN'T MEANT TO take it—it had been sitting out on her bedside table, and Celadon had never seen this piece of jewelry before in Arlo's collection, this ring that had caught his attention in a glint, and once he'd picked it up . . .

A simple band of gold, stamped with the sigil of a black serpent winding around a series of seven golden orbs.

It was exactly the same sigil that had been depicted on the leather spine of Nicholas Flamel's *Exposition of the Hieroglyphical Figures*, the book Celadon had stolen as well and kept in his bedroom, from the only time he'd ever been successful at infiltrating the carefully guarded palace vault; the book he'd been studying in his spare moments, attempting to decipher, combing through for clues as to what in all the realms was going on right now—a book that had been confiscated from the alchemist who'd nearly brought irreversible calamity to the world with his attempt to create all seven philosopher's stones.

The alchemist who was a direct descendant of the legendary Flamel.

It had horrified Celadon to discover Arlo in his bedroom those short few weeks ago, her nose stuffed into a book she had no idea would earn *her*, more than anyone else, such severe condemnation.

It had horrified Celadon even further to discover this *ring* out in the open in her room for anyone to find. Where it had even come from and *how* it had even come to be in her possession . . . Cosmin, but she had *no idea* how much danger she was in just owning this seemingly innocuous trinket; what the Courts would do to her, what the *folk* would do, if both the magical community's memory and records were restored. If they only knew what her *true* last name was . . . But that information had been erased by the High King's greatest weapon: Lethe. None but a few key people had been permitted to remember what Lethe had altered, and if it got back to his father that Arlo was in possession of this ring . . .

"Celadon?"

Lethe . . . despite the fact that he was in the High King's employ, that Celadon was High Prince and therefore of the highest clearance, he'd only met this particular Hunter personally on a handful of occasions. But he'd been . . . fascinating to Celadon as a child, in a way most people weren't. What's more, Celadon had been *fascinating* to *him*, the first Lethe had admitted to coming across in all his years apparently immune to his immortal talent of memory manipulation.

"Earth to Celadon . . ."

For all that Lethe had struck him as mysterious, manipulative, cunning, egocentric . . . beautiful . . . never had Celadon picked up on any actual *evil* in him; it had surprised him, therefore, to learn from Arlo that he was caught up in whatever was happening. That he was *helping* this plan of philosopher's stones along.

For what purpose, he wondered, gazing out the back-seat window of the car bringing him and Arlo back to the Palace of Spring. All the while, he toyed with the ring he'd slipped into his pocket on instinct when Arlo's return home earlier had startled him out of this very same thought. *What are you up to, and why does Arlo have—* "*Ack!*" he choked out, shedding his carefully manicured poise to rub his nose and work out the uncomfortable sensation of Arlo flicking its tip. "Excuse me, what was *that* for?"

He glanced to the side, half glowering, half pouting, to find a similar expression watching him back. "I was talking to you, Cel."

"Yes, that *definitely* explains this physical abuse, I understand now."

Arlo rolled her eyes before jerking her chin at the hand still hidden in the pocket of his trousers. "What are you playing with in your pants there?"

"Wrong answers only?"

"Oh my gods—give it." She reached over, shedding her own manners now to wrestle with his arm, and Celadon only put up a momentary fight, because really . . . when had he denied his cousin anything? And the only way he was going to get answers to his questions was if they talked. "I knew it!" Arlo cried when his hand was freed and she had prized open his fingers to reveal the ring in his palm. "You're like a magpie. More than half my jewelry always seems to wind up at your place."

"It's not like you wear most of it anyhow, and I *am* the one who buys most of it for you," he reminded. "Not this one though. Arlo . . ."

"Hmm?" She looked up from the ring, hadn't snatched it back upon its reveal, just sat beside him staring down at it . . .

Celadon watched her a moment for any sign of recognition—it was both a relief and mild irritation that nothing of the sort flickered across her face. "Where did you get this?"

For all the secrets he kept from her, things she just *couldn't* know even if he confided in her more than anyone else, Arlo very rarely kept anything from *him*. She hadn't brought this to him, and maybe that was simply because she didn't think it important. But still . . . it *hurt* to *think* that they were starting to grow apart, even a fraction.

"Lethe gave it to me," she replied in the very next instant before deflating with a sigh into the black leather of their seat.

More surprise—and at the same time, confirmation of what he'd already suspected. But he was glad that she hadn't made up some excuse, that she was telling him the truth—everything as it should be, Celadon and Arlo united against the world. "In the cavum factory, after I defeated Hieronymus. Lethe showed up, punched a hole right through his heart—it was awful." Her mouth turned down in a moue.

"Mmm," Celadon replied in a gentle hum of agreement, because Arlo had never been one for violence and gore. "I'm sorry I wasn't there."

Arlo laughed humorlessly. "You did try to be. I'm sorry I didn't let you, but we were on time-out from each other, and I'm sure someone would have caught you, and then us, if I let you follow."

"Which I did regardless," he pointed out. The moment he'd managed to pull from Elyas that Arlo had gone off with Prince Vehan, Lord Bessel, and the at-the-time highly suspect Nausicaä Kraken, and confirmed her whereabouts by way of the locator function on Snapchat, it was almost as though his heart had frozen in his chest.

He hadn't been able to *breathe*.

Arlo, the one person in the entire world who didn't *use* him for anything, who loved him for *him*, his *sister*, damn it, his best friend and dearest family—Arlo had been in danger, and Celadon hadn't been there to protect her. That was all he'd been trying to do from the beginning, since the dots he'd started connecting showed a frightening spiral that inched ever closer to *her*. "I stormed my father's private chambers to fetch him. Queen Riadne was already waiting at the Egress when we arrived to portal to Nevada, with news about her son's activities that corroborated mine about yours. But by the time we got there and made it down to that deities-awful chamber, Lethe was already gone . . ."

"Yeah," Arlo grunted in an even less amused scoff. "Yeah, he took off just in time. But not before tossing me this." She gestured at the ring. "He called it a *consolation prize* or something, pulled it off Hieronymus's hand. It's . . . I'm pretty sure it's meant to be a clue to figuring out who's really behind all the philosopher's stones. I was going to tell you, you know," she added, turning her head to slant him a pointed look. "I just haven't really had time to even think about it, let alone tackle what it means."

His thoughts dragged his gaze once more to the ring in his still open palm.

Lethe had given this to her.

He'd given it to her as a clue.

A simple band of gold, as pure as undiluted sunlight—and the way it glinted when he tilted his palm just so . . . the way light traveled around its edge, sharp as a flash of—

It wasn't until Arlo reached out a hand to snag his cloak that Celadon realized he'd thrown the car door open. That he was already sliding out onto the road, where they'd been stopped completely in commuting traffic for over five minutes now.

"Uh, Cel?"

"Your Highness!" The partition dividing the front of the car from the back retracted for his personal attendant, Ondine, to call after him. "Your Highness, what are you doing?"

Celadon turned to Arlo. "Come with me?"

No hesitation. No questions asked. Celadon had been all of three when Arlo had been born, had been the shut-away prince his entire life; even when it came to school, he'd only been permitted to attend a select number of classes and no extracurricular activities that bonded the rest of his classmates together. Celadon and Arlo—it had always been just them, two misfits in a gilded cage. Arlo knew him better than anyone, and trusted him enough to slide out behind him with nothing but a shake of her head.

"We'll meet you at the palace," was all Celadon explained to Ondine, who looked like she had a great many things to say about *that*, the least of them being that he *wasn't supposed to run around their Court like this*, but this was too important; Celadon had something to tell Arlo, and he had to do it *now*—any point after would be too late.

He closed the door.

Out on the street, cars were honking as though this would help speed up their situation; people milled about, most with their heads down and hearts intent on making it to their destinations as quickly as possible, but some had glanced their way. Celadon was used to attracting attention, even with his glamour, and certainly in his current, luxurious attire there were no doubt more than a few wondering if he was some celebrity they couldn't place.

"So . . . I'm in a dress and heels, I want to point out before we do . . . whatever this is," said Arlo, gesturing at her feet. "Is everything okay?"

She glanced back at the car. The phooka Celadon wasn't completely sold on actually being a phooka was still curled up on the seat as though they couldn't care in the least that their new owner had just taken off on them.

"Come with me?" Celadon repeated, holding out his hand.

When Arlo turned back to him, it was with a wry smile, like he was being absolutely ridiculous for questioning whether she would. "Just so long as this isn't your clever plan to make us late and insult the *queen* who's waiting for us," she replied, slotting her hand into his, and as soon as she did, Celadon tightened his hold.

And took off at a run.

"Heels and a dress!" Arlo cried, streaming behind him—and did she notice . . . how she was actually able to keep up?

Right on the cusp of her deities-damned Maturity . . . Nausicaä's words from the meeting earlier floated through his mind. He closed his eyes against them. There were too many things to be concerned about right now, but one thing in particular he needed to make sure Arlo knew, *before it's too late.*

Down the street, up on the sidewalk—in and out of pedestrians who called out in alarm as they streaked by. The city blurred around them, stone and steel blending together to smear their surroundings in shades of beige and gray.

Celadon *loved* the feeling of the air against his skin, the wind in his hair—his element, it calmed him, soothed the pent-up frustration inside him, made him want to run and run and *keep running* . . . just like the charge of a storm made his skin prickle, his pulse quicken, his fingers itch to reach out and—

He slammed to a stop.

Arlo slammed into his back, but she was the one to topple for it, bouncing off the impact and stumbling backward.

"*Cel,*" she growled when he came back to himself just in time to

140

tighten his grip once more and haul her back steady before she could actually fall. "What's gotten into you? Is everything okay? Why are we . . ."

She looked around.

Yonge-Dundas Square was perhaps one of the most recognizable spaces in all of Toronto, second to the CN Tower. Cars flooded the street that traveled the perimeter of the paved clearing at its center; people packed the sidewalks in droves. Directly above them was a stretch of open sky, everything else penned in by the cradle of towering shops and buildings, metal and glass and flashing screens that played advertisements for various human wares and depicted signage for the numerous other stores and restaurants and businesses.

Eaton Centre—one of Toronto's largest shopping malls—sat as pinnacle to it all, and it was here that he and Arlo had stolen to often over the years, snuck away from their respective schools to just be *them*, as teenagers, together.

"Are we seriously ditching the Seelie Summer Court to hunt perfume samples? Because—"

"Arlo Cyan Jarsdel."

Arlo froze.

She looked at him now—really *looked* at him, and something in his expression must have hinted at what was screaming in his head right now, because she tightened her hold on his hand as well. "Calix," she replied, so quietly even Celadon would have had to strain himself to hear it, but didn't have to, because he *felt* it.

Arlo was the only person in this entire world who knew his true name.

"I don't want you to go to Riadne's Court. I don't trust her, not at all, and whatever happened between her and my father aside, she's not known for kindness, Arlo. There is ruthlessness in Riadne Lysterne— *cruelty*. I don't want you to stay with her or to attend the Solstice ball with her. I think she's planning something, and I think it has to do with the philosopher's stones, and I'm afraid she's going to hurt you."

Frowning, Arlo considered him for a long moment before replying. "I know you don't like her."

He almost wanted to laugh for how obvious a statement that was.

"I know she isn't . . . well-liked in general."

This time, he couldn't help himself. Laughter came without his permission.

"I still want to go, Cel. I'm still going to do this because for all that you're a freaking celebrity with adoring, devoted fans, neither of *us* is well-liked either by a lot of people. Because this is the first person other than you and Mom who's tried to include me in my own culture. Because if she *is* involved with the philosopher's stones—which, I don't know how you got that from a ring or whatever, but *still*—even in all the unlikeliness she's involved in this, wouldn't it be better to go than to stay behind? Who else is going to look into that if not us?"

Shaking his head, Celadon sighed.

Certainly not his father, who was already so far gone that he could barely keep up with the present for more than a few hours at a time.

Celadon didn't want to do this. This felt like a point of no return, like whatever lay ahead of them once they started down this path . . . there would be no coming back from it.

But Arlo was right. He didn't want either of them to do this, but she was right—if they didn't, who would?

"You're so stubborn, you know that?"

With the crack of a grin, Arlo tugged on their clasped hands. "Who do you think I learned that from?" Her grin softened into a smile, as gentle as the Season she was Maturing into. "We'll be all right, you know? I think a lot of people forget that Riadne . . . she's just one person. A *mother—Vehan's* mother. She's not a monster, I really feel that. And between all the guards I'm sure they're sending with us, and you, and Nausicaä, I also dare someone to *try* to hurt me."

"True," Celadon mused, allowing a bit of better spirits to lift his tone. "Your girlfriend and I would make a formidable pair if we were to team up . . ."

"Er—she's not—"

Grinning now, too, at the blush that flared bright across his cousin's face, Celadon lifted his other hand and placed it on Arlo's shoulder. "But just in case . . ." He jerked his chin at his surroundings. "You remember what I told you about this place?"

Another glance around—Arlo took her time now, studying the Square.

"You are the blood of the Viridian royal family," he reminded her. "You are a child of Spring. So long as even *one* Viridian stands to call this place our home, you will *always* be safe here."

"The Circle of UnSeelie Spring."

Celadon nodded.

With the Sight stripping it of its glamours, Yonge-Dundas Square was almost exactly the same as its human image—save the fourteen sky-scraping statues arranged in a ring among the buildings.

Each Court had a Circle within their territory, a patch of land guarded by the Court's former Heads, whose ashes were mixed in with the enchanted stone that made these gargantuan Sentinels. If anything threatened the blood of the current Head, their Circle was where they'd be untouchable. These Sentinels were designed to protect the reigning royal family; so long as any member of that family stood within their ring, they would be safe—*Arlo* would be safe, from Riadne and from whatever plan she had in store for them. They'd never had to test it against the might of a philosopher's stone, but Celadon would rest easier knowing there was someplace in this world where Arlo would stand a chance, if the worst came to pass . . . if something were to happen to him during their stay.

Arlo had her reasons for wanting to believe that Riadne had goodness in her.

But Celadon wouldn't drop *his* guard.

Reaching down, he began to work a circlet off his wrist—thin and polished and smooth as marble, but the exact same shade of slate as the Sentinels around them. "Promise me you'll come here if there's trouble. *Directly* here."

If Arlo had been granted the Viridian name, she would have been gifted a bracelet just like this. One more thing she'd been denied, but Celadon wasn't taking any chances. This bracelet, once activated, would teleport her right back here as swiftly as Nausicaä could.

He held it out to her.

Once she took it, however hesitantly, he added, "'Termonn'—that's all you have to say, while touching the stone, and it will take you to safety."

Termonn—an Irish Gaelic term meaning "sanctuary."

"You know I don't really want to—this is *yours*, Celadon, and I feel like where we're going, knowing you, you're going to need it more than I do." She narrowed her gaze on him. "But . . ."

"But I'm not taking it back, so you'd better wear it."

"Yeah, I figured. *Fine*," she sighed, jamming it onto her wrist, and then with a touch more intimacy added, "Thank you."

He nodded. It was a relief to know that whatever he discovered while poking around the Seelie Summer palace for proof that Riadne was the mastermind behind the creation of the philosopher's stones, Arlo was going to be okay.

That was all he could ask.

That would have to be enough.

"All right, come on," he said with a brilliant smile, slipping back under the mask of poise—ease, charm, nonchalance—to offer his cousin the crook of his arm. "We should get back before Ondine has the Wild Hunt *Mark* me for punishment."

"You really shouldn't give her such a hard time, you know. Ondine is—"

"Very scary."

"Mmm, yeah, but I think she loves you, too. In her own way."

"Everyone loves me," Celadon replied, tossing his hair before dropping a wink that did normally earn him more than a few sighs from fans, but from Arlo never failed to earn—

A poke to his side.

"Guess we're going to find out, aren't we."

Celadon laughed, happier in this moment than he'd been in quite a while.

CHAPTER 10

Arlo

"ARE YOU READY, LADY Jarsdel?"

Arlo tore her gaze away from UnSeelie Spring's Endless Egress to look up into High Lord Morayo Otedola's
smiling face.

Lord Morayo was a towering, robust man. Fairer earthen brown
to the deep lily-black of the man who stood by his side—his husband, Lord Lekan—with a broad nose and clean-shaven round face
that dimpled when he smiled. Where Lord Lekan kept his long, curling hair unbound and a striking silver, High Lord Morayo's hair was
close-cropped to his head.

As the High King's Left Hand, it fell to *him* to oversee anything the
High King couldn't attend to himself. These days, his list of respon-
sibilities only grew longer. Arlo could see the fatigue of his job in the
strain around his dark brown eyes, the same sort of strain her mother
wore as the High King's Right Hand—the same exhaustion *everyone*
in the palace seemed to be showing signs of lately, all working hard
to keep up with the High King's changeable moods and increasingly
difficult demands.

Drawing on a deep breath to fortify her nerves, Arlo nodded
resolutely.

She'd never been in this room before, had never traveled anywhere
by UnSeelie Spring's Egress. It was kept in the topmost part of the
palace, a circular room made entirely of black marble, thriving ivy
that climbed the walls and dripped from the ceiling, and gleaming
windows that provided a panoramic view of Toronto. In the middle
of the dark moss that carpeted the floor stood the Egress. The mirror

shimmered like silvery starlight, the frame made of the deepest black onyx and accented with carvings of yet more vines and flowers.

"Excellent," said High Lord Morayo, clapping his wide hands together. His smile deepened; his dimples grew more pronounced. A highly attractive fae of considerable Court importance, Morayo earned no small amount of flirtation wherever he went, and Arlo wasn't the only one deeply amused by how his husband—well known for his steady, mild manner—still got a little flustered and blushing-blue in the face whenever Morayo pulled out one of his many charms. "Well, Your Highness," he continued to Celadon. "Lord Lekan and I will go through first with the guard to announce your arrival. You'll follow next, and Lady Jarsdel after you. There'll be a bit of flourish and pomp, then we'll check your accommodations, and inspect the Luminous Guard and the Seelie Summer attendants chosen to care for you during your stay. We'll remain with you through dinner and after that, part ways. There *will* be a few of UnSeelie Spring's guards remaining behind with you, though. The High King's strict orders."

Celadon, who stood at Arlo's side, nodded along with these details. They were nothing new. Arlo's mother had already gone over numerous times with her exactly what would happen today, and no doubt Celadon had been well-apprised of the day's proceedings too.

High Lord Morayo turned next to the four guards who stood behind him and his husband, two for Celadon and two for Arlo, in full ceremonial armor. The Verdant Guard was a deadly team of folk trained in a wide range of combative arts from the moment they were old enough to walk. Many felt the same way about these silent, veritable assassins as they felt about the Wild Hunt and the magical community's actual assassin's *guild*, the Grim Brotherhood—which was to say, *terrified*. More than anything else going on, it was the way the Guard stared blankly ahead that made Arlo the most nervous.

One of the two ordinary palace guards standing on either side of the Egress nodded to High Lord Morayo. It was time, Arlo gathered. Morayo gave his own sharp nod, and the Verdant Guards fell into graceful motion, sweeping forward, filing one after another toward the Egress, where they stepped through the glass without hesitation.

As Arlo watched it ripple around their bodies and swallow them whole, admitting them through to the Seelie Summer palace, a peculiar, tight sensation caught in her chest, almost like foreboding.

Which was ridiculous; it was probably just Celadon's little talk in the Square starting to get to her.

Yes, they were on the cusp of a new Season in which the Summer Courts would be at their strongest.

Yes, the Seelie Summer Queen might be after the Bone Crown and was *definitely* going to make good on her Challenge this year, given how poorly Arlo's great uncle was doing. And it would certainly put her and Celadon in a precarious position if she did that while they were staying with her, might even play to her advantage to have two UnSeelie Spring hostages to keep the Courts in line during the resulting transfer of power.

She wasn't a fool; Arlo knew why everyone around her was suspicious of this invitation, now of all times.

But honestly?

She'd said it twice now: this was Vehan's *mother*.

Arlo and Vehan were *friends*.

As someone whose mother was *also* considered a threat purely because she was powerful and female, Arlo (however stubbornly) refused to believe Riadne was after anything more here than an attempt at smoothing over future relations. But still, this feeling inside of her . . . this might be as simple as the most extravagant summer vacation she'd ever been on, but she couldn't deny that it felt a little bit like standing on the cusp of great change.

She wished more than ever now that her *own* mother was here to see her off.

The guard at the Egress nodded again, and High Lord Morayo exchanged a few more quick words with Celadon and Ondine, who would be accompanying them as well. Then he and Lord Lekan stepped through the glass too, and it was just Arlo and her cousin left behind . . . Ondine . . . and Luck, of course, in their glossy black cat form, seated still and watchful beside Arlo, their tail flicking side to side like the stick on a metronome.

Celadon turned to face her.

Eyes as bright as ever, her cousin smiled gently as he lifted a hand to place it on her shoulder. "It's not too late to change your mind, you know. We don't have to go. We could find you an alchemist in the Market, get up to all sorts of fun all on our own . . . just the two of us. Like it's always been."

Yes.

Celadon was *definitely* feeling it too. Like the moment in the Faerie Ring when Luck had told her she stood at a crossroads, she somehow knew that once they went through the Egress, they'd be setting something into motion. If they stayed behind, they'd be setting off something else.

Arlo smiled back at her cousin. It wasn't often *she* was the one to console *him*—usually, it was the other way around. "It's still going to be the two of us, Cel. It will *always* be the two of us. It's just that now, it's the two of us with other people. And remember." She held up her wrist, showing off the bracelet he'd given her. He'd been trying to pawn this off on her for a while now, but she'd always refused. Celadon needed it more—he was the *High Prince,* a much bigger target for danger than she'd ever be. She was glad she had it right now, though, for the way it made a bit of her cousin's tension dissolve as soon as he caught sight of it. "It's going to be okay."

A twitch of quiet amusement in the corner of his mouth—Celadon tugged on a strand of Arlo's hair. "Very well, the two of us with other people it is. As long as you're sure."

"I'm sure."

"Your Highness?" Both Arlo and Celadon turned to the guard who'd spoken. "When you're ready, it's your turn to go through."

"Right." He pulled at his sheer shirt to smooth it of nonexistent wrinkles. "Time to impose myself on my least favorite Court."

Maybe they *should* sit this one out.

Queen Riadne might not be out to harm them, but Arlo doubted she'd forgotten any of the tricks the spitting image of her greatest nemesis had pulled on her over the years.

"Why is it all the people in my life are the type I have to tell to behave when I'm not around?" Arlo sighed.

Winking at her over his shoulder, which earned him a click of the tongue from his attendant, Celadon stepped forward. He put a hand up to the glass, and when it rippled, stepped through just as calmly as the Verdant Guard had done. Ondine did the same and disappeared just as quickly.

"And then there were two . . ." Arlo frowned down at Luck. "At least *you're* with us. How bad could things get with *luck* on our side?"

Luck turned their face up to her and grinned.

"Oh, okay, now *that*? That wasn't comforting," Arlo said as the cat-titan proceeded to rise primly to all fours and bend themself in a deep stretch. They padded off toward the Egress, leaving Arlo behind, and whatever the guards on duty thought of her panther-like "pet," neither of them so much as blinked when Luck sat back down by the glass and turned an expectant look back at her.

Arlo stepped forward, then paused.

Even though she'd had a brief phone conversation with her mother on her way to the palace, confirming that Thalo wouldn't be here and that she was sorry. Even though they would FaceTime later tonight before her call with her father so that Arlo could tell her all about how everything went, a part of Arlo still hoped to see those doors slide open and reveal that her mother had come after all.

"Miss Jarsdel? I mean—*Lady* Jarsdel. Apologies. It's your turn to go through," the palace guard prompted. Celadon, who was very quick to remind folk when they weren't observing the "respect she was due" in using a title instead of "miss" in his presence, would have been extremely displeased by the guard's slipup just now, especially given how coolly he breezed over the correction. But Arlo had never been bold enough to reprimand anyone herself—was too used to this sort of slight, unintentional or otherwise, to bother getting overly worked up about it anymore.

With a subtle shake of her head to dispel her worries and wishes of what could have been, Arlo turned back around. "Right!" She nodded forcefully, and walked ahead with renewed purpose. Luck rose to standing once more. Just as Celadon had done, just as *she'd* been instructed to do, she extended a hand and placed it on the shimmery glass.

It was cool to the touch, a bit like placing her palm on the smooth, still surface of pond water. Then it rippled, and parted like shifting sand to let her through. It was better than traveling by Nausicaä's teleportation by far in that she felt no disorientation or nausea when she exited the other side, but it was still a curious sensation she wasn't too sure she liked.

"Ah." High Lord Morayo's resonant voice was the first thing she registered once all of her made it through the Egress. "And here she is. I present to you your guest of honor, Lady Arlo Jarsdel. Lady Arlo— the queen of Seelie Summer, Riadne Lysterne."

CHAPTER 11

Arlo

~~~

RLO!" CALLED A VOICE, and before Arlo could properly
get her bearings—were all the Seelie spaces so *bright?*—
there were arms around her pulling her into a crushing
hug. "You're okay."

This last part was spoken much quieter, in such profound relief
that it left her speechless. Who did she know apart from Celadon and
Nausicaä who'd get this worked up about her safety? But this aura,
it was familiar; this fizzling, citrus and gingery magic was uniquely
Vehan Lysterne, however much weaker it seemed from the last time
she'd seen the Crown Prince of Seelie Summer—tired, diminished, an
undercurrent of something Arlo could only label as *off* at the moment.
Her curiosity over the why of this was quickly usurped by another
realization: the last time she'd seen the Crown Prince of Seelie Summer had been in the bowels of Hieronymus's laboratory, both of them
only narrowly having escaped a gruesome death.

"Vehan," she breathed out, pulling back to look him in his sun-
tanned, blue-eyed, sharp-jawed face. "You're okay too!" she exclaimed,
then lunged into an even tighter hug.

This might have seemed ridiculous to everyone else watching,
because of *course* they were okay, they'd seen that themselves in Hieronymus's arena right before Arlo was whisked away by her mother and
Vehan by his. But this was their first time seeing each other since then.
Arlo had no idea if Vehan could say the same, but she'd written so
many drafts of texts over the past couple of weeks, wanting to check
on him, but awkwardness and anxiety refused to let her send a single
one, because she was just Arlo . . . and Vehan was . . . well . . .

A throat cleared behind them that reminded Arlo they weren't alone.

Drawing back once more, a blush heating her face, she dropped her arms and stepped away from Vehan to bow to him as technically she was supposed to have done before anything else.

Heck.

Not five minutes into her stay and she was already treading on important royal fae customs. She was going to wear out her welcome well before the Solstice, at this rate.

Vehan gave an awkward chuckle. "Ah, that's okay. You don't have to . . ."

"How come *I* didn't receive a hug on *my* arrival?" Celadon sniffed, and when Arlo lifted her head again, saw that her cousin had his arms folded petulantly across his chest. Vehan's eyes grew wide, as though even the *thought* of being so forward with the High Prince was deeply scandalous to him.

"Y-Your Highness," Vehan began with a stammer, but movement behind him stole everyone's focus.

Prior to their brief meeting in the cavum factory, Arlo had only ever known Queen Riadne Lysterne through gossip, random internet and magazine photos, and the occasional public appearance that was televised on Folk News. Though the Seelie Summer Queen had been present for the meeting that had taken place two weeks ago, Arlo had been too preoccupied with trying not to pass out to pay her close attention. But just like in their first encounter, Arlo's immediate impression of Queen Riadne was that of someone not to cross.

It was the way she held herself as she glided forward over the white marble floor; it was the power both her posture and aura radiated. She stood spine straight, chin directly parallel to the floor, not dipping in the slightest toward her chest as Arlo's often did in the unconscious desire to make herself smaller. Queen Riadne moved with the confidence of someone who was secure in their importance and ability, and the concision of someone who held themself to utmost strict standards.

Even her beauty was austere. She looked to Arlo a bit like carved ice with the sharp, fine lines of her features, the freezing intensity of her arctic-blue eyes, and the way her black hair contrasted the frosty morning glow of her snow-fair skin. But her smile was wide and genuine on her deceptively young face, and as she came to a halt in front of Arlo—Vehan bowing back to admit her by—Arlo felt . . . strangely calm.

"Hello again, Arlo Jarsdel." Queen Riadne reached out a hand just as delicately as she'd done everything else, and in the barest of touches, tilted Arlo's chin until she rose out of her bow.

Their eyes locked.

There was something behind Riadne's gaze, something fathomless and primal and oddly . . . otherworldly; something Arlo couldn't exactly label, but flashed like a red sheen, the same sort of shade as what she'd witnessed in Cassandra, the young ironborn girl who'd died in the Good Vibes Only café just over a month ago and set Arlo on the path that had led her *here*.

Their eyes locked, and *danger* sounded off in Arlo's head in an instant, and *yet* . . . still, she was only calm.

She could certainly feel the enormity of this moment, of meeting a fae as old and strong as this queen, who at just over three hundred was considered one of the oldest-living sidhe fae in the magical community, yet still looked like she could be in her fifties. But Riadne's aura was just too soothing, too clean and as fresh as an early winter morning, as ozone-fragrant as the air just before a storm; her arctic-blue stare was just too mesmerizing for anything like worry or concern to take root in Arlo's brain.

There was only calm.

"There." Queen Riadne released Arlo's face, withdrawing her hand completely. "The ground is no place for your gaze, my lady—certainly not one as lovely as yours."

Arlo blushed. "Um . . . thank you?" was all she could think to say.

Riadne shook her head. Still smiling, she swept a hand out behind her toward her son and the others who'd gathered for this reception.

There were random Seelie Summer officials she didn't know, Nayani and Gavin Larsen of the Fae High Council, palace guards, and what Arlo could only assume were a few of the Luminous Guard as well, judging by how similarly to the Verdant Guard they were dressed, though the bone-white of their armor made them look a bit like skeletons, frightening in a whole different way.

There was Aurelian, whom she nodded to in greeting, and who nodded politely back. He didn't look too pleased to see her, which made her remember *his* attempt at warning her off coming here as well.

With his dyed-purple hair, multiple piercings, and sleeve of leaf tattoos peeking out under the right arm of his Seelie Summer white blouse, which he'd rucked up to his elbows and left a few too many buttons open around his collar, his entire appearance suggested rebellion against something he'd never choose to wear of his own volition.

The boy beside him . . . Arlo *didn't* know him, but his prettiness was in perfect keeping with the sidhe fae theme, which he very obviously was. Curiously, his aura gave off the same sort of dawn-soft glow as Vehan's did, indicating royal status, but Vehan didn't have any brothers . . . did he?

"My son you already know, and his retainer, too—our Court's future steward, Aurelian Bessel. I think perhaps you may *not* know my other esteemed guest for the summer." Curling her fingers inward, she summoned the boy Arlo couldn't name, and his face split into a wide smile as he moved a step forward and bowed.

"Lady Jarsdel, it's a pleasure to meet such a beautiful girl. And now I know why Prince Vehan has kept you such a jealously guarded secret from me."

Aurelian rolled his eyes at this, which made it even harder for Arlo not to burst out in nervous laughter, but the boy continued. "My name is Theodore Reynolds. You, of course, I absolutely *insist* must call me Theo." He ended his brief introduction with a wink, and Arlo wondered if her face was just going to be distinctly red and warm throughout this entire vacation.

Reynolds—she knew that name, thanks to her lessons with Celadon. Theo was a member of one of the two other sidhe fae royal families. Aurelian didn't seem to like him much, but there was an air of fondness to the way Vehan scoffed at Theo's teasing spectacle.

"It's a pleasure to meet you too," Arlo replied, in a much smaller, softer voice, bowing deeply once again. Riadne clapped her hands together, drawing attention back to her; Arlo felt herself practically *snap* to face the Queen at the sound. "My son and I are so glad you agreed to spend the summer here with us, and I *greatly* look forward to our getting better acquainted. I am certain that, by the end of your stay, a bond will exist between the Courts of Seelie Summer and UnSeelie Spring stronger and more productive than any we've previously known."

It was only because she could see her cousin in her periphery, standing just behind the queen, that Arlo noticed the barely perceptible way Celadon's brow pinched together and his eyes narrowed in suspicion on Riadne's back. Celadon didn't like her, trusted her even less, and the fae were all so much about *layers*—they enjoyed slipping important subtext and clues under seemingly *un*important speeches.

Was there an entire conversation going on beneath the one Riadne was holding out loud? More than likely.

Did Arlo have any idea what that was? None.

So she clasped her hands in front of herself, gave the queen another quick bow, and answered, "Thank you for inviting me and my cousin. I look forward to getting to know you better too," as politely as she could, as she'd practiced in front of her bedroom mirror during any sliver of time she'd had alone there these past few weeks.

And it was all the queen expected her to say, apparently. She nodded and turned back to Celadon, High Lord Morayo, and Lord Lekan. By the time she did, Celadon's open skepticism was completely replaced by a mask of equal ease and charming civility, but a *touch* of what he truly felt about all this gave his gaze a slightly darker gleam. Riadne must have caught it. She paused, ever so briefly. Arlo couldn't see the look that passed between them, but the spark that zipped through Riadne's aura fizzled uncomfortably in Arlo's nose.

It was there and gone in a flicker, and Riadne was wholly composed once more. "Your belongings, Your Highness, have already been delivered to your rooms, as have your cousin's. I imagine you'd both like to get settled in before anything else—shall I show you to your accommodations?" She held out an arm, intention clear, and Celadon slid his own to wrap around it as though they were perfectly good friends.

"You honor me with your personal attendance." Perhaps not *perfectly* good; stiffness threaded the way Celadon said this. Arlo—who'd spent almost all her time with him—was probably the only one who could detect it for how subtle it was, but if she wasn't, no one commented or gave any indication they could hear it too.

"Vehan?" Riadne called over her shoulder, a casual snap of her fingers to prompt him into some unspoken action.

In an instant, he was back at Arlo's side. "Well, Arlo, shall I honor you with my personal attendance too?"

Biting the inside of her cheek to keep from grinning, Arlo looked back up at Vehan's lopsided smirk. Both he and his mother wore matching silk robes of stark white and gold embroidery, their emblem of a sun with lightning-fissures for rays sewn into the back of each, shimmering and crackling with the electricity woven right into the fabric—which they could draw on to fashion their weapons if no other option or source existed, Arlo knew.

The queen's ensemble beneath this robe was white linen trousers tied high around her cinched waist and dazzling golden feathers overlapping and wrapped tightly around her torso, to form a bodice over a tucked-in blouse, which at first glance looked to be made of lace but glinted a bit like frost. It was the same indefinable substance that made her semi-opaque white stilettos.

Vehan was only slightly less extravagant. His burnished gold pants were almost as tight as the ones Nausicaä favored. The buttons on his loosely fitted white linen shirt were the same shocking yellow as some of the jewels on the circlet in his charcoal-black hair, the ornament impressive for how artfully the golden bolt it was made to resemble wrapped around his head. But otherwise, despite how unfairly attractive he was, he was much less intimidating to stand next to than the queen was.

Arlo felt grateful for the outfit Celadon had dug out of the depths of her closet and talked her into wearing today, a thing that was far more luxurious than her normal attire, if admittedly pretty simple: a hunter green chiffon dress Celadon himself had designed and made as a previous birthday present for her, with its ebony black windflower embroidery at the hem of its fluttering skirts and thin onyx straps that Arlo had desperately wanted to put a cardigan over for how much of her broad shoulders they showed off, but Celadon had threatened to disown her if she did.

She dropped her gaze to his extended arm. "All right," she replied, still too quiet, but this was all somehow so much more than she'd been expecting. In theory, she'd known she was going to meet a queen and her prince son, and a whole host of other very important people who were all here specifically for *her*, when up until now, the sidhe fae elite had gone out of their way to pretend she didn't exist; in practice, it was overwhelming.

She was used to being invisible—she would even go so far right now as to say she maybe preferred it.

Vehan tucked her in closer to his side as soon as her arm slid through his, and with his other hand, he patted the one she vise-clutched him with. "It's okay, just breathe. I promise the majority of our summer will be much more low-key. And you're going to *love* the room my mother set up for you, just wait."

The procession set off, led by Riadne and Celadon.

Arlo chewed her lip, then said in a quiet rush as she and Vehan slowly made to follow, "She really didn't have to. I mean, thank you! But I really would have been fine sleeping pretty much anywhere . . ."

"No, no, she really did," Vehan explained, very matter-of-factly. "My mother? You might not have noticed yet, but give it a day or two. Even for a sidhe royal fae, she's a bit of a perfectionist. And I'm not even exaggerating; she'd rather *die* than let anything in association with her be labeled *subpar*."

Yes, Arlo was already starting to gather that.

The room Riadne kept her Egress in was a large, sparsely decorated area. In fact, there was absolutely nothing in it except the Egress. And somehow, despite this, it was still a work of art, every white granite column that supported the diamond-glass ceiling riddled with the same electric golden fissures as what streaked through the floor, so that every step made it look like a crackling energy flowed from the ground upward. The soapstone walls were just as white, just as bare, save for the intricate, pure gold sunbursts carved into a trim around the room, along with airy white clouds Arlo felt a deep compulsion to touch to see if they were actually as fluffy as they looked.

Out into the hall, Riadne led them on a winding tour down one corridor and up another. Everything was polished, pristine white stone and sparkling glass, elaborate gilded stuccowork and flourishing carvings. Many of the ceilings in this palace were magicked to reveal a perpetually sunny, robin's-egg-blue sky with perfectly shaped white clouds. The ones that weren't were inlaid with glittering sapphires and garnets and diamonds, opals and ambers and crystals, all of them varying shades of yellow and arranged into massive, stunning suns, which flared almost as bright due to the surrounding floor-to-ceiling windows, and the good deal of natural light that filtered through to strike them.

"The Luminous Palace isn't really in Las Vegas," Vehan explained, when he caught Arlo peeking curiously out one of the windows they passed, at the sprawling gardens of yellow and white flowers and enormous willows, and the mazelike stretch of sculpted hedges that kept the distant pine-tree forest and jagged spine of mountains beyond it at bay. "Think of it like a door. On one side is the Vegas Strip." He held up his free hand in demonstration, palm down. "That side changes with each new monarch and is the only point of access to the palace apart from the Egress. It wasn't until my mother that this portal entry moved to the Bellagio hotel." He flipped his hand, palm facing upward now. "But the palace is actually rooted elsewhere, by the Titan's Maw—the Rocky Mountains, as humans call it, I think—and *this* side is so heavily warded with magic that unless you're the High Sovereign, with all the Courts' power to bolster you, you can only get to it by coming here through that portal on the Strip. All those hedges out there act like a barrier, repelling anyone with magical blood, and transporting any stray non-magic being from one side directly out through the other, bypassing the palace altogether."

Arlo nodded along with this explanation.

The Seelie Summer palace wasn't the only one to hide their true location away, using random access points throughout the world as entry. In fact, UnSeelie Spring was one of only two that were bold enough to plant their entrance in the same place as their roots, the other being UnSeelie Winter.

Onward they walked.

Arlo picked up bits of the overly polite conversation Celadon and Riadne were holding, asking after the weather, and how the annual tithe had gone for Spring, and commenting on the pieces of artwork they passed.

High Lord Morayo and Lord Lekan were far more interested in the answers Riadne gave than Celadon was, though as a fae he couldn't help the natural draw he felt to eye every tapestry and sculpture and painting, many of which were human in production.

They came at last to an elevator.

Arlo didn't know if it was enchanted to expand to suit the size of the group that wished to board, or if it was always this big inside, but every wall was a mirrored panel and the floor a ceramic mosaic of various white and yellow tiles that made up yet another sun with lightning-bolt rays.

Up the floors they traveled.

Down another bright and airy hall.

They came at last to a halt outside a pale oak door trimmed in white limestone, the handle of which was a lemon quartz gem the size of Arlo's fist, cut and smoothed and polished into an oval.

"This will be *your* bedroom, Arlo. His Highness's is just down the way. But I'm sure he'd also like to inspect the suitability of your quarters, so why don't we start here," Riadne explained, and as she spoke, extracted herself from Celadon to reach for the handle.

She opened the door.

With an eager nod, Vehan released Arlo to follow as the queen stepped inside the room with Celadon close behind, and he hadn't been lying—the Seelie Summer Queen had outdone herself with its decor.

More marble floors, still polished-glassy and ivory white and riddled with golden veins. The walls were still white too, detailed with the same sort of golden embellishments as the halls leading here, and the white granite pillars holding up the ceiling boasted pure gold capitals carved with yet more suns. But all around the room, intermingling with Seelie Summer's accents, were nods to *UnSeelie Spring*—potted plants and twisting ivy, sofas and chairs upholstered in butter-soft sage, onyx black tables, and floor-to-ceiling arched windows curtained with fluttering emerald sheets, each one open to allow the floral-scented fresh air to waft in.

There was a balcony entrance framed in thicker, darker green curtains, a massive black flat-screen television mounted on the wall, a black piano, and an unlit fireplace trimmed in gleaming obsidian.

Arlo stared.

Part of her wondered where she was supposed to sleep; the other part of her was too entranced by the emerald and black railing to her right, where a marble staircase trailed *down* to some lower floor and what Arlo suspected was her own private *pool*, given the way watery light swayed on the just visible upper parts of the sunken room's walls.

"Your entertainment room," said Riadne, as though this were something Arlo had in her everyday life.

No big deal.

She strode across the room to the twin gilded doors at the far end. Arlo followed in something of a daze—and yes, there *was* a pool down that staircase, she confirmed as she passed by. When the queen threw open this second set of doors, it was to reveal moss-green carpeting and more sage sofas, dark-stained furniture, a platform-raised four-post bed complete with more emerald hangings and raven-black bedding, and a ceiling enchanted into a forest canopy like the one in UnSeelie Spring's palace, with more potted trees and plants tucked around to add to this illusion.

A set of glass doors pressed into the wall of open windows to Arlo's left offered another entrance onto her private balcony, and the doors to her right—

"Your bathroom." Riadne turned and smiled down at her.

Arlo could do nothing but gape. "This is . . . all for me?"

She came from a wealthy family—her mother was fae *royalty*—and she'd spent a number of sleepovers in Celadon's quarters, but *still* this extravagance amazed her. It was something more appropriate for the High Prince, not his virtual nobody younger cousin.

"Do you like it?" Riadne asked, simple as that.

Arlo nodded vigorously. "I do!"

"Then yes, this is yours. And I hope it will provide a comfortable stay for you, but if there's anything else you should need . . ." The queen clapped her hands, and Arlo startled. She hadn't seen the three folk standing against the far wall, who stepped forward at Riadne's beckoning. "Your attendants, Zelda and Madelief."

She pointed to each as she named them: Zelda, a cheerful-looking, plump, and full-figured young fae woman, with candy-floss-pink hair tied in an elaborate knot behind her head, soft white skin, and green, cat-like eyes; Madelief, another young fae, slender as a birch tree and just as papery pale, with daisy-yellow hair that hung in a wavy sheet to their narrow hips and brown eyes so dark they almost seemed black. Zelda smiled sweetly at Arlo before bending in an eager bow. Madelief was far more reserved, far more formal, bowing with a dancer's grace.

The third beside them struck Arlo as familiar, but she couldn't remember how she might know her.

A dryad, with lavender eyes and rosewood brown bark for skin, and a pin-straight curtain of pansy-black hair that fell like a mourning veil around her thin face and slim shoulders. She was beautiful, only slightly older than Zelda and Madelief in appearance, but there was something about the tired, brittle way she held herself that made Arlo suspect this youthfulness stopped at looks—dryads could live for a handful of centuries quite easily.

When and where could Arlo have met this woman? She tried to think back on it. Luck, who only now padded their way into the bedroom, sat down beside Arlo and cocked their furry head at the dryad too.

Now isn't this an interesting turn of luck . . . *but for who, I wonder?*

The voice in her head—in only her head, she surmised from the lack of reaction in anyone else present—sounded far too darkly amused for Arlo's liking. She frowned, but before she could ask Luck what they'd meant by that, Riadne crossed the room and settled at the dryad's side. "And this is Leda. I interviewed a few ironborn for the position of your tutor, all who were brave enough to come forward at the request we put out and willing to adhere to the High King's conditions, but *none* impressed me quite like Leda did. I think that together, the two of you will achieve tremendous things with your alchemy."

She ended on a smile that bloomed across her face with such wide intensity, Arlo had the feeling many would mistake it for vicious.

But now she noticed it, the subtly metallic note under Leda's rose-water aura, the same as what Arlo's and every other ironborn's magic possessed.

Leda inclined her head.

Arlo dipped into a much deeper bow—this was her *alchemy tutor*! She knew she wasn't supposed to want this, wasn't supposed to be trained in this at all and was only receiving this training so that she wouldn't die in a Rebound if she Matured. Plus, having just seen first-hand what evils alchemy could be put toward, she was also a little afraid of the art. But this was *magic*, the sort Arlo was apparently *good* at, and she'd be lying if she said she wasn't looking forward to learning how to use it.

"Thank you," she gushed, beginning to ramble both to Riadne and Leda. "I really appreciate everything you've done for me so far. I'm sure you picked an *amazing* alchemist, and—"

A throat cleared behind her.

Arlo paused.

She knew without looking who'd just stepped forward, could tell by the agitation that rippled through his aura that something the queen had said had rubbed Celadon as *unfriendly*—and she'd known all along that it would only be a matter of time before the act of civility between them was put to the test.

She just hadn't thought she'd have to worry about getting chucked out of Seelie Summer so soon.

CHAPTER 12

Aurelian

~~~~~~

AURELIAN WOULD HAVE PREFERRED to wait in the hall along with Theodore and the Councillors, the people who didn't need to inspect the extravagance Riadne no doubt hoped would awe Arlo Jarsdel into a false sense of importance to the queen, make her feel *special*—because that's what Riadne did. It's what she'd done when he and his family first arrived. It's what she did to all her guests, and new "employees," and even her own son. She'd find out what they liked and wanted most and then use it to lure them into her *game*, where the only way out was to play through to the gruesome end.

So he would have preferred to wait outside, but he had to know. He had to see exactly what they were dealing with and how Arlo responded to it all. That, and High Prince Celadon had wrapped himself tight against Aurelian's side after Riadne had released him (much to Aurelian's surprise, along with everyone else's). While Aurelian was *definitely* rude enough to shake him off, High Prince or not, there was something to the glance the prince had cut him just before pulling him along into the room that made Aurelian go along with it.

It was the same expression he wore now as he stood in the middle of Arlo's bedroom, Aurelian still pinned awkwardly to his side; glaring down the Seelie Summer Queen.

It was a look that said quite plainly, *I know.*

And despite the way the entire room had seemed to hold its breath, Aurelian couldn't remember the last time he felt as relieved as he did right now.

"*Tremendous* things." Only the barest trace of the High Prince's former courtesy remained in his delicate alto voice. "You think Arlo will accomplish *tremendous things* with her alchemy?"

It was . . . completely novel to hear someone speak to Riadne not only with so much authority, but the thinly veiled contempt of a person who knew full well she couldn't punish them for challenging *hers.* "Hmm. Well, between you and me, I think this outright ban on alchemy is ridiculous. I'd actually love to see my cousin—and every other ironborn, for that matter—flourish as they were meant to. But while I'm very curious what *tremendous things* your *personally selected* and no doubt Seelie Summer–loyal alchemist could coax out of Arlo, we'll stick probably with the basic training my father, the *High King*, permitted and leave it at that. You know"—he smiled, and just like the one Riadne had given Arlo, its intensity bordered on mean—"just so that my father doesn't start seeing threats where there aren't any."

No one moved.

No one spoke.

The High Prince's words hung in the air like a quivering guillotine, and whether it dropped would be determined by the way Riadne reacted.

So many things the High Prince had just said: admitting that the High King was as unstable as they all suspected; warning Riadne that anything viewed as an attempt to turn Arlo against UnSeelie Spring could be branded as treason; that the only thing preventing this conclusion was what the High Prince was willing to excuse during his stay here. But best of all was the general reminder that High Prince Celadon was a level of opponent Riadne was not used to dealing with and would have to work much harder to dupe, control, or eliminate from her board.

And Aurelian was *relieved.*

So relieved, in fact, that it escaped him without his permission: a laugh. A so *incredibly* poorly timed laugh. Aurelian could see in Riadne's glacial stare that she'd taken great insult to it. Arlo's eyes grew wide, and Vehan off to the side looked equal parts horrified and appalled, but Aurelian laughed because *finally* . . . it wasn't only him against the unfair, deadly, insurmountable odds he'd been struggling against all alone for years.

Thankfully, High Lord Morayo came to his rescue.

His booming laughter joined Aurelian's, which he couldn't stop now that it had started, and he finally pulled out of the High Prince's grasp to double over with it. An elbow to Lord Lekan's side prompted his immediate echo of amusement too, and then it was Riadne's slightly cool, far-too-light-to-be-genuine laughter ringing out, and the tension began to dissolve.

"His Highness cares deeply about you, doesn't he, Lady Arlo," said Riadne around the last of her arctic chuckling—and oh, but *that* made Aurelian's laughter stop.

The High Prince had played his card, had flexed the security in what his High title granted him, but it had come at the cost of *another* card he should have kept far out of Riadne's reach: the one that revealed Arlo as the heart of his concerns . . . and vulnerability.

Arlo, who looked wholly unsure of how to respond to anything at the moment, merely gave an awkward nod and a, "He does, Your Highness. I'm sorry."

"Nonsense." Riadne waved a hand. Did anyone notice how brittle her gentleness had become? How many of her teeth showed in her grin? How blue her eyes had flared? Aurelian chanced a glance at the High Prince, but his face had closed off entirely to what he was thinking and was now nothing more than a carefully arranged mask of mild contrition. "No apologies needed; of course His Highness would be confused by my poor choice of words. Rest assured, my only aim is to see you sufficiently trained, Arlo, by the best the Courts can offer—as a Viridian, you deserve nothing less. But come now." Riadne clapped her hands together, and Vehan wasn't the only one conditioned by now to instinctually snap to stiff attention at the sound, nor was he the only one to turn a little glassy-eyed when the queen met every gaze in the room.

Even Aurelian felt the *curious* effects, though he was able to shake them off much quicker for his awareness of what was happening.

"High Prince Celadon, you'd like to see your quarters."

It wasn't a question.

It wasn't even a suggestion.

And Aurelian knew that no matter what the High Prince felt about being ordered around like this, there'd be no disagreeing with what had trickled into Riadne's voice and layered itself overtop of her cut-glass words.

"Vehan," Riadne added, turning her bright gaze now on her son. "Would you be so kind as to—"

"Lord Aurelian will escort me," the High Prince interrupted, and Aurelian was once again caught off guard by *relief*.

The High Prince sounded a bit dazed—and oh, if he only knew—but it was a *very* good sign that despite this, he'd apparently kept enough of his wits and willpower to prevent Riadne's complete command of the situation.

Weaving his arm back through Aurelian's, he continued, "You're quite right, I would like to see my quarters, but there's no need to trouble the prince, not when Arlo looks so happy to see him."

Arlo, still caught in the throes of her own stupor, made no comment on what her cousin had just said, but her eyes did widen a fraction further, as though underneath her *unnatural* calm she would very much like to be left out of this confusing conflict.

"Lord Aurelian can escort me while you finish helping my cousin get settled in. We can reconvene after, and from there continue with our day's formalities."

"Very well." Riadne inclined her head, but her piercing gaze had fixed on Aurelian and didn't budge an inch. "An excellent suggestion. We'll catch up with you momentarily, then. Lord Aurelian, you heard your High Prince. Conduct him to his room."

She brushed a hand toward the door as though swatting away a fly.

Aurelian acquiesced.

There was no point in arguing, not when he'd already offended Riadne so badly with his laughter, which he knew she wouldn't forget anytime soon and would make him pay for, somehow or other. There was certainly no point in arguing with the High Prince, and honestly . . . this was the moment alone Aurelian needed with him.

Arlo would be all right.

Vehan was here, and Riadne still tried to keep from showing the full breadth of her viciousness in front of him. Not to mention High Lord Morayo, Lord Lekan, and the Verdant Guard who remained in Arlo's sitting room, in a staring match with the members of the Luminous Guard who had followed, all standing so stilly that even Aurelian's lesidhe senses hadn't been able to pick up on their presence when he and the High Prince passed them by on their way back to the hall. It wasn't until two of Spring's Guards had peeled away from the wall to fall into the High Prince's shadow that he remembered they were there.

The Councillors and attendants who'd been left outside the room with Theodore (leaning against the opposite wall, far more casual than the rest) all rustled excitedly, standing tall at attention when the High Prince stepped out to rejoin them, but the High Prince merely raised a hand and bid them a curt, "Remain as you are. Your queen will collect you shortly."

A few brows rose.

Murmurs churned in their wake.

Theodore's mouth twisted in brief but deep amusement, his dark eyes peering intensely at the High Prince over the perfectly manicured nails he'd been pretending to inspect in boredom.

Pretend . . . Aurelian couldn't say for certain just how much of Theodore was a performance, but he did know one thing: he wasn't at all what he appeared. What he was, what he was after, what he hoped to achieve in being here—all of this was something Aurelian would soon have to confront him on, because often Aurelian's impression of him was one of a scout having been sent in to gauge enemy territory before some devastating attack, and as much as he wanted to keep well out of as much danger as possible, Aurelian couldn't call himself Vehan's protector and let such a potential threat to the prince go unchecked for much longer.

Not to mention it gave Riadne one more edge against him if she figured out before Aurelian exactly who Theodore could be and what he wanted. She had to have guesses of her own—most likely better educated ones than his—but it all fed right back into *pretense*. Theodore pretended to be nothing but the spoiled son of one of the wealthiest fae families in all the magical community; Riadne pretended to want him here purely for the marriage prospects between him and her son, as well as the *generous donations* the Reynoldses paid her for the consideration.

The Reynolds family had to be pretending they didn't know Riadne was just as likely to carve this boy up for delicacies served at her upcoming ball as she was to actually marry him to her only son.

Pretending and pretending and *pretending* . . . The Seer in the Goblin Market those weeks ago had echoed a sentiment Aurelian had been feeling for years: for a people who abhorred telling lies, very little about their actions were truth.

Celadon Fleur-Viridian was an anomaly, a fae who was used to doing things his own way, used to folk—no matter how important— heeding his every command, used to flouting as he pleased the fae customs and traditions no one else would dare spurn.

Celadon was able to shed pretense whenever he wanted.

The trade-off, Aurelian surmised, was that it had earned him a reputation among the inflated egos of the Courts, who all relied on a certain order to stoke their self-importance and buzzed like angered wasps whenever it wasn't properly observed.

The Seelie Summer Councillors would *not* be happy with the dismissal they'd just received, this waving them off and denying them the opportunity to ingratiate themselves with the High Royalty.

"Is there any particular reason you wanted *me* to show you to your room, Your Highness?" Aurelian asked as they made their way down the hall to the door at the end, the High Prince's personal attendant following a few paces back.

He tried to keep the question light.

Distinctly aware that the last time they'd met, the High Prince had been in a spectacular mood Aurelian hadn't been willing to entertain, and maybe he didn't like Aurelian all that much for the way he'd talked back to him then—Aurelian didn't want to risk offending the High Prince a second time and ruining any chance of the best alliance he could hope to make in this situation.

But the High Prince said nothing.

He kept his arm tight around Aurelian's and walked with an air of ease beside him, and all the while his mask of perfect, polite indifference remained firmly in place. It was his eyes that gave him away.

Eyes that were exactly like Arlo's, Aurelian noted. The same shade of green, same shape, and most likely just as expressive to anyone who knew how to read them. Fortunately, what the High Prince was thinking right now wasn't too difficult to decipher—he was deeply confused by what had just happened, and fuming, but *he knew*.

He knew Riadne was far better at pretending than she led the world to believe.

Aurelian stopped them outside their destination and pushed open the door for the High Prince to step through, the High Prince waving off his attendant to stay her from following.

The room was just as extravagant as Arlo's had been. No doubt the ones adjoined to it were equally ostentatious, but the High Prince spared all of a cursory glance for the spectacle of marble and gold and emerald silk and twists of dark-leaved vines. Just as Aurelian closed the door behind them and turned back around, the High Prince whirled to face him, and now his gaze was as inscrutable as everything else about him.

"Do you know what my Gift is, Lord Aurelian?" was how he chose to begin.

Not every sidhe fae was born with a Gift, a quirk of their magic that correlated directly with their element. Some Gifts were harmless enough—the ability to fly, for example, or commune with woodland creatures. Some Gifts, like High Prince Celadon's, required registration with the Courts for the potential damage it could do if ever wielded against them. Even then, this registration was strictly confidential to the High King and the Fae High Council's records alone, and the upper elite were extremely tight-lipped about their talents. The only reason Aurelian knew anything at all about the High Prince's Gift was because rumors about this particular folk-icon spread like *wildfire* through the magical community.

But that was all it was, really.

Rumors.

Only a handful of folk—Arlo undoubtedly being one of those rare few, Aurelian was sure—actually knew what that Gift truly was, and their knowing this was no doubt guarded by a geas enforced by the High King's command.

Aurelian shrugged. "As I hear it, you can talk to the air."

As though deeply offended by the mild choice of phrasing, the High Prince's expression curdled slightly. He raised a brow. "I *talk* to the *air*?"

"Sorry. I didn't realize you wanted me to tack on the part where a lot of folk actually think you're just as mentally unwell as your father and more likely talking to *yourself* than the element of your Court."

"Oh, thank goodness." The High Prince's hand fluttered to his heart, and Aurelian was tempted to swear the relief on his face was genuine. "For a moment I thought I'd become too *boring* to gossip about."

"Yeah," Aurelian replied dryly. "Thank goodness."

The High Prince removed his hand from his chest to wave it between them. "I *do* commune with the air, though. Not in such a way as you might be guessing; it's more the air communing with *me* in the voices it collects. More or less, it captures conversations, and my Gift allows me to replay them at will, but I have to be in the place those words were originally spoken, and these captures only last a couple of days before they begin to break apart and fade, and I can no longer hear them."

A good Gift to have, if that was true, and no wonder the Courts had been so strict with their High Prince's registration. As Aurelian understood it, he wasn't even allowed to venture far outside his own palace anymore, and now Aurelian could probably guess this to be because of the things Celadon knew that could be pulled from him with the right pressure applied, and the things others didn't want him to somehow overhear. The High Prince was just as much of a liability as he was a potential weapon—to the fae and folk in general. The greatest wealth they had to trade was measured in the truths they tried to keep secret.

And it was all the more confusing to wonder why the High King had permitted him to come here at all—whatever Celadon could stand to learn from being here, there would be oh so much he could accidentally betray to Azurean's greatest enemy.

But . . . "Why are you telling me this?" was what Aurelian asked aloud.

"Because Riadne undoubtedly knows about my Gift. In the very least, she's overheard the rumors and is smart enough to believe them, and will go out of her way to keep me far from the spaces where she speaks valuable information. I don't think I need to tell you that I deeply mistrust the woman who's had it out for my father my entire life—who's spurned the whole Viridian family up until now, and whatever the reason she wanted Arlo here for the summer, I trust that even less. I'm telling *you* this because my Gift has made me fairly intuitive about certain things and certain people. I would not ask Prince Vehan to betray his own mother to me, but I intend to learn what Riadne Lysterne means to do before she makes her play. And I'm hoping I've read *you* correctly, Aurelian Bessel, in assuming you might be willing to help."

It couldn't be this easy.

Here Aurelian had been hoping he could use the High Prince's dislike for the Seelie Summer Queen as protection, a buffer between them, but it turns out the High Prince might be willing to go the extra step to help him thwart whatever terrible plot she had in store for the stage she'd been setting, piece by painstaking piece, for *centuries*?

High Prince Celadon was an intelligent fae, none of this should be surprising, but Aurelian was still too unused to having help to agree to anything without question. Riadne was a dangerous person who hid behind poise and overt acts of kindness; for as little as he actually knew about Celadon Fleur-Viridian, he could be dangerous too—*was* dangerous. The risk was in whether that danger would be to Aurelian.

"What sort of help are you after, exactly?" he asked, folding his arms over his chest and eyeing the High Prince with a hardness he could normally rely on to make Vehan yield in one of his more stubborn moods.

"Simply knowing where to look for the secrets I'm after would be a *tremendous* place to start, I'd say."

"If I agree to help you, it's a geas or nothing," Aurelian countered, his tone even harder than his stare. "I'll tell you whatever I can about Riadne and her secrets and do whatever is in my ability to help your plans where she's concerned. But in exchange, you'll take my family and myself *and* Prince Vehan under your protection. I can't risk the blowback from this should Riadne learn what we're doing without that assurance. An alliance, or we have no deal."

He held out his hand.

Aurelian didn't spend much time contemplating how attractive the High Prince was, not like Vehan had and probably still did, considering the posters he'd only just taken down and carefully (mournfully) rolled up to hide away in his closet so the High Prince wouldn't see them during his stay. It was a fact that didn't really need addressing. Magic was real. The sun rose in the morning and set at night. High Prince Celadon was extraordinarily beautiful. Delicately so, the same way Theodore was beautiful—and not Aurelian's usual type, but then . . . so far that type had been firmly Vehan and no one else.

And only because his mind had strayed in this direction did another errant thought make him wonder—who was the High Prince's type?

Aurelian watched him tilt back his head and laugh, then drop his chin to fix Aurelian with so much amusement that he then wondered if maybe there was some hole in the terms of his promise that he'd overlooked . . . until Aurelian noticed that amusement was also a little sad.

"It's tough, navigating perilous court intrigue all by yourself at such a young age, isn't it? Trying to keep loved ones safe from the things you're forced to do and be at the whims of others. Trying to keep the things you know from hurting the people who matter most. I'm sorry." The High Prince spoke with the gravity of someone who knew *exactly* what Aurelian had been bearing this whole time—most assuredly *did*, because Gifts like the High Prince's didn't just present themselves fully developed overnight. It might not have been until a mere handful of months ago that the Courts officially registered Celadon Fleur-Viridian as a Reader, but a Gift like that . . . they took their time in cultivating.

Aurelian couldn't say for sure exactly when the High Prince would have first started picking up bits of knowledge that he couldn't explain how he knew, but he would bet it was *far* earlier than what had been publicly admitted, clever wording and misdirecting truths allowing the Courts to conceal the lie that the High Prince had been . . . hells, a convenient little UnSeelie Spring spy.

One that might have played a key part these last few years in keeping that Crown on the Viridian patriarch's head.

But there it was again, that relief in the knowledge that he wasn't alone. This time, instead of laughter, the proof that it wasn't only him against what felt like the world made his eyes sting.

"I agree to your terms." Celadon took Aurelian's extended hand in his own, but this was just for show. A tingling warmth had bloomed in the center of his heart and wound itself around like a snarl of vines the moment Celadon spoke his assent.

The magic of their geas.

The High Prince would have felt it too, the warmth that burst to ensnare his own heart and bind him to his words.

The deal was struck.

Aurelian had his protector, the High Prince had his informant, and already there was something he needed to know before the queen came to collect them. Aurelian had been sitting on it for a while now, afraid to even ask around if anyone else had figured it out, because part of what made *this* particular Gift so dangerous was how easy it was to conceal and how virtually undetectable its usage was.

Aurelian had only noticed it at all because of a fluke.

The queen had been sloppy just once, in one crucial moment, and had misjudged how resistant Aurelian actually was to this sort of magic. She hadn't applied it strongly enough the first time she'd ever wielded it against him. And Aurelian *knew*. And knowing made his resistance stronger, but he had to keep pretending, just like everything else in his life, and just like every other piece of knowledge he possessed that he had no idea who to trust with.

Who would believe him? It was Aurelian's word against the far more *persuasive* queen's.

But now he had the High Prince on his side, and very clear to Aurelian was the fact that she'd just misjudged him, too.

"Riadne's office, that's where you should conduct your search. I can show you the way later, but while we still have the time . . . you felt it, didn't you? Back in Arlo's bedroom. She laid it on just a little too thick. You felt the Seelie Summer Queen's Gift—her *secondary* Gift, in addition to the radiance that makes her queen of this Court."

"Ah," replied Celadon, with all the air of a breeze. "Are we talking now about how Riadne Lysterne is apparently an unregistered Mesmer?"

Aurelian stared, slightly taken aback by the confirmation that the

High Prince had indeed figured it out—and so *quickly*. It had taken Aurelian *months* of research to come to this conclusion himself.

"Yes," Celadon continued, expression darkening. "I'd *very* much like to talk about *that*. Because according to records, there's a current grand total of three folk in the Eight Great Courts with persuasive ability profound enough to beguile even sidhe fae, let alone one of the High Royals like myself, *let alone* without drawing wider notice, and Riadne Lysterne isn't so much as an honorable mention on that list. So that's . . . concerning, I would say."

"Concerning?" Aurelian would have scoffed if he weren't so suddenly and incredibly exhausted. It was much, much more than *concerning*. "I tried to warn Nausicaä not to let Arlo come." A text to which she'd replied with a succinct, *fuck off, Legolas, she'll do what she likes*. "*None* of you should have come. I don't know what Riadne wants with your cousin, but I know *you* have no part in it. I know I'm expendable to her, we're *all* expendable to her, and if you think that whatever you've had to deal with in the UnSeelie Spring Court has been difficult? If you think your status is going to protect you here? Wait until you're ordered in to watch a serving girl—whose fault was drawing a bath just a *little* too hot for a visiting guest— hold *herself* under that water until she drowns, purely because the queen *suggests* it."

There was so much death and torture and horror stuffed into the five years Aurelian had been bound to this place, and still he saw it—the way that young faerie girl had thrashed against the magic that made her plunge her head into bath water heated to scalding, much hotter than the poor girl had mistakenly done, and keep it there until she went limp.

"You think you're ready for Riadne Lysterne. You think you're ready for her anger. But you've never encountered anger like *this* before. You've never encountered this sort of cruelty, I promise you."

And it was this *exact* underestimation she'd been using to her advantage for over three whole centuries. If ten thousand hours of practice in something made one an expert in a field, as the human adage went, the Seelie Summer Queen was as close to godhood in the art of deception as any mortal would likely ever be able to come.

None of them were ready.

And worst was that Aurelian suspected that none of them, no matter what they tried, ever would be.

Gossip had labeled Riadne many things over the years. Ambitious, intelligent, *talented*—the praises varied, but what folk tacked on at the end of these words was always the same, the condescending "for a girl" that implied that nothing they'd so graciously attributed her would ever be taken seriously.

The Seelie Summer Councillors, the palace staff, and random folk Riadne encountered whenever she went out—"she's such a wonder, *for a girl*"—for years those words had *grated*. They'd stung just as badly as her mother's blatant disdain. They'd sparked a rebellion in Riadne, pushed her to excel in everything she did, never mind if she made herself sick in the process or lost her already too-few friend-ships one by one. Her childhood had been consumed with the sin-gular need to prove herself equal to *any* of the folk, no matter their gender, no matter *hers*; to escape the pretty but insignificant box the world had packaged her up in, and pulled her out to ogle and cosset and then tuck her back away at their *amusement*, all because they *underestimated* who Riadne was.

The room in which she currently stood was carved entirely out of black granite stone.

The floors gleamed like a smooth wash of ink, the walls like the glittering cosmos.

Much like it did Riadne, the world might overlook this tiny hole in the wall as inconsequential. Anyone else who somehow found their way down into this highly secured vault might ignore the simple black marble pedestal at the room's center, the bell jar on top of it, and the misshapen chunk of obsidian black rock contained within.

Here in the bowels of the UnSeelie Spring palace, where the High King kept the most dangerous, legendary artifacts the folk had ever uncovered or forged—his privilege and duty, as the Courts' High Sovereign—there was so much *else* to dazzle the curiosity.

But the stone inside this bell jar . . .

Riadne reached to lift it and seize the prize within.

The moment her fingers made contact with the cool glass, she winced. A scene flashed across her vision, replacing the room for all of a moment with . . . something. A memory—not hers but the stone's, she was almost certain—and with it a feeling of such profound pride, such yearning, such *cruelty* . . .

A man sat sprawled on the floor of a darkened chamber, books and papers strewn around his weary body. In the middle of the room, an array—the most elaborate array, intricate looping, complex equations, lines and symbols all woven together in the shape of a butterfly, caught inside an alchemic ring.

Too dark—it was too dark to see anything other than the blood that dripped from his nose in dark red droplets onto the wood; other than the too-small corpse in the center of the array, twisted and warped by the magic that had drained their life to fuel this.

Smoke curled from the recently extinguished wicks of the candles all around—what had just taken place had cost very nearly all energy in the room, but the man sprawled on the floor . . . he lifted his head, took in the sight of the remains of his victim, where an obsidian black stone had bubbled up to break through flesh directly where a heart should have been.

"At last . . . ," the man rasped.

"Tsk, tsk, tsk."

Riadne gasped, broke free of whatever had stolen over her mind. Disoriented but not about to let herself fall prey to vulnerability, she whirled on her heels.

Someone had just been behind her. She'd been able to feel the presence of their magic brush ever so slightly against hers, and despite how quiet that mildly bemused *tsk*ing had been, her fae senses had picked up on it immediately. But when she turned around, there was no one there. She thought perhaps she saw something in the corner of the room flutter, the tail end of a black cloak snapping out of view, but as hard as she examined the entirety of this chamber—barely large enough to admit her along with its treasure—she saw nothing to suggest it was anything more than her mind playing tricks on her.

Frowning, still suspicious of what had just occurred, Riadne made to slowly turn back to the stone in the bell jar, but just as she did . . .

"Riadne?"

This voice she knew, and it wasn't her imagination.

"Riadne, what are you *doing* here? This place is expressly off-limits, I don't even know how you knew where to find it, let alone how you managed to—"

"Hello, Azurean," she greeted, turning to him with as lovely a smile as she could sculpt across her face.

She was careful to keep her words gentle, clear, concise—they were easier to magnetize that way, to make them and by result herself irresistible. It required very little magic to mesmerize a human. The majority of folk could do it with no more trouble than batting a lash. It was quite a different thing to be a full-blown Mesmer, a fae capable of wielding the electricborn Gift of Magnetism. *All* were susceptible to it, human, faerie, and fae alike—even immortals, they'd long ago learned—and with enough control and practice, this Magnetism could strip away free will almost as completely as dark magic could, leaving nothing but a *glimmer* of potential for resistance in the person it was used against.

All the reward, none of the immortal intervention and punishment, as dark magic warranted.

Given the potential magnitude of this Gift, and the danger it presented to the Courts, every sidhe fae with lightning in their blood was tested for it upon Maturity, and if Riadne had still been determined to impress a world so keen to overlook her at that time, she would have come forward with it proudly, as all the others had done, when it had first showed signs of manifesting. Mesmers were rare, and the grade of it in Riadne was what research assured her was unparalleled by any of her kind.

But why show this card at the Courts' demand? They only tested for Gifts within the first five years of Maturing. Why play her hand now when—quite anomalously—it had taken almost a full *decade* after Maturity for it to develop strongly enough in her to be classified as a Gift, as something a Reader could to pick up on in her mind if summoned back to test her again. Why reveal it when she'd come to realize just how much she enjoyed the *advantages* of the world's underestimation?

Standing in the doorway, Azurean regarded Riadne through thoroughly dazed shock. She didn't blame him. Just as he said, she wasn't supposed to be here, was *supposed* to be with her mother on a stroll through the indoor greenhouse with the High King, or luxuriating in her personal quarters, or taking tea with one of the numerous other nobles, as was all that was expected of her on this visit to the UnSeelie Spring palace.

Getting here required passing two sets of Verdant Guards, and this chamber specifically was only accessible to those of the High King's Viridian bloodline, and while both had been easily enough dealt with, of course Azurean would have no idea how she could manage it on her own.

He blinked down at his hand, which must be smarting, considering Riadne had magnetized him into slicing through his palm to smear the door with its asking price for admittance—a few drops of his royal blood.

"What's going on?" he wondered aloud, looking from his hand to the door, but before he could work himself into a state or start to draw any dangerous conclusions, Riadne raised her hands and clapped them loudly together at her mouth, directing his gaze back to her.

She didn't *need* this eye contact, but she'd found that it helped to center her intended target's focus and make them even more susceptible to her *charm*. Sudden, distinct sounds—such as the snap of one's fingers or the clap of their hands—were very good ways of claiming the attention she needed to work her magic.

"It's all right," she fairly purred. "You're taking me on a tour of the vaults, remember? What's one more secret between lovers, hmm?"

She leaned in, pressed her chest against Azurean's and a barely there kiss on his mouth. It was nowhere near the first they'd shared in recent years—what had started as sparring matches, sighs, longing looks had become stolen hours in out-of-the-way places, Azurean's hand drifting up the curve of her thigh as he kissed her breathless against the shelves of a darkened office; Riadne's teeth like a possessive vise as she bit down on his shoulder to stay silent and keep their budding affair from discovery.

She'd never needed her Magnetism to bend Azurean to her will in *that* respect—he very nearly *loved* her, she'd hazard a guess by now, and she . . . well, she very nearly loved him too, enough in return that she'd always wanted his affections to be his own choosing. What they got up to these days in addition to their matches and painfully cordial chats in public view . . . none of that had been false, and she suspected it was this mutual almost-love feeling for each other that made him so pliant to her secondary Gift.

To *this*, though, he wouldn't bend. Not of his own volition.

Riadne gave a coquettish grin as she reeled back, keeping their gazes locked all the while. Confusion weighed heavier on Azurean's furrowed brow. He was getting better at resisting Riadne's control and required magnetizing more frequently to keep him content and pliable to the things she wanted from him—simple things, nothing terrible. That *almost*-love she felt for him made her incapable of pushing him too far, but she'd wanted the practice, and his building resistance to her was just as valuable a discovery as anything else he'd unwittingly helped her learn.

She'd have to be careful how often she did this from here on out to prevent this immunity from building any further, but today would not be the day the High Prince found the strength to overcome this magic and realize what she'd done. "Right," he said, settling back into blissful ignorance, the tension in both his face and body melting away. "Right, the tour."

She liked him much better like this.

Silent. Subservient.

Every passing year, Azurean grew more and more lovely, and every passing year, Riadne grew more and more frustrated. A handful of decades had passed since they'd started up their affair, but still he was just as handsome as ever—jade eyes bright, cheeks flushed with sapphire color. A bit more of his father was beginning to peek through his image, though, in the russet hair that was long enough now to tie behind his head and the modest beard growing along his jaw.

It would be a handful of decades yet, a century easily, before a child was produced between his wife and him. Fae fertility was a sluggish thing—the price of their extended lifetimes, many folk reasoned. But folk already gossiped about this topic of conversation, when Reseda would provide an heir and how lovely their offspring would be. The High Prince of a well-established, well-respected family, Azurean positively radiated happiness, had everything he could possibly want and none of the condescension Riadne was constantly forced to bear.

No one ever said that *he* was "ambitious, intelligent, talented *for a boy*."

No one would blame *him* if their affair was ever discovered.

"This stone," Riadne prompted, stepping aside to give Azurean clearer view. "You spoke of it once before . . ."

"I . . . did?"

Riadne nodded. She recalled his letting it slip after one of their "meetings," a trinket more powerful than even the Bone Crown, if the stories were true. "Yes, a legendary stone that grants its possessor immortality and unimaginable wealth. The product of alchemy—which, incidentally, the Courts placed a permanent ban on the practice of, all for something some ironborn achieved that made them and their art intolerably dangerous in our Sovereign's eyes. What was their name again? Strangely, I find myself unable to remember."

Pain flickered across Azurean's gaze—no response. Very well, Riadne could try at a different angle.

"It was never revealed to the general public what that danger had truly been, but this is it, am I right? This is a philosopher's stone, isn't it, Azurean."

Most thought of the philosopher's stones as the invention of faerie tales and nothing more. If Riadne was at all capable of feeling shame, she would have been embarrassed merely asking the question aloud.

But Azurean walked forward, a man caught in a daydream. He peered at the object in question, considering it mildly. "It's more than that."

"What do you mean?"

His brows began to furrow again under some internal conflict. It was clear to Riadne that the question she'd asked had an answer he very much didn't want to give—or more likely, wasn't *supposed* to. Had he been sworn to secrecy on the subject? That would make this a little more difficult, but there were ways around such things if one was clever, and careful, and skilled at playing around with lies to make them sound like believable truths . . .

"It's okay, Azurean," Riadne soothed. "It's all right. This feels much like a dream, does it not? Perhaps it *is* one—and speaking this secret to a dream, why, surely *that* can't be forbidden to you?"

However much Azurean looked to be struggling against her sway over him, in his current befuddled state, he couldn't help but nod. "That's true," he replied, words heavy as molasses. "This does feel like a dream . . ."

"There's nothing to betray to a thing that isn't real. So tell me, go ahead. This secret you carry like a burden, *How is this object more than a philosopher's stone?*" Riadne repeated, applying so much of her Magnetism to the question that Azurean gasped, lifted a hand to dig the palm of it into his aching chest, where no doubt a geas throbbed its warning, but magic was a funny thing. So long as Azurean *believed* he wasn't breaking his promise . . . "It's a philosopher's stone," he rushed to comply, his tone gone breathless and trembling. "But it's more than that. It's the soul of one of the Seven Sins, the demon princes of old. This one is Pride, and he doesn't only grant his possessor immortality, but amplifies their magic to such a degree even the Bone Crown can't—"

He cut himself off in another gasp.

The spell Riadne had cast over him was breaking, nearly worn off entirely—the geas, likely, working to keep itself protected, and Riadne wasn't good enough yet to push any harder against what stayed Azurean's tongue. If she tried in this moment, he'd only find her out.

But it didn't matter.

He'd told her all she needed to know.

Something that could amplify magic to a degree even the Bone Crown couldn't contend with it?

One of *Seven Sins*?

The *power* she'd felt pouring off that stone even through its glass container—oh, but she wouldn't be overlooked with *this*. And with the Bone Crown *and* this rare magical artifact, well, her mother would *have* to acknowledge Riadne's talents *then*—her mother, and everyone else.

Riadne's renewed determination tucked itself beneath a wide and lovely grin. She slipped her arm to weave around Azurean's, folded herself delicately against his side. Appealing to the fraction of his lingering magnetization, she purred again, "What would you say to a sparring match, Your Highness? We haven't had one of those in ages—not in their *literal* sense."

And as she led him back out into the hall, Riadne cast one last look behind her, at the stone she'd pour the next however many years it took into replicating. What she didn't see—and wouldn't again for quite some time—was the figure who stood behind it, rendered invisible by his equally legendary cloak.

Acid green eyes . . .

Teeth as sharp as a shark's bite . . .

Starlight-shimmering and driftwood warped and hauntingly, almost horrifically beautiful . . .

"Tsk, tsk, tsk."

CHAPTER 13

Vehan

~~~~~~~~

THERE WERE A TOTAL of *four* dining rooms in the Luminous Palace, all of various sizes, and three of them were specifically designed to impress even the haughtiest of visitors the Seelie Court of Summer had ever played host to. Much like every other space in Vehan's home, no detail had been overlooked, no expense spared. Everything was gilded and dripping yellow jewels, offset by stark white stone and elegant ivory flourishes, and armed with delicate china and solid gold utensils.

Riadne Lysterne had a certain standard—nothing less than perfection—so Vehan felt his surprise was justified when, instead of one of those other extravagant three they normally used in these occasions, she'd led their UnSeelie Spring guests, High Prince and all, to the fourth and smallest dining room, where he and his mother alone shared their everyday meals.

But of course, as ever, his mother had known exactly what she was doing.

This space was fairly modest, much more *comfortable* than the others they had to offer. Its decadence was limited to a cream and gold Kashan rug laid out in the middle of the marble floor; a long and hefty mahogany table situated atop it, with matching chairs, tiny suns and miniature bolts of lightning carved into their backs; and a massive marble fireplace along one wall, currently unlit, flanked by twin glass cabinets filled with crystal decanters of the queen's favorite liquors, ports, and liqueurs.

It was the floor-to-ceiling indoor waterfall spanning the entirety of the opposite wall that served as both the windowless room's only source of light and display of elemental prowess. Instead of water, an endless shower of sparks flowed down the pane of its white slate tiles, the brilliance of which could be easily adjusted with a snap of the queen's fingers to mimic day's intensity, or the softer glow of early dawn, or anything in between.

However interesting this display was to watch—soothing, really, Vehan often found—it would be spectacularly dull to someone like High Prince Celadon, High Lord Morayo, or *any* of the sidhe fae elite Riadne had ever entertained. But as soon as he saw the effect this relative *normalcy* had on *Arlo*—the way she relaxed into her chair when directed to her seat, the color that had returned to her face—he understood why his mother had chosen here instead of elsewhere.

Zzzt

Vehan *almost* jolted in his seat. The shock Theo had shot under the table at his leg had caught him unaware, and it was instinct to clench the muscle in his smarting calf, but he'd managed just in time to keep from reacting in any other way.

He cut a sideways glare at his friend, at the fae his mother had made no secret of preferring over however many other suitors she no doubt managed behind his back.

It had no effect.

Theo, who'd been seated on Vehan's right, wasn't looking his way at all. His body was angled away from Vehan, more toward High Prince Celadon on his opposite side, with whom he was in deep conversation. But apparently not deep *enough* conversation if he was starting up a round of the game many of them played in school when their professors weren't looking.

Oh, the professors knew it was going on, of course. It was something of an age-old tradition to shoot off sparks of electric magic at one another during lessons, or assemblies, or (and especially) detention. The aim being, naturally, to see who could be the first to get a rise out of their friends. It was a harmless enough sport—the sparks weren't ever strong enough to do actual damage, and "losing" was just a teacher catching them and slapping them with classroom duties for the disruption—but then Vehan and a few of his . . . *cockier* friends took it a bit more seriously than that.

They pushed their magic to be a lot rougher with each other, got a little "carried away," as their principal had often phrased it.

Vehan might be too powerful to suffer any lasting injury, but Theo was powerful too, and the shocks the two of them *occasionally* ended up sending each other when their competitiveness got away from them were often hot enough to leave welts and actual burns.

His mother never cared.

In fact, Vehan suspected it actually pleased Riadne to know her son didn't shy away from such trivial pain. Once, though, the marks on them both had been so bad that Aurelian—in his unforgettable horror—had actually *shouted* at them, in loud and genuinely angry words that rang in Vehan's ears long after Aurelian had stormed off, leaving him and Theo stunned.

They tried to dial it down a bit after that incident.

And ever since the mountaintop when Vehan had failed to call down even a piddling fizzle of lightning, he'd noticed in a way he couldn't ignore that his magic was acting *unusually*—or rather, not acting at *all*. Whether he'd burnt out his core on that mountain or slammed into some mysterious wall inside himself, he couldn't summon even an ounce of it from his core, no matter what he or the palace head MediFae tried. So it wasn't as though he could retaliate right now.

Rest, the doctor had ordered. Vehan would be fine after rest. It was Theo who'd proposed, mere days ago, their school game as a way to help Vehan overcome this strange magical blockage, because so far "rest" was doing exactly nothing. They figured, perhaps, if they could trick his magic into responding, Vehan would be able to push past whatever was holding it back.

But while Riadne might look the other way whenever Vehan came home with a slip of admonishment from his teachers for his "overenthusiastic" participation in this "foolish behavior," he knew without a doubt she wouldn't appreciate it interrupting their evening tonight.

"Cut it out," Vehan whispered, kicking his foot against Theo's heel. "Not *now*."

"Vehan?" Riadne cut in, sharp as the edge of cut glass.

There was a certain protocol to follow, as far as seating arrangement went for meals. As the High King's steward, standing as representative in his place, High Lord Morayo and Lord Lekan sat at the end designated for the visiting Heads of the Courts. Riadne occupied the other end, with Arlo given the seat of importance at her left and Leda placed beside her, Aurelian, as steward in training, next. After the tension back in Arlo's bedroom—and honestly, that hadn't been surprising, given the past between the High Prince and Vehan's mother—he'd expected Celadon to be a little more offended by this deviation. Normally, *he* would be placed where Arlo was sitting, but he seemed quite happy for the distance right now, an eager participant in his conversation with Theo (though Vehan did notice the way he assessed in frequent glances every new interaction between the queen and his cousin).

Vehan lifted his gaze, turning it from Theo to the head of the table. To his mother, prim in her seat, wineglass in hand and a benign smile on her face that shrank a little with every ticking second Vehan didn't reply.

Ah.

Was it possible Theo hadn't been toying with him? That he'd been trying to nudge Vehan out of his thoughts?

He cleared his throat. "Yes, Mother?"

A moment passed in which Riadne merely stared at him over the rim of her wine glass. The electric waterfall illuminated the room to a warm, evening gentleness, but the way the shimmering light played off both her pale white wine and her freezing blue eyes lent a glint of something sharper to the atmosphere, and Vehan knew immediately that his distraction had made him miss something she'd said.

His mother greatly disliked repeating herself.

Instinct made him want to glance at Aurelian to gauge the situation. He could always tell how foolish a blunder he'd made was by the level of stoniness in his retainer's expression, but doing so right now—breaking the gaze his mother held—would only make things worse. She disliked being ignored even more.

"Sorry, I . . . didn't hear the question."

Another moment passed.

Vehan bit his lip. Had he missed something *important*? His mother wouldn't be pleased. *A king does not get distracted*, she'd taught him. One of her many, unflinching rules. *Distraction costs valuable control. No matter what or how much is going on around you, you* must *keep aware of it all at all times.*

But just when the table's watchful silence started to take an awkward turn, Riadne's smile replaced itself, wide and unconcerned. "I was just explaining to Arlo the modest schedule to her summer—apart from her alchemy training, I thought she might appreciate your guidance through a few dance lessons? And if she'd like, your additional tutoring on some of the guests who will be in attendance at the Solstice."

"Oh!" Vehan brightened, a smile of his own spreading across his face, slowly for how bizarre it was that his mother had dropped his unintentional rudeness without a word of admonishment. "Yes, of course, I'd be happy to help you with anything you'd like, Arlo."

"There." Riadne turned her smile to Arlo, who nodded gratefully and thanked both Vehan and his mother profusely.

And just like that, an entire minor crisis had been adverted.

Riadne delved back into conversation, asking after Arlo's favorite foods for future meals and things she might be interested in seeing during her stay with them.

Vehan watched them talk.

He watched the way his mother leaned ever so slightly toward

Arlo as though they were great friends catching up after some long parting; the way she laughed at the things Arlo said, encouraged her to continue at every stop; the way she drew Leda frequently into the open and easy dialogue between them, joked with the High Lord and his husband, and even nodded graciously whenever High Prince Celadon broke from his own conversation with Theo to contribute something.

This behavior was . . . not *common* for Vehan's mother. It was more how *Aurelian's* mother behaved in the once-upon-a-time when he and Aurelian had been closer, and Vehan used to join the Bessels for any meal he could. And he could still recall with perfect clarity the moment it had hit him—that not all mothers were distant and hard and strict with their sons, as Riadne was with him, as he'd simply assumed all mothers to be, until he'd seen firsthand how close Nerilla Bessel was with her children.

It was . . . nice to see this side of his own mother.

Maybe this visit would be good for them. Maybe it would thaw a bit of whatever had frosted over a clearly profound friendship that had once existed between the Viridian and Lysterne families. Maybe this was a glimpse of the woman Riadne could be once everything settled, the mother Vehan had *wanted* ever since learning that mothers were actually supposed to *care* where their children went and what they did beyond their royal obligations—

Zzzt

"*Theo*," Vehan hissed, gritting his teeth. He clenched his fist on the table, bit the inside of his cheek—that had *hurt*, damn it, and he wouldn't let it show, but why in the hells was Theo shocking him *this* time?

Theo's head dipped back a fraction in a throaty laugh at something High Prince Celadon had said, something that made Arlo roll her eyes and High Lord Morayo boom out laughter too. The corner of even Aurelian's mouth twitched in that highly controlled way of his that said he was amused but didn't want Celadon knowing.

Unable to shock Theo back, Vehan slipped a hand under the table and pinched him hard on the side.

Caught off guard, Theo grunted and slapped the table with the palm of his hand, turning a bewildered, slightly menacing look on Vehan. "What was *that* for?" he demanded, and then, with a glance at the queen, added stiffly, "Your Highness."

Vehan wasn't buying it for a second. In fact, the confused outrage on Theo's face only served to worsen his mood. "Cut. It. *Out*," he snapped under his breath.

Turning fully to Vehan now, Theo narrowed his glare even deadlier and replied in a much quieter (but no less annoyed) tone, "Cut *what* out, you inbred *troll*?"

"Don't give me that. You know exactly what—"

"Listen, train wreck, this is not your station. Day care is *Aurelian's* business, so pack up your damage and bring it to him, because I'm *trying* to have a conversation right now and whatever *this* is isn't helping."

The nerve of him. Something fluttered across Vehan's heart, a lot like what he'd felt on the mountain when Aurelian had tried to stop him from pushing himself into a Surge. Dark and poisonous and angry, it was a feeling that *lurched* inside of him, but wasn't at all his own.

The intensity of it . . . it left Vehan breathless as it washed over him, as it flooded out everything but the singular, all-consuming desire to lash out at his friend—to *hurt* him, physically, for daring to speak like this to him, and *Urielle,* this wasn't at all a healthy reaction to this relatively minor conflict.

The magnitude of this feeling that wasn't *him,* not at all, frightened Vehan, and yet he still only *just* caught the way his hand had instinctually tightened around the butter knife on the table out of the corner of his eye—

There in the blink of a moment, gone almost as soon as it had come.

As soon as Vehan realized what his hand was doing without his consent, the peculiar anger passed. His emotions were his own again, and sure, he was a little incensed by the implication that he used Aurelian in any such way, yet that was still *him*.

But anger like that . . . cruelty like what had flashed across his mind just a moment ago, that *wasn't*.

He swallowed.

Attempting to regain his composure before Theo realized something was wrong, he glowered at his friend, and frosted his tone almost as coolly as his mother could manage. "Conversation, yes, I see." His gaze flicked briefly over Theo's shoulder to the High Prince. "Keeping your options open, are you?"

"Absolutely. Because if you pinch me again, you're dead, and I'm going to need a new prospective husband."

"Shock me again, shadow prince, and *you'll* be—"

The doors at the back of the room sprung open to reveal the arrival of dinner, cutting off Vehan and the comment he'd barbed with an insult many whispered unkindly behind Theo's back as well as to his face: *shadow prince*, a royal without a throne, a prince without a crown, forever cast in the Lysterne family's shadow.

It was a low blow.

Vehan hadn't meant to actually say it. That unusual anger hadn't left him entirely yet, it seemed, for him to spit it out. And the hurt that flashed in Theo's gaze before he could shutter it away made Vehan feel wretched. He was glad for the interruption of dinner.

In walked several fae and faeries, each carrying a piece of tonight's feast. Their skin had been painted with glittering gold dust, their attire the bone-white uniform that designated them serving staff— straight-cut, high-rise trousers; molten gold heels; a tucked-in white silk blouse; and a long-tailed, form fitted jacket overtop.

Riadne's standard of perfection, down to every detail.

"Excellent," Vehan's mother exclaimed, draining the rest of her glass. The moment she set it down on the table, it was whisked away and replaced with a fresh glass, this one for the red wine she'd chosen to complement their meal.

One of the servants—Islas, Vehan recalled quickly, because the queen knew the names and faces of *each* of the people under her employ and expected Vehan to do the same—made his rounds, pouring out a healthy portion of wine so full-bodied and deeply red that it looked a great deal like human blood. Vehan didn't blame the mildly squeamish expression on Arlo's face when she covered her own glass to decline and stick to water.

Piece by piece, their meal was laid out before them on polished gold platters: leafy salads and baskets of fresh, fragrant bread; ruby-skinned potatoes slathered in coarse salt and melted butter; lushly pink smoked salmon on crisp cucumber rounds, topped with lemon-zest and dill cream cheese; tender roast duck breast with rosemary and figs and fried garlic; mouth-watering, marbled cuts of steak cooked to the juicier side of medium-rare; tureens of golden saffron risotto and vibrant mixtures of fire-roasted vegetables.

A human meal.

Riadne didn't eat like this—fae didn't need to eat much and usually stuck to lighter fare, like fruits and sea creatures and cakes and pastries, the sorts of things Aurelian's parents made. Many sidhe felt this was more in keeping with fae tradition, however much in secret they actually liked heavier, meatier meals.

Vehan's stomach rumbled.

"No more shocks," Vehan warned, pointing at Theo around Peregrine, the servant responsible for distributing cider and onion soup garnished with shredded cheese and apples sliced so thin they curled like flakes of snow in the bowl.

"I have literally no idea what you're talking about," Theo deadpanned—perhaps a little *too* stonily for Vehan's previous insult—and once Peregrine moved on, reached over to pinch Vehan back.

What ensued was the briefest and pettiest of battles kept low beneath the tabletop. It lasted until Riadne cleared her throat and

Vehan noticed how very close he was to pushing her over the edge of her patience with him this evening. He quickly yielded, wincing when Theo scored his winning point, and tried his best to ignore the way that stung too.

He chanced a glance at Aurelian.

That expression was as guarded as it always was, but the way he just sat there, *staring* at Vehan, in no way acknowledging the servers he'd normally thank individually, spoke volumes about the thin ice Vehan's behavior so far had skated him to.

Drawing a breath, Vehan willed himself to relax. He picked up his soup spoon, smiled widely, and with the air of someone completely untroubled, said to Arlo, "So, I haven't had a chance to ask yet—how's Nausicaä, Arlo? I hear she—"

Zzzzt

"—made a quick recovery, and if there's anyone who could—"

Zzt, zzzt, zzzzzztt

"—*who could walk off a stabbing like nothing, it's her.*" Vehan paused to draw another breath, to steel himself against the actual, shocking *pain* that shivered up his leg, down his arm, across his *back*. Pain he really shouldn't feel from a simple shock, as a Seelie Summer fae.

This wasn't Theo.

There was no way Theo would take the game this far, even if he could somehow manage these angles without anyone seeing, and even if he thought he might be helping.

Arlo cocked her head, looking at him oddly, because of course she noticed something was wrong, as undoubtedly the rest of the table had. "Um . . . Vehan—I mean, *Prince* Vehan? Uh . . . Your Highness? Are you okay?" she hedged in that gentle tone of hers.

"Fine, yep. Everything's fine."

ZZZZZZZT

Vehan clutched his chest, gritting his teeth against a groan.

That shock was different. *That* shock had pierced his back like an arrow straight through to his heart. It made his entire body seize, and much like in the bathroom after that embarrassing failure on the mountaintop, Vehan felt an ache radiate from the array on his chest—a throbbing, a dizziness, and a vague sense of nausea churning in his gut.

He shot up in his seat. "May I be excused, Mother?"

Riadne looked at him blankly.

"Bathroom," he clipped, because that vague sense of nausea was no longer all that vague, and he didn't want to chance more speech than necessary right now.

"Go on, then," Riadne bid in careful, delicate words that told him she was deeply displeased and he'd hear about it later, but so be it.

He couldn't stay here, not with whatever was going on.

He had no idea what was wrong with him, where these shocks were coming from; who that anger of before belonged to and why *he* had felt it. But his mother wouldn't appreciate the blood he could feel beginning to fill his nose, nor the unnecessary worry it would engender in their guests.

According to her and the MediFae she'd had look him over, this was all Vehan's body attempting to sort out his "ridiculous arrogance" in spending so much energy on playing with lightning back on that mountain. Making a scene in the middle of dinner when already there'd been quite enough theatrics for the scant hours Arlo and the High Prince had been here would not go over well.

At his mother's nod, Vehan extracted himself from his seat.

He passed by Theo, whose head had turned in examination of the electric waterfall behind them, with curious contemplation weighing on his brow.

He passed by High Prince Celadon, who tracked his movements with a concern that might have made Vehan feel a little fluttery if he hadn't been fighting back the urge to throw up on the floor.

He passed by Aurelian, who'd actually made to stand as well, but was frozen midway in the action by Riadne's "Let him be. I apologize, my son hasn't been feeling well lately. Arlo, how *is* your friend doing? How thoughtless of me to neglect asking after her health . . ."

Out into the hall.

Up several flights of stairs.

Down what felt like endless corridors.

Vehan had to wave off every well-meaning employee who tried to fuss over his obviously unwell state, had to clamp his hand over his nose by the time he made it to the elevator that would carry him up to his floor.

He burst into his bedroom, stumbled his way to his bathroom, collapsed on the marble tile, and retched into his toilet, finally releasing the sob he'd been containing for how suddenly, wholly, bone-deep *ill* he felt.

Blood dribbled down his face.

It splattered in sapphire bright splotches behind him as—once the nausea had subsided—he dragged himself to his sink to scrub his face with water.

"What's happening to me?" he rasped at his deathly pale, blood-smeared reflection.

The array on his chest gave another, albeit less painful, lurch. Vehan yanked his shirt up over his head, discarding it on the floor behind him.

There was no denying it now, his scar was much darker blue than before, parts of it even beginning to blacken around the edges. Could it be glowing? He couldn't tell, couldn't see anything other than the raw stamp of it. It was magic only Arlo or Aurelian would have been able to notice, and neither of them had said anything, but this wasn't *normal*. His magic was acting up, and had been for far longer than just since the mountain. His chest was hurting. And now these phantom shocks? Or . . . he recalled that Theo had been looking at the waterfall of sparks behind them when Vehan was leaving—had Vehan's magic been reacting to it? Had it been reaching out for the electricity there? If a fae's magical core was dangerously low on the element that sustained it, it did tend to latch onto any presence of it.

That would explain why he hadn't been strong enough to entice the lightning from the sky, but his magic couldn't be *that* depleted . . . He hadn't even *used* it, really, since his confrontation with the cava . . .

Had Hieronymus caused permanent damage to Vehan in whatever he'd done to block their magic?

Most of the blood trickling from his nose had stopped now, but Vehan snatched up a cloth as he stormed out of his bathroom. Somewhere in the back of his consciousness, he suspected he'd been on the way to seek out the palace doctor.

He didn't make it.

The last thing his awareness could grasp was the sound of laughter—his own, he would swear, but far too cold and unnatural to belong to him. He staggered, collapsed with his cloth on the bed, and just as creeping black began to eat away at his vision, he thought he saw a figure leaning against one of his bedposts.

Watching.

Blurred.

Nothing but shadow and glowing red eyes.

"Who . . . ," he tried to ask, his words sticking to his tongue. But he didn't need to ask who this was—he knew.

Somehow, he knew who was standing over him, felt no confusion or shock over the impossibility of staring at the shadow of *himself*, if only because, right in this moment, it was so perfectly clear to him what was happening . . . what was *going* to happen once Vehan's mark finally claimed him.

The Ruin he'd become . . .

"*Tsk, tsk, tsk*, Little Light. I'm beginning to think I can't leave you untended at all," said a second voice, cool as still water, from the opposite side of Vehan's bed. "What a pathetic state. The tedious things I'm reduced to for a bargain."

He knew who this was too—*Lethe*. But how was he here? Why was he here? What was he even going on about? Vehan wanted to ask after this, as well, but even before he could make the attempt, could turn to search out acid-green eyes and the glinting-sharp grin he was sure to find, Lethe extended a hand.

"How many times I've had to erase you figuring out your *fate* ahead of schedule . . . Tedious."

Fingers traced a ghostly touch across Vehan's temple, and just like that, his world—and memory of this entire exchange—dissolved at last into blissful nothing.

CHAPTER 14

Nausicaä

~~~~~~

BALCONIES. THERE WERE A fuck-ton of *balconies* to this palace. Nausicaä was no mortal plebeian, whatever her current appearance suggested. The considerable enchantments placed on the Luminous Palace weren't nearly strong enough to keep *her* from gaining entry any way she chose, but these deities-damned balconies . . . Teleporting herself onto the one belonging to Arlo for a surprise reunion had seemed like a better idea in Nausicaä's head until she saw this particular feature was apparently Riadne Lysterne's favorite piece of fucking home decor.

"*What love can do that dares love attempt—tch.* Romeo can eat a *whole* bag of—oh, for the love of *friggin* Fate, *finally.*"

Nine tries.

Nine balconies Nausicaä had popped herself along in search of the pretty little redhead she'd come specifically to see. There'd been a bit more planned to her grand entrance than her collapsing against Arlo's window in dramatic, irritated relief, but that was before all the effing *balconies.*

"Red," Nausicaä whined, banging her palms on the glass, the open curtains allowing her clear view of the room's interior. "*Reeeddd*, let me *iiinnn!*"

Arlo, who'd jolted in fright upon hearing this, sat cozy on her bed in lily-pink silk pajamas Nausicaä had never seen before. For a second she simply stared back at her, frozen. Propped on her lap was her computer—she'd been in the middle of a conversation with someone, one of her parental units, Nausicaä would hazard a guess, and she could hear Arlo ask whoever it was to *wait a moment* when

Arlo's shock dissipated enough to allow her to process what was going on.

Setting her laptop aside, she slid from the bed and padded over to the balcony doors. Nausicaä peeled herself off the glass, ran a hand through her hair to shake out some of the tangles and make herself look *somewhat* presentable (and immediately felt ridiculous for doing so, like it mattered at all what her hair looked like—*tch*).

Arlo threw the doors open.

"Hey, Red," Nausicaä greeted casually as she leaned against the doorframe, as though she'd been perfectly composed this entire time and this was a normal occurrence. As though Arlo had been expecting her.

And ah, but there was that hint of exasperation that weighed on one side of Arlo's mouth alongside the curl of amusement that perked up the other, which Nausicaä was discovering she *so* enjoyed to see. "How's it going?"

"Nausicaä, it's almost half past eleven."

"You know, I was actually pretty cool with 'Nos.' You can keep using that, if you'd like . . ."

Arlo blinked, nothing of what she thought readable in her expression. Then, "Nos," she amended, as easily as that, "it's almost half past eleven." And then she noticed. "What are you *wearing*?"

Nausicaä beamed.

It never failed to *fascinate* her how little Arlo was fazed by how undoubtedly "inhuman" and "generally terrifying" every one of Nausicaä's smiles, smirks, and grins had been labeled over the years. Nothing about Nausicaä seemed to frighten her like it did so many others. This wholesome, mildly timid, well-mannered girl didn't so much as bat a lash at her scary new friend, a being even the most gruesome of the folk would consider *monstrous*.

When she nodded at the room, asking Arlo's permission to enter, Arlo merely rolled her eyes in that barely concealed fondness for Nausicaä that was *also* very . . . *intriguing*, and stepped aside to let

Nausicaä through, closing the balcony doors again as soon as they were both inside.

Nausicaä turned around, grinning even more deeply at Arlo and sliding her hands into the pockets of the starry black cloak she'd worn over her usual leather-and-combat-boots combination. "Oh, you know, just a bit of vintage clothing." She dropped a wink. "But before my fancy, impressive news, how did day one of the Seelie Summer boot camp go?"

As though reminded by the question that she'd been talking to someone over video chat, Arlo raised a finger—"Hold on a sec"—and darted back to her bed.

With a soft snort, Nausicaä watched her bid good night to apparently her father, whom Nausicaä had only seen in the pictures she'd lazily scrolled through on Arlo's phone one evening but was determined to meet in person . . . if only to pinpoint why he seemed so familiar to her, more than his obvious relation to his daughter.

It took her a moment to notice the third presence in the room, the large black cat that was roughly the size of a miniature panther stretched out on the end of Arlo's bed. Their head was propped on daintily crossed paws, their eyes unnerving in their all-consuming cosmic black, pinning Nausicaä with their void-intensity, and—

Nausicaä stiffened. "Holy shit, Red."

Arlo's laptop closed with a quiet *snap*.

Her head shot up, gaze tracking from Nausicaä to her bedtime companion. Luck, a whole-ass *titan*, here in the Mortal Realm. Here in the Luminous Palace. Here, right in front of Nausicaä, a stark and sudden reminder of a past she couldn't figure out if she wanted to escape or cling to and never move on from; a barrage of memories and feelings she *definitely* wanted to *not think about right now*.

Of course Luck was here.

They'd given Arlo one of the Star Dice. They'd promised to train her in the new role she'd traded for. If there was anyone who could circumvent the laws keeping immortals out of the mortals-only clubhouse, it would be this particular titan. Nausicaä shouldn't be this surprised—but there was knowing a thing and there was experiencing it, and the two were drastically different.

Unbidden, Eris's words from earlier that day returned to her.

The same hand that delivers fortune is just as capable of the opposite. Do not go out of your way to earn their ire.

". . . Hey," Nausicaä greeted, now uncomfortably aware of the Hunter's cloak she was sporting, and the things she had to tell Arlo that maybe she shouldn't say in front of someone who was most certainly in on the whole "let's literally bring down the heavens" plot in one way or another.

Luck lifted their head.

Arlo, who'd slid back off her bed, seemed to vibrate now with everything she had to say in answer to Nausicaä's previous, offhand question, and had nowhere near the same amount of qualms about doing so in front of her titan *pet*. "Yeah, so, a lot has happened. As you can see, Luck's here. They're going to start training me this summer, but to keep that on the down low, they're pretending to be my cat. And I met my alchemy tutor! And Celadon almost started a fight with Riadne over it. And my bedroom, have you *seen* my bedroom? It's a *mansion*. And everyone's been really nice, but it's all sort of overwhelming, you know? And now they're all gone, and mom couldn't talk long, and I think Vehan's sick because he had to leave dinner early tonight and was acting really weird, and . . ." She deflated, standing on her mossy carpet floor, barefoot and very . . . fragile, Nausicaä concluded. More so than her mortality often made her seem. "My dad went on a date tonight—he was just telling me about it. With another professor from his school. I don't know how to feel about that, but apparently it went really well because he seemed . . . happy."

Nausicaä frowned.

First at Luck, then at Arlo.

"Sounds, uh . . . like a lot," she replied, as delicately as she could, because hells, when was the last time she cared enough about someone to attempt genuine empathy?

But Arlo merely sighed. With a nod, she trudged forward until her forehead pressed against Nausicaä's forearm. Arlo sagged a little against her, and now Nausicaä was even *further* out of her element and had absolutely *no* idea what to do at *this* point. "It *is* a lot," Arlo muttered, her dejection muffled by fabric. "Why are you wearing one of the Wild Hunt's cloaks?" she added just as softly.

"It's . . . uh, mine."

Arlo peeled her forehead off Nausicaä's arm. She blinked up at her in doe-ish confusion that made Nausicaä's stomach do an odd sort of jittery leap that she was never going to tell *anyone* about, thank you, and made her briefly want to poke Arlo's nose, which was a useless feeling, why the hells did she even want to do *that*—ah, and Arlo was still staring at her.

Nausicaä cleared her throat and tried to summon a bit of her usual arrogance to shape a boastful grin. "From the good old days," she explained, waggling her brows. "It's *my* cloak. Eris gave it back. Apparently, I was a very good girl, my time-out's over, etcetera, etcetera. He's made me an honorary Hunter again."

It was hard to keep all trace of how *excited* she was about this out of her voice, how much this seemingly insignificant gesture had actually meant to her. No one would care, not like Nausicaä did. Anyone who knew why she'd lost this honor in the first place would say she'd deserved to have it taken away and that Eris shouldn't have given it back, that Nausicaä had no place among the immortals in any way anymore, even this.

The ones who didn't know a shred about her couldn't possibly care more than distaste, because folk still recognized these cloaks if nothing else and associated nothing good with the sight of them.

Arlo wouldn't understand why this meant so much, and that wasn't *her* fault, because how could she? Nausicaä went out of her way to keep *everyone* at arm's length. Not to mention Arlo's only encounter with the Hunt so far had been *Lethe*, who didn't exactly make the best case for his kind. But for some reason, Nausicaä still felt herself erecting walls, shoring up her defenses against what was going to be an underwhelming response to this monumental news.

Arlo stepped back.

She cocked her head and considered Nausicaä, looking her over from head to toe.

And Nausicaä's grin began to shrink, her heart began to drop, because she wasn't anywhere close to as apathetic as she pretended to be, damn it. She *wanted* someone to care, to be happy for her . . . and she was *really* starting to want that someone to be Arlo—Arlo, whose entire face proceeded not to darken in contempt or fear for the Hunt as would have been entirely understandable, but *brighten* with a mixture of awe and elation.

"Eris . . . he's the leader of the Wild Hunt, right? He made you a *Hunter*? Nos, that's so *cool*!"

Nausicaä could only stare, the breath she'd been unwittingly holding slowly beginning to ease out. "Uh . . . yeah. It is."

This wasn't the response she'd been expecting.

It *was* cool—no one, not even Tisiphone, had seen it as such.

"It *is*." Arlo nodded vigorously, beginning now to circle Nausicaä in closer examination. "I mean, also terrifying—the Hunters are all pretty much nightmares incarnate—but . . ." She came to a halt on Nausicaä's opposite side, peering up at her from the handful of cloak she'd been scrutinizing. "You *are* happy about this, right?"

It was a little galling that, for the abundance of words and blithe sarcasm Nausicaä had for pretty much any situation, all she could manage right now was a nod.

"Then *I'm* happy about this, and happy for *you*. It's awesome." Releasing the cloak, Arlo stepped back once more, tapping her chin in more serious contemplation. "You said he gave it back. . . . Why did he take it away?"

"Oh, you know . . . ," Nausicaä replied when her tongue finally decided to be of some use. "The whole 'not playing nicely with the other children' incident. It . . . cost me certain privileges."

She almost winced.

This wasn't the conversation she'd intended to have tonight. This was dangerously close to the "feelings" department, the heart-to-heart she'd been avoiding for over a hundred years, the reason she cycled so quickly through the brief stint of therapy that she'd forced herself to seek purely because it had been an outlet *Tisiphone* had desperately needed and been denied. This was the reason Nausicaä hadn't *dared* let anyone close since her banishment, not anything more than the casual hookup when loneliness threatened to get the worst of her.

One hundred and sixteen years and she still wasn't ready to talk about what had happened.

She wondered if she ever would be.

"You mean when you were banished here?" Arlo hedged softly. Here it was, the moment Nausicaä would have to shut her down, and Arlo would be offended in the politest way possible, would start to question whether Nausicaä was worth it—what other secrets she could be hiding if she couldn't even talk about *this*, and how little she must trust Arlo that she wouldn't. "I'm sorry," Arlo added, in that even gentler, Canadian way of hers that Nausicaä had come to associate with the Vulcan *I grieve with thee*. "Well, I'm glad he gave it back to you. Congratulations, Nos!"

And that was it.

Arlo dropped the matter entirely, pressing no further.

She didn't even look put out over the half-assed answer she'd been given, but neither did she look indifferent to it. She stood there in those doll-pink pajamas that were clearly a gift from the palace, her red hair in a freshly washed and slightly puffy cloud around her, with far too much trust and acceptance and *caring* in those big green eyes of hers for someone who'd been kicked around by the world as much as she'd been.

"You're so weird," Nausicaä muttered.

Confused by the statement, Arlo cocked her head. "What?"

"You're *weird*," Nausicaä repeated, louder, this time in a teasing sort of tone that was far easier to navigate than whatever touching moment this had been veering toward. "In a good way, of course. All the best people are weird."

"*You're* weird."

"See?" Nausicaä winked, and Arlo rolled her eyes, huffed a laugh, and shook her head.

"So, does this mean you're like . . . a Hunter now? Like one of the *Wild Hunt* Hunters? Do you have to live at the palace and answer to the High King, and—"

"Nah, nothing like that," Nausicaä replied, moving across the room to relax against the ebony-wood vanity, where Arlo's modest collection of makeup and hair products were carefully arranged. "A cloak does not a Hunter make, but they've asked for my help. Or Eris has, at least. The ironborn—the ones who've been marked with philosopher's stone arrays—they're still out there and still *dying*. Only now there's no Reaper running around to conveniently connect these deaths like dots to one another. None of the ironborn's hearts have withstood the Sin's magic, but there's no purging the stain of this sort of darkness completely. Turns out, even failed stones make handy little amplifiers, and a few have already found their way into folk possession. Which, you know, *not* good. It's not really the Wild Hunt's function to run around after the shit that goes on in this realm, not unless the High King sends them on a chase, so they've asked me to step up instead and confiscate these shiny new toys like some professional schoolyard bully! My resume groweths."

She shot another glance at Luck, still watching from their perch at the end of Arlo's bed. What they made of her words, she couldn't tell, but she'd been careful to leave out the parts about Lethe being the one to more or less nudge them along in this. Her cousin seemed to be playing any side of the field most attractive to him at any given moment, and if Luck had thrown their lot in with aiding the immortals' return to the Mortal Realm, she didn't want to tip them off that Eris wasn't fully sold on a similar allegiance.

She liked Luck—she stood by what she'd said before, they were one of the better immortals. But until she knew their position on this plot unfolding around them, if they even had a position at all, she wasn't going to let that good opinion lure her into a false sense of security.

Certainly not where Arlo was concerned.

"Anyhow," she added, folding her arms over her chest and sagging a little deeper against the vanity. "I already have my first mission: some wood imp in the English countryside. Doesn't sound particularly difficult, but hey, I'll take my excitement where I can. I asked if it was cool to bring you along, and Eris said that if you wanted to come with, you could. *Originally*, I was thinking we could do this tonight, but yeah . . . I guess you're right, it's kind of late for you, and all that stuff you mentioned that happened today . . . We should Netflix and Talk about that instead. Countryside imp can wait for tomorrow. So, who do I have to threaten around here to get a matching pair of those jimjams?"

But Arlo threw a hand into the air. "Um, excuse me, I don't want to Netflix and Talk, I want to go to the English countryside and help you track down faeries."

". . . S'cuse me, what?"

"I want to help you track down faeries!" Arlo repeated, already flying over to her dresser to rummage around for a change of clothes. "You said ironborn are still dying and their hearts are falling into the wrong hands. I don't want that to happen, I want to help stop it! We can go tonight, there's plenty of time."

"Uh . . . it's half past eleven," Nausicaä reminded, still a little bewildered.

"And I'm UnSeelie—night is in my blood. Listen, I just got off the phone with my dad—the man who hates magic *so much* that he divorced my mother and voluntarily wiped his memory of the entire thing, and would probably definitely hate me too if he ever remembered why—and he spent the last half hour telling me all about this wonderful woman he's gone on a date with, who he's never mentioned *once* before now, and apparently she has a daughter too, and I'm kind of freaking out because this is all verging a little too much on *I'm replacing you with a whole new, much better family* territory, so either we run around after thieving faeries or I lie in my bed for hours panic-spiralling, but no matter what, I'm not getting much sleep tonight."

Nausicaä stared.

Before she could think of the right thing to say, like how she highly doubted Arlo's father was going to replace her—although, for all she really knew of the man, and her own experience with family, he could be, but that was definitely not the constructive sort of comment Arlo needed to hear right now—Luck leaped off the bed.

Transforming midair, they landed on two very humanoid, very long legs. Their olive-green skin glittered faintly. Their shamrock-green hair fell long and waving around a strong face full of high-flung and proudly cut features. Twin horns, blunted and obsidian black, protruded from the sides of their head and curved backward to a point at their chin. Their eyes, gleaming black as infinite space, were the only tells that here was no human, no faerie, no *mortal*, and no insignificant nothing *im*mortal, but the rest of them looked so spectacularly normal that Nausicaä almost laughed.

Mint-and-lime-green runners.

Tight black jeans.

A pink-and-emerald plaid shirt.

Luck looked like a woodsy *teenager*—distinctly masculine-aligned tonight, though no matter what gender they visibly expressed (if any one at all), they were still only to be addressed as "they" and "them," Nausicaä remembered learning in her previous life.

They'd even scaled their age down to match their image.

"You know," they said, crossing the room to help Arlo choose an outfit that would probably make her older cousin gag to see her in. And Arlo, *completely unfazed* by even this, looked Luck over in all of a glance before shuffling aside to allow their help. "This would be an excellent time to start your Hollow Star training."

"Hooray! Two against one—you lose," Arlo called over her shoulder, bunching the articles of clothing Luck shoved at her in her arms and heading for the bathroom.

With a shake of her head, Nausicaä watched her go, more amused than anything. "How am *I* the voice of reason right now?" she called after Arlo. But if this was what Arlo wanted, this was what she was going to get.

The county of Kent, in South East England, was eight hours ahead of Nevada time and seven ahead of where the Luminous Palace was actually located. As such, dawn had already spilled in gray rain-cloud light, over the horizon when Nausicaä, Arlo, and Luck arrived at their destination: a patch of densely populated forest full of towering, mossy, narrow trees twisting and bent at oddly warped angles.

Magic curled like mist between their trunks. Its gentle tinkling sound, as light as rain on glass, was unmistakable for how familiar it was to Nausicaä. And the way it sparked against her magic, pulled at her core, and stoked her adrenaline like shoveling coal into a furnace—it was nowhere close to how pure a concentration magic was in the Hiraeth, its very vein of life, but for a moment, she'd forgotten why they'd come. Out here, in the patch of Wild territory, this sliver of freedom between Court borders, was a reminder of what the immortals had lost to their greed and unkind rule long ago when the folk had pushed them out.

They might be goddesses, gods, and deities.

Their lives might stretch for eons, their bodies and homes and kingdoms shaped by the elements of the many worlds and parallel universes.

Immortals might be powerful, but Magic was just as much a living entity as Luck and Fate and all the Others . . . boundless, rule unto itself, and *here* in this quiet bit of mortal nowhere, there was a closeness to it that Nausicaä had never felt in all the sprawling Cosmos or Chaos she'd ever roamed.

Magic might be free to go wherever it wished, but it was the Mortal Realm where it chose to *live*.

Worship was the only thread that connected the immortals to what they'd once been so talented at wielding, their only means of utilizing the power that had chosen to reside on *this* side of the divide—perhaps in punishment for how arrogant the immortals had become with full access to it, or perhaps because Magic simply enjoyed the way everything here felt a little more . . . finite, and therefore precious.

Even Luck seemed subdued by its presence.

Maybe they wouldn't have been so quick to ruin what they'd had, if immortals knew how cold and detached they'd become so far removed as they were now from this progenitor-of-all. How dull their lives would be, compared to what they'd once been able to do on their own, now reduced to living off the goodwill of the Courts, and the trickle of sustenance it sent them with prayer.

Maybe they would have still.

"All right," Nausicaä said, turning to face Arlo and Luck with her hands on her hips. "Midnight, dawn, midday, and twilight: These are the hours of magic's zenith, the points of day when folk of the Courts and in *particular* the Wild are at their strongest. It's also, therefore, when their mischief cranks from a five right up to a fifteen. Every species of imp is nocturnal, and not usually more than a nuisance as far as destructive capability goes. But the one we're after has a failed stone and, from the sounds of things, if we come stomping along all *easy prey-like* through their territory, it doesn't matter what time it is, they won't be able to resist the little prank they've been pulling on the dick-ton of people they've already targeted."

Luck raised their hand, a curl of wry humor to their lips. "I am unfamiliar with this unit of measurement."

"Really?" Nausicaä waggled her brows. "Because from what I've heard about Your Husband His Supremeness Lord Cosmin's *endowment*—"

"So what *have* they been doing, exactly?" Arlo interjected, a look on her face that definitely warned against the joke Nausicaä had been about to make. "I mean, it has to be something really nasty for the *Hunt* to notice, and this is the Wild. Technically, we aren't supposed to interfere with things out here."

"Right you are," Nausicaä replied, pointing to Arlo. In her white Converse, black leggings, and long, sage-green T-shirt, she looked less like a "faerie hunter" and more like she and Luck were a hipster couple on some backpacking vacation through Europe. But when most of Nausicaä's ensembles consisted strictly of leather and black, she didn't have much room to judge. "We're not here to punish anyone. This isn't Court business. We're here to catch an imp for a face-to-face chat, and, you know, steal their stone—but that's it. Unless they want to be difficult, in which case, I have a variety of pointy objects that will illustrate why that's very much not in their best interest. As for what they've done . . ."

She turned back around, facing the depths of the forest.

That gray-cast light peeked through the narrow gaps in the trees, but it wasn't bright enough to chase away the darkness entirely. Shadows played with the forest's shape, its ebb and flow and sway. Eyes of various luminosities and sizes peered back at her from the foliage, watching, waiting, curious what had brought a Fury into their midst. None of their owners were in any way foolish enough to obstruct Nausicaä's business here, though.

The larger, meaner things that no doubt called this space home were either hiding away much deeper in these woods, or smart enough to pack their bags and take a holiday, putting as much distance as possible between them and the foul magic that the failed philosopher's stone would be giving off.

Unnatural.

Dark magic.

"For even a failed stone's catastrophic potential, what they've done is actually not that much. Like I said, they've mostly been tricking people off their paths, luring them away from their tasks, and the people they snag have apparently disappeared completely and have been missing for several days now. I'm liking it to the strongest patch of faerie grass the Mortal Realm has ever seen for our imp's modus operandi there. But I guess we won't know until we take a look."

Stray sod. Lone sod. Foidin Seachrain.

Nausicaä had picked up all kinds of names for faerie grass, which was almost as straightforward as it sounded: a patch of earth that a faerie enchanted to make any who walked across it lose their way. Of course, the enchantment was a little more complicated than that— if woven strongly enough, it could actually absorb whoever walked across it into a secondary plane, which the majority of people couldn't see and barely even knew about.

The spectral dimension.

The realm of ghosts.

It was lain like a film over the primary plane, where they were currently. And others overtop of it.

This bit of fun did more psychological damage to people than physical harm . . . most of the time. When the faerie who cast the spell grew bored of their prey, they were almost always released back to the primary plane, understandably shaken and probably much more watchful of where they went from then on, but otherwise . . . relatively okay.

Physically.

Mentally . . . again, probably not so much, and hence why the Courts forbade this trick, Nausicaä suspected, along with so many of the others the folk had once been free to utilize at will.

The enchantment an average wood imp could weave wouldn't be at all strong enough to do much more than disorient a person into walking in circles for a handful of hours, a day at most. It was more or less what a phooka could get up to. But a wood imp with a philosopher's stone, even a faulty one . . . Nausicaä had seen a great many sights during her stay in the Mortal Realm, but she'd never been whisked up by anything powerful enough to spirit her away to the ghost plane before.

Forest detritus crunched under Arlo's shoes as she walked up to Nausicaä's side. She peered into the woods' murky depths, squinting slightly, an action that made the bridge of her nose crinkle. Nausicaä's stomach did that stupid jittery leaping again.

When Arlo turned her gaze up to meet hers, a question in her spring-warm eyes, Nausicaä realized she'd missed something Arlo had said.

"Hmm?"

"How do we tell faerie grass from normal grass?"

"Ah." Giving herself a minute shake, Nausicaä crossed one arm over the other and tapped her chin in thought. "Well, anyone with the Sight can usually see the warped, shimmery presence of magic in the air around it. Which should be more than enough for us. At full, phenomenal cosmic power I could track it down like *that* by its aura—faerie grass would have a deeper, earthy scent to it, and it would be tinted by the imp's magic, plus, you know, the coppery, rotting, fleshy scent of ironborn death that's a *screaming* giveaway of a philosopher's stone, but—"

"Oh, so it's this way, then."

And just like that, Arlo was off, leaving Nausicaä standing stunned in her wake.

"Wait. She can . . . sense auras?" Nausicaä asked, bewildered, looking first to Luck, who merely shrugged unconcernedly, then once again after Arlo, now picking her way through the brush to their left, heedless of the creepy-crawly faerie nasties who might not *dare* touch Nausicaä, but would have no reservations about taking their shot at an Unmatured Court fae.

Shit.

"Arlo, wait!" She took off after her. "You were just never going to tell me you can sense auras?"

"Huh? Oh, yeah! Sorry, didn't I mention it? It's like my *one* talent. *Super nose.* We've been practicing it for years, Celadon and I, and I'm getting pretty good. I mean, it's not that fancy, nothing like you could have probably done, and definitely not up to Hunter standard, from what I hear. Basically, I can tell faeries apart from fae, and everyone has a unique scent to me. Sometimes I can even *feel* someone's aura if it's close enough to mine, but that's pretty much it. Did you know you smell like woodsmoke and metal? Fire and swords—it's very you."

Arlo paused, completely oblivious to the woodsprite her trailblazing had disturbed, and Nausicaä had to dart out a hand to catch the tree branch they'd been about to sling into her face.

"You can *scent* auras?" Because that very much bore repeating.

"Uh-huh. Lots of fae can do it."

"The lesidhe, maybe, but not like that they can't. That's . . . a highly unique talent, Red."

Between the haze of morning light and Nausicaä's exceptional eyesight, the embarrassed-pleased flush that spread rosy-faint across Arlo's cheeks was easily spotted, but she ducked her head, shrugging off the comment with a "Yeah, well, load of good it's done me so far," and carried on stomping her way through the brush. "This is the first time it's ever actually been *useful*. Come on, it's definitely this way."

It wasn't until Luck came up just behind her that she realized she hadn't moved.

Arlo could scent auras . . . She could *track* . . .

Her Gift of windborn swiftness . . .

Her clever mind and her *lucky* potential . . .

"What exactly does Lethe want with Arlo?" Because she was starting to suspect that Lethe's fascination with Red ran deeper than passing interest in someone Fate had labeled up for immortal grabs. That her original, destined potential had been a little more *legendary* than what Luck had probably let on in their trade.

She turned her head. "What does Lethe want with Arlo, Luck?" she repeated, in a darker, firmer tone.

Once again, Luck merely shrugged. "I couldn't tell you."

"Can't, or won't?"

They considered her with those fathomless, dark eyes, otherworldly—even to Nausicaä—but that was titans all around. They were older than immortals, made of far more ancient, stronger stuff—elements that no longer existed, stars that would never be again. "Won't," they replied after a beat. "I choose no side but *Arlo's*, divulge no secrets. You do well to remember that. All that matters is that Arlo has my favor now. I will guide her growth into whatever she chooses, be that what Fate originally intended or anything else. Hero or villain, and the whole realm in between—it is entirely up to *her* now. Lethe . . . Cosmin, even . . . every other immortal with their eye on our girl . . . in the end, it doesn't matter what they want, only what Arlo Jarsdel *chooses*."

Nausicaä bristled. "*Our* girl? Hey, when did this become a team exercise—"

"Are you two coming or what?" Arlo's voice floated back to them.

"She should, perhaps, cease shouting in the middle of the Wild, though." Luck observed with a pointed raise of a fine green brow.

Grumbling under her breath about supercilious, tight-lipped titans and pretty, timid girls who weren't actually all that timid underneath their manners, Nausicaä flicked her cloak out behind her and plodded off after "their girl."

It took even less time than originally anticipated to track down and confirm that faerie grass really was what the amplified imp had been using for his sport. Arlo led their group through the trees—up and over their fallen, decaying carcasses, and around and through snarls of dense undergrowth.

It was unwise to wind so far off the woods' beaten path.

If it weren't for Nausicaä and Luck, Arlo wouldn't have made it a handful of steps without attracting at least a dozen of the folk who called this place home—and with the careless way she stomped the twigs and dried leaves under her heel, the angry way she batted at low-hanging branches and snaking vines, she'd be lucky if a dozen was all that slunk out of the shadows and snatched her up to introduce her to the proper Wild Experience.

She was very clearly working through some understandable frustration.

Nausicaä sympathized.

She'd been *literally* replaced by her own mother upon expulsion from the Sisterhood, another Alecto chosen to assume *her* name, and a hundred years wasn't enough to soften that particular sting.

But just when Nausicaä wondered if maybe she should say something or warn her that her blustering might be having the opposite effect of what they intended, Arlo came to another abrupt halt.

Pausing a moment to examine the ground, she then pointed off to their right, and sure enough, there it was: faerie grass, a patch of mossy soil incongruous with the rest around it for the warp of magic, shimmering in the air like heat off the surface of hot black pavement.

"Well done, Red!" Nausicaä congratulated, clapping Arlo on the shoulder. "All right, time to go bag our weapon of mass magical destruction."

"Wait!" Arlo called, stopping Nausicaä midstep. When she looked behind her, she found a bit of Arlo's more typical hesitance had returned as she eyed the faerie grass with a grimace of mistrust. "We're just going to . . . go in?"

"That was the plan, yup."

"Isn't that dangerous? What if we can't get back out?"

It was tempting to laugh. Nausicaä had never had to worry about the things mortals did—it was a wonder, really, that they weren't *all* anxious bundles of hesitation, given how much of their realm was designed to hurt and torment and kill them—and Arlo wasn't a Fury. No part of Arlo's physical body had been made to withstand the things Nausicaä could.

"Don't worry," she consoled as gently as she could. "Between my teleportation and the actual *titan* we have on our side, we'll get back out just fine. But . . . come here."

Arlo stepped forward as bidden, and Nausicaä took a few steps closer as well until they were just far enough apart that she could have rested her chin on top of Arlo's head, but instead she reached for her hair.

Soft—Arlo's hair was so much softer than she thought it would be. Given its puffy and currently tangled volume, she'd expected something a little coarser, but the strands that slid over Nausicaä's fingers as she ran them from top to end were extremely fine and almost silken, and once again she found herself forgetting her initial intention for the way rosy red spread over Arlo's face.

"What are you doing?" Arlo asked. Had her voice gone breathy? What *was* Nausicaä doing?

Right.

She cleared her throat, raised her other hand, morning light glinting off the gold that leafed what was visible of her wrist. With deft quickness she wove a braid into the side of Arlo's head, then plucked a strand of hair off her own head to tie the braid off at the bottom. "A faerie braid," she replied when she was finished. If her breath had gone a little whispery too, it was only because she was a deities-damned schoolgirl at heart, apparently, and whatever was gleaming in Arlo's eyes made her *vividly* remember the kiss she'd stolen in the murder factory elevator . . . and definitely wanted to steal again.

And then, quite suddenly, a pair of arms wound themselves over and around Arlo's shoulders.

Arlo yelped in surprise. Nausicaä jolted a step backward.

Luck rested their chin on Arlo's head just as Nausicaä had envisioned doing, a curl of amusement plucking the side of their wide, full mouth. "This is what I think would be termed *cute*, but we're burning valuable morning. Our imp awaits us. Shall we get going?"

"*Least* favorite," Nausicaä growled.

"Pardon me?"

"You heard me, demon cat. You are now my least favorite immortal. I'm shunning your temples." She aimed a kick in their direction, but they'd already moved off, Arlo's arm linked with theirs. The faerie braid Nausicaä had given her would protect her from the faerie grass's disconcerting effects—would shield her from it entirely, given the hair that had been used to seal the ward came from an immortal such as her. But Luck in hand would be the ultimate buffer between them and any nasty they could possibly encounter, and Nausicaä slipping her arm around Arlo's other meant less chance they'd be separated hopping planes.

So she'd forgive this interruption, *this time*.

"Everybody ready?" Nausicaä asked once they were all in position. When Arlo nodded, they stepped forward as one.

CHAPTER 15

Arlo

～⌒～

THERE WAS A GREAT amount of speculation on the secondary plane—the "ghostworld," or nega-verse, as folk more commonly referred to it.

Some thought it the space between life and death, that anyone who ventured here might somehow cross accidentally into the afterlife. Some thought it was a trick of the mind, magic that caused such severe befuddlement that those who came under its spell weren't actually transported anywhere but instead merely suffered the magic like a powerful psychedelic. And others argued there were even more than just the *two* planes, that whole species of folk yet undiscovered existed right beneath the primary plane's nose, and "ghost sightings" were really just brief glimpses through weak spots into these alternate dimensions.

Arlo didn't know what she believed, but she could safely say the nega-verse was *creepy*. The grayish light of the cloudy morning had taken on a sickly green glow, the same shimmering distortion that had swirled around the faerie grass now stretching to blanket everything. It rendered the world a bit like a funhouse at the amusement park that Arlo's dad had taken her to as a child, the way the ground tilted here and there, and it wasn't quite clear if entire pockets of the forest were actually reflections of adjacent spaces, or nothing but empty illusion.

She was glad to have company.

Glad for the braid Nausicaä had woven into Arlo's hair, which no one but Celadon had ever done before—understandably, given how intimate a faerie braid was considered in folk culture, as the strength of its protection relied directly on how deeply its weaver cared about the one they marked with this ancient tradition. Arlo was about as well-guarded as anyone could be in this place. However much simply standing felt like trying to balance on a tiny boat in the middle of the sea, however hauntingly the slightly off-tune tinkling magic danced around her, trying to lure her away from the group, Arlo's head was clear. Her anxiety was manageable. She wasn't *alone*.

Unbidden, her gaze slid to her right, up the length of Nausicaä's profile, even sharper and vulture-wraithlike from this angle. In this otherworldly glow, the vaguely skeletal, monstrous truth of what she was beneath, her glamorous beauty was even easier to glimpse . . . and it was weird that just *looking* at this girl should make Arlo feel so calm (if also a little fluttery) when it was Nausicaä she should probably fear even over the all-powerful, enigmatic titan to her left.

A Fury *and* an honorary Hunter.

"We stick together, yeah?" said Nausicaä, turning her scrutiny of the woods on Arlo. "No wandering off. I've never actually been here before, so as much as it revolts me to have to say this—seriously, I can *feel* the chunk of my withered soul that just peeled off and died— better safe than sorry."

She frowned as though the words of caution had been genuinely vile in her mouth, and Arlo bit her lip to keep her laughter hushed. She nodded. "We'll stick together," she promised, and when Nausicaä reached behind to clasp Arlo's hand, she took it gladly, offering her other to Luck.

They peered down at it.

Even in their mortal guise, they reminded Arlo strongly of a cat, the way their right brow rose a twitch, the left corner of their lips curled apart in a delicate moue. When they slipped their hand into hers, it was strange how warm it felt—how *normal* it was—but she didn't comment. Just rolled her eyes at their haughty hesitance and proceeded to tug them forward when Nausicaä did the same to her.

"All right, so how do we find our imp?" Arlo asked once their trek was fully underway. "I can sort of sense them? But it's harder. Their aura's all over the place, probably because they're the one who opened this portal between the planes or . . . whatever the enchantment did to bring us here, right?"

"That's a pretty accurate summary," Nausicaä replied, lifting a tree branch out of the way and holding it for Arlo and Luck to walk under. "It's more or less what they did—opened a portal. Again, way too much skill for your run-of-the-mill wood imp, so this is either our mark with a stone or some other Big Bad that it wouldn't hurt to look into. It shouldn't be too hard to find them. We'll just follow their trail of mass terror, and they're bound to be hanging around somewhere close by, watching over their fun."

Trail of mass terror?

It didn't take long for Arlo to understand what this meant, for her to realize just how grateful she had to be for the seemingly simple braid in her hair.

They were few and far between at first, the victims of the imp's faerie grass. A young woman curled up by the base of a tree, sobbing into her hands, muttering in the death-rattle gasps that filled the space between her tears.

A Falchion officer, roaming around to Arlo's left, swatted fiercely at the air and something only he could see, *screaming* names of probable teammates as whatever he fought seemed to be gaining the upper hand.

They passed a boy slightly younger than Arlo, his arms clawed to shreds, the blood and bits of flesh packed under his nails as evidence that he'd done this to himself, and the vacancy in his wide eyes was almost as unnerving as the way he staggered silently along, little better than a walking corpse.

"We . . . we have to help them!" Arlo almost cried when she tried to break formation to go after this boy, but Nausicaä caught her firmly by the elbow before she could. "We can tell them we're here to rescue them and bring them with us. They're so *scared*—look at them! We can't just *leave* them."

"And yet you'll have to."

It was Luck who replied, shaking their head when Arlo turned her watery gaze on them.

"They are under the imp's spell. Between whatever ire sparked the particular degree of this prank and the dark influence of the stone our imp has used to enact it, none of these people will hear your attempts to console them. And if they see you at all, their terror will twist you into part of the nightmare they've been spelled to live out."

"We *will* help them, Arlo," Nausicaä added. "If we catch the imp, the spell will be broken, and they'll all be free to go home."

With a heavy sigh and a stiff nod from Arlo, their trek continued.

Deeper into the distorted forest they plunged, over massive rocks, under roots that swept like formidable arches overhead.

It was a little like the Hiraeth, Arlo noted, the way the earth tilted one way and then drastically the other in as little as the next step. Magic was thick in the air, but it wasn't calming, and it felt as though many pairs of eyes were trained on her at all times even though no one seemed to notice their presence.

They passed many more victims in what felt like the hour they'd been walking.

An enormous troll lay facedown on the ground, their grunting words muffled by the earth as though they'd given up on their struggle for freedom and gave themself over to whatever horror their mind made them see. There was a pixie Arlo couldn't look at long for the painful, too-still way they hung from one of the trees, tangled up in a mess of vines that had broken their fall from the sky, along with their neck.

Perhaps they'd hoped they could fly away?

One, at least, they'd been too late to save.

A quartet of gnomes sat around a puddle, none of them aware of the others but all of them holding arguments with themselves that sounded so much like a response to something the others said that Arlo's sinking mood latched onto this bit of humor, and a bubble of laughter escaped her.

Folk and humans alike were littered about in varying states of hysteria. Running around, scrambling on all fours, stomping through the brush, crying and begging for home, or shouting and muttering threats.

There was a darker side to faeries, to the tales people spun about them. As ironborn, as half-human, Arlo was fully aware of that. She'd been taught from a young age how careful she needed to be around them—but this felt somehow more horrific than any of the stories she'd been told. *Evil*, almost. Sinister, most definitely. This was so much more than someone's disturbed idea of a prank. This was dark magic, that thing Nausicaä had spent her life monitoring; it was no wonder she barely batted a lash when one of the victims, a little lesidhe girl in a dress made entirely out of sunflower petals, knocked into her as she tore through the woods screaming so fiercely for her mother that her voice had grown cracked and ragged.

Nausicaä's and Arlo's eyes met.

It was the briefest of flashes, but Arlo saw it then, that she *wasn't* as unaffected by this as she pretended to be. That this weighed on Nausicaä more heavily than she let anyone see.

When Nausicaä wheeled around to carry on, Arlo reached out and latched on to the back of her starlight cloak, making her pause. Arlo opened her mouth—maybe she'd been about to console Nausicaä, maybe she'd been about to ask just how much horror she'd been forced to witness over the years.

What she said instead was, "There," in a voice so quiet she was certain only Nausicaä could hear her, and Luck just behind them.

Because *there*, indeed—just off to her left, up in the trees, crouching low on a branch and watching closely—was the wood imp.

Arlo had never seen this particular species of imp outside of pictures, but he was much larger than she'd imagined in her head and than the other varieties she'd encountered in the city. He was almost as tall as she was, with spindly limbs and rags for clothes, giant leaves wrapped around his feet like boots and stringy black hair that hung like wisps of web around his completely flat face.

There was no nose, his nostrils carved into his head like a snake's, and his mouth was a thin, stretched line, his eyes spaced more toward his temples, wide and shaped like a bullfrog's.

Nausicaä looked up.

Luck did as well.

Arlo had been staring for a full minute now—at the dull, glassy red that glowed behind his eyes, the same as what glowed flickering-faint in the heart of the stone he clasped in his right hand . . .

The same color as— "Ow!"

Arlo winced, the memory she'd just tried to grasp tearing itself from her recollection as painfully as a crack to her skull with a metal bat.

There and gone—she couldn't at all think of what she'd been about to remember just then, and forced herself to recover quickly when Nausicaä's gaze dropped to her in alarm.

"I'm fine," Arlo assured her, though Nausicaä continued to survey her, eyes narrowed.

The imp cocked his head from side to side, examining them back, wondering perhaps how they'd come to be here and why they weren't befuddled and scared like the rest.

It was then that Luck raised their hand, and just like that, the forest fell still.

The tinkling of magic subsided. The cries and screams and rustling of brush quieted to nothing. The imp sat frozen in his tree—only Arlo, Nausicaä, and Luck remained mobile, and when Arlo realized what had happened, she looked to find the titan staring at her.

Or, more precisely, the pocket on her shirt where she'd been keeping her magic die.

Cluing in, Arlo retrieved it, its numbers already blazing gold, the jade it was made from warm and ready for use.

"As I said, this is an excellent time to conduct your first lesson," said Luck, lowering their hand. "Before we begin, it's important you know, Arlo Jarsdel, what a Hollow Star is. Under Fate's command, you were meant for a different path, one—as I mentioned—that would have put you in the position of a hero to your people. Under *my* command, your paths become many. Simply put, you are nothing and all. Just like your die, you are infinite possibility limited only by your understanding of what you can do and who you wish to become." Their gaze bore into Arlo's, never once leaving her face, and exactly as it had back in the Faerie Ring, her heart lurched in a panic-flutter to hear what fate she'd been born with.

Arlo Jarsdel—a *hero*? No way.

"At this moment, you know little of your ability; the rules that govern you, therefore, will seem more constricting. But only in understanding our limitations can we find a way to work *with* them and *around* them, and so, your limitations are where we'll begin." They paused and nodded off toward the imp. "Arlo, I'd like you to try to shoot him with an arrow."

Arlo's hand closed reflexively around her die. "*Shoot* him?"

She looked to the imp, who sat in his tree like a statue. What he'd done to all these people was unforgivable, but did he really deserve death? Was *she* really the one to deliver that to him?

"With an arrow." Luck nodded.

"But . . ." Arlo's brows furrowed in a mix of confusion and hesitation. "I don't have an arrow."

The smile that spread across their face glinted a hint of some deeper intention, something Arlo was missing, but Arlo couldn't figure out what that could be. Limitations, they'd said . . . Arlo didn't have to shoot to kill. She could shoot the imp in the leg or the arm and make him drop his stone. Maybe this was what Luck had meant? She had to try. Closing her eyes, she settled her focus, drew a deep breath, gave the die a squeeze, and said aloud, "I shoot the imp in the arm with an arrow and make him drop the philosopher's stone."

There.

Simple. Concise. Arlo opened her eyes, expecting to find glittering gold writing in the air and a number over the imp's head, designating what she had to roll to complete this action.

Except . . . there was nothing there.

The die was still warm in her hand, the number still golden hot, but the move she'd called hadn't worked.

She frowned, looking back up at Luck.

"You said it yourself, dear. Do you *have* an arrow with which to shoot your imp?" they asked, all baritone innocence and grinning wide.

Ah.

Arlo understood them now. She shook her head. "No, I don't."

"No, you don't," Luck repeated in agreement. "So naturally, that move wouldn't work at all. You can only use the skills you know and the tools you have available to you. The same for offering assistance— if Nausicaä had an arrow, you could aid in heightening her current level of luck, but without one, this move is useless. What skills *do* you possess?"

That was a very good question.

According to Nausicaä, she could run pretty fast. She was good at alchemy. Were either of those things useful in this situation?

Nausicaä raised her hand like a student answering a question in class. "She's a windborn fae. Her element is air."

Oh . . . right. Arlo wouldn't exactly describe herself that way, since she hadn't really done anything to classify herself as either fae *or* a proficient elemental. But back on her rooftop, when she and Elyas had first started playing around with this mysterious die, she'd managed to get the wind that had been ripping around the city that day to stop completely.

"She's a windborn fae," Luck echoed again, that smile of theirs drawing deeper. "A windborn fae with the budding hint of your element in your core, as you've recently discovered. Air will be easiest for you to use your luck toward manipulating. As you've yet to hit Maturity, there's only so much this die can boost for you, but the little you currently have access to will still be enough to utilize tonight. With time you'll get better and your power will grow, giving you a much wider arsenal to work with. For now, let's see what would happen if you tried to use the wind to blow each of the imp's victims back to the faerie grass that led them here."

Nausicaä's expression had turned noticeably wary, but Arlo trusted Luck. Titan or not, they wouldn't go through all this just to let her kill herself on something so underwhelming as basic training.

Then again, this may be their way of weeding out potential from the weak. If she only had access to a *little* of her fae magic—*fae magic*, that "what if" feeling in her trilled—wouldn't blowing *everyone* to safety be a bit beyond her capabilities right now?

She wouldn't think about it.

There was only one way to find out.

Closing her hand once more around her die, she focused her thoughts on her instruction, considered the specifics of the phrasing she'd need, and called out her move. "I use the wind to blow us, all the imp's victims, and the imp himself back to the faerie grass that will take us back to the primary plane."

There, she felt it now, the clunk of the world coming to a halt. Of course, everything was already frozen, but when she opened her eyes, it had drained of its scant color, and golden words scrawled her familiar options: *Roll, Assist,* and *Escape.*

Assist was grayed out, as there was no one currently to lend a bit of her luck to.

Escape gleamed as brightly as *Roll.*

She still didn't have the best grasp on what *Escape* would actually do for her, but as rolling to boost her own luck was what she was after, she'd save that particular question for later.

For now, the number twenty glared bright red, hovering in the air just above her options.

A very difficult roll, it seemed—would she fail? Was this the part of her lessons where she'd finally find out what happened if she didn't meet the requirements of a roll?

"Dang," she muttered under her breath.

"Wait, what happens if it doesn't work?" Nausicaä asked in a threatening demand that anyone *other* than a titan would definitely think twice about ignoring.

But Arlo didn't wait. She dropped her die, watched it bounce off the dirt and roll over dried leaves, and stop on the number . . .

"Eight."

Dang.

The reaction was instant.

A great gust of wind reared up around them, swelled and gathered into a tidal wave wall of air. Nausicaä darted in front of her, and Arlo threw her arms up to shield her face, but it made no difference. The wall blew through Nausicaä, hitting Arlo with what felt like the force of *bricks*, or perhaps a train, but either way it *hurt*. She tumbled backward . . . and backward . . . and *backward*, until the wind let up and she was deposited much deeper in the woods than before, flat on her back.

Winded, lying on the earth, blinking up at the dense canopy—she could only really exist in this moment, her entire body throbbing with pain and exhaustion like she'd never known before.

A second passed . . . followed by another.

When the third passed, Arlo was finally able to gather enough of herself to dare lifting her head. She winced with how it made her head pound even worse but was in the very least pleased to note nothing seemed broken.

"*Urgh*," she groaned, shifting upright gingerly. "Well, that sucked."

"—ever do that again, I'll reach down your fucking throat, rip your shriveled little titan heart out, and use your esophagus to tie it up in a pretty bow for your fucking dickbag husband piece of sh— Oh, *Arlo*! Are you okay?"

She was still a little too dazed to comprehend this as quickly as she normally could. Nausicaä and Luck were suddenly there when they hadn't been anywhere in sight just a sluggish blink ago. Nausicaä had her fists balled in the collar of Luck's plaid shirt, spitting mad, her nose an inch from theirs, and was it Arlo's possible concussion or had that face hollowed out a little? Were those teeth Nausicaä bared more like fangs?

Black smoke swirled behind Nausicaä, trickling in tendrils out of her back, forming a skeletal shape of wings Arlo kind of wanted to touch—but then, in a flash, Nausicaä abandoned whatever she'd been about to unleash on Luck to hover over Arlo, worry clear on a face that was just as ghastly gorgeous as always, no sharp teeth in sight.

"I'm fine," Arlo replied, wheezing slightly. "I'm okay, just got the wind knocked out of me, I think."

"Trash bag fucking titan deity of fucking dicks," Nausicaä growled under her breath as she helped Arlo sit up, and Arlo laughed, because it was funny if also touching how bright blue in the face Nausicaä had become in alarm. For *her*.

And Nausicaä called *her* weird.

The snap of Luck's fingers was all the warning Arlo received before the ground fell out from beneath her. She shrieked, lunging instantly for Nausicaä, wrapping her arms around her neck and burying her face in her shoulder. But the sensation of falling was short-lived. The ground rushed up to meet her again, a little too forceful considering the blow she'd just sustained, and she grunted when there was solid earth beneath her once more.

Pulling her head back a fraction, she realized they were back with the imp.

And that Nausicaä was grinning, razor-sharp and gleeful, her steel eyes sparkling with flirtatious delight. "Well, maybe they aren't *all* bad," she purred, pressing just a little bit closer.

With a yelp, Arlo shot to her feet, regretted it immediately, and almost toppled back over again. She was incredibly aware of how sore she was, but the *exhaustion* that hit her as soon as she was upright . . .

Rising much more gracefully, Nausicaä stalked back over to Luck, glaring them down the whole way. "She's mortal, remember?" she rumbled. "Be *careful*."

Luck frowned back at her, but wisely refrained from commenting whatever they definitely wanted to shoot back. The spot of silvery color on their left, high-swept cheekbone . . . it almost looked like a bruise. Had Nausicaä . . . had Nausicaä *punched* a *titan*? In the face? For *her*? No. Even Nausicaä wouldn't be that reckless. Surely.

"Please don't smite my friend," Arlo pleaded in a quick breath, because she had no idea what a titan could do, but it was probably a lot more than a Fury, and she didn't want Nausicaä to get into any more trouble than she was usually in.

But Luck shook their head and waved a hand—all was well . . . enough, at least. A little more rumpled than before but just as unfairly and ethereally stunning, they tossed Arlo's die back to her. She caught it with no problem, which meant she *probably* didn't have a concussion. Hopefully.

"I apologize for the necessity of that lesson, Arlo. The exhaustion you feel, the ache . . . not every failed roll will harm you. Some will harm you far more than that. It's important, especially in your current state, that you exercise care in your decisions—I can only protect you from so much. Luck is not the absence of misfortune, after all, but how well you weather it. And the more you have of one, the greater the odds of attracting the other. I'd be doing you a disservice to grant you too much of my favor. Now, come." They motioned again at the imp, still in his tree, still frozen in time. "Let's see what would happen if you aimed your magic a little more practically. It requires too much power from your current level to carry us all to safety, but your wind can be bent in other ways. Try using it instead to trap the imp."

There was a lot Luck had just told her.

Arlo filed it all away for later consideration.

For now, she did once more as instructed, closed her eyes and called her roll, asked the wind to form a cage around the imp and hold him in place. It was harder to get her thoughts to focus. She was so *impossibly* tired right now that as soon as her eyes had fallen closed, she feared she might fall asleep. But when she opened them again and saw the number nine shimmering pale green above his head, she dug deep within herself, forced herself to focus, called out, "Roll," and tossed her die in the air. She caught it on the way down and opened her palm to reveal—"Nineteen!"

That's more like it, she thought with a weary grin.

The earth lurched back into gear.

Just like before, the air around her surged. It gathered together, in a much smaller wall this time, and blew not toward her but the imp, who had little time to respond, couldn't leap fast enough down from his branch and was caught midway. Cradled by the bars the wind had formed, he was eased to the ground, where they closed around him, binding him up in a cage just as Arlo had instructed.

The imp *shrieked* at them.

He pounded his fists against the churning, translucent bars, bared his teeth and snapped at Nausicaä when she prowled over to try to wrench the stone out of his hand.

"Hey!" Nausicaä barked, withdrawing her hand. She kicked at the imp's cage hard enough to make it rock, and excited even more shrieking from within.

"I did it!" Arlo cheered weakly, pumping a fist in the air, which felt like it took almost the same amount of energy as lifting a boulder. "I trapped the imp! I *did it*!"

She almost regretted her celebration for the wave of *Exhaustion-NauseaLowBatteryPain* that swept over her now, the full toll of both using power at all and the roll she'd attempted and failed.

"You did very well," Luck allowed, nodding their head.

"I'm so freaking *awesome*," Arlo continued, her words slurring. She was definitely less energetic but still perhaps a little carried away on the rush of adrenaline she felt, having actually *succeeded* at something instead of messing it up royally. She raised her hand, intending to give herself a high-five, but another's hand slapped against hers before she could.

Nausicaä stood across from her, grinning now too.

Her fingers were much longer than Arlo's, her palm a bit wider. Like Luck's, it was warm against her skin—*really* warm, as though Nausicaä had been holding hers close to a flame, and it was only now that Arlo noticed the pearly scarring that riddled her flesh like veins.

Couldn't immortals heal themselves?

A Fury certainly could, Arlo had seen it. The stab wound on Nausicaä's chest was nothing now, not even a speck—so what had hurt her so badly it had left *these*?

She bit her bottom lip. Was it bad form to ask? Nausicaä was a highly private person. She didn't like talking about her past, and that was fine, but Arlo kind of wanted to hug her every time a bit of Nausicaä's significant trauma started peeking through all that bravado.

She caught it just in time, the flicker in Nausicaä's steel-gray eyes, awareness of what had captured Arlo's attention.

And that hand fell away.

"Well, I think I'm going to take this guy to Eris," she said, crossing back to the caged imp and balling her hands on her hips. "Let him sweat out his mood and the stone's dark magic before a nice long chat with the Hunters about why this wasn't very nice of him and where he even got that stone of his to begin with."

With a sigh, Arlo nodded. She glanced down at the hand that had just been flat against Nausicaä's, still warm and slightly tingling from the contact. It had been . . . strangely nice. Nice in a "hey, I think you're becoming my best friend" way or "hey, I'd really like to kiss you again" way, she had no idea, but the fluttering had started up once more in the pit of her stomach.

Why did *everything* in her life have to be so *confusing*?

Movement out of the corner of her eye stole her focus. Luck transformed back into their panther-cat body, loped toward Arlo, and sat at her feet, gazing expectantly up at her with those big black eyes of theirs that made Arlo feel a bit like being swallowed by space if she stared into them too long.

"What, do you want me to pick you up?"

Luck said nothing.

"Oh my deities, you *do*." She rolled her eyes and bent down with great difficulty to retrieve them. "Spoiled. You know I feel like complete death right now, yeah?" she muttered, but just as she gathered them into her arms—and goodness, this cat titan was *heavy*—she noticed something on the ground. Something incongruous with the rest of the forest. Something *wet* and mildly briny . . . "Seaweed?"

Shifting Luck into the crook of one arm, she picked the plant up off the ground for closer examination.

Seaweed. "Hey, Nos, look at this!" She held it out for Nausicaä's inspection.

And Nausicaä returned.

Took the seaweed from Arlo's outstretched hand.

Held it by the end in front of her face, the right corner of her wide mouth quirking in confusion. "One of these things is not like the other," she sang softly to herself. "Hmmm."

Nausicaä looked to Luck, squirming in Arlo's arms while she tried to get a more comfortable hold on them. If Luck had an answer for why this was here, they made no comment. Arlo would have thrown it away—there was a lot here out of place, and who was she to say it was out of place at all, given how little they knew of the secondary plane. Maybe seaweed just grew here—but Nausicaä pocketed it.

"All right, well, that's been enough excitement for one night. Time to get you two home and tucked up safe in bed—which is a whole lot questionable, I'm going to add, that you're sleeping in her bed, ancient timeless old-ass titan."

Luck turned up their nose.

I have no interest in teenagers, *thank you. Where would you like me to sleep, the* floor?

"Cosmin forbid," Nausicaä snorted. "O-*kay*, come *on*, bedtime. Chop, chop."

It wasn't until much later, in her bed that was more like a decadent cloud, it was so soft beneath her, when all the lights were off and Luck was curled up fast asleep on the bottom far corner and Nausicaä had gone off back to Eris with their catch, that Arlo realized there'd been something else about that seaweed—the scent of magic sickly sweet, like rotting flowers.

She was far too tired, though, to recall why the scent was so familiar.

CHAPTER 16

Aurelian

O
NE OF AURELIAN'S EARLIEST, clearest memories of his time together with Vehan was of them at fourteen. He and the prince had been playing where they shouldn't, by a lake in Wild territory, which they'd snuck off to through the palace portal because they were young and foolish. Aurelian had been so *proud* of himself for finally figuring out how to override this bit of magical technology from preapproved to unsanctioned coordinates. All he'd wanted was to test it out, and Vehan had been more than happy to tag along.

And just like too many of their "adventures" lately, it had nearly cost the prince his life.

Too preoccupied with finding the best place to hide for the game they'd been playing, Aurelian hadn't noticed when Vehan had wandered too close to the water. And neither of them had been aware that a kelpie had chosen this spot for its home. In what was almost a blink, the crimson-eyed faerie with its ebony coat, stringy black mane, and double set of yellowing teeth like tiny shards of broken glass, had managed to lure Vehan onto its back.

And into the lake.

Not a thrall, exactly, but Vehan had been young enough that even his fae nature hadn't been able to guard him against such tempting magic as what a kelpie could wield in its voice. It would have drowned him so easily if Aurelian hadn't gone in after him, singlehandedly wrestled the prince out of the kelpie's grasp, and then dragged him back to shore.

But Vehan had sustained a vicious bite to his side in the process.

For some reason, nothing any of the Seelie Summer MediFae tried could get the wound to close. They'd applied spells and balms and salves and even forbidden alchemical potions to expedite Vehan's innate fae ability to heal, but the injury kept reopening, as ugly and fresh as when Vehan had first received it.

It wasn't until Aurelian came to check on him one morning, earlier than usual, that he discovered that Vehan had been *keeping* his wound open by gouging his fingers into it and tearing at it with his own nails. Aurelian had been *horrified* to learn this, and even more so to catch him in the middle of the very act, a cloth pressed just under the wound to soak up the blood before it could drip onto the bed. Vehan had burst into fat tears when Aurelian *threw* himself at the prince to knock his hand away. He'd barely been able explain himself over how hard he'd been crying, begging Aurelian not to tell his mother on him, and Aurelian could recall quite vividly his own tears over the matter.

It was the first time he realized Vehan Lysterne wasn't as unaffected by his mother as he pretended.

To this day he still didn't know what was worse: the fact that Vehan had been doing this at all, as it said very clearly that Vehan was not *well*; or that what drove him to it—the awful, desperate reason Vehan had been willing to actually *rip himself open*—was the fervent desire to extend for as long as possible the piddling ounce of affection Riadne had given him during his invalidity, coming daily to check personally on her son's well-being instead of sending a surrogate to do the task for her.

In the end, Aurelian had felt wretched enough that he'd agreed to keep Vehan's secret. And in return he'd made Vehan promise never to do *anything* like that again. To his knowledge the prince had kept his word, but it didn't stop Aurelian from worrying about what lurked beneath Vehan's easy laughter and charming smiles.

I've done my best to keep him lonely, to keep him starved for affection . . .

I brought you here to break him . . .

. . . And it won't be useless love *I use to rebuild him.*

Standing at the side of Vehan's bed, Aurelian stared at the balled-up cloth the prince clutched in his hand, stained dark with splotches of sapphire, with more blood smeared beneath his nose. He felt his own hands start to shake.

More and more, his anger began to build on itself.

More and more, he was losing the ability to control it.

He clenched his trembling fingers into fists and *squeezed*—

"Knock, knock!" a voice whispered from the doorway, accompanied by a gentle rap of knuckles on wood, alerting Aurelian to the fact that he was no longer alone in Vehan's night-drenched bedroom.

Lifting his gaze, he watched as Theodore entered the room of cream white carpet and floor-to-ceiling arched windows, gilt and golden chandeliers and sunny yellow furniture, all of it muted in a wash of navy shadow, and none of it as captivating as the night-haired boy to whom it belonged—Aurelian's bias, perhaps, but he had a feeling many would agree.

Theodore crossed the room in long, graceful strides, came up beside Aurelian, and peered with a sigh down at Vehan as well. "Another nosebleed?"

Aurelian grunted his reply, nodding his head curtly.

"Hmmm." The Reynolds heir eased himself down onto the edge of Vehan's bed, careful not to disturb him. He reached over to pry the bloody cloth out of his hand, his warm brown eyes never once leaving Vehan's face. Aurelian was struck by the image of them . . . the casual intimacy Theodore was perfectly free and encouraged to show; the intimacy Aurelian had been forced to guard for *years* now.

He wasn't jealous.

He *wasn't*.

So long as he didn't attach to that sentiment what he wasn't jealous over, so long as he didn't say it out loud, he was able to think this untruth just fine, but it was just about as effective as the one he used to remind himself that he also wasn't angry.

"Are you in love with Prince Vehan?"

It wasn't until Theodore looked up at him that Aurelian realized he himself had been the one to blurt out the question. But he'd been wondering this for a while—or rather, wondering what Theodore felt for the prince in general.

What was his intention with Vehan? Did he even *want* to marry him? Because Aurelian was certain that whatever everyone was *pretending*—whatever Riadne had promised to get this boy here under her careful watch and control and whatever the Reynoldses got out of allowing their only heir to risk his life in staying here—Theodore was far too ambitious to content himself only as arm candy to a fae crown prince.

Riadne had a deeper reason for keeping him close, and Theodore had his own secrets too, but the tenderness with which he often treated Vehan . . . if he really did want to marry Vehan, was it love? A crush? Did he fancy himself the happy future husband of a powerful king? Would he be good to Vehan, or was he only in this for a crown?

There were so many mysterious variables when it came to Theodore Reynolds. The spare prince of Seelie Summer, a beautiful boy *anyone* would be lucky to have for a partner—wealthy, powerful, handsome, articulate. A royal fae who seemed to flourish under the pressures of court life and political intrigue and would be more than a match for any of the Councillors who thought they could turn him into their puppet. But if there was anyone here as good at guarding themselves as the queen, it was Theodore. Aurelian would have sought him out as an ally in a heartbeat . . . if he'd ever been able to glimpse even a *hint* of where his loyalty truly lay.

For a moment, Aurelian thought perhaps Theodore wouldn't answer his question.

In fact, he didn't expect him to, and if he did, his reply was sure to be some runaround response that was no answer at all.

Then Theodore grinned at him—a delicate, lopsided thing that only a *trace* of darker amusement could flicker through—and he drew himself a little straighter. "In what way?" he asked. "Do I love him like *you* do?"

Aurelian's eyes widened a barely perceptible fraction. His heart tripped over a beat. "I—"

"No, I don't," Theodore continued, saving Aurelian from scrambling for a reply of his own to that condemning statement. "And I don't think there's anyone in this world who does, considering the lengths I know you go to keep him safe, even from you." He paused to hold Aurelian's gaze, and Aurelian refused to look away, glaring back at him, jaw clenched. He wouldn't answer, and it would be an outright lie if he denied Theodore's accusation now, besides. But this whole charade only worked so long as Aurelian never admitted aloud how he truly felt. "I do love him, though," Theodore picked up again in the weighed silence. "Differently. As a friend. A companion. As someone who can see the man this boy has the potential to become."

"A king, you mean?"

"Well, sure, but no. *Good*, Aurelian. Vehan Lysterne is a *good* person. He'll be a good man. A good husband—I could do far worse . . . if that was what I actually wanted. If that's how I genuinely saw this ending." And there it was again, that darker, secret amusement flickering beneath a benign smile, and Aurelian was still no closer to understanding it than before. But . . . "You're a smart fae." Theodore tilted his head, almost daring Aurelian to chase after his building curiosity, the things Aurelian had suspected but never voiced, a truth that would be incredibly detrimental to Theodore if Aurelian leaked it. So what was Theodore playing at here? "You don't think for a second that the only role I serve in your lives is to decorate your prince's throne, and you certainly shouldn't. Because the people I work for desire a certain level of camaraderie between their organization and the fae woman who we're all very aware *will* become the first High *Queen* in Court History."

The people I work for. So there it was.

Theodore watched his face carefully as he continued. "There are things my people need, and to determine whether Riadne will be amiable to that or whether she needs to be . . . *dispatched* before she becomes untouchable, well, *that's* why I'm here. It has nothing to do with love and nothing to do with what my family pretends is simpering elation, just to be considered for Vehan's hand in marriage like everyone believes—like I've *encouraged* them to believe. But not you. *Not* you, so don't be droll."

He fixed Aurelian with a brief but very stern look that Aurelian felt cut straight to his core. "You've known who I am for a while now. It was no mistake on my part, of course. I've *allowed* you to know. But for all the reasons why you shouldn't, a part of you, however small, also knows you can trust me."

Theodore looked back to Vehan now, and there was that affection that Aurelian could see Theodore truly felt. Aurelian doubted that *liking* Vehan had been a part of Theodore's plan, but Vehan was very difficult not to develop an attachment to, Aurelian could say from firsthand experience. "It's that part, that sliver of trust, that's stayed your tongue in the trade you could definitely offer Riadne for a bit of your freedom returned—after all, Riadne suspects I'm a spy. She suspects I'm here to learn her weaknesses and even perhaps to be the one to deliver her killing blow if she's deemed a threat. She *doesn't* yet know who I'm doing the spying for. You do—or at least you should, considering I never kept it secret from *you*."

Aurelian frowned.

This was all true, he'd suspected right from the beginning that Theodore wasn't this pretty, this intelligent, this perfectly suited to Vehan all by *coincidence*. Which at first had been largely due to stubborn bias, a refusal to believe anyone could be so naturally and genuinely better for Vehan than Aurelian. He'd watched Theodore closely in an attempt to discover the agenda this Seelie prince had to be hiding behind his clever humor and easy charms, but for all of this, and though he eventually conceded to the decency in Theodore's aura, it had still been a surprise to Aurelian to learn that he was *right* to second-guess Theodore's motivations.

It had all come down to that damned tattoo . . .

Small and magically concealed was a tiny circle, inset at the top and bottom with two canine teeth. Aurelian had never thought it was an accident—he knew from first glance that Theodore had *allowed* him to catch a glimpse of it, because such was the magic that inked this symbol that permission was the only thing that made it visible to others.

It was, after all, the mark of the Grim Brotherhood—some amount of care had to be considered when stamping this organization's followers in such a distinguishable way. The only reason Aurelian even knew about it was from his own fits of rebellion in the past.

Theodore Reynolds was without a doubt a member of the magical community's league of assassins, the folk's veritable mafia that controlled the Courts' underbelly. It was possible that the whole Reynolds family was. Whether Theodore was a full-fledged assassin himself or just a spy, he was certainly one of the deadliest people in this palace purely for that damned tattoo, but what bothered Aurelian the most was that he couldn't pin down *why* Theodore had allowed him the glimpse of such a condemning thing.

Did he not care at all that Aurelian could bring this information to Riadne? What sort of reward did Theodore stand to gain from so big a risk?

Transferring the cloth from one hand to the other, Theodore brushed a few errant locks of Vehan's raven hair away from his brow. "He's a good person," he continued. "Not difficult to love at all. In the grand scheme of things, my family is entirely unnecessary—we really are at best decoration and at worst a threat to the throne. I was never going to marry for romantic love. I'm too valuable an asset not to be paired up with the best political match, regardless of what or *who* I might want . . . so if I did love him, if we *did* marry, I could have done so much worse than this kindhearted boy."

"You'll protect him, then?" Aurelian finally allowed himself to speak.

So many reasons to mistrust this fae, but so long as Aurelian could believe that it wasn't *Vehan* whom Theodore had been tasked by the Grim Brotherhood to "deal with," Aurelian had no reason not to keep Theodore's secret.

"In your stead, you mean?" Theodore replied with a teasing bite.

Aurelian said nothing, held his tongue against the spike of irritation those words provoked. Only when Theodore glanced back up at him did he give another curt nod—because yes, in his stead. Any day Riadne chose could be Aurelian's last, and Theodore had said it himself: *no one* cared about Vehan the way Aurelian did. When he was gone, who would be left to keep Vehan safe?

"He has no idea how much he owes you," was all Theodore replied, sounding somewhat sad, which was just as irritating to Aurelian as everything else this evening.

He opened his mouth, intending to tell him that Vehan owed him *nothing*, but Theodore interrupted. "For the record, Vehan's magical core is dangerously low. Back in the dining room, he was complaining about shocks. I think his core was desperate for a jump start and latched onto the electric waterfall behind us. That was likely his problem on the mountain, too—his core was too depleted to call on pure, undiluted energy, and some innate defense mechanism must have snapped into place to keep him from overloading straight into a Surge. It would have been so easy . . . so *quick* . . . He would have fried himself instantly, the fool." Theodore shook his head, looking far more serious for what he'd just said, and Aurelian . . . he didn't want to think about it. The truth in Theodore's statement frightened him. Because the fact that Vehan had pushed himself on that mountain despite what had to have been screaming inside him, warning him *not* to . . .

"Aurelian, there's something *wrong* with Vehan's magic. You feel it, right? Those lesidhe senses of yours, you have to have noticed. There's something wrong, and I'm willing to bet it has to do with . . ."

Theodore's hand shifted down from Vehan's forehead to his bare chest and the alchemic array marked there.

Once again Aurelian was reminded how intelligent this sidhe boy was—far more so than people gave him credit for, which was saying a lot, considering how highly they spoke of Theodore's every quality. He was intelligent, and he was watchful, and by his own admission, he was here to *gauge*. So he'd undoubtedly seen the mark on Vehan's chest at some point—even if he couldn't see the magic of it, even if he didn't know the array's true purpose, he'd know it was no ordinary scar.

But how much else did he know about what was going on here?

Somehow, this first real conversation they'd ever had filled Aurelian with more questions about Theodore Reynolds than before—but at least he wasn't the only one concerned about the state of Vehan's magic and convinced there was something off about it. He'd been able to sense it for a while now, growing more profound since his confrontation with the cava.

Something dark—something *cruel*—had begun to thread through the pure light that Aurelian had always seen at his core.

But once again, Theodore spoke before he could, and once again, the subject was changed.

"Her Highness sent me to 'play vigil' at Vehan's bedside tonight. Something about winning points of favor with him. You should go, get some sleep. It's the middle of the night, Aurelian. You're no good to your prince or yourself exhausted."

Well, that explained why Theodore was here in white silk pajamas and a blazing crimson sleep robe tied overtop. Riadne must have roused him, more concerned about playing matchmaker than what had caused her son so much distress at dinner that he'd had to leave the table without eating.

And Vehan already ate so little as it was . . .

"Make sure he gets breakfast," Aurelian replied by way of assenting to Theodore's dismissal. However much he would prefer the other way around—to send Theodore back to his room and be the one to sit with Vehan through the night—that wasn't his place. He wasn't Vehan's, not like Theodore was supposed to be, and it would ruin all the hard work he'd put into placing distance between them.

Plus, Riadne would definitely use it to her advantage if by chance she came to check on her son and found Aurelian mooning over him.

Theodore nodded.

That was that.

With one last look at Vehan's face, he turned for the door and left. It grated to have to leave him to someone else's care, but that was Aurelian's issue, not the prince's.

Out in the hall, he headed down the corridor for the elevator that would take him to the wing designated for him and his family. *Lord* Bessel—what an absolute *joke*.

He was so wrapped up in his thoughts that he almost stepped out of the elevator when it eased to a stop and the doors slid open, only to notice that this wasn't his floor at all, and someone was barring the way.

"Does no one sleep in this place?"

Aurelian's gaze shot up from the mosaic-tiled floor. "Celadon?" He winced. "High Prince," he corrected. "What are you doing here?"

Much like Theodore, the High Prince was dressed in *his* pajamas, as well. Emerald silk instead of white, CFV monogrammed in onyx thread over his heart, with a sheer black robe that seemed a little too indecent for casual wear, more like lingerie, slung over his sharp shoulders. His eyes were bright with exhilaration and whatever mischief he'd been up to or was currently aiming to cause.

Maybe Aurelian *didn't* want to know what had drawn him out of his room at almost midnight.

The way the High Prince grinned as he wafted into the elevator told him that he was going to find out anyhow. "Gathering intel," the High Prince replied, waggling his brows and sliding into place beside him. "Would you like to help? Since you're up and all."

Not really. "Riadne's secrets are no less guarded after nightfall," he pointed out.

The door slid closed, and the elevator began its descent once more.

"Yes, but there are fewer people around to clutter the air with non-sense and spy on what I'm doing. And I'm an UnSeelie fae, Lord Bessel. Nightfall is when my Gift is strongest."

"Aurelian," Aurelian corrected.

"Celadon," Celadon countered.

That was more than fine with him. The fae elite and their *titles*. Aurelian wasted so much time trying to keep up with them all. "I'm assuming, then, you'd like me to show you where Riadne's office is, *Celadon*?"

"If you could be so lovely, yes, that *would* save me time."

The elevator glided to another halt, this time on the correct floor. But with a roll of his eyes, Aurelian reached out and pressed the button to close them again, then another number that would take them almost all the way to the top of the palace.

"You know, I did wonder if maybe Riadne invited Arlo here this summer to try to set her up with her son. They're the same age, after all, and both come from Founding families. And the prince certainly isn't hard on the eyes, Arlo just as beautiful. They'd be a good match, all things considered, but Arlo's already spoken for. Plus, there's Lord Reynolds, and the queen does seem to like the two of *them* paired off. Which I'm sure doesn't sit well with *you* at all. Impressive love triangle you have going on in the Seelie Court of Summer."

Frowning, Aurelian wondered why *everyone* seemed to think it was their business to speculate on his love life—and even worse, was his affection really so painfully obvious to even the High Prince, a person he'd met only *once* before today?

"You don't talk much, do you."

"It's night. I'm a Seelie fae," Aurelian replied dryly, echoing the High Prince's—*Celadon's*—words and earning a laugh that . . . wasn't unpleasant. It reminded Aurelian a bit of the chimes his mother once kept in their garden back home.

The floor where Riadne kept her office was fully dark—or, at least, as dark as anything ever was in the Luminous Palace. The chandeliers that hung from the ceiling had all been doused, and the world beyond the windows was steeped in night. But between the way the hall's jeweled adornments were angled and all the highly polished white marble, moonlight refracted off every surface to light up the space quite brightly.

"Patrol will be by," said Aurelian, following Celadon out of the elevator. "Riadne leaves nothing unguarded. Whatever you have planned for tonight, you should do it quickly or you *will* be caught."

They approached the office door in absolute silence. Even by lesidhe standards, Celadon's movements were quiet and precise. "Here," Aurelian whispered. He lifted a hand to the wood of the door, could *feel* the pulse of magic that protected it.

Lesidhe magic.

"This is the place," Celadon murmured. It wasn't a question, but Aurelian nodded.

"You're better off trying to slip in during the day. The way it's locked down right now, I doubt even an immortal could break their way in. The lesidhe magic I could counter, but the *blood* magic . . ." Only Riadne would be able to open this door—or Vehan, but he was currently indisposed and wouldn't likely help them snoop through his own mother's things, besides. "No one goes into that room unless they're invited."

Celadon eyed him in a brief but guarded glance. "And I'm assuming that's an invitation I don't want."

Aurelian had to repress a shudder. "Very much no."

"A good thing, then, that I'm far from *no one*."

The way Celadon said this—the sour veneer glossed over words that meant far more than Aurelian could currently guess—drew Aurelian's gaze. He considered the High Prince for the length of the silence that stretched between them, because there was something there, something jaded. High Prince or High *King*, Celadon wasn't getting through that door, except . . . the way he pondered the door handle . . . the *DisgustHorrorResignation* that flickered quick as blinking across his face . . .

"Dispel the lesidhe protections for me?" he asked without looking, and Aurelian's mouth turned down in a frown.

"You won't be able to get inside—"

"Just do it . . . please."

Aurelian paused. If he did this, she would know it was him. His magical signature would be stamped all over the door. Every shred of self-preservation inside him screamed at him not to be this foolish, to keep a low profile and not draw the queen's attention.

But it was the High Prince asking him to do something . . . Celadon had already vowed to protect him and his family. If Riadne asked, he would tell her he was simply following orders.

Besides, it wasn't as though Celadon *Fleur-Viridian* would actually be able to do anything with the *Lysterne* blood magic in place . . .

Sighing, Aurelian inclined his head. "Sure." He raised a hand and pressed it flat against the upper middle of the door, closed his eyes, and concentrated on what had been spun here.

A moment's concentration—blue sparks rippled out around his hand. Like a stone being dropped through the glassy surface of a still pond, the magic laid over the door shuddered. Aurelian pressed a little harder, applying a little more force to the next ripple of sparks from his hand . . . and *there*, a shattering; the protection broke with a tinkling like thousands of shards raining down on the ground, and the door was at last bared . . . to the even stronger blood protections beneath.

"The guard will be along real soon, you realize . . ."

Celadon nodded, still deep in thought, his lower lip caught what had to be painfully between his teeth.

He reached for the handle.

Alarm rumbled in the back of Aurelian's throat, his hand darting out to catch Celadon's before he could make this grave mistake— if anyone dared to mess with something protected by blood, there would be consequences. It wouldn't end well; often, what it "ended" with was a *curse*.

But the High Prince's hand closed around the handle, and . . . nothing. The pair of them stood motionless for a moment, Aurelian in deep confusion, and Celadon with a stoniness that was almost frightening, it left him so unreadable.

"I don't . . . understand," Aurelian breathed.

He looked between Celadon and the handle.

Another second ticked by, then another, and still nothing happened, negative or otherwise.

No way. "She forgot to place the blood spell," he uttered through his next breath, and he just couldn't believe it . . . the *luck* of it all, that tonight of all nights Riadne had been so careless exactly when they needed her to be.

Wordlessly, Celadon twisted the handle—and to Aurelian's further surprise, it *opened*, the darkened depths of Riadne's private office revealed to them.

"*Tellis*," Aurelian swore on the earth goddess's name. "She really forgot."

"Yeah," said Celadon, his tone just as stony as his expression. "She forgot."

There was something very different about Celadon currently standing next to him, unmoving on the threshold of exactly what he'd wanted in coming here—so what was the problem? Granted, this had all been a little too easy. Maybe Celadon was already contemplating what Aurelian should have, that Riadne hadn't forgotten her security measures at all—had been counting on the High Prince to attempt getting into her office and had somehow turned this all into a trap.

Aurelian peered a second time into the waiting gloom, now for a proper scan of the office interior.

Nothing seemed out of place apart from the eclipsing wrongness of the columbarium opposite the doorway they filled. All those hearts trapped within . . . their beating stopped by ill-deed . . . Death clouded the room so thickly that it was almost impossible to push through it to whatever lay behind it, if anything at all.

"Are you even going in, then?"

Celadon said nothing, although the slight edge of exasperation Aurelian hadn't been able to keep completely from his voice seemed to make him bristle and shake himself out of whatever thought had immobilized him.

He stepped inside the office, a modest room of off-gray carpet and butter-yellow walls and, by all accounts, unremarkable furnishings: a large bay window to the far right, a slate fireplace, pale cabinets and solid gold bookcases and a small sitting area marked by stark white sofas.

"There," Aurelian said, pointing to the columbarium. "That's what you'll want to investigate. Her *trophy* case. There's something behind it, I can *sense* it, but . . ."

"Mmm." The High Prince issued a soft hum of interest. Ignoring the rest of the room's contents, he moved quietly around Riadne's stately oak desk—where Aurelian was tempted to rifle in search of anything that could connect her to the countless atrocities he suspected she was behind—and made for the slab of black slate set into the wall, where dozens of compact niches kept all that remained of the people who'd dared and failed to keep up with the Seelie Summer Queen's sport.

Aurelian watched him as he leaned in to inspect the wall of unmarked graves. There wasn't anything he'd be able to find, no inscription of any kind to give away what lay behind this looming reminder of Aurelian's own fate—Aurelian had been "invited" here on too many occasions for his lesidhe eyes to have missed anything that could be found.

"There *is* something behind it," Celadon confirmed, straightening once more to tap his chin in thought. "The air back there . . . there's a room, I can *hear* it. But how to get in . . ."

That . . . didn't make much sense to Aurelian. He had to suppose the High Prince meant that his Gift allowed him to hear hints of things spoken in the air within that secret room, but before he could ask for clarification—before he could even open his mouth—he noticed something . . . something he'd never seen until now because he'd never had he been on *this* side of Riadne's desk.

"Is that . . . your father?"

Celadon whirled around. If Aurelian weren't so anxious about what they were doing, it might have been funny, the look on the High Prince's face like he truly thought for a moment that the High King had just walked through the open door. But no . . . Aurelian crouched down, picked up the photo that had fallen on the floor—a carelessness Riadne didn't *ever* demonstrate, a once-in-a-million mistake in their favor, though how it served them he couldn't say.

He looked at what he clutched in his hand. Celadon drew fast to his side, peering down at the picture as well.

It was High King Azurean, there was no mistaking it—younger, but *Tellis*, Celadon looked *exactly* like him, to an almost impossible degree. Aurelian might have commented on how bizarrely identical the prince was to the man in this photo if it weren't for what else the image depicted.

Celadon.

Celadon as a baby, no older than one or two surely.

Judging by the ceremonial attire swaddling Celadon's infant body, Aurelian would hazard a guess that it was Celadon on one of his earliest birthdays, and it was such an innocent thing—there wasn't anything at all exciting or monumental about it, just the High King and his youngest son, so why on earth would Riadne have this, let alone keep it for so long?

He gave way easily when Celadon tugged on the photo to take it from him and study it more closely with just as much confusion.

Aurelian had no idea what to say—apart from the fact that perhaps Celadon should be a bit more careful, if Riadne had kept this like some sort of reminder of the intended targets of her anger—but before he could think up something, anything, to put an expression on the High Prince's eerily blank face, he heard a sound that made him freeze: the whirring of mechanics . . .

The elevator was coming to this floor.

"The guards—they're on their way. Your Highness, we have to leave. We can come back another night when this is better timed."

To Celadon's credit, he didn't second-guess the issue. A touch of frustration tugged at the downward turn of his mouth, but he pocketed the photo.

"We can leave now," he nodded, already retreating to the door. "This has been . . . enough for one night. I have other places to wander, and I imagine you'd like to get to bed. You can replace the protections on the door?"

"Easily," Aurelian replied, "but we don't have the time." He jerked his chin to the elevator and the lights climbing up to their level. No matter what, Riadne would know that he'd been here tonight. This had been damned reckless. He shouldn't have come, shouldn't have let the High Prince talk him into letting him in that room—but it would be worse if they were actually caught in the act.

"Come on." It was definitely an order, Aurelian grabbing onto the High Prince's upper arm to tug him toward the opposite end of the hall, where another elevator would be able to take them away from the scene of their crime perhaps just in time.

Whatever Celadon had to say about being led *anywhere* as High Prince, he allowed it, following Aurelian without further prompting.

And Aurelian was all too happy to put distance between them and that office for more than just the desire not to be found there. If Celadon only knew the horrors that had taken place inside over the years, he wouldn't be so blithely keen on investigating it, but perhaps that was for the better. *Someone* needed to check it out to get to the bottom of what was going on, and if that someone wasn't conditioned to associate that space with death—

"Oh dear."

Aurelian blinked.

He looked at Celadon's face, then back to the front . . . to the elevator they'd finally reached, just in time, Aurelian had thought, right until he noticed . . .

This elevator was on the rise, too, climbing upward from the floor only just beneath.

A glance behind them again revealed that the elevator at the opposite end had continued on past their floor, which meant the Luminous Guard making their rounds, *seconds* away from catching them, weren't coming from that direction at all . . .

"*Shit.*"

"Permission to be extremely and regrettably forward for a moment?"

Looking once more at the High Prince, Aurelian nodded numbly.

He had no idea what Celadon had just said for the ringing in his ears, but he'd agree to just about anything right now that would salvage this situation. And in the very next moment that resolve was tested by Celadon twisting his fingers into Aurelian's shirt, pushing him back against the wall and crowding in close. The High Prince was *just* tall enough to slam an arm over Aurelian's head, caging him against his chest—*looming* over him.

His face pressed close, close enough that their noses touched.

Close enough that Aurelian could taste his breath on his lips when his tongue darted out instinctually to wet them.

Was Celadon going to kiss him?

The elevator doors slid open, and the next thing Aurelian knew, a low whistle cut through stunned stillness, followed by a chuckle. "What do we have here? You two know you're out of bounds, right? Should probably take this rendezvous somewhere else."

Clearing his throat, Celadon straightened.

His arm peeled off the wall and he turned around slowly, keeping Aurelian shielded from view while grinning in feigned embarrassment over his shoulder at the pair of guards. Aurelian could see only well enough to notice the way they stiffened upon realization of who they'd been speaking so casually to.

"Y-Your Highness! I apologize for the rudeness— I didn't—"

"It's all right," Celadon consoled, his tone gone noticeably breathy but impossibly firm at the same time. "I'm the one who should beg forgiveness. I didn't realize we'd stepped out of bounds. I've been a little . . . distracted."

It was the second guard who peered around Celadon, eyes growing even wider when he noticed who Celadon was with, but he was wiser than his companion. He didn't say a word—not that Aurelian expected even his Luminous training would hold his tongue once his shift was over.

"We'll remove ourselves," Celadon continued. He nodded to the guards, who nodded warily in return, still too taken aback to question the High Prince any further, and thank goodness.

With steady hands, Celadon guided him away from the wall and into the elevator, and Aurelian supposed he had to be thankful for that too, given the way his knees suddenly felt both coltish and leaden.

It wasn't until the doors slid closed and they were alone again, the elevator plunging back down to the Bessel wing, that Aurelian collapsed against the back wall and ran a hand anxiously through his hair.

"I'm sorry," Celadon apologized, quiet and still facing the doors. He sounded genuinely contrite. "There will be rumors. I didn't mean to make your life any more difficult. It was just the first thing I could think of that would be quickly ignored, and everyone already thinks I'm a reckless playboy—apparently, as my father was in *his* youth, they like to tack on. People buy far easier into the things they already believe."

Aurelian stared at him.

His posture was stiff—he didn't look at all comfortable, definitely like he would rather have used any other form of escape.

"I don't care about rumors," Aurelian replied. If his voice was a little rough, it was probably because his heart had been trying to leap out through his throat during that entire exchange.

He didn't care about rumors at all—he cared about getting

caught someplace he wasn't supposed to be by Riadne's people.

For some reason, the comment made Celadon laugh.

Whatever he found humorous about it, Aurelian was glad it deflated some of his tension. "Yes. And I'm sure you're quite used to them, too," Celadon said.

It didn't take long to reach Aurelian's stop. The air between them was a little awkward, and despite everything that had happened tonight, despite the worry in the back of his head over the attention Riadne was going to focus on him for the next little while, trying to figure out what he'd been up to, Aurelian found it impossible to keep from sneaking glances at the mouth that had been so *close* to his just moments ago.

When the door slid open one final time, and Aurelian stepped out, Celadon was nothing but his perfect, unflappable charm. "Thank you for accompanying me tonight. I promise to uphold *my* end of our bargain just as attentively. Rest assured, you won't take the fall for any grievance Riadne should have with whatever she learns of tonight. Good night, Aurelian. Sleep well."

"Mmm." He nodded, fully aware of how distinctly warm his face had grown. "Good night, Celadon."

The doors slid closed. The elevator left, carrying the High Prince off to his next destination. Aurelian watched the light climb through the numbers for a full minute before he shook his head and turned to leave—and something else crept over him that would keep him awake for the rest of the night, if nothing else did.

Whatever talk spread come the morning, Vehan was going to be upset to hear that Aurelian had been caught in a darkened hallway, kissing his childhood crush.

The question was, *how* upset would Vehan be . . . and did Aurelian want to use this to his advantage to ensure that whatever existed between them was well and truly over?

CHAPTER 17

Celadon

~~~

I T TOOK A MOMENT for Celadon to surface enough from his mired
thoughts to register where his aimless wandering had brought him.
A door . . . but not his own.

It was certainly the right *floor*, but *his* room was farther off down
the hall. This one belonged to . . . "Vehan."

Celadon frowned.

The young Seelie Summer Prince hadn't seemed to be feeling all
that well at dinner, had disappeared from the evening altogether before
he'd even taken a bite of his food. Was that unusual behavior for him?
So far, he'd come across as a rather sunny person, but there was much
Celadon didn't know about the boy who a great deal of the magical
community liked to "ship" him with in their fandom rankings.

She forgot to place the blood spell . . .

Celadon frowned, his hand squeezing around the crumpled
photo—the one of *him*, as a baby.

Why Riadne had this . . . well, if it were just this picture on its
own, Celadon wouldn't have a guess in the world.

She forgot to place the blood spell . . .

Celadon was so *tired* of secrets, of things he *didn't want to know*
but somehow or another always found out.

It *was* possible—and most likely of all the explanations—that
Riadne had "forgotten" to place the blood protections on her door.
It was possible she'd done so out of the desire to see what Celadon
would try to get away with, what sort of adversary she was up against.

Just as possible, though, was the one thing Celadon's mind hadn't
wanted to contemplate, *wouldn't* have contemplated if it weren't for

the sudden, inexplainable spark of *what if* . . . because it would just be too awful, too absurd, too *cruel* of fate to make reality.

Reseda wasn't his mother. He'd worked that much out from his father's episodes and rants, the odd comments he'd occasionally made over the years, and the way Reseda had always denied him the same affection she gave his siblings. But tonight was the first time he'd ever been given an *ounce* of cause to suspect that the person that title truly belonged could ever *possibly* be—

His thoughts scattered as the door across from him opened, too quickly for Celadon to gather himself under his usual masks, the likeness he pretended to a woman who'd never wanted to be his mother despite the fact that she was the only one he actually knew.

"So there *is* someone out here slinking around after my husband. First Aurelian, now *you*. I'm going to have to invest in a broom to start fending you all off, aren't I."

"Prince Theodore?" Celadon blinked, taking in the sight of . . . well, *a* prince, but not the one he'd been expecting, Theodore in a bright crimson robe that hung a little provocatively off his left shoulder. "I'm sorry, I was only—"

"Teasing," Theodore half sang, hushed but no less amused. Folding his arms across his chest, he eyed Celadon from head to toe and back again, and ah, but Celadon supposed he probably looked a bit indecent himself in *his* attire, too. "But you *were* coming to check on him, which begs the question: Do you have a secret stash of posters with *his* face on them as he does of yours?"

"I do not," Celadon reassured, a little horrified, because *that* relationship would spell disaster if what he was beginning to worry about was true.

Cosmin.

He drew himself up tall, jutted his chin—he was never one to throw around the weight of his title unnecessarily, but he needed to chase these thoughts out of his head, because it *wasn't true*. His birth mother was one of Azurean's past conquests, a trifling affair with a pretty commoner his family had no doubt paid off in silence.

That was what Celadon had come to believe, and that's what he was sticking to. This photo of him in his pocket had just been something his father had sent in attempt to keep cordial with the queen who'd once been his good friend.

Who'd once *been his good friend* . . . Celadon shook his head.

"Curiosity was all, I assure you. Your fiancé is an important friend to my cousin, and for her sake I only wanted—"

"Pity. I could have used a crush against you. Very well then, come here."

Before tonight, there was only one person in Celadon's life whom he allowed to *grab* at him and lead him anywhere, and she was safely tucked up in bed right now, fast asleep. Aurelian had been forgiven in his earlier instance if only because his tugging had been necessary to make a quick escape, but *Theodore* reached out and without so much as a "please" or "forgive me," latched onto Celadon's arm and pulled him rather unceremoniously into Prince Vehan's room.

He was the *High Prince.*

"Ex*cuse* you—" Celadon gasped, rounding on Theodore once he was released to Vehan's dark bedroom.

"Thank you," Theodore replied, either insensible to the fickle mood of Spring-born fae or obnoxiously unconcerned. He closed Vehan's bedroom door, then leaned against it to grin at Celadon like a cat at a bird in a cage that had just miraculously sprung open. "Why are you here, Celadon Fleur-Viridian? And before you try to charm me with nonsense, why are you really *here*, in the one place you are perhaps *least* welcome in all the Courts, and certainly the most dangerous?"

"I did wonder when I'd finally meet the *real* you," was Celadon's immediate reply, frost beginning to lace his tone. This wasn't at all the boy he'd actually liked at dinner, but it had been made very clear to him then that Theodore was more than he seemed; he wasn't surprised to be meeting his truer side now.

"I'm sure. That doesn't answer my question."

Folding his arms over his chest to match the boy across from him, Celadon peered back at Theodore with disdain.

Unspoken threat for unspoken threat, the pair of them stood in a silent, petty battle of wills for a minute . . . two . . . "I could ask the same of you." Celadon jerked his chin at Theodore's hand, at the tattoo he'd obviously been allowed to glimpse there at dinner, though he supposed he was soon to find out why. "You can't possibly think she isn't aware that you're in league with the Grim Brotherhood."

The grin on Theodore's face curled even deeper. "The thing you have to understand about Riadne Lysterne is that she's an incredibly proud fae. She *likes* keeping her threats and toys alike right under her thumb. She likes her *games*, the same way she likes letting up on Aurelian's leash just enough for him to think there's hope of escaping her. But surprisingly, no, I'm actually fairly certain she has no idea yet that it's the *Brotherhood* I answer to. A sidhe fae prince trained by the most infamous criminal guild in all the Mortal Realm? Whatever possibly for? And I think this because it's kind of my job to assess people and the things they know."

"A fairly garbage assassin, don't you also think?" Celadon cut in, feeling himself grow warm around the collar and ears, because hells, but Theodore was a smug bastard, and where Celadon had navigated many conversations steeped in self-entitlement and superiority, for some reason *this* one grated against his current mood. "The way you so casually announce you're one to a complete stranger. And what do you think's going to happen to you when your queen gets bored of playing this game with you? When she reveals that she's known all along who you are because she's *hundreds* of years old and you're just a *boy*."

"Oh," Theodore replied brightly—and *urgh*, Celadon kind of wanted to slap him. "She absolutely will get bored of this. And I honestly don't expect I'll have any real shot at either bargaining with her or dispatching her until she does, so I'm *counting* on her boredom.

Boredom engenders recklessness, and recklessness is when people start slipping up."

"And Vehan just allows this, does he? He's fine with all this?"

The little that Celadon *did* know about the Seelie Summer Prince was that, despite the rumors and the evidence and perhaps even the ill treatment he himself suffered at her hand, Vehan was protective of his mother.

Celadon could relate.

His attention drifted, gaze sliding across the night-drenched pale carpet to the door of an inner chamber where Celadon was certain he'd find the prince fast asleep. He could relate to Vehan's desire to protect his family—Celadon did it himself every day for people who didn't love him at all, or if they did, couldn't remember who he even was the majority of the time. Because those people . . . they were all he had in the world, and Celadon discovered on almost a daily basis how much a person was willing to put up with and ignore just to not feel *entirely* alone.

Vehan wouldn't take any kinder than Celadon would to Theodore poised like a wound-up trap in his home, so he couldn't know, which meant . . . "You don't really intend to marry him, do you? I'll warn you only once—don't dare think to turn your *talents* on *him*."

An elegant shrug met this question. Theodore didn't look concerned in the least that he was baring himself completely right now, and *that* irritated Celadon too, because *why*? "I have my main objectives, and underlying ones depending on how well things go. I have to account for a wide variety of outcomes—and you do too, Your Highness, for whatever you're after. I'll be sure to tell Vehan you threatened me over him, though. I'm sure it will *thrill* him to know he has that much of your attention."

Celadon's gaze snapped back to Theodore to study him for a long, suspicious moment. He weighed his options. Celadon already had an alliance with Aurelian. He didn't need Theodore to spell it out for him to see that he was offering one, as well.

Poorly.

Celadon had never been propositioned in such an infuriating, conceited way before, and where Aurelian was an easily read entity to him, Theodore was an entirely unknown risk.

"I imagine we might be after the same thing," he finally replied. "Theoretically."

Because whatever, *whoever* Riadne was, she was after his father's Crown . . . and that was a thing only won over death. If that death was to be delivered at the Solstice like Celadon feared . . . he had a very finite amount of time in which to stop her.

Theodore's grin gained a sharper edge. "Then I *imagine* we might be able to help each other. Theoretically."

Theodore stepped back from the door and pulled it open once more. "I know a particular group of people who'd be *deeply* interested in meeting you, Your Highness. Someone with a Gift like rumor suggests of yours . . ."

Yes.

Celadon was certain.

He'd even been approached by members of this "particular group" once before, and this attempt to recruit him now would not be the last. But Celadon had been playing UnSeelie Court spy for too long, knew too well the toll it exacted—the exhaustion, the *weight*—to wish to tie himself to that lifestyle professionally.

"Not interested," he replied, and strode for the door.

Theodore slapped a palm against Celadon's chest at the threshold, and when Celadon looked down at it, noticed a matte black playing card trapped between them.

He didn't need to take it to know what it was—the only identifying markers on this card would be the same symbol that was tattooed on Theodore's hand and the word *Elysium*, visible only in certain slants of light—but he reached for it anyway.

"In case you change your mind."

CHAPTER 18

Arlo

~~~~~~

THE TABLE IN ARLO'S sitting room was laden with a variety of foods. There were berry scones and flaking pastries and slivers of fresh toast; jams and syrups and creams and mounds of butter whipped into delicate swirls; crisp bacon, fried hashbrowns, sausages, eggs, and an entire stack of golden-brown waffles; a pitcher of orange juice, and one of water garnished with bits of fruit; and a flute of what looked to be a mimosa had been set beside her plate, along with a platter of yet more fruit and cheese.

Arlo had never gone hungry, not once in her life. Not to mention that, between her childhood sleepovers with Celadon and the nights when her mother had no choice but to stay late at work, and Arlo with her, she was no stranger to this level of breakfast extravagance. But to see all this laid out for *her*, intentionally, not simply because she'd been around and *not* feeding her would have been too blatant of an insult even for the palace? It made her feel . . .

Happiness, most likely.

At the moment, struggling to surface from the haze of sleep, she was having enough trouble comprehending the food itself, let alone any deeper emotions about it. Eight-thirty in the morning, while not exactly a lie-in by vacation standards, wasn't all that horrible when Arlo considered that most Seelie folk were up at the crack of dawn. If she hadn't decided to run around last night with Nausicaä, chasing after faeries and philosopher's stones, she might have been able to do a little more right now than simply sit and blink down at her plate like she'd never seen one before in her life.

"We weren't sure what you liked," Zelda signed, Madelief translating what she said when Arlo's protracted silence no doubt started to make her anxious. "We opted for a little of all the basics. Please do tell us if there's something you do or don't want for tomorrow, though— we'd be happy to make the correction!"

Giving her head a minute shake, Arlo lifted her gaze from the table. "No, no, it's great," she attempted to assure, however thickly. She was so tired her tongue didn't even want to work properly. "Sorry, I'm just sleepy. This is really great. Thank you."

"Lady Arlo!" said a *definitely* awake, eager voice to Arlo's right. She jolted slightly for how the voice seemed to come out of nowhere, and when she looked to her side, it was to find a young male pixie stepping forward with a tray of tea.

Or rather . . . he *looked* to be young. Pixies were one of the few folk who stopped aging visibly altogether once they hit Maturity. A little taller than the average four feet, with beautiful wings like stained glass in a pallet of different hues, vibrant blue skin and powder blue hair and a cherubic face set with a delicate nose and wide eyes so dark a navy they verged on black, he could be anything from Arlo's eighteen years to the two hundred that was their typical lifespan.

He was also immaculate in the same attire as the serving staff from the night before, a bone-white uniform from head to high-heeled toe, and a gold powder shimmering on the exposed bits of his hands, arms, neck, and face.

A power move, Arlo had concluded when she'd noticed this last night.

The powder was probably *real* gold, and Queen Riadne wasn't the only royal fae to get creative with her display of wealth.

"Uh . . . just Arlo, please." Back home, the only time people called her "lady" anything was when fae etiquette strictly wouldn't allow otherwise, and Celadon or her mother were in earshot. "Um . . . ?"

"Gentian," replied the pixie, setting his tray down beside her plate with a smile just as eager as his tone. "Like the flower. But everyone simply calls me Gent, and you're free to do so too, if it pleases you.

I'll be one of your usual attendants this summer. Nothing fancy, I just bring the tea, but it's something I'm quite knowledgeable in! So, if you have any questions about the daily selections or anything you'd like to try, I'd be happy to supply you with answers—or tea! This morning's brew is a simple breakfast blend, nice and strong. It'll wake you right up with its hearty aroma and long finish on the tongue."

It was hard to get a word in edgewise, the way Gent continued and continued and *continued*, all while pouring dark tea into a delicate cup and setting it down by her plate. But Arlo didn't mind the chatter that much, even if it was hard to keep up in her current state. Gent seemed friendly and *very* passionate about tea. Arlo—as a barista— could appreciate that.

"You'll have to try the cheese and cherry Danishes," Zelda joined in, stepping excitedly toward Arlo's opposite side as though emboldened by Gent's disregard for whatever propriety they were expected to observe as royal attendants. "The way the pastry just *melts* in your mouth, it's divine. They were made by our queen's personally selected pâtissiers—Lord Aurelian's parents, Nerilla and Matthias Bessel—and I promise you, you've never had a better delicacy in your life."

Peering down at these highly exalted Danishes, Arlo considered this new bit of information.

Had she known Aurelian's parents were pastry chefs? Come to think of it, did she know *anything* about Vehan's friend besides the fact that he was very devoted to Vehan and extremely kind beneath all his surly broodiness . . . and that for some reason, he and Nausicaä got along about as well as oil and vinegar.

Arlo looked up once more from the table.

"Do you want one?" she asked. Zelda was hovering beside her with such gentle, genuine enthusiasm on her dimpled face, looking a bit like a Candyland princess with her puffy pink hair, blue-rose cheeks, and the pastel-yellow apron she wore over a cream white dress. There was so much food on this table, and so many people around her, and it was rare lately that she had someone to share a meal with.

Zelda's pink brows shot upward in alarm. "Oh, of course!" She turned to Madelief, who was still translating her signing for Arlo. "How careless, we should have tested the food in front of you so that you can see it isn't poisoned!"

"Uh . . . that's not what I meant . . ." Arlo started, but Zelda wasn't looking at her to read her lips.

"Forgive us, my lady. Madelief, try one of the pastries to test it for pois—*wait*." Madelief trailed off, their eyes narrowing to slivers as their translating caught up to what Zelda had signed. "You want *me* to test it?"

Now that they were no longer translating, Madelief's voice fell into a much flatter, deeper tone, and they looked spectacularly unimpressed with the flurry of things Zelda was currently saying. Arlo knew how to say "thank you" in sign language and that was just about it, but she could read the mood just fine. It was clear that an argument was now underway, Madelief rapid-fire signing back at her.

"Don't mind them," said Leda, as though Arlo had known she'd been at the table this entire time instead of just realizing it now.

She startled slightly—goodness, how much of this morning had she completely spaced on?

But Leda, who either didn't notice Arlo's alarm or didn't care that she'd been wholly edited out of Arlo's awareness, carried on, engrossed in her contemplation of the teacups on Gent's tray. She didn't once look up at Arlo. "The two of them are always like this."

Leda had a calm, methodical way of speaking that was almost like Queen Riadne's, with all the thought and decisive precision of a general plotting out war. But it was softer. Even last night at dinner she'd struck Arlo as the sort of person who didn't tolerate nonsense, but it lacked austerity. Much like her weary air and appearance, it was more that she seemed too tired to care one way or another about it and just preferred not to get caught in the crossfire.

At last, she chose her cup, one with a blue floral print and an elaborate gold-painted handle. Gent was quick at the ready with his pot to pour out her tea. "You've a faerie braid in your hair," she stated, changing the subject completely. "Who gave it to you? It wasn't there at dinner."

Again, no real curiosity touched her tone, but the question was far from cold or unkind. It was a statement, nothing more—if Arlo answered it or chose not to, she doubted Leda would mind either way.

Reaching a hand up to her hair, Arlo felt around for the braid she'd completely forgotten about. It was still there, the ward's magic securing the strand of Nausicaä's brighter, white hair that kept it from unraveling.

"Oh, ah . . . a friend." How did she explain it? First of all, how did one even approach the complexity that was *Nausicaä*, and second of all, people weren't supposed to be able to pop in and out of the palace unless it was through the front door or the Egress. She'd have to lie. "And I had it at dinner, just . . . hidden, I guess. I have a lot of hair. She gave it to me before I came here."

Leda smirked to herself as she arranged her now full teacup and saucer—as an ironborn dryad, not only would she be capable of lying as well, but more conscious of others' ability to do so themselves.

But instead of calling Arlo out, all she said was, "Some friend, to have gifted you such a profound protection. Faerie braids are quite intimate—more commonly exchanged between lovers, in fact. Is this the same friend His Highness the Prince asked after last night? Nausicaä?"

"Well, yes, but . . . we're not *lovers*!" Arlo gave an awkward laugh, waving her hands. Was it warm in the room? It had to be that. A kiss didn't make people *lovers*—didn't mean Nausicaä even wanted that, and here Arlo was, back at the crux of the problem: Was that what *she* wanted? "She's just a friend. I think. I mean, we haven't really . . . talked about it, but I'm pretty sure the Dark Star could have her pick of a *lot* of people, so she wouldn't choose *me*—"

Leda's teacup clattered on its saucer as it slipped from her fingers, the sound jarring both Arlo out of her rambling embarrassment and Madelief from their argument.

When Arlo glanced around to see what caused this, she found Gent *staring* at her as though Arlo had just sprouted another head that had told him tea was just flavored water.

"The *Dark Star*?" Leda repeated.

Oh—crap, yeah, Arlo had forgotten.

Nausicaä was more than just a sometimes angry, sometimes arrogant, all the time hilarious and secretly very big-hearted and accepting person. That, and surprisingly soft, Arlo knew from the one time she had thrown her arms around her, when all that muscle should have made it feel like hugging a very shapely rock. Nausicaä was fierce and loyal and blazing bright against a backdrop of cold tradition and rigid structure, but . . . she was also the Dark Star.

People *feared* her, and for good reason.

The rumors of what she could do, of what she *had* done—whether they were exaggerated or true or completely fabricated, and whether people believed she was even real at all—they were terrible enough that the odder reaction would be for the room to take the casual drop of the name in stride.

"Um . . . yes."

Leda's eyes swirled with emotions too numerous and confused for Arlo to make sense of them. But her tone grew a fraction harder, and all that brittleness seemed to have locked itself up into a shield between them. "*Nausicaä*?" she asked, as though struggling to reconcile the fact that the Dark Star had a name . . . or maybe that she called herself something other than the one she'd originally had.

How old was Leda? Arlo found herself wondering.

Was it possible she was old enough to remember Nausicaä when she'd been Alecto? How long ago had Nausicaä said she'd been banished here—over a hundred years . . . one hundred and sixteen? How long did dryads live? Leda looked to be around Arlo's mother's age, but it was possible, like pixies and almost all the folk, that she could be considerably older.

That dryad there, do you see her?

That dryad knows the answers to the questions that brought you here tonight—how fortunate *you are* . . .

Arlo cocked her head. A memory was starting to piece itself together, coming back to her slowly. It spoke in Luck's voice, but the when and where and context of the words had yet to fill themselves in.

There was a chuckle in her head—and that was Luck too, but here in the present. When she looked around, she saw them curled up on one of the ottomans in a collection of sofas, head down but eyes open, and they were fixed on her with gleaming amusement.

"Burner of ships?"

Arlo's head whipped back around to Gent, who'd grown several shades paler from the last time she looked, and the way he gripped his teapot was like a man overboard, holding fast to his only lifeline.

"Uh . . . what?" she asked.

Gent laughed.

It wasn't a joyful sound.

"Burner of ships, that's what that name means. Your friend—*Nausicaä*—I know the Dark Star. I know what she is, what she got cast out of her *family* for, and she *named* herself after it?"

"Um . . ." Her morning wasn't going at all how she'd expected it to, and yeah, it wasn't every day someone went around claiming to be best friends with the magical community's most dangerous poltergeist, but Gentian's reaction seemed . . . a touch personal. "I know she's . . . done some stuff. Some not good stuff. But she's not a bad person, and I think a lot of the rumors about her have—"

Gentian's laughter stopped. Its abrupt end was just as unkind. "She's *killed* people. She killed them very horribly, and then named herself after the deed, and that is *not* a rumor, it's *fact*. And since coming here, she's done nothing but cause even more mayhem and hurt." He fixed Arlo with his navy black gaze, fingers clutching so tightly to his teapot now that the china was starting to crack. "People have a way of telling you exactly who they are, Lady Arlo, without once ever speaking the words. The Dark Star is not your *friend*."

"Gentian," Leda interrupted. She hadn't lowered her defenses at all, and Arlo still couldn't read anything of what she thought or felt about this situation, but Leda's tone had regained a bit of its steadier softness. "I think the Lady's had enough tea for the morning."

Gentian looked to her.

He looked back at Arlo.

Then, with a sigh, he relaxed his grip on the fractured teapot and dropped into a deep bow. "Apologies, Lady Arlo. I didn't mean to offend. If you'll excuse me . . ."

He didn't wait to be excused.

Arlo watched him go, her head reeling, her face feeling distinctly hot but for once not due to embarrassment. Gentian didn't know Nausicaä, not like she did. To him, on the outside of things, it probably *did* look like Nausicaä had acted out of malice and nothing more, but Arlo knew better . . . didn't she?

Hey, Red.

You're weird.

A dark and hollow star, remember?

Nausicaä wasn't the monster the folk made her out to be—what she herself insisted she was . . .

People have a way of telling you exactly who they are.

"Never mind Gent," Leda consoled, and Arlo turned back to find her placing a Danish on her plate. She then placed one on another for Zelda, and one for Madelief. With a wave of her hand, she motioned for them both to sit down and join the table. "Some injuries take longer to heal than others."

Arlo considered this statement. "I don't understand. Did Nausicaä . . . *do* something to him? Is that why he doesn't like her? Because I know she's caused some trouble over the years but . . ." She shook her head. "It's not what people think. *She's* not what people think. Nos isn't the person rumor makes her out to be."

Leda considered *her* statement now for a long, closed-off minute.

Then she shook her head. Arlo didn't miss the way her unreadable expression wavered slightly, the way her gaze dropped briefly to her lap and her hand paused in the air, as though all the frail energy to her had finally drained away. "No, I imagine there's more to the truth than what we've been led to believe." With a breath, Leda recovered. "It's true what they say about pixies: they're incredibly headstrong and good at holding onto grudges. Gent's heart is in the right place, he's just . . . like I said, never mind him." She smiled gently, settling back into her seat and reclaiming her cup as though nothing had been wrong just a moment ago, as though this entire exchange had never happened. "Eat, drink your tea—I'd like to assess your alchemic standing today to get an idea of where we should begin. Better to not go into that hungry."

There was something deeper going on here, a more personal reason than mob mentality for disliking Nausicaä. And the feeling that Arlo *knew* who Leda was, had met her before yesterday—that barely there memory of Luck pointing her out, but unable to place *where* and *why*, as though that piece of the memory had been snapped off from a larger whole—was stronger than ever inside her.

The way Leda had faltered, and her immediate reaction to Nausicaä's pseudonym . . . Nausicaä might not have done anything to Gentian, but perhaps Arlo had asked about the wrong person.

Your memory has grown quite unreliable *lately, have you noticed? One would almost think it's been tampered with . . .*

Reaching for her Danish, Arlo shot a warning glare at Luck before replying to Leda, "Really? That's great! I've been looking forward to starting my training."

Leda's smile dimmed a little, as though the statement reminded her of something unpleasant. "You might want to keep that excitement to yourself, my lady."

Arlo winced. "Right, yeah, I'm sorry. I know we aren't supposed to be doing this. It's not something I'm supposed to *want* to do. It's just . . ."

But Leda shook her head. "It isn't that." She looked up from her teacup, but the smile she forced back onto her face was as brittle as the rest of her. "You'll see. Eat. And just remember that you're in Her Majesty's care right now—anyone who wants to give you trouble will have to go through her to do so."

CHAPTER 19

Arlo

~~~

THE REST OF BREAKFAST was considerably lighter as far as conversation went. Not at all used to having other people bathe and dress and ready her for her day, she politely excused Zelda and Madelief when their meal was over so she could do these things on her own. They yielded only so far as the bathing went—she couldn't dissuade Zelda from doing her hair (curled and half tied behind her head with a black satin bow), or Madelief from choosing her outfit (another one of Celadon's pre-approved selections: high-rise emerald shorts and a black, square-neck, puffy-sleeved top paired with her favorite gray high-tops).

When she was at last deemed appropriate to be seen by others, and after stopping briefly over at Celadon's room to see if he'd awoken yet—he hadn't, Ondine informed her, answering the door; he was still holed up in his dark room, blackout curtains closed firm against the sunny morning—she was finally free to begin her day and trail after Leda down the floors to the workshop that had been allotted for their lessons.

"*Deities*," Arlo exclaimed, following Leda into the room. "*Look* at all this!"

She could hardly believe her eyes.

The room was fairly enormous, and so well primed for alchemic experimentation that Arlo would have suspected the queen made regular use of it if the very idea wasn't totally absurd and completely laughable.

Despite how big it was, there was a quaintness to its setup unlike anything Arlo had seen anywhere else in the Luminous Palace. Instead of marble, the floor was narrow strips of dark wood, lacquered to protect it against any spills. The wall to Arlo's left had been devoted entirely to a coal-black chalkboard, and along its edges were pinned numerous scrolls and posters of symbols; some Arlo didn't know at all and others she recognized as the periodic table of elements, with minor adjustments. The other wall was lined with cabinets and book-cases, all of them full to bursting with thick, leather-bound tomes and jars and bowls of curious ingredients, and even more herbs and flow-ers. Other bits of forest flora were strung from the ceiling, some dry-ing and others fresh in many more jars and vases and baskets around the room.

It was the solid oak table that caught her attention. Stationed at the end of the room opposite the door, it sat directly in front of a set of windows stretching to look out over a quiet patch of the garden behind the palace, with many more cheerful flowers arranged around a sprawling pond and the forest beyond spilling over the tops of the neatly trimmed hedges.

The table was huge and looked quite heavy, foreign symbols and rune-like shapes carved into its stately legs. On its surface were arranged a wide array of instruments of varying degrees of elaborate-ness, gleaming in the warm daylight.

Arlo walked farther into the room, hands clasped in delight as she took in the space.

The woody-floral-metallic scent that clung to the air . . . Arlo had never studied alchemy, but simply walking into this room was a bit like *coming home*—it felt *right*, so much so that it overwhelmed her slightly and made her blink against a sudden hot stinging in her eyes.

"It's perfect," she said in soft reverence.

Leda, closing the door behind them, nodded. "Not every Head holds the same view on alchemy as the High King does," she replied in that careful, methodical tone of hers that gave away nothing of what she was really thinking. "Queen Riadne is surprisingly supportive of the art for a sidhe fae of royal standing. Of course, she keeps with the

High King's laws, but Seelie Summer lets far more ironborn alchemists go with warnings rather than with the strict punishment they would receive elsewhere, all for doing something no more harmful than help the ill with a potion."

Alchemy was forbidden, and so Arlo assumed that was just the way of it, because everyone had to follow the rules outlined by the Courts' High Sovereign, and anyone she'd ever heard even mention this art in any way did so with a certain air of scorn.

It didn't occur to her until just now that certain *sentiments* might not extend as strongly outside the High King's immediate control as they did within UnSeelie Spring.

"I see," she replied, turning back to survey the room once more, a little subdued. Her great uncle—Arlo's own *blood*—was the reason an entire people continued to be persecuted for the form of their magic. "Well, that's good. I'm glad it's a little safer here for ironborn."

Leda came up beside her.

With a gentle touch beneath Arlo's chin, she turned Arlo to face her and gave a sympathetic smile when their gazes met. "I can hear your thoughts just fine without speaking them. Come here, I'd like to show you something." Retracting her hand, she strode across the room to the table.

Arlo followed.

When she reached her side, she peered down at a sheet of curling papyrus that was pinned to the table by small glass weights at its corners.

On it was sketched a diagram Arlo had never seen before—a diamond of sorts, *Chaos* written in flourishing cursive at the top, a scattering of shapes in a row below labeled: *Earth, Water, Air, Fire, Electricity, Ice, Wood, Death*, and *Spirit*. Below that, three more shapes, these ones labeled: *Salt, Mercury*, and *Sulfur*.

"Alchemy is a vast and intricate magic. It's quite different from what any of the other folk can do, though it all comes from the same place—from energy itself." She slid a long finger to the top of the diagram. "From Chaos." Her finger slid down to the second line. "The fae, both sidhe and lesidhe, can dip a little further into that well, deep enough that their magic has attached itself to a singular element, and while that does grant them considerably more power, it also restricts them." Over to the label *Spirit* her finger traveled. "The lesidhe draw from a more versatile well—the spirit is a highly mutable power. It's life, ether, possibility, the very *matter* of things. It is also where *our* magic draws from. There is, however, a notable difference."

Leda's finger traced down to the final row, sitting just below the symbol for *Mercury*.

"The iron in our blood, it opens up a different channel and allows us far more variety and control of our element in three significant ways: Salt—the body or host of a thing. Through this, we can transmute shape, such as warping a metal pole into a chair. Mercury—the soul or heart of a thing. Its character. Through this we can transmute purpose, lend enchantment to a sword, for instance, or create a flame that burns cold instead of hot. And finally, Sulfur." She tapped on the final word. "Sulfur also represents spirit, but in a different way than our element—it's the vital force of a thing. Through Sulfur we can transmute intention, craft a potion that heals grave injury, or—far darker—reanimate the dead."

Arlo swallowed, recalling the cavum factory and the atrocities Hieronymus had committed with his profound grasp on alchemy.

"Yes," said Leda, noticing the serious turn in Arlo's mood. "Alchemy is dangerous, in the wrong hands. The same can be said of anything, though. There are fae in our history who could draw fire from our very sun, faeries who could speak with such mesmeric ability that even the long-ago immortals of our world were subject to their whims. There is danger in alchemy, but there is also great beauty."

"Unfortunately, the former far outweighs the latter."

Arlo stiffened.

She knew that voice, hadn't heard even a whisper of movement from its owner when they'd entered, at which point in the conversation Arlo could only guess. But it didn't matter. Suddenly, she knew exactly what Leda had meant when she said she'd have to guard her enthusiasm for these lessons, and of *course* the High King would want someone to observe what she learned to make sure it wasn't too much or that Arlo wasn't being turned into some weapon against him, as Celadon had hinted at the day before.

Of *course* Councillor Briar Sylvain had been the one he'd appointed, the man who'd been so set on expelling Arlo from the magical community during her Weighing. He'd probably even *volunteered* for the position, never mind that his domain was that of Seelie Spring, and Seelie Summer was the Court of Head Councillor Larsen's husband, and Arlo would have preferred him by far.

She snuck a glance up at Leda, whose mouth twitched briefly in distaste before her expression smoothed over back to her usual composure, and she turned around.

Arlo did the same, though judging by the Councillor's subtle shift—the way he tilted his head to jut his jaw just so, the way his eyes flashed and arrogant triumph curled his upper lip an almost imperceptible fraction—she was nowhere near as successful at concealing her own dismay.

"Councillor Sylvain—good morning." Leda inclined her head with the greeting.

A moment ticked by.

Sylvain gave no indication of even hearing Leda, didn't acknowledge her or her words in the slightest. He merely stood in the doorway with his arms folded over his chest, staring Arlo down, his gaze growing harder by the second.

Finally, Arlo realized what he was waiting for. "Oh—uh, good morning, Councillor Sylvain," she echoed, dipping into a quick but formal bow. "I . . . take it you're here to watch my lessons?"

Smug superiority returned to Sylvain's face as he entered the room fully now, closing the door once more behind him. He cut an intimidating figure in his emerald-and-turquoise robe, with Seelie

Spring's sigil of a singular leaf entwined in a twisted cage of branches embroidered above his heart. His bark-brown hair swept back from his alabaster face in a way that only accentuated its hard, proud lines and dark eyes—eyes that had yet to leave Arlo's as he advanced on her.

"I am," he replied, smooth as his movements and condescending as his expression. "As thoroughly *uninspiring* as I expect this task to be, his High Majesty wishes to ensure your instruction keeps strictly to his pre-approved outline, which I have kindly gone out of my way to send in advance to your . . . *tutor*." At last, his gaze cut to Leda, his lip curling in an even more blatant show of disgust—with Arlo, he might have to pretend some cordiality, but for an ironborn *faerie* with no relation to his sovereign, there was nothing to hinder his prejudice. "I will be watching *very* closely, Miss Jarsdel." He came to a halt in front of her, so close that Arlo was forced to press herself uncomfortably against the table behind her to keep a breathable space between them. The way he glared down his nose at her was just as openly hostile a look as what both High Prince Serulian and her uncle Malachite often wore for her. "Alchemy is a dark art, its practitioners little better than leeches on the essence of true magic. It very nearly cost the folk *everything* back when fae magnanimity allowed its use—you will do well to remember it's that same magnanimity that permits your mockery of our laws in these lessons, and I can strip you of it like *that* if you give me a single reason to do so."

In other words, Arlo wasn't going to learn anything more than the meager basics under Sylvain's supervision.

Anger flared up sudden and hot inside her.

It was just as Leda had said, alchemy *could* be used for dark, terrible things—she'd seen some of those things firsthand. But that depended entirely on the person, and those people . . . Arlo refused to believe they were the majority.

And Arlo *needed* this, Nausicaä had said so herself; if she didn't give her magic an outlet, it would very likely Rebound on her if she ever came into her fae Maturity.

However likely *that* was, Arlo didn't want to take any chances. Plus, she had the High King's permission—Councillor Sylvain was angry she'd made it through her Weighing and was taking any opportunity he could to punish her for it, but there was nothing he could do if Arlo played by his rules.

There was nothing he could do with both the High King and Celadon on her side, as well as Queen Riadne.

You're in Her Majesty's care right now—anyone who wants to give you trouble will have to go through her to do so.

Queen Riadne is surprisingly supportive of the art for a sidhe fae of royal standing.

She took a breath, lifted her jaw, forced herself—however difficult and all-around panic-inducing as it was—to match the Councillor's stare with unflinching steadiness. "I understand. Thank you."

Another moment of silence passed.

Councillor Sylvain snorted. "See that you don't forget it, Miss Jarsdel." *Miss* Jarsdel. Sylvain would never use an honorific for Arlo, even if she wore the Bone Crown and sat on the throne as High Queen. "But come," he continued, in a tone so much lighter and more congenial that he seemed like a different person entirely, however obviously false his cheer was. "Carry on as though I'm not here at all. I'll just be over here observing. A sprite on the wall, as the saying goes." He waved off to the side of the room, to a comfortable armchair upholstered in ironborn red crushed velvet, and removed himself from Arlo's space.

The anger, while not completely smothered, receded significantly when she was able to properly breathe again.

Leda watched the Councillor go with a tightness around her eyes before doing just as he'd instructed, ignoring he was there at all to turn to Arlo and place a hand on her shoulder.

It was a gentle touch—*Is all well?* it seemed to ask, and Arlo nodded.

With a nod in return, Leda guided her around to the scroll and drew Arlo's attention back to the symbols of salt, mercury, and sulfur.

"As I was saying, alchemy is dangerous, but with proper use and understanding, its capacity for goodness far outbalances this."

Councillor Sylvain snorted, but said nothing when Leda snapped her gaze to him.

"Salt. Mercury. Sulfur. These three elements are the basis for every array. They can be paired on their own with an array's other symbols or blended together, a mixture of two or all three, but there must be at least *one* present for an array to work. You can't force iron to change its shape, for example, without the presence of Salt. You can't fortify a potion's ability to heal without Sulfur. You can't turn water into wine without Mercury—that one always seems to be the favored starting point with young ones," Leda added, and though her tone remained unaffected by humor, the wink she dropped made Arlo exhale a quiet laugh. "As I hear it, you've already managed to power an array of intermediate difficulty."

The door to the cavum factory, yes, she was sure Leda had been filled in on that.

Was that an intermediate array?

What, then, was the one she'd activated to drain Hieronymus of his magic considered, and did she mention it to Leda or keep that particular success to herself?

A quick glance to Sylvain in his chair watching Arlo so intensely told her *no*, she didn't want to mention it just yet. He already suspected her of dubious intent enough as it was, knowing she could activate an "intermediate" array; she didn't want to know how he'd react to learning she could do more than that, *had* done more than that.

And the High King might arrest her after all, because Sylvain would *definitely* run back to her great uncle with that bit of news.

Arlo gave herself a shake. Leda was still speaking, and she didn't want to miss anything. "—But like I said, this isn't technically a lesson; I only want to get a feel for your current level of knowledge to determine where our lessons should begin. You have power, that much is evident, but not until you understand each and every symbol at your disposal will you truly be able to make something of that potential."

She crossed the room to the chalkboard.

With a piece of white chalk, she drew a symbol on the board that looked a lot like the human symbol for the gender of male, but with an elongated arrow.

"Can you tell me what this symbol is?" Leda asked when she was finished drawing.

Arlo nodded. It was the exact same symbol as what had been on the door to the cavum factory, and Nausicaä's brief introduction to alchemy. "It's iron."

"Correct. How about this one?"

She drew another symbol, this one with three long arrows shooting upward from a small, triangular base.

Arlo had no idea. She'd only really been taught the one. Except . . . *three arrows shot the moon, and fell to the earth again*—"Silver," she blurted, immediately confused over how she even knew that and why the folk nursery rhyme she'd been taught as a child, about a man and the legendary werewolf he'd hunted down, securing his place in the Wild Hunt, had popped into her head.

Why were all these bizarre half-memories spoken in her father's voice?

"Correct again," said Leda, raising a brow in new esteem of her student. The comment stole Arlo's focus, and in that second of distraction, the memory she'd been contemplating slipped away. "Impressive. How did you come by this knowledge, if I might ask? These symbols aren't widely circulated, certainly not anymore."

Arlo shrugged, uncomfortably aware of the Councillor's eyes boring into the back of her head, as though he could see right through to her thoughts and find the answer for himself. "Uh . . . honestly, I just guessed."

Leda accepted this answer with another delicate nod, though Arlo could tell she didn't wholly believe it. While she had no real reason for any sort of loyalty to Arlo, that she obviously disliked Councillor Sylvain a great deal made them allies, and this was what Arlo suspected kept her from pressing any further. "A very good guess, then. All right, one last symbol. Can you tell me what this one might be?"

Another symbol was drawn on the board. It looked a fancy rendition of the letter Z, its bottom line struck through with the number seven.

Arlo shook her head.

"I don't know."

"Can you take a guess?"

"Uh . . ."

She *could* take a guess. The harder she thought about it, the louder the whispers in the back of her head grew, but hearing her father speaking things in her mind that he'd never said aloud to her nor could have even known was frightening.

She shook her head even harder.

"Lead."

It wasn't she who'd spoken.

Her gaze snapping over Arlo's shoulder, Leda conceded this point to Councillor Sylvain. "Correct. It seems you've done your research, Councillor."

Arlo looked over her shoulder now too.

Sylvain was looking away, a brief respite from his penetrating stare, but he seemed distinctly irritated as he glared down the floor instead. With what, Arlo couldn't say, but his answer had been abrupt enough that maybe he hadn't meant to say it. His boredom must have gotten away from him, and his irritation seemed to stem from the fact that he had to know this answer at all—probably to make sure Arlo wasn't learning anything too dangerous. This suspicion was conformed by his rather acidic reply of, "Much to my dismay."

Leda ignored him. She looked back to Arlo. "Iron, silver, and lead—these are the easiest symbols for ironborn to learn to command off the start. They're generally considered the quickest to bend to iron-born magic. I'm going to give you a few sheets to study between our lessons, depicting the symbols for the basic elements, planets, and procedural commands that we'll be using most frequently. I'm afraid it will be mostly theory for the next little while, but—"

There was a knock at the door.

Sighing deeply, Leda bid this second interruption to enter, and immediately straightened her posture when they did.

Councillor Sylvain rose from his chair, bending at the waist into a deep bow.

Arlo could only gape.

The queen stood in the workshop's doorway, glowing as radiant as ever, her ink-black hair pulled back in a simple tail. Even though she was significantly dressed down compared to what she'd been wearing to receive them, she looked no less glamorous in her riding habit of cream white, sleeveless turtleneck, and skin-tight gold trousers that gleamed like they'd been made from mermaid scales, black leather riding boots pulled up to her knees.

"Arlo," she greeted, as warmly as Arlo's own mother would have, and as she spoke, she peeled off the leather gloves she'd been wearing with elegant fluidity. "I see you've been hard at work, and on your first day with us, too. Perhaps you'd like to take a break and join me for tea in the conservatory?"

She ignored the Councillor as she walked past him to approach Arlo. Arlo could see how little he appreciated being snubbed like this, but as Riadne was Head of this Court, well above him in station, he would be a fool to mention it.

"Leda?" she inquired, turning a pointed look to Arlo's tutor, and Leda sprung in action.

"Yes, of course, we're just wrapping up. Here." She moved to the table, gathered the sheets she'd mentioned, and handed them to Arlo. "I'll come seek you out in a few days for our first real lesson, but in the meantime, look these over. And it wouldn't hurt to give this a read, either." She turned again, grabbed a book that had been sitting on the desk, and held it out for Arlo to take as well. "A beginner's guide to alchemical theory. His High Majesty has graciously permitted you to borrow it from the royal collection. We'll be using that a lot this summer."

"Thank you," said Arlo. It was impossible to describe the feeling that washed over her as she stood there clutching all these new materials like the world's most valuable treasures. "I'll see you in a few days, then."

Leda nodded, smiling gently. Perhaps she understood this indescribable emotion, this overwhelming feeling of holding a physical piece of her own heritage for the very first time.

Giving herself a minute shake, she turned to the queen. "And thank *you*, yes, I'd love to join you for tea."

"Wonderful." The queen clapped her hands, then waved them outward, and both Leda and the Councillor melted away, Leda to collect her things and Sylvain to retreat to the door and wait for Riadne to take her leave first before he could. "Wonderful," Queen Riadne repeated, more sincerely than before, and reached out to place a hand on Arlo's shoulder. "Come, I want to hear *all* about your first ever alchemy lesson."

Arlo, whose own mother hadn't been half as interested in or agreeable with the subject, couldn't help the small and private smile that pulled at the corner of her lips as she followed the queen out into the hall.

CHAPTER 20

Vehan

───✦───

I T WAS THE GENTLE murmur of low, familiar voices that drew Vehan out of sleep. The first bit of awareness that managed to fight through his drowsy haze was that one of the speakers was undoubtedly Aurelian, and immediately upon this realization, he felt a sense of *calm*.

If Aurelian was here, there was no cause for alarm.

No harm could touch him with his retainer nearby, and this surety was his second awareness, followed a moment later by the identification of the person Aurelian was speaking to—Theo—and the warmth against his face and eyelids—sunlight.

Then it was a flood of situational input: the silk-soft cushion of his bed, which meant that at some point last night, he'd stumbled into it, but he couldn't recall that particular journey; the sunlight that was just a little too bright, which meant it was much later than six a.m., his usual time of waking. Most surprising was how uncommonly *good* Vehan felt. He couldn't recall the last time he'd slept through the entire night without waking.

It was an amazing, energized feeling—did normal people walk around feeling like this all the time? No wonder they were able to get so much done, while Vehan shuffled through his days a bit like the zombies in the human horror films Aurelian had made him watch when they were kids (that had given Vehan nightmares for a full month straight).

He stretched in his bed, humming softly in contentment.

As much as he'd like to stay here, comfortable and warm and safe in his bed, it was incredible to him that his mother hadn't sent someone to wake him yet. *The future king of Seelie Summer does not loll about in bed all morning,* he could hear her scold in his head—but then, Aurelian was here, and so was Theo, and perhaps that was exactly the reason.

He'd pushed his luck enough as it was.

"Mmmm, morning," he greeted, stifling a yawn.

It must have been a *deep* sleep, given how sweaty Vehan realized he was as he peeled his face off his damp pillow and ran a hand through his equally damp, disheveled hair. "Sorry, how long was I out?"

Shifting himself into an upright position, he blinked at his friends.

Aurelian was back to his more typical attire—black skinny jeans paired with an earthen brown shirt that stretched so loose around his collar, it showed off just a bit of the similarly colored leaves tattooed up and over his shoulder.

The lavender in his hair had been recently refreshed, his hair a bit disheveled too, but that was more how Aurelian liked it. He didn't look as rested as Vehan felt, with dark circles under his eyes as though he hadn't slept at all last night. But it said quite a lot about him (and Vehan's complete "lack of chill") that Aurelian was no less attractive for it.

Probably more so?

Vehan wasn't going to examine his tendency to gravitate toward "mess" right now.

Theo was as radiant as ever, dark eyes bright and not a single tight curl out of place. He was casually dressed too, in loose bronze-silk pants and a silvery white, long-sleeved shirt that looked a bit as though it had been spun from the clouds—Sylvan made, then—and its plunging v-cut neckline was outlined by a single band of gold that shimmered with a hint of electric magic.

The Sylvan folk—the celestial fae, many called them—were some of the rare few folk who lived up in the Wild Court of Air, but the material they made from the clouds they lived among was highly desired and only something the wealthiest could afford.

Vehan owned precisely one outfit made of this beyond-expensive material—a gift from the Reynolds family for his coming of age, which he already knew he'd be wearing to the Solstice.

Theo owned *several*, some—like this—merely for lounging around in.

The Lysternes might sit on the Seelie Summer throne, but it was the Reynolds family who controlled the majority of not just *this* Court's wealth but all the Courts as a whole, and it was just one more tick in their favor if Vehan couldn't demonstrate the power required to maintain his position.

"Good news," Theo replied, turning to face Vehan fully. "It's just about noon, so even though you slept straight through breakfast, you won't have to go hungry for long."

"It's *noon?*" Vehan exclaimed, scrambling out of bed. "How come nobody woke me?"

It was Aurelian who replied, stepping forward to steady him when Vehan's foot snagged on his duvet and he nearly fell face-first into his carpet. "We tried."

Aurelian had *biceps*—which was a ridiculous observation, because of course he had biceps, everyone had biceps, but Aurelian's were very *firm,* Vehan noticed when he instinctually reached out to grab them as he fell. "Sorry, what?" he said a bit thickly, and it took a moment for him to tear his gaze away from the smooth, Seelie-warm and black-inked skin beneath his fingers.

"I said we tried, but you wouldn't wake up."

"And you were bleeding last night," Theo added. "Not to mention how *weird* you were acting through dinner. Are you okay?"

Vehan looked from Aurelian's blank expression to Theo's very open concern. He reached up to feel beneath his nose, but there was no trace of blood now. "Uh . . . honestly? I don't really remember. I mean, I feel fine now. Fantastic, even. Maybe I just really needed some sleep? But I don't remember much of last night from dinner on. I don't even know how I made it to my bed."

A flash of antifreeze-green surfaced in his memory, and Vehan winced.

Aurelian stood too close not to notice it, and Vehan recovered just in time to see something ripple across his face, but it was swept beneath indifference too quickly for him to pinpoint what it had been. "I'm okay," Vehan nodded, forcing a small smile. Straightening, he patted Aurelian's arm in thanks for catching him, then untangled himself from his retainer and stepped back before he could do anything more embarrassing than ogle his tattoo and deceptively strong muscles.

"Hmm." Theo considered him for a long minute, not at all convinced by Vehan's statement. But apparently not to question his prince, he let it go. "Well, I'm glad you're feeling better, at least. We should keep an eye on those nosebleeds, though, and if any more holes in your memory appear, we should have a chat with Narwell."

"Nigel," Vehan corrected. Nigel, the palace Head MediFae, already thought the majority of Vehan's ills were made up for the attention. "And thanks, but I'm *fine*."

"I believe that *you* believe that," Theo sang, waving him off and heading for Vehan's closet. "I noticed last night that those shocks you were complaining about might have been coming from your mother's electric waterfall."

He'd been complaining about shocks?

Vehan lifted his hands, examining them as though they'd be able to confirm what Theo was saying, or more important, hint whether his magic was starting to return to normal.

"You've been off since the cavum factory," Aurelian said.

He looked up.

His retainer was watching him closely. Those molten gold eyes, *always* on the intense side of beautiful, never failed to make Vehan feel a bit warm when they fixed on him, but they seemed a little brighter right now, a little sharper and warier than usual . . . which was saying a lot. Aurelian was wary of a great deal these days.

Vehan shrugged.

For some reason, he didn't want Aurelian to know how genuinely bothered he was by the state of his magic. "Seems like that was the start of it, yeah. Maybe I just needed rest."

"That's what I was hoping," Theo interrupted, coming back out of Vehan's closet with an outfit in hand—dark gold pants that shrank to paint themselves like a second skin when Vehan put them on, and a snow-white linen tunic top, just on the decent side of transparent, its collar and hem embroidered with spun-gold suns and fissures of lightning and intricate looping design.

Much like the band of gold around Theo's collar, this embroidery would light up in accordance with the strength of electric magic of the one wearing it. On Vehan, it was normally *dazzling*, but when Theo pressed the articles of clothing into Vehan's arms, they remained their significantly duller, ordinary gold.

"Hmm," Theo hummed again.

Vehan tried to keep the way his heart fell from showing on his face. "It's only been one night. Maybe with a few more . . ."

"Maybe . . ." Theo didn't sound so sure. "I wonder . . ."

But whatever Theo had been about to say, he was cut off by a knocking at Vehan's bedroom door, and everyone stiffened.

Had his mother come to collect him at last? She was bound to have *much* to say about his choosing today to sleep in so long, the first proper day of Arlo's stay.

"Come in!" he called.

The door swept open.

And it wasn't Vehan's mother who walked in at all but someone far worse—someone who made Vehan's eyes grow wide with distinct awareness that he was in his pajamas, and when he'd put *those* on he had no idea, but High Prince Celadon Cornelius Fleur-Viridian was standing as bold as day in his bedroom. *Hells*. He sent a very fervent prayer to Urielle that he hadn't missed taking down one of his many "Celadom" fan club exclusive members-only posters.

"Uh . . . ," said Vehan, his brain beginning to short out. "Hi. You're in my bedroom."

Theo elbowed him sharply in the side, rolling his eyes when Vehan, gritting his teeth against the grunt this startled out of him, glared.

The High Prince cocked his head, observing all of this, and no, Vehan didn't like it any better that those famously jade eyes were examining him even closer now. "Hello again, Your Highness," the High Prince greeted, far more articulately. "How are you feeling? You seemed unwell at dinner . . ."

"Fine!" Vehan practically chirped, his voice had shot so high. "Fine, I'm fine! Was just . . . a little under the weather, but I'm completely fine now. Did you come all this way just to check on me, or was there something I can help you with, Your Highness?"

"Please, just Celadon will do."

"Please, just Celadon" would *not* do. Vehan stared. He could feel how wide his eyes had grown, and when one moment became two, became three, and still he said nothing in reply to this, the High Prince—*Celadon*—tilted his head the opposite way, and began to very visibly wonder if Vehan was as all right as he claimed.

There was another elbow to Vehan's side, Theodore once again reminding him how much of a *fool* he was being. "C-Celadon, then. And you . . . uh, can call me Vehan. If you like."

Deities, and he'd been so irritated that his mother had been running around behind the scenes setting up dates and "arrangements" and bribing Theodore's parents to send their son to stay with them for the summer. He didn't realize until now how much he clearly needed that help.

"And me, of course, Theo," Theo added, as though the two of them hadn't been chatting it up the night before, that much Vehan *did* recall. "So, now that we're all friends, because apparently you and Aurelian have gotten to know each other *very* well . . ." He paused to waggle his brows, first at the High Prince, then at Aurelian, and Vehan had . . . no idea what to make of that.

"For the last time," Aurelian scathed, rounding on Theo, finally speaking up after what felt like an eternity of silence. It was rare to hear this much emotion in his voice, but he sounded genuinely upset right now. Vehan didn't miss the way his gaze cut briefly, almost . . . anxiously to him. "It's none of your business."

"You were caught kissing the High Prince in a darkened corridor last night like a pair of forbidden lovers in a human's gothic romance," said Theo in a surprisingly dry tone. "People saw you. It's *everyone's* business *now*—"

. . .

Vehan held up a finger.

. . .

There was this sudden, steady, high-pitched ringing in his ears, and he needed it to pass before they continued this conversation, as it was impeding his ability to hear properly. Surely Theo hadn't just said the words "kiss" and "the High Prince" in a sentence attached to Aurelian's name.

Because . . . no.

The ringing in his ears grew louder.

"Mmm," the High Prince intervened with a hum of discontent, and an unreadable look fastened on Aurelian, which . . . *no.* "If Lord Aurelian doesn't want to talk about it, I think it's best to respect his wishes."

If the High Prince intended *this* to defuse the situation, he had a long way to go toward understanding Theo. His entire expression lighting up as though he'd caught a bolt of electricity, Theo grinned. "*Oh?* Is that the distinct lack of denial I hear?"

The High Prince raised a hand. "This isn't what I came here to discuss, actually—"

"What *did* you come here for?" Vehan heard himself ask—practically snap, in fact. The ringing had finally cut out, and in its wake, a flood of something uncomfortable washed through him, something oily and bitter and *dark*, a lot like jealousy, except he wasn't jealous. He didn't need to be jealous. Aurelian wasn't *his*. Neither was *Celadon,* for that matter. "You still haven't answered that."

But it was jealousy all the same.

Jealousy, and . . .

The High Prince pursed his lips, looking Vehan over a little more critically this time. If he wanted, he could reprimand Vehan dearly for the rudeness he'd just demonstrated—he was the *High Prince,* for Urielle's sake—but as quickly as it sealed around him, his stoniness crumbled, and the High Prince sighed. All at once, he looked extremely uneasy, had even grasped his own wrist as though to wring it. "Sorry," he apologized, his accent Canadian-heavy on the vowel. "Actually, I came here to ask if you wouldn't mind joining your mother for tea."

As though this entire morning was in competition with itself to see how many surprises it could pack into one hour, Vehan found himself staring once more. "Well, I mean, of course not. But why?" And why would his mother send the High Prince to beg this of him?

The High Prince's expression warped even further in unease. "It's Arlo. I'm informed your mother invited her for tea in the conservatory, and . . . well, I'd really appreciate if someone else was with them. It wouldn't go over well if *I* barged in uninvited, but if *you* went, I'm sure Her Majesty would like to know how her son is doing after last night, and Arlo wouldn't be on her own, and I'd—"

Vehan raised his hand exactly as the High Prince had done, calling boldly for silence. "You want me to interrupt my mother's tea with Arlo because . . ."

Aurelian looked . . . uncomfortable.

Even Theo, who was a master at keeping his thoughts to himself, seemed to be thinking quite hard about something that wasn't sitting well with him.

The High Prince was *anxious*.

All because Arlo was with his mother?

"Your Highness," Aurelian hedged, and for goodness' sake, could he just stop shooting *glances* at *Celadon* for half a second?

And there was that jealousy again, entwined with that darker, oily *wrongness* that wasn't . . . him. That *anger*, the same he'd felt on the mountain that made Vehan want to lash out, made him want to *hurt* something with a level of violence he didn't even know he could think up, let alone enact . . .

Damn it, it was one thing to know Aurelian had had boyfriends in the past. In the recent past, even. Vehan had even *met* one, and though the boy hadn't lasted longer than a couple of days—they never did—Vehan had hated him just as much as he'd hated all the others. Yet never once had he actually wanted to hurt *anyone* for it, for being allowed even a taste of the one thing Vehan couldn't have.

"Your Highness," Aurelian continued, ignorant of the *ringing* in Vehan's ear and the anger he was trying to swallow down. "I think we need to have a talk about your mother's private office, and the fact that—"

Vehan wanted to *scream*—instead, he laughed.

It was full and loud and not exactly good-humored, and when he stopped, he glared at all three of the people in his room in turn, in the same look his mother pinned to the people who began to wear on her patience.

When he spoke, it was with the same quiet iciness, too. "High Prince Celadon. I understand that you and Her Majesty have something of a *tumultuous* background. I would like to remind you, though, that she is my *mother*. She is my *family*, and she managed to raise me just fine, thank you. Arlo is in no danger here. *Also*"—he didn't know where all this boldness was coming from, but it was the High Prince now caught by surprise and staring, and Vehan had to admit . . . *that* wasn't a horrible feeling—"you were extremely rude to her yesterday in Arlo's bedroom. This after she's gone out of her way and put herself at risk of upsetting the High King *your father* by inviting the both of you here and finding Arlo a tutor to help control a magic that, as I understand it, might Rebound on her. I'm not going to interrupt them. Arlo is *fine*. My mother is no *monster*. And

I hope you'll apologize to her the next time you see her."

He turned around.

Mostly because the enormity of what he'd just done had started to settle in, and he had a newfound respect for his mother, who managed to speak with this authority in the face of anyone, no matter who they were.

"If you'll excuse me, I need to get dressed."

No one said a thing.

And because the headiness of his words had finally started to drain, but his strangely potent jealousy and anger had gone nowhere, he added, "*All* of you. I can get dressed on my own."

It wasn't until he was alone in his room that he deflated. That his heart fluttered uncomfortably and he breathed a sigh that was more a gasp as whatever dark feelings that had just come over him finally, *blessedly*, washed away in a single flush that left him drained to his very core.

This wasn't normal.

His magic, the mountaintop, the holes in his memory, the inexplainable rush of sinister emotions that weren't *him*—none of this was normal. He was tired of it, tired of everything in his life being so *dysfunctional* . . .

You were caught kissing the High Prince in a darkened corridor last night . . .

Blinking away the hot sensation that had begun to prickle in his eyes, Vehan shoved his legs into his pants and threw on his shirt.

Aurelian could kiss whoever he wanted.

And his mother *wasn't* a monster, damn it. She was strict and powerful and set impossible, unflinchingly high expectations, but she would never *hurt* Arlo or take advantage of her naivete. Arlo was *safe* here.

She wasn't a monster, his mother . . . she couldn't be, because if she was, that would mean Vehan was well and truly alone in this deities-awful place. That there existed *no one* who actually cared about him.

The muted spark of pain that bloomed in his left temple—there and gone in an instant—told him all he needed to know about how much he was starting to doubt the things he told himself to get by . . . how much his untruths were turning into outright falsehoods.

"She's *fine*," he whispered to himself. "I'm fine. We're all . . ."

He wouldn't check on Arlo.

The High Prince's request didn't bother him.

The throbbing again at his temple was a headache from over-sleeping.

None of this was a lie.

CHAPTER 21

Arlo

~~~~~~~~~~

THE CONSERVATORY QUEEN RIADNE had chosen for their midday tea was every bit the spectacle of magic and radiance Arlo had been expecting.

Its checkered-tile floor, which appeared at first to be nothing more than ordinary white marble and the palest gray slate, operated much like pressure pads. Whichever ones she and the queen stepped on lit up with a starburst of shimmering gold light that faded only when they moved to the next.

Its enormous arches, which had been stamped into the soft beige stone walls, had been filled with glass so impossibly thin and crystal clear that it wasn't until a warm breeze came along to morph them into fluttering sheer curtains that she could say for certain there was anything there at all.

Its ceiling, which had been made of yet more glass, boasted whole panes that were held together by nothing more than bluish-white, raw electricity that undoubtedly served as the room's only source of light come nightfall.

Jutting out into the surrounding palace garden, the ferns and spider plants and potted trees, the bone-white flowers—lilies, roses and massive hibiscuses, camellias, amaryllises, and delicate orchids—had all been arranged in a way to create the illusion that there was nothing separating this space from the outdoors. At the same time, Arlo felt hidden away entirely from the world, isolated, secure.

Comfortable.

When the queen indicated the sofa she wished Arlo to sit on, Arlo's awe snapped from examining the room itself to the furniture: the swan-shaped high-backed chairs and golden upholstered divans. The seat she sank onto, it felt a bit like sinking into the fluffy clouds that were carved all over the palace, here included. Between all this and the gentle tune a rather handsome goblin was playing on the ivory white piano in the far corner, Arlo would happily spend her entire vacation in this room alone.

"Ah, good, and here's our tea," the queen said as soon as she took her own seat and glanced up at the glass doors they'd entered through.

Arlo looked over as well.

After the turn their conversation had taken this morning, she felt a little awkward when she noticed Gentian pushing a golden trolly laden with porcelain bowls filled with a variety of hand-rolled pearls of tea leaves, along with an elegant bone-china teapot with matching cups. But when Gentian caught her gaze, he smiled, as wide and eager as he'd done upon their meeting.

The fae boy behind him Arlo didn't know.

Tall and softly curved, his molten gold eyes marked him distinctly lesidhe, but it wasn't only this that made her look a little closer. Unlike Gentian, he wasn't dressed in the kitchen uniform but tight, dark gold jeans and a simple white cotton shirt, the only hint of "otherness" to it the massive sun wrapping around his right side, a pearly shade of white a fraction darker than the material it had been set against, and visible only under certain slants of light.

Someone of status?

Arlo didn't know enough about the hierarchy here to say for certain, but it seemed a bit like the way everyone in this place with a sliver of importance to their name dressed.

And there was something about him . . .

He was younger than Arlo by a couple of years—fifteen, she guessed. Sixteen at the most. His long, dark brown hair had been gathered back behind his head in a messy bun, wisps of it left to flutter around his pointed ears and highly pronounced cheekbones, on a face that was so *familiar*, with its full lips and pretty but strong construction. If Arlo had to hazard a guess, she'd say he was . . .

"You're already well acquainted with Lord Aurelian," said Queen Riadne, practically beaming at the young fae boy. "This is his younger brother, Harlan. *Harlan* is training under his parents to become a pâtissier himself, and I have to say, I suspect he might just surpass even *their* mastery." She dropped him a wink, her smile growing even wider, and Arlo didn't miss how Harlan seemed to stand a little taller for it. "He's quite good, aren't you?"

"Thank you, Your Majesty," said Harlan, dipping into an eager bow over the handle of his own golden trolly. His voice, it was so different from Aurelian's, so full of *emotion*. If it weren't for the fact that they very much looked like brothers, Arlo would never guess they were related. "I hope you like what we've prepared for you today."

Petit fours.

A mountain of them.

Arlo's mouth began to water just looking at the tiny squares of cake, each cloaked in dense white fondant, the gold piping on them exquisite, the delicate white sugar-orchids crowning each so real Arlo would almost swear she could smell a floral sweetness on them. And intermixed with this lot were equally small fairy cakes, sprinkled with powdered sugar, topped with fluffy mounds of whipped cream and strawberries so brightly red they gleamed as though candied.

"You *made* these?" Arlo gasped, watching as Harlan offloaded his trolly and helped Gentian arrange their spread on the sandstone table.

"That's right, my lady." He winked at Arlo.

Queen Riadne laughed again. "Harlan is quite the charmer, Lady Arlo. Be warned, he has half the women on my staff sighing over him already. I imagine there will be quite the train of broken hearts when he Matures."

"I can't help that you employ so many beautiful ladies, Your Majesty," Harlan replied with a grave air of feigned solemnity. His next wink was for the queen. "Just like they can't help but pale in comparison to the one they serve."

Arlo snorted before she could help herself.

She could just imagine the horror on Aurelian's face if he were here to hear his brother speak like this to their queen. Her great uncle was a handsome fae, as were all his children, yet she'd had never known a single one of their staff to be as bold in their appreciation of their Head as Harlan currently was.

"All right, you've had your fun," Queen Riadne dismissed, a touch of fondness to the look she shot him as she waved him off. "His poor mother," she added once Harlan and Gentian had finished pouring out their tea, setting the table, and bowing themselves out of the room. "So much charm, none of his brother's temperance. *Quite* a handful indeed." She shook her head, then perked up to smile again at Arlo, an intimacy in her eyes like they'd been close friends their entire lives. "Well, Arlo, it's just the two of us now. Tell me: How did your lesson today with Leda go?"

"Oh!" Arlo sat a little straighter, replaced the teacup she'd just picked up back on its saucer. "It went very well, Your Majesty, thank you for arranging it, and for everything you put into that *room*—"

"No, no." The queen waved again. "There's no need for such formality between us. You are a Viridian, Arlo. We are in equal standing. And I confess, I envy your mother. Sons are all well and good, but I would have liked to have had a daughter, too—one like you, so pretty and intelligent. These chats are never the same for mothers with their sons. Now tell me, honestly." She leaned in a little closer, folding her arms on the table and grinning almost conspiratorially. "How was your introduction to alchemy?"

Arlo found herself at a momentary loss for words.

She might be a Viridian by technicality, but she certainly wasn't treated like one back home. And she was also certain she'd never heard anyone say they envied Thalo for a daughter like *her*—pretty . . . intelligent . . . these weren't the words the majority of the fae in her life had ever used to describe Arlo, not with the thickness to her thighs and arms, the plumpness of her face and figure, and her inability to

300

keep up with the fae academy. The queen was just being kind. But because she'd done so much for Arlo already, Arlo cleared her throat, pushed past the awkwardness she felt at being complimented like this, and did her best to answer how the queen wanted—with honesty. "I loved it."

The admission was quiet.

Leda had warned her to keep her enthusiasm to herself, but she'd also said Queen Riadne was *different*. The queen was the one who had arranged this, after all, and she wanted the truth, and Arlo *had* loved it. Her first taste of the life she would have had if alchemy hadn't been banned by the Courts, if she and her magic were *respected*—that had been worth even Councillor Sylvain's presence to Arlo.

"I thought you might," Queen Riadne replied, drawing back to relax a little more comfortably in her seat. "Especially considering these lessons come on the Dark Star's rather insistent recommendation. Which does make one curious, I have to say: Whatever has Nausicaä seen in you that the rest of us have not yet been privy to? You must be something special, Arlo, to have earned such a legend's regard."

Arlo's gaze shot up from her teacup, her own insistence on the tip of her tongue—a lie that Arlo had no idea what made Nausicaä so determined to fight for her training, her instinct to keep secret both the scope of what she'd managed in the cava factory and her titan-gifted die trilling in her head like an alarm.

But as quickly as her anxiety flared, it was just as easily soothed when she met the queen's gaze and saw a hint of understanding there, and no sign of desire to push the subject right now.

Sure enough, the queen pressed on. "It's an interesting art regardless, alchemy. So complex with all its many symbols and formulas and intricate arrays, the careful balance of science and magic necessary to power it . . . It's rather beautiful, don't you think? More so than this."

She raised a hand, curled her fingers inward slightly.

As though a shadow had passed over the sun overhead, the light in the room grew dimmer, the electricity holding the ceiling together dying down to fizzling threads. When she relaxed those fingers, the shadow passed, the electric forcefield replenished, and the room flared bright once again.

It was just as beautiful, in Arlo's opinion.

"I apologize for Councillor Sylvain," the queen continued, changing the subject. She folded her hands on her lap and peered a little more seriously now at Arlo. "The Courts are right to fear what alchemy is capable of—were presented a very difficult choice to make back when it had been turned so violently against them."

Yes, Arlo had seen what a philosopher's stone could do, the havoc even a failed one could wreak. Between Hieronymus Aurum and the imp in the woods, she had a little better understanding why the Courts had acted so drastically. But . . .

"But it doesn't excuse the prejudice that has built up around the ironborn and the magic they practice. It doesn't excuse the unrelenting strictness of our laws. It does *not* excuse the Councillor. His High Majesty wishes your studies monitored. I am his humble servant, I can only acquiesce, and I've already pushed the extent of my favor with your great uncle in choosing your tutor. I assure you, though, if Briar Sylvain makes himself an unbearable nuisance to your instruction, there are older favors I can call on to have him replaced with someone more agreeable."

That alone made Arlo breathe a little easier.

She *did* wish she could have someone else playing overseer in her lessons, that Queen Riadne would have him replaced for her next lesson. But it was true what she said, there was only so much sway *any* of the Heads had with the High King. In the end, what he wanted was what they followed, and at the moment, he was incredibly hard to work with.

She'd stick it out for as long as it was bearable. She was grateful she was even being allowed to study alchemy at all.

And it was relieving to know that if he overstepped his boundaries too greatly, there would be *someone* in her corner against Councillor Sylvain.

"Thank you, Your Majesty. I appreciate that, *really*. But I'll make it work. Councillor Sylvain has never liked me much anyhow. It's . . . nothing new." She chuckled awkwardly.

Queen Riadne's grin took on a sharper edge just long enough for Arlo to catch it and wonder what she'd said to spark this change in her mood. "Briar Sylvain has never liked alchemy. Which is . . . *amusing*, considering . . . well. Hatred is a complicated thing, I suppose."

Considering . . . what?

Arlo had no idea what the queen was implying, but Riadne shook her head, and once again the conversation switched tracks and carried on. It was all Arlo could do to keep up. They drifted into easier things, then—the human school she might be going to in the fall ("the University of Toronto"), what her father did ("he's a chemistry professor"), what she liked to do in her spare time ("play video games, or read, or watch shows on Netflix—just typical human teenage stuff, I guess").

She probably had no idea what half of the stuff was that Arlo told her about, especially when she asked which video game Arlo liked to play, and Arlo launched into an explanation of the Final Fantasy franchise. "Ten was where the graphics really changed, so a lot of people have only played the installments from then on, but they're missing out. The early Final Fantasy games were some of the best, in my opinion, especially Seven—that one's my favorite. Seven, and . . ."

She trailed off with a wince.

She hadn't realized how long she'd been going on about this subject, but it was definitely well past the point when most people got a glazed-over look in their eyes and very clearly hoped she'd be done soon.

It was a tick in Queen Riadne's favor that she didn't seem bored at all. In fact, she'd nodded and even asked a few questions here and there, engaging in the conversation, *paying attention*, with a focus that nobody save Celadon, and now Nausicaä, really spent on her. But Arlo was very familiar with busy, important women. Even if her mother did listen to Arlo's enthusiastic chattering—"I *like* to hear about the things that make you happy, sweetheart, even if I don't understand them"—Arlo was always conscious of how much of her mother's limited time she took up with inconsequential things.

How much time had passed since they'd first sat down for tea?

Arlo had eaten a number of cakes and had consumed two whole cups of bergamot and black tea, so she'd been talking for at least half an hour, by her estimation. And there Queen Riadne sat, completely unbothered by this. She hadn't once glanced at a clock or the door or anywhere except Arlo's face, despite the fact that she was a *queen* and undoubtedly had *something* else she should be doing instead of listening to teenage fangirling. She didn't want to press the queen's magnanimity any more than she already had.

Setting down her teacup, Arlo folded her hands on her lap and bowed her head in sheepish gratitude. "Sorry, I get carried away sometimes."

"Is that something you regret?"

Arlo bit her lip while she weighed what to say. "No, but—"

"Then I certainly don't. I wouldn't have asked after your interests if I didn't want to hear about them. And like I said"—Riadne set her cup down as well and fixed a gaze on Arlo that wasn't exactly warm, but was nowhere near as icy as her overall appearance suggested—"it would have been nice if Vadrien and I had had a daughter before his passing."

"May Light keep him," Arlo murmured, as she and all folk had been taught, in respect to Seelie folk who passed—a prayer of sorts, that when the deceased were reborn, it would be again as Seelie. For the UnSeelie, the prayer offered them up to Darkness instead.

"May Light keep him," Riadne echoed, however woodenly. She had to be tired of repeating this refrain every time she mentioned the late King of Seelie Summer. "Anyhow, I understand that we aren't that close, and perhaps you find me a bit intimidating. But I hope that will change a little over the summer, that you'll join me for tea as often as you can, and we can get to know each other well enough that you won't be shy to tell me *all* about this Cloud Strife and Lightning Farron you like so much."

Arlo almost laughed out loud for how bizarre it was to hear the Seelie Summer *sidhe fae* Queen name characters from a human video game. "You're nicer than I was expecting," she blurted out, then realized too late what she'd just said. "I mean—!"

Queen Riadne laughed.

"I expect many assume I am not."

Wincing again, Arlo hurried to explain herself. "I just meant that things aren't . . . as good between our Courts as they could be. And I know rumor makes up a lot; I know there's some bad history between you and the High King, and it's definitely none of my business! You don't have to explain or anything. It's just that a lot of people were worried about sending me here, and I kind of grew up hearing you were . . ."

"A bitch, to use the term?"

This was the opposite of smoothing things over.

Arlo should just stop talking.

Groaning, she planted her face in her hands. "That's not what I was going to say," she mumbled between her fingers, even though yes, that was exactly what she'd heard about the Cruel Queen of Light. There were *many* unflattering things said about Riadne Lysterne.

But Queen Riadne took this in stride, too, with another laugh. "Yes, I grew up hearing the same, don't worry."

"I'm sorry," Arlo gushed, lifting her head once more. "Really, I just meant that in general, for a queen, I was expecting to feel more awkward around you than I do, and it's *nice* that I don't. Or didn't. I'm feeling a bit more of that now."

Her face was hot.

She should leave, and probably hide for the rest of her stay in her bedroom, where she couldn't accidentally offend anyone and certainly not someone who could have her beheaded if they really wanted.

A hand pressed smooth and cool over that back of her own.

Arlo looked down.

Riadne had reached over the table to *pat* her, and it was a curious sensation to feel both better and worse for it. "It's all right," the queen said gently. "Things *aren't* as they should be between our Courts. There is hurt on both sides, and these wounds have caused deep rifts. Don't let it trouble you, Arlo. I'm sure, one day, what is wrong between our families will be made right."

Arlo's gaze snapped back to Riadne's face, and it was just in time—she caught it, the barest slip in the queen's composure. She wasn't as unaffected by rumor and gossip as she pretended, nor by the state of things between the Viridians and the Lysternes. Anger . . . grief . . . Arlo couldn't say for certain, and it wasn't her place to pry, but it also wasn't the first time she'd wondered what exactly had gone on between Riadne and Arlo's great uncle to result in so profound a falling out.

There had to be something more to that story than Azurean beating her to the Challenge for his father's Crown.

Fae were experts at holding grudges, but the animosity between UnSeelie Spring and Seelie Summer ran far deeper than merely that.

"And now I think our tea is over. My son has come to steal you away, but I hope we'll be able to do this again soon."

"Huh?"

"Arlo! Mother—*here* you are."

Arlo startled, suddenly aware that she'd been staring rather deeply into Queen Riadne's gaze, and she felt a bit disoriented for it . . . muzzy, as though surfacing from a mild stupor. Blinking, she turned to the source of the voice that had interrupted the queen, and it was indeed Vehan breezing into the conservatory, bright-eyed and unfairly striking in all that gold and white. He looked much healthier than he'd appeared last night.

"I'll take my leave," said Riadne, rising to stand.

Arlo rose as well and bowed.

Whatever had happened in the past, she was more certain than ever that this vacation and invitation to the Solstice was Riadne's attempt to make amends. Arlo, who knew full well how lonely and awful it was to be the subject of Viridian contempt, was determined to help her in any way she could.

"Thank you for the tea and cake. I look forward to next time, too."

Riadne smiled.

To Vehan, who finally arrived at the table, she frosted. "You're looking unwell still. Recover for tomorrow—I will have your corpse reanimated if you think even death will excuse you from your dancing lessons. Your tutor was *expensive*."

Only when she was out of the room did Vehan sigh and say, "Trade you—you can be the Crown Prince of Seelie Summer. I'll be the iron-born daughter of the High King's Sword."

"It's not as great as you think it is," Arlo replied with a shake of her head.

Vehan sighed again, even deeper. "Nothing ever is."

A powerful burst of wind sent Riadne stumbling through the doors of the Luminous Palace's Grand Ballroom, and it didn't let up. It was the sliver of opportunity Azurean had clearly been waiting for, but Riadne had been waiting for it, too—Azurean was always his most vulnerable right before he lunged for the win, and usually that win was secure. The Crown Prince of UnSeelie Spring was an incomparable swordsman and a clever strategist. He only pressed the advantages he was certain would play out in his favor, only struck his "killing blow" when he was certain the fight would be his.

But Riadne was clever, too.

How many years had they been training together, sparring each time they met, learning each other's strengths and—more important—their weaknesses?

Azurean was *long* since married now, had just produced a pair of twins to carry on the Viridian lineage.

Riadne herself was engaged to be wed to a fine, respectable husband—Vadrien Hanlon, whom *all* of Seelie Summer seemed to adore for both his looks and his renown as the war hero Emiradian Gaumond's hand-selected protégé.

So much time had passed.

Azurean knew full well by now how brash and starved for victory Riadne was, never once having won a single of their matches.

Riadne knew how *complacent* this had made him.

"I have to say, this is the hardest you've ever made me work for my victory." Azurean flicked his wrist, readying his sword.

He advanced on her, would sweep her legs out from under her the moment he was close enough.

It should have been easy.

His wind continued to blow in a stream directly at her, forcing Riadne to raise her hands and center all her gravity just to remain upright. She should have been too preoccupied with maintaining her balance to stop him, as she had every other time he employed this maneuver to drop her on her back and pin her throat beneath the point of his sword.

But not today.

Years had passed. So much *time*. Riadne had proven herself to be a creature of habit, stubborn, unwilling to yield even the small losses to gain the war. *This* was what Azurean had learned, what everyone who watched them spar had learned—exactly as Riadne had been hoping they would. All she had to do was bide her time, wait until Azurean defenses were truly lowered and no glimmer of suspicion remained that she could change her ways.

So much time . . . and in it, Riadne had discovered just how much she enjoyed playing games.

She dropped her hands.

Giving herself over to the blowing wind, she wished she could have seen Azurean's face as she sailed farther back and out of reach, as she curled in on herself when she was far enough that the gust wore thin, and rolled out of the way.

She gave him no quarter.

Before he had time to comprehend what had happened and redirect his magic, Riadne threw out her hand, drew on the electricity in the overhead chandeliers to channel a beam of it his way, hitting him square in the chest.

It would smart, to be sure.

Azurean seized with the pain of it and collapsed to his knees, gritting his teeth and putting up a good show of fighting through his paralysis.

He'd be fine—he was tough. Riadne had no reason to relent where others might, and Azurean wouldn't have wanted that, regardless.

"Have you been working hard, Zure?" She laughed, snapping her electric beam to her side, where it shaped itself like the tongue of a whip and lashed out at her fallen sword. The beam wrapped around it, dragged Riadne's sword back to her, and in an instant, she was armed again. "I've barely broken a sweat."

She lunged.

No longer caught in her beam of light, Azurean was able to climb to his feet just in time and raise his sword to catch hers, but this she'd anticipated too.

His sword caught nothing.

Riadne dropped.

She swept out a leg and toppled him once more, and quicker than it took him to blink up at the ceiling, she was there on top of him, pinning him down, sword-point at his throat.

Azurean could only stare.

For a moment, this was all Riadne could do as well.

Their match had begun where it always did, in the Crystal Atrium. Fewer and fewer people gathered to watch as the years wore on, but there'd still been something of an audience today. It had followed them out into the hall and through the palace as they unleashed their *everything* on each other, knocking each other into the walls and swinging blows with so much force that Riadne could already feel the bruises forming on her body.

They'd never given as much as they had today to one of their battles.

Today, there had been an edge, inexplicable to Riadne, but building like a storm behind both Azurean's actions and gaze.

The longer their battle wore on, the bigger their audience grew, and it wasn't until the stunned silence at the Ballroom's entrance *exploded* into applause that Riadne realized she'd done it.

She'd *done it*!

Azurean lay beneath her, panting just as heavily as she was, his eyes just as wide and darkening with the dawning realization that he'd *lost*—for the first time since he'd outgrown his instructor, Azurean Lazuli-Viridian had lost a match, and Riadne had *won*.

She sat back.

And stared.

"We're finished, Riadne."

And *stared*.

"It's over—we're done."

Azurean's tone was unflinching, however breathless his words. That edge he'd been sharpening his mood on all day was practically glinting now, impossible to miss or mistake for anything other than firm resolve, and Riadne could only *stare* down at him. "I'm a married man with children, and you're soon to be wed to a husband of your own. I *love* you, Riadne Lysterne—I will always love you, but you and I . . . we were never supposed to be. Each of us Heads of separate Courts . . . no marriage could exist between us. It would throw the very Seasons we command into too great an imbalance. And we've been so careful, but if a child *ever* came to be from our dalliances . . ."

He closed his eyes against this comment, as though he couldn't bear the thought of how difficult a life as the child of *both* Spring and Summer's sovereigns would be. The control the Courts would insist they be placed under, the constant careful eye, because if that child showed even a flicker of too much power—gods forbid, if they inherited the Gifts that could make them Head of *both* Seasons—control would turn into a target painted on their backs. It would be a reward no self-respecting member of the Grim Brotherhood could pass on.

The Fae High Council would put the target there themselves; power, once tasted, was difficult to give up, and the consolidation of Seasons, perhaps even the dissolution of the Courts . . . no. Azurean wouldn't ever view that torment as a risk worth taking for them.

He was too soft-hearted for such a thing.

"I'm sorry, Riadne. This is what I came to tell you today. I truly do wish things could have been different. I will miss you terribly, all my life, but we need to end this."

Riadne's attendants were upon them before she could pull herself from her shock, followed closely by Azurean's, everyone helping them both to their feet, completely oblivious to what was going on—to the fact that Riadne's entire world had just shifted.

They were . . . *done*?

Just like that?

At Azurean's say-so, never mind her thoughts and feelings or anything *she* wanted, because once again, who was Riadne, really? What were her needs compared to those of the *High Prince*?

Riadne's mouth fell open, but what came out was not a sob, because damn it all, somewhere along the line she'd fallen in love with Azurean too. She hadn't realized until just now, until that love was being snatched away and her shock and anger and *heartbreak* welled up in her eyes—but she wouldn't cry.

She was too practiced at keeping such useless things as grief and loneliness penned away that Azurean wouldn't receive the satisfaction of her tears.

Her mouth fell open, and Riadne *laughed*. She laughed even harder when Azurean shook himself free of the fuss around him and bowed to her with an impersonal, "A very good match, Your Highness. This victory was well deserved," then turned to whisk himself away.

To *run*.

Riadne laughed.

He was done with *her*, was he? She'd served his purpose to him, had she? Entertainment while she was available, but now that he had his quaint little family, she was suddenly too much of a risk?

Now that she had *beaten* him . . .

What need did she have for philosopher's stones? Research on that front had proven frustrating, to say the least. Even if the stones could be used by anyone, they could only be created by an alchemist, which she was not. That alchemist also had to be *exceptional*, which none of the ones she'd tracked down so far had been. It was difficult magic, dangerous magic, and quite possibly nothing more than myth built up around a deranged ironborn man.

But she didn't need a stone, after all, and apparently she didn't need Azurean's love, either.

Riadne was ready.

She had beaten Azurean all on her own, and she could beat his father, too.

She laughed, and she laughed, and then it was her mother laughing, later that night when the entirety of the Luminous Council burst into the dining room to inform them Azurean had just issued a Challenge to High King Enfys.

He'd defeated his father.

He'd claimed the Crown.

The Eight Great Courts of Folk had a new Sovereign, and Riadne had lost after all.

"You should see your face," her mother positively wheezed in her vicious delight over her daughter's embarrassing failure.

Azurean Viridian was now High King.

Riadne might have been able to beat him today, but she was no match for the power the Bone Crown imbued him with, and now . . . she'd lost *everything*.

"You really thought you'd had him! *Ridiculous* child. Oh, how hard you worked, whoring yourself out, *training* with him, and for *nothing*."

Arina Lysterne drained her wineglass and laughed some more, then stood and motioned for her flock of sycophantic advisors. "Come, we've a new High King to ingratiate ourselves with. And *you* have an apology to make. The way you *disgraced* yourself in front of him today, we'll be lucky if our generations of intimate fellowship save any of our good standing. I'm sure his wife thinks absolutely *nothing* of you, tumbling her husband in the shadows every chance you get. Foolish child, what your *weakness* has cost us . . ."

"I will not."

Arina halted. "Excuse me?"

"I will not go," Riadne repeated without looking up. She relaxed back in her chair with her wineglass, taking a casual, unhurried sip. "I will not apologize."

The dining room emptied out.

The table was cleared.

Every light save the glow of the flame in the fireplace beside her had bowed to the full onset of night, and Riadne's face stung where her mother had struck her for her impertinence. Where she'd struck her a second time when Riadne still didn't move, and a third when that had done nothing but split her lip with a rivulet of sapphire blue.

She would not go.

She would *not* apologize.

Used . . . discarded . . . reduced to a joke, *betrayed*—Riadne would burn into her memory the image of Azurean pinned to her ballroom floor, burn into her bones this utter, profound *humiliation* she felt right now for letting herself lose everything that had ever mattered to her.

The Crown . . . her dignity . . . She would never know this degradation again, would not permit another to swindle her in such a way a second time.

"To *love*," she murmured, lifting her wineglass to the quiet dining room. To herself, in fervent promise. To Azurean, the man she'd once considered her dearest—and now, with all the frost in her heart and electric heat in her veins, the man she vowed to utterly *destroy*.

CHAPTER 22

Vehan

~⁓~

"HOLY *CRAP!*"

Vehan looked to his side, where Arlo stood in wide-eyed astonishment, taking in the room they'd just entered.

The palace library was a place where he'd spent almost as much time over the years as he had the training grounds. As large as a stadium, it was *filled* with books on all manner of subjects, folk- and human-written alike, many for study, others purely for entertainment. There were rows upon rows of pale, handsomely carved oak bookcases to contain them all, the entire stretch of every wall inlaid with even more and spanning all the way from the white marble floor to the glass ceiling above.

Like any other library, there were tables and chairs and sofas, tucked-away corners stuffed with enormous satin pillows and more practical, boxed-in working spaces for those looking for more privacy. There was also a tree, rising from the center of the room and stretching up like a support beam. This was a common feature in palace libraries—real or fake, trees were a symbol of great power to the fae, and Vehan had visited enough royal palaces in his eighteen years to know each Head displayed theirs in their own unique way.

Here in the Luminous Palace, their massive oak was made entirely of the same glass it branched out of and fused with at the ceiling, shocks of real, harvested lightning contained to curl and dance and fizzle within.

None of the staff, scholars, or NFA students looking to get a head start on elective or remedial summer lessons paid much attention to their decadent surroundings—they were too used to coming here, as was Vehan, but the visible awe on Arlo's face made him smile . . . and reminded him of the first time he'd ever excitedly pulled Aurelian into this part of his personal tour.

"Yeah," Vehan agreed, looking back now at the room—the tree at its center, more specifically. "Pretty cool, right? It *was* originally solid crystal, back when my grandmother was Head of Seelie Summer. Mother is . . . well . . ." He angled a grin at Arlo. "It's definitely a power move, just like that iron staircase of hers in the grand foyer, because bottling up that much lightning is *really* dangerous and practically impossible for someone who isn't at *least* a registered Three lightning wielder. I'm sure she expects me to be able to maintain it when I ascend the throne."

His comment trailed off into a frown.

As little as mere weeks ago, he would have added the boast that this would be no problem, that he had Class Three in the bag and that keeping *all* his mother's displays running hot would be easy enough.

Now, however . . .

"This isn't what I wanted to show you, though." He tilted his head in silent question, and Arlo tightened her grip on his arm, fastening herself a little closer and nodding agreement to let him lead her inside.

He'd wanted to show her around, yes. It wasn't until after successfully stealing her away from his mother that he realized he hadn't actually spent any time with Arlo alone. He didn't even really know who she was—they were more or less strangers, everything he knew about her was the by-product of Celadom updates and the investigative mission that had thrown them together in the cavum factory.

He did want to get to know her, though, and a tour seemed like the best place to start, but not until he began to lead her in the direction of the library did he decide this moment might be the opportune time for something *else*, as well.

"There's a lot of people here," Arlo commented as they wound their way to the back of the room, nodding shyly here and there to the curious glances cast their way. "Is your library open to the public?"

"More or less," Vehan replied through a bright smile at Gisa, one of the librarians on staff who . . . didn't quite trust him not to be getting up to trouble anymore, the amount of times she'd had to chase him off from restricted content over the past little while. "There are areas that are out of bounds without official academic permission, of course, and a whole section you need both my mother's *and* the FHC's permission to even *think* about. But yeah, it's pretty much open to general study—there's a street entrance off that way that you can access through different portals around the territory. But it's up to security at each to determine whether your need is *important* enough to warrant entry, or something the actual public library can provide just as well."

"So . . . pretty much it's just the sidhe fae allowed in, isn't it."

Vehan bit his lip. That was . . . a fairly accurate assessment, and Arlo wasn't the first to point it out, nor to take issue with it.

"Sorry," she amended quickly, her face beginning to flush as though she hadn't meant to speak her previous comment out loud. "I didn't mean to—"

"No, don't apologize." He shook his head. "We're friends, yeah? We infiltrated a murder factory together, to use Nausicaä's term. You can speak your mind to me, Arlo. And besides, I'm . . . aware that there are things that need changing. Things that maybe now that I'm Mature, my mother and her council will be more likely to listen to me about."

"The price of privilege, I guess."

Once again, Vehan's gaze snapped to the girl on his arm, the girl who looked about as soft and timid as a mouse but had a way of saying things that shot the bullseye directly each time. "I . . . what?"

And once again, Arlo's face heated with embarrassment. "Sorry! Sorry, I keep doing it. With your mother, too, and just . . . *ugh*, I think I've just had a wild few days and my filters are all shot right now. All I meant was . . . well, it must really suck. Having to be the one to worry about and find solutions for all this stuff when you're just a teenager. I don't really know everything you have to do, but I've known Celadon forever, and he's *always* had his plate full with things I couldn't even *begin* to imagine juggling, and he's not even the Crown Prince of his Court like you are so . . ." She trailed off with a shrug of her shoulders. "It must suck. I'm sorry. But at the same time, I guess it comes with the territory, eh? Being the Crown Prince. There's a lot of things you won't ever have to personally worry about as someone with wealth and support and security. As a royal sidhe fae. The price for that security, I guess, is that you're a little more responsible for making sure the things you can fix that *need* fixing are made right."

All Vehan could do was look at her for a long moment. "That's . . . very true." And then, with the *slightest* quirk of his brows, added, "Eh?"

Arlo rolled her eyes. "Oh my gods—"

"Don't be shy, I think your accent is adorable."

"*Oh my gods*," she repeated, side-eyeing him—and it was then that something else caught her attention. Vehan noticed her half-hearted irritation morph into curiosity, and she paused, bringing them both to a halt just steps away from Vehan's destination. "Are those your parents?"

He turned to look, confused until he spotted the canvas painting mounted in the gap between shelves on the wall to their right.

How he could have forgotten about it when he'd come here so often as a child just to look at it specifically—this, the only of two portraits in the entire palace of his parents together, and the only *one* where his mother actually looked *happy*.

It still hurt to see his father.

At this point, the only real image he had in his head of Vadrien Hanlon was that of a reproduction. Vehan had a few memories of the man, but over time, his father's likeness had faded into oils on canvas, and it *hurt* to know that pictures were all he'd have to remember him for the rest of Vehan's life.

"You really look like him," Arlo said in a soft voice, pulling Vehan out of his reverie. "But also your mother. I'm sure you hear that a lot." Her laugh was a touch nervous as she patted his arm. "She looks really happy in this painting—all that glowing . . . but it's the smile, too, I think. Celadon has almost the exact same little curl when he's really happy about something . . ."

"She was pregnant."

"Aw," Arlo began, her face lighting up, but Vehan shook his head. "Not with me. Their . . . first child. My older brother."

He could *feel* Arlo's gaze on him, didn't need to look away from the painting to know she was baffled by what he'd just said. Because *no one* talked about it—Vehan himself hadn't even learned of this family tragedy until one of the librarians let it slip during one of his many visits.

And Arlo didn't need to ask it. He could feel her question, too.

Vehan shook his head.

"He died at birth, I'm told. Mother was . . . devastated. She doesn't talk about it. I tried asking her once, and all she said was that she *lost* him. Still couldn't even bring herself to say that he died. Obviously *I* wasn't born yet, so I wouldn't personally know, but I'm told it really changed her. That she used to be a bit warmer before it happened. A bit less of the ice she's encased herself in now . . ."

Everyone thought his mother was hard, cruel, a monster—they didn't see what Vehan saw: a grieving mother who'd lost a son, and then a husband, and had to face the whole of their cutthroat and generally nasty people in a position of power where everything about her as a single mother was viewed as a *weakness*.

Perhaps it *had* changed her, but Vehan didn't know anyone who could go through all his mother had and come out the other side unaffected.

"I'm so sorry . . ."

Again, Vehan shook his head. "Gods, no, I'm the one who's sorry! This isn't at all what I wanted to burden you with—"

"But you *do* want to burden me with something?"

He appreciated how easily she allowed him to change the subject. "Yes." He winced through an apologetic grin, and nodded off to the row just ahead. "Do you mind?"

She shook her head, and Vehan led her on, around the bookcase and down the row to another gap in the silk-papered wall.

This one bore no decoration.

There was nothing to set it apart or mark it as what it was, not a mere wall but a *door*. "Aurelian and I have been coming here a lot recently. It's a panic room, meant for the royal family, in case we're under siege or something when I'm in the middle of doing my home-work, I guess. Mother doesn't come here herself, so it became the perfect spot for Aurelian and me to sneak off with restricted books and browse without getting in trouble."

He placed his hand on the wall and swept it downward in a zag-ging bolt.

With a soft whir of magic, the wall pressed in on itself—slotted back and slid apart to reveal a set of stairs descending into a darkened chamber.

"After you, my lady," he demurred, stepping back to bow Arlo through with a flourish. She bit her lip against a laugh, and shook her head at him in passing. "Be careful on the steps," he added. "It's normally better lit, but . . ."

But with Vehan's magic as thoroughly uncooperative as it cur-rently was, the overhead glasswork that would have normally swelled with electric light lay dormant; the only sources of light now were the muted torches on the walls that had sprung to flickering life as soon as the door had sprung open—enough to see by, but vexing to his sense of pride.

Downward they wound, a short journey to the bottom, where the room opened up into a quaint space of gold-carpeted stone, wrap-around bookshelves built into windowless walls, a modest fireplace, and a plush, cream-colored sofa where he and Aurelian had spent *hours* together in the past few months, Aurelian absorbed in their hard-won forbidden reading and Vehan absorbed in studying *him* over the top of his own books.

You were caught kissing the High Prince in a darkened corridor last night.

He frowned.

"Are these . . . *alchemy books*?"

Startled, Vehan returned his attention to Arlo, his gaze snapping from the sofa to follow as she made for the table that commanded the center of the room.

Cluttered with papers and books, pens and dried inkwells and— ah, the empty mugs of hot chocolate Mrs. Bessel had kindly made for their late night "study sessions," where she assumed they'd been brushing up on four years of learning for the examinations that would soon take place.

He watched for a moment as Arlo selected one of the heavy, leather-bound tomes that he should probably return soon, before inventory was checked on the section it came from and the book was discovered as missing. "Nicholas Flamel's *Exposition of the Hieroglyphical Figures*, yeah. A copy—one of the few. The original's either been destroyed or locked up by your great uncle."

"Yeah, I've . . . read it," she replied, holding the book in her hands and looking down at it in a mixture of astonishment and the sort of intensity of someone attempting to piece something difficult together.

"You've read a copy, you mean?" Which was a surprise in itself, because there really were only a few of these left in the world, and only because the Heads of the Courts might *pretend* they follow the High King's commands to the letter, but none of them wanted to risk being the only one without such an important and powerful piece of knowledge. No one but Vehan, apparently, would leave one just lying around for anyone's perusal, and certainly not in the High King's own palace. "Where?"

Arlo frowned, turning the book this way and that in her hands, examining the spine. "There was one in Celadon's room. A copy too,

I guess, but it . . . looked different. There were pictures. And on the spine there was . . ."

She trailed off.

Something had occurred to her, Vehan could see that clear on her face—whatever she'd been trying to piece together had finally slotted into place. "On the spine there was . . . ?"

She shook her head. "Oh, um, there was this symbol? A snake winding through a series of orbs. It's the exact same symbol that was on a ring that Hieronymus Aurum was wearing—I couldn't place where I'd seen it before until just now."

Once again her gaze dropped to the book, and his with it. Vehan stepped toward the table as though *pulled* by the object in Arlo's hands. To be honest, he'd attempted reading it himself, but so much of it didn't make any sense to him. Half of it was so roundabout and unnecessarily floral that he couldn't quite make out anything the writer had been trying to say, and the other half was like reading the world's driest cookbook, with all these complicated ingredient lists and equations and instructions. None of it had seemed relevant to what he needed to know. There was nothing there about philosopher's stones.

"Hieronymus . . . he'd been wearing a ring?"

Arlo nodded.

"With a symbol you've seen on a copy of this book?"

"Mm-hmm."

"So this is a *cult,* then."

She looked up at him, a very critical expression in her eyes that matched almost perfectly the calculating look Celadon had fixed on Vehan's mother.

Arlo was intelligent.

She was vastly more intelligent, Vehan would wager, than anyone gave her credit for, including herself—it was all in the sharpness that was there and gone in a flash, like a resurfaced memory sinking back into forgotten fathoms.

"What do you mean?"

"Well," said Vehan, reaching for the book as he spoke, and Arlo handed it over easily. "If you're right, and there's a copy of this book out there with the symbol you just described, it's a symbol associated with great power. If that symbol is showing up on other things, that means others associated it with great power, too. And if it's now showing up on other things that are all related to one another—Hieronymus, using alchemy to create a stone, which is exactly what Flamel was known for as the first to do; Hieronymus, also not the true mastermind behind what's going on, but a *follower*—that means this isn't just a couple of people banding together to achieve some personal goal. It's a *group*. A dangerous one."

Urielle, what had they gotten themselves into?

They'd barely been a match for *one* power-thirsting villain with a philosopher's stone—but a whole cult?

Urielle.

Perhaps she could sense Vehan starting to spiral or perhaps she needed a change of conversation herself; regardless, when weighted silence began to press a little too suffocating around them, it was Arlo who relieved it with, "What exactly did you want to show me here?"

A different problem.

So many issues piling up in Vehan's life—there was the price of privilege, sure, but his was starting to cost a little too much.

"Ah." He set the book down on the table and reached for a sheet of paper: a drawing of the array on his chest. "So, you're starting alchemy training now, right?"

Another silent nod answered his question, Arlo watching him carefully.

"Right, so . . . I'm wondering if you might help me with something, as a side project. As further training. Here, in private—just between us, of course. This array on my chest . . . I've done a lot of research and haven't discovered a *thing* that even approaches what it is or how it got here. Thanks to Nausicaä and what we learned in our investigations, I've been able to work out that yes, it *is* a philosopher's stone array. Somehow, someone marked me with one. I'm not iron-born, neither is anyone else in my family, but reasonable deduction leads me to believe that this doesn't matter. Clearly, anyone can be marked with one of these arrays, but they only *work* if there's the ironborn balance of iron and magic. I only possess one of those two requirements, so my heart didn't turn into a philosopher's stone. But I'm thinking that the reason this stamp hasn't gone away, the reason it *hurts* sometimes, is that I have just enough of the magical requirement to keep it alive but starved."

"Because this is dark magic." Arlo nodded, reaching an under-standing now too. "It requires life to be created, so it's *dark magic*, and dark magic is a living thing, so it *feeds*."

It was Vehan's turn to nod. However much it made his skin crawl to imagine this array like a parasitic worm feeding off of him, he forced himself to remain focused on the task at hand. "I want it gone."

"I don't blame you." Pulling the paper toward her, Arlo examined the sketch. "You want me to help, don't you?"

"You dissolved the array on the cavum factory door. And you haven't said it, but I know . . . I *know* you interfered with that array in the arena where we found you."

"This is the most complicated array I've ever seen, though," Arlo replied, sighing. She didn't bother denying Vehan's statement, which was a good sign, because she was the only one here who could outright lie. "I mean, keeping in mind I've seen all of, like, four or five tops. I've only *just* started my training—have you asked Leda? Between the two of us, she's—"

"Not the one I trust not to tell anyone."

About this room . . . about his research . . . about his *knowing* what this was, and the resulting suspicions that his mother might, too, and if she *did* . . . no. It had to be Arlo. Arlo was his friend, and . . . *Urielle.*

Arlo was his *friend.*

He could count on one hand how many genuine friends he actually had, and still have fingers left over.

"Oh."

Arlo looked at him, understandably confused.

"You're my friend," he blurted out, and immediately felt his face grow hot.

Arlo's gaze darted downward at this admission, and damn it, now they were both uncomfortable and awkward. She probably thought he was trying to bribe her, guilt her into helping him, or worse—was it worse?—she pitied how pathetic he must look right now, standing in his junked bolt-hole, realizing for the first time that he now had one whole friend besides the boy who'd apparently already moved on from him, and the other boy who may or may not only be in this for Vehan's crown.

"Sorry, I—"

"I'll help."

His eyes widened. When his gaze had wandered to the floor as well, he didn't know, but it snapped up to Arlo's face and found her smiling gently. A little rosy red in the face, but . . . well, was it wishful thinking that she seemed happy?

"You will?"

Vehan watched in amazement as she folded the piece of paper he'd given her and slipped it into her pocket. "I'll look it over," Arlo replied with a nod. "There has to be something in this I can disrupt with a little more training. We'll get this off you, Vehan. I'll help—of *course* I'll help. We're friends."

That gentle smile turned into a beam.

"Oh," said Vehan. Then, "Thank you."

And his face split into a smile too.

CHAPTER 23

Nausicaä

~~~

THERE WERE MANY THINGS a Hunter's cloak could do that made one such an enviable, priceless possession, not least of all the ability to render the wearer completely invisible at will. Certain folk could weave their glamour strong enough to camouflage themselves with their surroundings. Places such as faerie cafés and the Palace of Spring utilized multiple glamours to dissuade human notice, forcing the eye to skip over its location. But *true* invisibility—erasing something completely from the planes of existence—was something only a select few could do without the assistance of Otherworldly artifacts.

It was thanks to this unique, Otherworldly magic that Nausicaä was able to lurk as she was currently, on the sidelines of a large, open room with dark hardwood flooring and pale oyster walls, against which had been pushed the handful of sofas, divans, potted plants, and tables that served as the room's only decorations.

Balls of electric light glowed like fireflies around the crystal chandeliers above.

The blush of sunset spilled in with the floral-scented breeze through the series open windows.

She hadn't meant to spy like this.

When she'd arrived at the Luminous Palace and found that Arlo wasn't in her room, she'd been all too happy to use this as an excuse to poke around the Seelie Summer palace as she'd *never* be allowed to do without the cover of her cloak, certainly not considering what she'd done to the queen's foyer only little over a month ago. On her arrival, her resolve had been to snoop until she discovered Arlo, then steal her away on another hunt, but in coming across her, she felt that resolve waver to something else.

Here, in the middle of what appeared to be a dance lesson with a bony and pinched-faced nymph instructor, Arlo stood paired off with the Seelie Summer prince, her cousin and a boy Nausicaä didn't know dancing beside them, and Arlo looked . . .

Happy.

Celadon was as much himself as ever in his impeccable emerald, sage, and obsidian embellishments. His partner was equally resplendent in white and gold. Vehan cut that dashing "prince charming" figure, all smiles and easy laughter and casual charm as he led Arlo this way and that, spun her around and dipped her into low, sweeping maneuvers that made her burst into delighted laughter as well. Nausicaä could only stare for how far she outshone the stunning fae elite around her.

In black nylons, a short emerald romper, and lime green high-top shoes, all her red hair swaying around her like flames, *here*, in the heart of a Court famed for its brilliance and light, Arlo was absolutely *radiant*.

She put them all to shame.

It was a little difficult to render into words the feeling that fluttered through her chest, made her smile, breathe out laughter too in echo every time Arlo did—it was impossible to define the sight of Arlo dancing in the twilight, but Arlo was happy, and for a moment, Nausicaä was as well.

Happier than she'd been in a very long time.

Happier, perhaps, than she'd ever been.

Vehan spun Arlo outward.

It was instinct that drew Nausicaä away from the wall she'd been leaning against, watching, *enthralled*—instinct, or longing, or a bittersweet mixture of both. Nausicaä stepped forward, and as she moved, she shed her invisibility. All she could think when she raised her hand to slot against the one Arlo held in the air, her other slipping to wind around the dip in her waist, was: *oh*.

Followed by: "You're beautiful."

It was a little unfair just *how* beautiful this girl in her arms was, especially when the shock of Nausicaä's sudden appearance was replaced on her face by a smile that bloomed even lovelier than the flowers of her Court.

"Nausicaä!" Arlo gushed, a little red in the face for the rather breathless comment Nausicaä hadn't realized she'd spoken out loud. "When did you get here? I didn't even notice you come in."

Did Riadne know an eighteen-year-old ironborn girl from UnSeelie Spring could light up a room better than she could?

Nausicaä grinned around the fluttering that refused to quit and tugged Arlo a little closer. "Would you believe me if I said it was magic?"

"Impossible. Magic isn't real," Arlo teased in return. The way her body yielded to Nausicaä's hold, how she fit just a little too perfectly into her arms as Nausicaä usurped the prince's place to lead her through their dance, the shyness in the curl of her fingers around Nausicaä's slightly larger hand, and then the absolute, comfortable surety of it . . . *Nausicaä*, she scolded herself, *get your head in the game.*

"Hey now, be careful," she teased out loud, her grin growing sharper. "Haven't you heard the theory? That every time someone says they don't believe in magic, a faerie loses their wings, and that's why so few of the folk have them."

"*Pah*—faerie tales." Arlo stuck her nose into the air. "I'm far too old for such nonsense."

Nausicaä laughed.

In a gentler, more serious tone, she asked, "Having fun, are you?"

Arlo nodded, her expression smoothing out into another smile. "I am. I'm glad you're back, though. I know it's only been a couple days, but I have so much to tell you! And my first full alchemy lesson is tomorrow—"

"You two, enough talking—focus!" the nymph instructor snapped.

"Prince Vehan, pair yourself with Lord Reynolds. Your Highness, with Lord Bessel if you could."

The boys were quick to sift apart and reassemble with their newly appointed partners.

Nausicaä hadn't realized Aurelian was here at all until he peeled himself off the far wall and strode briskly across the floor to Celadon, where a brief battle of wills to lead ensued in which, oddly enough, for what she knew of him, the High Prince eventually yielded.

The unknown boy—Lord Reynolds, Nausicaä figured, by process of elimination—seemed happy enough to comply with this rearrangement, but Vehan was glaring rather stonily at his partner's chest, quite opposite to the mood he'd been in while dancing with Arlo, only it wasn't Nausicaä he shot what she was tempted to label venomous glances at but *Celadon*, and Aurelian, too.

"I've missed something, haven't I."

Arlo sighed. "*Yes*. Oh deities, so apparently Celadon faked kissing Aurelian to get themselves out of trouble—don't look at me, I don't know, he watches too many dramas. Anyhow, of course the *faked* part is for some unknown reason what we're *not* talking about, according to Celadon, so the whole palace is convinced they're dating now, which Celadon says they aren't, but . . ."

"Ah, a *love triangle*. That explains Prince Rain Cloud, then. You do realize you've only been here, what, three days? Chaos just follows you everywhere, doesn't it?"

"It really does."

"Young lady," the instructor interrupted, when the rounds she made in observation brought her to them. "I don't know who you are, but so help you if you don't straighten that posture." On her way by, she snapped her crop against Nausicaä's back, and Nausicaä's eyes widened, more at the audacity than in any real pain.

"How dare you strike the infamous Dark Star."

Nausicaä looked down at Arlo in surprise.

"Insignificant mortal worm," her tiny fireball companion continued in a low-pitched, hushed mockery of what Nausicaä gathered was supposed to be *her*. "I could end you with the flick of my sword!" She paused, then, adopting her usual tone once more, said, "That's what you just thought, wasn't it?"

Nausicaä frowned around the urge to laugh. "I'm subtracting two hearts from our relationship meter."

"*Aww.*"

The next half hour passed in what felt like minutes.

Nausicaä had been to her share of parties, some of them even by invitation, but it had been ages since she'd danced like this—a proper dance, with set maneuvers and steps to follow, for no aim other than to enjoy the closeness of someone else, and of course the way Arlo's breath seemed to snag in her chest, the way she held Nausicaä's gaze when Nausicaä eased her languidly into a particularly low dip only to snap her quickly back upright, bringing them so much *closer* for an infinite *heartbeat*.

This was . . . not what she'd come to do.

It was fun, regardless.

And then it ended, far too quickly. Arlo stepped back, breathing a little harder and flushed in the face with what Nausicaä hoped was more than just exertion, and it felt like Arlo had taken something with her as she did—but that was mushy and sentimental, and Nausicaä was just going to ignore that she'd ever thought something so soppy.

"Room for improvement, whoever you are," the instructor sniffed in passing at Nausicaä. "You will return for the next lesson. I won't have it said *any* student of mine is anything less than perfect, even the intruding ones."

Nausicaä wrinkled her nose, but the comment she'd intended to bark back at . . . who the hells was this nymph anyhow? Celadon saved her from Nausicaä's wrath, regardless. "Where in the realm did you get *this*?" He came up beside her, picking at Nausicaä's cloak, an expression on his face so very *Arlo* that it took a moment for Nausicaä to respond for how much it threw her.

"Wouldn't *you* like to know, weather-boy—don't touch."

"But that's a *Hunter's* cloak," Celadon pressed. "I should know, I've seen them enough times with my father to be able to tell."

From the corner of her eye, she saw Vehan actually *cringe* at the mention of Hunters.

Right.

Arlo was a bit unusual—Nausicaä was spoiled by how unflappable she was when it came to the world's most frightening nasties. A Fury, a Reaper, *Lethe*; Arlo had stared down some of the absolute worst that both the Mortal and Immortal Realms had to offer, this timid, tiny teenage girl. People like Nausicaä and the Hunters were more used to being met with shivering, shrieking, curses, and vulgarities. Hells, someone had once even tried to chase Nausicaä out of a tavern with a deities-damned *broom*. They were beings to fear, not the sort that folk built their romantic tales around unless to feature them as the monster that beautiful princesses needed rescue from.

A very loud part of her screamed *good*, let them fear her. Fear meant she'd be left alone, and alone was what she wanted.

The quieter part that this screaming drowned out was the voice that whispered *please don't*.

"*Anyway*," Nausicaä said, pointedly moving on with the conversation *and* this train of thought. "Red. If you're finished playing Barbie in the Land of Faerie Princes, there's another hunt you might be interested in joining . . ." She slinked forward, slipped her arm through and around Arlo's, and knitted herself close to her side. With a waggle of her brows, she staged a whisper to add, "It involves the merfolk."

"Oh!" Vehan shot ramrod straight, recovering quickly from his aversion to Nausicaä's cloak for his hand to fly into the air. "Oh, I want to go! Whatever this hunt is, I want to go too!"

Nausicaä shot him a cool glance. "I wasn't offering to take *you*, Lightning McQueen."

"Are you just saying *words* at this point, because I have no idea who that—"

"If Arlo's going, I'm going," Celadon joined in, folding his arms across his chest and frowning like the whole-ass child he actually was. "A Hunter's cloak and a Hunter's mission? Whatever you're involved in, Nausicaä Kraken, if you bring along my cousin, you bring along me, too."

"If His Highness goes, I do," Aurelian chimed in, casting a glance at Vehan, but Vehan, who wasn't looking and clearly took the title to mean *Celadon,* dimmed by several voltages.

All of them were being the absolute worst right now.

"Arlo," Nausicaä growled. "I like precisely *none* of your friends."

"Oh, *wow.*" It was the unknown Lord Reynolds boy who'd spoken, blowing out his cheeks and shaking his head despairingly. "I don't even know who this is and even I can still see what's going on here." He prowled forward, slotting himself firmly between Vehan and Celadon and gripping them both by the arm. "Arlo, do you want to go with the pretty blond lady to terrorize some mermaids?"

Arlo, looking a bit like a doe caught in headlights, glanced from Lord Reynolds up to Nausicaä. "Um, well, I *do* want to go with you. I don't exactly want to *terrorize* anyone, but—"

"There you go," Lord Reynolds announced, and yanked on the arms in his grasp. "Enjoy your date, you two! Your Highnesses, Lord Aurelian, I'm suddenly feeling very desperately like a night out on the town and require all three of you for company. Come with me."

He proceeded to drag them away, which Nausicaä suspected very few people other than Arlo were brave enough to do to Celadon, and it was most likely the shock of this audacity that made him comply— she didn't miss the wide-eyed affront he stared Lord Reynolds down with as he stumbled along behind him.

"I like precisely *one* of your friends," Nausicaä amended, turning her attention back to Arlo. "Lord Reynolds—plus one relationship heart."

"Why do I get the impression you actually *have* a friendship chart you're keeping track of this tally on."

"Do you not?"

Arlo rolled her eyes, but there was a fern-curl hint of a grin in the corner of her mouth that betrayed her amusement. "Okay, well, I guess I'm ready to go when you are. Unless . . ." She paused to look down at herself. "Do you think I should change?"

Reaching up to tug on the braid she'd put in Arlo's hair during their last hunt together—a braid that would remain there until Nausicaä herself unwound it—Nausicaä replied, "Not a thing."

Another bit of sappiness that Nausicaä's bitter sarcasm and angry defenses recoiled to hear her utter, but it was worth it for the way Arlo ducked to hide a much softer, more private grin, and reached down to snag Nausicaä's hand in her own. Warm fingers slid gently between hers, a featherlight caress that made Nausicaä's magic tingle with the contact. They interwove, locking the two of them firmly together. For a moment the world narrowed down to this, and Nausicaä felt as though nothing in *any* of the endless realms could break them apart.

She cleared her throat.

Get it together.

"All right, let's mosey, flower girl," she said aloud, and teleported them away.

CHAPTER 24

Arlo

~~~~~~

I T WAS FULLY NIGHT wherever Nausicaä had taken them. Poor as her fae senses might be, Arlo was still UnSeelie; only in the Faerie Ring's disconcerting stairwell had she ever encountered a darkness so dense she couldn't see through it at all. It *did* take a moment, though, for her eyes to adjust to this particular gloom, and once they finally did, it was still like looking at the world through a shroud.

What she saw made her draw in a quiet gasp of surprise.

They were by the sea.

She'd been able to tell immediately from the salt in the sharply fresh air, but it was mildly alarming to realize it was *inches* from her feet, from the rocks they'd teleported onto at the base of a jagged cliff. That cliff rose high behind them, sweeping out to unfurl like wings around their modest alcove and the even murkier depths of a grotto off to Arlo's right. The ink-black water was so still it stretched like a single, endless pane of glass off into the distance. Where the sea ended and that horizon began was difficult to say. A forbidding canopy of storm clouds loomed overhead, blotting out the moon and stars. It was this that made it so difficult for Arlo to see, but none of it was what had trapped her breath in the back of her throat.

"*Nausicaä*," she exclaimed in hushed wonder, and took a small, unconscious step forward.

The *merfolk*—they were *everywhere*.

Coral pink, shell brown, anemone yellow, tropical blue—they were so many tones and so viciously beautiful, their bodies either soft and plump or bony and built a bit like spindly seahorses, the way their joints and vertebrae jutted under shimmery skin, but all of them possessed a driftwood-warped quality to their frames.

Seated along the clifftop's ledge, perched in the gaps of its face, or disembodied heads bobbing atop the water's surface, all their lamp-like eyes were wide and glinting in the gloom. Some had hair that dripped like tar around them, some wore braids, and some had masses tangled around crabs and wriggling minnows and bits of bone.

Barnacles climbed up their limbs.

Starfish and muscles and tiny white shells stuck to patches of skin.

Their clothing was varied: on some, strips of netting, kelp, and fins that had been plucked from numerous different fish; on others, a mismatch of treated leather, trousers, tunics, and boots that had undoubtedly belonged to someone else first.

All wore teeth and bones like jewelry; all the ones whose legs could be glimpsed were covered in iridescent scales from toe to hip; all had ears that pointed like Arlo's did, but longer and shaped like fins.

None seemed to want to come any closer to her and Nausicaä than they currently dared.

Arlo turned around, still unable to find the words to express how absolutely *amazing* this was, how *thrilled* she was to be standing here.

The merfolk were fae, just as much as the sidhe and lesidhe were, but as part of the Wild Courts, they were outside the High King's domain. Most of the Wild faeries preferred to keep to their respective spaces, but the mer were probably the most reclusive of all—and Arlo would argue, from the stories she'd heard about their power, violence, and insatiable taste for flesh, that they were easily the most dangerous.

What child of magic *didn't* know the legend of the merboy, a far-too-young prince of his people, stolen from the waters by a cruel human king whose wife could have no son of her own? Depending on the teller, this particular story was rife with torment and abuse, the pain the merboy was forced to suffer to become what the king had desired: a fearsome warrior who could ensure the king's throne stayed his forever.

Who didn't know the cautionary myth of that mer prince's revenge, the brutality he'd unleashed on them that had leveled the entire once-upon-a-time kingdom of Atlantis?

The merfolk were subjects of both immense fear and fascination to magical kind. Arlo had been obsessed with them growing up, had read as much about them as she could and even once camped out all night with Celadon by Lake Ontario to try to catch a glimpse of one, but she'd never met *any* before this moment, and here she was standing in the midst of what had to be nearly a *hundred* of them.

"Yup," Nausicaä announced, folding her arms over her chest and grinning cheekily at Arlo. "Called it—*weird*. Proper, quiet little Red, a *monster* lover."

She leered when she said this, but it was no insult. There was no bite behind it. In fact, Nausicaä seemed pleased more than anything, her vulture-like features standing even sharper in relief against the shadows, her silver eyes moonlight bright.

"Yeah, well," Arlo mumbled, wondering if Nausicaä's terrible beauty would ever stop catching her off guard like this, "not *all* monsters are bad."

"Indeed."

Nausicaä's grin widened. Arlo rolled her eyes. She forced herself to turn back to the sea and gesture out at the mer in the glassy water. "Why are there so many of them? Why are they so far away and just . . . watching?"

"Well," Nausicaä replied, a hint of excitement in her voice as though she was *very* glad to finally explain what was going on. "There's a siren in that grotto over there. You know what a siren is, yeah?"

She did, to a degree.

The merfolk were reclusive, but that didn't mean they couldn't venture onto land when they wanted.

Many did.

Their magic granted them legs for a while, but if they stayed too long away from their seas or oceans or lakes or rivers, they'd lose their fins altogether. Their bond to the water would be broken, and they'd never be allowed to return. But the water would miss them and cry out for what it had lost, and supposedly the land-bound mer would be able to hear it—would *always* hear this mournful song and wouldn't be able to stop until it drove them mad, warping their minds and turning them into feral creatures bent on death and destruction: sirens.

Eventually, it would pull them back into the water, and they would die—turn to sea foam the moment they did.

Sirens were a bit like high-functioning zombies, was Arlo's understanding of it. They were the things the worst of their legends were based on.

They were what the mer prince of Atlantis was said to have become before he sank into the sea along with his devastation.

"The seaweed you found on our last hunt, it led us here. *Lethe* led us here. I don't think I've mentioned the reason I joined up with the Hunt in the first place, other than the stones. Lethe was the one to send me that invitation a few days ago, just before you came here. Not the High King. And we've been trying to track him down for a while, but doubly so since. He's been scattering breadcrumbs, leaving us clues to . . . something. The answers I need, I hope. I'd say he's trying to help us catch the alchemist responsible for what's going on, but Lethe is a bag of wet cats, so whatever his motivation is, it isn't *only* to help. There's something he wants us to see, though, and that's a start. And once we do, I'm willing to put my money on his finally coming out of hiding. Anyhow"—she turned to the cave, gesturing at its gaping black mouth—"the siren that's taken up residence in there, she's been wreaking a bit more havoc than your run-of-the-mill mer should be capable of. A lot of people have gone missing, and I can smell the death on this place. And I'm sure you've noticed how dark it is here?"

Arlo nodded.

Much too dark, and she could sense it too, now that Nausicaä mentioned it: the sickly sweet stench of blood that wafted from the grotto, human and folk alike; the wriggling wrongness in the night air; the sour bite of dark magic, so abrasive against her own that it made the hair on the back of her neck and arms stand on end.

"The mer have been concealing this space from human notice, trying to keep potential victims from falling into their sister's grasp. There's not a lot that would make them ask your great uncle for assistance, and of course the rare honor of being useful to them comes at a time when *he* can't do jack all anymore, so here we are in his stead, problem outsourced, and lo: another failed stone."

Her gaze drifted from the grotto to the merfolk in the sea. Something about her expression had changed, a flicker of deeper feeling she didn't often let show through her many masks of sarcasm and disdain, anger and aloofness and cool apathy—masks that were just as much weapons as the blades she carried. "I'm a Fury, Arlo. The *Dark Star*. That siren in there is one of their own. It doesn't matter that she's fallen; they're still here to protect her. They're still family. They won't let her die alone, if she has to die tonight at all."

Grief.

That deeper feeling was grief, and something else—envy? Wistfulness? Arlo was getting better at reading the things Nausicaä tried to keep buried, but she was no expert yet. Grief was something consistently close enough to her surface, though, that it was the easiest for Arlo to spot, and had welled up so profoundly in her voice that Arlo found herself reaching out to take her hand once again. "She might not have to, though, yeah? I mean . . . we didn't kill the imp. If we can just take away her stone, she'd go back to . . ."

"Regular zombie doom? Yeah." Nausicaä sniffed a laugh, and just like that, was herself once more. "I mean . . . she's using an artifact of dark magic to *kill* people. She should be brought in for justice, but *my* sisters, it seems, have been otherwise preoccupied. And I'm not about to do jack-shit for them. Game plan is we march in there, flash some muscle, I wrestle down whatever that siren's got in there to throw at me—you're appropriately impressed, of course—and boom, bam, take away her weapon of mass magical destruction and dump her on Eris to deal with." Grinning once again now, she tugged on

Arlo's braid as playfully as she had in the practice room earlier. "You still have your faerie protection, so her voice won't have any affect on you. Just stay by the grotto entrance and you'll be fine."

"What about you?" Arlo asked.

Were Furies immune to a siren's voice?

A mer's voice could enthrall any within hearing distance, but a siren's song was deadly. It didn't just affect men, as the old human tales suggested. It took the tone of whoever the victim loved most and lured them off into blissful demise, usually to be drowned or ripped apart and eaten.

Nausicaä, eyes glinting even brighter, leaned in close enough that only an inch kept their noses from touching. "Why?" she husked. "Are you going to give me one, too?"

Swallowing down her urge to dip her chin under the flare of heat in that stare and ignoring the warmth that flushed through her, Arlo matched Nausicaä's gaze. Squared her jaw. *Dared* her to say something when she reached up and, quick as her fingers could manage, wove a braid into the side of Nausicaä's hair. Plucked a hair from her own head to tie it off and activate the charm.

She expected something like, *It has to mean something for the braid to work, Red.*

She could hear very loud in her head—*you like her, you like her, you like her.*

But Nausicaä said nothing.

She only stared.

"Just in case," Arlo said, very small and very quiet, and still Nausicaä *stared.*

She stared until Arlo wondered if maybe she shouldn't have done what she just did, if maybe she'd overstepped some boundary. Whatever she may or may not feel for Nausicaä, it didn't matter one bit if Nausicaä didn't like her that way back, and maybe that kiss in the cavum factory had been a spur-of-the-moment, we're-most-likely-going-to-die-soon sort of thing that meant nothing more than that.

Nausicaä was . . . *Nausicaä*. Fire and glory and power and ethereal beauty.

Arlo was Arlo. A little bit of a lot of things, none of it very impressive.

"Sorry—"

Nausicaä held up a finger.

"I'm—"

She held up a second.

Arlo bit her lip, waiting out the moment for Nausicaä to gather the words she needed to let her down gently, an "it's not you, it's me," which Arlo had never experienced herself because she'd never been bold enough to tell anyone she liked them.

"Challenge accepted."

It was Arlo's turn to stare. "Wait . . . what?" she spluttered.

"Challenge accepted!" Nausicaä repeated, turning abruptly and beginning for the grotto's entrance. "You're smooth, I'll give you that," she called over her shoulder, "but I'm definitely going to out-woo you!"

"That . . . that wasn't a *challenge!*" Arlo called after her, unsure how to even take this. Nausicaä liked to tease. She had a deeply flirtatious side to her. It was hard to know which things were serious and what was just banter and deflection.

When it was evident no reply would be forthcoming, Arlo heaved a weighted sigh and sprung into motion, following Nausicaä across the uneven rocks. It was much slower progress for her. The tide was steadily rising, and the stone was slick with the dampness in the air. She was never one hundred percent sure of her footing, but she was *not* going to be left behind.

At last she made it to the grotto, where Nausicaä already stood waiting for her to catch up.

"Ready?"

Arlo nodded.

"Remember, stay as close to this entrance as you can. I'm not sure what we'll find in there, but a pissed off super-siren is a handful enough. Also, try to stay on land."

At the mention, she looked down.

She couldn't make out any bottom to the pool leading into this seaside cave, not in this current gloom, but it was definitely deep enough to drown in. Arlo was a strong swimmer, but there was no telling what lurked under the water's surface, eager for her to fall in— the mer were all keeping well away, but they weren't the only folk of the Wild Court of Water she had to watch out for.

"Noted. All right, go on, impress me, *Dark Star*."

Nausicaä's delighted bark of laughter trailed behind her as she stepped into the waiting dark.

Arlo inched forward, too.

There was a noticeable difference in the air here—cooler, wetter, and that foul odor of blood and decay, brine and damp stone, malice and dark magic was so strong that it hit Arlo's senses like a physical wave.

One step.

Two.

She couldn't see a thing—not her hand in front of her face, nor Nausicaä just ahead, nor the rocks she walked over. Every step she had to feel out, and much like she'd been forced to do in the Faerie Ring's stairwell, had to rely on her hand on the uncomfortably slick wall to guide her way.

Another step.

Four.

This was dangerous. She wished she had her phone, or even her die—why hadn't she stopped to grab either? She'd been too distracted by Nausicaä's arrival and the giddy excitement of going along with her on another hunt, and now she was going to pay the price for it.

"Nos, I can't see *anything*."

A single spark cut through the darkness.

Arlo watched it shoot up from some unseen source and starburst into a ball of flame.

It grew and grew, sailing higher and higher above her head, filling the grotto with a warm light that made Arlo wince for how suddenly bright it was. Once again, she was forced to wait for her eyes to adjust to her surroundings, and once again, when they did, she gasped.

But not in amazement.

The grotto was a gaping wound gouged deep into the cliffside. The pool in its center was fathomless, its pale turquoise water crystal clear and yet Arlo could still see no hint of a bottom. A rocky path carved a steadily widening ledge that traveled along the grotto's wall, climbing up and up to spiral to the top, and Arlo counted: one, two, five, nine, eleven skeletal corpses dotted along the way.

Their flesh hung from their bones in the same state as their ragged, bloodied clothes.

Humans . . . fae . . . there was a pixie boy, a dryad girl, a satyr even, all of them standing as still as statues in various states of decomposition . . . but all with eyes wide open.

Reanimated corpses, *dark magic*—this was undoubtedly the work of a stone.

Arlo closed the distance between her and Nausicaä, who stood with her hand outstretched—the fireball was hers, Arlo realized. She didn't startle when Arlo latched onto the back of her cloak despite how intensely she stared down this scene, but she did sweep out an arm to keep Arlo back and tucked safely away from the water.

"Arlo," she said in a low and very careful voice. "Stay here."

Arlo couldn't move, anyhow.

Her eyes followed the spiral of corpses all the way around the grotto to the ledge tapered into a platform high above its entrance.

There, seated on a pile of bones as though it were some grand throne, was the siren they were after. She gazed down at them, her body as pale and translucent as the creatures only found in the deepest pits of the ocean, all her organs and her fragile skeleton visible beneath. She wore tatters of a pale blue silk gown. Her hair spilled like a clear, filmy oil around her; her legs oozed with sapphire blood, the pearly scales on them beginning to flake away, picked apart and plucked and scratched in patches, the same bloody score of nails on her arms and face.

Her aura was madness, and rage, and salt, but she sat there, haughty as any queen, those pale, wide eyes fixed on them.

"Actually . . . you should probably move back a bit," Nausicaä urged.

Finally, Arlo shook free of her shock. "Will you be okay?"

"Perfectly." She swung out a hand, and smoke shot out from her palm to shape itself into a sword. The shadows solidified into steel, glimmering in the firelight, and when she angled a glint toward one of the corpses, they shrieked, flinched back, and *hissed* at Nausicaä.

Nausicaä chuckled deep in her throat.

"All right, then."

Arlo made to turn back for the grotto's entrance, but paused once again.

The hissing had grown louder, caught on.

One by one by one, the others began to join in, and as they did, they stomped their feet. Every thud of their heels on the rock was like the beat of a war drum, and Arlo couldn't help it, she glanced back up at the siren.

The siren smirked back—at *her*.

What happened next was a progression of events that transpired too quickly for Arlo to process in time.

A rushing groan flooded the grotto. Nausicaä whipped around, the both of them gaping at the water that rolled in from the sea, gathering to build itself into a wall over the entrance, sealing them in.

The stomping grew louder.

The hissing turned into growls and gnashing teeth and garbled, rumbling words—rather, one word, to be precise, but just when Arlo realized this and tried to channel her focus to listen, something cold and smooth and slippery crept from the water and wrapped itself around her ankle.

She looked down.

"Uh . . ."

"Arlo!"

Nausicaä lunged, but even she wasn't quick enough.

The tentacle around her ankle *pulled*, and Arlo had just enough sense to throw out her arms to keep from bashing her head against the rock as she was dragged from the ledge into the pool.

Panic—it was the first thing to filter through the immediate daze of being so suddenly submerged.

Darkness; quiet; *water* pressed in all around her.

She couldn't breathe; the tentacle secured to her ankle continued to pull her downward, and no matter how hard she struggled and kicked at it, it wouldn't let go.

Down.

Down.

Down Arlo sank. Was it even possible for this pool to be this deep? This had to be some form of magic, but she was beginning to struggle with other things that were now much more concerning than this.

She was running out of oxygen.

A good thing, then, you're a windborn fae.

That voice . . . it sounded like Luck.

Luck . . . her die, she wished more than ever that she had it right now. She could use the help, could practically see it in her mind dropping through the water to her rescue like a cruel taunt of what could be, but no, she'd been too careless, too eager to jump when Nausicaä said jump to remember to bring it.

It was getting harder to focus, her lungs were *burning*, and any second now her brain would force her to draw a breath and she would *drown*.

A good thing, then, that you can manipulate air. *Goodness, do I really have to spell it out for you?*

That voice, it was definitely Luck's, and they sounded so close— not trapped in her memory and regrets but *here*, in the present. It was a foolish hope, but Arlo's eyes drifted open. When they'd closed, she didn't know, but that didn't matter because Luck was nowhere in sight.

But there, just in front of her face, almost exactly as she'd pictured it in her mind, a very small object sank through the water with her.

Her die!

Could it really be?

Your next lesson. Seems as good a time as any. You can summon your die to you at any point. It will answer your call regardless of where you are, even here. You do not need spoken words to give it purpose. If all you want to do is roll for a singular action and your desire is simple enough, it is possible to expedite the process . . .

Her die—Arlo's hand darted out to capture it.

Use your surroundings to your advantage.

Use her surroundings to her advantage? Her die would work, even here, even if she couldn't speak?

What she needed right now was air, and there was none here but plenty above the water. Luck had given her a hint, they'd mentioned her ability to manipulate it . . .

What if she could bring the air out there down here?

Arlo closed her eyes again.

She pictured it, the air pulled down from above, shaping itself like an oxygen mask over her face.

And just like that, the world chugged to a halt.

She threw her die upward, watched as it churned sluggishly through the water before sinking back down level with her face. When the churning stopped, it seemed to lock into place, and whatever number faced the surface, Arlo couldn't see—she could only wait and *hope* it was enough.

The second that ticked by while Arlo waited for her fate to be decided felt like an eternity. It had been simple enough, hadn't it? Her declaration? She'd learned from the previous lesson not to push too extravagantly beyond her ability, but a bubble of air to serve as an oxygen mask, that wasn't so outlandish . . . right?

And then . . .

Something slipped over her mouth—a curious sensation underneath the water, like nothingness against her skin, and Arlo *gasped*.

Spots of black danced across her vision, ate away at its edges, but she gasped and gasped and drank in *air*—finally! She'd done it.

Unfortunately, you're still in a bit of a bind.

True.

If only you had a sword . . .

She drew a few more breaths, forcing herself to calm and focus. Then, closing her eyes again, she pictured her die dropping back in front of her face. Sure enough, when she opened them once more, it had returned, and she grabbed for it.

She couldn't make a sword from nothing, so that ruled out a blade of steel, but that wasn't want Luck wanted to her do, anyhow. No, they'd said specifically this lesson was about using her surroundings to her advantage—the air, her mother could wield it like a whip. Any sidhe fae whose command over their element was strong enough could forge it into weaponized shape.

She thought of Vehan's electric sword . . . closed her eyes again . . .

Instead of crackling energy, she re-envisioned *her* blade as one of churning wind, bubbling streams of air trickling down from the surface to build it before her.

She threw her die, once again trusting it would roll what she needed.

The world clunked back into gear.

At first, a peek—then, her eyes flew open.

Just as before, what she'd pictured in her mind unfolded identically in reality. She watched in awe as a lethal, translucent blade took form, solidifying when she reached out to grasp its hilt.

She slashed a downward stroke at the tentacle holding her captive.

A shriek even louder than what the corpses had issued rent the water and sent a torrent of bubbles up from below.

Arlo slashed again, and inky blue bled into a cloud around her.

The tentacle released her ankle and recoiled.

With furious kicks and great sweeps of her arms, she propelled herself to the surface, racing against the unknown creature of the deep's recovery. There was no hesitation when she took hold of the hand that plunged below the surface to help her the rest of the way, and *finally*—she broke the water.

Despite the fact that she'd been able to breathe just fine—her oxygen mask had apparently been self-replenishing—she still inhaled a ragged gasp as she clambered back onto the rock. The mask dissolved, along with her sword. She spluttered and choked and gagged on residual panic, but she was *okay*, and strong arms heaved her up to safety.

Someone patted her back, smoothed the hair out of her face, tilted her chin upward when her breathing began to settle at last to make way for sniffling and the threat of tears.

She'd almost *died*.

"You did very well. On your first try, too. I'm actually looking forward to the things we might be able to accomplish together, Arlo Jarsdel . . ."

Luck.

She'd never seen this feminine-appearing face before, but it was them. Those cosmic black eyes were unmistakable, as were the obsidian horns that curved from their temples to their chin. As though dressed for the occasion, they looked distinctly *merish*—their bones jutting under olive-green skin scaled like a fish, their hair pouring like squid ink down their front and back, leather and shells and bits of coral forming a cuirass overtop some fluttering black material, the skirts of which hung from their ample hips in ragged shreds.

"Where's Nausicaä?" Arlo rasped, looking wildly around. There was no sign of her, and the corpses had stopped hissing. At some point, the siren had stood from her makeshift throne, and all were staring down at the pool. "Where's Nos?" she repeated, slightly more frantic, scrambling to her feet.

Luck eased back into a sitting position. "Oh, she jumped in after you—which really does say a lot, I think, about the bond between the two of you. Nausicaä is a creation of fire. I doubt she's ever been overly fond of water. But I wanted to give you a proper shot at learning to summon your die so . . . I may have tampered a bit with her *luck* in reaching you."

They waved a hand at the pool as though undoing some spell. Arlo felt a shift in the air, a nonexistent breeze rippling out from Luck's hand, and no sooner had it swept out over the water than the ghost of another shriek reverberated through the very rock they stood on.

A dark cloud of blood bloomed toward the surface. A moment later, a very angry Fury burst from its murky center, and the hissing started again, but this time in the key of deep displeasure.

"Nos!"

"Un-*fucking*-believable," Nausicaä growled. Arlo couldn't recall ever seeing her so furious. "This is why nobody *fucking* likes you."

She glared down Luck as she swam to the pool's edge, rivulets of blood that thankfully weren't her own running down her face. Arlo offered her a hand to help her out, and Nausicaä took it, grumbling the entire time.

"Always wondered," she gritted as she slammed her sword onto the rock and heaved herself out of the water, "why I never found even a single deities-damned shrine dedicated to *your* worship."

There was no pause in her momentum. With Arlo's help (however much Arlo suspected she actually didn't need it), she clambered back to her feet, marched right past them for the horde of corpses now hobbling forward on the attack.

"Why is there no actual temple for good old Luck?" she continued, louder so they could hear her as she swung her sword in an angry swipe, clean through the first corpse she encountered. In pieces it slid apart, half of it collapsing on the rock, the other tumbling into the water to darken it further. "Of all the stars-damned deities, why is it *Luck* the mortals were so quick to turn their backs on?"

Blow after blow after vicious blow, Nausicaä carved her gruesome path up the ledge to the siren. Were it Arlo leading this assault or even someone better trained, neither would have fared so well against what she was sure was quite a difficult enemy, but they dropped like dolls at Nausicaä's feet, squelching and crunching under her boot as she stomped over them to the next.

"Wonder no more, Nausicaä!" she shouted now, her outrage echoing around the grotto. "Luck's a little fucking *bitch*. We're going to have *very loud words* after this, you doucheboat shit excuse for a titan!"

Luck sighed.

"Um . . . again, *please* don't kill my friend," Arlo attempted to bargain, as she'd done back in the nega-verse woods, breathless in horror more over Nausicaä's repeated insult to this ancient, all-powerful being than all the so many other dangers around them.

"Hah!" Nausicaä's barking laughter cut even sharper than her blade through the air. "Good fucking *luck* with *that*. And *you*," she added scathingly.

At last, she'd made it to the top of the rocky spiral.

The siren had marked her progress with increasingly wide-eyed anger and fear, tension building in her body.

She clutched something to her chest—Arlo couldn't see it, but she knew it was most likely the stone she'd been using to pull off reanimation of the dead and manipulation of the water.

"Hand it over," Nausicaä demanded.

"I will not," the siren growled, skittering back. She had a beautiful voice, melodic and placid, and Arlo understood fully for the first time just how grateful she had to be for her braid in *this* situation—without it, she suspected that voice would have ensnared her under its spell from the very first syllable the siren spoke. There was an eerie warp to the tune of it, Arlo was able to notice in her clear state of mind, a haunted madness similar to what infected the siren's magic. "It's mine, I found it! It's the only thing that will help me!"

Sheathing her sword, Nausicaä raised her hands to show she

meant no harm. It was surprising how quickly she deflated from her previous anger, how deftly she slipped behind a mask of calm.

Her magic dialed back to something as close to unthreatening as she could manage.

Arlo watched her take another step forward, and freeze when that pushed the siren to retreat a step back, too close to the edge of her platform for Arlo's comfort.

If the siren fell, it would be straight into the pool, and she'd be done for—sea foam the moment she broke the surface. Nausicaä seemed very much to want anything but that outcome, as well.

"How is it going to help you?" Nausicaä asked, not unkindly, but like she genuinely wanted to talk. "Help you return to the *water*?"

"*Yes*," the siren hissed.

Nausicaä shook her head, sad but firm. "It won't. I'm sorry. Maybe a proper stone could, for a little while, but that one you've got? It's not strong enough, and you've used it almost all up on this sanctuary here. It can't help you."

"You're lying—it *can*."

Another step back.

"Nos . . . ," Arlo called, unable to help it, her heart jumping into her throat. "Nos, she's too close to the edge!"

"It *can* help me return to the water . . ." She trailed off, glancing over the edge with such grief and longing on her face, Arlo's heart ached even more to see it. Doubt crept into her tone, and it only served to make her sadder. "I *want* to return to the water. I want to go *home* . . ."

"Hey. I get it," Nausicaä tried to soothe, but Arlo could hear a touch of panic lacing her words. "I *get* it. But that stone isn't going to help you. I'm not lying to you. You know it won't. Just give it here, and we can . . . talk. I can help you. I *will* help you, I swear it—"

"No," replied the siren. Her words crumbled into despair so softly spoken that Arlo almost couldn't hear them. "You can't."

Once again, what happened next was so quick that it was surreal to watch.

Nausicaä made another plea for the siren to see reason, and the siren deflated. Pitched her stone at Nausicaä, where it struck off her chest and clattered dully to the rock. She took another step backward.

"I'm tired of fighting. I just want to go home."

"No, listen, you can't just—*no!*"

The siren jumped.

Nausicaä lunged with a strangled cry.

Arlo gasped.

On instinct, she flung the die from her hand, picturing what she wanted its help to do. It was simple enough, *urgent* enough that she didn't have time or room to feel doubt over its successful execution. She envisioned a gust of wind welling up to catch the siren as she plummeted. The world didn't slow to a halt, no actions or numbers printed themselves into the air. What Arlo wanted passed like a clear and concise flicker before her eyes, and as soon as her die rolled to a halt on the rock, it happened.

The air above the water softened into a cushion and caught the siren just as Arlo had imagined it doing. As soon as it did, she darted forward, up the ledge, eyes not on the siren lying stunned on her airy cloud but on Nausicaä's death-white face as she clutched the ledge, golden arm outstretched in a failed attempt to catch the siren.

Arlo ran.

All she could see was the *horror* in Nausicaä's shocked expression, her lips moving in a quiet whisper: the same two words, over and over, and only once Arlo reached her could she hear what they were.

"Tisiphone . . . *no.*"

"Nausicaä, it's all right! The siren's all right!" Arlo tried to console.

Tisiphone . . . Arlo recalled meeting Nausicaä's sister, Meg, the Fury who'd said she would have preferred that their *other* sister could have survived over Nausicaä.

But why was Nausicaä calling for her? What did Tisiphone have to do with . . .

Oh.

"Nos?" she called, a little softer, kneeling at her side.

Nausicaä shook.

It started as a tremble in the center of her shoulder blades and vibrated outward—a panic attack? Arlo had experienced enough of these herself over the years to recognize the signs. "Nos, I'm going to hold you, okay? Just . . . it helps. If you're okay with that?"

"NO!" Nausicaä roared, but not in reply to Arlo. "No—*damn it!*"

Arlo had to lurch to keep her from tipping over the edge.

She didn't need to look to know what had just happened.

The siren had recovered from her daze and had decided she didn't want saving—the resonant *splash* was all Arlo needed to know how this siren's story had ended.

She didn't look at the foam that floated on the pool's surface where the siren had rolled off her cushion and into the water she so desperately wanted to return to. Nausicaä didn't need to look either, but Arlo couldn't pull her back any farther or force her gaze away. All she could do was hold Nausicaä as she shook, and *shook*, and called her sister's name once more through a wetness that wrenched Arlo's heart.

Arlo could only hold her in shock of her own over what had just occurred . . .

Staring . . . not down at the water, but off to the side—at a snow globe, of all things.

A curious object all the way up here, where there was nothing else but rock and bones. A snow globe, broken, its plastic bits of snow spilling out around to shape an even more curious miniature frozen wasteland.

. . . Staring, and breathing in the subtlest scent of rotting flowers that clung to the air.

The snow globe—another clue, just like the seaweed that led them out here. But how many more were they meant to uncover? And how much more could they afford to pay to get to the end of this gruesome trail, Arlo wondered, when tonight's toll alone had cost so dearly, and Nausicaä was closer to breaking than she'd ever seen before . . .

CHAPTER 25

Celadon

~⌒~⌒~

I'M MISSING SOMETHING," CELADON concluded, because he simply couldn't make sense of why Theodore would bring them to . . . whatever this was supposed to be, an enormous steel door slapped into the bland, pockmarked face of a cement building, no signage to even *hint* at what could possibly lay on the other side.

He'd been to a fair few shady locations over the course of his teenage years, rebelling whenever he could against his father's strict control, but they were in *Las Vegas*. This city was full to *bursting* with casinos bejeweled in flashing lights, and nightclubs pumping music like a hypnotic heartbeat through the streets, and shopping malls and Michelin-starred restaurants and fantastical outdoor displays, *any of it* a better introduction to the "City of Sin"—as even the folk called it—than . . . "What are we looking at here?"

"The *real* Vegas experience, of course," was Theodore's cryptic reply.

Celadon turned a skeptical look on him.

He'd only been to the Seelie Summer Court precisely twice in his twenty years—once to attend the funeral of the late King Vadrien, and once a few years later when his father had surprised him with permission to accompany him to the Summer Solstice ball years back, even though he hadn't been Mature yet. Celadon had squandered this opportunity on a pack of Pokémon cards and a *harmless* trick that Riadne Lysterne hadn't much appreciated being the target of.

So when Prince Theodore had suggested a night out "on the town," Celadon had to admit . . . he'd been interested.

Not enough that he would have traded of his own volition following Arlo on whatever business Nausicaä had whisked her off on, but once again this *boy* had caught him off guard, pulling him away from his cousin, and Celadon just found himself stumbling after. Theodore had even laid into him once out in the hall, along with Prince Vehan and Aurelian, about letting "two young women be gay together in peace for *one evening*, honestly."

Before Celadon could really comprehend what was happening, a change of clothes had been thrust upon him, and here they were on some crowded, narrow side street that shot off the Strip, and for all that it was a hive of nightlife activity, every single building looked like it was on the verge of being condemned.

Theodore beamed at him and wound his arm around Vehan's, fastening himself to his "intended." Celadon didn't miss the way Aurelian's eyes flashed at this, but much like when Aurelian had curiously chosen to allow his prince to believe he and Celadon had kissed, Celadon held his tongue.

This was not his secret to reveal, nor his drama to get involved in.

"What's the matter, Your Highness?" That smile sharpened to match the glint in Theodore's eyes. "Are you scared?"

Celadon snorted.

He was *not* scared, thank you. He'd done far more *unadvisable* things than what Theodore undoubtedly had in store for them tonight. It was only that he honestly didn't want to be here, and it certainly didn't help that the murky depths of the alley smelled distinctly of garbage and urine.

But if he backed out now and returned to the Luminous Palace to wait for Arlo's return, Theodore would *never* let him live this down—and why that should matter at *all* was beyond him, but he chalked it up to pride.

"Well, I'm going in," Vehan announced, squaring his shoulders like he, too, would have chosen a different way to pass their evening but wasn't about to give Theodore motive to question his mettle as well. "Aurelian and I have been almost *everywhere* in this city but never once down here—"

"For good reason." Aurelian's comment was stiff, even for him.

He looked even less impressed to be on this street than Celadon, but with an air of familiarity—a pointed lack of interest in his surroundings—that suggested *he'd* been here once or twice before, sans his far naiver prince. And Celadon recalled then the thing or two he'd learned about *Lord Bessel* prior to meeting him . . . the rebellious stint of his own just a couple years back, a stint not many could say they'd managed to pull themselves out of before experimentation became *addiction*.

Ignoring his retainer (which Aurelian didn't seem to appreciate, judging by the way his golden eyes flashed again in warning), Vehan untangled himself from Theodore and stepped toward the steel door, and not for the first time since meeting these two did Celadon wonder how long this push and pull between them would last.

An idle curiosity, of course. He knew firsthand how exhausting it was to have outsiders interfering in personal matters; much like he was certain Vehan was used to, there was a *great* deal of speculation on Celadon's own love life. He tried his best to stay out of the depths of the "Celadom," the fanbase that had built itself around him, and which he did enjoy for the most part. It was nice to know people liked him, that they cared about how he was and supported his modeling, his fashion designs, and the self-care vlogs he threw together on occasion.

But there was a darker side to this adoration.

The side that seemed to forget that Celadon and the people associated with him were exactly that—*people*.

It was difficult, being young and trying to sort out both his genderqueerness (he'd determined for now that he wasn't only male, but that was still a pending subject for him) and his asexuality (which he'd figured out the better part of a decade ago now) *without* adding "High Prince" and "Court Idol" on top of this. All of a sudden both of these things were up for public debate, something to dissect and hold up against others of the same identities, as though there was one set of guidelines on how these identities were supposed to look and be, and if Celadon didn't follow the course, he always paid a price.

Often, that price was whoever else had been drawn under siege along with him, those hard-won relationships, romantic or otherwise, that eventually decided the invasion of privacy and stress simply weren't worth it—*he* wasn't worth it.

Vehan and Theodore . . . no doubt they were used to similar gossip and similar losses. The two of them together made *sense*. They had a lot in common from Celadon's viewpoint, a lot between them that would be understood without words. They were also pretty popularly backed by the majority of the folk, as a matter of fact, and yet . . .

The wants of the Courts and the wants of the heart were often two different things.

Theodore released Vehan, paused only a moment before following after him to shoot Aurelian a cheeky grin, and to Celadon a look that could only be described as a challenge.

And oh, but the *glower* on Aurelian's face as he watched him go . . .

"You *could* always say something," Celadon hedged, ignoring his vow to keep out of others' love lives just this one time. How Vehan didn't realize the depth of Aurelian's feelings for him was beyond Celadon, but all it would take was Aurelian clarifying that they hadn't kissed—that they'd faked it to get out of trouble, and the entire thing had been Celadon's idea to begin with—and Vehan would be sunshine and smiles with him once more, he was sure of it.

He placed a hand on Aurelian's shoulder; Aurelian shrugged it off almost instantly. "It's better this way," was all he replied, and stalked off for the door as well.

With a sigh, Celadon brought up the rear, hoping it at least smelled better *inside* the "real Vegas experience."

Theodore knocked on the slab of steel—a peculiar knock, one like a code, and as soon as he finished, a narrow slot in the door peeled back to reveal the bulging, olive-green eyes of a goblin on the other side.

"It's *you*," said the goblin, with no real affection or dislike, hardly any inflection of emotion at all.

"It's me," Theodore replied like silk.

"Prove it."

He shot the goblin his middle finger, and Vehan choked on a mixture of horror and humor. Whether anyone else saw it, Celadon couldn't say, but *he* had—the way the action flashed the tattoo inked on the inside of that finger, a tattoo Celadon apparently still had permission to see.

Damn it.

This was *Grim Brotherhood* territory.

No wonder Aurelian looked a little nervous and fidgety—if he'd gotten tangled up at *all* with the Brotherhood during the worst of his drug exploration, they'd definitely have a hook in him they could pull on whenever they wanted. And Celadon . . . the *one group he'd been actively trying to avoid* . . .

He could sympathize with Aurelian's anxiety.

The goblin disappeared like falling through the earth, the slot snapping shut as he dropped. There was a heavy *clunk* and the scraping of a stool, and the next moment, the steel door creaked open. The goblin—on the shorter side of only four feet, sharply dressed in a sleek black suit, and exceptionally well-groomed—peered around its edge at them.

When he noticed Celadon, his eyes grew ever so slightly wider. "Well, well, well, the Madam might actually be pleased with you tonight, Master Reynolds." He paused to give his words more weight, but still they were void of feelings any which way. If Vehan or Aurelian found it odd that Theodore was a *known* entity here, neither of them said. Did either of them suspect who Theodore was? What he was associated with? Vehan, he doubted, and would Aurelian really be so casual about a trained assassin so close to his prince? But then, both seemed a little too preoccupied with their own thoughts to even register this exchange of words.

"Audience or participant?" the goblin added, changing subject rather quickly, and it was then that Celadon knew.

Damn it, damn it, *damn it*—he'd been *tricked*.

Theodore had made it no secret to him during their last conversation that he worked with the Grim Brotherhood, that he'd be willing to align himself with Celadon against Riadne and whatever was going on in the Courts, but only if he met with his *employers* first. Celadon had wanted *nothing* to do with that . . . but here he was, just the same.

Sure, he could leave, could just turn around and walk away and circumvent this entire situation, but status among the sidhe fae was a fragile thing—very susceptible to gossip and aspersions, and depended greatly on one's reputation. Celadon could walk away from this, and by morning the Courts would be whispering about him, the vicious elite armed with one more weapon to wield in knocking the Viridians out of power.

But it was more than that.

It was the *look* on Theodore's face as he spun around to lock eyes with Celadon—the *dare* behind his mischief-bright gaze, the challenge in the way the right corner of his mouth curled upward ever so slightly . . .

The almost entirely nonexistent plea behind it all to give him this, and acquiesce.

Damn it.

Had Celadon always been this susceptible to his pride? Right now, he couldn't recall. All he knew was that he'd never met someone who infuriated him as wholly and immediately as Theodore did, and something about losing to him . . . *disappointing* him . . . Cosmin, it made Celadon bristle—made him reckless.

You're a gods-damned fool, he chided himself, as he replied to the goblin in Theodore's stead—"Participant."

"Oh?"

Theodore looked *delighted* in his surprise—and his gratitude; that only made Celadon bristle more.

"Do you even know what you're participating *in*?" Aurelian scolded low at his ear, and Celadon had been a little distracted himself now, glaring at the group's apparent ringleader, but not so much that he missed the way Vehan glared at *him,* probably for what looked like a display of intimacy between him and the prince's retainer.

"I'm also participating!" Vehan declared rather abruptly, and Aurelian actually *growled* at him—surged forward as though to grab him by the shoulders and possibly shake some sense into the Seelie Summer Prince.

Even Celadon snapped out of his anger to gape at him, but luckily, Theodore intervened.

Rolling his eyes, he fastened himself to his prince's side once again and tugged him into motion. "Another night, darling. Let's see how His Highness fares first, hmm?" Over his shoulder, he called to Celadon, "Good luck, *weather boy*. We'll be cheering for you!"

His laughter echoed in the stark cement hallway that conveyed him and a fuming Vehan toward another door.

Aurelian hurried off after the pair.

Celadon scowled.

He didn't need anything from Theodore Reynolds, least of all his *luck* . . .

On second thought, he could use a little luck right now, even if it was Theodore's.

What had he gotten himself into?

What had *any* of them gotten themselves into? Because when Celadon closed his eyes to get a grip on the nausea swelling inside of him, he saw that ridiculous *gratitude* on Theodore's face when Celadon agreed to put in an appearance here, like maybe—just *maybe*—he wasn't as indifferent to whatever bound him to the guild as he pretended and was just as tangled in danger as Celadon was . . . as Aurelian was . . . as Vehan was, and Arlo, and Nausicaä . . .

And oh gods, he'd volunteered himself for the damned *Colosseum*—he was going to *throttle* Theodore Reynolds!

"First time, huh?" said the massive faerie man beside him.

Celadon lifted his head from his knees.

All the other combatants clearly just saw was a slim-boned *boy* in pale-mint linen pants and a plain, tight black T-shirt when they looked at him, because why in the hells would their High Prince be participating in the Grim Brotherhood's very illegal and incredibly deadly underground battle arena, all the way out in a Court to which he didn't belong and was famously unwelcome to visit?

One or two of the staff had given him a second, harder look on his way down to the combatants' zone.

The rather gruesome-looking ogre leaning against the wall opposite the bench where Celadon sat had been staring rather fixedly at his face the entire time they'd been waiting here, clearly trying to work out why it was so familiar.

Las Vegas was the seat of the Grim Brotherhood's power, but its reach stretched far and wide. There were no Court borders to contain it, no enterprise they didn't shy from dabbling in at least once, and no spot of criminal activity that happened in the magical community passed without their notice—and often, their permission.

The Colosseum was just as infamous as the Faerie Ring, a place where folk could pit themselves against one another, no holds barred, no powers denied, no tricks too dirty to secure their win. And a *win* was highly sought after—the payout alone was tremendous, enough to set anyone up very prettily for quite a while if they could make it all the way through to the end of the night's participants.

It was also the only way to earn an audition with the Madam—head of the Grim Brotherhood—to join the Brotherhood ranks, and exactly the reason Celadon should have held his Cosmin-damned tongue and left while he had the chance.

"First time . . . yeah," Celadon replied, perhaps a little weakly, but he'd navigated many a daunting task in his short collection of years before now. Masking himself with nonchalance was almost second nature at this point. "Don't worry, I'll try not to bruise you up too badly."

The faerie man laughed.

Celadon didn't blame him. He'd laugh too if he were as large as a troll and corded with muscle, with great elephant's tusks protruding from his upper jaw.

But it was either feigned confidence or throwing up on the floor, because damn it, damn it, *damn it*—he'd been so *careful* to avoid the Madam, to keep from giving her even a moment's opportunity to hook him like she did *all* her other catches, and here he was participating in the Colosseum, just *handing* himself over to her on a platter.

Because if he won, she'd capitalize on this as permission to seek him out and meet with him to entice him into her fold.

And if he lost, he'd get the absolute hells beaten out of him. Possibly, he could die. If no one recognized him, they wouldn't hold back—and if they *did* recognize him, they would double down on their blows out of dislike for the High Royalty, the sidhe fae in general, or purely for the boasting rights, because most of the people here were in some way, shape, or form *adjacent* to the law . . .

And it was hard to say which was worse—the Madam or looming death.

"Gotta admit, I'm havin' a hard time pinnin' down what you're even doin' here, little guy."

"I don't look like the battle arena sort to you?"

The faerie man laughed again, a robust sound that filled the room. It might not be so bad, if he had to fight whoever this was. Celadon might survive, at least—but again, just surviving the match was grounds for the Madam to seek him out.

"Are you hoping to join the Brotherhood?"

Celadon shook his head, and for some reason, that only made the man happier. "The love of the fight, is it? I respect that! Name's Jerald, by the way. This is my fourth competition!"

He held out a massive hand that enveloped Celadon's entirely when he shook it. "Cel. Fourth time, eh—ever last the whole night?"

"Not a damn time!" Jerald boomed out more laughter. "But don't go thinkin' that means anything. Tonight's a grab-bag tournament—my favorite; no climbing ranks, just fighting until you can't fight no more, and nothing but luck to decide how many opponents you have to outlast. I always do best on the grab-bag tourneys. I don't tire easy, little guy!"

"No," Celadon heard himself chuckle, and despite his anxiety, began to relax for the conversation. "No, I'm sure you don't—"

The competitor's zone door slammed open to reveal another goblin. The same goblin who'd been coming to fetch them one by one from this ugly, compact cement room.

The rest of the Colosseum's interior had been *beautiful*, even Celadon had to admit.

As soon as they entered through the door at the end of the entrance hallway, they'd stepped into a massive room drenched in bloodred velvet and softly glowing crystal chandeliers, servers and attendants milling about with trays of sparkling wines and deep amber liquors, all of them dressed in the same black suits as the goblin bouncer had worn—elegance more reminiscent of an opera house than a glorified kill-box.

The competitor's zone was just as bleak as the Colosseum's streetfront, though, and it hadn't eased his nerves any when he'd parted ways with a joyfully waving Theodore, a worried Aurelian, and a stone-faced Vehan, who seemed very upset with him at the moment, but he couldn't deal with that right now.

Each time that door opened, Celadon's heart leaped into his throat, his stomach bottoming out simultaneously.

Each time, the suited goblin selected the next competitor, and it was never Celadon. At first that was all right, but they were getting down to the bottom of the barrel here. It was him and Jerald and the ogre across the room, and the longer this wore on, the likelier whoever he had to face was going to wipe the arena floor with him.

"You."

The goblin pointed to the ogre, even bigger and thicker than Jerald, with a bald head and a squashed faced with storm-gray, merciless eyes. The ogre peeled off the wall and prowled to the door, never once removing his gaze from Celadon. Celadon sent a fervent, quick prayer to Cosmin that he wouldn't be facing him next—if he had to get his ass handed to him, he would prefer it be by Jerald, who didn't look at him like he wanted to break every bone in his body.

The ogre left.

The minutes ticked by.

The goblin returned—this was the pattern of Celadon's night, and he never got to know who won or lost; part of the "thrill" was *not* knowing, he supposed.

"You," said the goblin, and once again it wasn't Celadon.

Jerald grinned at him, offering another shake of his hand. "Hope to see you out there, little guy."

"Yes," Celadon replied, with every bit of composure as he could muster. "Let's hope. Good luck."

Jerald laughed—and then there was one.

"You," the goblin said, when far too soon he returned for the final time. Celadon chosen at last, and he was willing to bet the entirety of the UnSeelie Spring fortune that the Madam had orchestrated this—that she knew he was here and had intentionally rigged her own system so that he'd have to contend with the strongest opponent of the night.

Jerald had undoubtedly lost.

He had a sinking feeling it was going to be the ogre who greeted him out in that cage.

Sighing, Celadon stood from his bench.

With legs that felt more lead than flesh, he followed the goblin out into the hall. "Rules are simple," he told Celadon as they walked. "Try not to die. Sign here."

At the end of the hall now, the goblin turned abruptly to face him—

held out his clipboard, and a waiver that absolved the Colosseum of any responsibility if Celadon snuffed it here tonight.

Another sigh—he signed the form *Celadon Fleur-Viridian*, because why the hells not when the Brotherhood already knew he was here?

The goblin looked down at it. He looked back up. "Oh . . . ," he replied. "Are you . . . uh . . . sure about this?"

Finally, it was Celadon's turn to laugh. He'd never been so *un*sure about anything in his life. But he nodded, and the goblin bit his lip, looked like he might almost try to stop Celadon from going out there, and that was honestly more kindness than he expected in this particular place . . . but it was also risking the Madam's wrath if he did.

The Madam and Riadne Lysterne . . . Celadon had never met the former, but wondered idly which one of *them* would survive a round pitted against each other in this cage.

"Good luck," the goblin muttered, and stepped aside at last.

The loading bay door behind him reeled upward, and Celadon's senses *exploded* with both light and sound—cheering, shouting, so much *noise* as the announcer wound up the crowd for this final event.

Strobe lights flashed.

Beams of multicolored light roamed around the room.

Celadon winced—it took a moment for his eyes to adjust, and when he walked out of the bay door into the cage . . .

He couldn't see a thing beyond it other than the first few rows of people, pressed against the wire mesh, clawing at the links, climbing them for a better view. If Theodore and Vehan and Aurelian were still out there in the stands beyond, he couldn't make out their faces, but at the moment . . . he was too distracted to look for them, anyhow.

It *wasn't* the ogre who'd survived the match.

In fact, it was the ogre's sapphire *blood* that smeared the cage's white-padded floor—the freshest of the smears, at least, and judging by the stain of it splashed down Jerald's front and bits of gore hanging wetly from those tusks . . . Celadon had misjudged the more dangerous opponent.

"Hello, little guy," Jerald boomed over the crowd, and there was that *laughter* again, but this time there was no mistaking the edge of mania that would have warned Celadon earlier, if he'd been paying better attention. "The Madam must be smiling on me tonight—the main event, all mine for the *tasting* . . ."

A flesh-eating faerie—*wonderful*.

The Madam's work once again, he would bet. Celadon couldn't throw this match, make himself seem underwhelming to the things the Brotherhood wanted from him, because there was no walking away from someone who wanted to *eat* him. Celadon would have to win, or he would die, all because he hadn't been able to bear *Theodore* thinking poorly of his courage.

Wonderful.

Would Jerald go easier on him if he knew who Celadon was?

"—the final event you've all been waiting for!" the announcer thundered overhead. **"We've a rare treat in store for you tonight—our very own High Prince of UnSeelie Spring, CELADON FLEUR-VIRIDIAN!"**

Booing erupted in the crowd—hissing, *jeering*. Someone threw a bottle at the cage hard enough that it shattered, spraying the mat inside with shards of glass and foaming beer. None of this was surprising to him. It was part of the reason he kept his identity secret when he snuck into places he shouldn't be. There was a great deal of tension within the Courts lately, and no small part of it was owing to the things the sidhe elite had done to elevate their kind over all the rest and supress faerie traditions.

He wasn't expecting to be liked here at all, but his focus narrowed on Jerald—how would he react? As the one who'd potentially deliver the killing blow, it was one thing to call Celadon names in a crowd and another thing to have his murder on one's hands.

"A *royal* little guy!" Jerald grinned, showing off every one of his blue-stained and bone-crushing teeth. "Talk about *fine dining*."

So . . . no, Jerald didn't care in the least who Celadon was. *Wooooonderful.*

He was going to die.

The announcer said some more words, none of them anything Celadon's brain could hear over the ringing in his ears. He tried to calm himself, tried to inhale a deep breath and use the air to push down useless things like fear and anxiety. Those wouldn't help him right now, and Celadon had been trained in combat by some of the best warriors the Courts could offer—by Thalo herself, even—but never had he actually had to fight for his life like he'd have to do now.

Breathe in, breathe out. Focus.

He might not have size on his side, but Celadon was powerful in many other ways. He could do this.

"Combatants, take the center!"

Numbly, Celadon stepped to the middle of the ring.

Jerald did too.

He towered over Celadon, near seven feet in height and just a little taller than Nausicaä. The smell of sickly-sweet faerie blood clung to his breath and clothes, wafting over Celadon so pungently it made his stomach roil.

But Celadon was a Viridian—his own High King Father had personally trained him too. He stood in the middle of the ring and matched Jerald's gaze with unwavering determination, and that was just about the last thing he remembered before his vision *exploded* with stars.

He staggered backward, a ringing in his ears now that had nothing to do with his galloping heart.

It took a moment for him to register that the left side of his jaw felt like it had just been struck by a bull-troll—Jerald, who'd started the match a little unfairly, before any gong or bell or instruction could be issued for them to begin.

Unfairly, but there was no such thing as *fairness* in this cage.

Celadon spit out blood on the mat, lifted his head just in time to catch the next blow on his cheekbone, and was sent stumbling even farther.

Fae were made of stronger stuff than humans and many other faeries. Plus, a High Prince was protected by certain magics no other had access to. But *gods,* he still felt pain. He felt his cheekbone fracture, and his power leap to heal it over as quickly as possible, but not fast enough.

To *hells* with this—Celadon righted himself, curled his hand around the air, and gave it a hard lashing. As he did, his magic pulled the element he controlled into the forked-tongue of a storming, violent whip.

Another lash—Celadon's whip caught Jerald around the ankle. With a forceful tug, the flesh-eating faerie was toppled, sending quakes through the cage the moment his back hit the floor.

More booing erupted in the crowd.

Celadon was not the favored win tonight, but it hardly mattered. He was too used to battling against dislike to be bothered, and right now, he was too focused on getting out of this foolish decision alive.

Jerald was felled, and Celadon acted without hesitation. He spun to wind his whip up tighter, and with all his fae strength, *heaved* the faerie off the ground to fling him roaring across the cage.

If he could just knock him unconscious, Celadon would win the round. Easier said than done, but—

"You sidhe fae and your flashy, cowardly *tricks!*"

Like he hadn't punched Celadon in the face before their round even began.

Hauling himself up from the ground, Jerald wasted no time in barreling straight at him, a glint in his eyes that was pure mania and bloodlust and the promise of painful death, no trace of his former humor remaining.

Jerald had brawn on his side to be sure, but Celadon was significantly more agile, all the more so for his gift.

He spun again, deftly dodging another blow that aimed itself at his head, then darted swiftly in the other direction to bend himself around the blow directed at his stomach.

The goal was to tire him.

All that muscle and blustering, all that heavy force behind each blow—if any of them caught Celadon, he would lose the sliver of advantage he'd managed to win, but it came at a price. Everything came at a price. Celadon could dart around this cage for hours if it took, but Jerald could only keep swinging the way he was for so long.

Another blow—missed.

A swipe at Celadon's head—through air.

A lunge for him around the middle—Jerald stumbled and crashed into the wire mesh, the barbed twist of it catching skin to tear it open and splatter the floor with his blood.

The crowd cheered.

They might not like Celadon, but they *loved* a good show.

Ripping away from the cage, Jerald made another lunge for him. There was no outmaneuvering a *windborn* fae when it came to agility, but Celadon's luck had finally worn thin . . .

The glass and beer from the broken bottle—he'd forgotten it was there, his foot slipping on the slicked surface, and while he caught himself quickly, it wasn't quick enough.

Jerald *slammed* him into the cage's wire, and Celadon's face, his hands, his arms—everything tore as it dug into his flesh, and the faerie behind him chuckled darkly.

"You smell so good, little guy; fear might toughen up the meat, but the way it spices blood . . ." He buried his face against Celadon's neck and inhaled deeply, and it was both the creepiest and most disgusting thing anyone had ever done to him when a tongue darted out to drag itself through rivulet of blood that trickled from his face.

Celadon cringed.

Instinctually, he tried to flinch away—to buck against the faerie man, kick backward at his shin, *anything*.

Trapped by Jerald enveloping him from behind and beginning to panic for the suffocating feeling of being pressed so hard against the wire, the crowd surging closer to claw at him, grab his clothes, spit in his face and throw more drinks—he'd never been so abused and degraded in his entire life.

Something in him *sparked* with ire.

It *surged* through him, hot and fizzling and weirdly electric— Celadon's magic, storming instinctually to his defense, but this wasn't how the wind at his core normally felt . . .

Suddenly Jerald was gone.

Blown away? Normally that would be the case, but the flesh-eating faerie leaped back with a howl, his muscles convulsing as if something had *shocked* him.

Celadon didn't have it in him to examine this right now. Gasping, his eyes flew open. Bolting straight, he intended to pry himself from the wire, to regain his composure and possibly his edge in this match—but the face his sight found first in the crowd immobilized him entirely.

Antifreeze-bright green eyes . . . gunmetal black hair . . . black leather and wicked silver fastenings and a cloak that made him almost impossible to see through the gloom, yet—

"I'm going to enjoy *breaking* you, little fae *prince*—"

Shit—Celadon snapped back to his senses, whirled around to maybe, hopefully defend himself against whatever Jerald was about to inflict on him, only to find . . .

The entire arena fell under a hush.

Everyone stared, Celadon most bewildered of all.

He had many talents—producing knives out of nowhere wasn't one. But that *was* a knife, a heavy silver dagger lodged *deep* to its hilt in Jerald's throat. The precision of such a throw, to make it not only through the gaps in the wire cage but to hit its mark with such deadly accuracy . . .

Jerald stood, eyes wide, simply staring at Celadon.

A moment later, he fell to knees. Gagging, spluttering, his hands scrambled for the knife. He pulled it out, and sapphire blood *poured* into a pool at his feet.

The crowd stood in stricken silence only a second longer, and then . . .

"I don't believe it!" the announcer called. **"We have ourselves a champion, folks! The winner and last faerie—er, fae—standing: CELADON FLEUR-VIRIDIAN!"**

There was booing again, but it was far quieter this time. Once more, the crowd proved what it craved most of all was entertainment—and Celadon had provided exactly that.

What he received for winning, he never found out.

Numb and trembling slightly, he didn't feel the barbed wire cut into his hands when he reached behind himself to grab hold of something steady.

He *did* feel the hand that wrapped around his, though.

Turning, he had just enough time to catch antifreeze-green eyes, so much closer than before, right in front of his face—and then . . . the world dissolved into black-like-tar, as if the very cosmos were melting around him, swallowing him whole and spitting him out . . .

In an alley?

An alley that reeked of garbage and urine.

"You *fool*," Lethe seethed, because, yes, it was Lethe, the Hunter no one could find. The Hunter who'd betrayed the others, and Celadon's father . . . but the Hunter who'd just rescued him?

That dagger, had it belonged to *Lethe*?

"What in the *Star's* name were you *possibly* thinking, you *foolish*—"

"*—don't understand why you won't help me.*
You have just as much reason to hate her as I do;
your sister is dead because of her!"

"*—arrogant—*"

"*Yes, Iliana is dead. Because of that creature's actions.*
My sister's fiancé died by her hand
and the despair she fell into . . . the way she wasted away in mourning . . .
Yes, I am angry about that—still, even after all these years."

Yes, I hate her for it. In fact, just weeks ago, if you'd come to me
with this,

I was in a low enough place that I might have even agreed to what
you want from me, because a part of me will always blame that creature
for what happened.

I'd seen her for the first time in years in the Faerie Ring,
and thought to myself, why not, she's right there, she deserves it.
She deserves to pay."

"—tedious *boy!*"

"Then why won't you help me?
Is it because of that girl you've taken on, your little protégé—"

"Do you have *any* idea how many times I've had to save your
worthless neck? The *cost* to me in doing so—"

Lethe was *furious.*

Celadon had never had such a close or personal conversation with
him before, that oddly warped face so close he could almost taste Lethe's
breath on his lips. But he couldn't focus. He couldn't concentrate.

Lethe was furious, scolding him like a child, and perhaps Celadon
did deserve that, but his mind was reeling with what he'd just survived, his entire body shaking with exhaustion and residual adrenaline
and heart-racing fear.

He was so out of sorts, he couldn't even block out the conversation
that the air in this alley had only *just* recorded, judging by the strength
and clarity of the voices it spoke in.

His Gift . . . There were different types of Readers. Some could
read minds, some could read auras like an open book on any given
person's life and destiny. Others—like him—could listen in on what
was left behind in the air.

None of them were trusted, by others . . . by themselves even, as
the older they got, the *better* their Gifts became, and the worse the
lines between past and present, reality and *thought* began to blur.

Gossip whispered that Celadon was losing his mind, just like his
father.

There were times—like now, standing in this filthy alley trying desperately to sort out reality—when Celadon wondered if he actually was.

Secrets, information, *burdens*—he tried so hard to push this power down, this "Gift" that made him so different, so dangerous, so untrustworthy to the Courts that he couldn't even leave his damned palace without permission. He didn't *want* to know things he wasn't supposed to know. He didn't *want* to be his family's puppet or a spy for the Grim Brotherhood. He didn't want to use his Gift any more than he had to, but in his father's palace, he was caught in a dangerous web that would get so much worse if he *didn't* pretend.

He didn't want to hear any of these whispers right now, but the voices . . . he was *sure* he knew them, if he could only just *focus* . . . But he was so overwhelmed in his current state, and he felt a little like passing out. His face hurt quite a lot, too—gods, he couldn't *concentrate* . . .

"I won't help you because even if my sister deserves revenge,
I don't deserve what it would do to me to enact it.
What you do with that poison you bought tonight is up to you, Gentian—
I will have no part of it, because it solves nothing.
It heals nothing. It doesn't bring anyone back.
I would only lose more, in fact—like that little protégé, *yes;*
that one girl who might just be the first real hope the ironborn have
of regaining what the Courts have stolen from us . . ."

"You will *not* do this again."

Celadon nodded, blinking to try to clear away the voices.

Lethe slammed a fist against the brick wall just beside Celadon's head. Not quite as tall as Jerald had been, or nearly as broad, he should have still been intimidating . . . but perhaps it was just that Celadon was too numb to the world right now to care. Regardless, it served to ground him fully in the present, the voices he couldn't place falling quiet. "You will *not*."

"I won't," he heard himself breathe.

"*Celadon?!*"

Ah, that was . . . Theodore? Aurelian? Vehan?

"Thank you," he blurted, because Lethe had stiffened, his head snapping toward the mouth of the alley, and all Celadon could think right now through the fog settling over his brain was that it was nice that someone cared. Another person other than Arlo. "Thank you for saving me."

Letting him go as abruptly as he'd snatched him up, Lethe peeled away. There was a sour look on his face, a mixture of irritation and regret but also . . . surprise? Not many people thanked him for things, Celadon had to assume. The High King certainly didn't. Was he going to pass out now? He felt like it . . .

"*Celadon*—there you are!"

"You're *welcome*," Lethe spat. It was the most appalled Celadon had ever heard anyone sound while uttering those words, and he couldn't help it . . . he laughed. The *look* he received just before Theodore reached them and Lethe was reabsorbed into the night . . . Celadon wondered idly how many could say they'd survived a glare like *that*.

CHAPTER 26

Arlo

~~~~~~~

S HE DIDN'T SEE NAUSICAÄ again for *days*.

The incident at the grotto weighed on Arlo's spirits, had given her nightmares and stolen her appetite and made it even more difficult than usual for her to rouse from bed in the mornings. This was the second person who'd died in front of her, and it was no easier to process this time around, but adding to her distress was Nausicaä's unusual and complete absence.

She wouldn't respond to any texts, didn't answer phone calls. Arlo had waited up until the sun rose for three whole nights on the off chance that Nausicaä would teleport onto her balcony, but never once had she showed.

The stillness about her . . . the alarming flatness of her aura . . . the apathetic *nothingness* in her expression when Nausicaä had peeled herself off that ledge, taken Arlo in hand, and teleported them out of the grotto back to the Luminous Palace—it worried Arlo. She couldn't help seeing it every time she closed her eyes.

She worried so much that she couldn't focus on anything for nearly a week—not on the array Vehan had asked her to find a way to dissolve, nor the alchemy lessons that had finally begun, nor the dance practice she glided muzzily through like a ghost every evening, nor the study sessions in the palace library that Vehan, Theo, Aurelian, and Celadon all gathered to host for her, to teach her the names and notable bits of background of all the important folk who'd be at the Solstice at the end of the month.

Tisiphone . . . that was Nausicaä's sister's name, Arlo was sure of it. Judging by her reaction to the siren's death, her sister had likely also died by suicide. There was a connection here, Arlo *knew* there was, to the reason eleven people had died and Nausicaä had been expelled, but there was so much else she didn't know and wanted to.

Whatever Nausicaä was to her, she was in the very least *important*. Arlo wanted to know why there was so much hurt and grief inside her friend, and why she did everything in her power to play up the monster the world accused her of being. Because Nausicaä *wasn't* a monster. If the grotto had taught Arlo anything, it was that Nausicaä possessed a much gentler soul than the fire and bluster she pretended, that she felt things *deeply*, that she was *good*, and people like that . . . they didn't break for nothing.

They didn't lash out for no reason . . .

"I'm afraid I can give you no insights, Lady Arlo," said Leda in her ever-gentle, vaguely weary tone. She frowned at the chunk of iron Arlo was meant to be learning how to transmute into a perfectly shaped square—beginner's lessons, just about all Arlo would be allowed to perform with Sylvain keeping watch over her (though currently he dozed in the sunny corner, giving Arlo the first bit of privacy with her tutor since arriving here).

In Arlo's distraction, so wound up with worry over her friend and finally able to talk to someone who seemed to know something of Nausicaä's past, she hadn't been monitoring her skill.

A *touch* overboard, she realized, when following Leda's line of sight made her find that her chunk of iron had taken on the more intricate shape of a sharp-pointed star.

"I cannot pretend to fathom the way the Dark Star's mind works. Nor, I admit, do I wish to."

Arlo liked Leda. She didn't ask unnecessary questions and seemed more delighted than anything whenever Arlo proved to be a bit more alchemically inclined than what she was willing to demonstrate in front of their *supervisor*. Arlo wanted desperately to get to know her better, because Leda was the first ironborn she'd ever been able to talk to on any personal level. There were so many things Arlo wanted to know, to ask, to learn from Leda . . . It was difficult, though, to befriend her. Because Leda, for all her grace and delicate airs, existed behind an impenetrable steel wall.

She had many opinions on Nausicaä. She *knew* things about Nausicaä that Arlo didn't. But Leda betrayed nothing, not about her or her past or anyone else's, for that matter, and Arlo couldn't blame her for that, even if she *was* disappointed to be kept all the time at a distance.

"She isn't a bad person," Arlo reminded, perhaps a little forcefully, but Leda didn't seem to mind the edge to her tone in the least. "I might not have known her for as long as you have, but I know her well enough to say for certain that her heart . . . it's in the right place. Nausicaä isn't a bad person just because she hasn't always done the right thing."

"True, Lady Arlo. The world isn't split into good and evil, and neither are its people. Still, the *Nausicaä* you know and the one from my past are two different entities." She looked up from Arlo's star to smile—a placating gesture, sure, but Arlo could tell there was genuine feeling buried deep within it, and it made a bit of her frustration yield. "She is very lucky, though, to have you on her side. Such a staunch and compassionate defender . . . not many can boast that they've ever known the loyalty you show for her . . ."

"—and *Leda* won't talk about it." Arlo complained later that day when she was free of her lessons and lying flopped on her bed. It was sometime after lunch. Vehan and Theo were off training somewhere. Celadon and Aurelian were gods knew where—and Celadon had seemed rather subdued lately anyway. That evening they all had plans to explore the Las Vegas Strip, because Arlo had never been, and it would be amusing to see Vehan and Theo and Celadon marvel over the most basic human things.

For now, though, she'd been left on her own to relax and "enjoy her vacation." She'd intended to go for a swim in her private pool on the floor below, but the water caused her thoughts to circle back to

Nausicaä, and she'd made it as far as pulling out her swimsuit before collapsing on her bed with a sigh.

"Gentian isn't an option at *all*."

He disliked Nausicaä so much that she doubted he'd give her an unbiased account of anything he knew.

"And it's almost like she can *sense* I want to talk about it, so of course Nausicaä isn't around to ask herself. But *you* have to know," Arlo said to the ceiling—to Luck, curled on the bed beside her and dozing in their cat form.

She turned on her side.

Luck cracked open an eye to peer at her.

"You knew Nausicaä before she came here."

I did.

"You know what happened to cause her expulsion."

I do.

"So . . . ," she hedged. "Can *you* tell me?"

Luck lifted their head, mouth stretching wide in a feline yawn that showed off all their very impressive teeth. *I think it's time for another lesson.*

Rolling to her back once more, Arlo groaned. "I don't feel like any more lessons today, Luck." She wasn't in the mood, not after the last one, and everything that had resulted from it.

You wish to know about Nausicaä?

"I do, but—"

Another lesson, then. Summon your die—now that you know how, I will no longer do it for you.

With a frown, Arlo pushed herself upright. She closed her eyes, picturing her die clearly in her mind, and called out to it just as she'd done in the grotto.

Very good.

Arlo opened her eyes. Her die had appeared beside her on the bed, face up on the number four.

It's time to teach you about a few very important features of that die.

You must remember, this is an instrument of chance and nothing more. The only magic that object possesses is a boost to your allotted luck. You can channel that luck in a number of ways, toward yourself or others, but there are other ways to use it too. You will have noticed, I imagine, that the die resets each time to the number four.

"I have, yeah."

That is your number. Your lucky *number, so to speak. It is the first number you ever rolled, and it is therefore the number of times you can ask anything of your die, and your request will come to pass.* Luck stared intently at her, their fathomless eyes growing somehow even darker.

Anything, they repeated.

Think of these as wishes. No matter what you ask, if you will it to be so, the die will make it happen—but only if that wish pertains to you. *You cannot wish for something that directly affects someone else, and four times is all you get before this power will be no more. You must also wait a recharging period once a wish is made in order to use any of the die's functions again, so I suggest you use your wishes wisely.*

Frowning, Arlo looked up from the die. "I suppose you're going to say it's just *the luck of the draw* that I couldn't roll something *higher* than four . . ." It seemed to her a little unfair, that she was only allotted four wishes when she could have just as easily rolled a different number. She could do a lot with four wishes—she could do even *more* with twenty.

Luck's obsidian void eyes glittered with amusement. *In a way. But consider this—things have been coming relatively easily to you, haven't they? You've suffered very little negative blowback from using a device that alters the very fabric of woven fate. Four wishes may seem unfair against fourteen, but all things come at a cost. I wouldn't be so quick to despair of four—your lower number protects you. Now, take up your die.*

Pressing the issue no further, Arlo did as commanded.

She hadn't asked anything of it, but as soon as she touched it, the world around her froze to a halt, draining of its color.

Glittering gold writing scrawled itself in the air before her face—the usual options: Roll, Assist, Escape.

There was a fourth now, though, written beneath the others as simply: Four.

Should you desire to access this ability, there will be no need to roll. Simply reach out and touch the option, and Four will become Three, whatever you've asked for granted. I would caution you to be very specific, though, in what you ask—magic operates in a peculiar precision. Another reason why it's beneficial to have fewer chances to put something into action you may come to regret later. Choose your words wisely.

The writing burst apart and rained to the ground in a shower of sparks. The world thawed out, regaining both life and color. Arlo's die dimmed inactive once more.

"So, you want me to use one of these wishes to learn about what happened to Nausicaä? That seems like a bit of a waste."

Luck chuckled. *No. That's just one of the things I'd like to teach you today. A little less drastically, you can channel your luck to trigger certain events. I did tell you in the Faerie Ring that there are a variety of paths Fate set out for you to walk—choose one, lose the others. The better you get at using this magic, the more you'll be able to scrape together your favored outcome from all those things that could have been.*

Your success, of course, depends on how likely it is for whatever you want to happen to actually occur, and there are all sorts of exciting little benefits should you pull it off: tidbits of information or experiences or even skills that will come in handy later. Triggering events in this way is an exhausting roll—it will take quite a bit of your energy to pull it off. The higher the roll, the greater its toll, and Fate won't make it easy for you to best her, so be careful how you use this, too. And keep in mind: just as with your wishes, doing this might force certain other things to happen that you might not like.

But you want to know about Nausicaä's past? An innocent enough event. There are people here who could tell you. Roll your die. Ask it to lead you to one of them.

This was . . . Fine, so Arlo was a little more interested in this lesson than she'd originally anticipated. She scrambled from her bed to her feet, her die still in hand. She felt a *little* guilty about using magic to help her learn something she wasn't entirely certain Nausicaä wanted her to know, but this was important. The inciting force behind Nausicaä's greatest crime—eleven *murders* that broke her laws and struck her from the Immortal Realm—she had to know, had Nausicaä done what she'd done for a reason, like Arlo believed, or had it been in cold-blooded arrogance, like what everyone else she'd encountered so far seemed to be convinced of?

"Lead me to someone who can and *will* tell me what really happened to expel Nausicaä from the Immortal Realm."

There, that had to be specific enough.

The world froze over.

Her options scrawled themselves in the air, each occupying their space like points on a compass, and in the center: the golden number fourteen.

Moderate difficulty.

"Roll," she called out, and the option she'd selected was the first to shatter into dust. When the world rejoined with time, she tossed her die into the air and caught it as it fell, and in her palm was revealed exactly the number she needed. "Now what?"

Nothing had happened.

She'd rolled the right number, but everything remained as quiet and *uneventful* as before.

Now we follow.

Before she could ask what they meant, Luck hopped down from the bed, and it was then that Arlo noticed the glittering powder that had written out her die's options had lingered beyond the timestop. It trailed from Arlo's bed to her door like a patch of golden clovers: a path for her to follow. "Can anyone see this, or just us?"

Only us. Now come along, this path will not stay clear for long. You don't want to suffer this particular kickback for nothing.

Arlo recalled their first hunt in the woods, what it had felt like to fail at a significant roll, the hint of fatigue she *always* felt after using her die in general—would her kickback from something like *this* feel similar or worse?

Regardless, Arlo nodded and slid herself off her bed after Luck.

The clover path led out into the hall, down the corridor, and into the elevator, stamping itself on the ground-floor button. Arlo pressed it, and they made their descent without any interference. Out the elevator, down another corridor; the clovers brought Arlo to a part of the palace she hadn't been to yet, one that existed open to the elements, with a wide arena that looked like it was used for physical combat training.

The path carried on past it and dipped into a room just beyond. Arlo practically jogged the distance to it, but slammed to a halt on its threshold as the clover path dissipated.

There, in the room, was someone she'd never met before—a *mer*. He was gorgeous, shell brown and sea-foam-green-haired, his features toned down under a loosely maintained glamour. Having just encountered a number of his kind only days ago, she could see hints of who he really was in his overall build, driftwood-warped enough to suggest that his magic smoothed out his peculiar boniness, that his ears were shaped like elegant fins and his eyes were a little wider than what was normal if he were actually the human he was masquerading as.

"Hello," she greeted, remembering herself. The way she'd appeared out of nowhere only to stare at him was rude enough on its own, even if it hadn't also startled this unknown mer. "Um . . . I'm Arlo."

The mer stared at her for a moment longer. Something like recognition flickered over his face, to be swallowed up by rigid poise. He nodded to her in returned greeting but didn't give his name.

She took in his attire: a loose white tunic tucked into pale clay trousers, bracers and shin pads strapped to his arms and legs, and leather gloves on his hands. He'd been in the middle of choosing a weapon. . . . Had she interrupted preparation for practice?

Focus, she scolded. "Um, this is going to sound . . . like a weird question but, do you know a Nausicaä Kraken?"

Again the mer simply stared at her. He looked down at Luck, who'd seated themself beside Arlo and had proceeded to clean their ears with their paw. He looked back up at Arlo and shook his head.

Well, that didn't mean he didn't know her. A lot of people, she was learning, didn't know Nausicaä's name beyond her infamous title. "What about the Dark Star?"

Success—the mer's brows twitched a little higher on his forehead.

He signed something to her.

Magic made it so easy for the folk to pick up languages, to translate the ones they couldn't speak. Arlo's wasn't nearly strong enough for that, but thankfully, she had Luck.

I know the Dark Star, said the mer, with Luck translating in her head. *Are you in trouble? Is she here?*

Arlo shook her head. "No, it's not that. I was just wondering if you knew about her. About what happened to her? The reason she got expelled from the Immortal Realm."

The mer's brows furrowed now, clearly confused by the question.

I don't know what you mean. The Dark Star is an immortal?

Damn it, this wasn't who she needed to talk to.

Had she not been specific enough? Had she done something wrong? The path had certainly led her to this room specifically. The mer began to sign further to her, but whatever he'd been trying to say, he cut himself abruptly off to stand at stiff attention.

Someone had come up just behind Arlo without her noticing. A shadow spilled over her, along with radiance that could only belong to one and the telltale wintry aura to match, which informed her this new arrival was none other than Riadne Lysterne.

Arlo turned on her heel. "Your Majesty!"

The queen stared long and hard at the mer inside the weapons room, as though he'd done something wrong. But the look quickly melted into a gentler expression, and her attention shifted to Arlo. "Arlo—by all means, the palace is yours entirely to explore, but I'm surprised to find you out here. Is everything all right? You look a little flustered. If Commander Zale has done something to upset you . . ."

Recovering from her own surprise over the queen's arrival from seemingly nowhere, Arlo shook her head. "No! No, nothing like that, Your Majesty. I was . . . well, looking for someone to talk to about something, and Commander Zale was the first person I came across."

"Indeed? Whatever did you want to know that took you to my training grounds?"

There was a peculiar quality to the way the queen spoke. It was just as gentle and pleasant as always, but there was an edge behind it, not quite threatening, but coupled with the way she'd practically glared down the Commander, Arlo wondered if she was unhappy about something.

And maybe it wasn't Commander Zale that her die meant her to speak to.

"Um, Your Majesty?" Arlo ventured with only the slightest hesitation. "Do you mind if I ask . . . Do you know the Dark Star? Nausicaä, I mean. I was wondering if there might be someone here who knew the truth about what caused her to be expelled from her . . . original home."

"The Immortal Realm, you mean."

Ah, so she *did* know, at least more than Commander Zale. Perhaps Arlo was on the right track after all.

Queen Riadne stepped easily past her into the chamber. She strode purposefully over to the wall, where a rack of swords had been strung, gleaming in the sliver of a window that ran clear around the room like trimming. She passed by Commander Zale on her way, who drew even stiffer for her proximity, and only because it had been so stark against the tang of silver and steel did Arlo pick up on the sour turn to his brine-drenched aura.

Fear.

Why was the Commander so afraid?

Was it of Riadne? But why should he feel such fear for his own queen?

"Do you practice, Arlo?"

It took a moment for Arlo to understand what she meant. "With swords? No, I've never. Celadon—I mean, the High Prince was trained, but not me. I don't live in the palace."

Riadne took her time perusing the wall.

Commander Zale's tension only built.

At last, she selected her weapon: a small blade, long and narrow and white as starlight from pommel to point. When she turned, the Commander flinched, and the queen didn't miss it—neither did she miss that Arlo caught it, too. "Would you like to learn? I would be happy to show you, and this one I think will suit you perfectly. Come, take it, let me see if I've chosen correctly."

Arlo had the distinct impression that she couldn't refuse even if she wanted to.

The sword was light, she discovered upon taking it from the queen's outstretched hand. Lighter than Arlo had been anticipating, almost as though it had been forged out of foil.

"Yes, that does seem the right fit for you."

Arlo held it up for a closer inspection. "It's . . . very nice."

"Consider it yours."

"Oh!" she exclaimed. "That's—you don't—"

"I insist." The queen smiled congenially at her, and turned to select another blade from the wall with far less consideration. The matter was settled.

As soon as she was armed, Riadne made for the door. She paused only to frown down at Luck in passing. Whatever she made of Arlo's "pet," it was clear she had no love for cats *or* the phooka she probably mistook Luck to be as everyone else did.

Riadne continued on, and with a glance to Commander Zale, who looked a little sickly pale and refused to meet her gaze in return, Arlo followed with building trepidation out to the arena.

It wasn't *forbidden*, was it? To ask about Nausicaä's past?

It would be ridiculous if that were so, but there had to be *some* reason why the Commander was so afraid, and why Riadne was acting . . . well, not strange, exactly, but something was off.

She remembered Luck's warning. Doing this might force certain other things to happen that you might not like.

But what could she be forcing with such a simple question?

It was bright daylight out in the training grounds. The arena was a simple circle of cleared earth marked by a perimeter of wooden fence. Riadne made for its center in long strides, the dry dirt crunching under the heel of her boots. Neither of them was dressed appropriately for this, but the queen didn't seem bothered in the least by their apparel when she turned to face Arlo.

"You wish to know the truth about your friend. I understand that desire. Where there is truth, so is there trust—a crucial element to *any* relationship." She fell to the ready, drawing her sword between them almost as effortlessly and elegantly as Nausicaä wielded her own blades. "We'll begin with your stance—do as I do, and I'll assess your posture and correct where needed."

Arlo complied.

She studied the queen as she tried to mimic exactly what she was doing. Once she was in position, Riadne rose to circle her slowly. "Very good—a little firmer here, a little less tension *here*." She placed her hand on Arlo's shoulder, a featherlight touch, but it sparked *almost* uncomfortably against her magic. "Nausicaä Kraken—I was a younger woman when she was cast from the Immortal Realm. None of us were told any particulars. Any who knew more than they should were wise to keep their suspicions to themselves, lest they attract unwanted attention both from the Dark Star and the immortals who spurned her."

"So *no one* knows what really happened?" Arlo asked, watching closely. Riadne made one final adjustment to her stance before moving back to the center of the ring.

"Oh, give me a little more credit than that." Riadne grinned. She settled back at the ready, flicking her sword upright once more. "I do not look it, but I'm only a few years younger than your great uncle. I know many things I should not. Now, I wish for you to come at me, attack me any way you know—let me judge where best to begin next with your instruction."

Only because the entire magical community knew how lethal Riadne Lysterne was with a sword did Arlo comply without hesitation—that, and because a quality had crept into Riadne's voice too alluring to ignore.

Arlo swung her sword.

The queen caught it in a single snap of her wrist and deflected it to the floor.

"My understanding is that Nausicaä learned a truth that did not agree with her. *Several*, in fact, that peeled away the rosy tint to her life like paint over rotting wood. Again," she commanded, and Arlo swung her sword again, a little more forcefully, almost as though the sword acted on its own.

She stumbled when the queen sidestepped the blow, but Riadne spun her about face with a simple tug to her upper arm.

"Trust was betrayed. One of Nausicaä's sisters died. The mortal seen as responsible for this was one of the eleven your friend extinguished. Nausicaä exacted a revenge against him that made her *legend*. Whatever other deeds to her name, I will tell you, I never once begrudged her what she did. I, too, take betrayal *deeply* to heart— betrayal, and lack of trust."

At the word, she touched the tip of her sword against Arlo's chest, where *her* heart lay just beneath.

"I hope you will soon confide in me, darling, what it is that makes you so special. Now, have I answered your question?"

Arlo swallowed—winced against how suddenly bright the halo-glow of Riadne's radiance flared around her, not warm and pure as Vehan's was but *harsh*, like a glint of direct sunlight off polished metal.

She nodded, even though Riadne hadn't. Not really. In fact, most of what Riadne had told her had been a riddle, a vehicle for something else that felt a bit . . . like a *threat*. And then there was the actual threat of Riadne prodding at the secrets Arlo kept about her abilities that, for some reason, she just couldn't bring herself to share yet, even though Riadne probably deserved to know for all she'd done so far to help Arlo. But still Arlo nodded, because it was clear that the queen expected her to, and she didn't want to disappoint—she'd made a misstep, displeased the queen, that much was obvious. Arlo *was* sorry she couldn't share yet the full extent of what she could do. After all her kindness to Arlo, displeasing Riadne was the last thing she wanted to do.

The glaring light subsided just as quickly as it came.

The queen's sword-point fell away.

Arlo didn't know why she was breathing so heavily. They hadn't done much at all, but Riadne dissolved into delicate laughter, and like a storm clearing from the sky, settled into a calmer demeanor. "I'm impressed, Arlo! You're a natural. Perhaps we ought to add sword practice to your schedule this summer. If you'd like, my son would be happy to have you join his lessons. Please do come again!"

What did we learn? Luck asked later, when Arlo had been freed to return to her room.

Back on her bed, extremely sore and beginning to feel the leaden exhaustion that was the toll of what she'd done, Arlo heaved a sigh. "Well, I know one thing for sure: Vehan's mother? Kind of intense."

You should spend a day in the Immortal Realm if you want to see true intensity.

"No, thanks. I don't think I'd survive."

CHAPTER 27

Aurelian

~~~~~

AURELIAN DIDN'T REALIZE HOW terrible he was at distancing himself from Vehan until *Vehan* was the one distancing himself from *him*. Wonderful news for his genius plan to smother the affection that had fanned itself into far too big a flame between them, to make Aurelian a less attractive pawn on Riadne's deadly chessboard and keep the prince out of his mother's grasp for just a little longer.

Less wonderful news for the treacherous, closely guarded fact that Aurelian didn't *want* the bond between them broken, not even a little.

But Vehan was *angry* with him—something made abundantly clear after their excursion to the Colosseum. And a little rich, if Aurelian was being honest; even if the rumors about him and the High Prince *were* true, Theodore had been brought here expressly and very publicly as Riadne's favored suitor for her son. There was nothing official yet, and it was just as well-known that the Solstice would be any other hopeful partner's last shot at winning the prince's hand, but Theodore wanted . . . well, he wanted whatever he'd come here to do. What's more, Vehan actually *liked* him, and Aurelian couldn't ignore how gods-damned *well* they fit together, even if much of Theodore's persona was an act designed to help him burrow deep into the Lysterne household.

Theo would be an excellent husband to Vehan if he was even half of what he pretended, and probably an even better ruler of this Court. And worst of all (if only to Aurelian's pride), Theodore would be a much better protector at Vehan's side, wealthy and powerful and well-connected.

Aurelian was *jealous*. There, he tried his best to keep from admitting that, but in the spirit of all this honesty, Aurelian had been the one in love with Vehan for as long as they'd known each other, the one who'd stood by his side and did his *everything* to keep him safe—at great personal cost to himself, he might add—and he was jealous.

Yes, he'd intended to use the rumor of him and Celadon to his "advantage" to help him push Vehan away, but it was *working*, and Aurelian didn't . . . he didn't *like* that it was working. That here was Vehan, pairing off with Theodore for every dance lesson now. Seeking *him* out to study with Arlo in the library. Whisking *him* away for the excursions that Aurelian normally accompanied him on, and it had been Celadon in that deities-damned cage the other night, but still Aurelian's biggest concern had been Vehan and how he was much too happy to trot after Theodore into Grim territory, shaking off Aurelian's attempts to protect him like unwanted advances. And Aurelian couldn't even say what upset Vehan the most about the rumors that definitely contributed to this severe fracture in their friendship, the ones about him and Celadon; he couldn't say which one of them Vehan was actually jealous of: his first crush or his oldest friend.

And now Vehan and Theodore were off with each other again, some training exercise Theo had come up with in an attempt to help Vehan push past whatever was blocking his magic, and once again, Aurelian hadn't been invited.

He was *trying* not to take it personally—"I'm not competing with you for his affection, Aurelian. I just . . . think today will go better if you're not around to put him on his guard," Theo had said to him in an aside before whisking Vehan away on their adventure. He was trying, but it was difficult. Aurelian hadn't said anything to Theo's statement because he couldn't outright lie and say he wasn't concerned, that he didn't care. Anything else would be confirmation that Aurelian viewed himself as a competitor, and he *couldn't*.

But it was *frustrating*.

And all this pretense, all these twists of truth and painstaking maneuvers just to keep afloat in this *awful* place, today Aurelian couldn't deal with any of it.

Today, he was tired, and so it was in a noticeable mood that he stormed through the palace for the one place here that made him feel like he could *breathe.*

Aurelian pushed open the door to the Bessel family wing so forcefully that it cracked against the wall.

"*Fuck* off."

"Harlan!"

"He made me squish a cake!"

The door opened immediately into a large, white-tiled room outfitted with the highest-end gleaming copper appliances. It was as familiar a sight to Aurelian as the scene around the Bessel kitchen's central island. His mother and father, Nerilla and Matthias, were busy at work preparing tonight's royal dessert, his younger brother, Harlan, beside them, engrossed in a project of his own.

Nerilla Bessel was a shapely, diminutive lesidhe fae woman with a smile that lit up her entire face and a frown that made her more formidable than the sea. Under glamour she had thick ebony hair, fair-tanned skin, and molten gold eyes framed by thick, long lashes and strong features. Her husband, Matthias, was much taller and only slightly paler, his hair a softer shade of brown and lesidhe gold eyes more the color of champagne.

In stature, Harlan resembled their mother, but his eyes and hair were like their father's. It was the opposite for Aurelian, who took after their father's hair and height, his sharper build, but had their mother's eyes. They *looked* like a family, even if Aurelian had dyed out most of the brown from his hair in favor of purple, pierced his ears with poisonous metal, and tattooed the autumn leaves of his *true* Court up and down his arm and hand—even if he refused to don the lighter colors of Seelie Summer when he could help it, like the white linen dress his mother wore; the white linen pants and butter-yellow shirt worn by his father; the painted-on, high-rise, dark copper jeans and airy, ivory tank his brother currently sported.

They bickered like a family, too.

"Any particular reason for the dramatics, son?" asked Matthias, shooting Harlan a look that said very clearly *don't argue with your mother*.

Aurelian didn't answer.

Not that he disdained the question, or his father, but because there was a fourth at the counter on Harlan's opposite side, smiling back at Aurelian as pleasantly as though his being here were completely ordinary and something Aurelian should have anticipated.

Aurelian's mother, a shrewd woman, looked between her eldest son and Celadon Fleur-Viridian like she'd tackle the High Prince right out of this kitchen if Aurelian gave her any indication that he genuinely didn't want him here. And that was all it took for Aurelian's mood to soften, for him to remember it *wasn't* only him against the world, as it often felt.

His family had no idea how entwined he'd become in Riadne's plots, and he was going to keep it that way if it killed him, but it was nice . . . to feel for a moment like he was *safe*, an ordinary eighteen-year-old boy, and here under the normalcy and protection of his mother and father was the only place that was possible.

"Sorry," Aurelian apologized, flicking his hand at the door without looking. The crack clear down the middle mended itself in a shower of dancing blue sparks, which winked out of existence as soon as their job was done.

The High Prince . . . he had a smudge of frosting on his cheek, flour on his fingers. In his hands was a plastic pipe filled with fondant for the fairy cakes Harlan had clearly been in the middle of showing him how to decorate. He looked distinctly *human* right now, not at all one of the most powerful fae in the entire Eight Great Courts of Folk. Deep forest-green sweatpants sat low on his narrow hips, and his shirt—a slate-gray printed tee that said "Believe in Yourself" alongside a red, shark-like video-game character Aurelian only vaguely recognized—stretched tight across a chest he could tell even from here was well-toned.

Every fae fashion magazine Vehan had showed him, every article and advertisement, every media appearance and poster portrayed an *immaculate* character, a flawless eidolon of fae standards, beautiful down the finest, painstaking detail.

This was not the High Prince.

This was *Celadon—just* Celadon, even more casual than he'd been the night they'd gone to the Colosseum.

"What are you doing here?" Aurelian blurted, his brain slightly reeling and unable to reconcile the sidhe fae monolith with the *boy* in front of him.

Harlan snorted. "You're always so fucking rude," he replied for the High Prince with a shake of his head. It earned him another hiss from their mother and a smack from the wooden spoon she was using to mix batter. "Mom, my shirt!"

"You will *not* use that sort of language in this household, young man!"

"What *house*hold, you hag? This is a *palace*, and it sure as shit isn't *yours*."

Harlan cried out. Nerilla took him by the ear and pinched the cartilage, and the pair of them launched into rapid, heated German. Arguments were the usual fare among three of the four Bessels, particularly between Aurelian's mother and younger brother. Matthias, milder-natured and too used to his family by now, merely shook his head.

The High Prince bit his lip, glancing first at Aurelian's squabbling family with something in his eyes that looked a bit wistful, before turning them on Aurelian. He straightened his posture, put down his pipe, and bowed his head. "Sorry, your brother invited me to down to help. I . . . can't remember the last time my *own* family did something together like this, so I thought it might be fun, but I didn't mean to intrude. I can go."

Matthias leveled Aurelian with a pointed look.

Aurelian sighed. He was going to need a much bigger box for all the small and wounded little birds he was starting to collect. "No," he apologized. "It's fine. I'm the one who's sorry."

Of all the people who could wind up here, the High Prince wasn't the worst Aurelian had to fear. But this was still his space. This was still his family. This still felt a little bit like yielding one of the few things that was still solely *his* to the arrogant, cruel royalty who thought they owned everything simply because they wanted it—royalty which Celadon was included in.

Twisting out of Nerilla's grip, Harlan stumbled back to the island. "Your boyfriend's been *eating* more of the damn things than decorating them anyway," he grumbled to a peel of wind-chime laughter from the High Prince paired with a wince of contrition.

"I apologize for that, too. Also, again, we aren't in any relationship. Your brother is a fine person—*anyone* would be lucky to have him as their partner—but he isn't mine."

Matching the High Prince's laugh with one of his own, Harlan replied, "Don't worry, I never believed it anyhow. Aurelian has a type, and you're nowhere near oblivious enough to qualify."

Was there even a point to pretending he didn't like Vehan? Everyone seemed to know. Everyone but Vehan, so he supposed it wasn't a completely wasted effort.

Ignoring the obvious jibe, Aurelian watched Celadon watch *Harlan* resume his demonstration of the flower he'd been teaching the High Prince to build. Rapt attention tracked each of his brother's movements. The High Prince seemed to have no ulterior motive Aurelian could detect, so heaving a sigh, Aurelian relented and slotted himself into the space between Harlan and his mother, who'd rejoined them now as well.

It was something about the light in Celadon's eyes that made him swallow down what had lingered of his protest. The Viridian Spare, as unkind gossip had labeled the youngest of the High King's children, might not be trapped in this house of horrors like Aurelian was, but there'd been a flicker of vulnerability to what he'd admitted about his family, about how little quality time they spent with one another.

His ailing, dying father . . .

Siblings that had always seemed cold and distant with one another . . .

His Gift and High status separating him from *everyone*, even the cousin he clearly adored . . .

Aurelian was too familiar with loneliness not to recognize it on someone else. He could share his family, he supposed, just this once— for the sake of the fae who'd agreed to play their protector if anything happened to prevent Aurelian doing so himself.

"Bet I can frost more of these cakes than you," Harlan challenged Aurelian, brandishing his pipe at the tray in front of them. He met Aurelian's gaze, eyes gleaming.

Aurelian snorted. "And if you lose?"

"Ha! As if, Space Boy—*I'm* the one taking over the family business. *You* run around playing shadow to a prince and spend your free time reading books about rocket ships. But okay. If I lose, I'll watch *one* Star War with you."

"*Wars*," Aurelian corrected.

Harlan waved his free hand dismissively. "If *you* lose, you have to admit I'm better at baking than you are, and you have to let me film it."

Such innocent stakes.

This was what his life *should* be.

Aurelian swallowed around the sudden lump in his throat and nodded. Harlan cheered. Celadon became their impromptu competition's judge, and before too long, Aurelian had to admit he was actually having fun. He didn't spend much time in the kitchen anymore. His duties as steward in training, as Vehan's retainer, as Riadne's amusement always kept him busy with some thing or another, and he didn't mind learning that the family business had fallen mostly to Harlan now, but this was . . . nice.

Aurelian was happy.

To his left, his mother and father chatted about this and this and that. To his right, Harlan frosted cakes with all the skill of a seasoned professional. Celadon took his time with his own, laughing whenever he fumbled his pipe, or his fondant icing tore, eating more of it than he put on the cakes and grinning to himself whenever he thought no one was looking, quiet little smiles of simple enjoyment.

"Can I talk to you?" Aurelian asked, on the third occasion of glancing over to catch him doing this.

Celadon looked up at him. "Of course?"

"In private."

"Of course," the High Prince repeated, laying down his fondant pipe and straightening to attention.

Harlan glowered. "Forfeiture is still a loss, just so you know," he warned, and Aurelian nodded absently at him.

"Fine, fine."

He hadn't gone into this competition thinking he could win against his brother. Once upon a time, Aurelian had been better at this sort of thing, but this was Harlan's domain now. And as surprisingly pleasant as this was, he and the High Prince hadn't actually been alone together since their skulking around the queen's office a week ago now. There were things, he realized suddenly, that needed to be discussed, and who knew when they'd next get a chance like this to do so.

Aurelian laid his fondant pipe down too. With a jerk of his chin, he motioned for the door at the opposite end of the room, pausing to grab two ginger beers from the fridge before leading Celadon through to his room.

Posters of various planets and stars; human grunge, death, and heavy metal bands; an artfully drawn human periodic table of elements; dark wood furniture and shelves crammed with books on things like human scientific theory, space, and engineering—Aurelian's bedroom possessed little whimsy. Only the shimmery, enchanted wallpaper of an autumnal forest hinted that this space belonged to a member of the magical community.

He didn't care too much that a pair of jeans had been strewn over the back of the chair at his book-cluttered and paper-littered desk, or that his laundry basket was overflowing in the corner where it waited for *him* to wash them (he didn't need to give Riadne's staff an excuse to poke around his room). Aurelian led Celadon through his room and out onto the modest balcony that overlooked a stunning view of the forest and ridge of mountains in the distance.

Once outside in the warm summer's day, he felt himself relax even more. He cracked open one of the ginger beers he'd snagged and passed it to Celadon before opening his own.

"Your face looks better," he commented, motioning to Celadon's jaw. "Has Theodore stopped apologizing to you yet?"

As angry as they'd *all* been at him for what had happened the night of the Colosseum, Aurelian had to admit, Theodore's remorse seemed pretty genuine. He'd been beside himself when Celadon had stepped out into the ring to face off against a faerie man considerably bigger and meaner than him; had instructed Vehan and Aurelian to try to stop the match while he met with the Madam to *renegotiate their deal*, whatever that had meant. But no amount of their pleading with the staff or attempting to get close enough to the cage to even *speak* to Celadon had proved fruitful that night. Theodore hadn't returned (unsuccessful and sporting a nasty cut on his own face he refused to explain to them) until the very end of things, when Celadon had been whisked away by someone even *more* dangerous than anyone who'd entered that arena—possibly ever.

What Lethe had hoped to get out of playing the High Prince's rescuer, Aurelian was willing to bet it was nothing good. Celadon had been too confused, and probably a bit concussed, to illuminate that mystery for them, so mostly since finding him in the alley and every day since, it was Theodore following him around the palace, attempting (much to Celadon's building irritation) to do anything and everything for him in penance.

"I wish he would." The High Prince frowned. "I healed up days ago and now have lifetime boasting rights as Champion of the Colosseum. Sort of." He paused as though he didn't want that title any more than he wanted Theodore rushing over to fluff his pillows if he'd been sitting in one place for too long.

Aurelian got it.

He owed the Madam a favor himself, from a life that felt like someone else's now, and she could collect on it whenever she chose. The question was on his tongue—has she paid you a visit yet? But before he could ask it . . .

"Arlo had to force me to try this when we were little." Celadon added, pointedly changing the subject and peering down at the label of his drink. "She went through a stint when she was about ten where the only thing she wanted to drink was this."

"You and your cousin are close."

It wasn't a query. It wasn't a profound statement, either—everyone knew the High Prince and his ironborn younger cousin were better siblings than the ones he'd been born with. Inseparable. Arlo featured in many of the Celadom fan club posts, and if topics of conversation were scarce, if some of the members were feeling particularly aggrieved about something, those posts could get . . . a little unkind. Accusatory, that the reason none of their favorite High Prince's romantic relationships lasted was because of her interference; that the reason Celadon didn't seem to care much for those relationships to begin with was because of what they dubbed his "incestuous fixation."

A royal sidhe fae of high pedigree, they sneered in those sour moments, he wouldn't be the first to want to "keep it in the family."

"She's my best friend," the High Prince replied, expression instantly guarded. "We've spent our entire lives together. You have *your* people you want to protect. I have mine, and Arlo . . ." He frowned.

"I wasn't judging," Aurelian replied when it was evident the thought wasn't going to finish out loud. "It's good she has you."

"And that your brother has you."

Well, he didn't know about that. Aurelian would do *anything* for

Harlan, so he understood the sentiment. And the folk weren't nearly as fussed about gender and sexuality as their human counterparts were, so when Harlan came out as transgender and transitioned a few years back, he hadn't been met with any backlash from the people who'd known him before. Aurelian was still protective, but Harlan took *every* opportunity to prove he'd never needed him to be. Honestly, between the two of them, it was Harlan who would have fared better against Riadne—he wouldn't live long, as Harlan had a tongue on him that would get him offed pretty quickly the very second he used it against the queen, but he'd at least make a decent go of bringing her down with him.

"We should—"

"Listen," Celadon interrupted, turning to face him and leaning sideways against the stone rail that ran the perimeter of the balcony. "I really should apologize to you. I didn't think my actions through, and it's caused some upheaval in your life. For that I *am* sorry. But just so we're clear, so that there aren't any hurt feelings between us, so that we can continue our productive working relationship—"

"I never thought you meant anything by it," Aurelian interrupted right back. "I just haven't said anything because it isn't anyone's business."

The High Prince drew a breath, released it slowly through his nose, and as he did, eased back into a smile. "All right. Again, I just wanted to be clear."

"We are friends, though, right?"

Celadon looked at him.

"You and I," Aurelian clarified, nodding at him. "We're friends? We should be. Between all the people we're looking out for—my parents, Harlan, Vehan, Arlo, *your* family—it would be nice to have someone looking out for *us*, wouldn't it? We could have each other's backs, already sort of do with our agreement and all. And you aren't terrible."

"A glowing review." The High Prince chuckled. Turning to look out now across the scenery, he lifted his bottle to his mouth and took a delicate sip. "I don't really have any friends other than Arlo," he added, more in thoughtful bemusement than anything, but there was that hint of wistfulness Aurelian had picked up on earlier. "I *could* be terrible at friendship."

Aurelian snorted into his bottle. He raised a brow, glancing sideways. "Do I strike you as the sort of person who's good at it myself?"

"True." Celadon cheersed him. "So, friends, then?"

"If you'd like." They could both use with one.

"Then as my first act of camaraderie, would you allow me to overstep polite boundaries to be blunt with you on something?"

His brow rose a little higher in question, but Aurelian nodded nonetheless.

"In my experience, which has been very limited, I'll admit, *love* has never been a *weakness*." His gaze had wandered back to Aurelian now, and it was *piercingly* bright. "I won't pretend to know the specifics, but I can tell from our brief interactions that there's a wall you've placed between you and your prince. A wall you put there perhaps because of Riadne, and if that's true—if you think holding yourself back from Vehan will keep either of you safe—remember that this is assuredly what she wants. The two of you, separated. Her many other machinations aside, neither of you pose much of a threat to her apart. *Together*, though . . ." He indicated the air between them, their own newly deepened relationship as example. "Like I said, love has never been a weakness."

I've done my best to keep him lonely, to keep him starved for hope and affection . . .

I brought you here to break him.

I brought you here to die.

Riadne's words rang sharp in his head. Oh, apart *was* what the queen wanted, but only after the love Aurelian and Vehan felt for each other built them up like a stack of cards for her to light on fire and watch in vicious triumph as they rained to the ground as ash.

"Love is exactly why I've done it. It might not be a weakness, but I *won't* let it be our downfall."

"Yet here you are, and where is he? Out *there* somewhere, with someone else, as I understand, and you can't do a thing to protect him if something happened. But ah, you'd still *feel* it. Any less, for all this pretend?" Celadon raised a brow on his point. "No. He'd feel it too, if something happened to *you*, and the destruction you tried to prevent would still devastate. Maybe all this energy would be better spent on a united front than an unnecessary war against the wrong person. Something to think about, one friend to another," he ended, too lightly for all the intention behind his gaze. "Now, since we're alone right now, I think it's time to discuss breaking into that secret vault in Riadne's office. I could do it, provided a certain *someone* could buy me some time during the day? A little distraction, perhaps, that would pull Riadne away from that floor . . ." He waggled his brows at Aurelian, and it was abundantly clear that the *certain someone* was meant to be *him*.

Aurelian groaned, because yes, Riadne and the secret chamber in her office were exactly what he'd wanted to talk to Celadon about when he asked him to follow him out here. If they were going to investigate it before the Solstice, they'd have to act quickly. Celadon's plan was reasonable enough, but playing the role of bait for an extremely dangerous and volatile queen . . .

"Oh, come on, the distraction's the easy part—and half the job will be done for you, because our best shot at pulling this off will be when the guests start arriving for the Solstice. Thoughts?"

Oh, Aurelian had many.

Loudest was that this was going to be the longest summer of his entire life—and more and more likely his last one.

CHAPTER 28

Vehan

⟶⌣⟵

THE THUNDER PLAINS—VEHAN RECOGNIZED the place immediately, though he couldn't pinpoint *exactly* where they were in the expansive stretch of prairie, steppe, and grassland humans referred to as the Great Plains. Unfurling like a vibrant, rolling carpet of lush greens and sun-kissed browns, it cut almost directly down the middle of Seelie Summer territory, and despite its lack of forest cover, was a popular draw for the folk of this Court, particularly young fae looking to practice their elemental magic.

"*So*," Vehan drawled. "Here we are . . ." Quirking a brow, he turned his gaze on Theo beside him. Theo hadn't said anything about whatever clever plan he'd come up with for training that day. But he had the queen's permission, and with Arlo still sleeping and no plans for entertainment until later, it wasn't as though Vehan was going to argue with him.

And it was a few hours' excuse to avoid Aurelian without any effort on his part. However much it had thrown Vehan that they weren't bringing *anyone* along today, not even the guards that trailed him in absence of his retainer, he was silently grateful when Theo added that he wanted to do this just the two of them.

"Here we are."

"Are you going to tell me what we're doing here today?"

"You mean you can't guess?" Theo called over his shoulder, stepping forward. "A big old field with no one around and a thunderstorm overhead, and you need me to *tell* you what we're getting up to? Gosh. Maybe I was wrong about you. You're going to be a shit king—your Court will eat you alive."

Rolling his eyes, Vehan followed after his friend. The Egress's shimmery impression lingered in the air and would remain there until they were finished with their lesson to portal them back home. As requested, none of the guards standing sentry on the palace side had accompanied them through, but Vehan knew they'd be quick to their aid should any significant danger present itself to the two Summer princes. "I can hazard a guess," Vehan returned, with just as much attitude. "Except, see, I'm thinking you want to try the whole summon-lightning thing again, but A—we're not at all supposed to do that without supervision, and B—that would work a lot better if I could summon *any* sort of electricity. Unless you brought me along so *you* could practice and have someone to show off in front of, in which case go off I guess, but I'm definitely going to laugh if you fry yourself and not help you one bit."

"Ever the supportive husband."

"I try."

They ascended a small hill, the tall grass that blanketed it rippling like verdant waves in the wind. Everything was so green in this patch of the Plains thanks to the late spring Season that would soon tip into early summer, but ominous cloud cover overhead lent a dark slate tone to the world. Yes, Vehan could feel it—the storm brewing in the air. His magic might not be fully operational, but it was *somewhere* inside him, and he felt the energy of his element fizzle like gentle, inquisitive sparks against it, as though trying to nudge it to life.

Just as they reached the top of the hill, a faint *boom* echoed from the distance. Theo turned to him. "I've been wondering something ever since the night Arlo and His Highness arrived. At dinner, the shocks you'd been complaining about, they were coming from that waterfall, I'm *sure* of it—and you've been having troubles with your magic since before our lesson on the mountain, right?"

Vehan shrugged. "A bit. I noticed something was off with it after coming back home from Hieronymus's lab. Nothing *too* concerning at the time—my magic just wasn't as strong as it normally was, and it felt like I had to reach a bit deeper than usual to access it."

"Mm-hmm," hummed Theo, nodding along. "Then, after the mountain, it stopped working for you altogether. Also, you've been having headaches, and your chest has been hurting."

"I . . ." Vehan narrowed his eyes in suspicion. "Nice to hear you and Aurelian have been chatting."

There was only one place where Theo could have gathered this information, because Vehan didn't talk about the extent of what had been ailing him lately to just anyone—Aurelian, and only Aurelian, in fact, after the Head MediFae had been so convinced that all that was wrong with Vehan was fatigue.

"I feel like you'd know this if you weren't skirting around trying to avoid chatting with him *yourself*, but we'll come back to that in a moment. Headaches, your magic won't respond to you, and that *scar*—I'm *wondering* if it's more than just a case of you being low on fuel and needing rest to recharge. It was only recently that you encountered a very stressful event back in that lab, and between your Maturity kicking off the expansion of your core and the potential you've undoubtedly inherited from your mother, a Class *Four* elemental, what if what's going on is somehow tied to your array? What if it's draining you, siphoning magic in some way, and your body just can't keep up on its own?"

This was exactly what Vehan had been wondering himself, exactly why he'd asked Arlo to help him attempt to dissolve his array. But while he liked Theodore and considered him a very close friend, he still wasn't sure how much he should let him in on—namely, the full extent of what this array was.

"You think we should try to summon lightning again for me to absorb?"

"That thing on your chest? I'm not stupid, Vehan, even if you won't talk to me about it. It's dark magic, and I suspect it's leeching off your electric core. So, yes, I *do* think we should supercharge it with lightning. See what happens if we give it what it wants."

"Uh-*huh*."

It wasn't a terrible idea—if all he needed was to refill his well to get himself to a point where he could fight this, and someone to help him do that . . .

Well, it was a *spectacularly* terrible idea if something went wrong. Vehan now knew why they hadn't brought anyone along, especially Aurelian, who would have had a *lot* to say to Theo for even suggesting this course of action.

Vehan turned his contemplation skyward. Rain had begun to fall now in scattered, fat droplets. Thunder beat another *boom* at an even closer distance. It wouldn't be long before the storm reached them, and the charge of it in the air, it excited Vehan, made him *itch* to touch it, just as it had back on the mountain. "There's a very high chance one or both of us could die if we get this wrong," he reminded his friend somewhat absently.

Folding his hands in front of him, eyes dark for the itch *he* undoubtedly felt as well, Theo grinned. "You know what they say: nothing ventured is nothing gained."

"I'm trying to decide whether this is the world's *worst* assassination attempt or its boldest."

"Darling." Theo chuckled, something very real and sharp in the way he did so, like what Vehan had just said was more than amusing. "Trust me, if I ever decide you have to die, I promise you won't see it coming. So we're doing this, yes?"

"Oh, we're doing this." He dropped his gaze back to his friend, a grin of his own curling at the corner of his mouth.

A *flash*—lightning crackled in the clouds.

Vehan shook out his arms to try to dispense of a little adrenaline.

Theo did as well. "Good." He nodded, then moved to position himself directly in front of Vehan. "All right, game plan: I'm going to pull down just a *bit* of electricity and attempt to direct it at you. All you have to do is stand there and look pretty and do what you do best—"

"If you say *catch*—"

"Hush, bottom, and come over here."

Shooting Theo his finger, Vehan nevertheless followed his instruction, allowing his friend to guide him into place by the shoulders.

Once arranged, the two of them stood facing each other in the steadily increasing rain, the white shirts and loose brown pants standard for their training sessions beginning to stick to their bodies. Theo raised a hand into the air.

"Are you ready?" he asked.

And Vehan smirked in reply. "Bring it down, Reynolds."

Theo closed his eyes.

Thunder rumbled across the plains—so very close to them now. There was another flash, and like grabbing hold of it, Theo's fingers curled into a fist. Vehan watched his face closely for any sign of discomfort or struggle, but just as on the mountain, Theo seemed perfectly calm, well in control of the situation and focused on nothing but the energy he was reaching out to. Like a phantom touch, Vehan could almost feel it reaching back, the memory of weeks ago when he'd been in Theo's position flooding back to him with a crooning sort of longing.

His core was so dangerously low on magic—he'd been running on fumes this whole time. If their suspicions were correct, his array was beginning to drain more from him as his well of power deepened and as more stones were successfully made. He'd been lucky that he hadn't bottomed out completely and gone into Stasis—a coma of sorts that most never woke from—but he couldn't think about that right now. There was no room for hesitation here or distraction.

It was the very next flash that caught.

A *crack* rent the air, and Theo pulled down, not quickly or harshly but with concise elegance, as though he'd been doing this his entire life instead of only having learned this skill less than a month ago.

Theodore Reynolds . . . Not for the first time, Vehan was glad to have him on his side rather than against it.

A thread of white-hot electricity unraveled from the clouds. They hadn't had a chance yet to practice doing this with their tutors— diverting the power they drew from the heavens to some other source—but Theo made it look as easy as breathing. The whisper-thin fissure of lightning descended, and Theo swept it out toward Vehan, who raised his hands to catch it.

It had been a long time since Vehan had touched electricity too powerful for him, but in his current state, he was much more sensitive to it. In such a modest amount, this lightning still felt hot but not unbearable through gritted teeth and years of training under his mother to steady him. It was sparking-sharp, but nowhere near painful enough to make him want to abandon his first hope of being whole again in quite a while. As soon as it touched his outstretched hands, it sank into his skin and traveled up the veins of his arms, dispersing out across his body.

"How do you feel?" Theo asked, opening his eyes.

A good question.

He felt . . . better? Perhaps? Not a whole lot different, but he didn't feel worse. "More, I think. Can you do another—a little bit bigger this time?"

"I suppose," Theo drawled, as though Vehan didn't know full well he was keen for another go, that the electric charge felt good to him, too.

He repeated the process, grabbing hold of another flash and passing it off to Vehan.

And again.

And again.

Each time the bolts hurt less than the last. It was the fourth attempt that finally took, and just in time. Theo was starting to sweat, his breathing a little erratic. His own magic was growing tired, and Vehan appreciated the sacrifice of his energy, because at long last, *heat* erupted from his core. It poured through him, static-charged and humming, and Vehan saw himself grow brighter, the Seelie Summer Gift of radiance that marked him a viable heir to the throne flaring blindingly bright in the flex of his power before settling back into a modest glow to match Theo's.

Amazing how quickly he had forgotten just how *good* it felt to be running on full. He only now realized how muzzy, disoriented, and ill he'd been now that he was so suddenly *better*.

Good boy.

That voice, a deep purr in the back of his mind, where had it—

"*There* you are," Theo teased, low and rich in the back of his throat.

Eyes glittering with intensity, Theodore swept out his arms, slashing them through the air at his sides. As he did, in his hands formed twin daggers of pure white electric magic, their wicked-long blades humming as he spun them to arm himself at the ready.

An unspoken challenge.

Vehan accepted—it was the only way to test if he was truly back to normal, after all, and he and Theo were well matched when it came to sparring with their weapons. He'd have to save his worrying over voices in his head for later.

He swept out *his* right arm, and for the first time in what felt like ages, his own weapon answered his call. A beautiful sword, its blade was long enough to score the earth with its burning hot point.

"First to pin?"

"First to pin," he agreed, and it was all the permission Theo needed to lunge at him quicker than a shot.

Vehan only just in time deflected the dagger that came at him from above, shifting next to catch the one that aimed up from below.

"Nice to see you haven't lost your edge."

"It's only been a few weeks, you know," Vehan retorted.

"Ah," said Theo, whirling in a graceful arc to swing a dagger at Vehan's face. "But a lot can happen in just a *few weeks*."

They should be wearing protective gear for this. Vehan only just narrowly dodged the bite of that blade, but what was a few cuts between future husbands? Plus, fae could heal their minor wounds with as little as a thought.

Besides, his mother preferred when Vehan *didn't* wear the enchanted gear when sparring against his peers—*You might as well not even bother if you're so convinced you'll lose*, she'd said to him the first time he and Theo had ever fought in front of her audience, and he hadn't worn it since, much to Aurelian's *profound* disapproval.

Vehan pressed the advance he'd won by deflecting another blow.

"In just a few weeks, we've gained two guests."

Theo spun deftly to the side that Vehan hadn't been guarding. Too quick to block, and apparently toying with him, Theo might have been able to disarm him and pin him right there, but he settled for a swipe that sliced a fine line right through Vehan's shirt and skin beneath.

With a hiss, Vehan flinched away.

"In just a few weeks, you came so close to Rebounding that I had to seek out our resident alchemist and, in the alarmingly disagreeable company of Councillor Sylvain, ask in very roundabout terms whether what I suspected about your brand was true."

Oh, so he *had* done his research properly.

Theo lunged once more, this time from behind, once again too quick for Vehan—they were well matched with their swordsmanship, but this wasn't the first time Vehan had suspected the Reynolds line had UnSeelie Spring blood in it for how swift he was. He caught Vehan around the throat, and it was all Vehan could do to twist himself free, but Theo had left him an opening.

Press every advantage—that's what his mother had taught him during the hours she personally spent on his training, those occasions so rare Vehan was always happy to comply with whatever she wanted of him in exchange, even when those hours wore from dawn to dusk; through rain and snow and dizzying heat; through a faerie flu that had *ripped* through their Court, and Vehan had been so ill that he'd thrown up several times between rounds and actually passed out once, but *press every advantage, and learn how to push through any ordeal.*

Vehan hooked his foot around Theo's ankle as he wrenched himself out of his arm and jerked it hard.

Theo stumbled sideways, let go of Vehan, but he didn't fall.

"Bitch," Theo huffed, to the reply of Vehan's laughed. "But that brings us to our final point." He straightened, stretched, cracked his neck, and fell to his ready stance once more. "The other thing that's happened in just a few weeks."

He kissed the air, insinuation clear.

Vehan frowned.

"You've been very *pissy* lately, you know. And at someone who probably *least* deserves your little tantrum."

It was a series of swipes, jabs, and slices that flew at Vehan next.

He caught every one, the buzzing clash of their electric weapons drowned out by the storm that had drifted fully to them now, the rain picking up like a torrent.

Swing—"They didn't kiss, you know. It's just gossip."

Block, *thrust.*

Dodge, strike—"And even if they had, you don't own that pretty retainer of yours. You aren't in a relationship. Aurelian can kiss whomever he likes."

"I *know*," Vehan growled, matching the cut to his side with a nick to Theo's arm, and something in him stirred.

AngerJealousyViolenceHurt—that darkness that wasn't him, that made him feel too many things he didn't like, shifted inside him. He could feel it spread itself like a shadow over his heart, and if he didn't get a grip on it soon . . .

He knew he was being unfair to Aurelian. Just as Theo said, it wasn't up to him who Aurelian kissed or liked or *didn't* like. Even if it had actually happened, even if Aurelian and High Prince Celadon were an item now, it shouldn't matter to Vehan, but it did. It *did*, damn it. He'd been in love with Aurelian for so long, and he'd messed that up somehow. He *adored* his friend, but among the many things Aurelian resented him for, the dissolution of their friendship was definitely Vehan's fault, he knew that. But it still hurt.

It hurt, the reminder that Aurelian eventually *would* find a partner.

It hurt, knowing Vehan would have to pretend to be all right with that.

It hurt, because he *wasn't*; no matter how much he told himself he needed to let go of the past, he was starting to suspect he'd *always* love Aurelian.

"So when are you going to stop acting like a child and talk to him?"

It was one distraction too many—Theo caught his sword between the pincer clutch of crossed daggers, and with one good twist, disarmed Vehan so completely he simply . . . gave in.

Dropped to his knees.

The stirring inside him . . . it fell once more subdued, almost at the exact same rate as his frustration drained to exhaustion.

"I'm scared," he said, in a voice so quiet that if Theo hadn't been fae, he wouldn't have been able to hear him.

The tip of one of Theo's daggers slid to the soft of his throat, tipped his head up to meet Theo's gaze. "A shit excuse. You are the Crown Prince of Seelie Summer, future king of this Court, son of Riadne Lysterne—you are not afraid of *anything*. You will talk to him."

"And say *what*?"

"What you want to say, of course. What you've been wanting to say for as long as I've known you. What you've been saying all this time, in pretty much everything but the actual *words*."

Vehan swallowed.

Theo's dagger didn't relent.

What *did* he want to say?

I'm sorry.

I love you.

Please don't shut me out from your life completely, it's the only thing in this world I couldn't bear.

"You'll figure it out," said Theo, and dipping in to press the lightest, barely there kiss to his lower lip, retreated completely. Without pausing once to look behind him—as though Theo had kissed him numerous times before, as though this weren't the first time he'd ever shown even the slightest hint of confirmation that his true intention with Vehan *wasn't* the relationship Riadne wanted—he sauntered his way down the hill toward the Egress.

Sighing, Vehan stood to follow, wondering, always *wondering*, and second-guessing every conclusion, what Theodore Reynolds was really after under all the things *he* pretended, too.

CHAPTER 29

Arlo

~~~

THE FIRST HINT OF pale pink and vibrant blood-orange light spilled through the series of open windows in Arlo's bedroom, bathing it in dying day. It was just after dinner. Celadon, Vehan, Theo, Aurelian—everyone had gathered in her sitting room, lounging in random chairs, tossing around ideas for what they could get up to tonight on the Strip as they waited for Arlo to finish getting ready in the adjoining room.

I like Las Vegas, said Luck, a certain air of yearning in their tone. *No other place in this entire realm pays half as much . . .* devotion *to my* worship.

"Yeah," Arlo replied around a laugh. "You must be the only immortal with an entire city for a temple. All right, you can look now." She threw herself down on the backless settee bench pushed up against the end of her bed and pulled out a pair of the shoes she'd tucked beneath it.

Luck, who'd turned to face the opposite way while she changed into something more comfortable for tonight's adventure—a simple outfit of black shorts and a floral-print tank top—lifted their head. *Are you sure I can't come with*?

"As a cat? No, that would draw a lot of attention. And the boys—particularly Cel—would all want to know where I pulled this random extra person from if you tagged along in a more human form or met up with us somewhere. I'm sorry . . ." She looked up from the shoes she'd slipped on and added by way of further apology, "I promise to bring you back a souvenir?"

You had better. My favor to you has so far been met with a startling lack of offering and sacrifice. I'm sure the other immortals would never have to put up with this level of disrespect.

Reaching over, Arlo ruffled the fur on top of their head. "There, there," she cooed in false consolation, and Luck glared balefully up at her, wholly unamused.

I am a Titan.

"So, a *big* souvenir, then?"

The disrespect . . . Luck grumbled in response, and lowered their head back to the bed as though settling in for a nap, but none of this was a *no. Remember not to overexert yourself—you're still very new to your role and used a lot of magical energy today. You don't want to push yourself into burnout.*

"Got it," she replied, rising from the settee with a salute and laughing again when Luck merely sighed at her. Ready at last for her night of shopping, sightseeing, and general teenage fun on the town, she crossed the room to grab her purse and her phone. Her hand had just closed around the knob of her bedroom door when she noticed it—a fluttering in her peripheral vision.

She glanced to the side.

"Arlo . . ."

"Gah!" Arlo yelped in surprise, jumping back from the door. Her hand flew to her rapidly beating heart, staring wide-eyed out her open balcony at the figure on the threshold. "Don't *do* that, Nos," she scolded. "You *scared* me!"

It took her a moment.

And then she remembered . . .

"*Nos*—you're back!" She darted to her friend, throwing her arms around Nausicaä's very stiff torso in a tight embrace. "You've been gone for days! Are you okay? I was so worried . . ."

There was no return hug. Nausicaä stood awkward and still against Arlo like a deceptively muscular, woodsmoke- and steel-scented statue. But slowly, just as Arlo remembered more things—like her manners— and made to pull away, a hand rose to place itself on top of Arlo's head.

"Lethe's clue, it leads to Greenland. Another hunt through Wild territory. You don't have to come along, but you can if you want. I figured I'd at least tell you, so you could decide."

There was a strange, profound flatness to the way Nausicaä spoke that Arlo had *never* heard in her voice before. Her posture, her air, the steel in her eyes—it was all so *dull* right now, when Nausicaä had always been passion and fire and biting *life*. It was more frightening to Arlo than any glimpse so far of Nausicaä's formidable true appearance.

A hollowed-out carcass, that's what she reminded Arlo of in her current and total apathy; a blaze burned down to flaking ash. When Arlo looked up into her face, she saw nothing but how utterly *exhausted* Nausicaä was, had probably been for a very long time but now didn't even have the energy to pick a mask to conceal it.

"Nos," she whispered in a much gentler tone, and repeated her most pressing question, "are you okay?"

Nausicaä only looked back at her. "Do you want to come?"

"I . . ." There were four people waiting on her out in the next room. But this was more important. "Hang on, just let me tell the boys to go ahead without me. I want to come, just give me a minute, okay?"

She waited until Nausicaä gave her single nod before pulling away.

Nausicaä didn't relax against the doorway, or saunter into the room, or grin and make any form of sarcastic comment—nothing of what she normally did. She just stood there and watched Arlo back away, Arlo a little hesitant to leave, as though Nausicaä might up and vanish the moment she did and disappear for good.

"I'll be right back," she said again, and when her back met the bedroom door, she felt around for the knob. Turned it, dipped into the sitting room and explained to Vehan and the rest that Nausicaä had just turned up and something was wrong—something personal. She assured them that they didn't need to stay back too, just her, and apologized profusely for ruining tonight's plans.

She kept the news of another hunt and her decision to go along on it to herself. Celadon would fuss, would once again try to stop her or insist on going along too if she told him, and who knew what sort of mood *that* would tip Nausicaä into. This one truth concealed, they were gracious enough to excuse Arlo, to tell her they hoped everything would be okay with Nausicaä and that they'd bring her and Arlo and her pet phooka *all* a souvenir, and the five of them would hit the Strip another night.

Once she saw them off, she dashed back to her bedroom. Nausicaä was still in the exact same place she'd been when Arlo had left her. What was different was Luck.

Short, flaming red hair; pale white skin and a wide, sturdy build; bright green eyes—Luck looked like they could be Arlo's older sibling, and a perfectly human one at that, no hint of otherworldliness about them at all. With neither the horns nor the infinite black eyes they normally favored, she might not have known who they even were if it weren't for the telltale absence of the cat that had been curled up on the end of her bed just moments before, and the fact that she didn't actually *have* any siblings.

Arlo eyed their emerald cloak, its interior lined with thick gray fur that spilled over the collar in a fluffy cloud of warmth. "Are you coming, too?" she asked, hoping they were, if for no other reason than the added security, even if she wasn't up for any more Hollow Star training for the day. And because the cloak had thrown her a bit, she added, "Is it *cold* in Greenland during June?"

Luck flourished a hand, and over their arm, a matching emerald cloak appeared. They held it out to her. "You're going to want to put on pants."

It *was* cold in Greenland—or at least the part of it they'd teleported to, where icy ocean water, black under the starry night, lapped against the scant few miles of rocky coastline that stood between them. Giant snowflakes fell from the sky, swept this way and that by whistling wind. Their breath formed clouds of crystal in the air. Frozen, snow-dusted earth crunched under their boots. There was something immensely peaceful about this dark isolation, different from what they'd encountered at the grotto, but just as still, like this sliver of space had been carved out of time to exist on its own terms—or, perhaps more accurately, as though magic had balled it up in the globe Lethe had left for their clue.

"The North Atlantic Ocean," Nausicaä informed them, her tone gone even flatter, now completely bereft of feeling and as chilly as their surroundings. Arlo glanced up from the powdery snow she'd immediately crouched to examine upon their arrival; the look on Nausicaä's face could only be described as glacial. "This is Cape Farewell, the southernmost point of Greenland," she added after her lengthy pause.

Arlo considered this. "Does it normally snow here this time of year?"

"No," Nausicaä replied, shaking her head. "Cool isn't unusual here, but this isn't normal. This is a failed stone in the hands of an ice wraith."

Shooting upright, Arlo looked at her in astonishment. "An *ice wraith*?" She had learned just enough about ice wraiths to know they were the ghostly remnants of ice elementals—sidhe fae of Winter— whose anger and grief and torment over whatever gruesome demise had cut their life short gave them power to retain some semblance of form here in the primary plane. They were a curious balance of demon and folk, and an incredibly rare encounter, as cold was deeply necessary to their survival, the further below zero the better.

"Yup, so this is going to be pretty straightforward. Find them, kill them, take back the stone." She threw out a hand, pulling a sword out of the air. Arlo watched it fashion out of smoke into a weapon she'd never seen before—not quite fire, not quite steel. Its flat, curved blade glowed a flickering dance of white and blue and looked as biting cold as winter, but even from here, Arlo could feel the heat that poured from it. "I say *kill*," Nausicaä continued once armed, "but ice wraiths are already dead, and there's no reasoning with them. They probably have no idea what the stone they hold even is, but as long as they have it, this cold will spread. And if you think the Courts have enough trouble to deal with right now, wait until the things they thank their lucky stars keep to the ice and snow are able to fuck around wherever they please."

Finally, a glimmer of Nausicaä's better humor. Whatever was weighing on her, the thrill of hunting down an ice wraith was too exciting for her mood to ignore completely.

"All right, well . . ." Arlo turned to scan the dark behind them. The rockiness climbed quickly into mountains and jagged hills, shooting up like trees in a snowy-white forest. "Where do we start looking, then?"

"*Tch.*"

She glanced to the side, catching sight of the barest hint of a smirk Nausicaä angled at her before lifting her unarmed hand. In her palm, another ball of fire sparked to life, swirling hotter and angrier and larger by the second. When it had grown to roughly the size of a basketball, Nausicaä lifted it above her head, drew back her arm, and *pitched* her fireball as hard as she could at the nearest mountain. "They'll come to us."

Arlo watched the fireball sail like a comet through the air, a perfect arc of blazing light trailing behind it.

"You'll want this," said Luck on Arlo's opposite side.

A flare of orange light drew her attention. Warmth washed over her as Luck pulled a sword from the air as well and presented it to her, a near-exact replica of the one Nausicaä currently wielded, save for its solid gold hilt. She was surprised to find precious metal cool against her fingers despite the flames that formed its blade.

"No regular weapon will cut down this foe, but I expect it returned once this is over," they added, giving her a meaningful look.

Out in the frosty night, they seemed a little more ethereal than they had back in Arlo's bedroom, a little more obviously immortal. Wind swept their red hair around pale, flushed cheeks; shadow softened their harder features. Still curiously human, and yet the most otherworldly being Arlo had ever encountered, and they seemed to feel the frigid temperature no more than Nausicaä, the way they stood there all casual grace, hands slipping back into the pockets of their furry cloak when Arlo took their proffered sword.

She dipped her head in a nod of gratitude. "Thank you . . ."

Was she really going to need this?

Nausicaä raised a brow. "It's an ice wraith. I think I've got this handled. No need to put Arlo in any direct danger . . ."

"Mm-hmm," was all Luck replied, in a singsongy way that made Arlo suspect they knew something she and Nausicaä didn't.

And in response, Nausicaä's mouth turned downward in a spectacular frown, but whatever she'd been about to comment, her fireball interrupted. Exploding into a fiery burst against the distant rock, it dispersed with a muffled *boom*. When the rippling rings of flame and smoke extinguished and the night returned to whistling calm, they stood and watched, and the hairs on Arlo's neck and arms prickled to attention with the peculiar feeling of something watching *back*.

"Um . . . Nos?"

It began as a singular, swirling vortex of wind in the distant snowy air.

One became two, became three, became a pack of eight, Arlo counted, all of them blustering down from their perches to carve a path directly for them.

A touch at her shoulder—Arlo jumped, for how raptly she'd been watching the *multiple* ice wraiths draw nearer, but it was only Luck. "You learned something today in the event you forced to pass. A skill."

"I . . ." Arlo thought back on her day, looking down at her blade. "I . . . learned how to use . . . a sword?"

"You learned how to use a sword," Luck confirmed. "Another lesson, if you feel up to trying it. It shouldn't take too much of your magic, but you know your own exhaustion best. You've been using your die to enhance the luck of certain actions like boosting your windborn magic. It can be used to boost other things, as well. Just like with the wind, those other things are limited to skills you already know or possess. Today you learned how to wield a sword—not well, or even proficiently, but you gained a basic knowledge. That's all your die needs to enhance the ability for a set duration of time and to varying degrees, all dependent on what you roll."

Reaching into her pocket, Arlo extracted her die. "How?"

"All you need to do is tell it what you want. Command it to *enhance your swordsmanship*. You won't be presented with any options; time will not stop. Simply roll the die after speaking your demand, and the number it lands faceup on will decide the duration of your enhancement, counted out by hours. The number facedown will decide its strength. This can even," they added, glancing over Arlo's head at Nausicaä, their smirk drawing deeper, "be used as an assist for others. You can enhance *their* skill instead of your own."

In a threatening flash, Nausicaä's sword swung to point at the titan. "Don't you fucking dare. That's literally the most insulting thing anyone's ever said to me. My skills do not need *enchancing*."

Luck raised their hands. "I was only pointing out a feature."

Blowing out her tongue, Nausicaä shot them her finger before flicking her sword back to her side.

The ice wraiths were almost upon them.

A little uneasy, Arlo looked between her die and her sword. "I've never killed anything before," she admitted quietly. It was one thing to go along with Nausicaä on these hunts and wield her magic and her die to help subdue and capture their targets—it was another thing to "cut them down."

"Hey," said Nausicaä, a modicum of gentleness creeping into her tone. Arlo looked up to find her closer than before, and looking down at her. "You don't have to do this. I'll be fine to handle them *all* on my own. I'm sorry, I . . . forget sometimes that you aren't . . . well, that you're mortal. That things like this would understandably bother you."

Shaking her head, Arlo tried to force her expression into something a little more reassuring. "It's like you said, they're already dead, yeah? This is just like the cava."

"It is."

"Just like playing a video game," Arlo added, drawing a breath to fortify her resolve. She came here to help, not to be a burden.

"Exactly," Nausicaä agreed, and there, a glint of another grin. "Don't worry, I'll do all the hard work. Roll your die for your skill enhancement, but you most likely won't even need to use it." She ducked suddenly, quick as a lick of flame, and pulled Arlo to the ground with her, bending slightly to cover Arlo's head—and inches above them sailed a creaking ball of black ice magic that only *just* missed them. It shattered apart on the ground a few feet back. "And that's time—we're up, Red!"

She unfurled to standing, pushed Arlo back toward Luck, and leaped the opposite way when another ball of ice shot directly between them a moment later.

Catching her by the shoulders, Luck bent to speak directly in Arlo's ear. "Will you do it?" they asked.

The first of the ice wraiths materialized, rearing up in front of Nausicaä so much *bigger* than Arlo had imagined they'd be. Like a giant, the wraith towered over her, the rags of a former luxurious robe fluttering in the air around him, his flesh as bitter white as snow, decayed in places and hanging in others from the brittle bone beneath.

Frost dripped in icy shards from his wisp-blue hair and beard.

It caked his skin like scales.

When he opened his mouth, it was to *screech* down at Nausicaä with a war cry so shrill that Arlo flinched back against Luck to try to block it out. Baring her teeth, Nausicaä bellowed right back and swung her sword in one elegant, forceful arc to slice clean through the wraith quicker than he had time to comprehend.

Another screech pierced the air, and as Nausicaä's sword cleared through his opposite side, instead of sliding apart to the ground, he burst into a shatter of ice, a gust of wind, and creaking magic, and scattered to nothing in the wind.

Arlo stared.

The remaining wraiths paused as well.

Then—another shriek, followed by another, until all seven other wraiths materialized, armed with rage and revenge, teeth and talons as wicked black as the ocean behind them, as glittering and sharp as the points of tiny blades.

They blew toward Nausicaä, focused entirely on her.

"Enhance my swordsmanship," Arlo said, her mind made up in an instant, her voice pitched low but firm.

She squeezed her hand around her die; tossed it into the air; caught it as it plummeted back—*two*, was the number that gleamed bright and golden back up at her. Two hours of enhancement, and the one facedown . . .

"Nineteen," Luck observed with a chuckle of some private amusement. They nudged her forward. "Well, then, off you go. Let your instincts guide you. And Arlo?"

Arlo turned around.

"Good luck, my dear. My best to Lethe, when you see him." And grinning a Cheshire grin at her, they winked and *vanished*—gone in a snap, right before her eyes.

"Lethe?" Arlo mouthed, stunned by how suddenly Luck had left them, quite differently from how Nausicaä teleported around, no telltale hint of smoke or even a *pop* of sound. The titan's last words left her confused. Lethe, was he *here*?

Turn—Arlo wheeled around.

Let your instincts guide you, that's what Luck had said. Arlo felt a pull at her navel, heard her own voice commanding in her mind to turn around, stronger and fiercer than she'd ever spoken before. Almost as though her sword had taken on a life of its own, it swung upward, catching a blade that had been about to fall on her from above.

The clash of their weapons echoed through the night.

Arlo didn't have time to think about how massive the sword was, how long and brutal and deadly the shards of ice were that extended from the hand that wielded it. A sword like that could have *crushed* Arlo, broken straight through her skull.

"Arlo!" Nausicaä called out.

"I'm fine!" Arlo gritted back, and deftly deflected the blow.

The ice wraith that had separated from the pack and launched its attack on her hovered in the air before her.

Was it just because it was closer that it seemed bigger than the one Nausicaä had faced—bigger than the six others she was locked in battle against right now? Was it her imagination that made her see the frost growing in a ring around his head like a crown?

The wraith hissed at her.

Nausicaä called her name again, urging her to get back. "—the one! He's the one with the stone. *Arlo*, don't—"

Another blow, and once again, Arlo's instincts took over, made her raise her fiery sword to match its force.

One strike.

Two.

The wraith advanced on her, raining down a series of swings and jabs with cleaving force, and Arlo deflected every one.

Her feet followed a dance she'd never learned.

She bent herself back, dipping so low to avoid a horizonal slice it amazed her that her spine didn't snap in two; leaped with feline agility high off the ground, curling in on herself when the next swipe of ice aimed at her legs; fell back to the ground with such sure balance that one might think to watch this that Arlo had been training for this level of fight for *years* when she'd only picked up a sword for the first time earlier *that day*.

Strike after strike after strike—dodge, deflect, a series of strikes of her own.

A laugh burst from her when she blocked yet another of the

stone-powered ice wraith's attacks, and everything paused. The wraith glared down at her, swords locked, eyes like burning balls of blue fire in his head, and she could tell he was frustrated that this kill wasn't as easy as he'd been anticipating. Somewhere in the back of whatever mind he had left, he was realizing there was something just a little bit different about this prey.

And that's when the point of Nausicaä's sword blew through the center of his chest from behind.

The ice wraith looked down at it, bellowed at the wound in outrage.

Cut—instinct took over again; Arlo arched her sword back, and with one last powerful swing, swept it straight through the trunk of his neck, *cutting* it clean off his shoulders.

Much like the first wraith, as soon as his severed head hit the ground, it burst apart into a shower of ice. But the body remained upright, flailing on the end of Nausicaä's blade, trying to dislodge it—then Nausicaä's hand punched through its stomach, and clutched in her fingers was the dying ember of a failed stone.

She wrenched it back out.

The ice wraith collapsed into a heap of tinkling shards that ground themselves down to powder, and sifted away on the wind.

Arlo stared.

Nausicaä stared back.

"*Wow*, Red. That was—"

Arlo threw up on the ground.

"I just decapitated someone," she wheezed, dropping her sword to clutch her knees. The cold hadn't bothered her before, but she could feel it now, nettling at her, picking at her cloak, seeping through the exposed bits of her skin to settle into her bones and make her shiver.

It was *nothing* like playing a video game.

Arlo had felt the crunch of the wraith's neck giving way. There had been no blood—*he was already dead*, she tried to remind herself—but he'd still looked too much like a person, had once *been* a person, and even though he'd died, Arlo had just killed him again.

"Hey," said Nausicaä, stepping toward her, and just like before, her tone was flat but gentle. "Yeah, that was a lot. I'm sorry, Arlo—just breathe, okay?" She squeezed her hand over the stone she held and it slipped into her invisible inventory. Now free, she placed it on Arlo's back and rubbed in a small, soothing circle. "Just take a breath. You were defending yourself, okay? You did what you had to do."

Swallowing back tears, wiping at her mouth, Arlo nodded, but didn't yet uncurl from the ground.

She'd decapitated someone.

Already dead and in defense, the particulars didn't make this any easier to digest right now.

And then came the clapping.

"Well *done*," said a light voice steeped in bored amusement.

On instinct or irritation, Arlo couldn't say, but Nausicaä's hand ripped from her back to fling a fireball at their intruder—Lethe. Arlo would *never* forget that cool, singsong tone and was freshly reminded of the sickly-sweet scent of rotting flowers that belonged to his aura.

The fireball streaked through the air, and Arlo finally lifted her head, but Lethe was already gone. Together, they watched it sail, sail, sail out across the ocean. Lethe was gone, but something had been left in his place: a spill of oil on the water, which caught ablaze when the fireball sank directly into it.

The North Atlantic Ocean *burning*—it was a curious sight, right up until Arlo glanced back at Nausicaä to ask what that had been about.

She'd thought Nausicaä had looked tired before . . . It was nothing compared to the wretchedly hollowed-out *shell* that stood beside her.

"Nausicaä?" she hedged, straightening to take a shaky step toward her, and wrap a hesitant arm around her waist. "Nausicaä, what is it?"

"I know where he wants me to go."

"I'll come with," she said, barely above a whisper, but it was no less certain. *She* was no less certain. She'd just decapitated someone, and still she would follow Nausicaä *anywhere*, so long as she was welcome—these were the only two facts she could hold on to right now.

Nausicaä didn't look at her.

She barely seemed to realize Arlo was there at all.

She stood and stared out at the burning ocean, and Arlo could feel her body quaking with small, barely perceptible tremors. And then her arm wound itself around Arlo's waist in return.

"I don't think you should."

Arlo squared her jaw. "I'm coming regardless."

There was no reply and no warning. Nausicaä tightened her hold, and the matter was settled; they teleported away.

Riadne sat in her office staring down at droplets of blue. They seeped into the pale carpet behind her desk, a vibrant sapphire stain that spread like spilled ink, growing with each additional drop that trickled down the letter opener still clutched so tightly in her hand. The blade ate deeper and deeper into her palm, her knuckles white from the force of her grip.

Another drop.

What did you do to my son?

Vadrien had been *livid* when he'd stormed into this room only moments ago, their infant son cradled protectively against his side. She'd never seen him so angry. For someone so skilled with a blade, the passionate apprentice of a Courts-renowned fae warrior and darling of the Seelie Summer people, Riadne couldn't recall a single time before this that he'd ever raised his voice at her.

And technically, he still hadn't—his voice had been a deadly sort of calm, cooler than even her own could manage, and yet *sparking* with his ire.

I want to know what you did to my son.

What is this mark *on his chest?*

Did you have one of your alchemists brand *him, Riadne? Did you* experiment *on him? Has your obsession with this forbidden magic truly gone this far?*

Vadrien was young, much younger than she was. He didn't appreciate yet the meaning of true power, the sacrifice such an elusive thing required. And he certainly hadn't appreciated when, in response to his angry questions, Riadne merely breathed a scoff and turned her attention back to the report she'd been in the process of reading, before this interruption.

Yes, she'd branded Vehan.

One son had already been stolen from her—a son she hadn't planned for in her revenge against Azurean. She'd let him be the one to come crawling to her each time he missed her too greatly to keep away any longer, let him *beg* for her, all so that she could be the one to roll away after and dismiss him as though he were nothing. She'd been so careful, she'd thought—but in the end, it was foolishness that once again cost her too much.

She'd lost one son, a child she'd actually *wanted* despite the circumstances; she would *not* allow herself to lose another.

It was a risk to use this magic the world knew so little about on Vehan, but she'd been more than willing to take it—a risk, but no child of hers could ever be so weak as to not be able to withstand a bit of dark magic. Vehan would not die; he would be *remade*, and Riadne would have the power to make things *right* again. Finally, *finally*, she'd be able avenge herself on the man who had everything that should be hers.

Yes, she'd branded Vehan.

For the chance to *protect* him, to make him strong. Strong enough that no one would ever try to take him from her, too.

The amount of research she'd done by this point . . . But it wasn't enough, she knew that now. There was some crucial detail she was missing. She'd *thought* it had been enough, had been *sure* of it, had finally found a skilled enough alchemist with sufficient reason to keep his devotion to her and this cause quiet. And Vehan had been young enough; only children could bear the mark of a fruitful philosopher's stone array, she'd learned, and she'd been so sure she'd met all the other requirements too, but it hadn't worked.

The array wouldn't activate.

She was *missing* something, and it *aggravated* her because she was close, she could *feel* it . . .

Never mind it, had been her dismissive reply to Vadrien's anger. *Vehan is fine. A prince should have a few scars, besides.*

Not this, he'd hissed back at her. *Riadne, you've carved him like torture. What does this symbol even mean? Is it the philosopher's stone business again?* Please *tell me it's not.*

Answer me, Riadne!

What did you do?

How *could you do this? Why are you so determined to bring ruin upon this family? To have nothing to do with our High King—a man and a family who were once our greatest allies and now you won't even* speak *to them anymore, won't congratulate Azurean on his becoming Sovereign or on the birth of any of his children? His youngest, Celadon . . . he would be the exact same age as our oldest, Light keep him. He's only a few years older than Vehan, and with his older sister being the next in line for the throne, he's an* eligible *Viridian—he and Vehan should be more than acquainted, you should be considering their betrothal!*

Riadne, answer me!

Riadne had answered.

Without lifting her gaze, she told her husband once again to *never mind it,* and, *if that's all, I'm quite busy,* and Vadrien had been incensed.

This ends now, he'd bit at her, hugging their now fussing son even closer and glaring over the disheveled down of his raven hair. *No more, Riadne. If this doesn't stop, I* will *take what you're doing to the High King.*

And then he'd left, and Riadne hadn't realized until she looked over that her hand had curled around the dagger-sharp edge of her letter knife.

Another drop of blood oozed down the blade.

Riadne watched it tremble on the tip before joining the rest.

"The curse of genius," said a voice beside her, and oh, she looked up *now.*

She snapped to stiff attention, magic crackling immediate and hot beneath her skin. Her gaze went straight to the window, where a young man lounged, leaning casual-as-nothing against the glass.

In his hand he tossed into the air a glinting, mishappen black stone, catching it as it fell only to toss it up again.

Young was her first impression of this *boy*. Younger than her by far—he looked like a fae fresh out of Maturity, no older than his early thirties at most, but there was an agelessness about him that hinted at far older, and no mistaking him for anything human. Shimmery pale skin, long gunmetal-black hair, freckles like silvery starlight, boney and driftwood-warped in a way that was vaguely familiar to her, but she couldn't place, and those eyes—the brightest shade of poison green.

In all his black leather and silver trimmings, chains and clasps and buckles and belts, he looked very out of place in her office, yet comfortable. Like he'd been there a while. Like she'd been expecting him in the first place. Like this was *his* domain, not hers.

She lifted her chin a fraction higher, squared her jaw. "Who are you?" she demanded. "How did you get in here?"

The intruder caught his stone and kept it now, turning a grin on her that revealed shark-sharp teeth.

That's what it was—he reminded her of a mer. There was even a hint of finning to the structure of his ears, but nothing else. Perhaps he was simply that good with his glamour, or the mer in his blood had been diluted. An ancestor, then? Regardless, when he grinned, it was just as awful as it was beautiful, and she wasn't fooled for a moment that the delight in it meant anything good.

"Useless questions."

"I don't believe in useless questions," Riadne clipped.

The intruder breathed a creaking sort of laugh that made her shiver, and she'd never admit as much, but *nothing* had frightened her like that sound in a very long time. "And maybe that's why you've come this far—further than anyone else has in quite a while. Very well, *Riadne Lysterne*, you can call me Lethe."

Lethe . . . she knew that name.

Azurean had told her the names of the four Hunters who served the Crown, and the special Gift unique to each that made the High

Sovereign such a formidable ruler. Was this *boy* actually telling her he was immortal, and one such that even the other Hunters treaded lightly around him? A Hunter whose Gift allowed him to erase and distort memory at a touch. "*Lethe.*" She eyed him suspiciously.

Had the High King sent him to spy on her—hells, and Vadrien had just been in here, spewing her secrets with his vitriol.

"My reputation precedes me." He creaked another laugh, looking not at her now but the rock in his hand. His examination of it was purely for show. "That's new, I have to admit. There aren't many here who know that name well enough to attach it to meaning. I'm *impressed.*" He peeled away from the window to drop into a deep bow, but the gleam in his eyes when he raised his head and the glint of his sharp teeth was anything but deferential. "I've been impressed for quite a while. Hopeful, even—how close you've come to creating a stone, you've got it just about down. The array, the talent, the iron-born alchemists, a young and impressionable host. *Ruthlessness*, using your own son to grow your sins. My oh my, you really are the ice rumor says of you."

"What do you want?" she repeated, bristling. She wouldn't be taunted like this, intimidated, *threatened* in her own home. She hadn't done *any* of this to Vehan out of lack of feeling for him. In fact, it was more like she cared too much. With the power of a true philosopher's stone inside him, no one could ever take him away from her. No one would stand a chance against him at all.

And immortal or not, she would make this self-proclaimed *Lethe* disappear if he was here to ruin what she'd accomplished so far.

"What do I want?" Lethe rose, straightening from his bow, and swept like night across the floor. He positioned himself in front of her desk. Still he grinned . . . and held out his toy—not a toy, Riadne realized now, upon closer examination of it herself.

Not a toy at all.

She sucked in a breath.

"So *close*. I really am impressed. So impressed that I think I might just help you out, my clever little queen. What do you say—would you like to know what you're missing? Why your array didn't work on your *sidhe fae* son? Why you're going to have to push yourself to incredible new heights of *cruelty* to put it right? Your son, you thought you were making him strong, but really, you only made a mistake. A mistake that's going to cost him his life if you can't figure out a way to *change his fate* for something else . . . What do you say, Riadne Lysterne? Would you like to know *everything*?"

Vehan . . . he was going to *die*?

Riadne stared down the boy across from her, weighing what he'd said. The array hadn't worked like she'd intended, true, but Vehan seemed just fine. A little tinkering . . . a little more research to figure out what had gone wrong, and *surely* she'd be on the right track again to reforging her son into an *indestructible* power.

But . . .

What if . . .

Could she really take the chance that she was wrong?

Riadne stared down this Lethe. Immortal or not, helpful or not, *right* or not, Lethe would give her nothing without any strings attached—she was no fool, and he wasn't either, she could tell that right away. "Assuming you're correct, which I will neither confirm nor deny. Assuming I *have* done what you accuse and am interested in what you have to offer, what is it you want in exchange for your help? What is your price, *Lethe*?"

Had he been grinning before? It was nothing to what unfurled across his face now, so horrible and wide that it couldn't really be called a smile, more like his face had split clean in two. "I'm so glad you asked. What I want is really quite simple . . ."

CHAPTER 30

Nausicaä

～～～

A SHIP ROCKED ON THE ocean below; Nausicaä recognized it in an instant, turning an already horrible day into a deities-damned fucking *nightmare*.

The organ harvesters, the faerie grass, the suicidal mer, the ice wraiths in Winter's territory, that Court to which Heulfryn had once belonged—all along, she'd been starting to suspect, but this confirmed it: Lethe had been leading her to the stones, sure, but more than that, he'd been tormenting her, chasing her on, snapping at her heels so that she'd run through every one of his hoops designed to bring her right back here, to this *fucking* ship.

The *Dirge*.

Its crew.

The horrible things they'd done under its flag, and the tricks they'd used to see those things accomplished.

And what *she* had done to *them*.

She didn't question how this ship could be here. She didn't question how it sat bobbing atop the water as whole and uncharred as though plucked out of time, as though Nausicaä had never set it ablaze with Starfire, as though it shouldn't be lying instead in a still-flaming heap on the ocean floor.

She didn't question it because this space was now a Sleeping Hollow, a festering wound in magic where any manner of darkness was possible, even this.

It was an illusion. A good one. A *solid* one, but it would only last out the hour. Because she knew which night this was. She knew what the darkness here was replaying.

The moon climbed high in the cloudless sky, tipping one hundred and sixteen years in this hideous realm into one hundred and *seventeen*. Was it all one giant joke to Lethe, trotting her out for this twisted commemoration of the very worst time in Nausicaä's life? Was he really this much of an asshole, or was there some deeper reason for it—much deeper, because hells, but she couldn't even guess what digging at these festering wounds could even serve?

They hovered in the air, she and Arlo, kept aloft mostly by the scant magic she had left to her, the great, unfurled expanse of Nausicaä's wings mostly for show anymore. Still smoldering, ripped, and puckered with scars in so many places, they were less wings than they were rags, the reason she had to teleport everywhere now—they were only good for slowing descent for a small stretch of time. But Arlo clung to her, *gaping* at them like they were the most magnificent sight, blissfully insensible to the enormity of this moment and to what it was they were likely heading into.

Nausicaä shouldn't have brought her—*why* had she brought her?

What *was* it about this mortal girl that made Nausicaä want to keep her close when the resolve she'd stuck to for over a century had been to keep others as far away as possible? Arlo was pretty, but Nausicaä had met *countless* others who'd put that very word to shame. Intelligent, but naive in so many ways. Good, but the world was full of people like this. None of it should have grabbed her attention.

"I've never seen your wings before, not like *this*," Arlo marveled. "They're *beautiful*." She'd shifted her arms to circle Nausicaä's neck and held tight to keep from slipping, as if Nausicaä would ever let her fall. But then . . . that was the very thing Nausicaä was in danger of doing the longer she spent with *her*.

Nausicaä was a poison, a curse—this was clear reminder of that.

"Hold on," she replied, her voice sounding strained to even her ears, but Arlo didn't comment on it. She merely tightened her hold as instructed, and Nausicaä descended. It wasn't until they landed that she could make out the figure leaning tucked against the *Dirge*'s center mast.

"Hello, Nausicaä," Lethe greeted in his half-bored, singsong tone. "Glad to see you were able to make it."

He *did* look glad, but then again, Nausicaä had played right into his claw-tipped hand. When he unfolded from the post behind him, she stepped in front of Arlo, shielding her from his acid-bright view, but this only seemed to amuse him, judging by the upward quirk of his mouth.

"What the fuck do you want, Lethe?" she growled at him, squaring her jaw in defiance against each step he took closer, and closer, and *closer*, stalking them like some starving tiger. Under unobstructed moonlight, his many silver trimmings, venomous eyes, and wicked-sharp teeth all *glinted* lethality, but it was the look on his face that made her most afraid—*no one* made Nausicaä as afraid as this ancient Hunter did when that grin of his split wide. "I assume you didn't lead us through your jacked-ass Candyland adventure just to chat it out on a boat."

He paused right in front of her, forcing Nausicaä's head to tilt to continue staring him dead in the eye. With a creaking chuckle and a whisper of, "*Nausicaä,*" he lifted his unclawed hand, brushed her cheek with the back of his fingers, and before she could snap her teeth at them, he was gone.

Too fast—he slid behind them, behind *Arlo*, and Nausicaä wheeled around to find him standing there with his hands curled around her shoulders, his claws too close to her fragile body for Nausicaä's liking.

"*Get away from her,*" she snarled.

But the warning wasn't necessary.

Arlo—good and soft and mortal *Arlo*—threw an elbow back so hard into Lethe's chest that he grunted, creaked an even brighter, louder laugh, and released her to scramble back behind Nausicaä.

"Arlo Jarsdel," Lethe purred again. "How fierce you're going to be. I'm looking forward to the things you'll accomplish. But first . . ." A bit of his amusement finally drained away. His eyes slid back to Nausicaä, hardening on her. "How annoying that your protectors need so much *guidance* to be worthy of the role. Nausicaä, I assume you know where we are?"

The things she'll accomplish . . . worthy of the role . . . Lethe knew. He knew *exactly* what was going on, what would happen to Arlo, caught up in the entire mess, a rag doll for deities and destiny to fight over. He knew more than anyone, Nausicaä was sure of it now, and had been collecting the pieces of this very large puzzle longer than any of them. He was the only one other than perhaps Fate herself who could see if not the entire picture, then enough of it to fill in the gaps.

And she was more determined than ever now to win her answers from him.

He wanted her here? Well, here she was.

At her sharpening glare, he waved a hand, gesturing around at the ship. "But yes, I suppose you *do* want to know why I brought you here—after all, you have dulled so *pathetically* over the years, I'm certain you need me to spell it out."

"Get on with it, Lethe," she clipped. The faster they got through this, the better. She could already feel the *heat* his words had been purposefully chosen to spark.

He flicked the hand he'd been gesturing with at *her* now, and she had to leap back, sweeping Arlo along behind her to avoid what fell from the sky.

Point first, it lodged with a quivering *thud* in the wood.

Nausicaä stared, and what she saw caught her breath in the back of her throat.

"Such a beautiful blade. It doesn't belong at the bottom of an ocean, I think."

Erebos—the sword forged for Nausicaä upon her ascension to Alecto, made of the very Darkness of the Void itself, where the elements were born. The Void that birthed the Fire that made Nausicaä. This was *her* sword, the one she'd lost one hundred and seventeen years ago in order to see through her revenge on the *Dirge's* captain. Try as she might after that incident, she'd never been able to summon it and figured this meant that the Starfire had claimed it too, but here it was.

Long as the late-day's shadow, gossamer thin, and darker than any black beheld by this realm or any other, Erebos was indeed beautiful. Its crossguard swept in an elegant arch that sharpened nearly flat against its blade, like the twin fangs of a serpent, and in the center of its pommel was a stone as fathomless and cosmic black as a titan's eyes—*was* an eye, as a matter of fact, won from the actual being Nausicaa had been forced to fight for the right to use his element for her blade's creation. Erebos was no mere weapon, and Nausicaä felt such an overwhelming *longing* to be reunited with it that her own eyes had gone oddly watery.

"A being of Fire—of light and heat—chose cold, unflinching darkness for her greatest strength. A legend in her own right. You, A-Twelve, have *never* played by any rule held to you. You are here to remember that. You are here to remember what it feels like to lose *everything*." Lethe jerked his chin at Erebos, his expression whittled down to firm demand. "Take your sword. You're going to fight—you, on your own, without Luck or *darling* Arlo's interference—and if you win, I will tell you all the things you want to know about immortal plotting and the Sins and the Ruinous game we've *all* been drafted into whether we like it or not. Fight, and win. That's all you have to do, Nausicaä."

Nausicaä laughed.

It was a singular bark of disbelief, as hollow as she felt right now. Fight *Lethe* and win?

Right.

"You take Arlo home, if I lose." *If* she lost, like it was at all in question, like Lethe wasn't the deadliest fucking thing Fate had ever dared to make, and realized after *never again*. "You don't hurt her. She goes back to the Luminous Palace and to the safety of her cousin,

Celadon Fleur-Viridian. Those are my only terms—and you have to *swear* to it."

"Wait—" Arlo interjected, her voice pitched in audible unease. "Wait, if she loses . . . Nos, you're not going to *die*, right? This isn't a duel to the death, is it?"

"I accept your terms," Lethe nodded, ignoring the question.

He swept out his hand, the one with long, silver filigree claws capped on the ends of each finger, but no sword filled his hand like it would if Nausicaä had done this. Instead, those vicious claws began to *grow*, elongating, melting, twisting together until his adamant Reaper's Blade was the very extension of his hand.

Nausicaä stepped forward. "Don't worry, Arlo. Just keep back." She closed her hand tightly around Erebos. She wouldn't lie, wouldn't tell Arlo that this wasn't the end she'd been chasing for far too long, the Destruction even an immortal would fall to from a Hunter's specialized weapon. It was up to Lethe entirely to decide whether he delivered that fatal blow or not, and it was curious . . . after so long *wanting* this release from her many years of torment, here she was, fighting against the instinct to wrap herself around Arlo and whisk them both away.

Fighting against her instinct to *live*.

"Well then, Starboy. Let's have us a battle."

Lethe cackled. "Hah, *no*. I didn't say you were fighting *me*—this is just in case you don't prove up to tonight's main event."

His eyes flashed. It was the only warning Nausicaä received to whirl around and tug Arlo out of the way in one hand, the other lifting Erebos to catch the blade that swung at her from behind.

Her mouth fell open in a silent gasp—it was more shock than her opponent deserved, but he'd caught her so completely unaware . . . She hadn't expected . . . and she really should have, because on this, the anniversary of this Sleeping Hollow's creation, of course it wouldn't be just the ship cursed to replay its last few moments of life.

"*Heulfryn.*"

In the flesh.

His sunny tan had gone gravely pale in death, but his eyes were as icy blue as ever, his windswept hair still raven black, and his fae-cut features and handsome charms no less diminished—all exactly like Nausicaä remembered them. The vivid sight of him, so close and warm and *real*, was like gouging her fingers into an open wound and ripping it even wider.

She gagged on the sudden swell of emotions—agony, helplessness, anger, grief, *everything* she'd felt since Tisiphone's death compacted into a single blow far more devastating than any sword could inflict, and she stumbled.

The ghost of Heulfryn grinned. He had no idea what was going on around him—couldn't, because it wasn't really *him*, just the anger and bitterness and darkness of his death preserved to give his restless, trapped soul a husk tonight alone. But he grinned like he could comprehend what was happening anyhow, and took advantage of her vulnerability to rain down a series of strikes from all angles.

Even more frustrating to Nausicaä was that several of them landed. His sword bit into her arms and side and sliced through skin, and while her magic knitted them whole in a flash, they still hurt, still drew a hiss of pain, still rubbed salt into *emotional* wounds because these cuts meant she was *losing*—to fucking *Heulfryn*.

"Nos!" Arlo screamed.

Nausicaä threw a quick glance to her, at the same time deflecting another strike.

Lethe had drawn Arlo to the sidelines, where she struggled against him but was safely out of the way. It wasn't this she'd been trying to draw attention to, though.

Fire.

It had started on the starboard rail, traveling along the wood, spreading quickly to the rest of the ship—not fire, but *Starfire*, the same that Nausicaä had used to sink this very vessel. And like a memory springing back to life, ghostly figures materialized within their dancing flames. One, two, seven, ten; Heulfryn completed the set, the eleven souls still trapped here by Nausicaä's hand.

Panic crept like frost through her veins.

"You *deserved* it," she snarled into Heulfryn's face. "You deserved death for what you did! You and your crew, you were *disgusting,* the lot of you, and I'm not sorry at all!"

You are, said a too-cool voice in the back of her head, at once her own and not. *You killed eleven people. Cursed them to a life of torment. And for what?*

"For *justice,* and I'd do it again!"

She kicked at Heulfryn, knocking him back. Sparing no advantage, she slashed at him in the very next moment, cleaving him in two at the breast.

Heulfryn melted into a flood of water that washed over her feet, then pooled and grew itself into flesh once more, restored.

Still, he said nothing to her.

Baring her teeth in a flashing threat, Nausicaä launched back into her assault.

Blow after blow after blow—had Heulfryn been this skilled in life, or had death made him stronger? Every strike his spectral blade deflected fanned the anger building up inside her, and the Starfire only added to the blistering heat.

Arlo—she couldn't be here. This fire, even the ghost of it, might be able to *sear* through her and snuff her out in an instant. But when Nausicaä tried to look to where she'd last seen her, Arlo was nowhere to be found, and it was once again the distraction Heulfryn needed.

Another strike.

His sword sank deep into her flesh, and when he spun to yank it out, a spray of blue-black blood arched through the air, erupting into tiny flames where it splattered onto the ground.

Nausicaä dropped to her knees, clutching her side.

And what was it for?

You killed all these people . . . Were they any viler than you were? Than you are now?

"Stop," she choked out. Weaker than she should be and trembling, she heaved her sword off the ground, and it was all she could do to block the blade Heulfryn swung at her head. "Stop, I don't want to fight you anymore."

You killed all these people and blamed the rest, when it was you who failed your sister the worst.

Too easily, Heulfryn twisted his sword, swept it under Erebos and disarmed Nausicaä as though she'd been a child brandishing a stick. The irony of their reversed positions wasn't lost on her, how it was Heulfryn standing triumphant over her now, batting away her pathetic attempt at defense.

"Stop," she begged, quiet and wet. To herself or to Heulfryn or Lethe—all, or none, she couldn't say. "Please . . . I'm just so tired."

She was just so tired of feeling this angry.

Heulfryn's sword swung down at her.

The clash of the weapon that caught it echoed through the night— through the flames, which died down to smolder, then extinguished completely; through the souls presiding over this battle; through Nausicaä's head, and the voice bearing down on her thoughts.

For a moment, she wondered if this sudden stark stillness was death.

Her gaze wandered upward, to stars that the fire and smoke had cleared to reveal once more. She couldn't remember when she'd last found comfort in such a place, but they were strangely reassuring now, beautiful and closer than they'd ever felt before.

And there, just above her head, Heulfryn's sword crossed with that of Erebos in someone else's hands.

"I don't play by the rules, either."

"Arlo," she gasped in wonder, because that die of hers had finally taken its toll for the evening, and Arlo looked like she could barely stand.

But stand she did.

It was *Arlo* behind her, *Arlo* who'd saved her, her abilities still enhanced by her die.

Arlo, who'd been saving her all this time, piece by patient piece.

Heulfryn glared down at Nausicaä. Lethe came up behind him, reached out with one hand to take hold of his blade, and with the other, ran him through with his adamant sword. He splashed to the wood in another puddle of water, but this time, he didn't rise again.

The night fell even quieter still, even more watchful.

With a lethal *shiiiick,* the adamant retracted back into claws, and Lethe . . . he was *beaming.* "Fierce, indeed." He bent down in front of Nausicaä to look her level in the eye, expression growing immediately serious. "I've said it once before to you: your grief has made you pathetic. You were the Fury who bent the very darkness of our Cosmos to your command. Cower any longer from the trauma of your past, continue to wallow in despair, and it will cost you very dearly in your future. It will cost you *her.*" Leaning in closer, right at her ear, he whispered, "See you at the Solstice, cousin." With that, he peeled back to drop a wink and retreated into the night.

Nausicaä sat there, staring at the damp patch of wood before her, all that was left of a nightmare that had been haunting her for too long.

Hands slipped under her arms. "Up we go." Arlo—kind, soft, mortal *Arlo*—heaved her back to her feet with equally soft words. "There. We're okay, Nos. You're okay." She patted her gently as she spoke, and reached up to brush a few strands of sweat-slicked hair from Nausicaä's face. "Let's go home now, yeah? I think we don't need to be here anymore."

Just as wordlessly as Nausicaä brought them here, she pulled Arlo close, tucked her arms around her, and whisked them both away.

CHAPTER 31

Arlo

~~~

IT WAS DIRECTLY BACK into her bedroom that Nausicaä teleported them, not even a full hour from when they'd left. Here the sun had still to set, though now it flooded Arlo's room with an even deeper orange, the glow reminding her strongly of the blaze that had lit the ship they'd just whisked away from. And wherever Luck had gone, they weren't anywhere in sight. Her room was quiet and steeped in growing shadows, but they were finally alone.

Still clutching tightly to Nausicaä, Arlo looked up into her face.

A thin sheen of perspiration glossed her ashen skin. Wild tangles disheveled her hair. A blank *nothingness* dulled the steel in her normally disarming eyes, and under it all, Nausicaä looked so small and fragile and *lost*, like she was just a girl, just like Arlo.

Arlo reached down.

Gently, carefully, she eased Nausicaä's newly reclaimed sword from her grip, withdrew to the table just a few steps away to lay it on its surface. Nausicaä watched her like she couldn't really follow what she'd been doing, but her eyes tracked Arlo's movements away and back again regardless.

"So . . . ," Arlo floundered. What did she say after what had just happened? There were so many things tumbling around in her head, but none of them seemed appropriate right now. "Today was . . . a lot."

"I should get back to Eris," Nausicaä announced half a beat later, her voice as raw as if she'd been screaming this entire time. "You should get some rest, Arlo, you—"

"Hey," Arlo interrupted, softly and simply, but with no room for argument. "Don't. Don't go. Don't keep shutting me out. I think we should talk, Nausicaä. I—"

"I don't want to *talk*."

It was the deadliest she'd ever heard Nausicaä speak, let alone to her. Arlo swallowed against the swell of not-quite-fear but something just as oily and nauseating as it slid to settle in her gut. "Then *I'll* talk, because today *was* a lot, and I'm worried. I'm worried about what's been going on. I'm worried about *you*—you're important to me, Nausicaä."

"I didn't ask to be."

Much as in the early part of their acquaintance, Arlo felt her irritation bristle. "Well, you are, and I just want you to know that you can close me out of any part of your life you choose, can hide behind as many masks and sarcasm and insults as you can create, but I'm not going anywhere, okay? We're friends, and if you want me to—"

"What I *want* is for you to leave me the fuck *alone*, Arlo," she growled out, advancing a step toward her, and when Arlo shrank an instinctive step back, there was finally a flash of emotion in her gaze: vicious triumph, followed by regret.

Arlo swallowed. Barely above a whisper, she said, "I can do that too. I can leave you alone. I don't want to make you uncomfortable, Nos, I just want—"

"*Please*," Nausicaä snarled, *exploding* in her anger at last, surging forward to crowd Arlo's space. "Please, yes, what *do* you want, Arlo? Because it feels like *everything* in my life lately has been all about *you*, so why don't we make *this* about you, too?"

"That's . . . that's really unfair, Nos, I didn't ask to be—"

"What do you want, for me to tell you my whole fucking sob story?"

"Nos, no, I don't—"

"Because it's really not that exciting. It's just that my sister was depressed, and none of us knew how to deal with it, got angry with her about it—*I* got angry with her about it because I just wanted her to be okay and she *wasn't* and that *scared* me, frustrated me. And then she fell in with a charming fucking asshole who used her, made himself her whole world, and then ditched her for someone new, pushing her past her breaking point, and she *died*. She died by suicide. Threw herself into the Starpool right in front of me."

Ah, so she'd been right about the siren at the grotto. But Arlo didn't feel any satisfaction in having made that connection already. Instead she felt even more nauseated on top of the toll of using so much magic from her die tonight. "Nausicaä, please, you don't have to—"

"No, but I do, because you and everyone else just won't fucking leave it the *hells* alone! Tisiphone died by suicide, and it was my fault, and I couldn't fucking handle that, so I snapped and murdered the only shitbags I could take that out on. You seem to think I'm some wonderful, misunderstood *woodland creature* that just needs saving— that I don't deserve the hate and scorn and fear associated with my name, that I'm not a monster—"

"Because you *aren't*," Arlo snapped, surprising herself just as much as Nausicaä. And it was Arlo surging forward now, as agitated and defiant as Nausicaä. "You. Are. Not. A. Monster. There is *nothing* you can say that will make me believe that—"

"I *enjoyed* killing them—"

"—because I know it's just an act—"

"—I enjoy causing harm, and destruction, and *death*—"

"—and if you think for a *second* I don't know that you can lie just fine to my face—"

That landed a blow. Nausicaä bared her teeth. "I've never asked for anything from you. I don't need your pity, Arlo—"

"It isn't pity, it's *sympathy*! It's *friendship*, and caring, and I'm giving it to you anyhow, *Nausicaä*, because you're not the boss of me! Because you deserve it, and much more, and I can do what I like, and I—"

—*love you.*

. . . oh.

Arlo swallowed again, but this time, it wasn't in fear.

Tears welled up in her eyes, but not in frustration.

Her sexuality was still a giant question mark, but she knew one thing for certain: she loved Nausicaä.

"I'll only get you hurt."

And just like that, Arlo softened.

Nausicaä was angry. She was angry at *her*. But more than that, she was angry at herself, because Arlo was starting to suspect that she was just as confused about things as Arlo was, and when you spent so long shutting everyone out, the scariest thing of all was letting even one back *in*.

Arlo knew that too well herself, between her father, and the Viridian family, and the classmates that never wanted anything to do with her. She only had Celadon, only *ever* Celadon, and now suddenly, she had Nausicaä.

It was a lot to digest for her, as well.

She smiled. It was small and a bit watery, and Nausicaä looked a little stricken to see it, but Arlo smiled nonetheless, and said, "I seem to find plenty of ways to get hurt with or without you, Nausicaä Kraken. That doesn't scare me."

"It scares *me*," Nausicaä replied, deflating from rage back into exhaustion . . . and something a bit like surrender. "*What it feels like to lose everything,* he told me . . . Arlo, it scares me a lot. That I could lose you, too . . ." She drew a shaking breath, opened her mouth to say something else, but whatever it was, a knock at Arlo's bedroom door interrupted her. She turned to it with a scowl so intense that Arlo felt a bubble of laughter well up from her receding nausea, but she pressed her lips against it.

"Hang on," she said with a shake of her head. "I'll see who it is."

She only vaguely recognized the aura trickling under her door— one of her attendants, not Madelief's or Zelda's, she knew those fairly well by now, but one of the others. "Gentian!" she exclaimed when she opened her bedroom door and found him standing there, a tray of tea in his hands.

Ah, she'd forgotten—Gentian brought her tea once in the morning and once in the evening, both like clockwork, and at exactly this time. His face lit up to see her. When he stepped past Arlo and into the room, she expected that expression to fall. But it didn't. His beaming grin might have etched a little more brittlely on his face, but he only nodded at Nausicaä, and instead of shouts or accusations, looked back to Arlo.

"Tea," he announced, holding up his tray a fraction higher.

She could see that. *Two* cups, and a pot between them.

Gentian must have read the question in her eyes, because he added, "News travels quickly in the palace. One of the staff overheard you were staying in tonight to tend to an unwell Nausicaä. I figured tea might . . . help."

"Oh!" Arlo exclaimed again. "That's . . . really nice of you, thank you, Gent."

Leda must have spoken to him about their argument. This must be his way of apologizing. Indeed, the way he glanced a little guiltily at her confirmed it, and who was Arlo to try to get in the way of someone's attempt to make amends.

"Shall I put it over here for you, my lady?" he asked, indicating the table with Nausicaä's sword.

Arlo nodded, and away he went, pausing to eye the sword with a bit of hesitance before setting down his tray and pouring out the first cup.

"Here you are," he said, returning to her with his offering. He didn't normally go *this* far in serving her, but then again, Arlo normally sat for tea, and this was most likely another step in his apology.

She took the cup with a nod of thanks, glancing apologetically at Nausicaä when he turned to whisk back to the table and proceeded to pour one for her as well, and Nausicaä just stood there, a bit bewildered.

"You don't know how to read a fucking room at *all*, do you, pixie boy?" she said, when Gentian handed her a cup next.

Gentian laughed. "I'm not a boy. I'm actually almost a hundred and twenty."

"Right," Nausicaä replied. "You lot don't age at all. All right, well, thank you, pixie *senior*. You can . . . uh, *leave* now."

"Nos," Arlo reprimanded, taking a sip of her tea. An unusual blend—a little on the bitter side—but not altogether unpleasant.

Nausicaä heaved a dramatic sigh and rolled her eyes. "*Please,* pretty please, will you leave us alone now?"

But Gentian only shook his head. "Sorry, it's only that I've had this picture of you in my head for so long, and it's funny, but . . . you're really just a girl."

"Uh . . . *huh.*" Nausicaä glared at Arlo as though this was *her* fault. "Well, yup, sorry to disappoint you. In my defense, they say you should never meet your heroes."

"The Dark Star, who has committed so *many* atrocities . . . nothing but a spoiled little *girl.*"

Arlo opened her mouth to scold Gentian this time, and add her voice to Nausicaä's request for him to leave. But Nausicaä beat her to it, her own mouth downturned in an even deeper frown than before. "So . . . this talk is . . . not great, I'm going to be really fucking honest with you. Not great at all. I don't know who you are, *Gentian*, but I'm just going to go ahead and real life block you from this conversation now. Arlo?"

Arlo nodded. "Yeah, I'm sorry, Nos. Gentian? Thank you for the tea, but I'm going to have to ask you to leave now."

"Of course!" He bobbed his head in a nod. "I really only wanted to meet the legend that killed my father."

Nausicaä snorted. "Oh yeah? And when did I supposedly manage *this*?"

Gentian returned to the table. As casual as though he weren't in the middle of steadily darkening hostility, he set about gathering his tray, continuing on. "My father was one of the eleven people you murdered on that ship all those years ago. His death left behind my mother and my four older siblings, and well . . . she just couldn't make ends meet without him. Worked herself to death not long after, and then my siblings died, too, fallen to a faerie flu none of us had any money to cure, since we were already so poor, and starving, and forgotten little *pixie boys*. So I just wanted to meet you." He turned when he reached the bedroom door, and added with a smile. "Just wanted to return the *favor* you dealt so long ago. The perfect opportunity—I didn't realize until just a few nights ago how this had to go. Who had to be the one to pay to make you feel what I've been feeling for one hundred and seventeen years. Apologies, my lady," he added, looking now at Arlo. "It's unfortunate you had to get involved in this. In your next life, try to make wiser choices about who you align yourself with."

The soft click of the door behind him as Gentian took his leave was almost indistinguishable from the oddly throbbing heartbeat in her ears.

". . . Arlo?" she heard Nausicaä call, and it was weird, but she sounded a little distant, as though speaking to Arlo through a tunnel.

Arlo lifted her cup, sniffing its contents, not really understanding why, even as she did. It was in a jumbled mess of thoughts that Arlo realized why her tea had tasted so off.

A teacup shattered on the floor.

Nausicaä *shrieked* her name.

Arlo wanted to ask what was wrong, but she couldn't around the choking, and the horrible cramping that had begun to clench in her stomach, and the floor rising quickly to slam against her face.

Apologies, my lady—Gentian had *poisoned* her, and Arlo didn't even have enough time before black consumed her vision to worry about what that meant.

CHAPTER 32

Nausicaä

———◦◦◦———

MOVE, SCREAMED A VOICE in Nausicaä's head.

Move!

But she couldn't.

Gentian had left—had sneered at her and marched right out of the room as though he hadn't just . . . hadn't just . . .

"*Arlo!*" she cried in strangled alarm, but she *still couldn't move*, could only stand there stricken as Arlo collapsed to the floor, spluttering and coughing and gasping for breath. *Poisoned*—the pixie had *poisoned* her. Arlo was going to *die,* and Nausicaä couldn't move.

"Arlo?" called a voice, and Nausicaä's gaze snapped back to the doorway. "Arlo, is everything okay? I just passed one of your attendants—Gentian, I think?—in a bit of a hurry. It sort of looked like he was . . . fleeing."

It was Celadon.

Nausicaä couldn't move.

". . . Arlo?"

High Prince Celadon stood in the bedroom doorway Gentian had left open. Hadn't he been out with Vehan and the others for the night? It didn't matter; all that mattered right now was Arlo, who Celadon *stared* at as though he couldn't quite make sense of what he was seeing either: Arlo, unconscious on the ground, deathly pale and beginning to perspire as her body temperature flared to try to fight off the toxin she'd ingested.

Move, Nausicaä screamed at herself again.

Damn it, do something!

"ARLO!" Celadon exploded, and with that the spell was broken.

Both he and Nausicaä rushed forward at the same time. Celadon was closer, but Nausicaä made it to her first, throwing herself onto the ground and gathering Arlo in her arms.

"Arlo? *Arlo*, can you hear me? It's going to be okay, everything's going to be okay, you're—"

"What *happened*?" Celadon seethed. In his distress, his expression painted him so fiercely *wild* that Nausicaä didn't think she'd be able to ignore his question even if she wanted to.

"G-Gentian. That p-pixie! *Celadon*," she rasped out, voice trembling as much as Arlo's body had begun to do. "Celadon, he poisoned her. He *poisoned* her! We need—"

Confusion fluttered over Celadon's face before it settled into understanding . . . and something that looked like a dark realization.

"Pick her up," he ordered. "Come on, *pick her up*. She needs the medical wing."

The firm command in the High Prince's dangerously level voice was exactly what Nausicaä needed right now. The clip of it cut through her building panic, made her able to blink through the tears welling up in her eyes and reminded her of *purpose*. Clear, concise purpose—lift Arlo up; follow. Nausicaä could do that.

Out of the bedroom, into the hall.

A flicker of surprise passed over the faces of the useless Verdant Guards who'd been on duty, but they were quick to shutter it away, snapping to attention as Celadon issued orders and demands like a general at war. "You—find the pixie Gentian and bring him into custody. You—fetch Queen Riadne and her alchemist, Leda. Bring them both to Medical. They will come immediately or you will drag them by their *hair* to me, but they will be there. And yes, I do mean the queen as well. Go."

The Verdant Guard went.

Down the hall, into the elevator, out onto another floor.

Nausicaä cradled Arlo with all the delicate care she could manage as they fled the corridors to the Luminous Palace's medical wing, where the Head MediFae had better be able to save the only fucking person Nausicaä had to love in this entire realm, despite her vows to never let anyone mean this much to her again. "Come on, Red," she whispered into Arlo's hair, fervent and fearful and *pleading*. "You'll pull through this, you have to. I won't lose you—I *won't*."

The palace staff scattered, dropped into deep bows, pressed themselves as flat as they could against the walls as Celadon passed, a fury in his air that would have impressed even Nausicaä were she in the mood to marvel over anything right now but her own foolish *recklessness*. She only ever hurt the people she dared to care about, she'd warned Arlo. This was all Nausicaä's fault. If she hadn't retaliated against Heulfryn and his crew, Gentian would never have felt the need to do so against *her* . . . to take away the *only fucking person she had in this entire realm*—

They burst into the medical wing, startling the staff on duty.

With no one in the rows of beds that lined the walls, all they'd been doing was cleaning and routine checks of their equipment, but several pieces clattered to the floor in their alarm, and one even *whimpered*, retreating a step on frightened instinct from the storm the High Prince wore in his eyes and no doubt in his aura.

"The Head Physician," he clipped at the stricken nurses, snapping his fingers at them. "Nausicaä, here. Put her down." He indicated one of the beds.

Quick to comply, Nausicaä did as she'd been instructed, laid Arlo carefully out on one of the pristine white beds. She smoothed back wisps of fire-red hair that matted against Arlo's clammy, hot skin, and when Arlo issued a quiet groan, pressed a kiss at her temple. "You'll be all right. You'll be all right now. Celadon's here, and he won't let anything happen to you. I'm sorry, Arlo, I'm so *sorry*—" She choked on the apology, tears spilling out at last. "I'm sorry," she cried, and dropped to kneel at Arlo's bedside.

Too still, her breathing too shallow, her complexion too sunken in gravely white death—"I'm sorry, Arlo. This is my fault. I'm sorry . . ."

The Head Physician—an elderly fae with white blond hair and many lines and dark age spots in his alabaster skin—came out from his office, still in the process of righting the voluminous, stark white robes of his position. He must have been off duty for the evening, but a High Prince's command was law to *all* in the Eight Great Courts, and Nausicaä had never been so grateful for a person as she suddenly was for Celadon Fleur-Viridian.

"Y-Your Highness!" the Head Physician stammered. "Whatever is wrong?"

And at the same time, the medical wing's doors burst open once more, admitting the queen, her son, and someone Nausicaä didn't know at all—a dryad woman with rosewood skin and pansy-black hair, who wore a look of stiff disbelief on her face when her gaze settled on Nausicaä.

"Your Highness," said Riadne to Celadon, and Nausicaä was absolutely certain no one in this room had ever seen the Seelie Queen of Summer show the genuine fear that flickered through her eyes. Riadne was mildly *breathless* as she spoke to her High Prince—*good*, she *should* be afraid. How she could let someone like Gentian personally attend her guest of honor . . . but apparently, Celadon was thinking along the same outrage.

He surged forward, drawing so close to the queen that their noses were only a hair's breadth away from touching.

"My cousin has been poisoned by one of your staff. If she dies, the only crown of bone you'll get to wear will be the one I make from your ribs, *are we clear?*"

Queen Riadne looked at him.

Nausicaä recognized all too well the way her lip curled over her teeth. Riadne wasn't the sort of woman to grin and bear a threat like *that* on the chin, but Celadon . . . oh, his ire painted him *far* more intimidating, whittled him down to avian sharpness a bit like the ice wraiths she and Arlo had faced only a *sliver* of time ago. A bit like the hollow iciness of the queen across from him, in fact . . .

And he was the High Prince.

In response to his violent promise, Riadne could only reel herself in and nod, excusing herself so that she, too, could fly to Arlo's bedside.

"*Leda,*" Celadon snarled next, rounding on the dryad woman. "You recently met with Gentian in Grim territory. I didn't realize it was you until just now, but I'm right, aren't I? It was you and that *pixie* in the alley beside the Colosseum. You were heard exchanging conversation with him on the matter of grievance with who I now have reasonable cause to believe to be the Dark Star. You were heard discussing *poison.*"

It was almost curious, how Nausicaä could simultaneously *hang* off what was happening and yet be so wholly unable to process it. Celadon was speaking words. The air around him almost seemed to be *sparking*, an electric sort of rage that should only be possible to Seelie Summer fae, not windborn fae of UnSeelie Spring. Did anyone else notice? It meant something. It all meant something. But Nausicaä couldn't *focus* to sort it out.

Celadon took a step closer to Leda, lip beginning to curl over his teeth. "I suggest you explain yourself *now.*"

Leda's compliance was immediate. "*I'm sorry,*" she gasped in a rush of apology, dropping to her knees in front of Celadon, who towered over her. "I'm sorry, I really didn't think . . . Yes, I met with Gentian! At the Colosseum. He'd heard the Madam would be there that night, and if anyone could find him a poison strong enough to harm an immortal, it would be her. I've known him for so long—he's the reason Queen Riadne even thought to ask if I wanted the job of instructing your cousin! I had *nothing* for *so long*, nothing but anger and resentment and hopelessness, and he gave me a chance to be something again. I *had* to go with him to make sure he got out of that place alive. I'm so sorry, Your Highness. He hated the Dark Star. I hated her too. My sister, Iliana—"

"Iliana," Nausicaä repeated dully.

That name.

She knew it.

She'd even cursed it, once. Because that name belonged to the woman Heulfryn had replaced Tisiphone with. That name belonged to the woman Nausicaä had placed blame on, too.

Leda didn't raise her head, didn't look Nausicaä's way, but she stiffened to hear her speak. When Leda resumed speaking, it was with less an edge of hysteria and more the hardness of a long-held grudge. "Iliana. My little sister, she'd been so in love with the man the Dark Star killed. They were going to be married. He'd promised her, one last trip and they would be married. But then he—"

Nausicaä barked an unkind laugh. "He wouldn't have. Heulfryn was *shit*. He was never going to marry your sister—in fact, after I torched him and his ride and got shunted *here*, I learned that she wasn't even the only one he'd *engaged* himself to in the weeks since he'd dumped Tisiphone. Iliana . . . Giselle . . . Lysandyr . . . If he married your sister, it would have been for something he wanted, and he would have left her once he got it, the same way he'd left Tisiphone. I did her a *fucking favor*—and you poisoned an innocent girl for it?"

"Leda," Riadne interrupted, without looking once at Nausicaä, merely waving back the Head Physician and motioning the dryad forward. "You mentioned this poison was potent. Time is of the essence, then—can you identify what it is?"

Leda glanced to Celadon, who still stood standing over her. But he gave the barest nod of his head, and she picked herself up off the ground and fell to Arlo's bedside.

Only because there was a slim possibility this mortal could help did Nausicaä yield her spot at Arlo's side to back away and join Vehan where he hovered, bluish-white in the face and gripping the bed frame of Arlo's cot so tightly his knuckles gouged at his skin.

Nausicaä watched, half her attention on Arlo, the other half darting around the room for sign of a Hunter come to collect on a soul. She sent a silent prayer to deities she'd forsworn and offended so greatly in the past century that she was sure they only laughed to hear it, but she was desperate . . . and they owed her.

They owed her this. Tisiphone was gone. Arlo couldn't be gone too. And where the hells was *Luck* right now? Arlo could certainly do with their presence.

Luck is not the absence of misfortune, after all, but how well you weather it. And the more you have of one, the greater the odds of attracting the other. I'd be doing you a disservice to grant you too much of my favor.

Unbidden, the words they'd said to Arlo back in their first hunt together played out in Nausicaä's head.

Damn it, she couldn't let herself think like this, couldn't spiral yet. If this Leda couldn't help Arlo, if the Head Physician couldn't . . . Nausicaä would do something, *anything* to keep her just a little longer. She didn't deserve the kindness or the happiness she was only just starting to realize Arlo brought into her life, but Arlo . . . Arlo didn't deserve to die.

Not for her.

Leda opened Arlo's mouth and examined what was inside.

She checked Arlo's pulse, laid a hand inches above her chest to examine her aura next, then slid it down to her stomach. "I can," she replied after far too long, and with a wince of something that might have been guilt. "It *is* the poison Gentian procured from the Grim Brotherhood. He asked for my help—told me it was for Nausicaä. I didn't think . . . I never thought for a moment he'd turn it on . . . not Arlo." She swallowed. "I didn't want this. I didn't want any part of revenge against the Dark Star. I turned him down, but this is still my fault. I'm sorry . . . I'm so *sorry.*"

"You're *sorry,*" Celadon hissed.

Nausicaä appreciated the sentiment. When this was all over, she and Leda were going to have a long discussion about this, but now wasn't the time.

Thank goodness for Riadne, who unfurled back to standing, took charge of the situation in a far more productive way than punching this dryad in the face, as Nausicaä sorely wanted to do right now. "You've the remedy, then?" she asked in cool calmness.

"Right here," Leda replied with a nod of her own, and pulled a tiny vial of some blue potion out of a pocket in her long skirt. "I kept it on me just . . . just in case. I was . . . I was debating giving it to Arlo in one of our lessons and telling her to watch out for her friend. But what the Madam gave Gentian . . . it wasn't strong enough, I recognized it as soon as he showed me. At most it would have made the Dark Star very ill for a while, and maybe Gentian would then realize he couldn't exact the revenge he wanted. Honestly, I never thought he'd dare change targets." She made no further hesitation to administer it, uncorking the vial and pressing the lip of it to Arlo's mouth, tipping its contents down her throat and massaging the muscle there to help her swallow.

Nausicaä observed every moment, every action like a hawk tracking its prey, because if this Leda and her potion only made things *worse* . . .

"Apologies, Your Highness," said Riadne as her servant worked. "It's my failing that this was allowed to pass at all."

"Your *failing*?" Celadon looked her deep in the eye. He was trembling with how angry he was.

Arlo's breathing was still too shallow.

Nausicaä gripped the bed frame too, felt the metal warp under her ungoverned strength.

"I'd say it was your *failing*, yes. You *failed* to vet your attendants properly. You *failed* to keep my cousin safe—a Viridian royal, your guest of honor, and now I'm starting to wonder if this might have been your intention all along, to place Arlo in the care of someone so unhinged and begrudging of her partner."

Her *partner*.

Nausicaä felt more stinging, hot wetness well up in her eyes.

It was just Nausicaä's luck to realize she had a beautiful, vibrant, indomitable *girlfriend* when that girlfriend was right on the cusp of death.

"This is your failing. This is your carelessness. This is your *hatred* for my family. We were foolish to come, and you *will*—"

It was sort of a big deal that Celadon was getting as worked up about this as he was.

Nausicaä appreciated it, but she knew what it meant, in the back of her head still capable of something other than debilitating panic, that a High Prince was so outraged with one of the Heads of the Courts. With his Father as unstable as he was . . . she wasn't the only one who was probably wondering right now what sort of punishment Celadon's temper might be able to coax Azurean into delivering.

And it was just as big a deal that Vehan, a mere Crown Prince, a nobody fae in the grand scheme of things, drew himself up to full height and rounded on Celadon with so much ice in both his eyes and voice, it seemed ridiculous it wasn't his element. "Then you're welcome to leave," he frosted.

Riadne—the young prince sounded *exactly* like his mother right now.

"You're welcome to leave if you're just going to insult *my* family in front of me like this. Because you're conveniently leaving out the fact that my mother has been nothing but *gracious* right now—"

"*Vehan Lysterne*," Riadne gasped, in livid reprimand.

And Nausicaä cut them *all* off with a gasp of her own. "*Arlo!*"

She tore to Arlo's side, ripping Leda away to reclaim her place, Arlo still unconscious but heaving great, wheezing breaths into her lungs—*alive.*

"Arlo!"

"She'll be okay."

She'll be okay!

"She just needs rest."

She just needs rest!

Nausicaä looked up at Leda, then over to Riadne. "Thank you," she uttered in a breath, and then, everything that had happened rushing in at her at once, burst out into torrential sobbing. "I'm s-sorry I trashed your f-f-foyer."

Riadne didn't seem to know quite what to do with a broken-down and blubbering Dark Star, could only nod in response and edge a step back—and yeah, Nausicaä didn't blame her. She probably looked half deranged in her current state, but she didn't care. Arlo was going to be *okay*.

She cried.

And she cried.

And she buried her face in her hands to cry some more, great streams of tears and gulps of breath and soul-shuddering *weeping*, a deluge that had been building for a while and hadn't found outlet until now, and the harder she cried, the harder it was to stop.

Celadon hovered a moment, then whirled around and swept from the room, taking with him half of the Verdant Guard that had assembled by the door, leaving behind the rest for Arlo.

No one commented.

Nausicaä barely noticed.

She *cried*. This was both the best and worst anniversary of the night she'd been expelled, but none of it mattered because Arlo was going to be *okay*.

CHAPTER 33

Aurelian

~⟶~

THEIR ADVENTURE ON THE Strip had been short-lived. Aurelian had been too preoccupied with thoughts about Vehan to be decent company, and while Vehan had seemed in outstanding physical condition, he was no less preoccupied with *his* thoughts as well. And the High Prince had been what could only be described as *morose* over leaving Arlo behind, so Aurelian suspected none of them were all that surprised when Theo declared them all "hopeless" and announced he was going back to the palace for an evening swim.

Another man down, and the rest of them had simply followed.

This had been more than fine with Aurelian.

It was difficult to concentrate on the potentially *life-altering* decision he was trying to make with Vehan right beside him, indeed in better health than he could remember seeing him in quite some time. Bright-eyed and flush with radiance, his aura warm and fizzling and *strong* against Aurelian's; he was quiet—whatever had gone on between him and Theo earlier in the day, it had apparently left him with a lot to think about—but he was *himself* again, and Aurelian couldn't help his attention wandering to trip over things like the way his raven hair shone even darker against the city lights or the way the dying orange of day made all that blue in his eyes so much more *electrifying*.

It was unfair for Vehan to look so fucking *perfect*, as though the universe knew Aurelian was trying to choose between telling him about his feelings or cutting himself off from them for good.

Alone in his bedroom, Aurelian had thought he'd finally be able to focus.

And then his brother had burst in—without so much as a knock, like usual, no matter how many heated arguments this invasion of Aurelian's privacy induced.

He was spared the biting reprimand that had leaped to the tip of Aurelian's tongue. *The High Prince's cousin has just been poisoned*, Harlan had blurted out in shock. *Io just told me. Apparently one of her attendants put something in her tea, and she's in the infirmary now, and—hey!*

Aurelian leaped off his bed.

He darted past Harlan and *ran*, clear from the Bessel wing to Medical. He barged through its door, dreading what he'd find, *convinced* he'd find carnage, a furious Nausicaä in its midst, and Arlo dead in a hospital bed, with Riadne's plot to wound the Viridian family finally unveiled just as he knew it would be.

What he found instead was Vehan.

It was dark in the infirmary. The windows had been drawn open to allow for night to filter through, moonlight bathing the rows of beds in a soft, cool glow.

There were no nurses, no MediFae, no strewn bodies—Nausicaä wasn't anywhere in sight, and for that matter, neither was Arlo's cousin or the queen. It was *only* Vehan, slumped in a chair pulled up to Arlo's bed. Aurelian's rather dramatic entry had startled him, the prince's blue eyes fairly luminous in the gloom, and piercing as they tracked Aurelian's approach to the bed.

He swallowed tightly—Arlo, she was so pale, looked so breakable and small, too innocent for Court theatrics and political intrigue and all the horrible things she'd be drawn into if she lived the palace life full-time.

Innocent . . . just like Aurelian had been before coming to this awful place.

"I just heard. Is she . . . ?"

"She'll be all right," Vehan replied. "Leda gave her a potion to counter the poison."

Deflating with his breath of relief, Aurelian nodded. "Good. That's . . . good." He cast a glance around, suddenly realizing that they were alone together for the first time since Aurelian had run off through the Egress after the incident on the mountain, and Vehan had been the one to track him down. That felt like *ages* ago now. "Does Nausicaä know?"

"She knows. She was very upset. And so grateful when Leda saved her that she even *thanked* them, both Leda and my mother, too."

"That's—" *Good*. He'd been about to say "good" again, but Vehan cut him off.

"The High Prince was *furious* of course. He yelled at my mother and made such awful threats to her that I couldn't hold my tongue. I shouted back, and Celadon . . ." He breathed a humorless laugh. "He wasn't very happy about that. Left just after Leda confirmed that Arlo would make a full recovery. He went to the Unseelie palace, I think, so we're in a lot of trouble whenever he gets back, possibly with the Falchion and *definitely* with Arlo's mother. A lot of trouble . . ." He frowned, glancing back down at Arlo, at her hand, which he'd been holding in his own all this time. "Nausicaä went to try to mediate things . . . I guess as a further show of gratitude. We'll probably be in even *more* trouble for it, but it was kind of her to offer, and she looked like she needed something to do with herself."

Aurelian took a step forward, placing his hands on the frame of Arlo's bed, looking not at her but at Vehan, so consumed with his thoughts that Aurelian had never felt him so out of reach as he was now.

He opened his mouth, intended to ask something—how Vehan was feeling, or if there was anything Aurelian could do for either him or Arlo right now, *something*. Once again, he floundered, and Vehan was quick to pick up the slack.

"Do you think my mother had something to do with this?"

Aurelian stared at him. His gaze dropped to Arlo. "No, Your Highness. Not this." From the sounds of things, this was too novice a job, too much risk for too little reward for Riadne to bother. The amount of trouble she was in right now so close to the Solstice . . . If it had been *afterward*, he might have had to answer *yes*.

And then Vehan asked, "Do you think she's capable of it?"

He held his tongue.

Something about the way Vehan watched him said he didn't really need Aurelian to confirm what he already knew.

"I'm not stupid, you know."

"I never once thought you were," Aurelian replied in a whisper.

"I know what everyone says about my mother—I know how she can be in a foul mood. I know she has a heavy hand, and that she's strict, and sometimes vicious even with her own flesh and blood and *especially* with her staff. I know they call her the Iron Queen because of that stupid staircase; the Cruel Queen of Light; that they whisper I'm the *true* Light, fated to be the saving grace they've all been waiting for, and I'm just so *tired*, Aurelian." He groaned, releasing Arlo's hand to curl forward, folding his arms across his knees and dropping his weight onto them. "I'm tired. I'm so tired of it. I know what they say. I know how she is. I know there's something not . . . not quite *right* with her. But she's my *mother*, Aurelian. She's my mother, and I'm not stupid, I don't buy for a second that Zale lost his tongue to some gods-damned infection or that the staff who suddenly disappear without a word or trace just packed their bags to return home. I know my mother is an obsessive, violent person and that she wants so badly to revenge herself on the Viridian family, and I'm *tired* of feeling so *torn* because *she's my mother*, and I love her. I know she's capable of so much *good*, and I just want to protect her because one day soon . . . I'm going to be the only person who will."

Aurelian let go of the bed frame.

He took a step toward Vehan.

Silently, wordlessly, he lowered himself to crouching until he looked his prince in the eye. "I don't blame you for wanting to protect the woman who gave birth to you, Vehan. The only family you have left. I don't think *anyone* does. She's your mother, just as you said. I couldn't imagine a thing I wouldn't do for mine."

Vehan lifted his gaze just enough to meet his, and it made something *squeeze* around his heart to see the amount of exhaustion and pain there. "Theo told me I *am* being stupid about one thing," he said, even quieter than before, so quiet that Aurelian had to lean in just a little closer to hear him. "Seeing Nausicaä today . . . how upset she was . . . I couldn't imagine being in that place, with *you* in that bed instead of Arlo. We went to the Thunder Plains today to practice my magic—it's back now. I'm . . . better now, but that's . . . He told me I was being a right ass about you and the High Prince, that there was nothing there, asked me why I was throwing such a childish tantrum over it and what it was I really wanted. And I've been thinking, Aurelian . . . I didn't really need to, but I've been thinking it over, because the one thing I'm tired of more than anything else is pretending I never loved you, that I ever stopped loving you. I'm tired of feeling like I've lost my best friend. I've been too afraid to ask it, but I think it's time I know . . . You said you don't hate me, but I really need you to answer it now: Do you like me at *all* anymore, Aurelian? Is there any hope for us . . . or should I let you go?"

"Yes."

The answer was out of him before he could even think to give it.

Panic drove it—panic, because he couldn't lie; panic, because he still wasn't sure what he wanted, although apparently he did; panic, because this changed *everything* between them, and there was no going back from this moment.

Blinking at him, Vehan leaned heavily back in his chair. "Yes?"

"Yes, I still like you."

"You . . . you do?"

"*Yes.*" Aurelian nodded once, curtly, and didn't blame how suspicious Vehan looked of his conviction, because his jaw had clenched rather tightly, and he probably looked very angry right now.

"I . . . okay. That's good. That's . . . good. I . . . have to ask, though, if . . . Is there any way you could ever *more* than like me? More than a friend, I mean?"

"Yes." Damn it. "I already do."

Vehan had loved him all this time? Well, so had Aurelian—fiercely, wholly, irrevocably. If there was one thing he'd learned in his role as Riadne's plaything, it was that he loved Vehan with everything he was, and he was never going to *not* love him. His prince would always be the most important person to Aurelian. He'd given him his *true name*, after all, and he wouldn't have done that no matter what sidhe fae custom demanded.

He wouldn't have done that for anyone other than the person he *loved*.

"Um . . ." Vehan looked the picture of startled by this information, not at all sure how to process it.

Aurelian shot to his feet.

"Ah—wait! Aurelian, where are you going?"

He turned around and strode right back out of the room into the hall.

Vehan called again for him, flew to the infirmary's door. Aurelian didn't stop. He *stormed* down the hall, one thought in his mind, and didn't yield to anyone he passed asking what he was doing or where he was going.

"You there, halt! You can't go in there—"

"Did you have anything to do with the poisoning of Arlo Jarsdel?" he demanded to know, barging into Riadne's office and slamming his palms on Riadne's desk, bending over the wood to look her close and firm in the eye.

Riadne watched him coolly from her seat, where she'd been doing nothing but sip on a glass of wine, as though this palace weren't falling apart, as though one of her guests weren't lying in her hospital recovering from near death.

Slowly, delicately, completely unconcerned and unsurprised by Aurelian's entrance, she blinked at him. Then, with a wave of her hand, the guards positioned outside her office retreated and closed the door behind them, and Aurelian was left alone with the singularly most deadly person in the entire Eight Great Courts, and he *didn't care*, because he was tired too.

"You know Arlo is important to Nausicaä. You know they're close, and she slighted you by what she did to your foyer, and you've punished others for *far* less. Did. You. Poison. Her?"

A rush of air escaped the queen's nose in a gentle snort. "I did not."

"Convenient that you found someone who dislikes Nausicaä so greatly to attend the girl she quite clearly adores."

"Truly," Riadne replied, leaning back in her chair. "But then, when you set yourself against the world as she has done, you tend to make a *number* of enemies. I had nothing to do with this."

Baring his teeth, emboldened by the adrenaline rushing through him, Aurelian decided to press his luck a little more—after everything that had happened today, this seemed like as good a time as any to shed a bit of self-preservation. "You're planning something for the Solstice—I know you are. And I'm willing to bet whatever it is, you're hiding the secrets behind that columbarium. There's something back there, I *know* there is, I can sense it. What are you playing at, Riadne Lysterne? What are you planning—*tell me*."

"Would you like me to show you?"

Aurelian stared.

His expression must have shown a flicker of confusion then, because Riadne pitched her head to laugh. "What would you do with the information, I wonder? I know you were in here not long ago. Did you sneak in with the High Prince? Have you managed to win young *Celadon* to your cause?" She grinned, something about the comment amusing to her. "I have your entire family in my palm, and if I give it but a squeeze . . ." She raised her hand, curled it closed around the air between them, crushing it just as she would Aurelian's mother, and father, and baby brother. "What would you do with the information? I'm tempted to let you know, because on the one hand, I could destroy you so *utterly* if you ever dared to tell my son the truth. I could make you watch as, one by one, every person who's ever meant *anything* to you curses your name for the torture they'll suffer, oh yes, my Vehan included. I could make you feel so much regret if you dared to speak . . . but on the other hand, such an *entertaining* game you've given me to play. This exciting *what if* danger you present, because really . . . what do you have to lose when I've already told you my *other* secret, that I plan on sacrificing your life to make Vehan mine completely."

"He will *never* be yours," Aurelian snarled. "Has it ever occurred to you that Vehan might as easily *turn* on you as bend to the grief over losing me?"

The flash of distaste was almost worth the way the queen leaned in, folding her arms on her stately desk, close enough that Aurelian wanted to flinch away. He could feel her breath as she spoke. "Has it ever occurred to you that you don't love my son at all and have merely bonded to him in your trauma? Can I ask you something, Aurelian? Do you actually like him as you say you do, or are you simply trying to *rescue* him from me like no one in this world can *ever* rescue you?"

He tore away, and the peel of laughter that floated out of the office after him rang in his ears well after he was gone.

CHAPTER 34

Celadon

———◇———

F ATHER." CELADON FAIRLY *SNARLED* the word as he burst into the High King's private quarters, his aura like a brewing tempest, consternation churning in his wake.

At his heels were the Verdant Guards who'd followed him from the Luminous Palace; numerous of the Reverdie's guards, whom he'd passed on his journey here from the Egress; his siblings; his *mother*, all of them pulled from their doings as though magnetized to Celadon's presence, all of them shouting after him—

"Celadon, what's the meaning of this?"

"Why are you here?"

"Your Highness, you haven't been announced, you can't go—"

And all of them he ignored.

He entered his father's personal chambers and promptly spun around, slamming the doors closed against his unwelcome entourage, and the Verdant Guard would do their duty. They'd been assigned to *his* care, and until their dismissal from that task, it was *his* orders they'd obey, no matter what Reseda, or Cerelia, or Serulean demanded—for now, at least, but that was just as well.

Celadon only needed a moment.

Crossing the room in a brisk stride, he approached where his father sat on a small obsidian sofa, evening tea set out on the coffee table before him. None of it Azurean had touched or even really seemed to notice—he did notice Celadon, though. Tracked his advance closely with those jade eyes that were both a blessing and a curse to any who inherited them.

Whatever state he was currently in, whatever reality, he watched

Celadon with awareness, which was all Celadon needed to know that in the very least, the person his father *saw* was his son.

A son who came to a halt in front of him and didn't bend the knee as custom dictated, nor bow his head with the respect the High King's position was due.

Celadon stood in front of him, glaring down his nose at the tired old man who sat in place of his once glorious father. Part of his heart *ached* to wear out his anger on him in such a way; the other part was tired, too. "I request an audience," he said, in a voice as quiet and level as still air, and tossed a balled-up photo in his lap.

Azurean only continued to look up at him—for a moment . . . two . . .

He wore the guise of kingship well, wrapped in sage and onyx silks, adorned with gold and ebony and emeralds—a little thinner than even the last time Celadon had seen him, sallow, age weighing so heavily on him now that it pulled at his skin, but still there was the beauty he'd once been famed for. Still there was the unsettling parallel, like looking into a mirror and seeing exactly himself. Curling russet hair, the bow mouth, the sweep of cheekbones, the cut of their hard, bright eyes—Celadon and Azurean.

So alike, they'd always been accused . . .

Azurean looked down at his lap.

He unfolded the photo, smoothed it out, stared down at it in yet more silence, until—

"It seems," his father replied at last, in a measured but far from soft tone, "that you hardly require or want my permission. Why are you here, Celadon? You are supposed to be—"

"With my mother?"

There.

That put some shock into that bland expression. And where Celadon might once have felt bad, as he'd been raised—no, *conditioned*— to put his family's needs and feelings above his own—it was curious that right now, all he felt was rage. "What?" he drawled. "Did you think I wouldn't figure it out? After all the hints you've dropped that I'm not Reseda's son; after all the time spent keeping me *here* and well away from Seelie Summer; after finding that picture in a room locked behind *blood* magic that I was somehow able to break?"

Azurean continued to gape at him. His head flung to the side, eyes wide, as though terrified that someone might walk in and overhear what they were discussing.

He *should* be terrified—Celadon didn't care, not any longer, not after tonight. He wasn't leaving here without the truth.

"I'd always assumed my mother to be a commoner you were too embarrassed to make your wife. Take it off."

"Celadon, I don't—"

"TAKE IT OFF!" he bellowed, his anger consuming him. Of their own accord, his hands darted out to seize his father by the front of his elaborate robes and haul him closer. "Take. It. Off. You take it off *right now.* The *lies.* This *glamour.* The magic you wove, that *only* you can weave, that your status as High King allows you to get away with. My *whole life* I've been looking at *your face* in the mirror—you think I can't feel that something is wrong with my own skin? You take it off, whatever you did to scrub away what marks me as *her* son. You take it off, and you explain to me *how.* How did this *happen?*" His voice cracked. His hands began to shake. There was guessing at a thing and there was receiving the undeniable proof of it, and the way Azurean's expression *melted* out of horror and into grief was confirmation enough that none of this was in Celadon's head. "How did this *happen?*" he repeated, his father's robes slipping out of his fingers for Celadon to stumble back. "Take it off. I want to see, just once, who I really am. Please. You owe me that much."

"My son," Azurean sighed—deeply, a breath that heaved his entire chest, and with it . . . he raised his hand. "It was only ever to protect you. Everything I did . . . it was only ever to *protect* you."

As High King, Azurean was powerful beyond what most could comprehend. Even now, this miserable shadow of who he'd once been, his magic was still so strong that there was nothing Celadon could have done to unweave what his father had placed over him—a glamour so carefully comprised and expertly laid, so profound it could apparently maintain itself for months at a time without the High King refreshing it.

But it *was* a glamour.

For so long, Celadon had suspected he was just a little *too* much his father's son, but the way his heart broke to feel the cool, tingling sensation that poured from head to toe like the trickle of water from a spring, washing away magic and ignorance both . . .

He shivered—fled to the mirror mounted on the wall beside the unlit fireplace and watched in horror as curling russet hair brightened to the shade of copper that was so prevalent in the Lysterne line; as his features took on an icy sharpness, as one eye remained the brightest, hardest jade green that marked him a Viridian, but the other . . . the purest, shocking *blue*. "*How*," he asked again, the fingers tracing beneath his changed eye and sliding up into hair that blazed like the firey sun against skin that had taken on a snowy quality.

This was *him*.

Celadon Viridian, himself for the very first time, dawn and twilight *both* in his royal glow and a *pain* in his core, because suddenly—as though it were more than a glamour the High King had removed—a magic that he'd been completely blocked off from stretched out from its confines.

He *gasped*.

"It was only to protect you, Celadon. My son. My *Light*." Azurean rose from the sofa. It sounded like a difficult task, but Celadon couldn't tear his eyes away from the mirror to help.

Footsteps on the carpet. Azurean came up behind him, looked as though he wanted to place his hands on Celadon's shoulders but then thought better of the action.

"The fate you were born to . . . I wanted to protect you. You are my *son*, and I wanted to spare you the cruelty of the people who'd see what you're capable of and either try to use it for their own gain . . . or kill you for the threat your very existence poses to the natural balance of things."

"I don't understand," Celadon breathed, sounding more like a child than he'd ever been even when he'd actually been that age.

Azurean sighed once more. "Reseda has always been a good woman, a *beautiful* woman. I love her as much as anyone dear to me, but Riadne . . . Riadne was something else entirely. *More* than love; she and I . . . we were inevitable."

"Riadne Lysterne is my mother."

Saying the words out loud . . . Celadon couldn't tell if he wanted to vomit right now or scream.

"Riadne Lysterne is your mother." Azurean nodded solemnly.

"*How.*"

"How else *but* love? We were never meant to be, Celadon. As the future Heads of our Courts, we weren't ever meant to be anything more than friends. And yet, as love does, it came for us regardless. I did try to break it off—it was . . . consuming, what I felt for Riadne, but I did try to end it after the twins were born, when Riadne had become engaged and our families grew more suspicious of the time we spent together. I tried to end it . . . but I *loved* her, Celadon. I loved her so much. Being parted from her . . . it was indescribable pain."

Breathing felt difficult—unreal.

This entire exchange was like a dream, a nightmare. The truth was exactly as he'd expected it, but it still changed *everything* to hear it spill from his father's lips.

"I'll spare you the details of my foolishness," Azurean continued. "Riadne married. Our affair didn't end. There was an edge to it, though—time perhaps would have healed the rift between us, the hurt of rejection, but then Riadne became . . . *with child*. And that child was not Vadrien's. And the world would know with undeniable proof what we'd done as soon as that child was born. A child of Spring and Summer—if they ever showed even a hint of inheriting

471

both Gifts of Headship . . . of being able to take command of *both* Seasons? The other Heads would all fear that a child with that power could easily turn their thoughts to taking command of the *rest* of the Seasons. It would mean war. I begged Riadne to give that child up, but she wouldn't. She wanted them . . . she wanted *you*."

Every time Celadon had ever met Riadne flashed before his eyes in that moment.

None of them had ever left him with even an inkling that she *wanted* him, as her son or even around in general.

"I loved her. I could not deny her what she wanted so badly. But . . . it had to come at a cost. A compromise. Reseda had been with child herself, due just days after Riadne, by the physician's estimation. It was pure luck that made this possible, luck . . . and misfortune. You see, it had taken . . . quite a lot to get Reseda to agree to pretend that she'd given birth to another set of twins. You, and our son, who in the end died before he could even draw his first breath. Quite a lot, and our relationship was never the same since. But it took an even greater toll on *Riadne* to agree to pretend that you'd died in childbirth too, to get an ironborn physician to pronounce you dead and smuggle you here to us. A newborn babe, ripped from his mother's arms. Riadne . . . you wouldn't see it. You don't know her as I do. The despair it filled her with to have the child she wanted more than anything torn from her completely at birth. To never know her for who she truly is—your *mother*. But you couldn't know. No one could know, least of all you, because . . . you are exactly what we feared you'd be, my son . . . and *more*."

This entire story left him *reeling*.

Riadne . . . his *mother*. The deception. The hurt. The *secrets*.

Celadon looked down at his feet, at the fresh new grass growing from the carpet, spilling out around where he and his father stood, bluebells beginning to push through in happy little blooms.

It took him a moment to realize this wasn't his father's doing but his *own*.

"You have always stood out brighter than any of your UnSeelie Spring kin, my son. You have always possessed *both* the blessings of your Courts, might even possess the blessing of *Winter*, if your power was all left free. My magic kept all this sealed away in you. It protected you through your most vulnerable years. I beg you, Celadon—tell no one of this yet, not even your cousin. Keep this between us and us alone for just a while longer. Buy yourself a little more time—"

"And you?"

Azurean looked at him sadly. "I do not deserve your consideration for what I've kept from you. I hope you'll give it to me, regardless, and to your mother—your true mother. Do not reveal what you know before the Solstice."

And suddenly, this was all *too much*.

Celadon laughed—he laughed, and he *laughed*, until that laughter turned to tears, and he couldn't be certain whether it was really laughter anymore or crying. "Reseda never loved me. The family I was raised with, no one here *ever* loved me, and *this* is the reason—"

"Your sister and brother don't—"

"Oh, they know. Of course they know, of course Reseda would have told them—*them*, her *real* children." He wheeled around, anger rising once again to pull his shoulders back, straighten his posture, draw him taller than Azurean . . . and when had *that* happened? When had Celadon ever been the one to tower over the man he'd idolized for as long as he could remember? "Do you know why I came here tonight?"

Azurean watched him wordlessly, taking the brunt of Celadon's frustration on the chin without any fight in return, and that only served to increase his irritation.

"I came here because Arlo's been poisoned. Arlo—the only family who's ever treated me like family, who's never lied to me even though *she's* the one who's supposed to be able to! Arlo—your own blood—was poisoned, and it was Riadne's fault. *So much* has been

Riadne's fault, and you let her get away with *murder*. I never understood why until now. She's been this way for so long. You *know* she's
ill, that she's suffering from far more than *grief*. You know that whole
Cosmin-damned palace is *terrified* of her, and you won't do *anything* . . . because you loved her, and you still do."

Azurean only continued to watch him.

"You've known this whole time. You're hiding behind what that
Crown is doing to you—oh, you're sick, you're ailing. I've been shoul-
dering *that* burden too, but you know. You knew what was going
on with the ironborn community. You knew it had to do with the
philosopher's stone Nausicaä brought you. You've known this whole
time that something *awful*, the darkest magic, was going on in your
Courts, and you did nothing—practically forbade anyone else to do
anything, either—because you also knew all this time that Riadne
Lysterne has something to do with it. And you love her, so you didn't
want to see her punished for it."

A moment passed . . .

Two . . .

"The things I've covered up for you. The secrets I've kept. The
truth about the Jarsdel family—what happened to them, who Arlo
really is, who her *father* really is. I've kept so much . . . and you want
me to keep this too? Riadne is going to kill you," Celadon added
breathlessly, panting as though he'd just run for *miles* at full speed
without stopping.

And still Azurean just stared at him.

"She's going to kill you," he repeated, this time on the hiccup of
emotion, because damn it all, but this was his *father*.

Lifting his hands, Azurean clutched him at last by the shoulders
and drew him in. Celadon could feel the cool trickle of magic weave
itself around him once more, his powers gathered up and stuffed back
inside their boxes, his appearance scrubbed clean of any trace that he
was anything other than his father's son.

He was Celadon Fleur-Viridian once more, and as his Father

drew him in, he collapsed against him, hugging him tightly, sobbing because it was just *too much* for far too long.

"I am sorry, my son. Celadon . . . I am sorry."

He couldn't remember the last time his father had consoled him like this, or even the last time his father had this much self-awareness for consolation to be possible.

It was nice to pretend for a moment that everything was as it should be—that Celadon was just a boy going through a rough time, with parents he could depend on to care about him.

But such was his life that the moment was fleeting.

The High King's doors burst open once more to reveal the Verdant Guards doubled over in pain and the palace guards cowering in fear. Reseda . . . Cerelia . . . Serulean . . . no one else dared to attempt apprehending Commander Thalo Viridian-Verdell as she barreled into the High King's chambers, sword drawn in one hand, the air pulled into a writhing whip in her other. She was *seething*.

"An attempt has been made on my daughter's life. I will have punishment or *war*, but either way, there *will* be a queen at my feet before dawn. Decide now."

A blond head popped out from behind the enraged Commander—Nausicaä Kraken, and *Cosmin*, but that couldn't mean anything good . . .

"Hi," said Nausicaä, sounding a touch awestruck and looking up at Thalo as though at a goddess of vengeance given flesh. "Believe it or not, I'm actually here as the *mediator*, but I want it stated for the record that if this *does* end in bloodshed, I'm immediately siding with Team Arlo's Mom."

And now it was Celadon who could only stare.

CHAPTER 35

Arlo

⁓

ARLO'S RETURN TO CONSCIOUSNESS occurred in a trickle of stages. It began with awareness that she'd never felt so spectacularly awful in her life. A headache throbbed between her eyes, and weariness had sunk through uncomfortably sticky skin straight down to her bones, turning even the slightest of movements—every one of which sent shivers of dull pain through her entire body—into a Heraclean effort.

The next thing she realized was that she wasn't alone.

The sound of conversation floated around her, muffled for her muzzy disconcertion, but she could tell the speakers were trying to keep their volume hushed as well.

She was in a bed, she noted after that.

It wasn't her own, and something about the overly crisp feel of it combined with the uniquely sterile scent in the air, which her time spent tending to Nausicaä earlier this summer now associated with medical wards, made her suspect this was exactly where she was—the palace infirmary.

And it was this conclusion that reminded her at last of all that had happened to bring her to this moment: Nausicaä appearing in her bedroom, coming to collect her for one last hunt; the ice wraith; the battle on the ghost ship on the North Atlantic Ocean; Gentian; *the poisoned tea* . . .

Arlo gasped, eyes flying open wide—and gasped *again*, even more violently, pressing as flat as she could against her pillow bed when what registered in her immediate line of vision were the far too close and *shockingly* yellow eyes of a person she didn't know.

"You're so . . ." This wholly unfamiliar person mused on what she was, drawing back to consider Arlo at a more comfortably distant angle. Very long and lean and disturbingly wraithlike with xis too-sharp features, golden-starlight shimmering skin, ivy-green hair, and eyes that were all electric iris and no pupil at all. Arlo didn't need the distinct tone of rotting in xis aura *or* the black cloak xe wore to tell her xe was one of the Wild Hunt. But xe was so *young*—goodness, xe had to be younger than her, even, at least in appearance. "You're so *mortal*," xe finally announced.

Arlo blinked at xim, unsure of how to respond to this. "Thank you?"

Whoever this was waved as though xis comment had been a kindness xe'd been all too gracious to bestow on her. It was fortunately the extent of their interaction, though, because in the very next moment, Nausicaä physically tackled xim to claim xis place, and rushing to claim the other side of Arlo's bed was—

"Mom?"

"Hey, sweetie," Thalo cooed, reaching to help as Arlo tried to sit up in her bed. But both were interrupted partway through, and Arlo wasn't the only one to startle when the door to the infirmary burst open wide to *crack* against the wall.

Aurelian stood in the doorway.

He looked *wild* with whatever determination had brought him here, lavender hair stuck in odd directions as though he'd been obsessively combing and gripping it with his hands. His dark brown jeans and burgundy shirt were rumpled like he hadn't slept since the last time Arlo had seen him, had instead been on a very brutal run, judging by how sweaty he was, and through the surrounding wood, by how bits of debris clung to his arms and face and clothing.

It was bright enough in the world beyond the infirmary windows to indicate late morning—Arlo had been out for at *least* a full night; had Aurelian been gone that whole time? Regardless, it wasn't her that inspired his distress.

Aurelian stood there, heaving breath.

His eyes widened slightly—possibly, he hadn't been expecting so many people present, but there was Nausicaä, Thalo, three people Arlo didn't recognize at all but was willing to bet were the remaining members of the Wild Hunt, Celadon, Theo, and standing in the midst of it all, Vehan, too.

The Seelie Summer prince looked a little worn as well, pale, with dark shadows under his eyes. Apparently, he hadn't slept a wink either, and it was him that Aurelian's gaze settle on.

It was him he squared his jaw at.

It was *him* he marched over to without a word, grabbing Vehan by a fistful of his shirt, and—for a moment Arlo thought he was going to throw a punch with his other hand.

Instead, and far more shockingly, he hauled Vehan toward him, and in the middle of the crowded room full of the realm's most dangerous and important people, crushed their mouths together in a *kiss*.

Arlo stared.

The rest of the room stared too.

Vehan seemed to be frozen.

"What is *happening*?" Arlo cried, batting away the hand Nausicaä lifted to shield her eyes, her other held up over her own with a look of feigned scandal.

"*Finally*," said Theo with a shake of his head.

Mouth pursed and a little disapproving, Celadon merely nodded in agreement with this statement.

It was Thalo who cleared her throat and gave the boys a pointed look when Aurelian broke his *interestingly timed* kiss to murmur a sorry at his thoroughly stupefied prince, and then an even quieter apology to the room. With a glance at Arlo and nod in her direction, and something that might have been an "I'm glad you're okay, please excuse us," he pulled Vehan toward the door, still holding him firm by the shirt, and exited with him back into the hall.

"*Well*," said Nausicaä, looking from the door to Arlo. "On that note, congratulations on surviving your very first poisoning!"

Arlo collapsed back against her pillow with a groan. "Is this what *surviving* feels like?"

"No idea. No one's ever tried to poison me before, which is very rude, and I'm very jealous."

The glare Arlo angled up at Nausicaä softened quickly for what lurked behind her frankly lackluster grin. Guilt, anxiety, relief, concern—her emotions were so close to the surface right now that the sarcastic bravado Nausicaä normally hid such things behind couldn't properly mask them. Arlo was given the rare reminder that the harder Nausicaä tried to pretend she was unaffected by certain things, the more she actually was.

With a sigh that made her lungs ache—seriously, every movement was pain that didn't make a *bit* of sense, because she'd been poisoned, not hit by a freaking *train*—she lifted her hand a couple of inches and shot Nausicaä a very flimsy, very quick finger-gun. "Never say never."

"You're such a *dork*," Nausicaä replied, hiccupping on an emotion.

"Okay, you two," Thalo interjected, bending in to sweep wisps of Arlo's hair back from her forehead. "That's enough excitement. You need your rest, Arlo. You very nearly died last night." The mere mention of what could have happened made Arlo's throat constrict, but adding to that were the tears that sprung to her mother's eyes as she spoke. "I was so scared, Arlo. My baby girl . . . but you're fine now, you're all right." She leaned in closer and pressed a kiss to Arlo's brow. "Don't ever do that to me again."

"I'll try," Arlo replied with a watery laugh to lighten the mood. With a glance between her mother and Nausicaä, she added in a slightly more serious hush, "Why is the Wild Hunt here?"

"I don't really know," her mother replied in a dark but considering tone, withdrawing slowly from Arlo to sharpen her famous jade glare at them. "They haven't said."

Nausicaä clapped her hands together, steel eyes a little starry. "You should have seen it—as soon as we showed up here, she drew her sword and was all *You Shall Not Pass*, and I think I fell a little bit in love with your mom, I'm not going to lie."

Not that Arlo blamed her mother. As harvesters of souls and ferrymen for the dead, it would be alarming to *anyone* to see the entirety of the Wild Hunt turn up in a sickroom, and Thalo Viridian-Verdell was not a mild person. She wouldn't have taken kindly to the sudden threat of their presence *or* given up Arlo without a spectacular fight, and if any mortal could manage to take one down with them, Arlo suspected it would be her.

"Nausicaä and Celadon both explained what happened at the palace, why the Verdant Guard had brought in a pixie for capture, but your friend here didn't return with us. Didn't appear until a short bit ago, the Hunt in tow. I can't imagine why, when the High King left it to *me* to deliver Queen Riadne's reprimand for her carelessness with my only daughter." Thalo paused on a look that said volumes about her displeasure, both with the queen and the Hunt's mysterious presence, and Arlo felt her guilt ratchet up another level. It really hadn't been the queen's fault. How was she to know that Gentian held such a grudge against Nausicaä? "But never mind it, sweetheart." She turned back to Arlo, expression smoothing out into motherly care. "You just focus on getting better. I'm sure you feel awful right now, and this all only *just* happened . . . None of this is for you to worry about. We'll talk out in the hall."

Thalo stood, narrowing her eyes in suspicion at the three Hunters by the door.

Stark white eyes; shimmery, dark bronze skin; long black hair pulled back in tight braids that draped down his back; tall and lean and carved from pure strength, Arlo knew who the one in front was even though she'd never seen his face before now—the Hunter from the throne room, the first she'd ever heard speak, whom Nausicaä had called *Eris*.

And when he spoke now, that deep, rich baritone confirmed it. "It is Arlo we have come to talk with."

Thalo folded her arms over her chest, scowl deepening. "Why? She's only just woken up. I'm sure whatever it is can wait."

"We were told to come," replied the other Hunter whom Arlo didn't recognize, the one beside Eris, with violet eyes, liquid black hair tied in a knot atop his head, and a fawn-brown complexion that possessed an otherworldly, moonlight-pearly sheen.

"By whose *instruction?*"

"That would be mine," said a voice off to Arlo's left, deeper in the infirmary. It was a voice she knew quite well by now, though when she looked, it was to find a face she'd only met once before.

A different infirmary, a different time, when their roles had been reversed and it had been Nausicaä lying in recovery in a hospital bed.

Luck—they were suddenly sitting on the bed beside hers, in a form that was no one gender but very distinctly many. Their olive-green skin gleamed under a sheen of gold that reminded Arlo a bit of her die, and was branded all over with runes like tattoos; their shamrock-green hair fanned around their angular face; their glittering black horns curled from temple to chin in great, proud sweeps, and in their elaborate, loosely fastened robes of emerald, red, and gold not-quite-fabric, not-quite-air, they seemed larger than life, every inch the titan they'd always been.

Their cosmic eyes *consumed* the room's rapt attention.

Everyone stared, even Arlo; even the Hunters.

It was Arlo's fearless mother who took a step toward them, hand flitting to the pommel of the sword she carried at her side. "And who, by Cosmin, are *you* supposed to be?" she growled.

Luck tipped their head in polite greeting. "A titan."

Once again the room plunged into ringing silence, broken only a beat later by Celadon's gasp. He rushed to Arlo's bedside, glaring daggers at Luck, but Thalo didn't need metaphor to demonstrate how she felt about this information.

"An immortal," she snarled, and ripped her sword clean from its sheath, arming herself in an instant. "You *dare* to break the treaty between our realms right in front of me, a *Viridian*?"

Arlo's very mortal mother, prepared in the bat of an eye to wage battle with a *titan*—Arlo sighed.

Nausicaä, meanwhile, folded her hands together in the shape of a heart in Thalo's direction.

"Mine is the ancestor who drove you out. Mine is the High King who can summon you to this realm, and *only* him. Over my rotting *corpse* will you be allowed to stand there so brazenly. What do you want? Speak and leave or *die*."

"Mom, please stop trying to fight everyone. It's okay!" Arlo tried to intervene, rising onto her elbows. "This is Luck. They've been *helping* me."

"*Helping* you?" Thalo wheeled around to fix an incredulous look on her. "A *titan* has been . . . helping you? With *what*?"

Luck rose from their bed, stepping around the point of Thalo's sword to approach the end of Arlo's. They were so much *bigger* than anyone else in the room, and their aura . . . it was a dense pressure against her own, as thick and overwhelming as tar, ancient and powerful and sitting in the back of Arlo's nose a bit like gasoline—not entirely *good*, but not a bad scent either. Although definitely too much for her current, recently *poisoned* state. "As your daughter has said, you may call me Luck. Chance. Fortune—I go by numerous names. The purposes I serve are myriad; I tend to many threads in the tapestry of the various worlds. I am also Arlo Jarsdel's patron—she, my vassal. What I'm helping her with is up to her to let you in on." They looked now at Arlo, sizing her up, possibly wondering whether they'd made the right decision in choosing someone as fragile and easily duped as her. But then they bowed their head to her. "It is time for your final lesson, Arlo. I have gathered here in this room the people you can trust to keep your secrets. Two have . . . found themselves otherwise preoccupied at the moment, but as I've said, luck is ever and closely entwined with Misfortune. It's no matter. Before we begin, I'll give you the chance to dismiss the rest, or allow them to stay and listen."

Arlo considered the titan before her.

She looked around the room, at Nausicaä, the three Hunters, Celadon, her mother, Theo . . .

"A lesson?" she echoed faintly.

Luck nodded.

So much had happened in the entire span of ten minutes since Arlo had regained consciousness after having been *near fatally poisoned*, but she sighed again, allowed Nausicaä to help her sit properly upright, and nodded for Luck to continue.

"When we first met in the Faerie Ring, I informed you that you were at a crossroads. Do you remember?"

Arlo nodded.

"You approach another. From here on out, I will only appear to you when summoned, and even then, only if I can. You are now, and until you choose otherwise, under my favored protection. Through hardship and ordeal, I will be on your side, doing all that I can to see you through this phase in your life."

But.

"Nausicaä here has already guessed it—Fate has marked you with great potential, spun you not from the usual ingredients but from the stars that burn for immortalkind. You are mortal. You are ironborn. But you have been made with a magical core far greater in strength and capacity than what either could ever hope to wield. It is Fate who slipped into your destiny the possibility of our meeting. It is she who gave you the chance to break free of her original plan that would have made you a hero to the Courts of Fae. In doing this, she made it possible for you to become what immortals call a Wild Card—free of one set destiny, with potential to become a demi-deity among your kind."

Arlo, who had no idea how to respond to this right now, simply gaped at Luck.

"Under my guidance, as a Hollow Star you can choose to replace your original destiny with *anything*. You could still yet be a hero . . . or a *villain*; famous, royal, a troll, a mer, even a *Hunter*, like Eris, Vesper, and Yue here." They paused to share a look with Eris, who returned it with a slow blink. Arlo didn't know what to make of this, but was distracted enough by what Luck was saying to pay it little attention.

Luck continued. "You can choose to be anything with one of your four wishes, and that makes you special, makes you very important to the immortals, who will soon begin to present themselves to you in quest for your favor—and there will be your crossroads. The many deities will seek to make you a scion of their name, and in so doing, will activate that potential inside you, fill you with otherworldly power so that you may channel the worship necessary to make them sovereign of *their* realm just as your High King is here. And the longer the Bone Crown remains in this realm, the higher the likelihood that the one-day clash of powers brewing in the immortal ranks will come to pass. That future is up to you, Arlo Jarsdel. It is *your* favor that will decide the form it will take."

Arlo swallowed.

Thalo and Celadon both were speechless, staring between Luck and Arlo as though they'd been conversing in the only language they didn't know—and really, considering how much backstory they were missing here, that was more or less the case.

Extending a hand, Luck somehow spanned the distance that separated them without moving at all and presented Arlo with her die. It sat in their palm, jade that was the exact shade of her eyes, gold that glowed with inviting warmth and promise. "For one so small, so young and breakable, there is a great deal of resilience in you. A great deal of strength, and will, and fire . . . Mortals have long amazed me with what they're capable of accomplishing on nothing but a wish and determination to see it through. Whatever path you choose to walk, I will be *glad* to do so with you."

It meant a lot to hear them say this. It terrified her in no small way, everything she was supposedly intwined in, everything she'd have to face in her near future if she continued on as a Hollow Star. But knowing she had Luck on her side throughout it all . . . "At the moment, you are weak and tired and have only just survived grave injury. This is why I've chosen now for your final lesson, so that you understand exactly what is at stake and exactly what you risk in continuing forward.

"There will be danger. There will be death. There will be a great deal of suffering. There is war brewing in the Immortal Realm. A war dependent on your favor, as well as whoever claims the Crown that my husband cast into this realm in desperation to keep it from those who would misuse it in our own. You said it once, my dear: shedding destiny is much more work than allowing Fate to steer you, and as was the case back in the Faerie Ring, so it is now. Arlo, should you ever wish to leave this all behind you, I present to you the final feature of your die: choice."

They closed their hand around it, and the world around them stopped.

Nausicaä and the Hunters were the only ones who remained in full life along with Arlo and Luck, all of them looking on at the words that had scrawled themselves in glittering dust in the air.

Arlo's options. *Escape* burned so brightly it drew her immediate attention.

"The escape function will cancel any roll you don't wish to go through with. If you take up your die for an action, if you call it out and then decide against it upon seeing how high a number you need to roll, you simply need to announce *Escape* instead of *Roll* to call it off. But just as this can be put toward general use, so can it be used to bring this entire journey to an end. Should you ever desire out of your role as a Hollow Star, out of immortal fancy and this entire plot, all you need to do is pick up your die and declare that intention—announce it, call *Escape*, and like a factory reset, you will be restored to how you were before our meeting. You will have no memory of being a Hollow Star. You will not remember me or our time together or anything done with the die in your hand—those memories will be glossed over with alternative fabrications, just as they would be if you failed to pass your Weighing and were stripped of your knowledge of magic. If you ever change your mind, this is your way out, but once surrendered, your die will never present itself to you again. I will disappear from your life. You will not get a second chance at this role. Do you understand, Arlo? There is a price for all things."

Arlo reached out slowly and allowed Luck to tip her die into her palm. It was as warm as it looked, and soothing just to hold, like a part of her returned after being missing.

As frightening as things had been lately, as overwhelming as was what Luck had just told her, she felt a little better knowing she wouldn't be trapped should the path she was on ever become too much for her to handle.

Looking up into Luck's face, she closed her hand around her die and nodded firmly. "I understand."

Luck closed their hand around her fist and stared deeply back into her gaze. "It is not my nature to prefer any one mortal being. It invites misfortune to be careless with my favor. Still . . . my girl. The immortals will seek you out in many ways, will pit their cleverness against the treaty that keeps only their *physical* form out of this realm. They will do this at great personal risk, all to get to *you*. Be careful of their desperation. And Arlo . . . be careful of Moros."

"So it's *true*, then?" Arlo heard Nausicaä ask—*demand*, really—but in the span of time it took Arlo to blink, Luck was gone, and she had to wonder whether it was better or worse that the one person they'd dared warn her against was someone who made the Dark Star's entire face drain deathly white.

CHAPTER 36

Vehan

~~~~~~

"AURELIAN, WILL YOU JUST *wait*?" Vehan cried in frustration, following at a jog as his . . . well, he wasn't entirely sure *what* Aurelian was to him now after what had occurred in the infirmary, and really, over the course of their entire relationship, which had been one giant question mark after another the whole duration so far.

But that was exactly what Vehan would like to talk about, if his *whatever Aurelian was* would only stop and allow him the chance to catch up.

Great, powerful strides swept Aurelian down the morning-drenched halls, already lit up dazzling for the cloudless day outside.

He'd released Vehan's shirt the moment they broke out into the medical-wing corridor and, without looking back at him, prowled off in the direction of only gods knew where, leaving Vehan to scramble after him.

Part of Vehan was deeply irritated by this expectation, as though it had been *him* tormenting *Aurelian* with his are-we-or-aren't-we indecision these past few years and not the other way around, but the other part—the more predominate part, the part that drove Vehan on and made his heart leap so high it sat in the back of his throat—was simply bewildered.

Aurelian had *kissed* him.

Aurelian had kissed him in a *room full of other people*.

And only hours ago, he'd told Vehan he didn't hate him, that he *liked* Vehan, as more than a friend, and Vehan couldn't help how all this made him hope against impossible hope that—

Aurelian slammed to a halt so suddenly that Vehan, absorbed as he currently was in his thoughts, nearly collided with his back.

"*Thank you,*" he said in breathless fervor. "Aurelian, can we talk? Please?"

But Aurelian didn't reply. He merely stood there, staring at the marble floor, possibly wondering just like Vehan what the hells had just happened.

With a sigh, Vehan slipped his hand into Aurelian's and moved toward the closest door. There'd be no hauling Aurelian anywhere as easily as he'd done with Vehan; as lesidhe, Aurelian was so much stronger, a bit like an unmoveable mountain, nearly as solid and unyielding as trying to nudge *Nausicaä* anywhere she didn't want to go. But a quick glance around told Vehan that this door would lead them to a small, comfortable parlor where no one else should be right now, perfect for the conversation they needed to have.

Vehan stepped toward the door.

Aurelian didn't budge.

"*Please*, Aurelian?" he coaxed, all the conflicting things he was feeling right now slipping out with the words. "It's time."

A golden glance snapped in Vehan's direction—finally, his words broke through.

"I know—why do you think I dragged you out here if not to talk?" His expression set in grim determination, Aurelian sprung back into motion, tightening the clasp of their hands and pushing past Vehan through the door and into the room beyond.

And Vehan *had* been right, the room *was* a parlor. Cloistered away from the world by heavy cream curtains that had yet to be opened by the palace staff, its pale gray carpet and white furniture and marble pieces of art were bathed in darkness—darkness as much as could gather in any corner of the Luminous Palace. It was exactly what they needed right now, a place for them to just be *them* away from the many eyes of the Court.

Releasing him once again, Aurelian strode to a sturdy oak table standing off to the right, stained to highlight every line and whorl in the timber that made it.

He placed his palms on the table's surface.

Vehan closed the parlor door, then crossed the room cautiously, because Aurelian had been acting so strangely these last few days. And yeah, Vehan's jealous tantrum might have had something to do with that, but he could tell there was more to Aurelian's unusual skittishness, and he didn't want to spook him into fleeing once again.

"Aurelian?" he hedged.

He stopped just close enough that he could touch Aurelian's back if he reached out to do so, but didn't.

For a moment, he thought Aurelian might not answer, that he would have to be the one to start their conversation. Which was fine with him, but then . . .

"I'm also tired."

Vehan's head tilted a fraction in confusion.

"I'm so tired, Vehan," he continued, fingers beginning to curl against the wood. "I'm so tired of this place. I'm so tired of feeling like *nothing* is in my control. I'm tired of pretending I don't want this, that I haven't been in love with you since we were kids, that I don't want to be with you, *properly*, for whatever time I have left."

For some reason, despite their kiss and their earlier conversation, Aurelian's confession surprised him. He could do nothing but stare at the darkened silhouette of his best friend's back—Aurelian, the boy with whom he'd shared more of himself than he'd ever dared with anyone else, the boy he *loved*, standing there hunched in surrender, telling him he loved Vehan back.

That he wanted to *be with him* . . . It was a lot, after Vehan had all but convinced himself this moment would never happen.

"So," Vehan said, still breathless. Hope against impossible hope . . . "Does this mean you . . . Are you asking me to be your boyfriend?"

He almost laughed at how ridiculously underwhelming the statement was, because this moment was so much more than that. Never once in Vehan's life had he had a relationship that was so simply defined. Boyfriends, girlfriends—he didn't have them. He had *secret trysts* and *prospective life partners*, people who would have to sign contracts and receive lessons on how to act as said partner and bear the world's scrutiny before they could even start officially dating. Relationships had *never* been a simple matter for Vehan Lysterne, Crown Prince of Seelie Summer, Queen Riadne's only heir. Asking Aurelian this question sounded completely absurd to his ears, however *right* it felt to say.

Aurelian felt no compunction over laughing, apparently. It was harsh and quiet and more an escape of breath than anything, but it was a laugh. "Yes, Vehan, I'm asking if you'll be my boyfriend."

Unfurling, Aurelian straightened and turned to face him. Even in the room's dim light, his molten gaze blazed luminous, and Vehan had always felt like those eyes could see right through him, but for once, they didn't need to. He was certain his feelings were as obvious to spot on his face as his features. "I would like to be *yours*—but on one condition." He swallowed, pinned Vehan with even fiercer intensity, so that Vehan couldn't look anywhere else in this moment but directly into those burning eyes. "You have to swear to me on your name, your *true* name, that if anything happens to me, you won't let it be your excuse to forget who you are. You have to swear that you won't lose sight of your goodness and compassion and capacity for *love*, the things that I know are going to make you the best king this Court has ever known."

A thread of apprehension knitted through Vehan then.

He'd written off the previous comment—the *for whatever time I have left*—as a manner of speech, but now this . . . "Aurelian?" he said, hesitant to ask, but he had to know. "Is everything all right? You're not in any sort of trouble, are you?"

"You have to swear it," Aurelian repeated, ignoring the question.

"Not until you answer why."

"Of *course* I'm in trouble," Aurelian replied, agitation weighing on his brow. But there was something more; to Vehan, it looked a little like *panic*. "As the Seelie Summer steward or your lover, I'll always be at some sort of risk, and I want you to swear to me—the only contract I care about—that whatever happens, you won't lose sight of who you are. You won't let yourself become someone else's puppet. You won't—"

Vehan lifted a hand.

So this was it, then—Aurelian's uncharacteristic austerity, his stony indifference to Vehan these last few years, his stipulations, he'd just been worried about the *standard things*, the difficulties Vehan's entire way of life since birth had desensitized him to, prepared him to handle in stride, but were understandably far more concerning to someone not born with a target on their back.

He smiled gently. "I swear it," he said. Cutting off Aurelian's desperation, he took a step forward, closing the distance between them to a sliver. "On my true name, Julean Soliel Lysterne, I swear to you." Raising his hands, he placed them on Aurelian's chest, the sunny autumn warmth of him seeping through the cotton of his shirt.

Aurelian was beautiful.

There were times when Vehan looked at him and thought he was the most beautiful person he'd ever seen. Looking up at him now, at all the vibrant colors of him—the richness of his tan, the gold in his eyes, purple hair and black tattoos and gleaming silver piercings—this was one such time. Vehan was fairly stricken with his wonder over how so much perfection could exist in a singular boy.

He loved Aurelian.

He loved Aurelian with *everything* he was.

"I swear to you that I won't forget my goodness and compassion and capacity for love. Anything, I'll swear to you *anything*, if you'll be mine for as long as you let me have you."

Aurelian released a breath and dipped his head, and in acceptance of this vow, touched his lips to Vehan's in the featherlight trace of a kiss.

Finally, a voice inside him cried—his own this time, his elation and years of pent-up stress and worry and *pining* spilling over. Finally, what had once felt inevitable, and later impossible, was now immutable reality, and it wasn't until he tasted watery salt that he realized how much he'd *needed* this.

"Rel," he gasped against Aurelian's mouth, hiccupped a laugh as the endearment escaped him, something he hadn't called him in so long that it only made Vehan's tears fall thicker to do so now. *Finally*.

Aurelian placed his hands on Vehan's hips.

They gripped a little tighter when his kiss turned firmer against Vehan's mouth.

And when they traveled down the back of Vehan's thighs to *heave* him up against him, to quickly turn them about so that it was Vehan pressed against the table and Aurelian pinning him *hard* against the wood with the length of his long body, what started as chaste sentiment fanned into wildfire *heat*.

And Vehan gasped again—a different word this time—into Aurelian's mouth, hot and open and *rough* against his own. "Luka . . ."

Aurelian growled.

He *smeared* a kiss across Vehan's lips that trailed over his jaw and down his throat, slow and heady as full-bodied wine.

Vehan bit his lip, rumbled back when Aurelian slotted himself between his legs and crowded in even closer, crushed together what had grown maddeningly hard between this juncture for the both of them.

There were teeth at the hollow of his throat.

Lust curled delicious and languid around his core.

It was the middle of the morning and they were *devouring* each other on a parlor table, and Arlo had only just woken up from a near-death experience, and this was *not the time*, but *damn* it . . . "*Aurelian*," he groaned against his every desire to keep going. "Wait."

Aurelian paused.

Fae healed quickly, but they'd definitely have to wait a minute for the bruise he'd been in the process of sucking onto Vehan's neck to subside before leaving this room.

Slowly, Aurelian's mouth drew away. He stiffened slightly, as though he'd only just realized how far they'd gotten carried away with each other so quickly. "Sorry," he murmured in apology, wincing as he stepped back, no doubt as *uncomfortable* at the moment as Vehan was, though Vehan's pants weren't anywhere near as restricting as Aurelian's jeans.

"No," Vehan assured around panting breath—a little kissing and he was already this winded? He'd never been so immediately undone by a partner before, but then again, his heart had never truly belonged to anyone other than the equally breathless boy before him. "No, it's just . . . we really should be there for Arlo right now."

Commander Viridian-Verdell had given his mother a very loud and very *stern* talking-to about her carelessness in appointing Gentian as Arlo's attendant when it was well known to her that she and Nausicaä were close. His mother should have examined the pixie's background a little closer, Vehan did agree with that, but he was glad that the Commander seemed mostly concerned with getting back to her daughter as soon as possible, and as Riadne had put up no fight against a mother's wrath, the punishment for her part in this fiasco hadn't been anywhere as severe as Vehan had feared.

His mother might not appreciate being brought before the High King, made to prostrate herself in front of him and his Court, and beg for his forgiveness for the danger one of his blood had been put in under her watch—oh, she was sure to be *boiling* over this, when she returned—but for all the wicked potential of fae creativity, for a mother whose child had just been threatened, and for the formidable Right Hand of the High King, this was lenience.

Vehan didn't feel right, spurning that by ignoring Arlo to make out with his *boyfriend* in a tucked-away sitting room.

Thankfully, Aurelian didn't seem offended. "You're right," he sighed. Then, pinching the bridge of his nose, dipped his head back in a groan. "Give me a minute."

That was fine.

Vehan needed one as well.

Chuckling lightly, he slid off the table, pulling the rucked-up creases from his clothing and trying his best to think about something other than how good it felt to be pinned beneath Aurelian. "Poor Theo—I'm guessing there's no longer an engagement in our future."

"What do you mean, you *guess*?" Aurelian retorted, a playful edge to the gravel that was still present in his voice.

"Well, I didn't want to assume anything. It's one thing to want to bed a prince, another to want to marry one. You could just be in this for my stunning good looks and *endowment*."

He waggled his brows, earning a snort from Aurelian.

"Well, it's definitely not for your *brains*," Aurelian teased, but there in his eyes was the open fondness he'd always shown back when they were kids. Back when they picked on each other mercilessly for this and that and this, so wrapped up in each other that nothing had mattered, only them, and gods—finally, *finally*, a weight lifted from Vehan's chest.

He hadn't realized how suffocating it had been, hadn't realized how profoundly he'd *missed* Aurelian until just now, seeing that look in his eyes, his complete lack of guard.

Vehan swallowed against the urge to burst into tears again. "Good," he replied, brightening into a beaming grin. "I've gotten by just fine on my charms. Brains are what I have *you* for."

Rolling his eyes, Aurelian jerked his chin at the door. "If you're ready, Your Highness."

Vehan nodded, but just as he made to step past Aurelian, he was snagged into another—what could only be described as *filthy*—kiss. "Later, though . . ." Aurelian murmured directly against his mouth, and Vehan could taste every word.

"Later," he agreed in a sigh, then, blinking, stepped out of Aurelian's reach. "Come on. I'm sure Nausicaä is just *dying* to make fun of us for what you did in front of her. I feel like the longer we let her sit with that, the worse it's going to be."

Groaning, Aurelian fell into step behind him. "The things I do for you," he grumbled affectionately, and Vehan couldn't remember ever feeling happier in his life.

Riadne knew well before receiving the summons that pulled her from her office that something was going to happen tonight.

Guillotine-sharp foreboding trembled in the air.

On whose neck it was about to fall, she couldn't say for certain, but it would *not* be hers, of this she was determined. It was still with a tendril of dread, however, that she entered the clearing in the woods.

"Mother," she greeted, unsurprised to find her standing there.

It was late at night. The moon hung full behind a wisp-thin veil of clouds, casting its cool light on the world below and bending the shadows of towering trees into wicked, distorted shapes.

The air was thick with the scent of pine.

Dried needles and leaves and twigs snapped under Riadne's heels as she approached the Queen Mother, poised in the center of this tiny clearing where Arina Lysterne had long been tending to the runes of a shrine dedicated to some nameless, forgotten god.

Her mother wasn't a pious woman. Riadne suspected she more enjoyed the tradition, the repetitive simplicity of trekking out here every morning at the crack of dawn to care for the pile of carved and painted rocks arranged around a stone idol whose face and body had been worn down to indistinct features by time.

What did surprise her was Vadrien.

"Husband," she added, pausing only a few steps into the clearing. She considered him, paler in the moonlight, his hair like fallen night around his face, where sidhe fae features stood on cutting, full display. He was such a handsome man, had such a noble heart. In another life, where Riadne had time for such luxuries, where *her* heart hadn't already been squandered on someone else, she wondered if she might actually love him.

In this one, she did not.

Judging by the hardness in his dark gaze, the feeling—or lack thereof—was mutual, but this was still her husband, and Riadne was still queen. However newly crowned, it was audacious for *either* to summon her anywhere, and questionable to say the least to call her all the way out here.

In the middle of nowhere.

Alone.

"How clandestine. Are we plotting a murder?" she asked, lighter than both the mood around them and the one bleeding suspicion inside her.

Arina didn't turn to greet her daughter.

She merely stood in front of her shrine, the fingers of one hand outstretched to trace over the stone. In the other, only just visible in glints of light around her skirts, was the silver of a blade Riadne could say for certain she'd *never* seen her mother wield—swords were not in keeping with Seelie sophistication—yet she seemed perfectly comfortable with it; point biting into earth, she held it like a cane she most certainly didn't need despite her many years.

Plotting a murder indeed. Her husband . . . she was almost impressed with him for finally finding the nerve to tell the secret he'd been holding over Riadne's head for a while now.

Arina didn't turn, but she spoke in a voice as firm and clear as the day she'd once commanded. "Your husband has come to me with quite the story, daughter. Can you guess at all what it might be?"

Riadne was *queen*—she'd fulfilled all the requirements, been of age to rule for quite a while now and married a respectable partner. The throne had been conceded to her, almost like a punishment, but it was *hers*. Riadne had *power*, and she was far too used to Arina by now to show fear over idle threats. Folding her hands behind her back, she stared at her mother, serene down to her heartbeat. "I wouldn't dream of depriving you of the joy of telling me."

Another glint—breeze rustled her mother's skirts, revealing a clearer glimpse of her sword.

A moment ticked by in absolute silence, then, "*Alchemy*. A forbidden art, and not only, as I hear it, have you been dabbling in its practice and recruiting alchemists to your cause, but you've been enlisting the parents of ironborn children and trading our riches for experimentation on their newborn babes. You can imagine the story I've been told . . . goodness, what the High King would do to you if he were to ever find out."

She almost laughed in their faces. Azurean would do *nothing* to her; she could conduct these experiments right in front of him, and he would turn the other cheek for the cost of what he'd taken from her.

"*Riadne*," Vadrien interjected, an ardent whisper of her name that possessed more feeling than he'd demonstrated for her in some time. "Please, for once, I ask you to just be honest. I *know,* Riadne. I know what you've done, *all of it*. I know who you're working with. I know that if the High King finds out, it won't only be you he punishes but all of us. Lord Jarsdel, Riadne—the High King's niece has married a human man. They have an *ironborn daughter*. They'll show *no* mercy for what you've done, using *children* to foul the name of their magic, nor to me for not stopping you sooner, and *our* son—"

"As Vadrien outlines, you have found yourself in quite the predicament," Arina stated placidly, stealing back the conversation but *still* not turning around. "He knows. I know. I can only assume the Hunter assisting you will hold his tongue for now, so long as you play to whatever aim he's after in enlisting you—but be sure of it, it's you who's serving *his* end, not the other way around. You do not know who Lethe is, the destruction that once-upon-a-time dark prince of legend is capable of . . . You wouldn't have been so foolish as to accept his help if you did. You should not have entered a bargain with that godling siren, but the deed is done. Your secret is out. Two people know."

That tendril of dread grew into fluttering unease, but Riadne held her ground.

Vadrien knew, and so did her mother, but she had her unregistered Magnetism; this wasn't ideal, but it also wasn't unsalvageable.

Lurching forward, Vadrien slotted himself between her and her mother. Taking her by the shoulders, he leaned in close, as though to keep his words for her, as though Arina wouldn't be able to hear them. "Riadne. My wife. I swore myself as your other half. I am your husband and your friend, but more than that, I am your subject, and you are my queen. I will face this with you. There is still time—we can tell the High King together, admit this wrong and take our punishment and *stop this* before it gets out of hand. Please. It's not too late for us to be a family, you and me, and—"

It was Arina's sword stabbing through his chest that cut his speech short this time.

Riadne could only stare at him, could only blink down at the sapphire that spilled from his fatal wound—Arina's sword, right through his *heart* . . . He'd drop the moment she wrenched it back out, and Vadrien barely had time to gasp, to look down at the point sticking out from between his ribs in shock and fear and *anger* before she did.

And just like that.

Vadrien Hanlon-Lysterne collapsed to the forest floor and bled his life out over Riadne's boots.

Her husband . . .

Vehan's father . . .

She might have actually *loved* this fae, if things had been different for them, if that "fairy-tale" sort of ending had ever been in her cards . . .

Eyes grown a fraction wider, heart beating wildly in her chest, Riadne swallowed and looked up at her mother. Arina had finally turned to face her, was currently busied with wiping her blade on her gown, great smears of fae-blue blood stark against snowy white.

"You always did wonder whose shrine this was that I tended to—*why* I tended to it . . . ," Arina continued, as blithely as though she hadn't just run the king-consort through. "I'm proud of you, darling. You've finally managed to do something right." Looking up, she smiled at Riadne, a smile Riadne would have given *anything* to see at so many points growing up. It seemed surreal to receive it now . . . and laughably cheap, for what it had cost, how little it actually filled the void that had been growing inside her all this time.

Arina took a step toward her.

"I have been strict with you. I have never yielded where others would. I have molded you, groomed you, armed you for greatness, because it's greatness you were born to achieve and greatness you will claim."

Another step planted her right in front of Riadne, and Riadne could only marvel over the realization . . . When had she become taller than the mother she'd always feared?

"Greatness doesn't share itself with useless things. It trusts no one, values *no one*, and puts no one else's needs or desires above its own, not a lover's or a parent's or a *child's*." She lifted her sword, grin sharpening to a keener edge, moonlight flickering threateningly off her mother's blade. For a moment, Riadne was certain she was going to stab her just as she'd done Vadrien, but Riadne couldn't move. "I know what you've done, what you've sacrificed. I know the affair between you and the High King never fully ended, even after his Crowning; that this resulted in a child you tried to pass off as Vadrien's, but that was not to be. Now a child born of Spring and Summer lives when all think he died, taken in by his true father and nestled deep in Azurean Viridian's Court. What you've done . . . what you've *secured* . . . I am proud of you, my daughter. You are living up to the destiny I was allowed to glimpse in return for my care of this forgotten shrine—the fate you were promised, the legacy that will be our name should you manage to rise to the challenge."

At this, her mother reached up and gently stroked Riadne's cheek. "And you finally have."

Riadne's breathing quickened.

"You've finally learned the last thing I have to teach you, my daughter—the stark reality that not even your precious sons should stand in the way of what you will one day do. You are finally ready. You are finally strong. You, the Fated Queen of Light, have finally become what this Court *needs* for it to ascend in history as greatest of them all: *cruel.*"

She could feel it—this was building to something. Arina didn't speak like this, didn't treat Riadne with this kindness. Not ever. All these things that Riadne had wanted from her mother as a child were now suddenly hers, and the only thing she could think as her pulse quickened in wary anticipation was that Arina wasn't finished yet.

There was one more lesson she intended to impart this night.

And sure enough . . .

"It is time for the last gift I can give you—the assurance that there will be two fewer people in this world who could cost you what you've worked so hard to obtain. Now go, my daughter, and carve the Lysterne name into the very *heart* of this realm, as you were meant to do."

As swiftly and deftly as she'd cut down her son-in-law, Arina angled her blade at her own chest and thrust it all the way through.

It was far too easy to pass the deaths off as an unfortunate attack in the woods, to leave the bodies in the clearing and return to her rooms, scrub herself of blood, and pretend the next morning's news of her husband's and mother's fate was appropriately devastating.

But she was never going to forgive her mother or thank her for *anything* she'd said in those woods.

It *wasn't* Arina who'd made Riadne into what she needed to be. It wasn't prophecy, fate, luck, or any such nonsense. She *would* be great, and it would be her own hard work that made her so. The heart that now lay in her columbarium, the heart Riadne had cut out of her mother's chest back in that clearing, would forever serve as a reminder of this—and that was as much as Arina Lysterne was ever going to mean.

CHAPTER 37

Arlo

ARLO SPENT TWO WHOLE days recovering in the infirmary with a constant stream of company. Nausicaä and Celadon were permanent fixtures at her bedside, with Vehan, Aurelian, and Theo stopping by for frequent visits around their various duties. But it was Thalo whose presence Arlo appreciated the most right now, if only because this was the first time in very long while that Arlo could remember spending so much undivided time with her mother.

Sitting and chatting with Nausicaä about weapon specs and comparing war stories; bickering with Celadon like brother and sister over the littlest detail of Arlo's care, but laughing with each other as they traded gossip about various family members—Commander Viridian-Verdell had been completely switched off for fully activated Mother Mode.

On the final night of Arlo's hospital stay, Aurelian had brought in and set up his television and Nintendo Switch for them to all play Mario Party together, and Arlo learned that he swore worse than Nausicaä; that Vehan was spectacularly *hopeless* at gaming; that Theo was just as methodically vicious as Celadon when it came to strategizing, the very first person who'd ever been an actual match for Celadon in this game; that her mother, who'd never played something like this with Arlo before, would be a *horror* unleashed on any battlefield together with Nausicaä, the way they teamed up under the banner of general chaos to ricochet around the map, stealing stars and sabotaging mini-games, suspiciously always in Arlo's favor.

It was the most fun she'd had yet on this vacation.

She was therefore a little sad when the third day saw her released from confinement, and Thalo had to return to the Palace of Spring.

"My daughter," she said, standing alone with Arlo in the spartan room that contained the palace Egress. Gazing down at her, Thalo's eyes were just as gentle as her smile, a specific air of nostalgia about her expression that Arlo knew from past experience meant they were about to reminisce on her childhood. "I swear you've grown so much in less than a few weeks. Whatever happened to my baby girl?"

She reached out to sweep Arlo's hair behind her ear, pausing to examine the braid Nausicaä had put there, and Arlo, who didn't know at all what to say to the questioning look in her mother's eyes, brushed it off with an awkward laugh, however pleased she was to be the focus of her mother's attention for just a little longer. "Yeah, well, I'm sure you wouldn't be too thrilled if I stayed a baby forever."

"You were such a little thing," Thalo continued, letting Arlo's sarcasm slide. "So small . . . I was so afraid to even *hold* you back then. Swords and shields and hammers and spears—those were the only things these hands were used to. Leather and steel, *hard* things, *strong* things, not a fragile newborn girl. I made your father do *everything* in the beginning." She laughed, a little wetly, but Arlo didn't comment. "Changing diapers and feeding you and rocking you when you cried. I was just so afraid that I would hurt you. And then came the time when Rory had to go away for a conference, and the nurse we normally had stand in for him was ill, and it was just me and you for what felt like the longest night in history. You were only two years old, and you lunged right out of my arms after a bit of magic I used to try to entertain you, and you *fell*." She actually shuddered, recalling it; Arlo's steadfast mother, undone by a baby—Arlo wanted to laugh, but she'd never heard this story before and found herself too enraptured to do anything but listen.

"You *fell*, right onto the kitchen floor. It was my worst fears come true—I was a horrible mother and would only hurt you, *had* just hurt you, and there you were, on the ground . . . and you were laughing.

This far too little thing, I *dropped* you and you *laughed*, and pulled yourself up by my pant legs, reaching for me like you were all too eager to go again. You taught me a valuable lesson that day, Arlo. I whisked you as quick as wind to the palace, to the MediFae to check you over, and I could tell they wanted to laugh at me too for how concerned I was, but I learned something—I learned that you were so much stronger than you looked, and that you grow stronger every day. The young woman standing before me . . . It was the happiest day of my life when I gave birth to you, and I am *proud* of the person you've become."

Blinking back the sudden and overwhelming urge to cry, Arlo threw herself forward and wrapped her arms around her mom.

Thalo hugged her tightly in return.

"I'm still not *entirely* happy we have you practicing dangerous magic so far away from your home Court."

"I know," Arlo said against her.

"And I'm *really* not happy about this business you've found yourself caught up in—titans and immortals and magical dice? I know you didn't ask for any of this, but I'm your mother, and I'm certainly not going to let you go through it alone. We'll talk, yes? After your vacation, we'll sit down, you and I, and talk about what can be done . . . about what you want to do."

"Okay," Arlo said again into her mother's cloak.

Thalo squeezed her even tighter—however afraid she might have once been about handling her own daughter, she was no such thing now. "I love you."

"I love you, too."

"All right," Thalo replied, pressed one last kiss to her hair, and withdrew. "I expect things will be fairly busy here soon. The Solstice is only just over a week away. Make sure you get plenty of rest before then, and let me know if there's *anything* you need."

"I will, don't worry."

"Good. Oh, and Arlo." She paused in turning toward the Egress to look back at Arlo. This time, what gleamed in her eyes was a little darker, a little more amused, *definitely* teasing. "I wouldn't be *at all* unhappy to have your Nausicaä as my future daughter-in-law."

Arlo flailed. "Okay, mom—good visit! Thank you for coming, it's time to go!"

Trailing laughter, Thalo allowed Arlo to push her through the mirror and out of sight.

The days carried on quickly after that.

Before Arlo knew it, the week of the Solstice had finally rolled around, the entire palace transformed to receive the increasing trickle of early arrivals.

She'd discovered a new favorite pastime as guests started rolling in.

Nausicaä had been quite busy, both with helping the Wild Hunt track down Lethe's whereabouts and with her new self-appointed task of learning all she could about the mysterious immortal Moros (a being who, so far, she hadn't been willing to speak about, but promised to do so after the Solstice). She stopped in as much as possible, though, to check on Arlo, and join her, Vehan, Aurelian, Theo, and Celadon, too, as they spied on Queen Riadne's favored invites and extended Lysterne family.

First to arrive had been what Arlo could only describe as a very tall, bipedal stag in a crisp slate suit, chains and rings of gleaming gold strung from the wide flare of his horns. Arlo had expected him to have to contort himself to get through doorways, but the doorways contorted themselves to fit *him*.

Next was a formidable sidhe fae man, thickly built and as pale as ice, with frost-blue eyes and a neatly combed black beard. Vehan muttered something that sounded like "Uncle Dmitri" with a grimace before Riadne came along, sweeping Vehan with her to greet him. Around the man appeared a set of triplets, young women all with curling black hair and bright blue eyes, and a younger, white-haired boy around Vehan's age, glacier fair and just as brittle-boned.

Judging by the looks on Vehan's and Aurelian's faces, neither Uncle Dmitri nor his children were very well liked, but preferable— Arlo learned shortly after—to "Aunt Linnea" and her *seven* golden- -toned, amber-eyed, strawberry- and copper-haired spawn. These Lysternes were direct competition for Vehan's ascension, and poison was apparently the *least* offensive thing they'd tried so far to vacate Vehan from the throne. It was popular suspicion that they'd been responsible for the murders of the Queen Mother and Riadne's late husband, as well.

There was, after that, a *beautiful* faerie woman in light blue gauze for a gown, her skin an iridescent shimmer, with a fan of peacock plumage sprouting from the tail of her spine and fanning out behind her, and similar purple and blue and green feathers growing from her head like hair. For all that even her bone structure reminded Arlo of a bird, when she smiled, it was the sharp grin of a starving fox.

A redcap ogre arrived after that, in enough black leather that Arlo had to hold Nausicaä back from storming forward to challenge her over it. Sienna-orange and corded with muscle, massive tusks jutting upward from her lower jaw and violent blue hair growing wild around her strong features, the ogre clasped arms with Riadne like they were old war companions. Arlo eyed the hood she wore, stained red by human blood, and clutched Nausicaä just a little tighter.

Several more fae were next through the Egress and Las Vegas's portal, all from various Courts and relations to the Lysternes; a troupe of pixies, a few other faeries, and even a djinn couple, whom Arlo was *deeply* interested in—the djinn were some of the only immortals who chose to give up that title to remain behind in this realm, but were powerful enough to still reign like the gods they'd once been in the deserts they now kept to. Technically Wild, not part of the Eight Great Courts, it was only a tenuous truce between them and the Court of UnSeelie Summer that kept them from pushing their boundaries. Of course Riadne would be the sort of fae to invite even one into her home.

Mavren and Eurora Reynolds arrived two days before the Solstice.

They were just as stunning as their son. Theo had clearly inherited his full features and short, curling hair from his mother, but Eurora was bronze cast in cool night, darker than her husband, whom Theodore took more after in his warmer, lighter tone. They shared the same sharp, deep brown eyes as well. Mavren Reynolds—strongly chiseled and sinew-lean, his long ebony hair gathered up in a braid down his back—pinned Theo with piecing intent as he and his wife made their approach. He gave Theo a proper reprimand for "skulking back in the shadows when he should be the first to come and greet them." Theo rolled his eyes, scoffed at them, and shook off the immediate fussing his mother fell into over usual mother things, like the crease she spotted in his clothes and whether he was training properly, "because you're looking very soft. Surely you weren't this thin the last we saw you."

"A *month* ago. I saw you a month ago, Mother. Hardly enough time to go *soft*—and I promise I'm giving Prince Vehan a thorough whipping around the arena at least once a day."

Nodding, Vehan grimly confirmed, "He is."

With Nausicaä off only she knew where today and Celadon already arm-in-arm with Lady Eurora, prodding stories about her son that she was all too happy to tell (much to Theo's increasing mortification), Arlo was happy to follow along as the group led the Reynoldses to the rooms prepared for their stay.

She took tea with them (though she personally stuck to juice), and listened to everyone talk about everything from the comparison of UnSeelie and Seelie Court cultures to participants in the upcoming Court World Games—a competition that extended even to the Wild folk, the CW Games were much like the human Olympics, alternating through the four Seasons and occurring only once every five years; such was the passion for these Games that already the Courts had begun to choose their competitors for the usual things like swimming and figure skating and skiing, but also Elemental Battle, and

Capture the Stag, and a particular crowd favorite: the long-distance Faerie Race, where *all* the folk were thrown together to race through difficult and potentially deadly obstacles to a randomly selected finish line, and the only rules for winning were to survive both the terrains and fellow competitors to cross it.

The rest of the day passed just as pleasantly.

Dinner was a much livelier affair. Several of the queen's guests joined them for the meal, and while Arlo discovered that the Lysterne cousins were all about as interesting to talk to as a candlestick, the frost-haired son of Lord Dmitri Lebezheninov—"Dima," he introduced himself in a glacial-quiet voice—was much more entertaining. Not at all one for words, he was brilliantly talented with the Gift of Winter, and dazzled Arlo under the table with how quickly he could shape tiny figurines of ice in the palm of his hand.

After dinner, and content with her day, she'd been happy enough still to retreat to her room, even though it felt a little odd to do so alone.

It was curious how quickly she'd gotten used to having at least *someone* else around. The only child of a single parent, Arlo had passed plenty of days by her own devices, but then Luck turned up, and Arlo had come here, and suddenly she had *company*.

Luck was gone now, of course, back to wherever they normally kept.

Celadon, Vehan, Aurelian, Theo—they all apparently had something else to do this evening, and where Celadon at least could normally be convinced to let her lounge in his quarters, busy or not, this time he'd shooed her off.

But that was fine.

She had *more* than enough to occupy herself before bed. She hadn't talked to her father in over a week, she realized—did he even know about her poisoning? Probably not, and she wasn't going to be the one to tell him. No sense in worrying him about something she couldn't even explain properly.

She could also, finally, go for a swim. Her own private pool right below her bedroom and she hadn't even used it yet.

In decent spirits, she entered her sitting room, kicked off her shoes at the door, and padded her way to her bedroom, intent on digging out her swimsuit and changing—and stopped on the threshold.

"*Surprise!*" Nausicaä shouted, springing off the bed to her feet. "*Shit,*" she hissed, as her enthusiasm made her overbalance slightly and nearly fall.

Arlo wanted to laugh.

She wanted to laugh *very much,* but she couldn't tell yet whether she was meant to.

Nausicaä, standing there in the absolute most *hideous* dress, shiny pleather that looked a bit like a floor-length garbage bag tied tightly around her body, enormous white ruffles like a cloud of bunched-up toilet paper lining both the top of the monstrosity and the slit that cut all the way up her thigh.

"Uh . . . ," Arlo ventured, practically choking on laughter she *would not release* until she knew what was going on, because she'd never once seen Nausicaä wear a dress, and maybe she was . . . trying for something here. Arlo didn't want to discourage . . . whatever it was. "So, what's this?"

"It's me accepting your challenge and *winning.*"

Challenge?

Oh—Arlo recalled the moment they'd shared before entering the grotto, when she'd tied a braid in Nausicaä's hair and Nausicaä had decided romance, like everything else, was some sort of competition.

"And by winning, you mean . . ." Arlo gave her a critical look from head to black-heeled toe and back again, and Nausicaä chuckled far too huskily for Arlo's comfort.

She turned around, grabbed something from the bed to present to Arlo, beaming like a cat that had just dragged home a gutted rat for praise.

Another dress—this one made of cheap emerald satin and looking distinctly like a party dress plucked right out of the eighties. It had giant ruffled sleeves as big as Arlo's head and a matching, knee-high, pleated-ruffle skirt. Celadon would light it on *fire*—with her in it—if she ever dared to bring it anywhere *near* him . . . and this was the grain too much.

Arlo burst out laughing. "What *is* this?"

"It's prom, Arlo," Nausicaä declared, marching over to thrust the dress into her hands and spin her toward her bathroom. "You said you didn't want to go to *your* prom because the people you went to school with were straight-up bitches."

"That's . . . not exactly the words I used, but—"

"I promise you'll like *mine* much better. Go on, march! We've got a schedule to keep here, Red, time's a tickin'." She shooed Arlo on, hands on her hips when Arlo turned to raise a brow at her.

She hadn't been lying. It really hadn't bothered her not to go to her high school prom; she'd much rather spend her time with Nausicaä and the others than her now former classmates, but she had to admit . . . she was intrigued. Whatever Nausicaä had planned, at least they were going to look hideous together. "Fine," she sighed, around a rebellious tendril of excitement. "I *guess* I'll play along. For now . . ."

"Here, you'll need these." Nausicaä staggered back to Arlo's bed and grabbed a pair of emerald-green heels so glittery that Arlo winced when she handed them to her. "Your *slippers*, Your Highness."

"We have very different definitions of winning, I think," Arlo frowned.

But half an hour later, dressed and done up in the *worst* makeup anyone had ever given her, giggling the entire time as Nausicaä painted green in garish strokes around her eyes to match the massive blocks of solid black painted over hers, Nausicaä teleported them to her makeshift prom . . . and she had to admit . . . all right, Nausicaä knew a thing or two about victory.

"*Surprise!*" shouted Celadon, Vehan, Aurelian, and Theo as soon as she and Nausicaä arrived on a rooftop that towered over the Las Vegas

Strip, dazzling lights like multicolored jewels set against velvet night.

It was *horrible*—a mash-up of all the clichéd prom things: enchanted forest fairy lights and craft-store flowers and plastic plants, under-the-sea blue balloons and green seaweed streamers and *two* bubble machines at opposite ends of the roof, medieval masquerade masks provided on a table, red and black lacy decor and cut-out hearts for the romantic *Moulin Rouge* effect.

There was space cleared for dancing, tables devoted to all sorts of finger foods, two different punch bowls and red plastic cups, several ambitious bottles of rum and whisky and soda for mix, because what prom would be complete without underage drinking, and a wide selection of pop songs blaring from an expensive-looking stereo pushed against the balcony.

Arlo gaped at the scene, at the *boys*—they were all dressed in equally hideous outfits, Theo's suit an acid-trip of neon color, Vehan's the classic and ill-fitted powder blue, Aurelian's head-to-toe hunter's camouflage, and Celadon . . . what Nausicaä must have offered him, Arlo didn't know. Arlo had seen him a number of times in beautiful gowns for various photoshoots and casual-wear alike, but this monstrosity of a full-out flamingo-pink and vibrant orange ballgown, the skirts of which shone just as plasticky as Nausicaä's pleather . . . *this* dress must be *killing* him.

Turning to Nausicaä, Arlo was a little lost for words. Nausicaä grinned down at her, cheeky and so very proud of herself, and probably the most excited of the lot of them for the night she clearly had planned.

"You're such a *dork*," Arlo teased, echoing what Nausicaä had said back in the infirmary.

And Nausicaä's razor grin stretched wider. She winked down at Arlo, then sauntered on by her to the dance floor.

Arlo learned much more about her friends that night: that Nausicaä had spiked one of the punch bowls well before the party had even begun; that she and Aurelian were competitive in *everything*, right down to beer pong, but bizarrely good friends after a certain level of intoxication; that Vehan could *sing*, and knew every single Taylor Swift song to prove it; that Theo and Celadon had developed some form of recent truce where Theo *didn't* attempt to make up for . . . whatever had happened while Arlo had been at the mermaid grotto that none of the boys would tell her about. In exchange, Celadon, apparently, had agreed to relax a little around him.

Everyone danced together, shouted off-tune lyrics at one another, sat around at the tables in between, talking and laughing and playing random games with the cards Nausicaä had brought.

Arlo didn't drink, and it probably wasn't even advised, given her recent hospitalization, but she was just as good with her Coke and the virgin sangria bowl Nausicaä had left un-spiked, and she was having fun—normal teenage *fun* with *friends*, a better prom than she ever could have attended if it weren't for the girl over by the railing, where she and Aurelian were writing childish obscenities on paper they then folded up into planes and chucked over the edge.

Her golden-tanned face was awash in a mixture of rainbow city lights and shadowy, navy night. She was at perfect ease, no trace of the tension that had been weighing on her more obviously than usual lately. The infamous Dark Star—beautiful, vibrant, and the brightest point in Arlo's whole life.

"All right, Nausicaä," she said to herself, watching Nausicaä double over in barking laughter at whatever Aurelian had just written. "You win."

She would tell her.

She would confess her feelings to Nausicaä and throw all caution to the wind. If Nausicaä didn't feel the same—because Arlo *still* couldn't say for certain; this entire evening could very well be Nausicaä demonstrating friendship, or the inability to pass up a challenge, or showing how smoothly she *could* woo someone, not necessarily Arlo—then so be it. Arlo was going to tell her no matter what.

Not tonight.

She would tell her, soon, but *this* night Arlo wanted to keep exactly as it was: a memory she could look back on, full of hope, everything light and everyone happy, the first time Arlo truly realized just how *lucky* she really was to have so many wonderful people suddenly in her life.

CHAPTER 38

Vehan

~~~~~~

THE RADIANT THRONE OF Summer was a magnificent hall by any standard. Citrine quartz cut in fissures through the marble walls, traveling like bolts of lightning from the entrance to the four-tiered glass dais commanding the room's far end. The floor was made of glass as well. Several crystal-clear inches of it had been poured over stone so pale that crossing this surface always felt to Vehan like he was walking across pure light, because refracted in it was the crowning piece of this otherwise unornamented chamber. Not the solid white-gold throne itself—no, what inspired even Vehan's marvel every time he saw it was the *enormous* chandelier hanging from the ceiling. *Hundreds* upon *thousands* of precious gems and jewels had gone into this fixture's construction; yellow and red, orange and white, shards of various shades of sunlight, all strung with careful precision in the *exquisite* likeness and luminosity of a blazing sun, as though the very symbol of Seelie power had been plucked from the sky and mounted like a trophy over the Seelie Summer Sovereign's head.

And yet, for all the light this impressive adornment emitted, it was nowhere near as radiant as the queen who sat beneath it.

Here, in the very heart of her Court, in the seat of its complete control, it was almost *impossible* to look directly at Riadne Lysterne— but that was the point. No one Queen Riadne called before her like this was meant to stare her in the eye, not even Vehan. *Especially* Vehan, he occasionally got the impression. His mother, at all times as austere as the light she currently radiated in full and dazzling force . . . He didn't know what was the greater cause for concern: that her light was more glaring than usual or that, from what he could see of her, she was folded in what Vehan was tempted to label *insouciance*—elbow propped on the arm of her chair, chin resting on her palm, legs sprawled like a decadent king as she *observed* them in perfect silence.

And she'd been doing this for quite a while now, watching both Vehan and Aurelian. The quiet was starting to unnerve him even more than the initial summons to bring themselves before her here. Vehan knew one hundred percent without a doubt what she wanted to talk to them about—there was no way the change in his and Aurelian's relationship had escaped his mother's omniscience—but he might as well waltz up to the throne and slap his mother across the face for how insulting it was considered to speak before she did first.

Five minutes passed . . . ten . . . fifteen. Vehan had once (and completely by accident) broken a vase that Riadne was particularly fond of, and he'd been made to stand before her here for an entire *night*, just for her to tell him she was disappointed in him and to make sure he kept his roughhousing to the training ring, then send him on his way for breakfast.

He was prepared to wait much longer for what brought him here today.

But then . . . "He cannot be your steward and your lover both, you realize. The Court would consider it a conflict of interest."

This was . . . not exactly how Vehan had expected this to go. Riadne Lysterne didn't shout unless she felt it absolutely necessary to raise her voice, but the way she spoke now, it wasn't with the iciness that indicated offense or anger or *disappointment*—all the things he expected his mother to be feeling about his trading a prince for a Seelie Autumn commoner.

Instead, she sounded almost . . . *amused*, and completely unsurprised. Her tone was hard and clear, to be sure, but there was something about this situation that entertained her. Vehan hoped it wasn't anything more sinister than her knowing all along how thoroughly smitten her son had always been with the boy beside him.

"I understand, mother," Vehan replied, as firmly as he could force himself to speak through his rising nerves, because Riadne didn't like at all for him to ever sound timid or insecure. "I was hoping Theodore might be interested in the role, instead."

It wasn't husband to a king, but it was almost better, because as steward he'd have much more direct say in what happened in this Court than he'd ever have as Vehan's partner, and Vehan wasn't as oblivious in other areas of his life as he'd been where Aurelian was concerned: he knew that, whatever else Theo wanted, *power* was without a doubt highest on that list.

"Oh," said Riadne, in a breath like a laugh, "you *will* secure him to that role before I give my blessing for this. The Reynolds family *will* be tied to ours. They are a bank the Lysternes cannot afford to lose."

"Yes, Mother."

"And I will make nothing official until after the Solstice, which means you are still to attend with Lord Theodore, and you will still make the acquaintance of *and* dance with every suitor we've personally invited here to meet you."

"Yes, Mother," Vehan repeated. "Of course."

He'd fully expected to have to do this anyhow. They hadn't planned on approaching Riadne for anything official themselves until after the Solstice celebrations had passed, when he'd hoped his mother would be in a potentially more gracious mood, like the one she was currently in, it seemed, because this wasn't at *all* how Vehan had thought this conversation would go. At the very least, he'd been convinced he'd have to argue their case, but Riadne was so wholly unconcerned about how the Reynoldses might take this that he felt a little like laughing for how tightly wound around anxiety he'd been over apparently nothing.

She was his mother, after all.

It might be harder to see sometimes. She might not be like Aurelian's mother, or Theo's or Arlo's, or anyone else's he knew, but she wanted what was best for him, he was sure of it, his happiness included.

"Aurelian," she said next, and Aurelian drew just a little stiffer to attention. Silence returned, thicker than before, Riadne stretching out this moment long enough to impress upon the both of them that it was *her* they answered to, and her magnanimity that allowed this relationship to continue. "This is what you want?"

Vehan darted a glance to his side.

He was only just quick enough to catch the muscle leap in Aurelian's tightened jaw and the barest twitch of his fingers as though fighting against the urge to form a fist.

Something passed between his retainer—no, his *partner*—and his mother, but . . .Vehan must have misread it, because it seemed like a flicker of challenge.

"It is."

Riadne clapped her hands together—Vehan's attention snapped immediately forward. "Very well," she announced in a much grander voice. "You are dismissed."

And just like that, they were released from the throne room.

Vehan burst out into the hall with an actual groan of relief. However well that had just gone (and they probably had the Solstice only *hours* away to thank for that) it had also been nerve-rackingly intense. "I'm never doing that again," he declared, pressing a hand over his wildly beating heart. "It's you and me forever now, or bachelorhood until my mother's passing and the only person I have to ask permission to date is myself."

It was only a joke.

Aurelian had been in such an agreeable mood these last few days that he'd expected him to laugh and agree.

But when Vehan looked over at him, walking quietly at Vehan's side, he saw that same tension coiled in him as when Riadne had directly addressed him.

"Is . . . everything okay?" Was he worried about Theo? About Vehan? About *this,* their relationship? He was definitely worrying about something. Now that Aurelian had confessed to keeping his emotions guarded to make Vehan think he didn't care, he was no longer as good at it—or Vehan had just stopped second-guessing what he saw on his face. "Aurelian, hey."

He stopped them just before a bend in the hall, a hand clasped gently to Aurelian's elbow, coaxing Aurelian to look him in the eye, which he eventually—slowly—did. "It's going to be fine, I *promise*. You and I, we're going to be okay. It'll be a little tricky, sure. We're definitely going to face a bit of heat from the Reynoldses. I think they were very set on Theo marrying into the family, but it will pass. Because I also think *this* was more what *Theo* wanted. It's worth it, okay? *You're* worth it—you're worth *everything* to me."

Rising onto the balls of his feet and leaning in, he touched his nose to Aurelian's, and Aurelian softened in response—sighed, and slipped a hand around the back of Vehan's neck to draw him in the rest of the way. Thus ensnared, Aurelian pressed a full, lingering kiss to Vehan's mouth that left Vehan feeling slightly light-headed.

"Don't make promises you can't keep," Aurelian said against his lips, skin catching skin as he spoke, until speaking devolved into another kiss.

This was Aurelian all over—his boyfriend, intense in his own right, always concerned about others, as protective as he was wary of so many things, not least of all this relationship. But he was *Vehan's* now. This was no offhand promise; this was a *certainty*. Things *would* be all right, whatever hardship came their way. Now that Vehan knew Aurelian wanted him back, he would overcome *any* obstacle to keep him.

They would be okay, in the end—Vehan would make sure of it.

Fingers hooking through the loops in Aurelian's jeans, Vehan tugged him just a little bit closer, flush against him as he walked him slowly back against the wall, their kiss growing deeper the moment Aurelian's back touched stone.

It wasn't until the soft but awkward "Oh! S-sorry!" sliced through the dense haze of desire flooding through him that Vehan remembered they were in the middle of a very open hall, broad daylight all around, with Solstice guests arriving in droves.

Breaking apart in a gasp of breath, Vehan looked wildly to his side, excuses on the tip of his tongue that he hoped would be enough to dissuade the gossip at being caught making out with a boy everyone was meant to still think was only his retainer, and nothing more.

. . . and deflated with another groan of even shakier relief when he realized it was only Arlo. Arlo, who knew they were together and wouldn't betray a word of it to anyone, but was looking like she was about to skitter off at a run.

Vehan cleared his throat. "Arlo!" he exclaimed as cheerfully as he could manage. "Sorry, that was . . ." He glanced at Aurelian, still caught in shock of his own and staring unblinkingly at Arlo as though he didn't yet believe how narrowly they'd just avoided getting caught.

Arlo's hands shot into the air. "None of my business! That was none of my business, sorry! I'll just . . ." She pointed past them and made as though to sneak by, but Vehan shook his head and laughed.

"No, no, we really shouldn't have been doing that here. Just . . . well, new relationship and all . . . you understand."

He winked at her.

Arlo paused. She raised a brow, confused by what Vehan had implicated. "I do?"

"You don't?" Vehan shared another look with Aurelian, though *shared* was a generous term; Aurelian was still stuck on overcoming the surprise of being caught out kissing in the hallway. "I just thought . . . you know, you and Nausicaä *are* dating, right?"

Judging by how *immediately* red Arlo's face flared, they very much weren't, and now Vehan had gone and made things even more awkward.

Surfacing at last from his mortification, Aurelian rolled his eyes at Vehan's lack of tact.

"Ah," said Vehan, rubbing the back of his neck. "Sorry, it's just that you two are very close and you *look* like a couple, and after the party the other night . . ." Arlo's face was now so red that Vehan wondered if maybe she was going to pass out, or have a heart attack, or—

"No, it's fine. I . . . um . . . well, I *am* planning on asking her to be, you know, a c-couple? I guess? Soon? Haven't quite worked up to that yet."

Vehan's brow quirked in humor. "What, do you think she's going to say *no*?"

"Soooo, I don't know if you've noticed," Arlo replied, her stammer traded in favor of sarcasm that was a little bit a mixture of Nausicaä and Celadon. "There's *me*, and then there's Nausicaä, the literal Dark Star badass sword-wielding Fury of tight leather pants and destruction. So yes, Vehan, there is a *possibility* she might say no."

It was Aurelian who said, "Unlikely," and Arlo frowned at him in pointed disbelief. Glancing first to Vehan, he explained himself with a quieter, "The forest for the trees—you're too close to the issue to see how she looks at you."

Just as it had been for them.

This whole time, it had only been Aurelian for Vehan, and Vehan for Aurelian, and neither of them had been able to see that for the self-deprecation and doubt and worry, at least in Vehan's case.

Arlo . . . she reminded Vehan a lot of himself, sometimes.

"What are you up to right now, Arlo?" he asked, an idea coming to him.

Arlo wanted to ask Nausicaä to be her girlfriend and clearly couldn't see what Vehan did—what Nausicaä *definitely* did: that Arlo was a beautiful young woman with fire and passion of her own, intelligent and stubborn and, in Vehan's opinion, just as much a badass as her Fury, if perhaps in a slightly different way. Arlo Jarsdel, who faced down Reapers and alchemists and Hunters, who chased after the world's nastiest folk and kept the company of titans and wielded a magic *none* of them possessed. As though someone like that could ever pale in comparison to *anyone*.

Arlo shrugged a bit sheepishly. "Oh, you know. The usual." Dance lessons, study sessions, Arlo's alchemy classes—even spying on new arrivals had taken a back seat to their new obsession: trying to steal a peek at the ballroom Vehan's mother had declared off-limits until the Solstice to anyone but her and a chosen few, which for some reason included Leda and Councillor Sylvain but unfairly *ex*cluded her own son.

With a grin, Vehan clapped his hands together once, much in the fashion Riadne did. "You know what I think? I think we need to head down to the royal tailor and make a few adjustments to the gown he's been preparing for you. We can't send you off into battle without the proper gear, after all."

"Um." Arlo flatlined. "Which battle?"

Nudging her, Vehan laughed. "This is Nausicaä we're talking about. *All* things are a battle, including her affections. And how do we win battles, Arlo?"

"I'm not sure in this situation I'm supposed to answer *killing things*, but . . ."

He laughed again. "Actually, that might do the trick too, but I was thinking something more along the lines of making a few adjustments to what you'll be wearing to the Solstice."

"Oh! Umm . . ." Arlo worried a moment at her lip before darting forward and slipping her arm to curl around his. "Okay, well, pin that idea for now. Because actually, there's a different battle we should maybe talk about, and if you and Aurelian aren't busy . . ."

She glanced around, then leaned in closer and pitched her voice in a secretive hush. "It's about your array."

"*Oh?*"

That caught his attention. Vehan straightened, his playfulness vanishing in an instant. He didn't imagine there'd been much time, between everything going on and Arlo's hospitalization, for her to examine the drawing he'd given her of his array and work on a way to dissolve it. Surely there hadn't been much time to even study with Leda in general practice—he hadn't, therefore, expected this conversation yet, and a part of his heart *plummeted* just to hear this request because . . . she was going to tell him it was hopeless.

Vehan was stuck with this cursed array, and he was fated to spend the rest of his life scrambling to feed it . . . or *die*.

"Can we go to your study?"

Aurelian was looking oddly between them, and it was only now that Vehan realized how much had happened in the last couple of weeks that he hadn't filled him in on, *this* development in particular.

He nodded, both to Arlo and to Aurelian, and reached behind to snag his boyfriend so all three of them could go together. He wouldn't hide anything from Aurelian, not anymore. "I'll explain along the way," Vehan said to him, and it made him feel a little less terrified right now that Aurelian simply nodded back and fastened himself wordlessly to his side.

"You see this here?"

Bent over the worktable in Vehan's bolt-hold study, the lighting at full luminescence now that Vehan's magic had been (however temporarily) recharged, Arlo pointed to a symbol on the array he'd sketched for her examination back when first asking her to undertake this task. Both Vehan and Aurelian leaned closer to examine it.

"This is the symbol for iron."

"I remember from the cavum factory," Vehan mused, and then quickly brightened. "Would we be able to disrupt the array enough if we could dissolve even just this symbol? Because you've managed that well enough before!"

Could it really be as simple as that, this enormous weight . . . lifted that easily?

The sigh Arlo issued punctured the hope ballooning inside of him. "Yes and no," she explained through an apologetic look. "That's what I was thinking too, and in theory, yeah, it's actually simple enough. Dissolve the iron, disrupt the array—child's play, really."

Not really—he and Aurelian shared a look, but kept the comment to themselves. This was all so much more than "child's play." The fact that Arlo could even attempt to dissolve anything was far more advanced than a beginner's trick.

Arlo, meanwhile, ignored them, grabbed for a pen and a piece of blank paper. "We haven't been doing much in, like, only the handful of lessons I've had so far. Councillor Sylvain is—"

"Councillor *Sylvain?*" Vehan interrupted, then fell silent at the look Arlo shot him from her paper.

"—pretty adamant that I only learn the theory of things and practice the basics. Iron is a starter symbol, so it's basically all I've been allowed to play around with."

She drew up a quick array, and once it was finished, fished a small chunk of iron from her pocket, placing it in the center of her array.

Vehan watched in rapt attention as she then traced a finger around the array's seam, and like a flower bursting into bloom, a blue-white glow shot through the ring of it, lighting up the symbols and words and equations.

It happened quickly—once the entire array was activated, there was a sound like the *zap* of electric current. The air took on a strong metallic scent that burned in Vehan's nose. In a blink, the chunk of iron transformed from a simple, misshapen oval to a miniature but *exquisitely* crafted rose.

"Arlo, that's . . ." Beautiful. Talented. Difficult? It looked as though that should be difficult, and she should be extremely proud of herself for managing in weeks what sounded like (from what Vehan had read in his recent studies on the topic) something no ordinary novice should be able to do so effortlessly.

To manipulate shape and then take it a step further to give it such intricate detail . . . thorns and leaves and, goodness, it looked like there were veins in those iron petals that Vehan wanted to touch, because he could almost swear they weren't metal but *velvet*.

But Arlo, who'd just accomplished this *tremendous* feat, looked only annoyed.

She tapped the array again, the one that mirrored what was on Vehan's chest. "That's definitely iron, but it's tied in the most complex way I've seen to what I'm assuming is the symbol for *blood*, and a whole host of other things, and isolating it . . . I need to know what every symbol it's tied to is and how to work it before I can get it on its own and dissolve it."

It was an errant, habitual glance to the side to check on Aurelian that had him catch the way he was staring, not at the array like Arlo was and Vehan had been, but at Arlo herself. Very little about Aurelian was unreadable to him anymore, but there was something about his expression that was hard to place . . . as though Aurelian himself didn't know how he should be feeling.

"What aren't you saying?" he asked, speaking for the first time since coming here. "There's something bothering you. What is it?"

Arlo didn't look up at the question, but her frown deepened. She seemed to hesitate, wrestling with something internally, and just when Vehan opened his mouth to assure her that she didn't have to give them an answer, that Aurelian was just a very intuitive and curious person, she replied, "I've done this before."

"I . . . beg your pardon?" Vehan didn't understand. "You've done what before, Arlo? Dissolved an array?" Yes, the one at the factory, but that was different, that was *simpler*—much simpler than what surely went into crafting the brand on Vehan's chest, so she really shouldn't be this upset with herself—

"Yes?" she replied, her voice threaded with uncertainty. "No? Sort of? It's just . . . even back when you first showed this to me in the Assistance Headquarters . . . and then when you handed me this drawing . . . There's something about it." She shook her head. At long last, her gaze rose from the table, and oh yes, there was deep confusion there, but also . . . fear? Excitement? Perhaps a little of both. "I can't remember. I've been noticing a lot lately that there's stuff I can't remember—stuff I *should* remember—and then sometimes these memories come to me, pieces of information that I have no idea how

I know. It's not like . . . it's not a Gift. I don't . . . hear this stuff in the air or in people's minds, I'm not a Reader, but . . ." She sighed and folded her arms over her chest. "I know how this needs to be done. I just need a little bit longer. I need more lessons; I need to be *stronger*. I need, I think, to study *here*—would that be okay?"

"Of *course* it would be," Vehan replied, shooting upright. "Arlo, you can have anything you need! Even *attempting* to help me out of this . . . Urielle, I'm just glad you haven't looked at all this and told me it isn't worth the trouble. Whatever you need, just say the word."

"You're worth the trouble, Vehan," she replied, far more seriously than Vehan had spoken the secret fear he had about . . . pretty much everything. "We're friends. You're worth the trouble. But all right." A tentative smile spread across her face. It *was* excitement she'd been feeling. Arlo . . . she *enjoyed* alchemy—and she should, because she was good at it, especially if she could pull off what needed to be done. Vehan was more determined than ever to make sure that, when he became king, she could at least have a place within *his* Court to practice that all she wanted. "After the Solstice?" she hedged. "We'll set everything up after the Solstice and start from there."

"It's a deal." He held out his hand, and Arlo shook it, and as her smile grew wider, so did his grin. "Now, about that dress you thought you could distract me from . . ."

"Did it hurt?"

Riadne stood in the doorway of her office, simply staring.

In twenty years, she'd never *once* been alone with Celadon, had only a handful of times ever been given the chance to *speak* with him before relations between their Courts dissolved completely.

Twenty years . . . Riadne had almost feared it, when this boy she hardly knew asked to come along with his cousin. She'd almost been *afraid* of what it would mean . . . that at some point, the two of them would find themselves in each other's company with no one else between them to act as buffer.

She'd been afraid of it, because if there was anything in Riadne still capable of remorse, of regret, of *love* and all the other *useless feelings that would only unravel everything she'd worked so hard for* . . .

Riadne swallowed.

She lifted her chin.

In perfect, unruffled elegance, she stepped inside the office she didn't have to ask how he'd broken in to. The first time she'd allowed him this audacity, it had been to *feel out* how much he really knew. She hadn't forgotten to weave her blood protections, as Vehan's retainer-turned-*paramour* seemed to think, and she hadn't *this* time, either. But she'd allowed it then as she allowed it now, because Riadne might not know much *personally* about the boy before her, but every scrap of intelligence she'd gathered on him over twenty years . . . every magazine and picture and article and video scoured . . . just this once, even if this was the hardest thing she'd ever have to do, she wanted to see it in *person*—the astounding number of traits that made this boy *her* flesh and blood.

Weakness.

But if she was going to cut that part of her out, cauterize that gaping wound with searing electric fire and rage, she wanted to see it. *Just this once*, before whatever glimmer of hope still living inside him that Riadne might not do what he suspected she would died along with his father.

Riadne stepped into the room.

She closed the door behind her and fixed the boy seated like a tired rag doll on the edge of her desk with a raised brow and total, glacial apathy. "I'm afraid, Your Highness, that you'll have to be more specific. Did *what* hurt?"

Celadon's reply was quick; he paused only to *glare* at her through his disheveled fringe. "Did it hurt when you *lost your son*? Your firstborn—Gavriel, didn't you name him? I was told he died at birth."

Her heart lurched—he'd figured it out. She knew he suspected, but the way he looked at her, the careful phrasing of his words . . . he'd figured it out. Urielle, but the *frost* in those hideous green eyes . . .

"I wonder what you expect me to say here. Physically, it hurt very much. Childbirth is no easy feat even for the fae. Would you like me to tell you it brought me to tears?" She snorted.

Inside, she felt something *crack*.

Had it hurt? When she'd gone through *hours* of labor that felt like *dying* the way each contraction burned, and then finally, *finally*, when that child was born—so tiny but healthy and beautiful and whole— to have him *torn* from her before her fingers could even touch him, before she could even see his face and commit to memory everything that made him her boy . . .

She has no care for that boy of hers, she knew the Courts whispered. *She doesn't love him at all. Lucky that first one didn't make it . . .*

Lucky . . . How little they knew.

How much Riadne cared about *both* her children, what she was willing to do and sacrifice for them to *protect them* and ensure that they, too, reached the greatness they were *all* meant for—*three* Fated Lights, each with a destiny that every one of those whisperers could only dare to dream of possessing for their own.

She'd gone to the clearing her mother had kept for all those years and put in years of her own care after, all for one purpose: for the glimpse it had earned Arina, and finally her daughter, of the future. Because *everything* Riadne did was to ensure her boys could one day stand beside her in the world she'd create . . . a world where they were all safe and worshipped above all others . . .

Had it hurt, when Riadne had allowed Azurean to take her child from her, disguise him from all recognition, and foster hatred for her in his heart . . . all so that he could *live*?

Something inside of her *cracked*, but she held her tongue. Said nothing. Until Celadon rolled his eyes and slid off the desk to his feet.

Such a handsome boy . . . but then, he was meant to look exactly like his father at that age, all windswept rosy-blue in the cheeks, russet hair perpetually tousled, jade-green eyes, and a twilight glow. She wondered—often, often, so very often—what the real Celadon looked like underneath.

Because he might be his father's boy wearing that magic, but the cut of that glare . . . the glide of that deadly poise . . . the way he approached Riadne and squared his jaw at her the same way she'd done to everyone who ever tried to make her feel worthless and small . . .

He took her hand.

Placed something in the palm of it—a ring, the one she'd given Hieronymus Aurum in contracting him to her service.

How had Celadon come into possession of this?

"You're planning something for the Solstice."

Riadne shrugged. "That would be a given. It is both the vanity *and* prerogative of every host to ensure theirs is the Solstice that stands out in memory."

"You're planning on killing my father."

"A thing I've been planning for a great many years and have never once made secret. That is how the Bone Crown is won, is it not? Is there something I can actually help you with, Your Highness, or are we going to keep asking questions we already know the answers to—"

"What's behind your columbarium?" Celadon interrupted, and took one step closer.

A handsome boy—a *tall* boy. Celadon took after her in that as well; they very nearly matched each other hardened stare for hardened stare. "I was going to do the thing properly, you know. Bait you into distraction elsewhere so I could learn this answer for myself, but you know what? I want to give you the chance to tell me yourself. To prove to me you aren't the monster *everyone* says you are. Riadne . . ."

He paused, and Riadne felt her heart simultaneously *freeze* and *drop*.

He was going to say it—it was right on his tongue. Riadne . . . *Mother*, and the crack inside her grew even deeper in the glass that caged her emotions away—glass she'd foolishly thought was steel.

He was going to say it; she couldn't let him.

"Moth—"

Crack

Riadne's heart unfroze only to speed like a hummingbird's wings.

"Did it hurt to lose your son?" Celadon repeated a few ringing minutes later, in a small and deadly level voice, his head still cast to the side where Riadne's slap had snapped it.

Breathless, as though she'd just run *leagues*, she replied, "I have never felt a pain so intense in all my years before or after."

"Good." He pushed past her.

Riadne couldn't move, could hardly think, but she felt Celadon hesitate behind her, his hand on the door. A moment later, he added, "If you make a move against my father, I'll tell *everyone* you're keeping the philosopher's stones in that room back there. I might not be a Mesmer, but *you* were a little too careless, it seems, about the things you spoke in here with Lethe recently. The Solstice, Riadne. Whatever you've got planned... let it go. You probably felt giving me up was what was best for me? For once in your life, do something for me I actually *want*."

How long she remained standing there after Celadon took his leave, Riadne couldn't say.

His words echoed in her ears.

His warning grated against her heart.

It didn't matter what Celadon wanted—what he wanted and what would actually help him survive were two different things, and if he thought for a second that she'd come this far only to let him guilt her into hanging it all up on sentiment . . .

"You know, for a moment there, I almost lost faith in your nerve."

Lethe.

Riadne lifted her gaze from her palm, where it had been trained for . . . almost an hour? By the angle of light outside, at *least* that much time had passed in which, apparently, her immortal aid had been watching over her and (by the sound of it) her conversation.

She narrowed her eyes on him. "How foolish of you."

Laughing, Lethe peeled off the columbarium, where he'd been leaning invisible until now under that glittering cloak of his. He stalked around the table on long legs, slid like oil to stand just behind her, and with the slightest brush of his adamant claws, plucked at the ends of her hair that hung at the small of her back. "If you don't get my girl to promise you her aid before you move against your former lover, everything you've done will be for *nothing*—you remember what I told you, *yes*? You remember Fate's warning in doling out her little prophecy to you, how easy it is to *burn* when you fly this close to the sun? Arlo's allegiance, or it won't only be your precious Vehan whose fate will end in death . . ."

"You know," Riadne echoed, turning on her heel, shaving the ends of her hair off on the claw still holding a strand. "It's a little curious. I never contracted you to *Celadon's* safety, only Vehan's. *Son*, not *sons*— and yet Theodore tells me it was *you* who aided his escape from the

Colosseum. How very . . . *soft* of you. Don't tell me you really *are* growing attached to your toys?"

She cocked her head at him, grinned a little when Lethe positively glowered at her. It wasn't often that she got the better of him when they were trading threats, so when he whirled from her and vanished, she latched onto the feeling of triumph that budded in her chest and used it to repair the fissure that had *almost* broken her resolve.

The Solstice—she had work to do, and so little time in which to get it done. Not once had Lethe ever detailed the specifics of what she was supposed to secure from Arlo Jarsdel. Aid was such a vague and varied thing, and any time she asked, he would only (quite maddeningly) reply with the refrain, "You'll know when she presents it." The Solstice . . . so much to do . . . but soon the *world* would see. Soon it would know that she didn't need love; she didn't need her sons' forgiveness or affection or understanding. Cruelty was the only thing that had ever served her well, was the only thing that would complete what needed doing.

It would be what she used to break that sheltered, pathetic *girl* if she didn't yield what Riadne wanted.

It would be what cut down the man who had to fall so her heart could close for good.

And once it did . . . oh, the cruelty she'd show them *then* . . .

CHAPTER 39

Arlo

~⌒~⌒~

"LOOK AT YOU," ZELDA gushed, stepping back to allow Arlo a moment to marvel at her reflection.

In the tailor's quarters, when she'd first been shown the redesigned sketch of her dress, Arlo had been convinced she'd never be able to pull it off. She hadn't worn anything like this before: two narrow strips of void-black fabric cutting from her breast to her waist, the plunging neckline, and the bare back and shoulders, displaying so much she might as well not be wearing anything at all, which meant she *certainly* wasn't able to wear a bra to prevent herself from spilling out, but faerie enchantments kept everything firmly in their strategic placement.

From her waist down fell a cascade of material—layers upon layers of equally black silk and tulle spilling to the floor, tiny crystals like stars sewn in to the voluminous skirts. Much lighter than it should be, every swirl and movement sent her gown dancing like shadows in firelight, and it reminded Arlo so much of the swatches of midnight the Hunters wore that she could tell where Vehan had drawn his inspiration from.

It was an outfit Nausicaä would certainly appreciate, but more than that, Arlo *loved* it. The way her hair had been curled to resemble actual flame, and the color enhanced to burn just as bright; the smoky makeup around her jade-green eyes, and moonlight-shimmer brushed over her skin, and ash-pale gloss to her lips. With her glamours shed to reveal more sharpness to her facial structure, a bit more length and point to the tips of her ears, she felt . . . older. More confident. Like someone who could walk up to the absolute *enormity* that was Nausicaä Kraken and boldly declare her feelings.

Just like when she'd infiltrated the Faerie Ring, this gown was exactly the armor Arlo needed right now. At the same time, she felt wonderfully *herself* in it, the things about her she didn't always like too much—the width of her hips and shoulders, the thickness to her arms and thighs, the ample size of her chest, all of it bared to the world and yet, somehow, looked better to her eyes tonight than ever, as though all she needed was this boost to realize they'd been okay all along.

She was Arlo Jarsdel, a little bit human, a little bit fae, wholly *herself*, and if she wanted to pursue Nausicaä in a romantic manner she *could*, because for all of this she was—

". . . Stars."

Arlo whirled around from her full-length mirror.

There at the door stood Celadon. His chosen outfit for the night was cosmic-black trousers, a matching, high-necked black shirt, and ebony boots that rose to his knees with heels like five-inch daggers. It was the loose-fitted robe of Sylvan silk overtop that drew Arlo's attention. Half sage so pale it gleamed like moonlight, the other half so deep an emerald it was almost as dark as the clothing beneath. The burst of flowers patterning his side, and the bottom right hem, and over his right shoulder were all in fact *real*, growing from the fabric itself. And tying it all was a sash of leafy vines that dripped over his hip and down his leg, and flicked around him like a tail.

With his curling, russet-bronze hair and his own glamours shed to reveal his deep sapphire flush, with his avian-sharp features and all-consuming jade eyes, with the greens and blacks and silver paint and shimmer around his eyes and cheekbones, he looked like some forest-temple deity come to greet her.

She fidgeted a little as Celadon stood there, still as a cat and *staring* like he couldn't believe his eyes.

"Arlo," he gasped, and Arlo found herself holding her breath. Did he hate it? Celadon was very picky about his fashion, but surely this would pass even his standards? She would make him tell Vehan himself if he didn't like it. "You look beautiful."

"Oh," she said, and then her face burst into a smile. Looking down at herself, feeling no less awkward than if Celadon hadn't given his vote of approval, she started to ramble. "Good. I really wasn't sure at first—this is . . . a lot more of *me* than even my bathing suit shows off, I think, but turns out Vehan isn't the worst at fashion design."

"*Vehan* made this?" Celadon stepped into the room, making his way toward her. As he did, he nodded to Zelda and Madelief, dismissing them for a few minutes' privacy.

Arlo turned back to the mirror. "No, just the concept. It's seriously amazing how quickly the folk can throw something together, but it turned out well. I'm . . . happy."

She caught Celadon's expression in the glass. A little misty-eyed and grinning, he wore an expression that was fairly close to what Thalo had been wearing when they'd parted ways last week, and if Celadon started getting emotional on her now, she'd definitely cry and ruin her makeup. "Aren't you supposed to be down with Mom and the rest of the family?"

The High King and his Viridian company were already here, waiting with the others where Arlo, too, was meant to be. As the Lysternes' special guest, she'd been given the honor of making an entrance with Riadne's troupe, and even though she would rather face her first fae ball with her mother and cousin at her side, declining such a coveted invitation would be more than just insulting. At least Vehan and Theo would be close for moral support.

Clearing his throat, Celadon stepped behind her—reached around to string something around Arlo's neck, and now it was *Arlo* who could only look on, speechless, at what he fastened there, the collection of emeralds cut and polished into the shape of an UnSeelie Spring windflower, strung from a fine silver chain.

"I only came to give you this—an heirloom that's been in our family for generations. I was waiting until your Maturity to give it to you, but I think tonight . . . you ought to wear it. You *deserve* to wear it, because Maturity or not, you are and always have been a true Viridian, Arlo. The very best of what I think many of us have forgotten over the years."

"*Cel*," she whispered, tracing the emerald flower with a finger.

Damn it, she'd been trying so hard not to cry, and now her eyes were beginning to water so much she could barely see.

"Thank you," she said in a breath.

Smoothing out her hair, Celadon pressed a kiss to the side of her head, then took a step back. "You've never kept such a large secret from me before—all that stuff with Luck and you becoming a Hollow Star."

"I know," Arlo said, whisper-quiet. "I'm sorry. It wasn't because I don't trust you, Cel—"

"I know," Celadon echoed in reply, and it relieved Arlo that there was no hint of anger or disappointment in his tone. "But I hope after the Solstice, we can sit down and talk, and you can tell me everything you feel comfortable sharing—because Arlo? I love you. With my whole heart, I just want to support you."

Great, now she was *really* going to cry.

"After the Solstice," she promised, and meant it—because she loved him just as much in return.

Crossing to the table, he plucked the crown of windflowers—white with centers as black as Arlo's dress, an exact likeness of the one he too was currently wearing—and brought it to her. Royal families all wore crowns of the flowers of their Courts to celebrations such as this. She'd played dress-up so often with the ones her mother returned home with, but this was the first that had ever been made specifically for Arlo. "It's almost time," he said, lifting the crown to place it on her head. "Would you allow me the honor of escorting you down to the antechamber where our families are waiting?"

Drawing himself into the perfect picture of a fairy-tale prince, Celadon held his arm out at an angle for her to weave her own around.

"The *honor*?" she teased, still too overcome with everything right now for the words to have much edge. "I'm going to remind you that you said this, the next time we're fighting over who gets to play Link in Smash Brothers."

"Arlo, you're a precious treasure, truly the most valuable in my life, but I will pull rank *every* time when it comes to Link, don't even try it."

It was a quiet walk down to the Grand Ballroom's antechamber.

The closer they drew to the room, the greater Arlo's nerves began to roil, because this was an entirely new experience to her. The numerous guests she'd already met in the few days leading up to tonight had been deeply curious about her, stopping her in the halls or leaning over their dinner plates to ask her prying questions. Likely, they'd been interested only to compare what she answered to the things they'd learned from gossip about Commander Viridian-Verdell's ironborn daughter, but it would be like jumping out of their uncomfortable spotlight only to find herself beneath the microscope of their fascination as soon as she walked through the ballroom doors in Queen Riadne's train.

This was something she'd wanted for as long as she'd known about these parties that kicked off on the Solstice's Eve and wore on well through the week but were closed to her participation. An unrecognized royal scandal—that's all Arlo had been to so many of the folk before now. There would be *countless* celebrations occurring all around the world tonight, but *here*, in the Luminous Palace, only the select elite would get to ring in Summer with the Seelie Queen of the Season.

She'd wanted this, but now that it was moments from happening, Arlo was beginning to panic.

So many folk would be here, *important* folk, kings and queens and sovereigns, princes and princesses and royal heirs, every dignitary and well-connected aristocrat, Councillor, and Court Ambassador, A-list celebrities and fashion icons and anyone else Queen Riadne deemed significant enough to invite into this highly competitive and vicious inner circle of the Courts. No amount of wine or spirits, or dancing or other entertainment, would distract these folk from scrutinizing Arlo's every move, and if she messed up even a little, it would be on both the Lysterne *and* Viridian names . . . On her mother's name . . . Celadon's . . . the High King's . . .

"Deep breath," Celadon murmured.

They arrived at the antechamber but paused just before going in so that Arlo could take a moment to breathe as instructed and wind herself down a bit. "You're a Viridian, Arlo, remember that. You're one of us; you belong here. And I'll say this about Riadne—as her guest of honor and under her roof, no one is going to *dare* insult you to your face."

"Excellent," said Arlo dryly. "Behind my back it is, then."

Celadon laughed. "Yes, well, pettiness often can't exist without insecurity to drive it. And I always find something amusing when someone I wouldn't think twice about spends all that energy just to *gossip* about me."

"Yes, well," Arlo mimicked, "you're the High Prince. They could literally start the rumor that you're five gnomes in a trenchcoat and no one's going to chase you out of a store with a broom."

"First of all, I'm much taller than only *five gnomes*, thank you. Second of all, have *you* ever been chased out of a store with a broom?" He narrowed his eyes at her in skepticism. "Is this a human culture thing? Do they actually do this? Follow-up question: Did the folk *miss* whatever brooms did in human history to earn this much mistrust, because between this and the whole thing you've invented for witches, I feel like—"

"All right, I'm going in now," Arlo announced, rolling her eyes and pushing open the antechamber door.

A gasp caught her attention as soon as she stepped inside. "*Arlo,*" Thalo exclaimed, rushing forward to clasp her shoulders and study what Arlo was wearing. "A bit revealing," she mused, because Thalo might be fae, and fae had never been all that concerned with showing off skin, but she was still a mother. "But look at you . . . as beautiful as ever."

Arlo noticed the *exact* moment Thalo recognized what she wore around her neck, and bit her lip in anxious anticipation of what she would say.

Not that she worried her own mother would declare her a fraud and rip it off her throat, but it was a very bold statement on Arlo's part, especially paired with the protective bracelet Celadon had also given her that only those of royal status owned and wore . . .

The more Viridians that gave these things approval, the better.

When a wide, delighted smile unfurled across her mother's face, Arlo breathed a small sigh of relief, and smiled back. "As beautiful as ever," Thalo repeated, then stepped aside. "Don't you agree?"

For a moment, Arlo had no idea if she was talking to any one person, or the room.

There was High King Azurean—and goodness, he looked like he'd aged a full century in a month, his hair gone completely gray now and lines weighing down his handsome face—and his wife, Reseda, on his arm; the Crown High Princess Cerelia, next in line as Head of UnSeelie Spring, and a beautiful fae woman on *her* arm whom Arlo didn't recognize but was no doubt her date; High Prince Serulian and his wife, Elexa—Elyas was still just a little too young to tag along for this event, so he was most likely sulking in his room back home; Lords Morayo and Lekan Otedola; the Fae High Councillors of Spring and Summer and their respective families; Vehan, Aurelian, Theodore; Mavren and Eurora Reynolds; a handful of both the Verdant and Luminous Guard . . .

There were the Heads of Seelie Spring and UnSeelie Summer and *their* families, whom Arlo only really knew by way of her lessons in the library these past few weeks.

Spring and their company were all dressed in leafy and airy trimmings, and lush greens and exquisite blues, Summer and theirs in electric and flaming warmth and dazzling whites and vibrant reds.

Riadne stood in a halo of radiance in the center of it all, in a dress made entirely out of tiny, wicked-sharp shards of crystal-glass, fitted to her body like dragon scales and slotting like a glinting cage around a large gold stone sitting like a sun on her chest. Arlo could just glimpse the pommel of Riadne's infamous sword fixed along her spine.

Glitter and gauze, Sylvan silk and insect wings, velvet petals, melted gold and leaves and vines—others had ceremonial weapons fixed to them as well, displays of deadly beauty that fae so delighted in. All manner of materials went into making up this collection of folk as the immortals they'd long ago cast out, the powerful elite—but none of them were who Thalo had been speaking to.

None of them were who captured Arlo's attention as swiftly and entirely as though compelled by magic's thrall.

"Nos," said Arlo, the name escaping in a breath. "You're here."

They'd agreed to attend this ball together back in Arlo's bedroom, but it hadn't really been addressed since, not any more than Nausicaä's passing comments of looking forward to "getting trashed with the upper echelons" and seeing the looks on people's faces when Arlo—by Nausicaä's firm demand—introduced her to them as the Dark Star.

Arlo had just assumed she'd meet Nausicaä out on the floor.

Really, there was still nothing spoken or official between them yet, and asking Nausicaä outright to enter the ballroom *with* Arlo had felt too much like asking her out back when she didn't have the words to do so; back before the rooftop prom, when Arlo had made up her mind that this young woman in front of her was worth the risk of rejection; back before this dress and before seeing Nausicaä now, standing there like this had all been inevitable.

Nausicaä, in a suit as weapon-sharp as her features, black as the dress Arlo wore, her blazer left open to reveal nothing but a black lace bra underneath, and shoes as liquid silver as the shimmer painted on Arlo's skin. Her hair had been braided to the skull on one side, twisted around the braid Arlo had woven there and swept around to the opposite side, showing off the black star tattooed on her neck, and her full mouth, it was even wider for the *sin* that was the red that painted it.

She was *devastating*.

Arlo could only look at her, speechless, breathless at the sight . . .

And Nausicaä stared back, seemingly just as lost in the moment as she was.

"*Success*," Arlo heard Vehan whisper very loudly to Theo, and the spell broke.

Clearing her throat, Nausicaä pushed off the wall. She prowled toward Arlo and came to a halt in front of her, and when she didn't say a thing—which was most unusual Nausicaä behavior—Arlo's nerves cranked back to a ten, and she threw her arms wide with an awkward, "So . . . Dark Star approval?"

Nausicaä's eyes gleamed with some dark, unspoken thought. She looked Arlo over, a single sweep that Arlo felt like *fire*, traveling from the point of her heels to the crown of windflowers on her head, then settling to lock on her eyes. "Well, I'd like to formally invite you to *step* on me . . . ," she replied at last in a low, husky voice kept quietly between them, her words a little thick and sticking together. But then she faltered again. Humming low in the back of her throat, she seemed to be mulling over another thought, and Arlo found herself desperately curious to know, but maybe not in front of all this family.

Nausicaä bit her lip, dropped her gaze once more to catch on Arlo's chest and linger—the heat of her stare stirred something fluttering and delicious-*warm* low in Arlo's core, her breath arrested entirely by the consuming swell of feeling.

At some point, Thalo had wandered off toward Vehan. They were now the both of them grinning enthusiastically in the background, Vehan shooting her two thumbs up. Arlo only noticed them when her gaze began to drift down the golden expanse of Nausicaä's bared throat, but it was reminder enough that they weren't alone for her to gather herself.

And just in time. Arlo shook her head to clear it of the haze, and the very next moment, an attendant in full ceremonial garb entered the room.

"It's time!" he announced, and no sooner had he finished did *more* attendants filter in behind him to usher everyone into place and see to last-minute touches to their conceptualized looks.

Nausicaä held out an arm to Arlo, as perfectly poised as Celadon had been. "And *now* I can't wait to see the looks on people's faces when they realize the Dark Star brought the prettiest girl to the ball."

Rolling her eyes, Arlo laughed, but took the proffered arm regardless. "*Dork.*"

"I cannot help, fairest maiden, that the sight of you divests me of all reason."

Arlo fairly choked on her laughter now as Nausicaä lead them to their designated spot in Riadne's procession. "Oh my gods, *stop*," she wheezed. "I feel like I'm going to pop out of this dress if I laugh too hard."

"Chin up and tits out—that's my girl, assert that dominance."

Dominance? Doubtful. The folk had a tendency to get away with themselves whenever they gathered for a revel of any kind, but for a *Solstice* celebration? Arlo knew enough about what happened here that a slip of her dress would be nothing in comparison, would barely earn the bat of a lash, let alone begrudging respect. But there was an appreciation in the way Nausicaä watched her when she said this, that dark gleam returning, and a wolfish hint of promise curled her almost *profane* mouth, which Arlo couldn't help but look at . . . and couldn't look away from until a clock out in the waiting ballroom struck the first of eleven chimes.

The final hour of Spring was at hand.

Their procession began to move.

CHAPTER 40

Aurelian

~~~

THE SIDHE FAE AND their elaborate customs. To symbolize the transition of spring into summer, the High King Azurean led their procession out into the ballroom, King Beron of Seelie Spring linked arm-in-arm beside him. Queen Riadne and King Ishaan, as the Seelie and UnSeelie Heads of Summer, stood similarly paired at the farthest end of this very long line. They would be the last to make their entrance. Intermingled between were their families, which Aurelian figured was meant to signify equality and unity and respect. Of course, these were things they didn't feel at all for one another—certainly not the Lysterne triplets, who all glared daggers at the back of Aurelian's head, having clearly been hoping one of *them* would get to walk out of this room on High Prince Celadon's arm.

"Ready?" asked Celadon when their turn through the antechamber doors was only one pair away.

Eyes forward, both posture and aura at perfect ease, the High Prince had been to enough of these celebrations that of course he wasn't nervous right now. Aurelian had attended enough as well in his time in this palace, in this very procession as Vehan's steward, but there was that *feeling* that had been plaguing him for a while now—a certain foreboding that told him Riadne had something planned for this evening that none of them would forget.

Celadon had (almost suspiciously) called off his own plot to infiltrate Riadne's office, said he had the situation handled and no longer required Aurelian's assistance, that Aurelian was to drop the matter entirely, in fact.

But Aurelian . . . wasn't very good at letting go of things, and Celadon had changed his resolve so abruptly that it actually baffled him, because right up until a few days ago, the High Prince had been just as convinced Riadne was up to something, and that *something* was being kept behind that columbarium of hers.

Whatever changed his mind, Aurelian couldn't press it.

Celadon had issued the order to drop it in the tone of a High Prince, but *this feeling* . . . The air was thick with that terrible foreboding he couldn't shake, and maybe it was Aurelian keyed-up on too many years spent trying to stay just one step ahead of Riadne, of death, of looking at every scenario as a potential battleground, and this unease was all in his head?

Maybe nothing was actually wrong.

After all, would Riadne *really* sabotage this evening she'd been working day and night for *months* to prepare, just to make any sort of significant move *now*? Certainly not with the terms of her Challenge for Azurean's Crown still to be established.

That was one strict custom Aurelian was glad for right now, that whatever Riadne had planned for her undoubtedly dramatic usurpation, she couldn't enact it without officially declaring her venue and Challenger first, and giving the High King reasonable time to secure a Challenger of his own, if that was what he wished.

If Riadne had done this at any point over the last month, Aurelian would have heard about it. The magical community would have *exploded* with gossip and speculation. But there was plenty else she could get up to meanwhile, and he would breathe a little easier once this night was over.

"Ready," he replied tightly.

For better or worse.

A stately, booming voice announced the names of the pair in front of them—which meant that they were next. Aurelian couldn't help but glance over his shoulder at Vehan and Theo standing just behind him.

Theo had achieved a godly level of attractive with his wing-tipped liner and gold around his black-amber eyes, wearing an ivory-and-gold brocade suit that looked as though someone had poured it around his lean body, and with a diamond shimmer to his deeply bronze skin and a crown of pure white lilies around his head. But even so, it was only Vehan that Aurelian could see right now.

It was only *ever* Vehan he could see.

Vehan who, in Sylvan robes of porcelain white and brilliant gold, his tanned skin dusted with a fine powder of the same precious metal, his black hair swept back from his cut-glass features and smears of diamond and gold on his lips and around his electric eyes, looked a bit to Aurelian like the romantic fallen angels that humans often wrote about.

It was unfathomable to think that this might be the last time they'd have to enter any official function *separately*.

He was no fool. Riadne wouldn't make their relationship easy, and it was going to end in a very final way, for him at least. But she'd dangled the temptation in front of them back in her throne room, that after this Solstice, for however long Riadne allowed them, she might just grant them her blessing to present themselves as an official *couple*. Not as steward and prince but *partners . . .*

It was unfathomable.

She would never let Aurelian be that happy unless she planned on using that to *crush* him, but looking back at Vehan in this moment, he could almost see it—the glimpse of what things might be like if Fate hadn't written their story as a tragedy.

As though he could feel Aurelian's eyes on him, Vehan turned from the whispered conversation he and Theo had been having. The two might look made for each other, but it was *Aurelian* his impossibly beautiful prince had chosen, and when Vehan's face split into the widest, most radiant smile he'd ever seen him wear, despite Aurelian's doubts and fears and swirling thoughts, he couldn't help but smile back.

"—the UnSeelie Spring High Prince Celadon Cornelius Fleur-Viridian and Lord Aurelian Bessel of Seelie Summer."

Their turn at last.

Aurelian's gaze snapped forward.

The attendant in charge of pacing the procession waved them quickly through the antechamber's door.

From within, the world beyond had been a glowing convolution of indistinct shapes, flickering impressions, and the muffled trickle of chatter and tune. The moment he and Celadon walked out onto the top landing of the ballroom's grand staircase, Aurelian was struck with the impression of having crossed through a veil strung between two worlds, the way color and light and sound burst to a vibrancy such as only magic could effect.

"I'll give her this," Celadon muttered through his teeth as he beamed and waved at the overwhelming enthusiasm that received him as a Courts-beloved fae idol, "Riadne does nothing in halves."

She certainly didn't.

He'd been in this room before, but he'd never seen it like this. Tonight, the ceiling had been stripped away completely. They were at once both inside and out, the room's perimeter marked by its underlying framework of marble and gilt and elaborate stuccowork walls, the sort one would expect to find in any ostentatious palace. But thick, enormous oak trees made entirely of solid gold now stood in place of pillars in the traveling colonnade that supported a wraparound mezzanine, where numerous folk were gathered watching and several pockets of a faerie orchestra played music in perfect synchrony.

The branches of these golden oaks reached up and up and up into a sky suspended in glowing dawn. They spread a canopy of pure white blossoms overhead, the petals of which drifted in lazy freefall to the ground, and at the slightest touch burst into a shower of sparks to reveal they'd been nothing but illusion all along.

A nod to spring—once this final hour was up, this spectacle would no doubt cease. Whatever took its place would symbolize the start of summer. Aurelian could already see hints of electric-white fire beginning to catch in empty spaces.

Every gaping arch in the colonnade led out into the palace gardens. Silken sheets of yet more electricity-like-fire fluttered across the archways, snapping and crackling and extinguishing to a *zap* of nothing whenever someone passed through.

There was a gentle tug at Aurelian's arm to break his examination of their surroundings, Celadon spurring him back into motion. They descended the golden crushed-velvet carpet down the grand staircase, a profusion of lilies and black-eyed windflowers overgrowing the banister to sweep with the cascading steps to the ballroom's main level.

The folk here had cleared a path for the procession, so that pair by pair they could filter through to the middle of the room, where they were expected to kick off the night with the dance Aurelian and the others had been practicing for weeks now.

Just as in the throne room, several inches of thick glass had been poured overtop a pale marble foundation. Unlike in the throne room, though, whole bolts of lightning were trapped within it, crackling and spitting-mad, swirling in some intricate pattern he couldn't quite make out.

The bolts shifted through white and yellow and blue depending on the angle, and it was only because even Aurelian found himself drawn to watching this shimmering transition of color as they moved into position and waited for the rest of the procession to join them that he noticed something far more curious.

"What's been carved into the glass?" he wondered aloud, more to himself than to Celadon, who was likely the only person who could hear him right now.

Because something *had* been carved there.

It looked like a symbol—most likely some old faerie language they'd once spoken and was now forgotten—but it was hard to discern the clean, sharp lines of whatever it could be for the crowd and distortion of light around them. No one else seemed all that concerned about it, but Aurelian did wonder . . .

The orchestra stopped playing.

Aurelian looked up.

Riadne and Ishaan had taken to the landing at last, and as they stepped out into view, the entire hall fell to silence.

There would be no cheer for Summer yet, not until the eleventh hour of Spring had passed. None would bow them through to the circle of dancers, as they had done for the High King and Beron.

The Heads of Summer took to the very center of the circle, joining the Heads of Spring. Seelie beside Seelie, UnSeelie by UnSeelie, the two Seasons made no eye contact, acted as though mirror image of one another, parallel entities that didn't so much as brush cloaks when the orchestra began to play the first traditional dance of the evening.

And they were off, swept immediately into the swirl of complicated steps Aurelian had learned so well over the years that he moved on pure memory alone. His preference was to lead, but the upheaval *that* would cause, for daring to assert himself over a High Prince . . . Celadon *had* actually dared him to do it back when they'd been sorting through the logistics of pairings.

Aurelian had flatly informed him that he refused to be the first casualty of this party.

And he was glad for it now, so preoccupied with the floor as he was. He probably looked like he was a novice counting steps, but there was more than just the one symbol carved into the glass, and on their own they could be anything, but the way *some* were entwined with the most complex *equations* he'd ever encountered . . .

"Celadon." The word came slowly, stuck in his throat, a bit like trying to run in a nightmare where the very air turns as thick as tar.

Their waltz was at last over.

Celadon looked at him.

Before Aurelian could unstick his tongue and remember how to speak, the crowd erupted back into applause. Folk rushed forward, pairing off with each other take the floor now too, others flocking to the royals who were now free to be courted for more dancing.

Celadon had been swarmed the very second the orchestra ended their piece.

He smiled at everyone, greeted them pleasantly, laughed and winked and flirted with them, but even Aurelian could see he was carefully trying to disentangle himself all the while, no doubt aiming to get to his cousin.

This was Arlo's first ball. Nausicaä would protect her, but Nausicaä's temper was a very short fuse, and Arlo had just arrived on the scene in the royal procession with a yet-unidentified entity on her arm. There was no small crowd of curiosity beginning to gather around the pair of them, and when they found out who Nausicaä was . . . He didn't blame the High Prince for wanting to get ahead of it.

Vehan, then . . . but when he turned to find him, he came face-to-face with a young fae girl who had to be only *barely* Mature—anyone younger would find themselves ushered off to the guest-room quarters as soon as midnight passed.

"Uhh . . ."

"Hello," the fae girl greeted. "Would you like to dance?" Deep umber eyes, flowing onyx hair, youthful-soft features and desert-warm skin with just a hint of sapphire flush beneath. She'd been spritzed with something floral-scented and ruby-shimmery, and wore a crown of UnSeelie Summer jasmine flowers around her head. A pretty girl . . . as far as Aurelian could gauge prettiness in young women.

But before he could even politely decline, an arm entwined with his, snapping his attention to his right. Another fae, twice Aurelian's age, his features as carved from stone as his muscle.

"I think he'd much rather dance with me, wouldn't you, Lord Aurelian?" said whoever this was—someone from the Seelie Spring Court, judging by the roses in his crown—in a tone like Aurelian should probably be honored by the attention.

"Can I have a dance, Lord Aurelian?"

"Would you like to dance with *me*, Lord Aurelian?"

"Piss off, Teselle! I asked him first!"

"Yes, well, I'm sure if he wanted to dance with someone who smells like the hay you've tumbled half the folk here in, he'd rather a *cow* over *you*."

There were suddenly a lot of folk around him, almost in a blink.

He didn't know why it surprised him every time it happened— four times a year since he'd turned sixteen and taken on the role of steward-in-training. It didn't matter what gossip said behind his back. It didn't matter that Aurelian was stamped with human ink and iron piercings, that he was "Autumn masquerading as Summer" and probably a spy, probably Riadne's secret *toy*, and they were much more on the mark about that one, even if it wasn't (thankfully) as lewd as rumor suggested.

Aurelian could be thoroughly despised by the lot of them, and they would still flock to him in these moments, because he was still a lord and a stand-in for the one-day king of the Seelie Summer Court, and he was . . . not unattractive.

He was also an entire spectacle in his own right now, because Vehan had marched into his room this morning, and without so much as a word of explanation, presented him with something that was very *not* Seelie Summer white-and-gold attire.

It was probably the most luxurious thing Aurelian had ever worn, a brocade silk suit of earthen brown and coal black cut to such exacting measurements that it was almost as though he wore nothing at all. Paired with his burgundy waistcoat and the ruby-bright dress shirt beneath, whatever Riadne must feel about him donning the Seelie Autumn colors of home, he'd definitely made a statement.

Even more so, with the crown of lilies Vehan had insisted he wear with it—not the one he'd normally wear, but one that matched Vehan's own. The one that should be sitting on *Theo's* head if he were actually Vehan's intended, ornate and gilded and studded with lightning-yellow crystals.

He had Vehan to thank for the more than usual amount of attention right now.

The lesidhe fae boy brought in to play the prince's steward—they were probably wondering if that had been a ruse all along, and Vehan might announce tonight that he'd actually been his intended, which meant Aurelian might actually be *someone*: an illegitimate son of one of the Autumn royals, perhaps, or a distant enough relative that no one had heard much about them.

"Sorry," he murmured, distinctly uncomfortable and trying, much like Celadon had yet to successfully manage, to escape from the hands that bound him in place. "I'm . . . not in the mood for dancing right now. If you'd just excuse me . . ."

But the hands wouldn't let go.

In fact, none of his petitioners seemed to even hear him over the argument they'd devolved into, Aurelian trapped in the midst of it all like a toy between squabbling children. There was nothing else for it—lesidhe strength made easy work of jerking out of their grasp. A cacophony of startled yelps and moans of disappointment rose to chase him, but Aurelian plunged into the sea of folk before anyone could try to physically wrangle him back in.

He pushed his way through the crowded throng.

All manner of faeries and fae flitted and danced about, huddled around in groups, or showed off to one another their outfits and their partners and whatever clever accessory they'd paired with each, chatting about this and that going on in both their lives and the Courts.

Aurelian tried to ignore it all, kept his head bent and eyes to the floor to slip unnoticed between them.

He followed the carvings; there was a line in the glass spreading much farther out than the circle containing their previous dance. Heels caught on it, folk tripped over it, every one of them muttered about how impractical this bit of decoration was. Aurelian had to agree in some respect, but Riadne wasn't a superfluous person. It might not be the most sensible of her ornamentations, but it was far from pointless.

The line curved around the room.

Aurelian followed it. He had to know . . . *had* to know, and also didn't want to be right, because *why?*

The more people he nudged aside as he went, the more of the pattern he uncovered, and the deeper dread began to sink its claws into his heart.

Seeing the thing in snatches like this . . . if he could get to higher ground and observe the thing as a whole, he'd be able to tell if it was what he feared. He'd be able to see the design of it all . . . whether these looping lines bent into a shape that had haunted his sleep for years.

He *had a feeling* . . . but there were too many folk obscuring the carvings.

Skirts and robes and legs and tails—there was too much going on to be able to tell with certainty what anything was. Like collecting random pieces of an elaborate puzzle, Aurelian tried to fit them together, to picture there what his eyes couldn't see.

He slammed to a halt.

The symbol at his foot . . . He knew what this was.

He remembered seeing this just this afternoon, in the private study in the palace library, where Arlo had demonstrated a mastery over this very element.

He remembered seeing it, in the intricacies of that deities-damned *array* etched on Vehan's heart.

Alchemy.

This marking, it was the alchemic symbol for *iron.*

He could sense a little more of this poison in the air than usual, but it was negligible, really, with the High King's presence to dilute the effects and Aurelian's years of exposure to Riadne's horrible staircase.

What was she planning?

There would be quite the controversial show come the midnight transferral of power from Spring to Summer, Aurelian was almost positive of that now, and he finally knew why Leda had been one of the few allowed in this room to help with its setup and why Councillor Sylvain had followed in tow, to watch over this entire process like a highly prejudiced hawk.

The lines he'd been following, the symbols—an *array* had been carved into the glass, but if Councillor Sylvain knew about this, it had to have the approval of the High King, right? Of at least *someone* in the High King's council, or even the Fae High Council itself, which meant it had to be harmless enough, surely?

It *couldn't* be *the* array, the one that turned ironborn hearts to stone. Even Riadne wouldn't allow that sort of alchemy to be performed right under the High King's nose, but then again . . . it would be a clear demonstration to the people, after all, how ineffective and little respected their High King was now.

This could be one last dig at Azurean before she came for his Crown.

Her grand reveal . . .

And Aurelian couldn't shake the awful thought that had just occurred to him as he noted all the gold in this room, that if Riadne *was* in any way responsible for the philosopher's stone plot . . . if this wasn't an array that created philosopher's stones, she might still have in her possession *Hieronymus's* stone, the one that would allow her to transmute the precious metal gilding *everything* around them into a poison she'd been . . . *conditioning* herself to withstand ever since she put in those *iron stairs*.

A stone . . . that didn't require iron blood to utilize.

A stone . . . like the one transfixed in the middle of the dress she currently wore.

"Hello!"

Startled, Aurelian's eyes snapped up from the ground.

One of the serving staff stood before him. New—Aurelian knew pretty well everyone who worked the kitchens, between his determination to learn the hands behind the scenes here and his parents' occupation. He didn't recognize this young man—this *ironborn* young man. The longer Aurelian stared at him, the more obvious this became, the flush of red so genuine that no glamour could mimic, and a bend of the same metallic scent that stained the air sitting heavy in his magic.

It wasn't the fact that he was here that made Aurelian gawk.

It wasn't his presence alone that pulled at the thread of Aurelian's unease.

This young man, there was something *wrong* about him—about his aura, specifically. Something oily and dark and cold stretched beneath his magic like a yawning tar pit.

It was the exact same wrongness that he sometimes felt stir in *Vehan's* magic. It made him want to flinch away, as though he'd just stuck his hand into a jar of something slimy that he couldn't see.

And his *eyes* . . .

Aurelian was suddenly reminded of the young man they'd found dead in the park in what felt like ages ago now, the very first ironborn victim of an alchemic plot much vaster and more deadly than they ever could have imagined, and growing more complicated by the day.

At least, the first ironborn victim to be *discovered* by them.

There was no glowing in his veins—and surely he'd be a little more panicked about that, if there was—but there was something in this young man's eyes that was almost *worse* than that, a deeper claret sheen like finely aged wine . . . like the magic that had put that there had done the opposite of kill him, as it did the others . . . like it had taken successful, parasitic hold.

Like whoever this was, it was no longer the young man whose face it was wearing but a husk for the Sin that had been grown in his very heart, ready for the plucking.

Aurelian stared.

"Would you like a drink?" the young man asked, as though nothing were wrong. As though there weren't something just a little bit *dull* behind his voice, inhuman, which of course none of the folk here would pick up on, because what did they care about other than themselves?

He extended a tray of champagne so pale it gleamed like water in its elegant flute, sparkling like the electric fire that crept through the trees overhead.

Aurelian's stare transferred to the glasses. He shook his head.

One step.

Two.

He backed away from the ironborn man, who tracked his retreat with no more interest than the slightest tilt of his head.

All along . . . he'd been right all along.

The trepidation he'd been feeling all night wasn't unfounded.

The Viridians had all been gathered in one convenient place.

Riadne's Challenge to the High King . . .

Her clever, methodical cruelty and obsession with revenge . . .

He needed to find Vehan. They needed to get away from this room, to regroup with the others and *address this* before the hour was up and Riadne's plan was put into motion. He needed to—

"Tsk, tsk, tsk," said a voice, and Aurelian froze once more.

An arm slid to drape across his shoulders. Rot bloomed against his aura, that wriggling, crawling sensation of death that could only belong to a Hunter—and that voice, the cool, trickling lightness of it . . .

Aurelian winced as the hand that curled around him squeezed just enough to prick his skin with adamant claws—and if he was anything other than lesidhe, his magic tied so profoundly to exactly what stars were made of, what that metal was made of too, he wouldn't be able to heal it.

"She wouldn't be happy if you spoiled her game before it's won," Lethe drawled.

He marched Aurelian forward, toward one of the archways leading out into the gardens. Try as Aurelian might, he couldn't plant himself firmly enough to prevent this, could only struggle futilely and stumble along as Lethe led him farther and farther away—from the room, from *Vehan*.

"I thought you were just an *interested party*," Aurelian growled as they stepped out into the night. Because that's what this Hunter had said back in Hieronymus's lab, that he didn't serve any particular side of what was going on. "Why are you helping her?"

"Helping *her*?"

Lethe made an exaggeration of looking around. Pointedly finding the queen nowhere in sight, he turned a grin on Aurelian, and Aurelian didn't think it was possible to see anyone do so more terribly than Nausicaä, but if this wasn't worse, it was certainly tied.

A creaking laugh as they marched deeper into the garden, past fae and faeries already wrapped too intimately in one another to notice what passed through their midst, and Lethe drawled once more at him. "Well, here I thought I was helping *you*."

CHAPTER 41

Arlo

~~~

CELADON *HAD* WARNED THAT she'd attract no small amount of curiosity tonight. The folk in general valued knowledge over any gem, but the sidhe fae elite were *notorious* for their rapacious pursuit of this commodity. Royal luxury was a level of cunning and manipulation all its own, and when a people who were used to throwing treasures at things to get their way encountered something that couldn't always be bought, it lent an edge to their ruthlessness that few but their own could contend with . . . or survive.

Arlo making an entrance at her very first fae ball in the company of both the Lysterne and Viridian families would perk every pointed ear in the hall. They'd want to know how Arlo had earned such an honor, who she considered her friends both here and back home, what she'd been up to while she was here, what she liked eating, wearing, doing with her spare time. The slightest detail was all it took for alliances to be forged *and* unmade, after all, for gossip to find ground to seed, for lives to be ruined and family feuds to erupt, and could even set off wars between the veritable tinderboxes that were the Eight Great Courts.

Arlo hadn't been born into this life.

She didn't have Celadon's years of practice dealing with this brand of deceit and viciousness and wouldn't know until far too late down the line if she'd accidentally given any one of them leverage over her or someone she cared about.

He'd warned her to pay close attention to her conversations and avoid certain people, whose faces she'd spent a great deal of time committing to memory during their study sessions in the library—but she hadn't been expecting such a *swarm* of interest to crowd her and Nausicaä, as soon as their dance had ended.

"*Who* designed your dress, Lady Arlo, I *must* know."

"Is this lovely young woman here your girlfriend?"

"I hear, Lady Arlo, that you were invited here as a guest of honor. You and Prince Vehan must be *very* close then—come on, just between us girls, you've put yourself forth as a suitor for his hand, haven't you?"

Their questions were immediate and numerous, fired too quickly for Arlo to keep up with.

Hands plucked at her hair and dress and the flowers on her crown.

Folk fawned over her—if nothing else, this was the first time many of them were meeting the girl they'd only ever seen in random articles featuring her High Prince cousin, and they wouldn't let this chance to ingratiate themselves with him through her pass by.

Some of the attention seemed harmless enough: a faerie girl asking for a dance, or a sidhe fae not much older than she asking if they could take a selfie together. One skipped Arlo completely to confess to Nausicaä that she was the most beautiful person they'd ever seen, and Arlo had to agree with that, but Nausicaä merely scowled.

A glance to Arlo—Arlo gave her a minute nod, and it was all it took for Nausicaä to snatch up her hand, bark out the command to "Move," and plough straight through the crowd that parted easily (and wisely) for them to sweep back toward the grand staircase.

Up to the mezzanine, out onto a portion of the balcony where there was no one yet but them. Arlo drew a deep breath of the floral-fragrant night air and finally felt herself *relax*.

"All right, I'm going to say it," Nausicaä announced, turning to Arlo with her hands on her hips and a wrinkle of disgust over the bridge of her nose. "There is a *slight* chance, very possible, that I am maybe not a people person."

"But you hide it so well," Arlo deadpanned.

"I know, I know—I mean, easy-going, affectionate, loveable? These are all definitely the adjectives that come to mind at the mention of my name. Alas, beneath this convincing charade, I am but a curmudgeon."

Arlo laughed, more of a cackle really, low and deep in her throat. "Come here, curmudgeon," she summoned as she moved to the balcony railing.

It was dark out here.

The magic that made it day within hadn't been extended beyond the ballroom, but Riadne hadn't spared expense, even so. It was like looking out at the world through a fishbowl. Beyond the manicured gardens strung with fluttering white silk and dancing electric balls that drifted around like fireflies, beyond the strings of will-o'-the-wisp fairy lights and decorative fountains and white and yellow flowers, instead of the usual surrounding forest and Colorado landscape, what pressed against the hedges was a magicked view into the vaguely distorted majesty of the Las Vegas Strip at night.

"It's so pretty," she marveled, as soon as Nausicaä joined her.

She looked over at the breathy "yeah" of agreement this received only to find Nausicaä staring at *her* instead of the scenery, and just like that, all the things Arlo had felt when she first saw Nausicaä back in the antechamber—the sheer overwhelming *happiness* she felt any and every time they were together—swelled to such a crescendo inside her that Arlo could only swallow.

Clearing her throat, Nausicaä turned so that her back leaned against the railing, and Arlo was almost too distracted by the way this silhouetted her in a hazy glow of pinks and reds and purples and blues, cast shadows across her features and deepened the richness of her golden tan. Arlo's gaze snagged once more on those red painted lips . . .

"Nausicaä?"

"Hmm?"

Do it, a voice inside her urged. *Tell her you like her.* But when Arlo opened her mouth again, what came out was, "The argument we had . . . back in my bedroom. It got . . . pretty heated. I just

559

wanted to make sure everything's okay? I mean, of course it isn't. You went through a pretty traumatic experience with what happened to your sister, and all these hunts we've gone on recently opening up old wounds . . ."

"Arlo?" Nausicaä said her name gently, picking up where Arlo's hesitation made her trail off. She didn't know what to say, or rather how to say it, without potentially making things worse and ruining their entire evening.

"I just wanted you to know that nothing's changed between us. Nos . . . I know there's anger inside you. I know you've been struggling with it and so many other things for some time. I don't expect you to be happy all the time, to be able to pretend things are fine when they're not, or to know how to act in and deal with every situation perfectly. It doesn't scare me, okay? I like you exactly the way you are, and you don't scare me, not one bit. Whatever you want to share with me, whatever you want my company in dealing with, whatever you choose to open up to me about, *you* get to decide what and when and how that happens. I won't ever pressure you. Just know that I *want* to be the one you let into your life. Because you deserve to *heal*, Nausicaä, and you can absolutely heal on your own—you don't need a relationship of any kind to do that—but . . . you don't *have* to do it alone. Yeah?"

Quiet stretched between them for a moment, the only sounds those of the night and the party happening around them. Arlo could hear her heartbeat in her ears. She was so nervous about what Nausicaä's reply might be, if anything at all—maybe Nausicaä would brush her off and tell her to keep her nose out. She certainly wasn't looking at Arlo at the moment, staring straight ahead instead, but there was no trace of the fear or resentment or panic that Arlo had seen back in her bedroom the last time they'd broached this subject, so . . . that had to be a good sign, right?

"Listen, Red . . . *Arlo* . . ." She blew out her cheeks. Sighed. Dropped her chin to collect herself, and with a deep breath, tried again, but still she didn't actually *look* at Arlo. "I'm sorry. I'm not . . . used to other people yet. To letting them in. You're right, there's a lot I'm still dealing with, and it's been only *me* to deal with it for so long because . . . well, it was easier. I thought. To go at it alone. Turns out, not so much. And I'm sorry. I'm working on it, okay? If it's any reassurance . . . I really want the person I let in to be you, as well."

Arlo smiled, wide and overjoyed. "That's enough for me. Thank you, Nos."

"Yeah," she replied, soft and distinctly awkward, and Arlo had to swallow a laugh for the way her face heated with a mixture of embarrassment and pleasure. "So," Nausicaä continued, clearing her throat once more. "Is this everything you thought it would be?" She waved at the ballroom within. "Your first official Solstice party—you get to be a Viridian tonight, and all those fancy-ass fae in there who ignored you your whole life were just clawing at one another to be your new best friend. Kind of a dream come true, huh?"

"Nausicaä?" she heard herself blurt once more.

Nausicaä turned to look at her just as Arlo averted her gaze to her hands, folded over the railing's stone.

She drew a breath—*now, now, say it now,* her very heart seemed to beat.

Now, before she lost this chance, the only sliver of time alone they'd probably get all evening. Nausicaä could very well reject her, that was still a possibility, but if she *didn't* . . . And wouldn't it be nice to be with her tonight as the *girlfriend* Arlo wanted to be, to say *yes* every time she was asked that particular question.

Wouldn't it be nice to tell Nausicaä how beautiful she looked, always, but especially right now, and have Nausicaä understand what she meant by that?

And she couldn't let Vehan's dress go to waste . . .

Now, now, say it now—another breath . . .

"You are . . . ," she said in a very small and trembling voice. *No.* She gripped the stone railing harder, but straightened. She wouldn't confess what she felt to Nausicaä with anything less than the firm conviction this feeling deserved. "*You* are the dream come true, Nausicaä."

She lifted her gaze.

Nausicaä was staring back at her, still as the statues in the garden.

"I've been . . . struggling with how to word this. With what I *am*. I've never really thought much about it until meeting you. I've always liked boys, I know that, but it wasn't until recently that I realized I like more than this, too. Google has been a very useful tool lately." She choked a laugh, recalling how many nights she'd spent over the past few weeks researching various sexualities. "I think . . . I mean, for now at least, I'm pretty sure I'm pansexual. Gender doesn't necessarily matter to my attraction, and this label just seemed to fit the best? So . . . yeah, pansexual. But that's not—"

She was starting to digress, allowing her fears to overwhelm the moment, because *goodness*, even just claiming her sexuality out loud to someone for the first time was enormous, and still not the largest confession she intended to make.

Focus, she scolded.

She shook her head. "For the longest time, it's been just me and Celadon. He's been my very best friend, the only person who didn't make me feel unwanted or useless or like I was an extra in my own life. Just us for so long, and back then, that was enough, because it *had* to be enough. But then *you* happened, and I don't know if you realize how *amazing* you are to me, Nausicaä, how fierce and bold and brave you are, how *immense* you've always been . . . and bright, the brightest thing in my entire life."

Now that she'd started, it felt impossible to stop. Everything she'd been thinking since meeting Nausicaä poured from her. Her hands were shaking, her eyes were starting to water with emotion, but her tone was clear. She kept her gaze locked firmly on Nausicaä, and Nausicaä, still motionless, watched her back with something that looked fairly like shock . . .

But that was all right.

Arlo had started, and she was going to finish no matter what, because she needed to say this, and Nausicaä needed to know how much she meant to her.

"Being with you, I've realized those things I thought were only meant for other people—things like bravery, and fierceness, and strength—I can be them too, in my own way. Being with you, I've realized what that *own way* might be. Being with you . . . Nausicaä, it's like everything in the world just stops, and there's this incredible moment of perfect stillness, and you're the only thing I can see. There's this happiness that wells up inside me when we're together, and it's so overwhelming sometimes that I feel like I might explode with it, and I'm never really sure if I want to laugh or smile or cry to see you look at me sometimes like you understand. Like I'm that stillness for you too."

It wasn't until she gasped that she realized she'd started to cry, but she'd finally arrived at what she wanted to say.

She took a step forward, closing the distance between her and Nausicaä, then reached out and slid her fingers over the slightly larger hand Nausicaä rested on the railing beside them.

"I didn't realize it until you happened," she breathed, "but I've been waiting my whole life for *you*, Nausicaä. *You're* my dream, and I think . . . I think I love you. And it's okay if you don't love me back, but—"

"Can I kiss you now?" Nausicaä blurted—*choked* out the question, like she could barely speak over her own emotion—and almost as soon as the words were said, water welled over in her eyes. "Because I'd really like to do that at the moment."

A smile bloomed on Arlo's face, slow and stretching wider as she lifted her other hand to the lapel of Nausicaä's open jacket, curled her fingers around the fabric, and dragged Nausicaä down to press their lips together.

Arlo had noticed the first time they'd done this—kissing Nausicaä was like tasting *fire*.

It was searing and silken and all-consuming.

She was so very warm to the touch. Arlo's fingers brushed the bare skin beneath her jacket, and the flare of heat that scorched through her at the contact made her shiver in the cool night and that delicious, simmering feeling unspooled once more, spreading low and molten-hot in her belly.

She gasped, and Nausicaä took command of her mouth, deepening their kiss to a headiness that made Arlo *cling* to her.

Hands drifted down to her lower back and hauled Arlo up just enough to press them flush together.

A deft maneuver reversed their positions.

With *Arlo* against the railing now, and Nausicaä practically folded around her, they were so much closer than Arlo had thought possible and yet still too far apart.

Heat rolled through her in constant waves.

The simmering in her belly caught flame.

One of Nausicaä's hands slipped upward, traveled her spine to the back of her neck and sank into her hair. Arlo groaned a little in the back of her throat, tilted her head a fraction—had no real experience with kissing *anyone* like this, but she'd never wanted anything more. She met every touch of Nausicaä's wicked-clever tongue with just as much enthusiasm and defiance, because *of course* Nausicaä attacked her mouth like this, too, was a challenge she was determined to win.

It was impossible to know how long they stood there, wrapped up so entirely in each other. Arlo's fingers skittered over Nausicaä's golden-toned abdomen, and her smile bloomed again for how the barely there caress made Nausicaä's muscles twitch.

When Arlo's fingers reached her navel, Nausicaä gasped a laugh— peeled away from Arlo's mouth to chuckle again, a little more darkly, and rest their foreheads together.

Between the kiss itself and desire curling molasses-thick and languid through her, Arlo was more than a little breathless.

It was satisfying in a way she didn't know how to express right now to see that Nausicaä was just as affected, the pupils in her eyes blown wide and chest heaving for air.

"Magic is the *worst*," Nausicaä pouted, her voice pitched quiet and husky-deep. Lifting the hand wreathed in gold, she pressed a finger to the plush of Arlo's lower, black-painted lip, and dragged it provocatively over the far edge. "No faerie-enchanted lipstick next time—I was looking forward to seeing all this smeared with red."

She waggled her brows.

Arlo's face flared hot for the innuendo, however also pleased it made her to hear they'd been thinking about the same thing.

"So," Arlo ventured, "are we . . . well, what I mean is, are you . . . Will you be my girlfriend?" she finally decided on, blurting her words in a rush of hope and *what if* and still just a tinge of fear, because again . . . a kiss did not a relationship make, and Nausicaä could very possibly still want nothing to do with one.

Arlo's heart thudded in her chest as she watched Nausicaä raise a brow—what if she said *no*? That would be fine, she told herself. It would *have* to be fine. Arlo would respect that decision even if it would honestly leave her heartbroken, but maybe they could just be them, could just keeping doing *this*, whatever it was. And hey, what was young adulthood without a little one-sided pining?

"Arlo," Nausicaä replied, straightforward and simple. "I had *better* be your girlfriend, after all that."

She exhaled a sigh of relief. "*Whew*, okay, good. Because I really have to tell you, I sort of thought maybe you wouldn't want—wait." Arlo looked down from the sky, which her gaze had tilted to. "You're going to be my girlfriend? Really? *Mine?*"

"*Oooh*, trying out the possessives, are we? It really *is* the quiet ones you have to watch out for after all—I'm . . ." She trailed off, her eyes narrowing on something in the gardens below. When she stiffened, Arlo whirled around to see for herself what had caught her attention, but as hard as she looked, she found nothing there to explain this reaction.

Arlo turned back around. "What is it? What's wrong?"

"Nothing, I think," said Nausicaä, but she'd gone fully serious now and shifted a little around Arlo to get a better view. "I thought I just saw—"

"Arlo!"

Arlo wheeled around to the ballroom entrance to find a slightly harried Vehan.

His white-and-gold robes were in rumpled disarray, his hair a touch mussed. Arlo distantly wondered just how many people he'd had to fight through to get here, but the unease on his face sparked her concern.

"Nausicaä," Vehan added, stepping out onto the balcony now too. "Have either of you seen Aurelian? I haven't since the first dance, and it's not really like him to disappear for quite as long as he's been gone. Theo hasn't seen him either—*no one* has. I'm . . ." He frowned, bit his lip in a brief flicker of anxiety. "I'm a little worried."

Shaking her head, Arlo looked to Nausicaä. "I haven't seen him, no. We can help you look for him, though."

But Nausicaä was back to staring down at the gardens. She frowned. "Let's take a look outside. I could almost *swear* I just saw him down there with . . ." Her gaze snapped to Arlo. "Come on, we'll take the long way. Maybe we'll bump into him in the crowd."

She didn't sound too convinced by this, but Arlo didn't argue.

Vehan nodded, thanking them several times and apologizing for interrupting whatever they'd been doing, but Nausicaä merely waved him off and prowled past him.

"We'll find him," Arlo assured, as together they made their way back to the grand staircase. "He's *somewhere* in the palace. He's probably looking for *you* right now, and the two of you just keep missing each other."

"Hopefully," Vehan replied, back to worrying his bottom lip and scanning the ballroom closely.

"Arlo!" called another voice, and Arlo looked up—her mother, making her way from the opposite side of the mezzanine to the staircase.

She waved a hand at her and called in return, "Just a minute, Mom, we're looking for Aurelian! I'll come find you when we're done."

Thalo replied with something Arlo couldn't hear. A group of fae ascending the staircase had just cut between them and, distracted by her mother, Arlo hadn't been watching where she was going.

"Oh—!" she gasped when she collided with one. "Sorry, sorry, that was my fault, sorry."

She scrambled to secure whoever it was before they could topple backward down the stairs . . . and froze when her hands closed around their arm.

It was quick—a flicker at most. Arlo barely had time to make sense of what she'd seen. But she could swear the sidhe fae she'd just knocked into had *rippled*, his glamour knocked away completely. It wasn't uncommon. An ironborn that was magical enough to be ruled one of the folk in their Weighing had their status as ironborn expunged. They were then free to marry whomever they wanted, could have children with the other folk, and while those children might still be ironborn themselves, any indicators of this heritage would be subtle enough that they could be easily and *wholly* concealed by a well-placed glamour.

For some, this was considered a boon.

For some, they were *glad* to have their iron roots erased, to be considered faerie, and in even fewer cases *fae*. With such strong magic to fall back on, it was easy work for them to weave a glamour to hide whatever amount of red tinted their blood, to even mask the bitter zest of iron in their aura. Arlo could almost swear that when she knocked into this man, he'd been wearing one such glamour, that the perfect image of a sidhe fae, all sapphire-flushed and tanned, his hard, proud features avian-sharp and his carefully groomed brown hair crowned with a ring of Seelie Spring roses, had slipped for just the *sliver* of a moment.

And through it, Arlo noticed the barest hint of ironborn truth beneath.

Almost; she would *almost* swear.

Because when Arlo looked into the outraged face of the fae in question, if there was one person in this realm who she was firmly convinced was *not* her kind, it was *him*.

"Councillor Sylvain," she gasped. "Oh, gosh, I'm—"

"Sorry, yes, I know," he seethed. Tearing himself out of Arlo's grasp, he was entirely fae once more. With a glance to Vehan, who'd edged protectively closer to Arlo's side, he clenched his jaw and waved her away. "Go on, then, enjoy your evening, *Miss Jarsdel*."

Miss.

"Lady," Arlo heard herself correct with a boldness that had come from where, she didn't quite know, but she'd *said* it.

Holy crap.

"It's *Lady* Jarsdel," she kept on speaking through the ringing in her ears and the feeling that her heart was going to leap right out of her chest to escape this situation . . . but it was worth it.

For the way Councillor Sylvain just *stared* at her.

This wasn't worth her time, and Nausicaä was well ahead of them now, swallowed up by the sea of folk swirling across the ballroom. Arlo had other things to be doing than letting a tired old fae wear his prejudice out on her. With a clipped nod of farewell to the Councillor, Arlo wound her arm through Vehan's and together they continued down the stairs for the garden.

CHAPTER 42

Vehan

~~~~

AURELIAN WAS PERFECTLY CAPABLE of looking after himself. He was *trained* to be able to look after himself, and Vehan in addition, and furthermore was no wilting flower to be trampled on by the many folk here who'd be all too happy to do so.

But this *was* one of the largest social events of the year, gathering some of the cruelest and generally worst of folk-kind in one small room, and Aurelian was already target enough for jealousy and hostility, an Autumn lesidhe fae made future steward of a Court he had no ties to but his friendship with Vehan.

Even when they were most at odds, even when Aurelian was angriest with him, he didn't leave Vehan's side for long—certainly not in a crowd of people who looked at Vehan like a target as well—so he couldn't help this feeling inside him that something was *wrong*.

"I shouldn't have given him that stupid outfit to wear," he murmured, more to himself than Arlo as they walked out into the gardens. "He's just so proud of where he comes from, and he never gets to wear Seelie Autumn colors, so I thought, *hey, why not give him this one last chance to do so?* Because if he thinks he's lost his freedom as my retainer, wait until we announce him as my *partner*."

"And, you know," Arlo commented quietly, with only a *trace* of wryness to betray her teasing, "it has nothing to do with how good he looks in all that brown and red."

"So *good*," Vehan moaned in distress. "He looks so unfairly good in the colors of his Court. I'm just a man, Arlo, a man who's very weak to other men with long legs and a well-made suit."

"There, there," she consoled, patting his arm.

Arlo's humor and playfulness were subtle, easy to miss for how gentle everything about her seemed, but this gentleness was quickly shed in defense of her friends and in the face of danger others would have cowered before on bended knees.

He was glad for Arlo.

She was a good person in his life.

And a bit like Aurelian, the steadiness of her beside him helped to tamp down his spiraling panic. Arms linked, they ventured through the manicured beds of flowers, the marble sculptures and elaborate fountains and blossoming trees, much smaller in scale than the ones that enchantment wove in the ballroom. His mother was very proud of the palace gardens, and he could tell by the firefly lights that floated around them as they walked, by the dome of magic that painted the distance as the cityscape of Las Vegas, as though peering into it through a scrying glass; he could tell by the careful attention to detail, not a single twig out of place, or petal wilting, or blade of grass longer than the one beside it, that she'd put a lot of work into seeing it every bit the wonder as the ballroom was within.

"See anything?" Arlo called when they finally caught up to Nausicaä.

Nausicaä turned around, shaking her head. Vehan's heart sank a little to see the disappointment on her face . . . and confusion. "Nothing. Should have teleported—don't know what I was thinking." She paused then to look at Arlo, something passing between them that maybe Vehan wasn't supposed to know, so he didn't ask. Then, snapping out of her thoughts, Nausicaä recovered to add, "Have you tried just calling him? On his *phone*? I know you're shit when it comes to technology, but Aurelian isn't. I'm sure he remembered to bring his tonight. Here." She reached into her jacket and pulled out her phone. "I saved him under Legolas."

Vehan raised a brow. "Who's—"

"Vehan? What *are* you doing out here? Do you have any idea what time it is?"

He didn't need to turn around to know who'd just spoken, to see who was making their approach—his mother. He turned to her anyway and glanced from her stern expression to the clock on Nausicaä's phone.

Midnight was only a few minutes away.

It was just about time for the ceremonial transfer of power, where Riadne and the UnSeelie King of Summer would take to the middle landing of the staircase and receive the Seelie and UnSeelie Kings of Spring. They would clasp hands, another show of unity that no one actually believed, but it was tradition, and tradition was always observed.

The crowd would bow to their new dominant Season.

Then the party would truly begin.

As Crown Prince, Vehan was expected to stand on that landing just behind his mother. It would cause quite the stir if he wasn't there, because *tradition*. Any deviation would be muttered about until the Autumn Equinox as an ill omen.

His search for Aurelian would have to wait.

"Would you both call him for me, please?" he asked Arlo, holding the phone out to Nausicaä.

Arlo nodded. "Yeah, of course."

"Why was Lethe here?"

For a moment, everyone stared.

Nausicaä didn't reclaim her phone. She didn't look at Vehan at all. Her gaze was fixed on his mother instead, arms folded over her chest, jaw squared and steel eyes glinting dangerously.

Then . . . "I beg your pardon?" Riadne inquired, her tone encased in ice.

"Lethe," Nausicaä repeated. "Why was he here? I'm trying to give you the benefit of doubt in the spirit of having helped save Arlo's life, but literally the most self-serving, sadistic asshole in all the realms combined has been trailing after *your* son quite a lot lately. Lethe, who doesn't do a thing that doesn't benefit him in some way, has been playing knight-in-shining-armor to Vehan, rescuing him from one potentially fatal situation after the next; the goblins in the desert, the Sleeping Hollow, Hieronymus Aurum's murder lab . . . Sure, maybe Lethe just likes a pretty face, but then there's that *thing* on Vehan's *chest*, and your uncommon tolerance for alchemy. I'm trying very hard to pretend it wasn't once my specialty to connect obscure dots, but you're going to have to look me in the eye and tell me you have no idea what I'm talking about right now."

"Of *course* she has no idea what you're talking about," Vehan cried in exasperation.

Did *no one* trust his mother? Did they *all* suspect her as responsible for every little thing that ever happened in this realm?

Riadne showed very little concern over all these thinly veiled accusations being hurled at her—in fact, she didn't even seem like she heard them, the way her attention was fixed not on Nausicaä but on *Arlo*, and the look in his mother's eyes . . . like someone who'd just been presented a great opportunity and only had to figure out how best to reach out and take it. Vehan would never understand Riadne's complexities, but he did know one thing: his mother was flesh and blood, and though they were carefully guarded, she did have feelings that could be wounded. Whatever Nausicaä was trying to imply about her right now, she had just crossed a line.

Anger flared inside him, and this time he couldn't actually tell if it was that parasitic darkness growing in his array or his own emotion—and maybe that blurry indistinction should be concerning, but . . . later. For now, Vehan took a step toward Nausicaä, intending to reprimand her just as sharply as he'd done High Prince Celadon. He didn't care that she was some all-powerful immortal being of death and revenge who could strike him down as easily as flicking a finger. He wouldn't allow someone to hurl insults at his family like this, right in front of him, in his own house.

But once again, Riadne spoke, cutting him off before he could.

"*My son* has been branded," she replied to Nausicaä, her tone only growing colder. "That *thing* on his *chest*, you're absolutely correct in what you're thinking, it's the mark of alchemy. An array. It was put there when Vehan was newly born, something he only *barely* survived, and I've been working ever since to figure out a way to fix that. My son may not be ironborn; it won't turn his heart into a philosopher's stone's vessel—oh, yes, I know *exactly* what that branding is meant to do—but it will do something worse."

Vehan could only gape at his mother as she spoke.

This was the first time she'd ever confirmed it, the first time she'd ever shed her roundabout convolution to answer with the direct truth. That she *did* know more about what had been happening with the ironborn than she'd let on. Whether she'd held her tongue by the High King's orders or for some other, more *personal* reason, Vehan found he didn't much care right now. A ringing had started up in his ears, and his focus refused to unstick from one specific thing—what could be worse than becoming a vessel for dark magic?

"So no," Riadne continued, "Vehan may not have the iron blood required to properly fuel the array, but in his current state, that array on his chest *will* kill him if he is still in possession of it when all the stones in this plot are created and Ruin is summoned forth from their cage."

The ringing in Vehan's ears grew louder.

A shadow passed over his heart, the ghostly echo of magic's painful hold on him. It was something he'd felt clench in his chest so often over the years that he'd almost grown *used* to the flutter of ache, which had been calmer for the past little while, ever since his trip to the Thunder Plains with Theo. It had been so foolish of Vehan, so *naive*, to think that this might mean his brand was possibly healing—but it was just as he'd feared all along.

This mark was a ticking clock counting down the hours of his life.

This array . . . They'd been right. *Aurelian* had been right, to worry as he had.

Where are you? Vehan wondered, desperately now, his hand lifting to absently palm his chest where the death-stamp had been carved.

"Ruin?" Arlo asked, giving voice to things Vehan should be questioning but couldn't.

Riadne inclined her head. "A titan—their progenitor, I should say. I assume that Nausicaä has filled you in: The stones are *not* mere pieces of rock that bestow upon their possessors wealth and immortality. They are the vessels of the Sins, and each one successfully drawn into this world is part of a whole, one of seven keys necessary to unlocking this titan from what has bound them for eons."

"But . . . why? Why free them at all? What purpose would that serve? And who the heck even put this on Vehan to begin with?" Arlo turned to look up at Nausicaä, but Nausicaä was still fixed on watching Vehan's mother—*assessing* her.

"I cannot tell you, just as I cannot tell you why Lethe was here," Riadne continued, lifting a shoulder in a casual shrug. "Our relationship is not one that affords me such privilege into the full breadth of his plans. But I have looked to any avenue I can to find my answers—yes, even the Hunters. Lethe *has* been helping me. He, I felt, above anyone would know what was necessary to save my son."

Just as defensive as before, her jaw still squared, the steel in her eyes even *harder*, Nausicaä asked, "And what does *he* get out of this?"

"Arlo," Riadne replied, to something other than tense silence.

A flash of metal—this time not only in Nausicaä's eyes. The Fury had armed herself in an instant, tugging Arlo immediately behind her, and Arlo went easily, if a little shocked.

Raising her hands, Riadne made no hurry to explain herself, as though a Fury hadn't just leveled her with the point of a glittering sword that looked like shadow itself wrought into a blade. "Peace, Nausicaä. The trade was for Arlo's safety. I promised Lethe back when we first entered this alliance that if I was ever in the position to protect Arlo, I would. Just as he guards my son, I guard *his* interests. You are special to him, Arlo. Something about you wholly unique—"

It was then that Arlo stepped forward.

Vehan watched, a bit like this was one of Aurelian's movies and not his own reality, as she lifted a hand. Hesitantly—clearly not sure of her decision, but acting on some innate instinct—she unfurled her fingers to reveal in the palm of her hand an object Vehan had only seen in person once before.

"I think I know," she answered, breathless with whatever realization she had come to. "And I think I know how *I* might be able to help *you*."

CHAPTER 43

Celadon

~~~~~

"Y OUR HIGHNESS?"

Celadon turned around—or rather, he craned his head. Movement at the moment was a little difficult for the number of people pressing around him, clinging closer than they'd normally dare in hopes of stealing his attention for the night about as completely as that voice had just managed.

And when they all turned their heads as well, there was a collective gasp, a resounding silence; then a flurry of whispers and whimpers and even a shriek of alarm bubbled around him as every single one of the folk who'd been vying for a dance from him suddenly released him to skitter back.

He'd been trying for the better part of the last ten minutes since the opening dance ended to free himself from this cluster, to rush to Arlo and help her navigate if not her entire night, then at *least* the first and sharpest part of the interest that would spotlight her.

Every bribe, every silken world, every trick he'd learned over the years had been employed to win his escape, but apparently all it took was the arrival of one of the Wild Hunt—Yue, Celadon recalled, though Yue as he'd never seen him before.

His Hunter's cloak was just as impossibly black and starlight-glittering as ever, but it had been refashioned for tonight into something that resembled a kimono. His tar-black hair was gathered somewhat messily behind his head, his fringe left loose across his face, and his bright purple eyes stood out even more vibrantly.

He looked like he belonged at this party, and at the same time, looked so exquisitely out of place Celadon might have laughed . . . if he weren't a little afraid, himself.

Not exactly of this young man.

More . . . what his presence here tonight might mean.

Riadne—she couldn't. He'd sensed it in her, a flicker of regret for what she'd done, a caring that still lived inside her for him, and she *couldn't* . . . she couldn't betray him a second time.

"Yue," Celadon greeted with as polite a nod as he could manage through the dread that flooded his system. "I wasn't aware my father had requested your attendance tonight."

Yue stared at him with that disconcerting gaze. The daggers at his sides glinted in the shifting light of the room. The crowd that had been pressed so closely against Celadon had now cleared so much space around him that he could reach out his arms in any direction and still make no contact with anyone else, no one but Yue.

He should make his break for it *now*, while he had the chance.

He should take this gift of space that Yue had given him and locate Arlo, his father, *Riadne*, but caught in this Hunter's gaze . . . he found couldn't move.

Something was wrong.

"Our presence wasn't requested."

Our.

"Tonight, we gather for our original cause."

Original cause.

"Tonight, we come to ferry loss. To mark the end of this era's greatest warrior. To stand with her soul as it ascends to join our ranks. Do you understand what I'm telling you, Celadon Lysterne-Viridian?"

Yue . . . he wasn't here alone. Celadon threw his gaze around the room, from face to face to face, in search of the Hunters he now knew to look for, and only in knowing they were there was he able to pick them out. Vesper . . . Eris . . . another, and another, and another— more than just the Wild Hunt, there were *other* Hunters here tonight, other cadres. Celadon could tell them apart by the starlight in their deeper-than-black cloaks, by their vivid eyes and the starry shimmer to their skin. *Dozens* gathered here, hiding in plain view, biding their time to *ferry loss* and *mark the end of this era's greatest warrior*, and . . .

"Cosmin," Celadon swore, returning his gaze to Yue. "You're talking about my mother?"

His *true* mother.

Riadne . . . She was going to die?

Yue said nothing—most likely, he was breaking quite the serious rule in even speaking to him right now, handing him this convoluted *sliver* of a warning, but Celadon wasn't feeling generous. He wasn't feeling grateful. He was tired, and scared, and he had been pulled so deep into so perilous a scheme that he was starting to feel like he was *drowning* . . . and he'd only just learned the truth of who he was.

. . . who *Riadne* was.

"I asked if you're talking about my mother," he demanded in a much deadlier tone, advancing a step on Yue . . . who seemed not in the slightest intimidated by this.

It changed nothing.

It changed *everything*.

Riadne Lysterne . . . Until Yue spoke the words that condemned her, Celadon had only entertained her death in theory. Now that it was real . . . His *mother*—no, she couldn't die yet either, not until she explained to him *why*.

"Be careful, Your Highness," Yue murmured, sadness creeping into his voice. Suddenly, he looked much younger, more like the mortal he'd been in life—a boy not much older than Celadon. A brother? A son? A prince, too? Did Yue even remember who he'd been before this life? Did he remember *his* mother—is that why he was doing this? Giving Celadon this warning when Celadon knew that such a thing shouldn't happen in any shape or form. "Be *careful*. Tonight, your cousin takes her first real step in shifting destiny, and for it, change will ripple across the board. Some will die who wouldn't have before; others will live past their time. But this is so because *Luck* patrons Arlo Jarsdel." Yue paused for the briefest moment. "Of course, the one who patrons *you* is no less dangerous, no less twined with *consequence*, but far less protected against Fate's wrath for what they've done . . . and continue to do. It might tempt you to throw your allegiance behind them, but *take care* of what that will cost and what will happen if Fate's ire turns on you, as well."

Yue held out a hand.

In the hand was a book.

Simple black leather, icy cool to the touch when Celadon took it with a great amount of hesitation. He peered down at its blank cover. "What's this?" he asked, but upon glancing up, discovered Yue was gone.

Frowning, he looked back at the book he'd been given—opened it, flipped through pages filled with names, and names, and *names*, none of which held any meaning to him. It was an odd sort of gift, but this entire exchange had been odd, and he had no idea what to make of that warning. Someone *patroned* him? He needed to be careful? Riadne was going to *die*—his brain snapped back to that, because what by Cosmin was he supposed to *do* with this information? How was he supposed to *feel*? Riadne, who was so clearly cruel and unstable and violent, who would kill the father Celadon loved if she got the chance . . . she was also Riadne, his mother.

Did that matter?

He nearly closed the book, with its bone-white pages and looping, silvery cursive . . . but then noticed what it undoubtedly was that Yue had wanted him to see.

~~Celadon Lysterne-Viridian~~ — *Lethe*

His name.

~~Celadon Lysterne-Viridian~~ — *Lethe*

His name, on more than one page.

~~Celadon Lysterne-Viridian~~ — *Lethe*

His name, on so many pages, and each of them crossed out as though it were really that simple to strike him from whatever fate its being there would have destined him to.

Celadon Lysterne-Viridian—*Lethe*

Celadon Lysterne-Viridian—*Lethe*

Celadon Lysterne-Viridian—*Lethe*

His name on every page, each of them claimed by the same Hunter and stricken out. There was a note about the Colosseum attached to the very last entry, so apparently he hadn't been meant to survive *that*. What did any of this mean?

The realization suddenly *clicked*.

What this book was . . . and the names filling tomorrow's page, many upon many, and most of them . . . Cosmin, no.

Shit—

The clock over the grand staircase made its first chime, so loudly that Celadon startled.

Chiming—it was midnight already?

He looked down at his hands. The book was gone, almost as though he'd never held it to begin with.

"*Shit*," he swore again out loud.

He didn't know where the book had gone or who it had just returned to, though he could hazard a guess. But he didn't have time for this. He needed to get to his family; he needed to find his mother, his father, *now*, because whatever was going to happen . . . they were just about to tip over midnight, and Celadon couldn't, couldn't, *couldn't* let himself think for a moment that he was already too late—

The barest pinprick to the back of his neck . . .

An arm slid around his waist, securing him to someone's side like they'd just discovered each other and were happily about to whisk away for private conversation.

It took *seconds* for whatever had been injected into his system to take effect, and it couldn't be anything human, because not only was

Celadon fae and therefore incredibly resilient against such things, but he was also a High Prince—he'd been conditioned from an early age to withstand a certain amount of poisoning.

As though he'd imbibed an entire barrel of the royal reserve's best rum, Celadon felt himself grow . . . fuzzy. Relaxed. Numb all over, like a limb falling asleep if it was bent too long at a certain angle. He slumped against whoever had caught him as that person pushed quickly through the sea of faces that were starting to blur together.

"What's . . . ," he slurred. His tongue felt too thick for his mouth.

What's going on—he wanted to ask.

Let me go, I need . . . I need to get to . . .

"I'm sorry, Your Highness," Theodore Reynolds bent to whisper into his ear, as together they made their way to the ballroom's exit, leaving *everyone* Celadon cared about behind to . . . to . . . "I'm sorry," he repeated, "I have to bring you to safety. She made me swear it if I want to keep my parents safe, too."

She?

Mother . . .

Was he crying? His face felt wet, but he couldn't really tell. His heart broke, regardless, as they grew closer to the ballroom's exit, and darkness ate away at his vision. Because if Theodore had been instructed to lead him away, then Riadne had never intended to spare his father for him as he'd asked. She'd never intended to do this one thing, the *only* thing he'd ever requested of her . . . as her *son.*

Riadne hadn't changed.

She never would.

Celadon meant *nothing* to her.

And despite all this, he couldn't help that part of his grief was the fear that he was about to lose *her*, too.

CHAPTER 44

Arlo

~~~~~~

RIADNE PEERED DOWN AT the contents of Arlo's hand, her expression unchanging, just as placid as it had been throughout this entire conversation. "Oh?" she said, without looking up from the die Arlo held between them. Whatever she felt, whatever her thoughts about being presented such an underwhelming and confusing solution to her considerable problem, nothing of it showed through her poise.

Arlo, meanwhile, felt as if her heart might hammer right out of her chest.

She could tell by the way Nausicaä's hand tightened around hers that she didn't exactly agree with what Arlo was about to do. And Vehan—distinctly pale and a bit glassy-eyed in his shock—she'd filled him and Aurelian in on what they'd missed in the hospital wing, on her role and future as a Hollow Star, but right now he was too impossible to gauge for warning or encouragement in sharing that with his mother.

But this was the Seelie Queen of Summer.

She'd invited Arlo into her home to attend this famously exclusive folk ball when no one else had ever taken that risk for Arlo.

She'd given Arlo beautiful rooms for her stay, allowed Celadon to accompany her even though she and he were well-known as incompatible, found her an actual *alchemy* tutor, and permitted Arlo to study this forbidden art within the protection of her home, no matter what sort of gossip this would spread about her. She'd gone to such lengths to make Arlo feel comfortable and welcome, like the Viridian fae that Arlo's own family refused to acknowledge she was, and she had *saved*

Arlo's life! Or Leda had, but without Riadne having hired her . . .

If the Seelie Summer Queen needed a favor from Arlo—if there was *anything* Arlo could do to repay all the kindness she'd received from her—she would give it gladly.

And it was *Vehan* they were talking about . . . Vehan, one of the few people Arlo could now consider a friend.

Riadne said nothing further than this quiet, mild exclamation.

Her gaze didn't lift from Arlo's unfurled palm. She was *looking,* though; Arlo had her attention. And before she could lose it, Arlo took a steadying breath, moved another step toward the queen, and as though she *weren't* about to reveal her biggest, most crucial secret—a secret that she didn't need to be told could be wielded against her, if the wrong person knew—she plunged into betraying it.

"There's something we haven't told you, something I can do. This die . . . ," said Arlo, tilting it in the cast-off glow of Vegas lighting. Its golden numbers flashed up at her as though cautioning her *itself* against this course of action, but she'd already decided on its doing. The matter of trust aside, she would *not* lose Vehan because she was too afraid to use the only thing that could help him. "This die was given to me by a titan. It allows me to . . . alter the course of fate and play around with the outcome of things—more or less. The array on Prince Vehan's chest, there might be something I can do about that. The other alchemists might not have been able to dissolve it, but I might be able to! With this die, I can . . . I don't know, boost my alchemic ability? But better than that . . ." She took another breath. She didn't need telling by Luck or her die or anyone else to know this final part was the bit that could be the most dangerous, both to her and perhaps even the *world*, depending on what was done with the information. "Better than that—*surer* than that, I have . . . four wishes. Four things I can ask the die to make come true, no matter how impossible. The wishes can only be used on me, but if all we need to do to save Vehan is erase his array, I think I could . . . wish myself able to do it. I could wish myself skilled enough at alchemy to remove it."

She ended on as firm a note as possible, glancing up from the die where her gaze had fallen and back to Riadne's face.

It was only just quick enough—only *just* quick enough—to catch the lightning-flicker of *something* pass behind her composure.

Something . . . Arlo would almost call it *triumph* . . .

But then Riadne's expression smoothed out into a gentle smile.

She stepped toward Arlo, closing the distance between them, and Arlo tracked her every movement, stiffening much like Nausicaä behind her. But when the queen arrived in front of her, she merely reached out a hand and folded Arlo's fingers back over her die. She continued to smile, and in an equally gentle voice, replied, "I thank you for the offer of your *aid*, Arlo Jarsdel. Truly. That is more than I think anyone has ever so willingly given me in my life, and I appreciate the amount of courage and trust required to bestow it. You have a very kind heart, my dear. I can only imagine how *proud* you must make your own mother for it."

Like the release of a coil, Arlo's tension unwound to flood her with relief.

There was nothing to fear; she'd been right—Riadne wasn't going to use this information against Arlo. She was a *mother*, just like Arlo's, so desperate to save the life of her only child that she'd have been willing to make a bargain with death itself to save him. Lethe . . . Arlo hoped he hadn't been too nasty about it, that Riadne hadn't been made to suffer more than she already was, knowing Vehan was in such danger.

"I will not turn down this favor. Nothing . . . There is nothing I wouldn't do for my son," the queen continued, unfurling back to standing and looking down at Arlo was so much unguarded hope that Arlo felt her eyes grow warm to see it. She'd done something right, was finally *helping* a situation instead of getting in the way. "Would you do it, Arlo? Would you spend this invaluable treasure—this wish—on helping me save my son?"

"Of course!" Arlo blurted, nodding just as eagerly. "I really mean it. I'll wish myself better at alchemy—I can do it right now, even!"

I would caution you to be very specific, though . . .

Magic operates in a peculiar precision . . .

Choose your words wisely.

Luck's warnings rang in her ear. Nausicaä was radiating disapproval behind her. But this was Arlo's choice, and she wanted to do this—*could* do this—and honestly, there was something inside her that said she was *meant* to do this. Alchemy felt right to her, as right and easy as breathing, and of all the things she had the potential to become, skilled in this particular area was the only one that fit.

"I won't object," was Riadne's delicate reply. "I admit, I'm curious to see what this tool of yours can do. I'm curious to see what makes Luck's favor such a coveted thing. A die that can alter fate and grant wishes . . ."

"Arlo . . . ," Nausicaä started.

"I'll do it then," Arlo said, as firm as her grasp around her die. She ignored Nausicaä—she appreciated the impulse to protect Arlo from potential danger, but Nausicaä could do so many things for the people she cared about . . . Arlo could do only this. And Riadne wasn't evil. The world mistrusted her. It mistrusted Arlo, too, and it mistrusted her magic. She would prove it was wrong on *all* counts. She would save her friend for the woman who'd done nothing but try to hold her head high despite the nasty things whispered about her. "I'll do it. It will . . . only take a moment."

She hoped.

She looked to Vehan. Optimistic, cautious, confused—there was a great deal on Vehan's face, but he wanted that array off his chest so badly. He didn't want to die, and Arlo didn't blame him. She was the only one who could help him . . . This was the right decision.

She was going to use a wish.

Almost as soon as thinking this, the world around her slowed to motionless gray. The flashing lights, the party, even the breeze and the petals it sent dancing like rain from the trees—everything stopped but Arlo . . . and Nausicaä.

"Arlo."

A hand fell on her shoulder, and Arlo turned her head, eyes flying open to meet the profound worry on Nausicaä's face. "Arlo, this is . . . this is really fucking sus."

"Nos . . ."

"You never mentioned Luck was the one who gave that die to you . . ."

Frowning, Arlo turned herself a little more toward her *girlfriend*, angling away from the gold-dust writing that hovered in the air. "What do you mean?"

Nausicaä's gaze drifted from Arlo to settle much more severely on the time-frozen form of Riadne. For a moment, she said nothing, but just when Arlo was about to turn back to her task and call out her wish, she released a heavy sigh through her nose and shook her head. "What Riadne just said about wanting to see the power of Luck for herself—you never mentioned Luck being the one to give you this die. Riadne *knows* things. Arlo, I think she's known you can do this, or at least that you could do *something* to help her goals. I think she's been hoping you would do exactly what you're about to do for her. Hells, she admitted it herself, she's been working with Lethe—I'm willing to bet he told her all about what you could do as a Hollow Star and this has been their plan all along."

It was Arlo's turn to sigh. "Nos . . ."

"No, no, I get it, I do—she's been all kinds of wonderful to you. And the shitty thing is that not very many people have been wonderful to you like they should be, in my complete bias, so of course you're going to want to defend her. But, Arlo, *listen to me*." With more gravity than Nausicaä had ever let Arlo see, she took Arlo's hands in her own, cupping the die between them, and stared deep into her eyes. Despite the situation they were in, Arlo once again felt that feeling, that stillness, like it was only the two of them in the entire world.

And at the moment, they very nearly were.

"Arlo, everything in me is almost positive that this has been exactly what Riadne wants and that you'll be playing directly into her hands if you make this wish. I'm *positive* she has something to do with the philosopher's stones. I'm *scared*, all right? I'm scared this is going to cost you something big . . . and that it's going to cost *me* you, just like Lethe warned."

One breath . . .

Two . . .

Arlo smiled. She interlocked her fingers with Nausicaä's, taking a minute—just a sliver of time—to marvel at how warm they were and wonder once more about what had given her these pearly, raised scars. "I hear you," she said softly. "I still have to do this. For Vehan's sake . . . and for *ours*. Because if you're right? If you're all seeing something I can't, if the rumors and your suspicions are all true, then I'm going to need every ounce of alchemical skill I can get to take that on. Because fixing this mess is going to fall to us. It's been falling to us again and again, and I can't be the weakness of the group. I need to do this. I need to do this for *me*. And if I'm wrong about trusting her . . . at least I'll have the power to put things right."

"I can't stop you from making this choice."

"You can't. I have to do it. I have to at least try to do whatever I can to save Vehan. He's my friend, Nos."

"I know." She stepped back. "And I'll be right here beside you." She didn't look convinced that this was the right thing to do, but there was trust in the way she relented, nodded, and gave Arlo space to make the move that Arlo felt was best. "She's definitely catching hands if she tries to use you for this, though. And, Red?"

Pursing her lips in barely concealed fondness, Arlo allowed one last pause. "Yes?"

"You are *not* a weakness to this group."

For a moment, Arlo could only look back at Nausicaä, unable to say a word. It was . . . nice to hear that she didn't think Arlo was useless, as Arlo feared. Maybe one day she'd even believe it herself—a much sooner one day, if this wish worked out in their favor.

The time for stalling was over.

With a jerk of a nod—awkward, brief, but no less grateful even if she couldn't accept what Nausicaä claimed yet herself—Arlo turned back to her options written out in the air . . .

Back to the number four that hovered before her, gleaming just a little brighter than her other options, as though the die already knew what she wanted to ask of it.

I would caution you to be very specific, though . . .

Magic operates in a peculiar precision . . .

Choose your words wisely.

Here went nothing.

"I wish that I possessed enough skill in and knowledge of alchemy to be able to remove the array etched on Vehan Lysterne's chest."

The four gleamed even brighter.

Arlo reached out her hand and touched the number.

As soon as her fingers made contact with the golden dust that shaped it, it burst apart, rearranged itself into the number three, and then shattered along with the rest of the writing.

Arlo watched as the last golden speck winked out of existence.

She watched . . . and nothing happened.

"Did it . . . work?" she asked, with a glance first to Nausicaä, but when all Nausicaä did was shrug, she transferred her question to the die still clutched in her hand.

Dim . . . Cool to the touch . . .

The die sat completely inactive, no trace of energy or magic about it, no warmth of life she could usually feel when she held it. That was . . . a good sign, right? Luck had warned her that she wouldn't be able to use her die for a while after spending a wish. She'd done it right . . . *right?*

But then why didn't she feel any different? Why was the world still stoppered in frozen gray?

"Do you think I said something—"

The world gave a *lurch*, very different than it usually did. Arlo always felt it kick back into gear, but this time, the reanimation of time nearly threatened to topple her, it pulled so suddenly and fiercely at her core.

Time sped itself to catch up with the rest of the world around it. Vehan, Riadne, the party, the lights, *everything* burst back into vibrant life as Arlo straightened. She felt . . . *exhausted*. There was no other word to describe how tired she was so suddenly, and that lurch inside her very core left her feeling just a little unusual in other ways she couldn't name. But otherwise . . . Was that it?

Had it worked or not? She couldn't tell. Nothing about her felt different at all, aside from a deep wave of exhaustion that had hit her, and when she called on her knowledge to see if it was any more profound than before, she didn't feel like she suddenly had any deeper understanding of *anything*.

"Whenever you're ready then, dearest Arlo."

Arlo looked up into Riadne's face. Still patient, still watchful, still under the impression that Arlo had yet to do what she'd promised.

"It's . . . done," she said, a little thickly for her confusion. "I think. I guess we'll have to wait and see? If it didn't work, I can try it again when the die recharges."

Tilting her head in consideration of Arlo's words, Riadne's benign smile shrank to hesitation. "It's done?" she repeated.

With a nod, Arlo lowered her hand. "I made the wish. It . . . kind of stops time while I do, so you wouldn't have noticed the last minute or so. But . . . I made the wish. I've never made one before. Only time will tell, I guess, whether it worked . . ."

"You made the wish," Riadne echoed—and there it was again; relief, yes, but also that flicker of *triumph*, and a small, barely audible wail of alarm pinged in the back of Arlo's head . . . but no. She'd done the right thing. Riadne's triumph was merely that of a mother finally making progress in saving her son's life.

"*Thank you*, Arlo," the queen continued. "You have no idea how appreciative I am of what you've just given me."

And all Arlo could do was nod again.

Nausicaä moved forward, a sound in the back of her throat like she was at her limit with holding her tongue, like this final statement had been the one straw too many in the pile of suspicion she held against pretty much everyone.

But the comment she'd been about to make was interrupted—by an *explosion*.

Arlo's head snapped up, her eyes darting to the skies.

Nausicaä looked up as well, and Vehan, too, and Riadne. Where they were in the gardens was fairly secluded, not many other guests around, but the ones Arlo could see milling about had all stopped to gawk as well as fireworks took to the sky.

Brilliant flares and vibrant bursts of color rained around them, red and orange and green and blue, white and yellow and purple, all from the Vegas side of the dome.

Midnight—there were many humans who celebrated the Solstice as well, but this could just as likely be part of Riadne's planning, folk situated around the Strip to light off one of the few bits of human ingenuity that even fae commended them for achieving.

From within the ballroom, the clock began to chime.

One.

"It's time," said Riadne, as simply as that.

She dropped her gaze—Arlo did too, straight to the arm that the queen extended to her.

Two.

"Come with me, my dear. I'll escort you back inside. Vehan . . ." She cast a look at her son, threw out a hand to snap her fingers. At the sound, Vehan straightened, startled out of the panic he'd been struggling with, but Arlo could see it still trembled behind his scrapings of composure.

Three.

"Nausicaä?" Arlo turned to call, to make sure she was going to follow before Arlo accepted the queen's arm.

Together, they made for the ballroom, Nausicaä prowling close at their heels, Vehan drifting along beside her.

Four, the clock chimed.

Five.

Arlo could still feel Nausicaä's mistrust in her aura. They'd talk after the party, *all* of them, and if Riadne showed signs of trying to use Arlo's die to her advantage at any point hereafter, Arlo would concede to the same mistrust.

But for now . . . it was done. All Arlo could do was hold on to the hope that, just like her own mother, Riadne possessed a good heart beneath the toughened exterior she had to maintain just to keep afloat.

Six—they re-entered the ballroom.

She and Riadne were the first to step through the archway. When she heard a gasp, Arlo tried to turn around. Nausicaä started to call her name in an air that was both shock and alarm but was cut off halfway through.

"Eyes forward, Arlo," Riadne commanded, in a tone that Arlo found herself completely unable to ignore—like she didn't *want* to ignore it, she *wanted* to keep her sight trained forward, with only the barest cry of *no* in the back of her head, like thunder on the distant horizon.

It was a tone she'd heard enough before—clipped; unkind—but never directed at *her*. And for it, a thread of unease began to unspool.

Something was wrong.

Once again, Riadne lifted a hand in the air and snapped her fingers. Nausicaä had silenced completely now—in fact, Arlo couldn't even sense her aura, as though she'd disappeared entirely from the room. But replacing her cry was Vehan's "Mother? What is this—*hey*, let go of me!" as a pair of the Luminous Guards on duty peeled away from the wall to seize their prince . . . or at least, that was what Arlo had gathered from Vehan's confusion and outrage.

She couldn't see to be certain.

She couldn't look anywhere but straight ahead.

Sleep—screamed her mind and body and soul alike.

Wrong, wrong, wrong—screamed her heart.

"What's going on?" she asked, her anxiety growing thicker with every step. "Where are we going?"

"*Your Majesty,*" Riadne corrected through no small amount of frost. "What's going on, *Your Majesty*—and you will see, if you care to pay attention to something other than your miserable self-pity for once. Now *silence.*"

Arlo didn't need this added command.

Stricken speechless by this complete duality, by the queen so unlike how she'd always been with Arlo now dragging her through the crowd. Arlo could only gape, eyes still forward. She couldn't *stop* staring forward, and now she also couldn't speak. It was hard to tell what frightened her most in this situation: her inability to *do* anything, or the queen herself, or the cries that were starting to echo around the room as the Luminous Guard broke forward, combed through the sea of folk for their predetermined captives, and hauled them to the grand staircase.

As she and Riadne strolled through the unsettled crowd, folk parted before them, and silence that was born of either terror or wicked fascination—and in many cases, both—descended in their wake.

Like a virus, that hush began to spread until the chiming clock, Vehan's struggling, and the staccato *click* of Riadne's heels on the glass floor were the only sounds in the entire ballroom.

Petals no longer fell from the ceiling.

Arlo couldn't look up, but she noticed the trunks of the trees around them had started to change right before her eyes, draining of color and life from their golden forms into *iron*.

In the back of her mind, she knew what was happening, that this was the work of alchemy, so similar to what Hieronymus had done with his philosopher's stone . . . but *how?*

"Arlo?"

Her mother.

"Arlo!"

Vehan . . .

"What's the meaning of this? What's going on?"

The hush slowly grew into gagging and groaning as the air around them became thick with the poisonous scent of iron. Against so much of it, their ailing High King was apparently no match.

Her mother, Queen Reseda, High Prince Serulean, several other Viridians, Arlo couldn't answer any of them or beg them for help like she wanted. Whatever was going on, despite how much she wanted away from it, more guards had filtered into the ballroom and had herded the entirety of the Viridian family to its center.

Weapons drawn, they formed a formidable barrier around them, and they might be the Luminous Guard in *dozens*, but Thalo . . . she could have taken them.

Arlo knew her mother could have taken every single one of those soldiers at once, and *would have*, but there it was, the reason Arlo was kept hostage in the queen's clutches.

Her mother wouldn't move an inch and risk Riadne hurting her daughter in retaliation.

Arm-in-arm, Arlo and Riadne stalked through the crowd, circumventing the room's center to make for the grand staircase, where Riadne and the UnSeelie Summer King were meant to stand and receive the Heads of the previous Seasons—tradition, the folk were *strict* about tradition, yet the staircase was empty.

Theodore, his parents, the Lebezheninovs, Councillor Sylvain—a collection of others were at the base of the staircase, where there seemed to be something of a buffer between them and the iron clouding the room. Keeping the UnSeelie Summer King from charging from the crowd and taking the stage next to Riadne were two more guards, their blades crossed to bar the way up.

Guards at the doors.

Guards at every archway.

Riadne had something planned for this evening, and they were *all* meant to play witness to it.

Where was Nausicaä?

Where was *Celadon*?

Arlo was *frantic* with these questions, because so far she couldn't see either of them, and both would probably be *raging* against Riadne as Vehan was right now, demanding in a very loud and panicked voice, "*Mother*, t-tell me *right now* what's g-going on or . . . or . . . *Mother*!"

But still Arlo couldn't *speak*.

Still, she couldn't scan the room any more than what was in her immediate line of vision.

She was so exhausted she could barely keep conscious.

There wasn't a single person here tonight who could contain Nausicaä when she didn't wish to be, no one who could stand between her and Arlo if Arlo needed her.

Numerous scenarios sprung into her head as they made for the staircase, as the guards parted to admit them through and they made their ascension to the middle landing, and each possibility to explain what had happened to her *girlfriend*, damn it, was even more gruesome than the last.

"Your allegiance, Arlo."

Arlo's back stiffened. Riadne's voice as they climbed the stairs, every step slow and deliberate, cut through Arlo's dread like an icy blade. She couldn't ignore it; couldn't answer it either, but Riadne carried on perfectly aware—and indeed in preference—of this fact.

"I gave you several opportunities to place your trust in me. You'll give it to me now. You *will* lend me your aid. You will tie yourself to my service—you, and your little die, and all that alchemy you just wished on yourself. I demand all three, and in exchange for the contract between us, I will spare *one* of your family in this room tonight. I will even let you choose which. Nod your agreement, and I'll allow you to speak their name."

Spare her family . . .

Riadne was going to . . . what, *kill* them? The Viridians, all of them? But the Bone Crown . . . She might be able to flout tradition with the Solstice, but the Bone Crown was nowhere near as forgiving. She'd spoken her Challenge, Arlo had been there to hear it, but to her knowledge she'd never given any terms. If she killed the High King without following through with the strict outline of claiming his Crown, it would fall to whichever Viridian remained who was closest in line to ascension.

No matter how diluted the inheritance, Riadne would have to kill every single one of them to default the Crown to *her*.

She couldn't . . . she *wouldn't*. She . . . she couldn't be this person! Arlo had *trusted* her! Nausicaä, Celadon, her own mother—everyone, *everyone* had told Arlo to be careful with Riadne Lysterne, and Arlo had just wanted to believe they were wrong. Because if they were wrong about Riadne, they could be wrong about Arlo, too. If they were wrong about all the nasty things they said about the Seelie Summer Queen, then maybe Arlo *wasn't* a weakness, like her family often pointed out. Maybe she *wasn't* a stain on their name. Arlo was just Arlo, and maybe that could be enough, but . . . it wasn't.

Riadne had been kind and attentive and exactly the person Arlo had wanted so desperately to see, and everyone, *everyone* but Arlo had been right.

This wasn't messing up royally. This wasn't a simple mistake.

Arlo had just made the worst decision in her entire life, and it was going to cost others *theirs*. Her *family* . . .

She wouldn't agree to this. She would *never* agree to this! She wouldn't swear her allegiance, and if she had to die for that, so be it—she was going to do *one* thing right while she still could.

But then . . . they reached the middle landing.

The clock behind them struck its final chime.

Twelve—midnight.

Spring had passed. Summer's reign was now at hand. And when

Arlo turned around with the queen to face the room, she finally saw what she hadn't been able to before.

The trees were dead.

They stood like iron tombs around the room, licked clean by the electricity that hummed now in place of the flowers, stark imagery of what Riadne had planned for the Viridian's family tree.

Below their ravaged branches, the crowd was doubled over, slouched against the walls, too nauseated and disoriented to pay any real attention to what was going on around them. They shied away from the Viridian family almost on instinct to form a clearing from the stairs straight through to the Viridians in their sword-point *pen*.

Arlo hadn't noticed before—had been too wrapped up in Nausicaä to examine the room earlier. But now she could see the carvings around the room for what they were.

Leda had been *training* her to see them.

Alchemical symbols were *everywhere*.

An extremely complicated array was woven around the room, but Arlo had no idea what it was for.

Why her wish hadn't kicked in yet she had no idea, but she couldn't spend much time on wondering—it was the *second* array in the room's center that stole her attention completely, made her mouth fall open in a silent gasp.

Too beautiful to be something so deadly, Arlo recognized it immediately. Vehan definitely would—he'd seen it every day of his life, the looping, butterfly-like pattern of symbols and equations that made a philosopher's stone array—but he was still kicking and screaming and retching on iron poisoning as the Luminous Guard dragged him to the safety of the magicked zone around the staircase.

"MOTHER!" he shouted at her, so furiously that his voice cracked, but Riadne ignored him. The Luminous Guards only leveled the points of their swords at his throat and pinned him in place beside Theodore.

It was much easier to say that Arlo would never agree to Riadne's terms when she'd been facing the other way . . . when she hadn't been staring down at all these people she *loved*.

At her *mother*, who stared back not at the queen she should be watching, but at Arlo, like *Arlo* was the one in danger . . . like still, as always, it was Arlo who needed protecting right now.

The fear in her mother's eyes . . . Arlo had never seen such terror before in her life, and never, never, *never* would she forget the sight of it after this.

Whatever was after this . . .

And where was Celadon?

"Your answer, Arlo. Everyone's waiting. Nod and speak the name of who here you wish to save. Decline, and I will kill every single one of them."

Please, she thought in desperation, tears welling up in her eyes. *Please don't do this.*

Her die—if there was ever a time to use a wish . . . but she'd foolishly, *foolishly* already spent that, and it was still cool in her hands. Even if she could think through the fog of terror and *sleep, sleep, sleep* that thrummed like a heartbeat through her, she couldn't use her only power.

She couldn't roll and simply *ask* the die to whisk them all away, it had to be something that applied directly to *her*, and she couldn't teleport like Nausicaä could to be able to do the whisking herself.

What were her options?

Think! she screamed at herself in her head.

Sleep!

"I will not ask it again, Arlo. Nod, or decline."

The entire room had quieted now.

Everyone seemed to be staring up at them, at Riadne, waiting to see what she was going to do. Whether they could hear what she spoke in a whisper to Arlo, Arlo couldn't focus on any one expression to see—none but her mother's, only *just* visible between two guards.

Her options . . . All Arlo could think at the moment was that she had to stop Riadne. That she was running out of time, that *killing* her might be the only way to stop this terrible plan from unfolding . . .

Please, please *come back to life,* she thought to her die in desperation.

"Oh, yes, I almost forgot." Riadne took hold of Arlo's face in so tight a grip that her eyes watered further and she winced around the pain. Forcing Arlo's gaze to hers, Riadne said, "This should make the choosing easier in case that little *gift* of yours had a much shorter refractory period than you've led me to believe: you won't be using your die tonight, not even to make a wish."

Arlo felt like crying—actually whimpered with how much it hurt to fight against the pull of Riadne's order, but then her hand relaxed around her die, now even worse than useless to her.

She complied, but not without realizing at last something *else* she'd been foolishly ignorant to.

A Mesmer.

The Seelie Summer Queen was an unregistered Mesmer, Arlo was certain, because there was nothing other than that magic that could have made her surrender like this. And the sheer amount of power that she'd poured into ordering Arlo's compliance . . . Her Magnetic Gift would be easier to fight against in the future, but for now it was *impossible* to oppose.

"Well?"

Arlo nodded.

Tears streaking down her face, she nodded agreement to Riadne's contract. She could almost feel the terms of it close around her like shackles at her wrists, wouldn't be surprised to look down to find *actual* chains there, like the weight of what she'd just signed herself over to suggested.

She nodded, but she couldn't speak a name.

Her mother or Celadon—*where was he, where* was *he*—they were both so important to her, and the thought of choosing one made her heart break for the thought of losing the other . . .

"Good girl," Riadne purred, releasing her face to smile once more. It was Riadne as Arlo had always known her—beautiful, composed, intimidating but kind, strict but good-hearted.

It was a *lie*.

Folk were so much better at lying, for all that they couldn't do so in words. And Riadne . . . she was best of them all. Arlo had been so *stupid* to fall for what nobody else clearly had.

"And the name?"

Arlo opened her mouth.

Her mother or Celadon, and she couldn't even argue with the queen to spare them both.

She wanted to cry; she wanted to *throw up*; she wanted to slap Riadne across the face . . . and *more*. She'd never felt such a violent, dark desire before, like maybe she *could* kill this queen before her . . . but none of it happened.

Arlo looked past the queen, out into the ballroom, to once again find her mother's face.

She knew without a doubt what Thalo would want her to do, who she would want Arlo to choose, but bringing herself to actually do it . . .

"You would really let them *all* die?" Riadne fairly taunted. "Goodness, and they call *me* cruel. You're not at all your mother's daughter, you know—how ashamed she'd be. I wonder what she'd say if she knew you didn't have the strength enough to make such a simple—"

"Celadon," Arlo growled, because that comment had stung. She knew she wasn't anywhere near as impressive as her mother; this wasn't the first time someone had thrown in her face that Thalo must be ashamed of her, and to hear it now . . .

Riadne pitched her head back to laugh, so amused by something, but Arlo hadn't any idea in the slightest what. And she didn't care.

She'd just named a name, and she couldn't, couldn't, *couldn't* lose Celadon—but that name . . . it hadn't been her mother's, and the reality of that was setting in.

"So predictable. To think, if you were just a little less noble, a little less weak, and a little more clever, you might have been able to save them both."

No, *wait*—what?

"So be it. Eyes forward, Arlo—you don't want to miss this, I assure you." Drawing herself up to full height, Riadne turned her stare on the crowd—on one fae there, in particular—and in a voice that echoed around the entire ballroom, said, "Here and now, you and I. My terms, Azurean. Do you accept?"

As one, those in the room who were physically able all turned to their High King—and *erupted* into murmurs when Azurean ploughed through the Guards restraining him and his family, wild-eyed and aura blazing, and growling out loud enough for all to hear two simple words:

"I *do*."

CHAPTER 45

Nausicaä

~⟶~

HANDS GRABBED HER FROM behind.

An iron collar closed around her neck.

Nausicaä was no piddling mortal. This poisonous metal would never be enough to render her *completely* helpless, even in her sorry half-state of immortality. But it burned and itched and *ate* at her skin as soon as it clamped around it, and it was no simple band: this collar was a Hunter's tool, a blend of human and Otherworld ore that would require the whole of her strength to break it open—and interfered with her magic.

That was the most concerning bit right now, because this interference was all her mysterious assailant needed to capitalize on Nausicaä's momentary shock, and before reflex could kick in, she was whisked away from the ballroom—from *Arlo*.

Before Nausicaä could even finish calling Arlo's name, she was swallowed up by shadow and spat out again she had no idea where, as distorted bursts of sound and color and movement *exploded* around her.

She fell to the ground like a plummeting cannon, hit so hard against the cement where she landed that it cracked and caved around her.

A horn blared—several, in fact.

Her assailant had plucked her out of the Luminous Palace ballroom and discarded her right into the middle of the street spanning the Vegas Strip.

Nausicaä had just enough time to curl herself inward and brace for impact before a car struck her head on. She was, thankfully, more or less an immoveable object, a solid block of carbon steel against what amounted to the impact of someone chucking a frisbee at her. The car collided and crunched to a mangled halt, crumpling around her—another crashing into *it*, and another, and another.

All around her, collisions piled up to a cacophony of yet more honking, and alarms, and breaking glass; fireworks; shouting and screams and jarringly cheerful music playing out from the various stores and attractions around them.

Groaning, she unfurled herself to standing.

Her hands flew up once more to her fucking *collar*, scrabbling again to try to pry it back open. The people in their cars pulled themselves from their wreckage to shout some more, at one another, at *her*.

Nausicaä ignored it all. Someone had put this metal around her, someone who was strong enough to wrangle a Fury, even distracted, and *teleport* her away without her even noticing them coming up on her. She didn't need a single thing more than this to know who it had been.

She had to get this off.

She was no match for who'd done this even under the best of circumstances, but disadvantaged as she was . . . "Fuck," she spat, as her nails scored through bubbling, irritated flesh, and silvery-sapphire blood oozed in rivulets down her throat. "*Fuck!*"

"Holy shit, girl, are you okay?"

"What the fucking *hell* just happened?"

"Hey, asshole, where the fuck did you learn how to drive?"

Questions, panic, accusations, and suspicions hurled around her, and Nausicaä didn't have time for *any* of them, because she felt it now. She couldn't scent his aura, not like she once could, but she could *feel* it swell to envelop her, cold and deadly and wriggling, like maggots squirming in the washed-up carcass of a rotting sea creature.

"Tsk, tsk, tsk."

Her back to Lethe, Nausicaä stiffened.

Her gazed snapped up to the crowd of humans. Bleeding and

injured, staggering and coughing and dazed, most had switched their concern to one another, no one really paying attention to *her* anymore save the one who'd hit her directly. He climbed out of his car, approached Nausicaä with the absolute terror of having just hit a person. There was confusion, too, and Nausicaä sympathized with *that*, but there *wasn't time*. "Run," she ordered firmly. "Go, get the fuck out of here."

He didn't need telling twice.

The man who'd come to check on her took one look at what was amassing over her shoulder, froze, stumbled backward, and proceeded to run away.

There was screaming now for a different reason.

Other people began to run.

The scene cleared out. Lethe—the only way these humans would be able to see him right now was if he *wanted* them to, which meant he very much did, and this was one thousand percent a play for time. But with this iron fucking collar, if Nausicaä tried to teleport back to the ballroom she was clearly being kept from, there'd be no telling where she'd wind up or with how many body parts missing.

Worth the risk—Arlo needed her, and she couldn't let herself be waylaid or incapacitated any more than she already was. But there was no capturing Lethe unless he allowed it, and no escaping him without his permission, either.

Schooling her features, Nausicaä turned around.

There across their shambles of an arena stood Lethe in full Hunter gear—or rather, there he *sat* on the back of Pestilence, his familiar-in-death. In equine form, Pestilence currently towered as an *enormous* beast, with antifreeze-bright eyes and a gunmetal mane exactly the same shade as Lethe's hair, rotting water lilies tangled in both this and their tail like a super-charged kelpie.

Chains and hooks and clasps were strung from their saddle, serving as their reins, and wound straight through their bones and *gouged* their festering hide. Where Death—Eris's familiar—was ghastly white in color, Pestilence was a sickly green, with a grotesque iridescence to their hide like oil on the surface of swampy waters.

Nausicaä didn't blame the humans for fleeing at the sight the two presented.

Lethe glinted just as sinisterly as his steed, between his own silver trimmings, his midnight cloak, and his elongated claws already fused into that vicious sword of his. Its point touched down only barely against the cement, but it already scoured through it as though the rock were nothing but snow.

Nope, Nausicaä didn't blame them. She a little bit wanted to flee herself.

A lot bit, really—she didn't want to face Lethe, right now or ever, preferably, but certainly not when it was very clear he was here to keep her *occupied*. Arlo could be in danger, but there was still the matter of Nausicaä's deities-damned collar making her head a little fuzzy and her magic unpredictable, like a poorly tuned radio station.

So be it.

If it was a fight Lethe wanted, it was a fight he was going to get.

"You have five minutes to make this worth my while, Edge-lord," she called across the shambles of their arena.

Lethe laughed at her, *delighted*.

No doubt, the implication that Nausicaä could last that long against him had amused him. Five more minutes might be all she needed for her body and magic to stabilize, for her system to adjust to the poison coursing through it and her strength to recover. Five more minutes might be all she needed to break free of her collar and tele-port back to Arlo, but five minutes was a *very* long time to stay alive when the last she'd ever seriously fought Lethe had been in training over a century ago . . . and she'd barely held out a minute—longer than anyone else, but a far cry from this veritable, whole ass eon.

"Five minutes on the clock, then." He lifted his claw-bladed hand, pointed at a clock on one of the giant screens on the buildings.

Midnight—whatever Riadne had planned for tonight, Nausicaä

could only send a fervent prayer to Luck that Arlo survived it. Five minutes. *Just hold out for five minutes, Arlo.*

"And Nausicaä?" The point of his blade swung to her, and Pestilence reared on their hind legs. When their hooves stomped back on the street, the tremors of their impact were so forceful that Nausicaä nearly lost her footing. "I was given no instruction to let you live. Five minutes—and if you don't make it, I'll enjoy delivering that Destruction you so craved before."

Before.

Before *Arlo.*

Funny that it took staring her own demise in the face for her to realize that, at some point, Red had become much more than her *stillness* but her *reason*, too—for so many things, not least of all surviving this fight.

"Instruction, huh?" Nausicaä snorted. "Getting in good with the new boss, are we? Never knew the Great and Powerful Lethe was such a *kiss-ass*." As she spoke, her shadow-wrought sword assembled in her hand. Erebos—kind of Lethe to return it to her, when the Darkness that had forged it was one of the only things that could contend with his specialized adamant weapon, which in turn was the only type of blade that could actually Destroy an immortal as he threatened.

Almost as if he planned it so.

Another creaking laugh—it was all the warning Nausicaä received before Pestilence lunged forward, and Lethe swung.

His Reaper's scythe missed her head by a hair.

Nausicaä ducked; it was all she had time for. But she fell to the ground, and Pestilence galloped past, reared around, and charged forward once more.

Nausicaä dove for the side, and as she rolled, she shifted.

It was very impractical to fight like this, shirtless with only a bra and open jacket for cover, both of which were oddly restricting for how little there was to either article. And what did she need her glamour for if Lethe was prancing around like a West-End Ringwraith for everyone to see? At this point, her mortal masquerade was more of a hindrance than anything, and so she simply let it fall away.

Her suit morphed into leather armor that wrapped around her like a second skin.

Her skeleton grew until she towered nearly tall as Lethe; her body harrowed into something vulture-like in structure, boney and sharp underneath lean ropes of muscle. Her nails hardened, lengthened into glittering black talons, while her eyes turned to molten silver and her hair to white-hot flame.

When the smoldering, not-quite-leather, not-quite-feather mass of her wings flared wide behind her, Pestilence slammed to a halt and reared again with a whinny. Lethe seemed even more delighted than before.

"*There* you are, *exquisite* thing," he practically moaned in elation, nudging Pestilence off to her right to begin circling her, his blade cutting a ring in the ground as he went. "This is a much better look for you, you know."

If this were training, Nausicaä would have lunged at him. She'd never been much for tact or strategy when it came to fighting—her favored approach was coming in heavy and cleaning house, and that usually worked, but this wasn't her usual opponent.

And she needed to last.

12:01.

She needed to last four more minutes, so she had to buy herself time.

Lethe began to windmill his blade, closing his circle tighter and tighter, and forcing Nausicaä into the air—but this was no advantage.

Pestilence followed.

With a leap, they galloped toward her on invisible wings, Lethe's grinning madness gleaming as bright as his chains in the exploding firework display.

Higher Nausicaä flew, heading for the shower of sparks. They wouldn't harm either of them, but it would make it just a *little* more distracting for Lethe and his mount. Just before she could reach them, though, Lethe flicked his scythe at her.

The blade of it melted, reshaped itself, and solidified into a wicked-tongued whip that wrapped around Nausicaä's ankle. Before she could even struggle against it, Lethe yanked on the grip, *pulled* Nausicaä down from the sky, and hurled her back to the street.

She crashed through one of the abandoned cars.

There were sirens in the distance—the human police were coming, and no doubt the Falchion with them to manage the chaos and try to conceal the very obvious magical activity taking place. But what were they going to do when they realized the being who helped them erase and manipulate memories was the one causing the chaos?

No time to worry about any of that. Nausicaä scrambled out of the bed of warped steel that had caught her fall.

Lethe came down on her, having sprung from Pestilence to javelin-throw himself with his scythe into the space she'd only just vacated.

"*Fight* me, Nausicaä. I might just get bored and kill you after all, you know. Make this worth my while, and I'll return you to our darling girl . . ."

He *wanted* her to fight him?

"*Not* your girl," Nausicaä seethed, rounding immediately on Lethe's advance and swinging her sword at his neck.

It was a blow he caught easily, but Nausicaä hadn't expected it to land.

Her eyes blazed; her hair crackled, sparks dripping from its ends like the venom in her words. "I don't know what the fuck you think Arlo's going to do for you, but she's *not* your girl."

"Is she *yours* then?" Lethe teased.

With a cock of his head and a flick of his wrist, he deflected the blow he'd caught. Simultaneously, his foot came out to catch Nausicaä's, and in a blink, he had her flat on her back.

"Fuck you," Nausicaä spat.

She didn't bother trying to get up or out of the way. Instead, she threw her all into raising her sword between them to block the blade swung down at her with so much force that she *sank* into the pavement . . . but survived.

Her bones hurt.

She'd felt that impact with a worrying severity, but again there was no time to assess the damage done.

What was a struggle for her to keep that sword from crashing through her defense was a twitch for Lethe, another flick of his wrist. Nausicaä had never been disarmed so *easily* as when she fought against Lethe, both in training and now.

12:04.

One more minute.

A matter of seconds.

Erebos was too far away, and Lethe's claws were poised to strike straight through her heart.

Four whole minutes—a new record.

And if she was going out, she would do so in the way she'd always intended: fighting.

"In any case, alas, now it seems she will be only *mine* . . ."

Lethe's grin—*fuck* this guy.

She threw herself up at Lethe's face, a fistful of fire in her palm and fury in her eyes. She threw herself directly against Lethe's blade and felt it *rip* through her, not her heart but her shoulder . . . but still just as potentially fatal, because she couldn't heal a wound like this in time to keep from bleeding out.

Bleeding out she could survive too—she was *immortal*—but it would leave her a husk that Lethe would be able to cut down whenever he chose.

And it didn't matter.

Her hand sealed across Lethe's face, and he *shrieked* as her fire burned him—fire that wouldn't heal without scarring. Immortal though he was, Nausicaä's fire was the element itself. He would wear this mark for the rest of his life as a reminder that he wasn't as indestructible as everyone thought he was.

Nausicaä, the closest anyone had ever come to defeating this legendary Hunter.

"You should see the look on your fucking *face*," she gasped in a shaky laugh.

Lethe surged. He gripped her by the front of her leather, heaved her just a little farther off the ground and closer to his face.

He was incendiary in his anger, incandescent with it.

Nausicaä had never seen him so bare and livid before, and it was *frightening*, but dulled—what did it matter? What could he do? She was already going to die.

"Twelve-oh-five," he snarled in her face.

And Nausicaä could only blink.

Releasing her, Lethe tore his sword out of her shoulder. Nausicaä couldn't help then but scream. Touching the tender, raw burn on his face, Lethe *glowered* down at her. "Come, fae boy. Heal your friend. She has someplace to be. And quickly, please; *we* have someplace to be, as well."

Nausicaä could only blink again as, out from his shelter in a nearby store, the "fae boy" Lethe had summoned picked his way across the street.

". . . *Aurelian?*"

"Nausicaä," Aurelian rasped, throwing himself down beside her. His hands went automatically for her wound—lesidhe magic. Of course. It was linked so intrinsically with the primordial source of all things that it *could* actually heal her, could actually heal *this*.

"Are you shitting me?" Nausicaä coughed, wincing as she felt her shattered bone regrow and her muscle and flesh knit back together. "I can't believe I owe you my life *twice* now."

"Nausicaä," Aurelian urged again, ignoring her comments, hardly paying attention at all to the amount of magic he was pouring into healing her. "Nausicaä, you need to listen. We don't have long. You have to get back, you have to stop her. You have to get Arlo and Vehan *out* of there. Riadne, she's going to—"

"Oh, it's a little too late for that. She *is* going to, and likely by now has already done so. If you want to survive it, you had all better master what I've primed for each of you. But he's right about one thing . . ." Lethe lowered onto his haunches, reached out, and with all the effort of snapping a twig, broke the iron collar around Nausicaä's neck. "Take care, cousin. We'll see each other soon. For now, you really must be getting back."

Back . . .

Quick as she got her bearings, Nausicaä teleported back to the ballroom . . .

For a moment, Nausicaä thought she'd gone back too far, not just to the ballroom but in time itself, for what she teleported into was a scene plucked straight from nightmare and memory.

Fire.

Death.

Chaos.

Screaming—a sound that echoed what she'd never *once* forgotten in the one hundred and seventeen years since all the rage inside of her shattered her apart.

CHAPTER 46

Arlo

～⁀～

I DO."

Azurean prowled forward.

He was a fae remade. Arlo watched as he billowed across the ballroom, down the path his subjects cleared for him.

She hadn't known him like this in some time—possibly ever. This was Azurean with all the air and confidence and arrogance of youth that *Celadon* was attributed. She'd noticed plenty of times before how striking a resemblance there was between the two, but in this moment, she could almost swear it really was the High Prince advancing on the grand staircase, jaw squared and shoulders back, graceful as the wind they could both command.

But *there* was the High King the folk had praised for so long.

There was the intelligence, the cunning, the ferocity, and most important, the astute awareness that had been absent from his jade eyes for the past few years.

"Father!" shouted Serulian and Cerelia in unified alarm.

"Azurean!" his queen pleaded.

"High Majesty!" bellowed Arlo's mother, but they had no choice but to clear as much of the room as they could for the impending Challenge to take place.

Azurean heeded none but the call inside him, the centuries-long feud between him and Riadne Lysterne that would at last come to a head.

And here was Arlo, trapped as though behind glass, observing it all. She couldn't move, couldn't speak, couldn't do anything but look on as the guards at the steps admitted Azurean through; as the

Viridians and the crowd in general realized none of their magic would work properly—that the trees hadn't petrified into stone, they'd been transmuted into *iron*.

Some tried to flee.

They stopped trying once the Luminous Guard—their strength no doubt conditioned by constant exposure to Riadne's iron staircase, and likely more horrible things—began cutting folk down.

The Challenge was commencing, and *everyone* gathered would bear witness to it whether they wanted to or not.

As though none of them were there, as though he could only see Riadne, as though all along all he'd *ever* seen was her, Azurean climbed the steps of the staircase. "You think I don't remember this room? You think I don't remember what took place here?" he asked in a low, deadly voice. "You think because you beat me *once*, when I beat *you* a thousand and one times over, that you can do it again? That this room will help you? Riadne . . ."

He came to halt in front of her.

They were well matched, Arlo noticed, tall and beautiful and fearsome. Summer and Spring . . . In another life, they'd look good together as partners instead of enemies, but there was no love for Azurean in Riadne's twisting snarl.

Curiously, there *was* something like affection in Azurean's sorrow. "I have no wish to kill you, Riadne. I never wished that. I *loved* you. Always, I have loved you, and I've allowed you so much. I've done so much for your happiness, for your health. I never wished for you to know the burden that comes with this Crown you crave. I've asked you before, and I'll ask you again: *Why* do you want it so badly? The only reason I took it at all was to save you from its toll."

Riadne breathed an arctic laugh.

"I never asked you to play my defender, Azurean. *Why* do I want that Crown that means so little to you?"

She laughed, and she laughed, and the nausea inside Arlo swelled.

She wanted to call out to her mother, beg her to fight, to flee, to *look at the center of the room, oh gods, that's a philosopher's stone array*! More than anything, Arlo wanted to *scream*. To beg Luck to intervene—for assistance, for her family to live, even if she herself didn't . . .

But still Arlo could do nothing; still she was trapped; still she was silent.

Desperation swirled inside her, clawed at her seams, pounded like fists against the enchantment that bound her. She could feel its hold on her start to tremble, but it wouldn't give—why wouldn't it *give*?

"Why do I want that Crown so badly, asks the *man* who's wanted for *nothing* . . ."

In a single, deft movement, Riadne unsheathed her sword from the back of her dress. Like a sprung trap, all the shards of glass that made up the dress *shifted* into the deadliest of chainmail encasing her body with the points of a thousand glinting blades.

Armed in a blink, Azurean was no less quick to catch the attack she gave no warning of launching. She flew at him, and the High King lifted a hand—in it, he clutched his element, a wind-hewn sword just as famous and deadly as what the Seelie Summer Queen wielded.

Blow after blow, Riadne pressed an impressive opening sequence, advancing on the High King and pushing him back down the stairs he'd just climbed one step at a time.

There were murmurs in the watching crowd, but no one would be able to intervene or even *move* until the Challenge was over. They couldn't even look away. But many, much like Arlo, were surely nauseated with dread. If Azurean lost . . . if Riadne *won* . . . how many of them would walk out of this room tonight?

Like a charge in the air, Arlo could *feel* it as more and more began to wonder exactly this.

PLEASE! Arlo screamed inside her head as loudly as she could. *LUCK, PLEASE, I NEED YOU—PLEASE!*

It was then that Arlo noticed Councillor Sylvain stepping from the smaller group of fae contained by the staircase.

He skirted the edge of the room, and no one paid him much attention, but Arlo did—could do nothing else as the Councillor who'd always spurned her kind, who *hated* Arlo for her ironborn blood, who was rude and mean and so picture-perfect sidhe fae she almost wanted to laugh, knelt down and touched his hands to the outer array.

No . . .

Riadne and Azurean, meanwhile, had broken back out onto the ballroom floor.

Sword clashed with sword; wind howled each time it was struck, and the curious yellow blade that shaped the Seelie Summer Queen's famous weapon cried out like a haunted keening with every blow it rained, as though even her weapon didn't want what she was forcing it to do.

Azurean was *skilled*—he was every bit still the warrior who'd managed to claim the Crown on his head, but for some reason . . . he pressed no assault like what he defended himself against.

He aimed no cleaving blow of his own.

Nothing of what he parried, blocked, or returned was meant to kill, and he was going to *die* for whatever steeled him to this resolve, because Arlo could see it in Riadne's eyes: it was death she was after, his or hers.

The High King, meanwhile . . .

"Riadne . . ." Arlo heard him speak—curiously. He was so far away, but she could hear it just as easily as she could hear when they'd been almost directly beside her. "Riadne, I have mistreated you, greatly."

"*Why do I want it?*" Riadne scathed in return, and lifted a hand in the air.

The room began to hum as *energy* gathered in the Seelie Summer Queen's palm . . .

"Why do I want it? Why do I want the only thing that will give me the power and the respect I've *always* deserved?"

Arlo could barely breathe.

"Why do I want it . . . the only thing that will put all this right and give me back what's been *taken* from me?"

Electricity shot in a sizzling bolt across the room, and folk against the opposite wall shrieked and clawed at one another, scampered and scrambled and *trampled* their neighbors just to escape it as it scorched through the space where Azurean had only *just* been . . .

The ground began to quake.

Arlo's focus fractured *further*.

Councillor Sylvain . . . his hands on the array. It wasn't possible but . . . here it was.

He'd been *ironborn* all along.

And now he was helping Riadne destroy their world.

Why, she wanted to shriek, but the question in her mind drowned in horror.

As the quaking parted to crumbling stone and breaking glass.

To iron tree roots.

The tree roots lifted into the air, and there was more gasping now, a fresh and even more desperate attempt at escape that was met with the Luminous Guard's denial, because those razor-sharp tree roots . . . they weren't aimed at the High King . . .

"You took *everything* from me."

Another strike. Another block. More bolts of electricity and a distinct lack of retaliation from the only person who stood between the Courts as Arlo knew them . . . and whatever awaited them in their collapse.

"Riadne, I'm *sorry*. I did it for you—I did it for *him*. He *lives,* Riadne. That's worth any pain . . ."

Laughter.

Arlo would hear this sound forever after, she was certain; it was the most horrible sound she'd ever heard, so very far from amusement— so cold and dark and cruel. It was *evil*.

"You think you know what pain is? You have no idea . . . let me *show* you."

Councillor Sylvain pressed his hands even flatter against the array. As though this entire night was an act in some play and Riadne's threat a horrific cue, the tree roots shot out—

Toward the Solstice's gathered guests.

It was . . .

It was . . .

Arlo couldn't watch, and yet she couldn't look away.

Those iron tree roots, powered by the Councillor's ironborn magic, snatched up folk from the crowd and *rent them apart* before Arlo's eyes.

Impaled . . .

Crushed . . .

Folk—but not just any. The tree roots went for none but the Viridian royals—Cerelia, Serulean, Malachite, *all of them*, and Arlo could only watch . . . and watch . . . and *shake* in place on her landing as, one by one, iron claimed in brutal, gruesome finality her entire family line.

Sapphire rained down on the ground, spraying the panicked, scrambling masses fleeing to evade a similar doom.

"Arlo—"

Her mother, she somehow heard her voice above it all. Thalo shouted to her, in her very last breath, *"Survive."* And with all her might, she *hurled* her sword at the staircase, where it embedded itself in the stone, point down.

Her mother's sword.

And finally, *finally*, all the noise inside Arlo's head found its way without, tore from her throat just as violently as the iron root that punched through her mother's chest, hoisting her dead in the air with the rest of the Viridians to splatter the glass below with her life.

Somewhere in the midst of this all, Azurean fell to his knees.

Spring and Summer . . . This clash had been a storm of blood and violence, a dance more appropriate for this ballroom than the earlier festivities, and Arlo couldn't breathe right now—her mother, her mother, her *mother* . . .

"MOTHER!" Vehan had been crying too.

"MOTHER!" Celadon roared—and there, just at the back of the room, Arlo only noticed in an exhausted, stunned, out-of-body sort of way that the ballroom doors had been flung open wide with her cousin silhouetted in the doorway. The Luminous Guard rounded on Arlo's cousin . . . and halted immediately when they realized who it was.

Celadon was there . . .

Arlo was screaming, and couldn't stop.

She screamed in grief. She screamed in warning. She screamed as Reseda Viridian broken from what remained of the Verdant Guard and flew across the room to her husband's aid—only to be stopped dead in her tracks by an iron root erupting from her stomach.

And Arlo could only continue to scream as her great uncle saw this and *wilted*, watching his queen fall lifeless on the root that hauled her into the air to dangle her like a puppet on cut strings.

With a complete and total look of despair, the High King Azurean Viridian dropped his sword at Riadne's feet. Riadne stood over him, tall and unyielding and emotionless as carved ice.

"I would do it again, for him. For *you*—I love you, Riadne."

The queen hesitated for the briefest of seconds, but then . . . "I don't love *you*."

Riadne's sword plunged through Azurean's heart, so deeply that it was almost as though she'd reached her hand through with it. Folded over the High King, Arlo couldn't see her expression, but just for a moment, she would swear Riadne *shook* . . .

Azurean fell.

Just like that.

He sagged into Riadne's arms—their indomitable High King—dead as though flesh and blood and not at all the mountain he'd once been.

He sagged, and Riadne held him for all of a *second*, maybe two, before dumping him to the ground, her sword still stuck in his chest.

As he dropped, she snagged his Crown. As he too was claimed by an iron root and heaved up to join the others that haunted the tree-top graveyard, Riadne merely retreated a step, gazing not up at her hard-won revenge but at the twist of antler in her hands.

And suddenly, there was Nausicaä, teleported back from wherever she'd been stolen away, but Arlo could barely notice for the way she'd been screaming, screaming, screaming all this *time* . . .

"ARLO!"

She screamed . . .

"The ironborn servant—bring him here, Councillor Sylvain. It's time to create your stone."

And screamed . . .

"MOTHER . . . WHAT HAVE YOU *DONE*?"

And *screamed*.

Lethe

WHERE ARE WE?"
   Children.
   "What are we doing here?"
He'd been one once.

"Lethe, please, I just want to get back to Vehan. To Arlo—they need help. What do you need *me* for that you won't let me go to them? What are we *doing*?"

Arlo had been one once, as well.

He was no child any longer, hadn't been for quite some time. Arlo wasn't one either, Riadne had most likely made sure of that by now, if her plans had gone accordingly, which they *should* have. But then . . . mortals were woefully incapable of anything when he wasn't around to guide them by the hand.

"*Lethe!*"

The fae boy—Aurelian—he knelt in front of the kitchen counter where Lethe had seated himself. Why had he saved him when it had been Riadne's wish for him to die tonight as well?

Questions for later, if he felt like second-guessing himself. Aurelian was useful to his aims, aims that he'd been so patiently setting up—so much waiting, so much preparation, but not much longer now. They thought he was doing this for revenge against his father, and yes . . . in part, that was true, but he wondered what they'd say if they knew the truth: that he was just so *tired* of death and destruction, the only things he'd ever known . . .

He had one more piece to slip onto this board, one last pawn before the game he played could *finally* be set into motion, and Lethe . . . Lethe could be free.

He looked down.

People had knelt to him once, first in the mockery of his status, then as he cut them down at the knees and *forced* them to kneel.

Did he like it, to see this little fae *thing* doing so voluntarily?

Unbidden, his thoughts flashed to a certain High Prince, how perhaps he wouldn't mind someone kneeling before him if the person was—and he quickly forced *those* thoughts back away.

"Can we at least turn on a light?"

A hand darted out almost before Lethe could realize it was his own. The one that wasn't clawed, so the boy was lucky, as that hand took a hold of his oh so fragile jaw and tilted him this way and that, examining the moonlight that played off his bone.

"You are so . . . *tedious*." And then released him.

His fae boy straightened, working his jaw as he turned to the kitchen threshold like a cat that had just heard a curious sound.

The front door opened.

What were they doing here, the boy asked? Lethe grinned, just in time to greet the man who entered the kitchen and *froze*.

Fire-red hair, warm hazel eyes, and a freckled, pale face that was older than Lethe remembered it being—but then, humans did age so quickly.

"Who are you?" the man demanded, and for someone who had grown so soft, he didn't look too frightened to find this collection of leather and tattoos and chains and piercings making cozy in his house. Virtual strangers . . . but no, they weren't strangers at all, and Lethe could tell there was something in the back of the man's mind that remembered this.

Lethe had made sure there would be, after all.

"What do you want?"

"Don't worry," said Lethe, biting into one of the apples he'd plucked from a bowl on the table. "It's nothing you haven't already promised. You'll recall soon enough. I'm here to collect on a debt that's owed, to myself and to your daughter."

He chewed and took his time in swallowing, then smiled even wider.

"It's time to wake up, Rory Jarsdel. Time to wake up and remember who you are, my last but one *Flamel*."

ACKNOWLEDGMENTS

Two hundred thousand words went into this sequel, but it's these last few hundred that are the hardest to write. Because how do I sum up the experience of *A CRUEL AND FATED LIGHT*, drafted, revised, polished, and printed during the same pandemic I debuted in with *A DARK AND HOLLOW STAR*? This book is the epitome of "started making it, had a breakdown, bon appétit," and if it weren't for the people who've gathered to support both it and me, neither me nor it would have recovered from that "breakdown" stage.

First, as always, a thank you to my family: my mother, father, and stepparents; my grandparents; my siblings, cousins, and aunts and uncles. Thank you all for the love you've shown me throughout this entire journey. For believing in me during the times I didn't, for sharing in the joyous moments and patiently letting me vent when pandemic-wrought changes brought me down, for celebrating with me and treating these books like the enormous things they very much are to me, and above all else, for showing me and these characters the unconditional acceptance not everyone is fortunate enough to know.

Thank you to my agent, Mandy Hubbard of Emerald City Literary Agency. Mandy, I couldn't do this without you. From the very beginning, you believed in this story, and that support has never once wavered. Thank you for all the patient emails explaining all the facets of this industry. Thank you for the love and support, for checking in on me when times were tough, for celebrating with me when times were exciting, and for being the best agent I could ask for all the times in-between. I look forward to all the incredible things we'll achieve together: to finishing the Hollow Star Saga and launching into the new beyond.

Thank you to my editor, Sarah McCabe of Margaret K. McElderry Books. A million thank yous for being so open, approachable, and supportive. For understanding. For not giving up on me and this story when I could barely bring myself to get out of bed, let alone open my laptop. For once again seeing the vital piece this story was missing, and for the suggestions that allowed me to put into words something I'll never be able to otherwise express but deeply needed to say. Thank you. I couldn't imagine this story and these characters in anyone else's hands. You are incomparable.

To the entirety of the Margaret K. McElderry Books team at Simon & Schuster, including (but not limited to): Justin Chanda, Karen Wojtyla, Anne Zafian, Eugene Lee, Elizabeth Blake-Lin, Greg Stadnyk, Lauren Hoffman, Caitlin Sweeny, Alissa Nigro, Lisa Quach, Savannah Breckenridge, Anna Jarzab, Yasleen Trinidad, Saleena Nival, Emily Ritter, Amy Lavigne, Mandy Veloso, Nicole Russo, Jenny Lu, Christina Pecorale and her sales team, Michelle Leo and her education/library team. Thank you. So incredibly much. Thank you all for making this dream a reality, for all the hard work, long hours, and numerous tasks that go into putting a book out into the world. Thank you also to my Canadian team at Simon & Schuster Canada—including Mackenzie Croft, Arden Hagedorn, Laura MacDonald, and Randall Perry—for being equally badass, hardworking, and supportive from the very beginning. And thank you too to Molly Powell and the entire UK team at Hodder and Stoughton. None of this would be possible without any of you.

A book is more than just its (wonderful) publishing team, though. There are more people I have to thank for how far the Hollow Star Saga has been able to come, my found family, beginning as ever with Julianna Will—you have gone above and beyond to make sure this experience is infused with as much happiness as possible and I will never be able to say it enough, but I hope you know how much it means to me to have you in my life. Thank you also to Abi Alton, Colleen Johnston, Jess Flath, Jee Hewson, Jeryn Daly, Shana VanDusen, Laura Feetham, Julia Duenas, and Kyle Dixon, the best friends anyone could ever want, the most beloved hype team, and just all-around good people with whom I've been incredibly lucky to share these past years with.

Thank you to Melanie Delon for the GEORGEOUS cover art, and to the Canadian Council of Arts for the generous grant that made writing this book possible, and Natalie Naudus, Neo Cihi, Vikas Adam, Imani Jade Powers, and everyone with Simon & Schuster Audio for bringing these characters so beautifully to audiobook life.

Thank you to my partner, Kade, for filling my life with the love and laughter that makes this all worthwhile.

Thank you to the ladies at the Wine Rack, to Debbie for everything you did for me, to Kathy and my new work family at the Birdie's Nest.

A HUGE thank you to Final Fantasy VIIR for finally releasing and giving me something other than Final Fantasy XV to play. To my cat, Zack, Taylor Swift, and BTS for getting me through the day. To my writing community family, including the Toronto Writing Crew, Liselle Sambury, Louisa Onomé, Adrienne Tooley, Xiran Jay Zhao, Priyanka Taslim, Kat Enright, Sadie Blach, ZR Ellor, Brittany Evans, and Rebecca Coffindaffer.

And lastly, but certainly not least, thank you to all the people who've welcomed the Hollow Star Saga into their hearts. The readers and book bloggers and TikTokers and IG influencers, librarians and teachers and parents and teens—all the people who've picked up these books and loved them—I cannot thank you enough. You are the reason I get to continue to do this. You are the reason more and more LGBTQ+ content is finding its way to the shelves, and to the people who desperately need it. With my whole heart, thank you. I look forward to meeting you all again in book three.

WANT MORE?

If you enjoyed this and would like to find out about similar books we publish, we'd love you to join our online Sci-Fi, Fantasy and Horror community, Hodderscape.

Visit hodderscape.co.uk for exclusive content form our authors, news, competitions and general musings, and feel free to comment, contribute or just keep an eye on what we are up to.

See you there!

HODDERSCAPE

NEVER AFRAID TO BE OUT OF THIS WORLD

 @Hodderscape  @Hodderscape  /hodderscape